KU-412-981

C0052 15903

The

SEA GARDEN

Also by Deborah Lawrenson

Songs of Blue and Gold
The Art of Falling
The Moonbathers
Hot Gossip
Idol Chatter
The Lantern

The
SEA GARDEN

Deborah Lawrenson

First published in Great Britain in 2014 by Orion Books,
an imprint of The Orion Publishing Group Ltd
Orion House, 5 Upper Saint Martin's Lane
London WC2H 9EA

An Hachette UK Company

1 3 5 7 9 10 8 6 4 2

Copyright © Deborah Lawrenson 2014

The moral right of Deborah Lawrenson to be identified as the author
of this work has been asserted in accordance with
the Copyright, Designs and Patents Act of 1988.

All rights reserved. No part of this publication may be
reproduced, stored in a retrieval system, or transmitted
in any form or by any means, electronic, mechanical,
photocopying, recording, or otherwise, without the
prior permission of both the copyright owner and the
above publisher of this book.

All the characters in this book are fictitious, and any resemblance to
actual persons, living or dead, is purely coincidental.

A CIP catalogue record for this book is
available from the British Library.

ISBN (Mass Market Paperback) 978 1 4091 4618 6
ISBN (Hardback) 978 1 4091 4591 2
ISBN (Ebook) 978 1 4091 4593 6

Typeset by Input Data Services Ltd, Bridgwater, Somerset

Printed and bound by CPI Group (UK) Ltd, Croydon, CRO 4YY

The Orion Publishing Group's policy is to use papers that are natural,
renewable and recyclable products and made from wood grown in sustainable
forests. The logging and manufacturing processes are expected to
conform to the environmental regulations of the country of origin.

www.orionbooks.co.uk

There comes a murmur from the shore,
And in the place two fair streams are,
Drawn from the purple hills afar,
Drawn down unto the restless sea.
The hills whose flowers ne'er fed the bee,
The shore no ship has ever seen,
Still beaten by the billows green,
Whose murmur comes unceasingly
Unto the place for which I cry.

– WILLIAM MORRIS, *A Garden by the Sea*

GLASGOW LIFE GLASGOW LIBRARIES	
C005215903	
Bertrams	11/09/2014
F/LAW	£20.00
EL	GEN

BOOK I

~

The Sea Garden

1

The Crossing

Sunday, 2 June 2013

The island lay in wait, a smudge of land across the water.

From the port at La Tour Fondue, the crossing to Porquerolles would take only fifteen minutes.

Ellie Brooke put her face up to the sun, absorbing the heat. On the deck of the ferry, where she had a prime seat, there were few other passengers this late in the afternoon.

The young man had his back to the curve of the deck rail, facing her. It was his T-shirt that drew her attention: the lead singer of a heavy metal band thrust a tongue out from the boy's chest, an image that invited reaction but succeeded only in making its thin, blond bearer appear innocuous in comparison.

The engines thrummed and the boat nosed out into sea glitter and salt spray, then powered up to full speed. The island was already sharpening into focus when the young man climbed over the deck rail, spread both arms and then let himself slip down the side of the ferry, a silent movement so quick and so unexpected that Ellie was not the only passenger to admit that she had at first doubted her own eyes. No splash was heard in the churning water close to the hull.

Perhaps their shouts to the crew were seconds too late, the

choking of the ferry's engine not fast enough. The young man had gone over the edge too close to the bow to have had any chance of swimming away safely. As soon as he hit the water he would have been sucked under and pulled towards the propellers, it was said later.

In the moments immediately afterwards, though, in the calm as the engine noise died and the ferry drifted, it seemed quite possible that he would be fished out spluttering, shrinking with embarrassment at the gangling weakness of his limbs, the idiocy of his stunt. Someone threw a life belt.

On deck, more passengers emerged from the cabin to lean over the rail, asking why the ferry had stopped. They were drawn to one another, wanting to help but frightened of getting in the way as the crew set about a rescue procedure.

Ellie did not speak French well enough to understand much of what they were saying, but it was clear that the middle-aged couple with a small yappy dog, the man carrying a briefcase, and the elderly woman were united in their furious incomprehension of the young man's actions. The man with the briefcase was particularly vocal, and his tirade sounded like condemnation. A man in a panama hat and loose white shirt hung slightly back, making no comment.

'Did you see what happened?' she asked him in English, hoping he would understand.

'Yes.'

'One moment he was fine. It didn't look as if anything was wrong. The next he was gone.'

'It's terrible.'

'Was it an accident, or—'

'He climbed over.'

There were shouts from the water, but they were not cries for help.

'Don't look,' said the man.

She turned away. Bright sunlit sails slid across the sapphire sea. A small aircraft cut across the sky.

Waves slapped against the port side of the ferry. A dinghy was quickly joined by a police launch. Shouting cut through the buzz of the crew's electronic communications. Falling cadences of conversation on deck marked the transition from irritation with the delay to understanding. The fear felt by all was primitive: the oldest sea story of all, the soul lost overboard.

A hundred years ago the ferry boat had been summoned to the mainland by smoke signal – the fire of resinous leaves and twigs lit in a brazier outside the café at the end of the Presqu'île de Giens, she remembered. It was the kind of detail she enjoyed, culled from the reading she had done in preparation for the trip. Now, within minutes, invisible modern signals brought the emergency services.

Ellie stood up and went over to the rail. Not for the first time, she wondered why she had come.

As it was, her arrival on the island was bound up with more immediate questions from the harbourmaster and two male police officers who boarded the ferry when it docked. Her first impressions of Porquerolles' fabled beauty were shot through with shock and a sense of waste. Oleanders and palms waved a subtropical greeting from the quayside, while the passengers were asked to give their names and contact details and to make statements before disembarkation. What had she noticed about the young man? Had he spoken to anyone? Had he seemed agitated, nervous? It seemed trite to reply that she had paid more attention to the vulgarity of his T-shirt than to the person wearing it.

She showed Lieutenant Franck Meunier where she had been sitting on deck, and approximately where he had been standing.

'Did he shout as he fell?' The police officer was all sharp eyes, buzz-cut hair and controlled strength. Not as young, close up, as he seemed when he came aboard. His English was good, though heavily accented.

'No. At least, I didn't hear him say anything.'

'Was he sweating, perhaps – had he taken drugs? Did you see his eyes?'

'I wasn't close enough to see. I don't know.'

5

The white and steel needles of the marina extended out to the ferry dock. A warm breeze rang with clinks of metal rigging. This shore felt far more foreign than the one they had left, as if the sea voyage had crossed much more than the few miles of the strait.

'Where are you staying on the island?'

'A hotel on the Place d'Armes.'

'Which one?'

She pulled a piece of paper out of her shoulder bag and handed it over, uncertain of the pronunciation.

'L'Oustaou des Palmiers,' read the officer.

She nodded.

'You are on holiday?'

'No. Business.'

He frowned, rubbing at his crew cut. His head looked newly shorn. 'What business?'

'I am a garden designer. I'm coming here to look at a garden tomorrow and meet a prospective client.'

Had she been less driven to prove herself, she might have turned the job down months before, on the grounds of impracticability. Any number of garden designers and landscape architects were better qualified to take on the restoration of a garden on a Mediterranean island; someone who – unlike her – already knew the terrain and was experienced in the dry heat, rocky soil and exoticism of the Riviera would have been the obvious choice. But spring in England had been dismal, a fleeting glimmer of sun in March and gone by April; the subsequent weeks of grey skies and rain had been unbearable. It was the simplest of urges that had brought her this far, on the journey up to London and beyond, the flight to Hyères: the need for heat and the light. Of course she was curious about the job too, and lured by the flattering terms of the invitation.

'Who is this client?'

'Laurent de Fayols. At the Domaine de Fayols.'

Lieutenant Meunier considered this, then looked back through his notes. 'When did you first see the man go to the deck rail?'

For what seemed like hours, pinned down on the motion-less ferry, Ellie gave answers that could offer nothing in the way of insight and could save no one. From the dock she could see pale beaches and low, verdant hills berried with red roofs. The fort above the harbour punched up a fist of stone through green trees. The sun was dazzling.

Finally she was allowed to go. She wiped a hand over her forehead and consulted the information and a map outside the tourist office on the quai. 'Average temperature for June, 20 degrees Celsius,' she read. It was only the beginning of June, and almost seven o'clock in the evening, yet it felt hotter. She set off wearily towards the Place d'Armes. The wheels of her travel bag, weighted by a laptop, a box file of sketches and photocopied material from old books, scraped along behind her.

It was a wide, dusty square dominated by a church with a distinctly Spanish look. Three sides were edged with eucalyp-tus and the canopies of restaurants and shops. She made her way round, moving slowly from pool to pool of harsh light and shadow towards what looked like a hotel at the far end. It was not the Oustaou des Palmiers. Nor were any of the other establishments – the apartment entrances or art galleries, the souvenir shops, or the bar that looked as if it would be crowded later, outside which a jazz guitarist now practised. She walked on past fruit stalls stacked with watermelons, apples, strawberries, bananas, pineapples, until she was back almost where she started. It was only then that she saw she had missed the hotel by a few metres when she arrived at the square. The sign was hidden under a red canopy and succulent green creepers that shaded tables laid outside for dinner.

Inside, the reception desk was a cramped counter under the stairs.

'I'm Jean-Luc,' said a young man who looked like a student dressed for the beach, shirt hanging open to expose a smooth, bare chest. He handed over the keys without consulting any paperwork. 'Anything you need, you can come and find me.'

Mercifully he asked nothing about her journey.

'And there is a message for you,' said Jean-Luc. He smiled and looked around vaguely in the small space behind the desk, as if he knew he had put it somewhere. 'Ah!' He seized on an envelope and handed it over.

'Thank you.'

'I will take you up.'

He picked up her bag as if it contained only air, bounded upstairs.

The room was better than she'd imagined, with simple decor and a harbour view. Jean-Luc bounced across the room – he walked in that elastic way of the young and very fit – to show her the air-conditioning control and compact bathroom. When he'd gone, she threw open the windows and stood for a while, trying to reconcile what had just happened with the pleasure boats swaying at anchor and, beyond, the sea of scudding white sails. Slipping her shoes off, she padded across bare polished floorboards.

She looked around for the envelope she'd been given and found it on the dressing table. Her name was written in ink, the hand bold yet elegant. It was a long time since she'd received a message written in fountain pen. Or any handwritten message. It all added to the feeling that she had stepped back in time on this island. She slid out the card. Her hands were still trembling slightly.

'I am very glad you have arrived safely,' she read. 'I look forward to seeing you at the Domaine de Fayols tomorrow morning. I will send transport for you at ten o'clock. Enjoy your first evening on our lovely island.

'Cordialement, Laurent de Fayols.'

What had made him do it, the boy in the T-shirt – what disturbance in the mind, or sickness, or terrible event had induced him to go over the edge, and so quietly? Had he intended to kill himself, or only to attract attention?

There could be no comfort in solitary thoughts in a single hotel room. She put her camera into her shoulder bag and headed outside. A rough concrete road led away from the main square and crumbled into dust that sifted into her open shoes as she walked through pines and Mexican cypress tall enough to deaden any sounds.

Even in her darkest moments she had never considered suicide. Not even in the agonizing weeks after Dan died, when she was struggling to process the loss. Her business was life: the nurturing of plants and the innate optimism involved in planning gardens that would not grow to meet her vision for years, decades even. It had been hard, but she had turned her grief into determination. Self-reliance, too. She had simply worked harder, investing in life. But perhaps other people could find neither the strength nor their own versions of her beech avenues and sculpted borders to watch over.

Where the path split, the beach was signposted: Plage d'Argent. The scent of pines, intensified by a dense heat, mingled with the unmistakably salty tang of the shore. Dan would have loved it: Porquerolles, the island of the ten forts. As a dedicated army man, he had been fascinated by any kind of military history. A tear escaped. He's gone, Ellie told herself for the thousandth time. Let him go. She had to let herself go too, push herself out into the unknown.

The sea nibbled at bone-white sand. She stood alone, lost in thought, where shallow ripples nudged shells into lace patterns across the beach.

2

~∘~

The Domaine

Monday, 3 June

In the morning sun, the Place d'Armes was an empty white expanse. Activity was confined to the shops and cafés under the trees. Ellie bought a guidebook and a large-scale map from the nearest *tabac* and sat on a low wall in the shade to open out the map. When she couldn't locate the Domaine de Fayols immediately, an unwarranted spike of panic rose. But there it was, marked on the southern rim of the island, close to a cove and a lighthouse. Until then she'd had only the word of Laurent de Fayols that the place would exist when she arrived.

By ten o'clock she was waiting outside the hotel. No cars were permitted on the island, and most people who passed were on bicycles: dented, clicking, cumbersome machines of uncertain vintage, used by countless people on countless holidays. The only alternative was a horse-drawn cart. Ellie watched as the driver jumped down and ran inside the hotel. Minutes later he came out with Jean-Luc, who waved her over.

'This will transport you to the Domaine de Fayols.'

The driver pulled her up into the seat next to him, his work-callused hand rough against hers as they touched, then he tutted and murmured to the elderly black horse, brushing its flank gently with the whip. They set off, swaying high above

10

the road. The wheels winnowed up puffs of dust that trailed the cart as it jolted along the track. Ellie clutched her bag and folders tightly.

Neither of them spoke. The driver kept his eyes ahead. Scrubby evergreen bushes released a strong scent of resin and honey; forests of pine gave way to gentle south-facing vineyards disturbed only by the ululation of early summer cicadas. Sitting up tall on the seat, she craned around eagerly to see what plants thrived naturally.

It was a wild and romantic place, Laurent de Fayols had written, the whole island once bought as a wedding gift to his wife by a man who had made his fortune in the silver mines of Mexico. One of three small specks in the Mediterranean known as the Golden Isles, after the oranges, lemons and grapefruit that glowed like lamps in their citrus groves.

There were few reference works in English that offered information beyond superficial facts about the island, and those she had managed to find were old. The best had been published in 1880, by a journalist called Adolphe Smith. Ellie had been struck by the loveliness of his 'description of the most Southern Point of the French Riviera':

> *The island is divided into seven ranges of small hills, and in the numerous valleys thus created are walks sheltered from every wind, where the umbrella pines throw their deep shade over the path and mingle their balsamic odour with the scent of the thyme, myrtle and the tamarisk.*

She inhaled deeply.

They turned off the track and up a drive spiked by Italian cypress. Soon the driveway opened onto a turning circle in front of the house. Inside the circle, in front of the house, stood a venerable olive tree surrounded by a bed of lavender. On either side of the house, towering pines, eucalyptus and more cypresses stood guard.

'*Ici, la Domaine*,' said the driver.

'*Merci*.'

Ellie accepted his chapped hand, and climbed down. The facade of the house was rendered in pale terracotta with butterfly-blue shutters. It was a substantial property, three storeys high, under a traditional tile roof. Sculpted clouds of box hedge in galvanised planters lined the steps to the front door.

She had hardly started to take it all in when her host emerged, advancing down the shallow stone steps with his hand extended. Laurent de Fayols must have been in his sixties, not particularly tall but slim and elegant, with deep brown eyes that she knew at once would be persuasive.

'Come in, come in, my dear Miss Brooke – and welcome! At last you will be able to see for yourself what we've been speaking about.'

There was no doubting his enthusiasm. His tanned face looked young behind designer sunglasses that he pushed onto the top of his head. Despite the heat, he had slung a jaunty yellow pullover across his shoulders.

'I can't wait.'

He led her into the house, across a hallway and through the centre of the house. A few moments of relative darkness, and they emerged on a wide terrace of pale stone. The sharpness of the sun made her blink, then her eyes adjusted to a glistening panorama of sky and sea framed by palms and parasol pines.

Ellie went straight to the balustrade. The flat area immediately below was broken up into a formal pattern of beds containing oleander and more clipped clouds of box, a southern imitation of the grand parterres of aristocratic chateaux. A rose garden beyond was the first in a series of gardens created on descending levels, apparently linked by a magnificently overgrown wisteria. Dense lines of cypress hid any farther areas from view, including the memorial garden that was her special brief. As a whole, the garden was charming, luxuriant, but – from a professional point of view – dilapidated.

'A great deal of work needed, *non*?' said Laurent.

She relaxed a little. At least he was under no illusions. And his command of English was even better than she remembered from his phone calls.

'Now, you will take coffee with me? Come!'

She found it hard to draw her eyes away from the exquisite vista. The light brought semi-tropical flowers into keen focus: spiked and veined and pulsing with life.

Laurent de Fayols led her along the terrace and around the corner. He had the brisk walk of the older man who takes pride in his fitness.

'This is west-facing,' he said. 'We sit here in the evening.'

Flaking pillars formed a wide loggia, an inviting spot. One wall was smothered by jasmine. On a table sat a coffee pot, cups, a jug of iced water and an untidy pile of papers weighted down by several old books with metal clasps.

'And you can still see the sea!' She wanted to swim there, immediately – she had a childlike surge of excitement at the sight of water so clear the rocks at the foot of the cliffs looked like clumps of turquoise flowers growing on the seabed.

'Yes, the position is perfectly chosen. That's the Calanque de l'Indienne down there. And this is the book I told you about on the telephone.'

With an effort, she returned her attention to her host. He pushed a tome the size of an atlas towards her across the table. The leather binding was scuffed, but the marbled endpapers were a startlingly vibrant red with no sign of damage. It was a photograph album full of foxed images of the garden – and of its makers. The figures pictured flanking the dark arches and horticultural opulence were dressed in heavy clothes that seemed to deny the heat and the density of the humidity. Here and there were blank pages between which botanical speci- mens had been pressed long ago; flowers that in life had once been extravagantly scented and vibrantly coloured were flat- tened and bleached on the page. Yet the shapes of these brown, crisped flowers – the canna lily, the agapanthus, the rose – spoke of succulence.

She accepted the small gold-rimmed cup of coffee that Laurent handed her.

'It's going to be quite a challenge.'

'I would not trust anyone who claimed this was an easy job.'

He came round the table and stood next to her. 'This is the memorial garden just after it was laid out in 1947, in memory of Dr Louis de Fayols' – he turned to the right page with an ivory letter opener – 'and here it is in bloom for the first time in 1948, though obviously the Italian cypresses are still small and the boxwood has yet to establish. But this shows very clearly the spaces in the planting.'

It was a formal garden designed around a *bassin* edged in stone, a rectangular pool captured as a sheet of black in the photograph. A carved stone bench of Italianate design was placed at one narrow end. At the other stood two lichened statues, one that might have been Venus, the other Mercury, to judge from the wings on his ankles. A large stone urn was placed in each corner of the garden. No flowers had yet been planted.

'Typical of its time,' she mused. 'So many of the grand gardens were created when the Riviera was populated by rich foreigners – who wanted outdoor temples to wealth and the imagination.'

'I know you have the sensitivity to do this.'

It was not the first time Laurent de Fayols had invoked her sensitivity. She took note. Sometimes when clients spoke about her qualities, they were really speaking about themselves.

'You have a sense of history, too,' he went on. 'You respect that.'

'If you mean the Chelsea garden,' she said, knowing full well that he did, 'that was very different. It was a modern impression of an era, not historical fact – a stage set, if you like.'

The exhibition garden she had designed for the Chelsea Flower Show, gold-medal-winning and much admired in the media, had brought in more business than she could take on, and a host of misconceptions.

'Of course. You know I'm not looking for you to reproduce that. It was the small details in War Garden that spoke to me. The gramophone. The woman's jacket hanging on the spade

14

in the tiny vegetable patch. The crinkled photograph of the soldier, and the man's cigarette case left as a keepsake.'

She'd opened her mouth to protest when he pre-empted her. 'I know. That is not garden design, it is more . . . a piece of theatre. But trust me, I saw that you were the person I had been looking for. Young, with fresh ideas.'

'Well, it's a question of understanding the period, doing the right research.' And it was true, she did enjoy that aspect. 'I have been poring over old books in the British Library for references, but there are very few. The best I've found is a description of the island's indigenous plants in a Victorian travel account.'

It didn't amount to much, but it had probably been *Delphinium requienii*, *Genista linifolia* and *Cistus porquerollensis* that lured her here to discuss the commission.

He was looking out at the garden, where exotic tree ferns unfurled like frozen green fountains on a path down to the shore. Impossible to guess what he was thinking. The sea breeze lifted tendrils of jasmine. So close to the sea, the scent was intoxicating: a heady blend of salt and musky sweetness. Ellie felt a wave of conviction that it was all possible. The restoration of the memorial garden could be achieved, the realignment of the great archways and evergreen walls, the reinvigoration of the rose garden.

Laurent leafed through a few more pages of photographs and stopped at one that revealed a doorway cut into a hedge, edged by topiary of a monumental triumphal arch.

'That is spectacular,' said Ellie.

'It stands at the southern end of the memorial garden. It wasn't yet made in the first photograph.'

'Is it still there?'

'The remains of it – very damaged now, but I can show you the place.'

'I'm curious to know what's on the other side of the arch. It draws the eye in and makes the visitor want to walk through.'

He tapped his nose, then winked. 'Now you are interested, yes?'

She gave him a smile, feeling that they were beginning to connect.

This was the aim of an initial meeting with a potential client: to understand exactly what he hoped to achieve. The garden designer – like an architect – was the practical means of bringing the client's imagination to life. For that to happen, there had to be an understanding based on a clear sense of the pictures in his mind; but also, and perhaps trickier, there had to be a personal relationship. The connection between designer and client was crucial to the success of any project, and the lack of it very often a precursor to failure.

Laurent led the way back to the terrace. 'After you,' he said when they reached the first of two wide stone staircases down into the formal parterre. Closer up, the box hedging clipped into interlocking patches was brown and patchy.

Through the rose garden, the path ran straight ahead to the mass of mauve wisteria, now past its best. At ground level, Ellie could see now that it formed a tunnel leading deeper into the garden, gnarled trunks growing over a long wooden frame that was rotten in places. At the end was a green space the size of a large room, walled by a hedge of clipped myrtle. From all sides white trumpets of datura hung down, smelling faintly of coffee.

'I've never seen such a display,' said Ellie.

'My mother planted them many years ago. Moonflowers.'

'Also known as devil's trumpet.'

'Angel's trumpet, too. Or so she told me.'

One garden opened from another in a series of secret rooms. Stone steps were made treacherous by creeping ivy. As they walked on, rotting leaves seeped from unexpectedly dank corners. The temperature dropped. There were no more flowers.

'And this is the memorial garden.'

It was a temple of darkest evergreen, scattered with an artless arrangement of broken pillars and statuary. The statues of Venus and Mercury were bigger than life-size. Mercury no longer had wings on his ankles, only tumours of lichen.

'That's astonishing . . . like ruins left by the Greeks or Romans.'

'The doctor was a great classicist. Some of the wells we have here were sunk by the Greeks and then forgotten under the scrub. He was very proud of reviving them.'

The water in the stone *bassin* was a black mirror, then silver as she went closer. Its magnetic stillness drew her in.

'Tell me more about the doctor – he was your father, grand-father? – and how he came to the island.'

'My father's uncle, in fact.' He stared out again, as if picturing the old man in the grounds of his estate. 'You know already that Porquerolles has a long military history?'

She nodded. 'The island of ten forts, a strategic defence for the south coast of France.'

'Used for centuries as a retreat for old soldiers and army convalescents. During the Crimean War, it was a hospital camp for wounded soldiers, and there was an orphanage there for many years for the children of the fallen.

'A hundred years ago, M Fournier, the man who bought Porquerolles with the fortune he made in the silver mines of Mexico, began all kinds of agricultural enterprises. He planted the first vineyard. But he wanted to be a benefactor too. He kept open the convalescent centre and brought his own doctor to run it. When Fournier died in 1935, leaving a widow and seven children, the presence of the doctor was all the more im-portant for her peace of mind. The Domaine was built as one of the farms for the Fournier estate, but the widow Fournier set it aside for the doctor and his family.'

'Is it still part of the estate?'

'No, it was bought by the doctor after Fournier died.'

'It's a huge house – did he have a large family?'

'Two sons.'

He hesitated.

'Your father's cousins, then . . . did neither of them want to take on the Domaine?'

'Both were killed in the war.'

Ellie pressed her eyes closed. 'That's awful, I'm sorry . . .' It was a feeble response, but she never knew what to say, how to put her feelings into words to a stranger. What could anyone say? 'But this garden commemorates the doctor, not the sons?'

'That's right.'

'So who was responsible for creating it?'

'My father. And the man who had been the head gardener here in the golden era before the war. Both of them wanting to honour the past in their different ways. When my parents took over the property, it was in a terrible state. The island was occupied during the war, and all the Porquerollais and French were evacuated. First the Italians, then the Germans. They showed no respect, none at all. The islanders came back to find their houses plundered or blown up, furniture reduced to matchwood. Boats had been destroyed, vines pulled up, citrus trees scythed to stumps . . . it took a long time to restore and redress the balance.'

Ellie shivered. No wonder; she was standing in deep shade. She rubbed her arms and moved towards the few rays of sun that penetrated the overhang.

'Here is the doorway and arch in the photograph.'

It had once been cut with precision. Now the yew hedging was half dead. A cavelike hole gaped where the doorway had once been, and the dark pillars of cypress seemed to hide something behind them rather than stand guard, as they did elsewhere.

Ellie stooped and pushed through.

The grounds ran down to the sea, through wind-twisted pines, crumbling rocks and the unexpectedly lush green of the bushes and trees that held fast to every scrap of earth. On a cliff to her right was the lighthouse. Now she understood the way the house sat on its land, with the open sea to the south and the rocky bay of the Calanque de l'Indienne to the south-west.

The warmth poured over her like hot water. The wide blue sky and lustrous sea were all light and space. For a few heady seconds she felt a sense of freedom more intense than she had ever experienced.

They walked back slowly towards the house.

The sunlight could not quite dispel the difference in atmosphere now that she had seen the interior of the garden. It was as if a dark underside had been revealed that changed the cast of the whole property. But the whimsy of it, the way the eye was drawn down through every vista, the inventiveness, the fairy-tale quality, the melancholy of the lost gardens – it all excited her.

A summer dining room, shaded by a vigorous vine, had been created at the far end of the terrace. One long wall, perhaps the wall of the kitchen garden, was roughly washed with yellow ochre. A row of kumquat trees stood in glossy black pots, tiny orange fruit trembling in dark foliage.

Laurent pulled out a chair for her. The table was set for two.

A thin woman of about fifty came out to serve them. Silver threads shone in her black hair, pulled back severely with a large bar clip.

'Is Mme de Fayols not joining us, Jeanne?'

'She sends her apologies, monsieur.'

'I thought you said your wife would be in Paris,' said Ellie, conversationally.

'My mother.'

A muted clatter of lid and serving spoons.

'Is she unwell?' he asked in French, turning to Jeanne.

'No more than usual.'

At least that was what Ellie thought they said. Jeanne served a delicate tart of tomato and caramelised onion. A leaf salad with light tangy dressing. Grilled crayfish. She left the table.

'My mother will be disappointed not to be able to meet you straight away. But there will be plenty of other opportunities. Now, eat! Some wine? Water?'

Ellie took a small glass of rosé.

As they ate, her mood lifted again. She found herself warming to him, and to his enthusiasm. She sensed a dash of mischief. His wife lived mainly in Paris, he told her, close to her spiritual home of fine clothes and the arts, trips to the opera on the arm of a young walker, light lunches beneath crystal chandeliers. It was clear the arrangement suited them both. Ellie assumed that Laurent would have his own attachments in the south.

'This property is my passion,' he said, as if reading her mind disconcertingly accurately. 'If I have a mistress, she is here.'

He took a sip of wine and dabbed the corners of his mouth with a starched white napkin. 'So . . . tell me what more I can do to persuade you to accept the commission.'

'I'd like to walk in the garden alone this afternoon. I want to get a sense of the place, and to think about how the new parts and the restoration might work. Perhaps just look at the other plants, in the shade as well as the sun, to understand how it all fits together. Then I will do some preliminary drawings to scale.

'Also, I need to work out what irrigation is available. I'm assuming there is, or has been in the past, some kind of watering system. Everything is possible, of course, but with a job like this we have to start at the beginning, and the first investment may be to put in new irrigation pipes. We could spend a fortune on a library of the right plants, but without water we would lose them as soon as they go into the ground.'

He waved away that concern. 'There is a source linked to a channel under the first myrtle hedge. It's never been a problem before. I can send someone down to show you. Now, I must attend to some other matters. You are welcome to spend as long as you like here.'

The first task was to survey the site and take precise measurements. Then she photographed the memorial garden from every angle. Close to the house she found a ladder that she propped behind the hedge and climbed to achieve a view of the whole area. She downloaded the photos onto her laptop and began to make a series of loose sketches by hand on tracing paper.

Her instincts were to respect the set pieces of the garden

– the central stone pool, the high green walls, the position of the statues, the grand exit – but to soften the hard edges with planting that added a modern depth. It was important to stay to see how the sun set over the land, to walk up the hill and look down, considering which plants and colour schemes would be most effective.

Hours passed. Ellie made templates for more sketches and then lost herself in the garden. Now that she was on her own, undistracted, the grounds seemed so much larger than they had only a few hours before. Absorbed in her work, she felt calm. Was one of the attractions of garden design the imposition of order on an unruly natural world? If so, there was plenty to engage her here. As ever, once the client had left her to her own devices she could see more clearly.

The sound of footsteps approaching startled her. Someone had come into the maze of garden rooms. Anticipating the employee Laurent de Fayols had said would show her the water source, she was already smiling as she turned around. She waited, then called out, 'Hello? I'm in here!'

No one answered.

She walked over to the remains of the grand topiary arch, lured by the perfection of the view: the sea; the clouds of umbrella pines and cistus, with its evening fragrance of warm amber; the artful framing of the lighthouse. She was so quietly transfixed that when a bird cawed above she turned, too abruptly.

A jab of pain; a deep scratch to her arm oozed blood. She looked around. One struggling bloom of palest pink in the ragged green doorway revealed an old shoot of rose studded with vicious thorns.

The sun was setting behind a line of trees; it cast a great bird's wing halfway across the field when she finally headed back towards the house. In the warm shade of the first enclosed garden, the datura plants were already releasing pulses of their heady night scent. The coffee aroma of earlier was now a burnt chocolate and earthy spice smell that would deepen with the

21

night. Ellie felt a burning sensation in her nose, like mustard.

She met no one. The prosaic accoutrements of the garden – the lengths of hosepipe, ladders, wheelbarrow, rakes and rolls of twine – were left scattered along the way like clues to a treasure hunt.

The terrace was empty, too. She crossed into the semi-darkness of the sitting room. A flicker of movement drew her eye to a row of display cabinets to her left as she passed. Rows of exotic butterflies and moths were pinned fast to the velvet backdrops, their exuberant wings as regimented and inert in death as they would have been chaotic and fluttering in life. Ellie paused by their fragile corpses and felt a surge of irrational fear.

She rationalised it as the after-effects of what had happened on the crossing. In recent months her grief for Dan had lost some of its rawness; now it had broken wide again. If she were to be honest, she had felt on edge since she arrived on the island.

A fire was burning in the grate under a stone mantel. Who would want a fire in early summer? But she saw now that it was the reflections of this fire that had made the flickering movement on the glass-fronted cabinets. She stood still for a few moments, disconcerted by her own overreaction, wondering where to look for Laurent, whether to go into the hall and call out.

After the searing sun of the morning, followed by the enclosed dark shade of the garden in the afternoon, the light in this immense room pooled around set pieces of furniture. In front of the fireplace stood an armchair, a side table and an antique sofa. Beyond was a baby grand piano illuminated by a standard lamp. A painting was lit by an overhead light bar that spilled polished gold across a console table.

A tap-tap-tapping echoed on stone.

Ellie started.

'Qui est là?'

A very old woman was standing in the doorway, propped on a cane. Her breath came in waves of exertion, a sound like the sea breaking on the shore and receding.

22

'It's . . . I'm . . . Ellie Brooke – the garden designer.'

The woman tapped her way to the armchair by the fire. She was thin to the point of emaciation; the legs that took her across the room and lowered her tentatively into her seat were sticklike as a crane's. She waved away Ellie's offer of help.

Settled at last, she propped the walking cane against the side table. It had a striking horn handle, curving to a point.

'I thought you were long gone,' said the woman in English. Only the mouth moved; the rest of her frail body was a statue.

'I didn't realise it was so late.'

'You gave me a fright. Come closer.'

Ellie approached.

'Be so kind as to put that light on.'

There was a lamp on the table. Ellie reached under the shade and found the switch. The illumination burst between them. Ellie found herself staring intently at the deeply lined face in front of her. The eyebrows were pencilled arcs, very nearly hairless.

'Come back into the light where I can see you.'

She narrowed her eyes as Ellie did as she asked. Ellie felt the examination, every inch of it. The breath, too close, was dry and powdery with a sweet violet note that did not quite mask the rotten whisper of dental decay. Ellie resisted the impulse to pull back.

Mme de Fayols – for there was no doubt that was who she was – gave her a hard look, seemed to start to say something and then decided against it. A clock ticked loudly, and the fire cracked and popped.

'How will you get back to the mainland?'

'I don't need to, actually – I'm staying at a hotel.'

'Back to the village, then.'

Ellie hadn't thought.

Mme de Fayols extended an eagle's claw from her sleeve and rang a tiny bell.

The housekeeper came at a brisk trot. They conferred rapidly.

'Jeanne's husband will take you back.'

23

'Is M de Fayols here? I should thank him.'

'No, he is gone,' said Jeanne.

'Oh. Well, good night, then,' Ellie offered.

The response was a dismissive raise of the hand. There was no sign of Laurent on the way out. At the front door, Ellie wondered whether the horse and cart would be brought round again. But the driver who had collected her that morning roared up on a quad bike, pulling a small trailer in which two people could sit.

She climbed in, greeting him, but although he acknowledged her thanks, he remained as taciturn as ever.

The noise of the engine cut crudely through the tranquil evening. They passed pale sandy tracks, some that disappeared intriguingly into pine forest, others that reached down to the sea. Gradually the grey-blue outline of the mainland melted into the twilight.

The police officer from the ferry was sitting at one of the outside tables at the hotel. He was drinking a glass of wine and reading the newspaper. Ellie nodded to him in recognition, but it was only when he stood up and indicated the seat beside him that she realised he had been waiting for her.

'I have to ask you some more questions about the mortal incident,' said Lieutenant Meunier, without any preamble beyond a cursory inquiry after her day. 'The prosecutor at the Port of Toulon has requested more information.'

She was tired, in need of a shower and beginning to feel hungry. 'All right.'

Meunier was as bright-eyed and bushy-tailed as before. 'You may have seen in the evening newspaper that the dead man has been named. Florian Creys, nineteen years old. A student from Strasbourg.'

'I haven't seen the newspaper.'

'The journalist spoke to some of the passengers who were on the ferry. One of them now says that the dead man may have been pushed.'

'I don't think that can be right. He was standing alone.'

'The witness says that he was standing with a man wearing a straw hat.'

'That is not what I saw. But I was not looking at the . . . young man all the time.'

The lieutenant squared his broad sportsman's shoulders. 'So it could be possible that he was pushed.'

'That's not what I said. I am sure that I saw him climb over the rail and go over the side. He was alone then, but I suppose he might have been standing next to someone before that.'

'You were looking at him at the exact moment he went over?'

Ellie fiddled with the pendant around her neck, then stopped as soon as she realised what she was doing. 'He was in my field of vision. I wasn't staring at him, but he was part of the picture in front of me.'

'You are certain of this?'

'Well, as certain as I can be.'

Under close questioning, however, the picture in her mind did not seem as robust as it had been. She judged it unwise to say so. Best to go with her instincts that her memory was true.

'Did you see a man on the deck wearing a straw hat?'

'Yes . . . there was a man in a panama hat.'

'Did you see him standing close to the deceased man?'

'No.'

'At no time?'

'No.'

'Did you speak to the man wearing the hat?'

'Actually . . . yes. I did.'

'What did you say?'

'I can't remember. No, wait . . . I think I asked him whether he had seen what just happened. He said he had – he had seen.'

'And then?'

'He told me not to look.'

'What did he mean when he said that?'

'I thought he meant that something terrible was now visible in the water. Something that I wouldn't want to see.'

Meunier wrote it down. 'Do you know who this man is?'

'I only saw him on the boat.'

'Describe him.'

Ellie gazed past the policeman, feeling oddly detached from the tables and chairs under the red awning and the sparse sandy square that she recognised now as an old military parade ground. The Place d'Armes – of course.

'He was quite tall – about six inches . . . sorry, er . . . fifteen centimetres taller than I am. Dark hair, dark eyes, olive skin. Good-looking. Late thirties, early forties, that kind of age.'

'Nationality?'

'French, I assumed. Didn't you interview him?'

He ignored her question. 'Did you notice anything else about this man?'

She shook her head. 'He wore a loose white shirt, stylish in a very casual way. That's all. I wasn't really concentrating on him at the time.'

Meunier pushed his card across the table. 'If you see him again, please call me as soon as you can.'

She had intended to eat a quick supper and spend the rest of the evening working on her preliminary sketches. But once up in her room, she lay on the bed, exhausted. How could someone say that Florian Creys was pushed when she was certain he had been standing alone? Why hadn't the police interviewed the man in the panama hat while they were all still on the ferry? She tried to remember if she had seen him after he told her not to look at the water. Remembering the shouts from below made her shudder. She was looking away, as he had urged her, concentrating fiercely on the sailing boats in the distance, not quite able to subdue the horrors her imagination was producing. She did not speak to him again. Whether he was still on deck after the ferry restarted, she could not recall. In that case, he probably was not.

And if someone was saying that Florian Creys was pushed – he had definitely not been pushed, unless her memory was completely false – had that person also told the police that the man in the hat was responsible?

She shut her eyes, trying to still her mind. But the gardens provided the next wave of questions. Could she work with Laurent de Fayols? Was he as affable as he seemed; were his expectations realistic? Why hadn't he employed a French designer? If she accepted the job, would she be able to give effective instructions to the landscape contractors; would they be able to source the right plants? Then there was the encounter with Mme de Fayols. What was it about the old woman and that firelit room that had made her so uneasy?

Ellie pictured the dark yew garden room and felt its green walls closing in. She trusted her instincts, and was unsettled by the implications.

Inevitably her thoughts turned back to Dan, thoughts she failed to avoid. What were you supposed to do when someone you had been closer to than anyone in the world was no longer part of your life? When his absence was ever-present in empty seats and the cold, wide space in the bed, in the phone calls that went unmade, the observations unsaid and the landscapes unshared? Two years since he passed away, and his loss seemed harder than ever to deal with.

He had come into her life with the force of an accident, and left it with equal abruptness. Four years together. Not nearly long enough.

She hadn't been looking for anyone like Dan, wouldn't have known where to start looking, but when he stopped his car – stopped dead – in front of hers and ran off into the crowds on the pavement, she had no choice but to stop too, preferably before the bonnet of her VW went any farther into the boot of his Audi. She was late as it was for a meeting with a man called Ivell, an expert in rare British plants; Dan was only just in time to save the life of a man who was having a heart attack in the middle of Chichester High Street.

Ellie watched as Dan ripped open the man's coat and began to pump his chest, while a knot of helpless passers-by formed. 'Call an ambulance,' he shouted. Her mobile was already in her hand.

He was an army medic, a surgeon, he told her as they swapped insurance details.

'Hardwired for decisive action,' she said, trying not to flirt and failing. At least the patient was coming round as the paramedics arrived.

Dan grinned. 'We're a bit reckless with the machinery when we have to be. Sorry.'

Hers were not the only admiring glances, Ellie noticed. He was tall and blond, with a loosely confident stance.

'Can I buy you a coffee to apologise?' he asked.

'That would be great – oh, but I can't, I'm late as it is. It's work, and—'

'It's important, I understand.'

He was wearing a soft flannel shirt, the shade of a cornflower, which she would come to know as his favourite. Darker blue eyes crinkled in amusement.

'You've got my number,' she said.

Two months later, they moved into the cottage near Arundel together.

She twisted the ring on her finger. Rubies and seed pearls, bought in the Lanes in Brighton for her thirtieth birthday. She wore it always, along with the pearl pendant.

Even now she could hardly bear to hear the news from Afghanistan, the terrible roll call of the dead that would not stop. The dread had been ever-present that she would hear his name one day. When the Afghan shell hit the yard outside the hospital at Camp Bastion, he was coming off duty, having saved three lives on the operating table. Captain Dan Wensley, with his contagious good humour, the hair that always stuck up in odd places and the startling blue eyes, the mouth that always seemed on the point of a smile and could kiss her like no other, the broad shoulders and the manner that asserted without words that he was in charge and you would be safe with him. His life was taken in an instant. A freak incident. They happened, and they blasted the heart of families, relationships, normal life. There were still times when she felt only half alive, either too sensitive or too numbed to feel normal.

She woke at two in the morning, unable to understand where she was or why she was lying down in her work clothes. Something was wrong, but she didn't know what it was – then consciousness formed, followed by the same old heart-shiver and the leaden dread.

Dan. The boy on the boat. The garden. She was shaking slightly, just a tremor. At six o'clock she gave up on the idea of more sleep and went for a run. It was only when she was passing the empty reception cubbyhole that it occurred to her the main door would be locked and she might not be able to get out without calling someone. But it opened easily when she tried the handle.

The air was pleasantly fresh as she broke into a jog, map in hand. On the Pointe de Lequin, twenty minutes east along the coastal path, she stopped, allowed her heart rate to fall as she surveyed the strait. The hills of the mainland were sharply defined in the way the world can look after disrupted sleep. Somewhere close by was the eighteenth-century Batterie de Lequin and, farther round the headland, the Fort de l'Alycastre, built under Richelieu – two of the ten forts left that formed a defensive front along the rocky north coast against the island's many invaders over the centuries.

She resumed her run, pushing herself harder.

3

The Lighthouse

Tuesday, 4 June

Ellie ate breakfast outside the hotel under the red awning, concentrating on the pleasures of perfect flaky croissants and greengage jam with strong, rich coffee.

After the run, she felt more positive about both herself and the garden commission. Five days was a reasonable time to assess the plot and the landscape and the scale of the job at the Domaine de Fayols, and to present a professional folder of preliminary sketches; whether it was long enough to get the measure of Laurent de Fayols, she wasn't so sure.

The air was already hot and close. She stuffed a swimsuit into her bag along with her notebook and papers and marched down towards the harbour and the cycle hire shop. The machine they offered her had five simple gears and a comfortably well-used saddle. She nodded, pleased to have a measure of independence from the unpredictable modes of transport offered by the de Fayols estate.

A wide path led out of the village, past signs to beaches she had still not visited. She took the long way round, wanting to see more of the west side of the island and to work out exactly how the Domaine de Fayols sat in the landscape. The bicycle tyres crunched on small sandy stones as she followed the trail between green oak and pines: the Aleppo and the parasol pine. She spotted an *arbutus*, a strawberry tree, and pulled off the path to have a closer look.

On the south-western side of the island the path opened out into a small bay, reinforced by jagged rocks. All seemed at peace. It was too early in the year for tourist hordes; here was freedom from the modern world, for a while at least. There was a timelessness about being on an island so small that it seemed closed in on itself; the sense of being adrift, not quite connected to the rest of the world.

She pedalled along the coast path to the Calanque de l'Indienne. It was a small bay rather than a cliff inlet. On the west side was the lighthouse; on the other, the house at the Domaine de Fayols rose above the trees and green terraces of its garden. Ellie dismounted. Small brown crickets scattered as she walked the bike across tough grass.

On the sea below a boat was tied up by the end of a steep path; the turquoise water was so clear that the hull was fully visible over the pale ghosts of submerged rock.

From here, trees screened the high dark hedges that surrounded the memorial garden and the other outdoor rooms. Those gardens still puzzled her: the sense that they were the wrong structures in the wrong place persisted. Why would anyone have wanted to enclose gardens in this place of wide horizons in the first place? It didn't make sense, but perhaps she was overthinking. Perhaps there was no reason, or it was deliberately counter-intuitive. Perhaps not until the reconstruction began would the answers become obvious. She had only the faded photographs to work from, and they were like looking into tarnished mirrors.

Some of the sculptural elements clearly held some past meaning, plotting the line back to the past and the doctor's passion for ancient history. But surely that could have been achieved more naturally in more open spaces, like the classical temples built on hillsides surrounded by light and air? If it had been left to her to create from scratch, she might well have chosen the same site above the sea, but the design would have embraced the elements and announced itself proudly. As it was, the memorial garden was hidden away like a secret to be protected.

She made a few notes, a quick sketch of an arch that might frame rather than block the sea view, while alluding to the heavy original. When she looked up again, a man was watching her from the de Fayols side of the bay.

It might have been Laurent, so she waved. He did not respond.

The lighthouse was set on a great solid base, like a chimney rising from a bunker. What looked elegantly well proportioned when framed by the arch of the memorial garden was a monumental structure closer up.

Ellie pushed the bicycle towards it. Birds shrieked from high trees, among them the Wasp-eater, the Thin-Beak and the Stormy Petrel, according to the guidebook. Giant fennel plants, showstoppers of the plant kingdom, offered globes composed of hundreds of yellow flowers; the towering stalks of these relatives of the hemlock contained a resin that could sicken grazing livestock and even kill. There was no sign of livestock here.

She walked around two sides of the lighthouse before she saw the door. The handle was rusty, but it opened easily.

Inside was a tiny museum – or rather, as there were few display cases but a considerable number of photographs and framed information sheets on the walls, a simple room offering a potted history of the lighthouse.

Ellie reached instinctively for her notebook, already scanning the walls for a complementary mirror view across the bay to the Domaine de Fayols.

The largest photograph was garlanded with a draped French flag with a plaque bearing the date 22 August 1944. It showed the lighthouse dirty and run-down. To the left of this was a poster-size photograph, with a bilingual caption, of Senegalese troops led by General Magnan, breaching the beach defences to liberate the island under covering fire from

American marines in their corvettes. To the right was another large photograph, of a line of islanders walking into the Place d'Armes led by the Abbé le Cuziat. According to the caption, they broke spontaneously into a rendition of 'La Marseillaise', the song echoing in the still air as the stout abbot hurried to the bell tower from which he raised the tricolour. Several houses on the left side of the square, as well as the beautiful Fournier house known as Le Château, were still smouldering in the wake of the departing Germans.

On a glass-topped table in front of these was a large, open ledger filled with rows of dates and figures, open to August 1944. A pair of well-worn gloves was attributed to Henri Rousset, the guardian of the lighthouse and recipient of the cross of the Légion d'Honneur in recognition of his heroic wartime actions.

Ellie spent a few more minutes looking around but found no connections to the Domaine across the bay. She pulled the door closed after her and walked slowly to the edge of the cliff.

Patchy rock and scrub stretched out in the sun like old animals that were losing their fur. She almost tripped over a tall stone, so dazzling was the light. She looked down at her feet and saw that the stone had been placed deliberately by the path. Sunk into it was a lead plaque that read:

> *Angelo, bel Angelo Gabriel*
> *Se tu non festi un angelo*
> *Non vole resti in Ciel*
> *Chanson*

The sun pulsed ever warmer on her skin. Ellie stared down with a sudden sense of joy, which just as quickly dissipated, as if she had been on the brink of some profound understanding that fled from any scrutiny. It was the thought of war, she rationalised, like the death of the boy on the ferry. Everything led back to Dan. The loss and terror was the same, whether that war raged within the pages of picture books, fought with chariots and winged horses and pomegranate seeds against the dark powers of the underworld, or with cannonballs sent from ships to Napoleonic forts on islands, or in the searing deserts of Helmand.

She wished she believed in silent communication, in delicate signs that some spirits still burned, but she did not.

Yet something made her look back, up at the lighthouse lamp, and the words came into her head: *the light of the world.* The thought caught her by surprise. She had never been particularly religious, even less so after Dan.

The man was standing quite still, studying her.

He was about ten metres away, maybe less. His hands were pushed deep into the pockets of baggy trousers. It was hard to make out his features in the glare of the late-morning sun. Her first thought was that he had something to do with the lighthouse, that he had come to ask her whether she wanted to make a donation to the home-made museum. She opened her mouth to give a tentative '*Bonjour*' but replaced it with a weak smile when he backed away. His retreat was curiously mocking, his palms held up in apology. She felt stupid, as if she had made some groundless accusation.

She looked away. Could he be the man she had waved to across the bay? She tried to recapture the scene in her mind, but it refused to materialise.

When she looked up a moment later, he had gone.

'I had another idea last night. It came to me after you left,' said Laurent de Fayols. 'What do you think about a garden landscaped to be seen from the air?'

They were in a book-lined library, mercifully cool and softly lit after the harsh morning sun over the sea. Her photographs and sketches of the memorial garden were spread across a table.

'It would be a piece of fun, with a serious purpose,' Laurent went on, obviously enthused. 'You have heard, I imagine, of Jacques Simon? No? OK, so since the early 1990s he was involved with what they call land art. Jacques Simon planted fields so that their designs and pictures could be visible from the air. Mainly these fields were on land close to airports, so they came into view when the planes took off and landed.'

This was so different from what they had previously discussed that she was at a loss. 'You think you might want to try a design like that here?'

'There are many pleasure flights around here – it might even be a clever way of getting publicity for the wine we make.'

Ellie hesitated, feeling blindsided. He seized on her bewilderment to usher her out of the room, onto the terrace and down into the grounds. 'Come, come! You'll see what I mean.'

Instead of taking the wisteria walkway towards the memorial garden, he led her through orchards of apricots, peaches, nectarines and almonds, trying to explain his vision for this set piece as they approached the vineyard.

It would have to be cleverly done, she thought, with reliable plants, but why not? If it was done well, it would be the talking point of the garden, and would generate good publicity for her as well as the vineyards at the Domaine de Fayols. It would be a unique, modern creation. As a commission it had some distinct advantages over the historical restoration.

'All right . . . I'm just thinking out loud here . . . If you want to dream up the kind of picture you'd like, then I'm very happy to discuss the practicalities, how it might be achieved. You want this as an alternative to the memorial restoration?'

'No, in addition, of course. I'm not sure yet how I want it to look. It's just the beginning of an idea at the moment, you understand.'

'Of course.'

As she looked up, a small plane passed overhead. A white scratch opened across the dense blue of the sky.

'Gardens have always been about history and symbolism,' said Laurent. 'The earthly paradise, the enclosed retreat from a cruel outside world.'

'I agree. That's the fascinating dimension—'

'I knew you would see it that way!'

'But' – she struggled to find a way of putting it diplomatically – 'this is completely new . . . not at all what I was prepared for.' Only a day into the project, and Laurent was already revealing himself to be one of those maddeningly indecisive clients who constantly change their minds.

'But I believe in you, Miss Brooke. I have no doubt that you could achieve anything you wanted. And it is not impossible, is it?'

She pulled a face. 'It can certainly be done,' she said when she saw how optimistic he was. So it could be, though it would require considerable extra work. 'Can you describe what you have in mind?'

He rattled off ideas. He took her through the types of vines planted on the estate: *monistel, grenache, queue-de-renard, clairette-pointu, cinsault, rosé d'Aramon*. He proposed they taste the wines; she could study the subtle differences in their colour; it would be an amusement that she would enjoy.

But before they even reached the vineyard, Laurent veered off on yet another path. 'Come, I want to show you what remains of the Greek wells . . . That part of the estate opens up some most interesting possibilities . . .'

She left that afternoon with an aching head. Whenever she had tried to discuss the memorial restoration, Laurent had quickly reverted to his new agenda, to advertise the vineyard from the air. His vision involved a river of red and pink to represent the abundant flow of wine. An interesting idea, but Ellie had to consider the practicalities. Rivers of lavender had been done. Waves of red, though – planted with what? Roses, pelargoniums, dark red oleanders? The best designs were all about patterns and playfulness, though there was a line between creative ingenuity and silly excess. And what about the labour-intense maintenance each year, and the poor longevity of such a scheme? Even a river of lavender would only last for a decade or so without careful tending.

Close to the most north-westerly point of the island, the wooded path sloped gently to meet the tideless sea. The beach was empty. She swam at last in the sea, feeling herself revive in water that slipped around her limbs like satin sheets.

Birds pecked at the shoreline. At one point someone else came down to the sand, then a dog ran past. The next time she looked back, both dog and owner had gone.

Her arms felt strong as she made for the rocks at the arm of the bay. The water was so clear it was like a discovery of a silent new world of cave entrances and subterranean flowers. A deeper dive, and she would be able to touch the bed. A few kicks, and she went down. She was almost there when, from nowhere, the thought welled up that she might never make it up again. She stroked harder, watching her own pale arms draw closer to a constellation of starfish, a night sky above a coral garden.

A dull pain in her chest intensified. The water darkened all around her, and she panicked. If she didn't act now, she would lose consciousness. She turned back, in a sunlight-shattering, froth-churning, choking rush for the surface. As she broke the water, the thought came to her: you nearly drowned.

She splashed to the nearest rock and held on, panting, blinking the salt from her eyes. She was fine. How ridiculous. Nothing was wrong. Yet the feeling persisted, hardening into an image of her own body on the seabed, the only movement from her hair waving slowly like weeds.

To prove her vitality, she swam crawl and backstroke until the sky was catching fire.

Shops and restaurants lined the harbour waterfront like a string of amber beads in the gathering night. To the whicker of bicycles moving past, returning sailors leapt from their yachts and shouted greetings and gathered to relay news of the day's winds and triumphs.

Ellie parked the bicycle outside the hire shop.

'You want again for tomorrow?' asked the proprietor.

'Yes, please.'

'You have a nice time?'

'Very nice, thank you.'

She realised she was relieved to be among other people – people who were not scrutinising her – and to have a friendly, inconsequential exchange. Back in her room at the Oustaou, she checked the messages on her mobile as her laptop powered up. There were a couple of messages; she called the office first.

Her business partner, Sarah – the May of Brooks May – picked up on the second ring. 'At last! I've been trying to get hold of you, and it kept going straight through to voicemail.' It was reassuring to hear Sarah's voice, to visualise the red curls bobbing as she tried to do six tasks with her spare hand, still at the office attached to the nursery just outside Chichester.

'I was with the client most of the day.'

'So how's it going?'

'Well . . . not straightforward, but it's a stunning place. All sea and sky and light – except for the site of the restoration, unfortunately. But there's plenty of scope. It could be sensational.'

'But?'

'But . . .' How could she explain? 'There's no "but". The amount of work the client's talking about is a bit overwhelming – more than just the memorial garden. There's a lot to be done to the gardens leading into it.'

Sarah's silence on the line seemed to question whether it had been a good idea to take this on. But they had rehearsed all the arguments too many times: this was business, a game-changing opportunity to expand internationally.

'You don't always have to be so . . . tough, so hard on yourself, Ellie. You can say that it's too much.'

Ellie hesitated, then decided not to tell her business partner about the boy on the boat; reliving it would not help.

'Look, I'll call you in a day or so and let you know how it's working out here. There's a lot of mind-changing and . . . I don't know, a bit of a strange vibe. It's not going to be straightforward.'

'What do you mean?'

'Oh, I'm just . . . perhaps I'm tired. I can't seem to think.'

'Sure you're all right?'

'Yeah . . . I need to do some more research. It could be a

38

huge job for us, a real chance to prove ourselves, but obviously I need to be sure we can deliver.'

'Given the obvious difficulties, perhaps the most practical solution would be to offer some designs and let them arrange construction?'

'You may well be right. But to get full credit we'll need to oversee the whole project. I'm sure it can be done, but it will require some thought. Perhaps we could think about sub-contracting, or sharing the jobs of building and purchasing the plants with an established landscape company on the mainland.'

'Do you want me to come out? The Akehurst job will be finished in the next few days; I could get on a plane.'

'No, it's not worth it. I'll be home myself soon enough. But you might do a bit of research on landscape and garden firms based in Provence that we could approach.'

'But it might be helpful to—'

'No, really, the extra expense . . . Laurent de Fayols is only paying for one of us to get here. If nothing comes of this, we'll barely cover costs, and the office will be closed in the meantime.'

'If you're sure.'

' 'Course.'

She didn't go far that evening, eating dinner at one of the tables laid out under the Oustaou's red canopy. No sign of Lieutenant Meunier tonight. She felt the pocket of her jeans. His card was still there.

'You are very serious, thinking all the time,' said Jean-Luc as he placed a platter of Provençal hors d'oeuvres in front of her.

'Yes . . . Jean-Luc, do you know a man on the island who wears a panama hat, white linen shirt?' Even as she was saying the words, she felt stupid. 'No, forget it. There must be hundreds of men here it could be. I'm—'

'Sooner or later, you meet everyone here.'

He smiled as if he knew why she was asking.

She let him think what he liked. He was right, though: the Place d'Armes was clearly the beating heart of the island. In the slightly sticky heat, men played *pétanque*. The evening crowd seemed to be mostly families with younger children, and older couples, self-consciously dressing down. The few teenagers were of university age, roaming in well-behaved packs. The atmosphere was the same as any holiday island with good sailing: full of the quietly well-to-do and the bourgeois families, *bon chic, bon genre*, who had been coming here for decades, all meeting each summer, their children growing up together during long days full of healthy activities.

When she had finished her meal, Ellie strolled out among them, people-watching carefully. She lingered at the many ice-cream shops so as not to look conspicuous walking round and round the square. They sold extraordinary flavours: lavender, liquorice, apple tart, candied orange, bitter caramel and an unfathomable blue confection labelled 'Stroumph'. She did not try any, nor did she see anyone resembling the man she'd spoken to on the boat.

4

~⟡~

The Restoration

Wednesday, 5 June

She arrived at the Domaine de Fayols by nine o'clock the next
morning, hoping to show Laurent her preliminary sketches of
the memorial garden and get his reaction.

'He has gone to Paris,' said Jeanne.

'Oh.'

The housekeeper gave a smile as thin as her body. 'Did he
not tell you?'

'No.'

'He left some information for you.'

On the library table was a botanical dictionary dedicated
to the region, on top of which lay a note, again written with
a fountain pen. 'Another idea! An apothecary garden as part
of the memorial? The doctor experimented with growing the
medicinal plants he needed.'

That was all. No polite excuse or explanation for his sudden
absence. She looked up into a shaft of sunlight that fizzed with
dust motes. In the brightness Ellie noticed for the first time
how worn most of the furniture was, the faded colours of the
rugs on the tiled floor.

It occurred to her for the first time to question whether there
was enough money to pay for the restoration job, let alone the

41

daunting new projects Laurent now seemed to envisage. She stared into an enlargement of one of the age-speckled photographs with a rising annoyance. It would not be the first time she had been inveigled into wasting time on what had turned out to be nothing more than a fantasy of self-importance.

This time Ellie recognised the tapping on the stone floors. The sound of waves – breaths in, breaths out – preceded the entrance of Mme de Fayols.

'*Bonjour, madame.*'

The woman waved away her greeting, paused unsteadily and then approached with the irritating inevitability of a wasp to an August picnic.

'After the fire, I had to have someone to live here with me, or that was what the mayor decided when he came down to see me with his deputy and a woman from the commune I had never met. As if they felt I needed to be looked after like a child. It was only a small fire, but it left this room blackened to blazes.'

She rasped a strange laugh at her choice of words. 'It looked worse than it was. The couple who came to look after me covered it over with cheap paint, but I couldn't bear to be in there; the smoke marks didn't take long to break through the thin white skin, so the room was shut up.'

Ellie had no idea what to say.

'That was when Laurent decided to come back from Paris. He had to, for me, don't you see. Good of him, all things considered. But he has to go back now and then, to keep everything on track. We can't expect him to stay here all the time.'

'It's perfectly all right,' said Ellie. Though a hint of his intentions might have been polite.

'He's a gambler, you know, like his father. Sometimes he has a run of luck, other times . . . well, let's not dwell on the other times.'

Ellie shook her head.

'You make choices when you're young and you spend the rest of your life paying for them,' continued Mme de Fayols, with the same hard look as the previous evening. She pointed at the note and the open book on the table. 'That's what this is all about. Don't say I'm not being as helpful as I can be.'

It was an odd thing to say. 'Laurent told me the story of the doctor. I can see why you would want to preserve the garden in his memory.'

'There's always a price to be paid.'

'Right . . . I'm going to take these out with me, see whether there are any traces of the old landscaping.' Ellie shut the book, keen to escape.

'You do that,' said Madame. 'Though you still don't understand, do you?'

'I'm sorry?'

'Nothing. We have to watch out for the past. It can come back to bite us.'

'What do you mean?'

But the old woman only smiled.

The wisteria tunnel and the enclosed green spaces felt comfortably familiar as she wandered down to the memorial garden.

Four stone urns, which had not been there the previous day, stood one at each corner of the *bassin*. Were they the originals? She would have to check. Laurent must have asked the estate gardeners to get them out of storage or move them from another part of the garden. They were planted with lilies, the equivalent of house flowers arranged in vases – they wouldn't take root. Why bother? What a waste, when the grounds were under reconstruction. Were they some kind of message to keep her thoughts on the primary purpose of the garden?

At the head of the pool a stone bench had appeared, too, quite possibly the one from the photograph. It had been broken at some stage and badly repaired. The stone serpent that had once coiled across the front edge was missing its head, and one end of the seat was cracked. It seemed solid enough, though, and useful too. She pulled her laptop and sketchbook out of her bag and sat down. Whether Laurent de Fayols was here or not, he was paying for a week's consultation and would want to see something tangible for his money.

Staring into the green wall, it was easy to lose herself in an imagined version of the garden as it had once been. She drew quickly and scribbled notes on plants and light.

A movement across the pool caught her eye. From her seated position the water gleamed silver. But something had sent ripples across its surface. Curious, she got up and leaned forward, one foot on the stone rim of the *bassin*. From this angle the water was pewter grey. Her reflection was sharp and still.

The outline of a man slid up behind her.

Her heart seemed to jump out of her body. She spun round. 'Yes? Who's that?'

There was no one there.

Dizzy, she looked back at the reflection in the pool. She was alone. She went down on her knees, hands on the edge, to lean over the water. It was a serene, glossy blackness. As she pulled herself away, the shadow of a bird swooped across.

Then she was shaking uncontrollably. She remained sitting on the ground, dazed by her body's reaction. As her fright subsided and she consolidated logical explanations for what she had seemed to see, she was unable to shift the notion that the figure resembled the man who had slunk up behind her at the lighthouse. Stubbornly immune to logic, he took up position in her thoughts, each detail coming more clearly into focus: the assertive stance, the loose clothes, the stillness that somehow constituted a threat. But there was no one there – how could he have been a reflection behind her?

Her back prickled. Now that her imagination was working overtime, she could not shake the feeling of being watched. She let her eyes move from left to right. Apart from a creaking in the trees, all was quiet. She twisted her head slightly but saw no one. A shift of the light through the leaves raked light across the grass.

Unsettled, but cross with herself now, she tried to concentrate on the photographs. Under a magnifying glass she attempted to identify the plants Laurent had in mind for an apothecary's garden.

A shadow fell.

This time the figure did not dematerialise. It was stout, with a well-tended stomach over which blue workman's trousers were hitched. One of the estate workers, surely.

'Bonjour, monsieur.'

He wrestled with the possibility of ignoring the niceties, then ingrained politeness won out. 'Bonjour, madame.'

'Have you come to show me the water source?' she asked, speaking slowly in English. 'La source?'

'Non.'

He looked suspiciously at the photographs, her notes and her breasts. 'Pourquoi vous êtes ici?'

He launched into a tirade, much of which she could not understand. His accent was thick, and he snarled his way through his piece without looking her in the eye. But she got the gist. He and the other gardeners could not understand why she had been brought in. They could easily do what was required themselves. And Madame had never wanted the old garden restored; she enjoyed its savage dereliction.

His message delivered, he stomped off before she could begin to formulate a reply. Not an emissary sent by Laurent, then – but quite possibly by his mother.

As early as her conscience would allow in late afternoon, and with enough notes and sketches to justify her time, Ellie gathered her things. She was looking forward to finding another swimming cove, to getting back to the friendly ease of the Place d'Armes. She had almost reached the top of the terrace stairs when Jeanne came out to meet her.

'Madame would like you to dine with her this evening.'

Her mind blanked in search of an excuse.

'I'll show you up to a room you can use to shower and change.'

'I'm sorry, but I have nothing to change into. All I have are the clothes I'm wearing.'

'Follow me, please.'

They ascended a wide stone staircase. Along a dark corridor, Jeanne opened a door and went ahead to unclasp the shutters. As light came in, Ellie saw that a familiar bag had been placed at the foot of the bed.

'What on earth . . . ?'

'Madame asked me to arrange for your luggage to be brought from the hotel. She felt it would be easier if you stayed here for the remainder of your visit.'

'But—'

'The de Fayols know everyone on the island. It was very easily arranged.'

Ellie shook her head, knowing that she was beaten.

'Dinner is served at eight. Madame will receive you on the terrace at seven thirty for an *apéro*.'

The furniture in the room Jeanne had prepared was dark and heavy: a large wooden wardrobe and a matching chest of drawers, both ornately carved. A massive headboard, also carved to depict some complex scene, loomed over the bed, a small double, raised high off the floor. She tried it with a hand. It felt surprisingly soft. Her spirits rallied slightly.

First, though, she would leave a message for Sarah, to tell her – to tell someone – where she was.

She dug into her shoulder bag for her mobile. Then scrambled around deeper inside. It was not in her bag.

Heart pounding, she tried to think. Had she put the phone in her bag that morning? Yes, she remembered checking for it. Had she left the bag somewhere at any time? No, surely it had been with her all the time she was at the Domaine. Had she put it down in the village where some opportunist thief had dipped into it?

Her travel bags were there on the floor. But they seemed deflated. She ripped the zip open and saw that half her clothes were missing. Sat back on her heels, head spinning. Then she got up and opened the wardrobe. Her few dresses and clean trousers were inside on padded silk hangers.

In a bathroom across the corridor skulked a huge roll-top bath and a tiled shower. The latter boasted a complicated arrangement of levers and taps that had not been updated for many years. Steam hissed into the room. She reached towards the taps with one outstretched arm, prepared to pull back if the temperature was scalding. But the vapour was freezing cold. Chilled and puzzled, she fiddled with the controls to no effect. In the end she stripped and ducked briefly under the cold stream of water, shivering as she washed quickly.

She was shown into a side room draped in heavy fabric. A pair of ruby glass urns held lighted candles. Reclining on a chaise longue like an ancient odalisque, Mme de Fayols put a finger to a decanter that rested on a mat of fine crochet work.

At this gesture, Jeanne moved forward and poured a purple tincture into a heavy, etched glass, then passed it to Ellie.

'Eau de vie – flavoured with myrtle,' said the old woman. 'Try it!' She watched intently as Ellie raised the glass to her lips. 'Myrtle from the garden. I steep the berries with honey in the local firewater, but the secret ingredient is the flower, added for the final day. Such a pretty white flower it is, drowned in purple for just one day.'

The liqueur tasted of stewed plums. Not unpleasant, but very strong. It went to Ellie's head after the first sip.

Jeanne moved forward with an oil lamp, casting light over cabinets and ornate display cases full of curiosities. Heavy Chinese antiques, inlaid with mother-of-pearl, stood awkwardly with delicate glass vases and chunks of whalebone engraved with maritime pictures.

The old lady followed Ellie's glances around the room. 'The de Fayols family has lived here for three generations,' she said. 'The doctor was a great collector and traveller. Not only artefacts. Botanical specimens too. Did Laurent tell you there was once an apothecary garden here?'

'Yes, he did. You speak excellent English, madame.'

Each time they had spoken, Mme de Fayols' command of the language had become more fluent.

She gave an unladylike snort of laughter at the compliment. 'I'm not French – I'm British. Or I was, a very long time ago. Just as well you didn't say anything vile to Laurent, all the time thinking I couldn't understand, or had gone deaf or lost my marbles.'

'I wouldn't have,' mumbled Ellie.

'No, I don't suppose you would.' Some private amusement seemed to surge into her lizard eyes.

Now Ellie's ear was attuned to her accent, it seemed less foreign and more of an earlier era. The short vowels of aristocratic speech, rarely heard these days except in old British films and newsreels. 'Orf,' she said, for *off*. 'Said,' for *sad*. It was there, though barely more than an echo.

'Laurent is a very good son. He has had a commendable career in the civil service. Took his degree in *sciences politiques* at the Sorbonne in Paris, followed by one of the great admin schools so beloved of the French of a certain bureaucratic bent. His first wife divorced him, and his second wife is much younger, an arts administrator. Why would she want to give up Paris for a tiny speck of land off the coast? Fine for holidays but not much else. She is serious about her career, and more importantly for a woman, she is taken seriously.

'But when Laurent retired, he felt a pull to the island. And by then I could no longer live here alone.'

This was not quite the story she had told that morning. Then again, the old lady seemed more compos mentis now. Perhaps she had taken some medication that had restored her balance. 'How did you—'

'How did I end up here? That's a very long story.'

Ellie settled, expecting to have to listen for a while, but Jeanne stepped forward.

'Yes, you can get me the telephone now,' said Madame.

An old set appeared, its long cord snaking back to the landline socket. The housekeeper dialled the number.

'Laurent . . . the girl is here.'

She handed the receiver to Ellie.

'Hello?'

'Ah, my dear, I offer my apologies. I have been called away on business. Could not be helped, I'm afraid.'

'I see.'

48

Now she understood the excellence of his English, too.

'Promise me you will wait until my return. I'm sure you will be comfortable at the Domaine.'

'How long will you be?'

'Not long, only a day or so. But we must discuss the plans before you leave. It's never right if it's not done face to face with the drawings, is it?'

'That's true,' Ellie conceded.

'So that's settled then.'

'Well, it's—'

'Excellent. I will see you in a couple of days.'

The line was cut dead, without a goodbye.

Ellie handed it back to Jeanne, who was hovering, expressionless.

Dinner was a desolate affair, served at one end of a long table in a room that felt empty.

A chicken dish was served, but only to Ellie. Mme de Fayols refused a dinner plate for herself, then accepted the positioning of a side plate in front of her, and a sniff at the fricassee in the serving bowl, but waved it away.

'I don't enjoy eating any more,' said Madame. 'But you go ahead.' She smiled, either oblivious to Ellie's discomfort or enjoying her small social cruelties. Were they deliberate, or a natural result of being a very old lady in triple isolation: on a private estate, on an island, long adrift from her native land?

Though she was hungry, Ellie tried to eat as if she too disdained the practice.

Mme de Fayols sipped at a glass of white wine. 'You seem very young. You do realise that to create a garden is to work with time, don't you? It's possible for you to understand nature and growth and change and all the . . . science business – but those who make gardens to last must understand the past and see into the future.'

Ellie restrained herself from offering the retort she would have liked. 'What was it like when you first arrived here?'

'It was a wild place.'

'I'm trying to imagine how it was . . . the formal gardens overgrown? The citrus and olive groves and a lot of scrub, like the garrigue land?'

'Much of it had fallen back into garrigue, yes. But the structure of the formal gardens was well established before the war. The hedges were strong. Then there was the apothecary garden, of course, thanks to the doctor. He began that during the war, I believe, when there was no likelihood of receiving any medical supplies. There was a kitchen garden, naturally.'

'And it was you and your husband who first made the memorial garden?'

The old lady nodded. 'What do you think of it?'

'It's . . . intriguing.'

'It has a life of its own, our garden.'

Ellie nodded, trying to indicate that she understood while chewing on a sliver of chicken. Moths butted at the glass of the full-length window, closed to the night garden.

'Oh, you really don't know what I mean. This garden that reflects the misfortunes of others, it pulls you in. It has a hold. It doesn't let you go, even if you have to get away.'

'I'm not sure—' Was she referring to Laurent and his sudden departure?

'The greatest shock is to discover that the person you love is not what he seems. As more evidence emerges, it's hard to see him in the same way. And whatever the circumstances, it's always the small things that give us away.'

Ellie swallowed. Perhaps she wasn't supposed to understand. Mme de Fayols seemed to take pleasure in wrong-footing her.

Her hostess plucked at the slack of her shawl, pulling it tighter around her as if she were cold.

'I think you know all about that, don't you, Miss Brooke?'

Ellie was saved from having to find a response as Jeanne reappeared with a tray, set it down carefully and left the room without a word.

'A cup of tea, Miss Brooke?'

'Actually, that's exactly what I'd like. Yes, please.'

'Good, dark tea. It's the one thing that reminds me of home.'

The only sound was the tea being poured from a porcelain pot. Ellie's thoughts drifted off.

'It's haunted, you know.'

'I'm sorry?'

'It's haunted.'

'What is?'

'The garden. It was where he was shot. Executed.'

'He?'

'The good doctor. Did Laurent not explain?'

'No, he didn't tell me that.'

'Tell me, did you feel anything in the garden – any change in temperature, any sense of being watched?'

'The temperature is always very pleasant. It would be inside those high hedges, even in summer.'

'You didn't answer the important part.'

Ellie looked her in the eye. 'No. Well, apart from . . . there was someone, this afternoon.'

'Yes?'

'A man. I took him to be one of the estate staff. He said he was a gardener and that he could have done the work without any help from me. Or words to that effect.'

'Substantial chap, in peasant's blue?'

'That's the one.'

Falteringly, Madame took out a cigarette from a spring-loaded case and fumbled with a slim lighter. The cigarette wobbled wetly on her bottom lip until, after a struggle, it was lit and a thin stream of smoke exhaled.

'That's Picolet. He wouldn't manage the work. Well past it, these days.'

That was rich, coming from a woman of her advanced years.

Madame took another puff in a stagy gesture that might once have been alluring. 'No, I don't mean Picolet.' Exhalation of smoke with a tidal rasp. 'You are either peculiarly unobservant or you are a liar, Miss Brooke. You know exactly what I mean.'

51

'I'm not sure I do.'

'Do you ever sense spirits around you in certain places?'

'I don't tend to give such things much thought.'

The cigarette smoke coiled between them. 'Ah, what it is to be so sure. Except you're not sure, are you?'

'I don't believe in ghosts, if that's what you're asking.'

'You understand what is meant by haunting, though. How would you account for the phenomena that so many others understand as haunting?'

'I think . . . that these phenomena must be a sign of some inner disturbance.' Even as she heard herself saying the words, they seemed to be coming straight from her subconscious. As if she had no idea this was what she really thought. 'Anxiety, stress . . .' she continued feebly.

'I see. Anxiety could certainly come into it. But more likely to be a result of a haunting rather than a cause, surely?'

Ellie stared at her hands wrapped around the cup. Unease at the turn of the conversation and the way the woman had been able to insinuate herself into her thoughts hardened into an urge to escape.

'You can't run away from everything, you know.'

Ellie tensed. She put down the cup and sat up straighter. 'It's certainly possible to sense a mood in a garden, to read the signals planted there. Gardens can be laid out and planted to capture an atmosphere, just as houses can be furnished and dressed to reflect different tastes and moods. Key pieces, the way light and space are used. In the harsh light of summer here, reds and hard yellows stand out too much – they clash and unsettle the eye and our expectations. It's all about emotional reactions.'

'Ever the practical miss, with her logical explanation.'

Ellie felt drained. Some vital information was seeded in the strange misfire of communications that passed for conversation with the old lady. 'What else is there?'

'Do you believe everything can be explained?'

'Well, if you're talking in general terms, then no. But that is only because we don't yet have the knowledge to understand.'

Mme de Fayols smiled disconcertingly. 'On that at least, we agree.' She took a birdlike sip of tea. 'How long have you been interested in the war, Miss Brooke?'

'I'm . . . the Chelsea garden was a commission from a services charity. They came to me with the theme and some of the ideas, and I worked to their brief all the way through.'

The old woman subjected her to a withering assessment.

'You're not very happy, are you?'

Ellie gave her best professional smile. 'I'm fine. What makes you say that? This is a very interesting project.'

There was another long pause.

'I mean in general. Your life hasn't quite worked out as you hoped.'

Ellie stared back, not trusting herself to remain polite.

'The restoration of the garden was not my idea,' announced the old lady, with some malice. A disparaging expression pulled at the waxy creases of her face. 'But as my son was determined to go ahead, I thought we might as well have the right person to do it. Perhaps I have made a mistake in choosing you.'

'It was you who asked me to come?'

'I am the one who reads the English newspapers.'

'I'm still astonished how many people saw that piece and how many commissions have come from it.'

'But you're out of your depth here.'

'Why do you say that?'

'It's clear to see. I had hoped you wouldn't be, but – well, we can none of us predict exactly what we'll get, can we? Now I hope you understand that I am very tired. I shall say good night now.'

Mme de Fayols struggled slowly to her feet.

Ellie rose too, waiting to see how she could help but unwilling to touch the old lady. Why did you arrange for me to come here, let alone insist I stayed the night, when you don't even seem to like me? Ellie wanted to ask. Each encounter seemed to confirm that Mme de Fayols was suffering from some kind of psychological disorder. Ellie hesitated to attach a label to it, but something was clearly amiss.

'Good night,' she said.

Upstairs Ellie pulled open drawers, knowing that she had not put her phone in any of them, but at a loss to know where else to look.

The second drawer down on the right-hand side of the chest was heavier. She had to jiggle it to slide it out. At first she couldn't make sense of what she saw. Then her blood chilled as the shape seemed to come into focus.

It was a heavy steel revolver, obviously old. Ellie stared at the gun. She reached out instinctively, then pulled her hand back. She must not touch it. Had it been there all the time? Was it loaded?

Carefully she pushed the drawer back in and opened the one on the left. Inside, it too was empty, apart from one item. It was a pillbox with a glass lid. It contained a single tablet.

Through the window she had left ajar to let fresh air into the room, the garden was dark. A violent animal noise rode the darkness and then receded. A wave of sadness broke over her. It was sadness, she reflected, not shock or fear. If the stark presence of the revolver had forced her to confront herself, it revealed nothing to be ashamed of.

Yet was it intended to be a test? If so, it was one that said more about the oddness of the mother and son who had brought her here. Mme de Fayols' voice replayed in her head, along with the sense that she was being mocked. *You're not happy, are you?*

Was it so obvious? And what could she do to hide it? No, she wasn't happy, but she was allowed to be unhappy for a while. It would pass, surely. It had to.

An unspecific pain woke Ellie. For a moment she felt unable to breathe. She put a hand up to her face, and it spread wetness onto her mouth and cheek. She felt for the bedside light

54

switch and gasped as the bed was illuminated. Dark red stains blotched the white sheets.

On the back of her right hand was a wound from which blood was still seeping. A suffocating darkness bore down on her and a rushing noise filled her head. She forced herself to calm down. Somehow she had cut herself. She must have caught her hand on one of the protruding elements of the carved bedhead. She turned over to look, and it was obvious that was what had happened. A goat figure with viciously curving horns was well within reach of her right hand.

She got up slowly, slightly queasily, and ran her hand under the basin tap. There were tissues in her bag, and she wrapped several tightly around the wound. For a while she lay awake in the darkness as the panic subsided.

It was not until the morning that she dared to look in the second drawer again. It was empty. She stared, searching for an explanation in the dusty interior of the chest. She must have dreamt it, she decided; she had been trapped in a nightmare so vivid she was convinced she had been awake.

Her phone was still missing, though.

5

The Historian

It had been light for hours when Ellie went downstairs. At the foot of the stairs she listened for sounds from the kitchen, but all was quiet. For one odd moment she had the feeling she was the only person in the house. The sensation passed. If there was no one in the kitchen yet, she would make herself a cup of instant coffee.

As she crossed the hall, she looked through the main room to the French doors, closed now. At that precise moment something hit the clear surface with a dull thud. What were the chances of that happening just as she looked in that direction? Shakily, she went over to see what it was. A small black bird was lying on the tiles outside. It must have flown into the glass. The bird had made no sound of distress. It had knocked itself out. Or perhaps it was dead.

Ellie turned away.

There was no one in the kitchen. Surely Jeanne would arrive soon. It didn't feel all that early. She looked at her wrist and saw that she had left her watch upstairs. As she did so, a clock chimed softly. Seven – or was it eight times?

Ellie went back into the hall, then the sitting room, looking for the clock. As she did so another small bird slammed into the window. It was so quick and so upsetting, especially as the corpse of the first was still twitching, that she felt sick.

Out in the grounds, Ellie was determined to bury her anxieties by thinking about work. She had not yet seen the memorial garden this early, and she should do. Notebook in hand, she mapped the sequence of shadows in the anterooms leading into it and the angle of the sun in the main space.

Sitting on the low stone rim of the *bassin*, she sketched the archway and the precise proportions of the view of the lighthouse and the bay.

At first she thought it was birdsong. Then, when the melody was accompanied by words, she wondered whether one of the gardeners was singing as he worked. Though it was too high for a man's voice, surely. A child of one of the gardeners, then. She strained to get a fix on the source, but could not.

She listened for sounds of activity, but soon the grounds were quiet again. She continued her sketch, looking up quickly and regularly from the page. It was only when she put her pencil back on the paper that the impression formed in her head, as if her mind had only now been able to process the image, however indistinct. Had someone just walked across the view of the sea and through the gap in the arch? She sat completely still and raised her head. She was alone. The once-grand topiary arch rustled in a light breeze that shook loose dead leaves and twigs. The view was uninterrupted.

It was hard not to think about the previous night's conversation with Mme de Fayols. Her instincts were to dismiss the old lady's assertions about otherworldly sensations as a spiteful game. She seemed to enjoy finding ways to disconcert Ellie. It was pathetic, really; she should feel sorry for her. It occurred to Ellie only then that perhaps she was the one who was mad. Had the strange episodes over the past few days tipped her over the edge? All she was sure of was that she needed to talk to Laurent. But she would not be spending another night at the Domaine while she waited for him to return.

*

She would do it her way. Ellie cycled the most direct route back to the village and harbour, resolutely keeping her thoughts on normal matters: a late breakfast of coffee and croissants; checking at the hotel to see if anyone had come across her mobile. She was flushed with the effort as she pushed into the wind. When she saw a pay phone on the road leading into the Place d'Armes, she took the chance to use it straight away. Her fingers trembled as she got some coins ready and pressed in the numbers for Laurent de Fayols' office in Paris.

He was not there.

She gave a moan of frustration. Wait – his mobile number was on the first letter he had written her. The letter should be in her bag. She scrabbled. It was. She tried the number twice; each time it prompted a repeating electronic message that she guessed meant the number was out of order.

As she came out of the phone booth, she felt rattled. It was only a short walk to the friendly hotel on the other corner of the square, but she was grateful for the support of the cycle as she wheeled it. Her legs seemed to be trembling slightly, more than they should for someone as fit as she was.

The Place d'Armes no longer seemed so benevolent. The voices of young children running across the dust sounded from a long way away, as if in an echo chamber. She was gripped by the unpleasant sensation that had begun at the Domaine de Fayols: a profound detachment that placed the world beyond a film of gauze.

The sun was already oppressive, sapping her strength. Yet she knew she needed the safety of crowds. She headed over to a bustling café with tables set out under the eucalyptus trees and propped the cycle against the low stone wall before taking a seat in the shade.

It was frustrating to have come so far, only to find that the job was a dud. But these things happened. She flipped through the pages of her sketchbook. The scrawled notes seemed to jump, and the drawings looked like angry doodles. She pinched the bridge of her nose to dull the pain that had settled behind her eyes.

Her heart sank when the other chair at her table was pulled out.

'Do you mind if I join you?' A man's voice.

'Not at all.' It was an automatic response.

She hardly looked up as he took the seat by her side.

'Are you on your own?' he asked.

'Yes.'

'I can't understand why.'

Ellie gazed out at the square and fixed on the trees and the church until the lines began to melt.

'I'm sorry,' he said, when she failed to respond.

'What?'

He remained silent, looking at her. It was impossible not to look back. Eyes deep brown, with vertical frown lines above the nose. Straight eyebrows. The floppy dark hair and olive skin of Roman genes, she thought, though the process of forming impressions seemed to be too heavy for normal brain activity. She scarcely felt capable of any rational thought.

Ellie dropped her eyes to her coffee cup.

She was so close she could see the seams and the weave of his white shirt. Then the fabric seemed to swim in and out of focus. She thought she might be about to faint. The last thing she wanted to do was make conversation with a stranger. On the other hand, if she wasn't well, it felt better somehow to be with someone.

'How are you enjoying the island?' he asked.

She closed her eyes and dug her fingernails into the flesh of her palms. Her head felt thick, as if she had a bad cold.

'Are you all right? I'm sorry. Would you like me to go?'

His concern was real enough. She gathered herself.

'I'm fine.'

There was something her subconscious was trying to tell her. It almost became clear, then receded. The man smelled of tobacco, sweet and not at all unpleasant. The scent hung in the air between them like perfume.

'Do you live here, or are you on holiday?' she asked, the words ringing hollow as she said them.

59

He was deeply tanned, with beautiful skin for a man, smooth and unlined.

'My family has lived here for many years – many generations.'

'You work here?'

'Oh . . .' He raised his palms and pulled an expression that said, *Not really.*

'On the mainland, then?'

'No . . . I'm here almost all the time. I'm . . . a historian, I suppose you would say.'

'I see,' she said, though she didn't. 'What kind of historian?'

'Military history. I specialise in World War Two. And you?'

'I'm a garden designer. I'm doing some preliminary work at a property here.'

He looked over at the waiter, but the man was busy at the bar and didn't see him. It didn't matter, thought Ellie. Actually, it was reassuring that they could sit undisturbed.

The world slowed. She was starting to relax. In fact, it was lovely to sit next to this man. It didn't make sense, but it was as if she had come home after a long journey. Perhaps it was the intense atmosphere at the Domaine de Fayols; it was only upon leaving it that she realised how strange and overwhelming it had been.

He was telling her about the different beaches on the island, and the groves of mandarin and grapefruit that once grew all along the Langoustier road, trees brought from Sicily to start the citrus groves.

'It must have been a glorious place to grow up,' she prompted, enjoying hearing him speak.

'It certainly was. During the long, hot days we children found shady hiding places and made encampments, ramshackle affairs. When we roused ourselves from these cocoons, we filled up with apricots from the orchard, then walked for hours down the hill to dip our feet in the sea.

'We judged the time by the sun, tiredness and hunger. When we were parched and covered in dust, we would turn back to the farm.

'We lived in the open air, of course, all summer long. We ate at a long wooden table on the west-facing terrace. Each night the sunset, each night a different composition, in fire colours.'

The way he spoke, she could picture the place exactly.

It was as if all noise and movement had ceased around them. For Ellie, there was a sense of histories large and small unfolding.

'In the winter we hunted, the men and the boys,' he went on.

He didn't much like to hunt, though he learned how to do so effectively with gun and knife. They went after rabbit and pheasant, mainly. But what was the point of using up ammunition, when there was always also the constant risk of a stray bullet hitting a poacher child, of whom there were a surprising number? Better to hunt by night. Easier to track the prey to its resting place and wait, to creep up on a pheasant in the low branches of a tree and rip it from its nest.

'There was always more hunting by moonlight. Not only of game. The fishermen stole grapes at full moon to make their own wine, and it was understood by all that they would. Sometimes you could smell the bouillabaisse they cooked up on camping stoves on the rocks below the vineyards.'

She could see it all, the men with their tin bowls, the shimmer of silver on fish and sea. The cliffs rising steeply.

'If you like history, you should go diving,' he said, his words slipping insidiously inside her thoughts. 'The scuba schools are down at the harbour.'

'I've seen them. But I've never done scuba before.'

'You should learn. There are fabulous dives here – wrecked ships and subterranean cliffs. And there's a plane wreck on the seabed to the south-west beyond the lighthouse. You should ask about it.'

'It sounds very exciting.'

'You don't have to scuba – you can just snorkel. The Domaine de Fayols place is just by the Calanque de l'Indienne – that's as good a place as any to start. The water is so clear you can see right down to the bed in most places. But to make the most of it, you need proper equipment. Perhaps I could give you—'

'What's your name? I never asked.'

He smiled, and then stood up. 'Ah, well . . . it's a small place. Perhaps our paths will cross again,' he said.

'Perhaps they will.'

Ellie watched him walk away soundlessly on his canvas shoes. It must have been close to noon, for he had no shadow.

Where was he going? She tried to imagine his life on the island: a wife and children, perhaps; a mistress was a distinct possibility. Maybe he was going to see her now, in a house hidden among the pine trees, before returning for an evening with his family. The archetypal Frenchman and his women, his exquisite manners and pragmatic approach to matters of the heart.

His rolled-up sleeves and open-necked shirt, baggy linen trousers and old espadrilles. The panama hat he pulled on as he walked away. By the time she stood up to run after him, he had vanished.

Why hadn't she realised sooner? She should call Lieutenant Meunier. If she hadn't lost her mobile, she would have called him right then and there – wouldn't she?

'Where have you been?'

Mme de Fayols carved the air in the hall with the curved point of the horn handle of her cane. In the dim light her pupils were so huge that her stare was completely black.

'You are supposed to be doing a job here! You have to be here to understand. You can only learn so much from the books and the photographs. The rest you have to feel, sense, absorb. Or have you felt it, and wish you had not?'

Ellie said nothing, determined not to pursue this line of questioning.

'You feel it. I know you feel it.'

A deep breath. 'I went to the village because I needed to do something.'

'But you're here to work!'

'And I have been working on plans for the garden. You can see them if you wish, but you must understand that they are

62

preliminary ideas rather than plans ready for submission.'

A couple of impatient taps from the cane.

'Actually,' said Ellie, 'I've done as much as I can here. Now I need to refine my sketches, which I will do back at the hotel. I'll just collect my things and get on with that as soon as possible.'

Mme de Fayols looked as if she had been slapped in the face.

Ellie found Jeanne in the kitchen. It was an even colder reception than normal. Tersely Ellie told her about her mobile, still missing though Jean-Luc had assured her he would ask all the staff at the hotel.

'So I need to use the telephone here to call Laurent, please.'

The housekeeper indicated the telephone mounted on the kitchen wall. When Ellie rang it, Laurent's mobile was still out of service.

'Are these his numbers when he's away?' she asked, pointing to a list pinned up on the wall. Several numbers clustered around a simple 'L'.

Jeanne nodded.

Two calls rang and rang, and one was answered by a hotel concierge. Laurent de Fayols was not currently in residence.

'Will you be sure to tell him that I'm working back at the Oustaou des Palmiers, please? I'm going upstairs now to collect my bags.'

'I'll come with you.'

It was as if she was not trusted to be alone in any part of the house. Ellie wondered what on earth the old lady had told Jeanne.

Upstairs the lamp in her room was on – and lying sideways on the bedside table. Her small collection of cosmetics was strewn across the floor. Papers were scattered. Some of the larger drawings she had done were ripped to shreds.

'What on earth – what's happened here?'

Jeanne shook her head. 'I have not been in here today. This is how you left it.'

'I absolutely did not,' said Ellie. For the second time that day her vision blurred and she felt faint. The bed was rumpled, as

63

if it had been slept in. She knew she had made it that morning, remembered thinking that she must leave everything perfectly tidy to withstand any checking by Jeanne.

Her camera was on top of the chest of drawers, but switched on, draining power. She gave silent thanks that she had thought to take her laptop with its precious files with her into the garden that morning. There was no damage to the camera, but when she examined it there were no photographs left; they had all been deleted.

'Someone's done this,' she said to Jeanne. She turned to gauge the housekeeper's reaction, but she was no longer there.

Drip. Drip. Drip-drip. It took longer than it should have for Ellie to hear it. The drips sounded as if they were coming from a lazy tap or shower. But the bathroom was down the corridor. She found her travel grip and went over to the wardrobe.

Inside, her clothes were soaking wet. They smelled of the sea.

Drip. Drip.

She surveyed the wreckage. Then with shaking hands she stuffed her things into the grip, wet clothes onto dry. She pulled open drawers and swept out anything that was hers. Luckily it was not much. She glanced round for anything she had missed, hoping irrationally to see her mobile.

The light hit the headboard of the bed at an odd angle. It was only then that she took in what the carved scene depicted. It was a version of the garden with the topiary arch, in which some pagan dance was taking place. A devil's horns, shaved to a point. The cut on her hand throbbed.

She lunged for the door. For a mad instant she half thought it might be locked, but the handle turned easily enough. She almost fell down the stairs with her bags. There would be no horse and trap waiting to take her back. No option but to wheel the cycle with the luggage, even if it meant slow progress.

On a table at the foot of the staircase an hourglass was running. The sand flowed smoothly from one clear bulb into the other. Who had set that, and why?

A door banged.

'Miss Brooke?'

Madame was leaning on Jeanne as she came into the hall from the sitting room.

Ellie felt a trickle of sweat run down the back of her neck. Her heart thudded.

'You can't leave,' said the old lady.

'I'm afraid I have to.'

'What will I tell Laurent?'

'I left messages for him. I will speak to him myself.'

'If you go now . . .'

If she went now, then what? It would be the end of the French restoration project? Quite probably. There would be no prestige and quite possibly some bad publicity. But she had the terrible feeling that this was the end of something more than just one garden job, over before it had properly started; that events were taking place out of her control, but she had no idea what they might be. She took several deep breaths. Was this how it felt when a nervous breakdown began? Was that what was happening? Stupid, she told herself, you're making it worse by letting these ridiculous thoughts take root.

'I will speak to your son, madame. But after this . . . I can't see that I will be able to work here.'

When she got back to England she would take a week off, maybe two. She could relax and let herself recover. It was the incident on the ferry, the forts and the military parade ground, the talk of war and the memorial garden that had combined to bring on this nervous reaction, crisis, whatever it was, and revisit her grief over Dan more painfully than ever.

'I have to go.'

'If you do, it will ruin your career. I will say that you took our money and weren't capable of delivering.'

'I've been paid nothing yet.'

'Apart from your flight and a stay in a hotel. The hotel you had to leave and come here because we were worried about your extravagance, racking up huge bar bills and charging them to our account.'

'But that's not true!'

'Truth is the first casualty of war.'

Ellie shook her head in bewilderment. What was she on about now?

'Furthermore, you attacked me.'

'You know that I did not.'

'Who will the French authorities believe, though? That is the only aspect to concern us.'

'The room I stayed in last night was trashed when I went up just now. My clothes are dripping wet,' Ellie started, then faltered. What was the point? The woman was not well.

'How do I know you haven't done this yourself?'

'Why would I do that?'

'Are you saying there has been a break-in?'

'Well, perhaps there has. My phone has disappeared, but that went yesterday. But it would be a very strange burglar who decided to delete my photos but not take the camera and drench my clothes in seawater . . . I don't know what kind of vicious game is being played here, but I want nothing to do with it. I've had enough of this craziness!'

Madame swayed, seeming to shrink into decrepitude as the tirade went on. Jeanne frowned and moved towards the old lady protectively. 'We did not do this,' she said.

Ellie wrenched open the main door.

Of course the bicycle was not where she had left it. It was all so predictable that Ellie congratulated herself on guessing as much as she went down the steps. There was nothing to worry about – nothing at all. It was only a malicious game played at the command of a madwoman.

She could walk. The island was so small, no walk was too far. Without a glance back, she set off. The bag containing her laptop was heavy, and she had to stop frequently to change sides before trudging on. When she came out onto the main track she paused, half expecting to be stopped by a domaine worker in a vehicle. No one appeared. Then she began hoping that a vehicle would miraculously appear and offer her a lift, but that didn't happen either.

As she trudged towards the village, the tension in her

shoulders and legs eased a little. To the left of the path, the sea formed strips of sequins. Farther out, it was the darkest blue she'd ever seen.

Much as she had been determined to swim in the Calanque de l'Indienne, it occurred to her that it might be unwise now. As soon as the thought occurred, however, she longed for cold water on her body, that delicious shock on immersion, to float, eyes closed against the sun. She was so close to the *calanque*.

Without further thought, she put down her bags and broke into a jog, slowing only to pick her way down over the rocks to the sea. It was steep, and loose stones made her slip more than once. She was alone. Standing on a flat rock half hidden by a pine, she stripped off down to her underwear and let herself into the water.

She floated on her back, barely moving. She was fine; everything was going to be all right. Beyond the wide inlet, sleek modern boats skimmed across the blue, trailing white ribbons of froth. Too fast, too soulless, she thought; this was a journey to be taken slowly, a transition to be savoured.

The sudden weight on her chest seemed to compress her whole body. She was being both pushed and pulled down. Banks of trees seemed to tower over her, blotting out the sky. At least, she thought they were trees. The shapes were pushing her down. She was underwater now; she could see clusters of bright darting fish, and the pressure in her head was building as the water became colder and bluer and deeper. She could not breathe. Deeper, into black water. Nothing more to see. All was black.

Her head seemed to explode. Then she was in the light again. Her teeth chattered. She was cold, and then hot. Gasping, she found she could stand. She was still in the shallows. Yet she had been drowning. It had been so vivid. What had just happened?

Ellie made it, terrified, to the rock. She hauled herself onto it and tried to slow her inhalations. Gradually a hot, heavy stillness settled over her, and she found the strength to drag herself out of the water.

She had to be rational. It was the only way she could get through this. Had she fainted? Was this anxiety, a kind of panic attack following on from the first time it happened, and worse a second time? Or was there another explanation – an infection caused by that nasty thorn scratch, reopened by the gash from the bedhead? A plant she had come into contact with, maybe . . . those hanging bells of datura in the entrance to the garden rooms were witches' weeds, cousins to deadly nightshade and henbane.

The logical progression of thought steadied her. Even so, it was a while before she picked up her bags and started walking again.

Her watch said it was eight o'clock in the evening, but she was not sure how that could be possible. At the Oustaou des Palmiers, Jean-Luc looked surprised to see her, though she was sure she had told him she was coming back. There was a small room she could have. She would have taken a cupboard.

Up in a tiny bathroom in the eaves, she looked in the mirror. A startled wreck stared back, dirt and charcoal smudged across her face and hands and pinched shadows under her eyes.

Kneeling by the bed, she switched on the laptop, praying for a strong Wi-Fi connection. A search, and the answers to some questions, at least, were there at her fingertips. Most parts of the datura were poisonous, and the seductive scent masked toxic hallucinogens. Confusion, delirium and drowsiness were all symptoms of accidental poisoning. Coma, in the worst cases. Agitation and convulsions had also been reported. Muscle weakness. Memory loss.

Some sources claimed datura seeds had been used as a murder weapon, others that it was known in ancient times as a means by which whores might sedate then rob their clients, who would remember nothing.

Most of the cases discussed online concerned the plant's dubious use as a recreational drug. It was slightly worrying – but also made sense – that the trippy, lucid-dream states it induced could recur spontaneously over a period of several days.

Ellie sat back on her heels. It was certainly possible that she had come into contact with the datura in the garden. But she had not ingested the seeds, which accounted for most of the experiences requiring an antidote. She wondered whether she ought to ask Jean-Luc if there was a doctor she could see as a precaution, but actually, now that she was back in the safety of the hotel and in control again, she felt better. Whatever had occurred seemed to have passed. She drank four glasses of water in an attempt to flush out her system and curled up on the bed, desperate for sleep.

6

The Flight

It was a bad night. She woke constantly, feeling either nauseous or thirsty. The waking broke her thoughts into vivid
dream fragments: on a low rocky promontory a tower melted
on a crag; the ferry was waiting for her; crowds surged up from
the quay, but she was searching for the boy in the T-shirt. She
kept losing her bags. The man at the lighthouse was watching
her, face still hidden. At last she was on the boat, then she was
balancing on the rail over the sea, walking it like a tightrope.
Falling through blue air, trying and failing to fly.

As early as she could, she called Sarah from the reception
desk of the Oustaou des Palmiers. 'It's not working out. I'm
sorry. My flight home isn't until tomorrow evening, but I
might go back to the mainland and stay in a cheap hotel in
Hyères tonight – I'll see how I feel.'

In Sussex, Sarah was eating breakfast, swallowing rapidly.
'What's gone wrong?'

'I'll tell you everything when I get back. But don't waste any
time on contacting the landscapers out here. Oh, and I've lost
my mobile, so don't worry if I don't pick up.'

'Ugh, what a pain. Lost how?'

'It disappeared while I was at the client's place. Misplaced, stolen, taken as part of the game, I don't know.'

'The *game*?'

'Don't ask. I'll tell you when I get back.'

'Are you sure you're all right?'

Tears threatened to spill over. 'Fine. Just . . . I just want out of this. It's not what we thought.'

'OK, well . . . I'll wait to hear from you. Call me when you get to Hyères, yes? And Ellie? It doesn't matter. It's only one job.'

'I know. But thanks.'

'Speak to you later.'

A warm breeze ruffled the palm trees and drew soft clinking sounds from the sailing boats in the marina. Just a few miles away from the Domaine de Fayols, the island seemed a different place, full of light and life, cause for cautious optimism. The previous day was a world away, farther than a few kilometres, longer ago than twenty-four hours. She was relieved to feel relatively normal, if tired and gritty-eyed, as she walked down towards the ferry office to look at the timetables for the crossing back to La Tour Fondue. Perhaps she had been right about the datura, and all that water had done the trick. With a pang of guilt she remembered the hired bicycle. On the way to the ferry she should go into the shop and tell the man that it had been left at the Domaine. He could keep the deposit for his trouble.

On a quayside board the timetable showed crossings so frequent that the return trip would be no more complicated than catching a bus. She could turn up whenever she wanted. There was nothing more to worry about.

Signs advertised pleasure cruises, catamaran trips and visits to the other islands. A row of similar ventures was in healthy competition. Several dive schools offered lessons in using scuba equipment. Pictures of sunken ships interlaced with shoals of subtropical fish were placed as bait by an open door for those who were already qualified to dive and could be enticed on a guided expedition.

'You want scuba dive?' called a student type with long hair and a manner in which flirtatiousness did battle with lassitude.

Ellie remembered something.

'Do you dive over the wrecks?'

'Certainly, yes. Many ships on the bed.' He managed to make it sound quite lascivious.

'What about the plane wreck?'

He pulled a puzzled face.

'Aeroplane?' she asked.

'No plane. Only ship.'

'Maybe someone else does that dive trip?'

'No. There is no plane in the sea.'

'Oh. OK . . . *merci*.'

'You make a dive to see some ship?'

'Another time, maybe.'

A fishing boat nosed into the harbour, and two men spread out their catches: spiny crab, sea urchins, prawns and squid, as well as less exotic fish. It was surprisingly quiet, so close to the buzz of the village, the crowded marina with its pleasure craft and fishermen, the pastel stucco buildings with their bars and restaurants under red awnings. Porquerolles was an attractive place, no doubt about that. She wondered if she would ever return. Under different circumstances, it would be gorgeous. Now that the past few days at the Domaine de Fayols seemed a world away, she could be objective again. Frankly it was amazing that more approaches from prospective clients weren't a waste of time, wealthy, eccentric, unrealistic and demanding as those who could afford her services often were.

She walked aimlessly, just for some gentle exercise to test her muscle strength. The path to the east rose up through spiny bushes – *griffes de sorcières*, witches' claws, as she now knew from one of Laurent's botanical dictionaries. A few hundred metres farther, pine trees were gnarled and blackened, as if they had been scorched by a forest fire but survived.

Not long now, and she would be off the island. She could leave any time she wanted. The hills behind Le Lavandou on the mainland reared up in reassurance, so close that they seemed no farther than the opposite side of a lake. White sails skipped over the blue, and she watched them, thinking of the man in the billowing shirt, how sweetly serious he was at the café and how he had noticed and helped her when she felt unwell.

She walked on. Then, as if she had summoned him by the power of thought, there he was – or a figure that could easily be him – on the path ahead where it curved round a higher point in the direction of the Cap Medès. Or had seeing him sparked the thought, subconsciously? She began running, but when she emerged from a line of holm oaks, he was nowhere to be seen.

The disappointment she felt was entirely disproportionate. She tried to justify it; as a local there was so much he could explain: whether there had been any other news about Florian Creys, what his background was and why he had slipped off the boat in front of them; the oddness of the de Fayols family and their domaine; what was wrong with Madame, and whether everyone on the island knew she was a lunatic.

If nothing else, she would have liked to run into him once more, anyhow, to say goodbye and thanks. Apart from Jean-Luc at the hotel, he was the only person who had shown her real kindness during the past few days. There had been something about him she found calming.

She skittered to a halt. What was she doing, chasing him like this? Had she lost her mind again? She turned round to start walking back to the Plage de la Courtade. A handful of earth trickled from above, as if the higher ground had been disturbed. She looked up but could see only trees. Her train of thought half forgotten, she turned back the way she came. Her shirt was damp and cold on her back.

'How is your work going on the garden?'

As she reached the harbour, there he was at her shoulder. His battered espadrilles had made not a sound on the concrete runway of the quay.

'Oh! It's you.' Close up, she caught the aroma of old-style

73

French tobacco. 'The garden . . . it's not really happening now.'

'Problems?'

'You win some, you lose some.'

'I saw you over at one of the dive places.'

'Yes.'

'Are you going out on a dive?'

'I was just curious.'

He said nothing.

'I asked about the plane wreck, but they didn't know about it.'

'Not many people do.'

'I see . . .'

'It is there, even if most people don't know about it.'

She watched closely as he ran his hand up his right forearm. As the sleeve was pushed back, it revealed a contusion of red scars. 'It was you on the ferry, the day the boy committed suicide, wasn't it?'

'Yes.'

'There's a police lieutenant, Meunier, who wants to talk to you. They're still talking to everyone, trying to get an accurate picture of what happened. I've got his card somewhere.'

'Meunier? OK, no problem. I can find him.'

'Someone is saying the boy was pushed. Did you think he was pushed?'

'No.'

The sea shuddered in the wake of a passing boat, setting off a carillon of metal against mast in the marina.

'The trouble is, the more you try to remember exactly what you saw, the more you begin to doubt yourself.'

'First instincts are normally right.' He fidgeted with a heavy brass cigarette lighter he brought out of his pocket. 'So what happened over at the Domaine de Fayols?'

'I'm not taking the job – I'm going home today.'

'Good.'

'Good? Why do you say that?'

'There is something I want to ask you. Will you walk with me?'

'I still don't know your name.'
'Gabriel.'
'I'm Ellie.'

Slim tree trunks twisted like wrought-iron latticework, holding up clouds of acid-green foliage against the sea and sky. From the coastal path, the hills on the mainland were soft purple-brown mounds.

'How exactly did you come to be involved with the Domaine de Fayols in the first place?' Gabriel asked, in a tone that implied she was out of her depth there.

'Laurent de Fayols sent me an email. He'd heard about my work. We spoke on the phone a few times and arranged for me to come over to look at the garden. But then he went off to Paris, and Mme de Fayols informed me that she was the one who'd found out about my work and chosen our firm, yet she has done nothing but undermine me since I arrived. It has all been very strange – and to what purpose?'

'She has a certain reputation.'

'I am very glad to hear that.'

'She is crazy.'

Ellie laughed, and the tension in her shoulders began to release. 'Certifiably . . . or was that just a figure of speech!'

He did not reply.

As the trees grew more dense, a brown weave of needles on the path deadened the sound of their footsteps.

'So the memorial garden at the Domaine de Fayols will have to wait to be restored,' he said.

'I'm sure they'll find someone else.'

'I hope so. It's important to preserve it. It's special, the way it brings together the land, the sea and the sky – and the lighthouse.'

'I agree. The view of the lighthouse is integral to the garden.'

'You are very perceptive.'

'I went into the little museum there. I thought perhaps there might be a connection to the Domaine, but if there is, it's not mentioned.'

'Did you see the record book and gloves that belonged to the lighthouse keeper who remained on the island under the Germans during the war?'

'Yes.'

'Henri Rousset refused to join the evacuation, and the occupiers needed him. He was permitted to stay to operate the lighthouse as normal. A very brave man.'

'I saw the large photograph and the flag,' she said. 'I guessed it must have been something like that.' She shivered involuntarily as it came back to her: the feeling as she stood on the cliff looking up to the beacon that she was on the verge of making some important connection.

Gabriel was quiet for so long that she wondered whether he was going to respond. They climbed farther, following signs for the Fort de l'Alycastre, defenceless now, gnawed back to bare stone by birds and wind. Tufts of sea grass stole up the squat stone walls like a raiding party.

'Rousset put his life at risk to safeguard the lives of thousands of Allied men,' he said. 'Before the Allies landed at Saint-Tropez on the fifteenth of August, 1944, these three Golden Islands had to be neutralised. At the crucial moment, just before the amphibious assault, he disabled the lighthouse beam to confuse the German night defences. Meanwhile, another beam was set up farther along the coast to imitate the Porquerolles lighthouse.'

'How did he know what he had to do?'

'A Resistance agent managed to get out here to tell him. It was risky, but it had to be done. Allied intelligence agents in Marseille wanted to blow up the lighthouse, but bombing it from a plane would have condemned Rousset, a good man who had stayed on the island watching the Germans and waiting for his chance to act, to certain death – and risked the destruction of nearby properties.'

'The Domaine de Fayols,' said Ellie. 'I'm beginning to understand. But how did the Resistance get someone out to an occupied island, in an area that must have been heavily defended?'

'A light aircraft, flying at night.'

'That must have been extremely dangerous.'

'It was.'

'So the plan worked?'

'Up to a point. The objective was achieved. But Rousset was beaten senseless, had his head kicked in by the Germans when they realised they had been tricked. He never properly recovered, nor was able to remember exactly what had happened.'

They had stopped walking. Below was a beach of pebbles where three small boats rocked in the shallows. Even with one hand shading her eyes, Ellie could only see in patches of light and dark.

'But there was someone else who had stayed on the island, surely,' she said. 'The doctor. Louis de Fayols.'

'They told you that, then.'

'Madame de Fayols told me.'

'Yes, during the war the doctor continued to care for the convalescents, mainly Italian soldiers. Most were poor young conscripts who had done very little harm. The doctor felt a responsibility for them. When the Nazis took over, they sent the Italians to prison camps, but they realised the value of having a doctor on the island. He was ordered to stay, effectively a prisoner in his own house. They shot him there, in the grounds, on the night the plane landed.'

'But the Allies were so close, the liberation was about to begin – why do it then?'

He did not answer.

'I can understand how you became a war historian, trying to make sense of it all.'

He nodded gravely. 'So are you going back to London?' he asked.

She smiled at the assumption. 'Only passing through, but I don't live too far away. Why?'

Gabriel pushed a hand through his hair. 'Would you . . . consider doing something for me, to help me with my research?'

She was touched by the way he seemed hesitant about asking, this man who was otherwise supremely confident.

'I'll certainly help, if I can.'

'Some of the material I need is in London. The story concerns both France and Great Britain. It occurs to me that if I could find out in advance which archives hold the documents I need, then it would make my job quite a lot easier when I come over to England.'

'Of course. I'm sure I can do that.' It would mean keeping in touch, maybe even meeting up. She felt a smile spreading. 'No problem at all. Tell me what you need to know.'

They found a shady spot and sat down. Ellie made notes as he spoke. It was hard to tell whether his interest in her was romantic or just friendly. They did not touch, even by accident. When he had described the events he was working on, making sure she had enough useful detail, they spoke of other relationships and the difficulty of love disrupted by war. He seemed to understand her need to talk about Dan and, as she did so, it felt for the first time as if she was freeing herself for the possibility of another life.

The afternoon grew hotter. Gabriel leaned back on a tree and closed his eyes. Ellie began a small sketch of him, ready to snap the book shut if he stirred. At last she was living for the moment, seizing the day with an optimism she had not expected to feel again. There no longer seemed any urgency to catch the ferry back to the mainland.

At the hotel there were two messages. One was to call Laurent de Fayols as soon as she got back. She used the landline on the reception desk.

'What's been going on while I was away?'

She would have told him, but he continued without waiting for an answer. 'And you left your phone. Will you come over to get it?'

Reluctantly, she agreed.

The other message was that Lieutenant Meunier was waiting for her in the hotel dining room. Wearied by his persistence,

Ellie went to meet him. The door was open, and he filled the space by the window, alert and aware of his power, looking out at the harbour. It was very possible he had seen her with Gabriel.

They greeted each other brusquely.

He was going to ask her whether she had seen the man in the panama hat, she knew it. A question to which he already knew the answer.

'I thought you should know the result of our inquiries into the death of Florian Creys. It cannot have been pleasant for you to have this as part of your introduction to Porquerolles, but perhaps it helps to know. I have come to tell you that Florian Creys had a history of depression and drug abuse from the age of fourteen. He was diagnosed as schizophrenic a month ago. Last week he walked out of a clinic in Strasbourg and headed south.'

'So . . . it was suicide, then?'

'The prosecutor at Toulon seems satisfied that it was.'

Ellie peered at him, the narrowed eyes and bulky shoulders that made the room seem so small around him. 'But you're not satisfied.'

He made an expressive sound with his mouth. 'It probably is so.'

'Very sad.'

Just another sad story of a young man who found he could not deal with the world; he would not be the first or the last, the lieutenant seemed to imply. 'You say that he was standing alone when he climbed over the rail.'

'Yes.'

'You say that there was someone else who saw the same as you – but we cannot find this person.'

Now he was closing in on his point.

'I have seen him again – the man in the panama hat. I saw him today.'

'Where?'

'Here, by the harbour.'

'But you did not call me.'

79

She sighed. 'I haven't got my phone. I lost it. I gave him your name and told him that you wanted to speak to him. I'm sure he will call you.'

Meunier appraised this information. 'Do you know the name of this man?' He took out his notebook.

'Gabriel. He didn't tell me his surname.'

'You did not ask?'

'Well, no . . . he said he was attached to the university at Aix. I was going to google him,' she admitted.

He blew air out of his mouth, shaking his head.

'You could find him that way,' she pointed out.

'And you don't know where I can find him on the island?'

'No . . . I'm sorry, I—'

'This is a serious matter involving the death of a young man. In cases like this we have to be sure that all the witness statements support the conclusion. You do understand that?'

She nodded. It seemed to be more about paperwork than anything else.

Against her better judgement, she went back to the Domaine de Fayols. What else could she do? Her mobile held so much information; it felt as if more and more of her life was filed on that phone. Jean-Luc offered to lend her a bicycle from the hotel.

For once the exercise did not calm her mind. The warmth and colour of the landscape had faded. The atmosphere was changing; banks of dark cloud had massed on the horizon; trees whispered in the wind. Was it happening again? Why was it that any connection with the Domaine de Fayols provoked this anxiety?

Dusk was falling early as she pedalled up the drive. The house grew more imposing, its grand facade streaked by the last rays of sunset permitted through the clotting sky. Most of the shutters were closed, and as she looked up, another was pulled shut by an unseen hand, as if the inhabitants were locking themselves in, or securing the house to leave.

Ellie dismounted. She hadn't any time to waste, should have been on the ferry hours ago. She would go in quickly and get out.

The main door was slightly open. Even so, she rang the bell at the side and waited. When no one came after a few minutes, she pushed the door open and entered the hall.

'Hello? Laurent?'

Dance music from the 1940s swelled from somewhere deep inside the house, then stopped. A ticking grew louder, then faded, replaced by a light scratching from one side of the hall, as if mice were invading the wall cavities.

'Hello?'

A faint churchy smell, recent polish perhaps, hinted at order and respectability. She would do everything by the book. It would be foolish to provide the de Fayolses with any reason for finding fault with her professional services. She would not allow them the satisfaction. Returning to the portico, she pulled the door shut and rang the doorbell again, keeping her finger pressed down as she counted to five and released.

The noise continued to ring inside her head, drowning out any other sound.

After a few minutes, a familiar tapping on the flagstones approached the other side of the door and then stopped. Ellie's heart sank. The tapping began again, but was receding now.

It was a few more minutes before the door was opened.

'*Bonsoir*,' said Jeanne, no longer bothering to speak in English. '*Venez avec moi.*'

Ellie followed her across the hall.

In the large sitting room the doors to the terrace were half closed. The lamps had been lit. Outside, the taller trees were bending in an increasingly heavy wind.

The *tap-tap-tap* of a cane began again.

Laurent bounded in from the terrace.

'Ah, you're here! I was making sure the boat was moored properly. Better to be safe if there's going to be a storm.'

Relief at seeing him so unperturbed, so *normal*, allowed

81

Ellie to give him a genuine smile. For a moment he was silhouetted against a sickly yellow-grey sky as he moved towards the drinks tray.

'Will you take an aperitif?'

'No, thank you.'

He poured a glass anyway, and held it out. 'A kir made with our own rosé.'

She shook her head, then took it because there were more important issues to settle.

'My phone, do you—'

'Ah, yes.'

He made no move to fetch it, far less explain how it had left her possession. Instead he raised his glass.

'Let's talk. I want to persuade you to accept the commission. Surely you won't go without reconsidering?'

She watched him carefully, holding her glass but not drinking.

'I'm sorry I had to leave for Paris,' he went on. 'But now I'm back, we can resume our work, *non*? While I was on the move I had some good ideas, and there are various details that I think would appeal to you.'

'My week here is up, I'm afraid. I have a flight booked tomorrow, and commissions back home that need my attention.'

'But we can discuss further, at least.'

'Perhaps.' The lies we tell, she thought.

Tap-tap-tap. Ellie's heart sank.

'Maman,' said Laurent.

Mme de Fayols leaned on her cane. Her eyes were hollows in the candlelight. Laurent leapt over in time to steady the sway and led her tenderly to her high-backed armchair.

'You look frightened of me, Miss Brooke,' she said, staring at Ellie. Her head was skull-like.

'No, not at all. I'm tired, that's all.'

Tired of your games, she wanted to convey.

'I tried to tell you, didn't I?'

Ellie forced herself to stand still, though her legs trembled with the urge to run. She looked to Laurent. 'I really can't stay.

I just – want to collect my phone. Please.'

But he was in no hurry to indulge her ahead of his mother. She asked for her drink, and he poured a tiny flute of purple liqueur.

'We were like animals hunting at night,' said Madame, still addressing Ellie. 'It was all instinct. My instincts have always been acute.'

Ellie stood uneasily rooted to the spot, wondering where she had heard a similar phrase recently. She glanced at Laurent, but he was oblivious.

'We had to spot minute differences,' his mother went on. 'A glimpse, a flicker, a peep, did not carry the same weight as an observation or a stare or even a gaze. We were all deciphering symbols . . . these traps. But we all see in different ways.

'If you saw someone arrested, you had to pretend not to know them, to have no connection. It was life or death. We were silent and helpless in the countryside, where all the winds have names but none of us could whisper ours. Our names were not our own. Our lives were not our own. Can you understand that?'

Ellie shook her head. She had no idea what the woman was talking about.

'Secrecy was everything. It informed the shame of defeat and underpinned our fears for the future. I am old enough now to be cynical, but even then I knew that we all see things in different ways, even when we are on the same side.'

A clock ticked loudly, though Ellie could not see one in the room.

'You concern me, Miss Brooke. You don't seem to want to know about this, and you need to know it.'

Ellie sighed, looking impatiently to Laurent for help. But he was flipping through one of his books in the same way he had when he was searching for a particular image to show her, fired by another of his big ideas, no doubt. If she wanted her phone, she would have to interrupt.

'I'm sorry to have to—'

'He was a traitor, and she helped him. I hate them both for

what they did. It stays with you and poisons what comes after.'

The reedy invective broke with such aggression that at last Laurent seemed concerned. He came over and put his hand on her thin arm. 'Have you taken your pills, Maman?'

'The treacherous Xavier, who left me to fend for myself and betrayed so many others. He threw us to the dogs!' Mme de Fayols spat on the floor.

'Maman—'

As Laurent addressed his mother, Ellie saw the boy he must once have been, the enthusiasms, the eagerness to please, the incomprehension and, ultimately, the ineffectiveness.

Jeanne came in with a tray. Had she been listening outside, judging when to intervene? Was this the subject that marked the tipping into a barely contained madness and the trigger for intervention?

Mme de Fayols waved the housekeeper away imperiously. Her voice was becoming a snarl, shocking from so tiny a person. 'War is brutal, Miss Brooke. It unleashes man's inhumanity, shows a man's true character. And that's why any connection to Xavier had to be treated as suspicious.'

'*Madame, tenez!*' Jeanne held out a glass of water and a small porcelain bowl in which a selection of pills had been arranged.

The handle of the cane cracked down. Glass shattered on the stone floor, accompanied by a howl of fury from the old lady. The housekeeper took a deep breath but said nothing. She turned to go out of the room, presumably to fetch a dustpan and brush.

Laurent bent over his mother, his back blocking her from sight.

'Go. Go as soon as you can,' Jeanne whispered to Ellie as she passed.

'Where's my phone?'

'In the kitchen.'

'Did you take it?' asked Ellie incredulously.

'No! Why would I do that? Madame said she found it in the library.'

'What?' This was beyond exasperating.

84

'I will bring it now.'

In the flash of light that followed – was the storm finally breaking? – Laurent looked frail as he tried to calm his mother. For the first time, Ellie wondered whether he was more worried than he had seemed. His face, when he looked up, was drained of its colour.

'He's here!' cried Madame.

'Who is, Maman?'

'You brought him,' she said, pointing to Ellie.

'I came on my own. To collect my mobile.'

Madame looked past her, out at the terrace.

A slight movement beyond the doors could have been rain, or leaves or distant lightning.

'The priest came today,' she went on. 'He performed an exorcism. He said there would be no more trouble.'

The tang of incense in the hall. Ellie looked around, half expecting to see some ghostly figure. At last Laurent met her eye. He shook his head. More flashes of light – surely this was lightning – reflected on the polished surface of the table. Through the glass doors the night sky slipped past, riding the wind.

Mme de Fayols rambled incoherently, then screamed. Laurent tried and failed to calm her. Then the cries thinned. She dipped her head. Her bony fingers plucked at the folds of her skirt. In an instant Ellie felt nothing but sadness for her. Then—

'Oh please, no . . .'

Mme de Fayols was hardly strong enough to keep the gun level. It shook in her frail grip. Was it the same gun that had been in the drawer upstairs? As if that mattered. She would drop it at any moment. Laurent was quietly making his way behind her chair. A few more seconds, and he would take it from her.

'I'm so sorry,' said Ellie with parched throat. The weapon was no doubt all for show, but she had no intention of taking any risk. 'You're right. I shouldn't have come here. I've obviously upset you, and I didn't mean to. I'm sorry.' The words came out as a kind of sob that did not sound like her.

85

No response.

Ellie watched her. The rushing in her ears came again. Her muscles were flexed to run, but she was pinned to the ground as if in a bad dream. All I wanted was my bloody phone, she thought.

An explosion of thunder overhead seemed to crack the house open. A second later the room fizzed with an eerie brightness, and the gun fired. Her reaction was pure instinct. In the jolt of light and noise, Ellie ran. At last she was moving, throwing herself forward as fast as she could, out onto the terrace and down the stone stairway.

The garden was black. There was barely any light from the sky – no stars, no moon. The storm clouds were thickly banked. But the day's heat lay heavy on the ground, hotter now than it had been when she arrived, like the updraft of a forest fire. Another bolt of lightning plunged a shaft down into the tree line.

She veered round, trying to keep to the path. It was hard to decide what to do – was it crazy to ride a bicycle in an electric storm? Should she just keep running, or find somewhere to hide until the worst was over? More thunder rumbled overhead.

Her feet were no longer crunching on gravel but springing off grass or soft earth. Somehow she had lost the path. How could she have missed it? She stopped. Her vision was blurred.

She put her hands out. She touched foliage, a dense wall of hedge. She could smell the opulent death scent of the datura. She ran along the length of the dark wall, as if feeling for an answer. Her head felt tight. If she could reorient herself, she could find the long way round the house. Perhaps that would be safer anyway.

A rustle sounded up ahead. She froze. When she moved, she sensed other movements. She was not alone. It was as though she were being tracked.

'Ellie! Stop – come back!' It sounded like Laurent.

She fled, running faster than she had ever run. Lightning cracked – or were those more shots? She ran until her lungs were bursting. The ground was sloping downhill. Her muscles felt so weak she stumbled, but kept going. Ever steeper, the path plunged downward. If she stopped, she would fall. But she knew now where she was.

The sea was ahead, the choppy blackness of the *calanque*.

The lighthouse. Was that a beam of light?

She was jerked backwards. She had been caught. Hands out to push her invisible assailant away, she touched prickly branches. Her shirt had snagged on some small tree or shrub. She pulled away, tearing the fabric. Gasping for breath, she doubled over.

When she came up, she turned slowly, hardly daring to look behind. As far as she could make out, she was alone.

But then the clouds shifted, releasing enough opaque brightness to show dark shapes gaining on her. This time, she would not go back. On and on she scrambled. She was soaked through. When he caught her, his hands were slippery on her arms.

It was Gabriel.

He pulled her close with infinite tenderness. 'It's over now,' he said.

'Madame de Fayols – she tried to kill me!'

'It's all right, it's all right . . . I've got you, I'm here now.'

'You came to find me? How did you—'

He stroked her hair with a warm hand, easing away the fear. 'Shh . . . you don't have to worry about anything. I'm here. Whatever needs to be done, I can help you. You're safe now.'

She let herself fall against him.

They walked away from the garden by the sea. The storm had ceased. The clouds were lifting to reveal a flame-red sky; he held her by the hand. They were bathed in the sunset. A plane soared overhead, and she seemed to be taking flight herself.

'No rush now,' he said. 'We have all the time in the world.'

He was right. That was the moment she felt the past slip away, the longing for a man who was gone, along with the grief that had locked the door to her future. She could still feel the sadness, but it no longer held her down.

In this present hour, there was time for anything to happen, endless time.

So she continued slowly, with Gabriel, the man who understood the power of the past, towards the most westerly point of the island. Dark rocks stood waiting to be sculpted by the wind. Tiny seeds rode the air, waiting to fall and take root. Under the sea, corals formed and pearls hardened. Sap rose and juices fed along the vines. White trumpets flowered, and mandarins and lemons shone like drops of gold in fragrant groves.

BOOK II

~

The Lavender Field

1

<small>〜◯</small>

Provence

April 1944

Not a word should be spoken. The scent was the word.

Each week it was the same routine: the girl caught the bus coming down from Digne, no different from any other nineteen-year-old with a job to do. The bus pulled in under the plane trees in the village of Céreste, and she alighted. By a bench where she placed her baskets for a moment, she reached into her shoulder bag for the perfume bottle and carefully dabbed her wrists, applying enough fragrance for it to be unambiguous. Nothing suspicious about this, simply attention to detail; a charming advertisement for the Distillerie Musset, makers of soap and scent. A blue scarf secured her hair; tied around her waist, the lavender-print apron she wore to serve in the shop. Then she picked up her two heavy baskets and made her deliveries: one to the hotel, one to the doctor's surgery and one to the general store. She walked purposefully but would stop for a few minutes to pass the time of day with occasional customers. Then, when her load was lighter, she went on to various houses around and beyond the village and finally arrived at the café.

She would order a small glass of weak wine, and greet the regulars. It was important to acknowledge the Gestapo officers or the Milice at the best tables. She would drink the wine, turn to leave, and then hesitate by the man reading the paper. Sometimes she went over to the Germans to ask if they had any special requests, a present for a girl perhaps. She always gave them a heart-lifting smile, just the right balance of sunny nature and shy innocence, then took a few paces back to the table where the man sat with his newspaper. He was always there, a little unkempt, smudging his glass with dirty hands. Sometimes he read, sometimes he stared into space. They all knew that his spirit had gone. He drank too much. She ignored him, let the scent pass the message. It had warmed now on her skin, thanks to all the walking; her quickened pulse pumped sweet fragrances into the air between them. Lavender: come to the farm. Rose: we have more men to move. Thyme: supplies needed urgently.

She stood at the table, halfway between the counter and the door, making a note of any orders from the men who enjoyed their new powers so much. Smiling pleasantly, though all her instincts told her to spit in their faces.

She glanced up at the clock on the front of the Mairie to check that her watch was correct. Unwise to hang around too long at the roadside bus stop, with the eyes of the men in the café lingering on her. She thanked the café owner, then walked across the road to catch the return bus as the clock hand moved down to show half past three. A nice normal pace, all the way.

2

~⌒~

Wild Violet

1943

When the war lowered the whole of France into blackness, everyone spoke of shadows falling, the dulling of the sun. It seemed to Marthe that she was one of the few who already had the knowledge necessary to survive. She had never seen the occupation of France, but she felt its force pressing down like a meaty pair of hands around the throat; it weakened the breath and weighted the body. On Nazi flags dripping from official buildings, a sinister half-spider sat on a full moon against a background of blood, a sight surely no more peculiar to see than to imagine. Polished black boots rang on cobblestones, stamping authority to the streets, and harsh voices shouted in a language no one understood. The more Marthe heard, the braver it made her: she was no worse off than anyone else as the Germans and the despised Vichy regime tightened their hold on the south.

'Filthy collaborators!'

The insult flew at them like a hissing insect. Mme Musset and Marthe, walking arm in arm down the boulevard des Tilleuls in Manosque, said nothing in response. Marthe felt Madame's grip dig deep into her arm. Their pace picked up, but the older woman made no attempt to refute the accusation.

Marthe allowed herself to be steered along the street to the shop with its own small perfume distillery and soap factory at the rear. There they stopped abruptly. The morning jangle of keys preceded their entry into a calming billow of lavender. Madame opened up the shop, then oversaw Marthe's tasks for the day, providing two young girls to help her. They set to work in the shed at the back, making a fresh batch of rosemary soap.

'Is it true what they say, that we are collaborators?' Marthe finally asked Madame as they stood side by side in the shop putting together an order of *eau de lavande*. It was shaming to admit, even if only to herself, that she had never considered that they might be.

'We are doing the best we can for ourselves.'

'But when people say—'

'It's best to forget whatever you happen to hear.'

'So—'

'We all have to bend with the wind.'

'But—'

'No more questions, my petal.'

' "Nothing is to be feared, it is only to be understood." Do you know who said that?' persisted Marthe. 'Marie Curie, the great scientist – the great *woman* scientist. They told us that, more than once, at school, and I have always believed it.'

'And I cannot disagree. Now, make sure these stoppers are pushed in as tight as can be. I'll not send out leaking bottles.'

Marthe pressed her thumbs harder into the cork until it stuck fast in the glass neck. In the end, she rationalised, bravery came down to faith: faith in the Mussets' kindness and calm authority; faith in the knowledge that waves still broke on the southern shores, that spring buds would unfurl into flower and fruit would ripen.

Throughout the war the Distillerie Musset had continued to manufacture and distribute basic lines of soap and antiseptic cleaning fluids, and small amounts of scent. In most parts of France, a soap made of wood ash and clay was a luxury permitted only to those who had the dirtiest employments. In Provence, where olives still produced oil, and soap could be made from the most basic of local plants, the wartime mix was easily improved; the authorities demanded they continue, allowing Victor Musset to negotiate favourable terms for the supply of any excess.

'What's the alternative?' M Musset always said. 'Without work, we will all starve. With produce, we can at least barter. And if we do not work, what are we? We are dead trees, or fruit that falls unripened. If we have no respect for the land and the crops, respect for the olives and almonds and vines, then we have no respect for ourselves.'

Following their lead in this as in everything, Marthe allowed herself to embrace this comfortingly simple philosophy of life in the foothills close to the great lavender fields on the Valensole plateau. She had already left one home and found another, faced both her fears and then the terrible reality that they were not unfounded. This was the place where, against the odds, the loss of her sight had opened up a world she might never have known without her blindness.

The Mussets were clearly fond of Marthe, and she was so grateful to them for her apprenticeship at the Distillerie Musset that she never thought to question what they told her. They were a second family, and with that came absolute trust and acceptance.

The war had not yet begun when Marthe Lincel went to the perfume factory for the first time. It was a visit organised by the school for the blind in Manosque. If anyone were ever to ask her, she would tell him without hesitation that it was the day that changed her life.

She was eighteen years old, almost ready to leave the school, when she took her first careful steps towards the long table in the blending room at the Distillerie Musset, her hands in the hands of other girls, one in front and one behind. The girls walked in concert down from the school, through gusts of dung from the stables, past the ramparts of the ancient teardrop-shaped town, on past incense from the church and into the tree-lined boulevard des Tilleuls. At the door to the

95

shop, a bell tinkled, and moments later they seemed to enter the very flowering of lavender.

The scent was all around them; it curled and diffused in the air with a sweet warmth and subtlety, then burst with a peppery, musky intensity. The blind girls moved into another room. There they arranged themselves expectantly around a long wooden table, Mme Musset welcomed them and a cork was pulled with a squeaky pop.

'This is pure essence of lavender, grown on the Valensole plateau,' said Madame. 'It is in a glass bottle I am sending around to the right for you all to smell. Be patient, and you will get your turn.'

Other scents followed: rose and mimosa and oil of almond. Now that they felt more relaxed, some of the other girls started being silly, pretending to sniff too hard and claiming the liquid leapt up at them. Marthe remained silent and composed, concentrating hard. Then came the various blends: the lavender and rosemary antiseptic, the orange and clove scent for the house in winter, the liqueur with the tang of juniper that made Marthe unexpectedly homesick for her family's farming hamlet over the hills to the west, where as a child she had been able to see brightness and colours and precise shapes of faces and hills and fruits and flowers.

Afterwards, as the pupils filed past Mme Musset, each nodding her thanks, Marthe found she was speaking before she had even decided to. 'Could I come again, please?'

'You enjoyed this, my petal?'

'Very much, madame. I can't tell you how much.'

The line of girls was pressing into her back now, warm and softly solid.

'I will talk to your teacher.'

The movement of other bodies carried her along past the lilting voice that Marthe could have listened to all day, telling her so much she wanted to know and making sense of the world in a way that she understood instinctively.

'Till the next time, I hope,' said Marthe.

She could not speak on the way back. It was as though her

senses had fully opened and the smells of the town were not only distinct but living, complex but delicious puzzles to solve. Waves of vanilla cream from the patisserie danced with iron from the blacksmith's forge. As they waited to cross a road, she picked up powdered sugar and spring woodland.

Voices of young children sang out: 'Gathered today! Wild violets – only a centime a bunch!'

Marthe dropped the hand she was holding and plucked a centime from her pocket.

Mme Delphine Musset, wife of Victor Musset, owner of the small perfume distillery, also held the title of potions manager, which denoted a higher calling than the production of homespun fragrances. She was a mixer of country tonics and medicines. In a more southern, less industrialised country she might have been known as a wise woman, the kind who dispensed natural cures and used her powers with compassion.

She kept her word to Marthe. Over the following months, she arranged for her to come back a couple of hours one afternoon a week. Marthe washed bottles and stirred soap mixtures with the workers in the sheds of the courtyard factory behind the shop. She was there when deliveries of other essences were made from the farm: the grass-green herbs of spring and winter infusions of cardamom and ginger. But in the course of the many tasks there was always time to talk about which aromas combined successfully and why the addition of one could deepen the impact of another; and the more Marthe asked, the more she was allowed to do. When the time came for her to leave school, she had impressed the Mussets enough with her nose for fragrance to be offered an apprenticeship as a scent maker.

The war came, but life in the unoccupied south went on. For the first few years of learning her craft, Marthe lodged in a room of a house belonging to a friend of Mme Musset. It was close to the shop-factory, and her landlady would take Marthe's arm for the five-minute walk along the pavement under the plane trees to her workplace.

When Mme Musset spoke, it was in the true accent of the southern mountains. Every vowel proclaimed her ancestry in these rocky slopes. To Marthe, whose only physical contact with her was the guiding touch of her hands, Mme Musset was a stout person, with a wide, red-cheeked face. It was several years before Marthe was given a description of the strong bony features that gave her a touch of the witch, one of those elderly women in fairy tales who might be good, or might be evil.

'The kind who sets a trap,' said Bénédicte.

By the time Bénédicte told her this, Marthe was engrossed in the alchemy of perfume and the infinite possibilities it offered. Bénédicte, her sister, was fifteen years old, with little experience outside the farming hamlet where they had been brought up. She had loved to read from an early age; Marthe remembered her bent over an illustrated book of folk tales, the grotesque coloured plates showing wild creatures and wilder humans with distorted features, and she understood where this disconcerting image might have sprung from.

'That's not like you, to be unkind,' said Marthe.

'You told me that's what you wanted me to come for, so that I could describe to you what you couldn't see for yourself.'

'That's true. But—'

'I'm not being unkind. I'm doing my best.'

But Marthe felt her certainties fracture. Here was her sister, usually so good-hearted and loyal, speaking out of turn about the Mussets, her saviours. Mme Musset had seen something special in her. She had kept her word, and they had chosen her. More than that, Madame had given her a purpose in life, and a future she could scarcely have imagined but for the lucky chance of a school visit to the distillery.

'And Monsieur Musset, what do you think of him?'

Bénédicte gave a nervous laugh. 'He's the boss, and he acts like one.'

'He can be a bit distant when he's at work. And short-tempered, sometimes, when people make silly mistakes. "He doesn't suffer fools", that's what Madame says. It took me a while to gain his acceptance. But – oh, Bénédicte! – when he

98

is with his family, he is the kindest man. You should hear the terrible jokes, and how affectionate he is to his wife.'

She didn't need her sister to tell her that Victor Musset was a wide tree of a man – Marthe could sense his bulk and hear where the rumble of his voice started deep in his chest. When Marthe offered the Mussets her ideas for new perfumes, he might suggest a touch more refinement, but there was always expansive praise for her efforts. Madame's small sigh after an inhalation told her all was well. But Monsieur's heavy arm came around her narrow shoulders, and she would shine in his encouragement like a star in the firmament. She had had to work hard to earn his approval.

'He works harder than anyone, always on the move all day between the fields and the production line, the shop and the customers. At least three days a week he's out on the road in the old trap delivering the basic lines in soap and cleaning products. He says he likes to do it himself. He loves to eat, and talk and read, too. In the evenings he reads the essays of Montaigne, makes notes and reads aloud from them – so you see he is a man of culture. The pages of his book turn slowly, and his pencil scribbles. You can tell he is thinking deeply.'

Gradually she had relaxed in his company. The Mussets had no children, but there were always people around at their farmhouse up in the hills above Manosque – in many ways spending time there, as she soon did, was like coming home to the farmstead where she grew up. She missed her family, naturally, but what she was learning at the perfume factory was so absorbing that any misgivings or homesickness passed.

'I'll never forget the day Monsieur called me over to the chair where he was reading by the fire. "Here are some words for you, little one, from the wisest man I know," he said. He meant Montaigne, of course. "A straight oar looks bent in the water. What matters is not merely that we see things but how we see them." And ever since then . . . well, I've known he is thoughtful of others. He is a good man.'

Bénédicte took her hand and squeezed the fingers affectionately. 'It's obvious you're happy here. Maman and Papa . . .

it'll make them happy too when I tell them.'

'I am, yes.'

It was true: despite everything, she was happy. Sometimes it was hard to put such an elemental feeling into words. How was it possible to capture in words what the essence spoke for itself?

After her sister's visit, Marthe's head was brimming with new pictures: the fields of lavender at Valensole, all the subtle grades of blue and purple; the way twilight melted them all into one; the precise hues of the liquid distilled from each plant, the shape and colour of the bottles and a new understanding of the surroundings where she was learning her craft. Just as plant variations were bred together to create new hybrids – like the lavandin from the delicate wild lavender – this was what she did with the descriptions her sister had supplied; she grafted them onto the sights she remembered from childhood and reinvigorated them.

Somehow, though, in Marthe's mind the kindly pumpkin face she had given her mentor Mme Musset was always more dominant than the face that could be seen by others. Without sight, you had to understand what was beneath the surface.

Madame was a true and generous person who cared for her. The endearment had come so naturally – 'my petal' – a name not used for anyone else. The deft way she set out the essential oils for Marthe, always in the same order and the same place on the table, spoke silently of encouragement. The thoughtful cleverness in the way Madame had labelled Marthe's first experimental blends by using sealing wax stamped with letters from an old printing set, so that Marthe could identify each one by touch. Later, when the quality of Marthe's nose and invention was becoming more and more apparent, she was permitted to open the tiny vials of more exotic ingredients bought in Marseille before the war – orris root, amber, patchouli – and used drop by precious drop to add distinction to the homely fragrances of the landscape.

When Marthe's widowed landlady decided to close up the house and move to Banon to live with her daughter and grandchildren while her son-in-law was held as a prisoner of war in Germany, Marthe went to live with the Mussets at the farmhouse surrounded by lavender fields, halfway between the plateau and the town.

3

Almond Blossom

1943

The shepherd's body was found up on the steep slopes where the lavender made its last wild clutches at the mountain peak.

Each year the sheep were moved across the high meadows above the lavender fields. Here men still adhered to the old ways: hardy men with gnarled and twisted limbs, as if they had been carved by the same winds as the rock sculptures.

One of them was the shepherd Pineau. Alone under the blue citadel of the sky, he guided his flock from one ancient stone *borie* to the next. All the farmers knew him: old Pineau in his ragged clothes had been part of the landscape when the great surge in lavender growing for the perfume industry had begun, when the Mussets and others began staining the slopes purple. The shepherd was a man who knew every stone and tree of the ridges, a man who seemed part of nature: part mountain, part stream, part animal, living his life by the turn of the seasons, solitary with his sheep, walking from rocky ledge to pasture, valley to plateau, as they fed. He sang as he went, songs that had been sung for centuries.

That summer day in 1943, when small puffs of his flock broke away and drifted in lazy clouds down the hill, the lavender farmers knew something was wrong. In the uplands men and women had always relied on one another. They went up looking for him.

Urgent footsteps on the path, spitting stones, brought the news to the Musset farmhouse that evening. A hammering at the door, and Auguste burst into the kitchen, panting. 'Old Pineau's had it – they got him!'

Auguste Baumel was the Mussets' best supplier, son of the farmer who had planted vast swathes of the new hybrid lavandin on the plateau.

M Musset scraped his chair back. For a moment there was silence. Then Madame flapped into action, fetching glasses, telling him to pull up a chair, pouring from the bottle.

'I went up with a couple of the others to . . . check on him. I took my cousin Thierry with me,' said Auguste. Thierry ran a garage in town. Marthe couldn't think what expertise he might have provided up in the fields.

Auguste gulped down a drink, and it made him splutter.

'Take it easy, lad.'

The story spilled out. Looking back, it seemed to Marthe that they had forgotten she was in the corner of the room. She listened intently.

Inside the shepherds' hut, hardly more than a pile of stones with its lone chair and table, Auguste and Thierry found Pineau's tin drinking cup on the floor, abandoned. Outside, under the lone olive tree, the shepherd's last meal was still being devoured by flies and beetles. They called his name, thinking he might be injured, unable to move. They found him a hundred metres away, face down in a stream he had used for drinking and bathing. Blowflies hummed over sweet and sickly flesh.

'We turned him over to be sure,' said Auguste.

'And was it—'

'A shot to the head,' said Auguste. 'They must have found him as he washed his hands before eating.'

Silence.

Marthe didn't dare move, let alone speak. She felt the chill of the spring water as it filled the shepherd's nostrils, the stones pushed into his mouth by the flow. Twice dead, by bullet and by water. She remembered her sister describing the hills and mountains as waves on the sea, and the pictures in her head merged. Marthe told no one, but she had a dread fear of drowning.

M Musset paced the floor, his words coming as fast as Auguste's. 'Every barter is a risk. We put aside our differences for a common cause, but never forget that others have their own agenda. It is no longer possible to assume that any two people understand a situation in the same way or have the same loyalties. The natural order has gone, that is what we know.'

She could make no sense of it.

Perhaps one of them noticed her then, as she sat scarcely breathing in the chair by the window. Whatever prompted them, the two men headed for the door and went out.

Marthe's skin prickled. She wondered whether Madame would say anything, either to them or her, but she only clattered some pans and ran the tap.

The shock of Pineau's murder fused with the aroma of burning onions and garlic as Madame turned away from the stove. Insults in the street and the herbal astringency of rosemary soap. Memory and scent, so closely entwined. It can't have been long after that Arlette came to live with the Mussets, bringing a tin of real ground coffee beans. For years they had drunk only a bitter brew of acorns. The rich coffee fragrance was so intoxicating, so redolent of lost freedom, that it brought a tear to the eye. Rosemary, burnt onion and coffee; the lavender harvest; all combined and gave coherence to Marthe's memory of those precise few weeks in July 1943.

Arlette was Mme Musset's niece, daughter of Madame's sister who lived in Lyon. Her parents ran a drapery shop, but since the Germans had crossed the demarcation line and eradicated the *zone libre*, Lyon was considered as dangerous as Paris. Arlette, nineteen when she moved south, had a smile so wide it could be heard in her speech and made others smile in return. She was resilient and optimistic, and she was going to be an actress one day, though quite how she was going to achieve her dream in Manosque rather than the great city of Lyon wasn't altogether clear.

The first time Marthe heard Arlette's voice, it was singing. The song ended, but even when her chatter took over, it had a musical quality that seemed to brim with confidence and joie de vivre, the words barely able to contain the giggle that might erupt at any moment. Marthe had pulled herself back into the corner of the room, as if she might make herself invisible, fearing disdain from the laughing voice, steeling herself for resentment at her position as a cuckoo in the nest.

But Arlette bounded over to her. 'You must be Marthe – I've been longing to meet you! Aunt Delphine sent me some of your lemon balm scent for my birthday, and do you know, I've had women stop me in the street to ask what it is!'

Marthe could only stutter her thanks for the compliment.

'Your ears must be terribly singed.'

'I beg your pardon?'

'My aunt and uncle talk about you all the time – heaping the praise! Your ears must burn on a regular basis.'

'Well, I – that's very good to know, thank you.'

She might not be sincere, Marthe reminded herself.

But over the following months Arlette proved herself not only enthusiastic but practical and a hard worker too. She rolled up her sleeves to make soap alongside the other employees, as well as helping with the deliveries and going out with Monsieur to drum up more business. At the farm too she took on any job that had to be done.

Along the way she and Marthe became firm friends. The war was horrible, but they both agreed it was never a good idea to worry about anything you couldn't change.

'You can't go around asking "What if?" What is, that's the only thing that matters,' said Arlette.

'I had to learn that lesson too, but it was hard,' admitted Marthe. She had surprised herself by confiding the story of how she became blind to Arlette. How, as her eyesight worsened, she had focused – closely, unbearably closely – on what she could still see and feel: the heliotrope flowers on the slope outside the barn; the meadows; the smooth iron of the banister rail under her hand, the half-moons of stone stairs worn away by centuries of use; the tiles on the floor, which still bore the imprints of dogs' paws like fossils. The passages and steps and rooms of her childhood home were safe in her memory, the bedrock and template of all that came after. And then her parents had sent her away, to a new place she had never seen.

'Tell me. Tell me all of it,' Arlette said. Often that first summer they lay in a grassy dell by a group of wild plum trees, gorging on crisp fruit.

'I've never told anyone this before.'

But Arlette would wait for her to find the words. The hum of bees in the background intensified the tart honey of the plums as they sucked the stones clean.

And so Marthe would talk. She told how she had been taken to Manosque when she was eleven years old. Her parents explained that they had brought her to a school for girls like her, and then they left her there alone, struck dumb by the realisation that her worst fears had materialised. At the school for the blind everything around her was alien. Had her parents any idea what it felt like to be surrounded by emptiness, swirling and roaring?

'Were you very angry?'

'Yes. For a long time. I threw myself down the stairs once, furious because I didn't know what that stairwell looked like. I hoped my parents would understand and come and fetch me. But they never did.'

'That must have been terrible.'

'It was, but funnily enough it was the start of better times for me. The two girls who found me at the bottom of the stairs and took me to the matron became my good friends. Renée and Elise. They were so kind, but I'd been so wrapped up in my own worries, I hadn't even noticed before that they were there.'

106

'Friends make all the difference, always. And something good came of your pain.'

'You're right. But it was the fury at my situation that spurred me on. I had to learn how to read a new darkness by using all my senses. I had to identify each sound – think of listening to an orchestra and trying to work out which instruments are playing and in which patterns. I had to interpret the way the air felt on my skin and taste the seasons as they changed. If I thought of myself as anything, it was as a young dog exploring new worlds carried by smell.'

That was why, when they listened to the news on the radio or heard talk about the occupation, Marthe felt no different from the others. She heard what they heard. None of them had seen the events described. The most appalling acts of cruelty and inhuman barbarity were carried out unseen, experienced in absences and abstracts.

As autumn turned to winter that year, they gathered around the wireless each night, forswearing the propaganda of the Vichy government to listen illegally to the BBC broadcasts through storms of interference. From London, patriotic exiles sent out morale-boosting bulletins of Nazi reversals and re-layed the stern, growling drama of Churchill's speeches. And messages would come through, snippets of trite-sounding news from the exiles to their compatriots across the Channel, 'The French Speak to the French'.

By then Auguste often joined them for dinner first. He had taken to bringing pamphlets printed by the underground re-sistance, from which he was keen to read aloud.

'"The Vichy prime minister Pierre Laval is so desperate to keep his deal with the Germans on track, to place France at the right hand of the victor at Europe's top table, that he is sac-rificing the country's young men in ridiculously unbalanced numbers: eight young Frenchmen pushed over the borders to work in German factories for each prisoner returned."'

'I tell you, the Germans obviously hold Laval in contempt, but it's as nothing compared to the contempt I feel for the bastard. And as for Maréchal Pétain, don't get me started on that dangerous old fool! What the hell do they think they are doing? It's unbelievable . . . *unbelievable*! And people still think that he saved the country once before, in the Great War, so no one can doubt his patriotism! He may have been a patriot once, but he is no patriot now.'

A murmur of agreement went round the table. When the occupation began and the Germans assumed control of the northern half of the country, Pétain told the French people it was a pragmatic arrangement; that the French government at Vichy was protecting its people in the wider interests of the country. If France cooperated, he claimed, they would emerge stronger, in partnership with Germany, after this war was over.

A bottle of apricot liqueur was being passed around. Its fiery trail burned Marthe's throat, and she had only managed a few tiny sips.

Arlette was speaking now. 'My father says there are those who want to believe it, that they welcome the invaders because they fear factions of our own people more – the radicals and the Communists. They are secretly pleased that the Germans are stamping out all the disorderly factions.'

'It always astonishes how many different views and interpretations of the same facts there can be,' commented her uncle bitterly.

A guttural sound of derision from Auguste. 'So we're all supposed to read this, and then roll over and let them walk all over us? We must all do what the Germans tell us to do because Pétain did the right thing once? It beggars belief! He and his stooges are just as fascist as the Germans. Have you seen the posters they've put up all over town? Smiling boys leaning out of train windows on their way to work in German factories. They make it look so benign! They're all in it together, and I can't stand it, I tell you.

'And actually, I want to talk about what the hell we are doing, still selling soap to those bastards who are stamping all over us. I mean—'

'I agree with all your political sentiments,' cut in M Musset.

108

'But we have to hold our noses and do what we have to do.'

'And sleep the sleep of the just and the ignorant each night?'

'We do it in order to survive. And it's not so black and white! Sometimes it's the "collaborators" who are keeping people safe – have you thought about that? The clerks working at the town hall who try to intervene on behalf of others, they are the ones to put themselves on the line, negotiating and trading with the regime.'

'Is that what we're doing?'

'Yes. The Distillerie Musset is open for business so that we and many others can eat.'

This measured response was met by another snort from Auguste. 'When my father planted the first lavender fields on the plateau after the last war, it was to build a better life, to safeguard the people and their livelihoods here. He was not doing it to surrender the fields of the south to the old enemy.'

'Your late father was a fine man, and a good friend to me. He was also a good negotiator. Don't forget the two of us were once in partnership, as we are now. He would have taken the practical line too.'

'He would turn in his grave at the thought of the way you appease Kommandant Baumann and his bully boys every time.'

'It's a good contract. And if we do not work, what are we?'

'You know they call us dirty collaborators, don't you?'

'They can call us what they like. We have our integrity and our ideals in this half-life of broken promises and self-interest from our politicians! We've worked hard to build up our business.'

'I don't disagree . . . How can I? But – ah! I get so angry!'

Auguste had changed. It was as if, with the occupation, he had found what he had wanted all along – a purpose. He sparked and fizzed with energy. His actions made clean, de-finite noises: a bang of his glass on the table, clipped footsteps, single swishes of newspaper. Not so long ago he had had a reputation of trying it on with girls who were too young for him, whether that was an issue of self-confidence or not. But now he was sure of himself, surer than ever. His time had come, and he was going to seize it.

'Pétain is eighty-seven years old! He won't be around to see the hell of what he's done! I don't care if he was the country's greatest hero of the Great War, he's turned against his own people.'

Mme Musset's soft voice changed the subject to less troubling matters. 'How is your girl, Auguste? Is that all still on?'

Auguste's girl worked in a dress shop in Céreste. Pretty, according to Monsieur and Madame. Vain and proud, according to Arlette, though she conceded that her clothes were always pretty, when most people rarely had anything new.

'Why would I not still be seeing Christine?'

'I'm only asking.'

'Well, I am. It's just that I've been so busy lately . . . many things to be organised. She understands. You know how it is.'

'Of course, dear. Now, I expect you're hungry as usual, my dear idealist. There's hazelnut cake – surprisingly good, considering I've had to substitute grated nuts and carrot for flour and sugar. And Victor came back from Reillanne this afternoon with a rabbit, which I've stewed.'

Soon there was a soothing sizzle of courgettes frying in a pan.

Over dinner Auguste calmed down. When Marthe pictured him, he was the upright figure in the fields described by Bénédicte, sporting a dark waistcoat over a white shirt and baring the gold tooth that had commanded her sister's attention. Still a relatively young man who was not all he seemed, she had intimated. Marthe had always found him pleasant and sincere. You could tell a great deal by the tone of a voice, and while he was undoubtedly impulsive at times, his usual state was cautiousness. He was determined, and he felt things deeply.

And Marthe too struggled to put aside what had happened to the country and not allow it to spoil the pictures she retained in her head. That was what she found unforgivable as news of the first atrocities swept across the villages with the malevolent force of the mistral. No longer did the vista of a single olive tree by a *borie*, or a stream above a rolling sea of purple, signify serenity; after old Pineau's death, they were execution scenes, just as the first white almond blossom of spring was now redolent of death. From across the valley the orchards were easily mistaken for drifts of white mist; a shroud for the farmer and his family shot in the back of the head for sheltering escaped prisoners of war.

The violence had come closer. Marthe could sense the disintegration of what had been passing for normality. Week after week as the year turned, the soothing choreography of feet on the floor tiles, the routines and rhythms of the family, the regular appearances of the workers, all was changing.

Marthe was disconcerted by unfamiliar footfalls and low voices. Heavy objects were moved around the farmhouse and the outbuildings. Swishing noises came from the entrance hall for which she could not find a source. Almost every day there was a new sound to be processed.

'What's going on?' Marthe asked Mme Musset.

'Nothing for you to concern yourself with, my petal. Here, take these peas to shell – that would be a help.'

Peas to shell. Soap to wrap. A knitted jumper to unravel and rewind the wool to use again. There was always a little job to keep her busy. To keep her quiet and away from whatever was happening. With trembling fingers Marthe bent to her task, alive to the faintest clue.

Arlette tried to lighten the mood. She had gone back to Lyon to visit her family at Christmas and came back with some gramophone records. M Musset put them on, and suddenly the house came alive with music, Arlette singing along. One recording was played over and over again: 'Douce France', sung by Charles Trenet. *'Douce France, cher pays de mon enfance . . . Je t'ai gardée dans mon coeur.'* Marthe realised she was not the only one whose childhood country belonged to a vanished world.

The other great favourite was 'Boum!' It was such a jolly song about the way the heart beat when you fell in love. *'Boum!*

La pendule fait tic-tac tic-tac . . . et la jolie cloche din dan don . . . mais Boum! Et c'est l'Amour qui s'eveille!'

'Do you have a young man, Arlette?'

'No. I have several!'

'*. . . Quand notre coeur fait boum, tout avec lui dit boum . . .*'

'Are you in love with any of them?'

'Phooey, no! I just want to have some fun, and then when the war's over I shall concentrate on my career as an actress. I'm going to do it, you know, you just wait and see – I mean, sorry—'

'Nothing to be sorry about. I shall still see you in my way, you know that. I shall be the first on my feet clapping and cheering as the curtain comes down.'

'You'll have to travel . . . to Nice and Paris and . . . Biarritz and beyond. Rome! London! New York! You won't see me for dust here after this war is over! But I shall always send you the money and tickets, don't worry.'

'It will be wonderful.'

It was easy to be positive with Arlette. She had even persuaded her uncle to allow her to help him recruit more workers. 'Why can't a girl do it? In fact, I shall make it my mission to improve sales despite all the obstacles. I might even have certain . . . advantages when it comes to persuading young men to stay here and work for us instead of getting on a train for Germany.'

Auguste seemed more cheerful too. Marthe heard Auguste and Arlette, chattering and joshing, setting off to town together. He gave her lifts sometimes in the old hayrick they used to pull the cut lavender to the copper still in the fields at harvest time.

'You're not in love with Auguste, are you?' asked Marthe shyly.

'No! Not in the least. Oh, he's nice enough, but he's a bit too old for me. He's more like a much older brother, one you can tease.'

It was just as well there could still be some light-heartedness. Water coughed in the pipes. There were a couple of new workers in the lavender fields whom Madame had invited to have baths at the farmhouse. Marthe had heard the heavy tread of their boots going up the tiled staircase.

'That reminds me,' said Arlette. 'Aunt Delphine asked if we would finish washing some sheets that have been soaking.'

They linked arms and went to the outhouse. They talked as they scrubbed sheets at the washboard. They worked until the tips of their fingers were cold and wrinkling like seaweed.

'There seem to be an awful lot of sheets.'

'You're not wrong there. It's hard work.'

'I don't mind,' said Marthe.

'I know you don't.'

'This reminds me of chores at home, helping Maman. I like it.'

For a while there was nothing but the sound of evening birds singing and the wind in the orchard trees. Then Marthe said: 'Please don't tell me I'm speaking out of turn, but I've sensed things lately . . . sensed changes. Will *you* tell me what is happening here?'

She kept on working the cold sheet as if the steady rhythm would ward off her fears. Change frightened her. If the world changed completely, I wouldn't know it, she thought but did not say. In my head it will always be the world of my childhood, but the scenes will be obsolete, like the images frozen in woodblocks used to print pictures, or enamelled hard and shiny on old-fashioned ornaments.

'We have a few extra workers at the moment,' said Arlette. 'We have to billet them for now, that's all.'

'I know that. But—'

'Marthe . . . dear, sweet Marthe, it's better you don't know.'

'Please don't say that! That's what everyone says, and it just isn't true!'

But still Arlette would not tell her.

In the blending room at the Distillerie Musset in town, Marthe held a glass vial to her nose: a distillation of violet. She breathed in slowly until it seemed for those few moments the air was reduced to a powdery sweet-sharpness. This February, when the schoolchildren once again sold posies of wild violets on the street corners, Marthe asked them to bring all they had to the perfume factory and managed to extract a few drops of essence. Over the months since then she had experimented with other ingredients to intensify the fragrance, but now the addition of spicy acacia wood had deepened its distinctive sweetness (the scent that would always recall that first propitious visit to the Mussets) to capture its shaded woodland origins and the shy purple petals in the first shafts of spring sunshine.

Arlette clattered in. She had worn through her shoes with all the walking she did making deliveries in the towns and villages, and the cobbler had fitted wooden tips on the soles and heels. As ever, Arlette turned adversity to her advantage and announced her arrival with a little tap dance.

'Bravo! Monsieur Astaire of Hollywood will have you as his new partner yet!' Marthe giggled.

Arlette tap-tapped over to the tall wooden cupboards that lined the room. 'I thank you kindly, mademoiselle, and will perform an encore as soon as I collect some more of that new rose eau de toilette you mixed the other week.' Doors opened and closed as she helped herself.

'You're getting through that one,' said Marthe.

'It's proving very popular.'

'I'm glad.'

'What's so sublime is the way the true essence of the flower comes through so strongly and distinctly, and seems to grow as you wear it.'

'It's a soliflore. The simple essence of one flower, enhanced a little but absolutely itself.'

'That's right.'

'If you like that, come and smell this. Tell me what you think.'

Arlette sniffed at the glass vial Marthe held out. 'Mmm . . . it's violet! Unmistakable.'

'Unmistakably itself, but deepened by using an extract from the leaves as well as the flower, and with acacia wood. Can you

114

smell the cinnamon spiciness of the acacia? I've added a faint touch of orange and narcissus to sharpen it. Then a tiny hint of musky sandalwood too, which will help it develop on the skin and make it last.'

'It's just incredible. You know, we need a new, stronger fragrance . . . another single flower—'

'Do we?'

'—and this could work very well, as it couldn't possibly be mistaken for anything else in our line.'

'It's an old-fashioned perfume really, but romantic. Girls used to say that violets stood for modesty and humility. Would it work today, though? You see, the reason I've been making this was . . . well, it's silly and sentimental really . . . but this was the scent I smelled out on the street that first day I came to—'

An excited *rat-a-tat* burst from Arlette's feet. 'I've got to go! Marthe, you are a genius!'

'Where—'

But Marthe was speaking to the air. Arlette had waltzed off, as lost in her own world as Marthe was in hers.

The violet perfume was good, though. It would be quite special when she had it exactly right.

But later that night at the farmhouse, long after she had gone to her room, Marthe overheard the Mussets talking. She stopped outside the kitchen, forgetting about the water she wanted.

'She is safe, though, isn't she?' asked Monsieur.

'Can we trust her, you mean?'

'We must all be careful.'

'I'm not sure. I want to – but it's hard to judge. There's certainly . . .'

'So what are we to do?' asked Monsieur. 'If we say anything—'

'I know.'

'We'll just have to watch and wait.'

Marthe felt sick. How could it be that the family did not trust her? And had they taken her in only out of charity, after all, a hopeless case to whom kindness should be shown? Worse, did they consider her a liability? But surely there could be no conceivable question about her trustworthiness and loyalty!

'It costs money to do all this,' went on Monsieur. 'Money that none of us have. Fuel for the truck, the working hours lost.'

A murmur from Madame.

'I thought about selling some books, but that won't raise much. It will have to be my father's fob watch.'

'Take it to the pawnbroker, you mean?'

'No, that might be too obvious. It would have to be done on the quiet. I know someone who is willing to buy.'

'Who?'

'The Engineer. He's a wealthy man.'

Silence except for the ticking of the old clock.

'You can't sell that watch. But I could offer some bits and pieces from the jewellery my mother left me. I never wear the jade bracelet or that cameo brooch.'

'It's a kind thought, but that won't raise much.'

Another pause, then a light sigh. 'My pearl, then, as well. The setting, the chain – it's all good-quality gold.'

'But that was—'

'I know. But I don't need it any more to tell me you care. All the years since have told me that – my dearest, sweetest man.'

'Are you sure?'

'Of course. This way, we give it together to show we care.'

'But if Auguste can come up with a few things too—'

'We'll manage somehow. We have to.'

Marthe stood stock-still against the wall. The sense of elation at her achievement with the violet perfume had drained away.

In the days afterwards, as she tried and failed to decide what to do, the words went round in her head, humiliating her like a public slap. She was too frightened of what she might be told if she opened the subject herself with Madame, so she kept quiet, wanting to hold onto her job with the Mussets for as long as possible. There were many kinds of darkness, she realised then, and the most daunting was being cast off by those who had previously offered comfort. Marthe bore the secret knowledge as a fight she was not yet willing to concede, but nothing was the same. The water from the spring tasted bitter, where once it held flavours of thyme and mint. She ate sparingly, careful to take as little as possible at meals, and lay awake hungry, night after night.

The violet perfume was praised to the skies, but the Mussets allowed her to make only a very small quantity. Spring burst out and warmth returned, yet Marthe's world contracted tightly around her. She was more isolated than she had ever been before. Lonely too, in the most profound sense, as lonely as she had been when she first arrived at the school for the blind, but this was worse because once the Mussets had opened their magical world to her, she would always know what treasures were inside. She wanted to protest, but sensed that her only weapon was her pride. She would work harder than ever to prove herself.

Superficially, nothing had changed, but Monsieur was away on ever more frequent delivery trips, often taking Arlette with him. Auguste's role had changed to involve him much more in the product distribution, too. Madame often seemed preoccupied.

'Just the war, my petal,' she would say when Marthe asked her if everything was all right.

When winter returned for a few weeks, frost killing any green shoots, it seemed a reflection of the mood at the Musset farmhouse. Dank mist over the orchard trees muffled birdsong and reduced voices to echoes in the gloom.

4

Thyme and Fig

April 1944

At the farm on the slopes above Manosque, the clock on the shelf ticked too loudly. It always ticked louder than usual and much too slowly on Thursday afternoons as they waited for Arlette to return from making deliveries in Céreste on the bus. Only when the latch rattled on the back door and Arlette's voice punctured the tension did it slip back to its normal volume and rhythm.

The hour sounded: five soft hits on the bell mechanism. Mme Musset opened a squeaky cupboard door and then closed it again, as if compelled to find some mundane business for her hands. The chink of a glass, water running. Monsieur padded over to the range and struck a match. The thin blue scent of a poor cigarette.

'She's normally back by now,' said Madame, unnecessarily.

Each week Arlette returned from Céreste with tales of the lazy brutishness of the young blond soldiers who stood guard over Route Nationale 100 as it came through the village, of the *miliciens* kicking up the dust in the streets of the old quarter to harass the inhabitants of its narrow houses.

The Milice were a triumph of Vichy fascism, according to Monsieur. The French themselves had created this corruption of the military and the police, with the help of the Germans, as a paramilitary force to be unleashed against any dissent, in particular the growing influence of the Resistance. These *miliciens* soon became cruelly expert in executions and deportations. Some were criminals who were told their sentences would be commuted for this loyal government service. Some were the starving who joined for the regular pay and food. Many were locals recruited as part-timers, and all were more dangerous than the Germans because they knew the language and the terrain. After a year and a half, the vicious methods of the Milice were no better than the Nazis'. The old networks of families and neighbours had been corrupted. No one knew who to trust any more.

The quarter-hour *ting-ting*ed.

Seconds later Arlette's chatter preceded her through the doorway. There was a clumsy thump as she brought the large woven basket down on the table. The scent of a fresh loaf of rationed bread. A rattle of cups and plates. Quick, light steps and flurries of air nudged the room back into its usual rhythms.

'How did it go?' asked Musset.

'Fine,' said Arlette. 'No need to be worried. I did nothing, said nothing, out of the ordinary.'

She squeezed Marthe's hand in greeting. Rosewater softened the air as she drew close.

'What did you see? Did you notice any changes?' M Musset was already asking her. 'It's the smallest details that make the difference, even if you don't know what they mean yet.' He was here in the kitchen every Thursday when Arlette returned, eager to know what she had observed on her rounds. Needing to know that she was back safely.

'There are definitely more soldiers in uniform, going in and out of the Mairie and looking purposeful,' said Arlette. 'A couple of new ones in the café. Two young men I'd never seen before. One of them leered at me, like a pig with small eyes.'

'I hope you—'

'I smiled very sweetly, nothing more. The Milice were

119

counting the passengers on and off the bus from Aix, but not ours.'

'They say there are more soldiers coming, German and those they're putting into uniform from the east of Europe, more every week – read the newspaper. Baumann is boasting of doubling the garrison.'

'May the saints preserve us!' Mme Musset interrupted.

There was silence, broken finally by Arlette. 'That explains the next order. Here's the list, longer than ever.'

'Good girl. We will let them have what they need,' said Musset.

'They'll get what they need all right,' said Arlette defiantly. 'I hate them. Over at Castellet last week two families in the hamlet were shot outside the church on Sunday just for supplying food to the Maquis. They say there are six hundred Maquis in the hills behind Céreste – all of them hungry and impatient.'

'Some of them are young hotheads. They don't think before they act, though I admire their spirit.' Monsieur sucked hard on his cigarette and then ground it out. A tarry bitterness hung over the table. Each week brought more tales of subordination and sabotage, followed by retaliations, swift and brutal.

'More and more are joining them, now they sense the tide has turned,' said Arlette.

'Make no mistake, the enemy is always most dangerous when it is pushed onto the back foot.'

No one said anything.

Madame began to investigate the contents of the basket, rustling paper wrappings. Since food rations had been cut, their coupons brought less and less back to the table. But they were better off by far than many, with their orchards of fruit and nuts and olives, chickens and land to grow vegetables. On market day in cities there was often little more to buy than swedes and turnips and tough plucked crows on the butcher's stall.

She sniffed. 'That cheese isn't too bad.'

'Exchanged for a bar of lavandin-rosemary soap,' said Arlette.

'You've done very well, my dear.'

'Tell me what the Engineer had to say,' said Musset.

Marthe felt the imprint of Arlette's hand on her shoulder and then a renewed sense of loss when her friend walked away into the garden with her uncle to continue their conversation.

Afew days later Marthe was sitting alone on the terrace by the kitchen door, trying to separate the scents as they rode a warm breeze: thyme and lemon balm; the fig tree's spices, sweet as cinnamon milk in the drowsy afternoon heat. Madame had gone out to check on the chickens, hoping for eggs. A click sounded. It could have been the wind in the tree by the door. Marthe listened harder. Light footfalls came up the path and stopped in front of her.

'Who is it?'

'Christine.'

Auguste's girlfriend, who worked in the dress shop. Marthe tried to imagine what marvels of new clothing adorned her. All she could picture was a princess in an old book in a swirling puff of organza, and that could not have been right.

'Do you know where Auguste is?'

'I don't – I'm sorry,' said Marthe. 'In the fields, I would imagine. Either here or at one of the other farms.' Auguste had recently taken on a supervisory role at several other lavender farms, where workers were in short supply, linking them into a cooperative to keep supplies coming.

'And Arlette – where is she?'

'I'm not sure. Have you tried the shop?'

'She's not there.'

'She might be helping with the deliveries.'

'She might be. Or she might be with Auguste.'

'Well, I suppose she might. It's possible.'

'So are they somewhere together?'

'I've told you, I don't know.'

Christine reached across her. She picked up and set down various objects on the table: a candle lantern; a magazine; some papers under a weight.

Marthe stood up. 'I'm not sure how I can help you, Christine.'

'I am. You can answer my question: are they together?' Her tone was impatient, bordering on rudeness.

'I have no idea,' snapped Marthe.

A silence stretched between them. Then the other girl made a noise of furious frustration. She seemed to be focusing her anger on Marthe, but then swept past her and into the kitchen. The door slammed.

'Hey, you can't—'

She obviously had.

Marthe got up and stood in the doorway. Christine was opening drawers and cupboards. 'You won't find them in there!'

Without another word, the woman pushed past her. Marthe followed the movement to the wall of the terrace. Footsteps broke the path's crust once again, and the unsettling incident was over.

Marthe pressed her hands to her forehead and tried to recover her composure. She was trembling. She did not understand what had just occurred, sensed only that something untoward had taken place.

'Madame!' she called.

When there was no answer, she made her way down towards the chicken run, one hand on the wall that ran down to the stone barn. She knew every stone of the way. Lizards skittered. Sunlight seared her face and bare arms, then faded as if thick clouds had pushed in and absorbed all the heat.

A rustling noise caught her attention, then a low intermittent hum. She slowed, straining to hear, while creeping forward, keeping her steps soundless.

It was a voice, speaking in a low murmur.

She drew closer. At the edge of the barn she could hear male voices inside. She could not understand what was being said. Perhaps they were the foreigners who worked in the fields. Marthe had known for years that itinerant Spanish and Portuguese worked the lavender farms. But they should not be up here at the Musset farmhouse. They had their own large hut in the fields owned by Auguste's family.

Moving faster now, she worked her way round to the door. Already riled by Christine, she felt a rising anger that these men might have come to steal from the very people who were providing their work and shelter.

'What are you doing here?' she shouted into the space.

No answer.

'I know you're there. Answer me!'

Hay rustled. 'Caspian knows we are here,' came a whisper. A man's voice, oddly accented. So they were foreigners.

Her face was burning. 'Who's Caspian?'

'Keep your voice down! You know the rules. Caspian ... the Philosopher.'

'You're talking nonsense. I'll ask you again: what are you doing here?'

'Ssh! We're ... waiting for the moon ...'

Waiting for the moon? It was as though she had stumbled into another farm, one in fairyland perhaps. They might be tiny sprites, another set of workers with an unknown purpose. Marthe shivered now, completely at sea.

'There's no Caspian here,' she repeated.

'Sometimes they just call him the Philosopher. You think I would say this to you if I hadn't seen you here for weeks, working, eating and riding the pony trap with the family?'

Marthe backed away.

'I'm going back now,' she said, edging her way out. He did not try to stop her.

Her forehead was tight; her head was beginning to hurt. This man was no Spaniard or Portuguese, she realised, feeling for the top of the stone wall under her outstretched hand.

She had to act quickly.

'Monsieur! Madame!' she called as she approached the farmhouse.

No answer.

Before she reached the door, someone caught hold of her and she jumped.

'Whatever's the matter?' asked Mme Musset.

'I'm not sure, but you need to know . . .' Marthe couldn't form the words fast enough. 'Strangers in the barn. Some men.'

'Stay here, I'll deal with this.'

But when Mme Musset returned, she said not a word about the men. 'Here, I've picked some courgettes and a nice fat aubergine. If you'll give me a hand, we'll make a start on supper.'

By now, Marthe knew better than to ask.

That night, as usual now, she pulled away from the voices in the kitchen and sat in the corner seat with her Braille stylus device and her slate, writing to a friend from school. If she had to earn the family's trust once again from the beginning, then she was determined to do so.

'What are you doing?' asked Arlette. Perhaps she had been so bound up in whatever was going on that she had only just noticed that Marthe was also behaving differently.

'I'm writing in Braille.'

There was a pause. 'Show me.'

Marthe offered up the slate and stylus. 'Once you know the patterns for each letter, you use these to make the dot from the back of the paper, writing in a mirror image.'

'Is it hard?'

'Well, not once you've learned how to do it.'

Arlette ran her fingers over the page.

'Did you know that Braille was once known as night writing? It was invented for Napoleon, so that soldiers could read messages in the dark with no need to use a light,' said Marthe.

There was no answer. Then Arlette clasped her so tightly around the shoulders that it hurt.

'Uncle Victor! Come here quick!' she cried.

M Musset drew up a chair next to her.

She knew what came next would not be easy for him, but this was it: he was going to tell her to leave, that they could no

124

longer support her, and she began to prepare herself for the worst, to fling herself at him and beg him to reconsider.

'I am going to make a terrible demand of you, Marthe.'

She stood up to take the blow, however it fell, though she felt as though she were sinking through the floor. 'Please don't make me leave! You can trust me – you know you can!'

'Leave? Whoever said anything about leaving?'

'That's not what you wanted to tell me? I heard you talking, weeks ago – saying you didn't know whether I was safe or not, whether you could trust me,' she said.

'You heard that? We've never thought that! How could we?'

'But you said—'

There was a pause, during which she sensed silent communication.

'We weren't talking about you, my dear. Never.'

It was a struggle to contain her joy.

'Now listen, child . . . I'm going to ask you something, Marthe. It is very serious. But before I do, you must know that you have a choice. You don't have to do it.'

Marthe wondered whether he realised that she could never refuse any request he made of her.

'What I have to ask you is—'

'Yes. I'll do it.'

' 'Yes? You don't even know what I'm going to ask!'

'If it's you who are asking, or Madame, then the answer's yes, whatever it is.'

'That's very loyal. I appreciate that, I really do. But some demands, some actions, are extremely serious. There are grave moral implications. There might be danger of the very worst kind, my dear.'

'I don't care.'

Silence.

'All right. I hope what I say will not shock you.'

Marthe shook her head.

'Even now I cannot tell you too much. There are aspects I know nothing about. No one knows everything, except for the chiefs. Knowledge is a dangerous commodity in these times.

If we have kept certain things from you, you must accept that it was for the safety of all of us.'

They had begun by helping to repatriate Allied airmen and escapees. For weeks, sometimes months, the men were looked after at the lavender farm, gathering their strength in sunlight by doing light work in the fields, hiding in plain view while they waited for the local guides who would take them on to the port at Marseille. These British and American men, sometimes a Pole or Czech who flew for the RAF, were hidden among the Spanish and Portuguese and the other refugee workers who had moved south when this was still the *Zone Libre*. If the Germans ever came to check, their lack of good French could be explained away. But thanks to Musset's tightrope walk playing the collaborator, they were mostly left alone.

Over the past year, their links with the Resistance had strengthened. Auguste had drawn them closer into active circles. At Céreste there lived a man who in another life had been a poet; this gentle but passionate man had built up cells of resistance across the region, all playing their part, all in contact with other cells, all links in the chain. The idiosyncratic messages broadcast from London to friends and family in France on the BBC were coded instructions to the partisans.

'They confirm the imminent arrival of parachute drops and landings. The British send us weapons by air. Explosives. Clothes and shoes too, sometimes. Planes that land in the dead of night with no lights. We are all working together to regain our country. Now, I am only ever going to tell you only as much as you need to know.'

Marthe nodded eagerly, hardly able to believe what he was telling her.

'What we need is your expertise in communication.'

'My expertise?'

'After they got old Pineau, we knew we had to keep wireless communications to a minimum. The authorities can track the signals too easily. It's too dangerous to use radios between themselves – we have to keep our capacity to contact the British agents on the ground and for them to contact London. The fallback system has always been to leave messages in known locations, but many of these are now unsafe. There's no such thing as a safe house any more, and we can't put more people in danger.

'Anything written down, even in code, would be suspicious. But if we designed a wrapper for the soap, containing no additional note or markings – any visible markings—'

'Braille.'

'Yes, exactly so.'

'Just tell me what you want me to write, and I will do it.'

'Good girl.'

'But what about a translator?'

'That's the other matter for which I need your help. Who can read Braille that you know you can trust absolutely?'

'Which area?'

'Over towards Apt, ideally. Aix. Sisteron.'

Her mind was already working through her old friends from school. Renée, of course. And Elise too. She could trust them.

'Renée lives in Apt now. She has a job in the music shop.'

'Good. That's a very good start. All the best drops have plenty of people legitimately going in and out.'

'There will be others . . . Elise is at Forcalquier now, and there's another girl, Jeanne, who comes from Aix. We will all work so diligently – we were taught well at the school!'

The prospect of the months to come was thrilling. Her tasks would be as absorbing as they were mysterious and exciting. But first there were other questions she needed to ask. 'The men in the barn . . .' she said.

'We decided to bring some of our . . . foreign guests up here last week. It won't be long now until they can move on, and it's safer that they are here while the final arrangements are being made.'

'They said they were waiting for someone called Caspian who was a philosopher.'

There was a loaded pause. 'I am Caspian,' said M Musset.

'We don't use our real names, it's too dangerous. Also known as the Philosopher. I will have to speak to them. We've made a narrow room for them behind tall stacks of hay, and they are supposed to stay completely quiet if they hear anything at all outside. But obviously they have not been as careful as they should be.'

At last she understood.

'It won't be long now,' said Monsieur. 'We're waiting for the full moon. When the moon is full, a plane is coming for them.'

Resistance. What was resistance but the will to survive? Like roots in the winter ground, they had been dormant, but when the sun warmed the soil, they would push up to emerge into the air again, every cell remembering the blueness of the sky, each tiny bud coiled tight and ready to burst out.

'I wore your violet perfume today,' said Arlette. 'Violet for modesty, to tell our people at Céreste that all is quiet but well. It sent a beautifully clear message. There were many compliments. Even our man Candide, pretending to be drunk as usual in the café, sniffed appreciatively.'

'I am learning so much,' said Marthe to Arlette as they said good night. 'But I'm not frightened.' That was not quite true. But she had been far more frightened of being cast adrift by the Mussets.

It was extraordinary, thought Marthe, how they had adapted to living in constant terror of discovery. At first it was exhausting. Then exhaustion and tension became normal, it seemed. It was extraordinary; yet another way the human body and mind adapted to circumstance.

There were two of them in the barn, and they were both Americans.

Arlette took Marthe with her when she brought food to the men. Arlette stood guard by the open door while they wolfed chickpea stew. It was the best they could offer that day.

Marthe sat on the straw. After a while they spoke to her. At first it was a conversation *in rondo*, one of those songs where the same tune and words are sung at different intervals. Their responses clashed and misfired. One of them could hardly speak French, just single words he had picked up. But the other could speak surprisingly well after months on the run through France.

His name was Kenton Attwater, and he was a twenty-three-year-old navigator in a plane called a Fortress that had been shot down somewhere close to Grenoble. He had managed to bail out, and his parachute brought him down uninjured but for a few gashes and bruises.

'I was lucky. It was a wild, remote place. There was no one watching me come down.'

He had buried the parachute and run into woodland where he hid until it was dark. At night he walked south. When he became so hungry that he had no choice but to take a chance on an isolated farmhouse, he was welcomed and fed.

'That was my second piece of luck. They let me rest in a barn, and the next day they brought a man to see me. I thought he must have been OK because he carried a British gun. He brought me that night to the next safe house.'

It took two months of resting and moving on at night, each time with a different guide, before he had arrived at Auguste's lavender fields.

'When we came over the hill there was a great cliff high in the sky but deep in shadow. It was a threatening place – the whole mountain was looming over us, purple and black. But in front of it was a smaller hilltop with a church on top and a very few houses, and this small hill was lit gold by the sun like a spotlight. I'll never forget it. I couldn't tell you why, but I felt safe.'

'You *are* safe,' said Marthe. 'There are so many complicated ways the mountains and valleys and plateaux link together here – that's our secret weapon. And you know, some of these farms and houses were built in the time of the Romans. The thick stone walls are defences, and the drystone walls that drop down the terraces provide secret enclosures. We can see who is coming up here, and we can be ready.'

'From a flying fortress to an old one,' the American said grimly.

'How long were you at Auguste's farm?'

'Almost a month. That's where I ran into Scotty.'

'Who's Scotty?'

'My friend here. Gunner Scotty Davis from Detroit. He's been in a prisoner-of-war camp. He managed to escape – that's quite something! He's lucky, too. He got a pack of playing cards in a food parcel. So he started a poker school. Two days later there's a letter telling them in code to drop the cards in a bucket of water. Turned out the cards were a fifty-two-part map of the route to Switzerland. So he started figuring out how he could use it.' He laughed. 'And would you look at that, there he goes again, taking his chances!'

'What do you mean?'

'He hasn't wasted much time with Arlette over there!'

'I can't look at that.'

'Sorry?'

'I can't see that. Or anything else.'

'You're blind? I didn't know. I mean, now you tell me, I can see it, but I – ah, no, I shouldn't have put it like that – I . . . I'm sorry.'

'You mustn't feel sorry for me. I don't.'

In some ways they were all the same now. So many people stumbling around in the dark, just as she was. All across Europe there were secret roads along which men and women were moving, some towards safety, others farther into darkness. One false step. Lives in the balance. So much unknown.

Work at the perfume factory continued at a frenetic pace. Marthe spent hours each night at the farmhouse with her slate and stylus. The packages of soap with their embossed wrappers, different scents bearing different messages, were delivered to a hotel in Apt. The messages were transcribed and passed on verbally at the music shop a few narrow streets away. In Céreste, the Poet generously gave board and lodging to a blind refugee. He too was an eager recipient of soap, and wasted no time in organising his own distribution network.

The end was nearing, they could feel it. On 6 June millions of Allied soldiers had landed in Normandy and were breaking through from the north. But the dangers had increased. In Reillanne a medieval convent on the hill had been used for several years as a hostel for those who had fled the north, and other foreign workers. In an act of pure viciousness, fifty-four Jewish workers who had lived quietly among them were deported. In the nearby village of Saint-Michel the inhabitants were woken by pounding on their doors and ordered to gather in the square in front of the Mairie. A senior officer of the Milice stood on the steps and read out a transcript of Pétain's speech: 'People of France, do not worsen your unhappiness with acts that risk calling tragic reprisals upon yourselves . . .'

On 4 July a Gestapo officer was killed by a sniper in Aix, and only a matter of hours afterwards every one of the inhabitants – men, women and children – of the hamlet of Les Figuiers was either gunned down or burned alive in their homes.

There was despair among the resistants that the raid on the convent at Reillanne had taken place before they had any chance of stopping it. But there was also a terrible suspicion that factions within the Resistance, specifically the Communists, had their own political agenda; and that it suited their purposes to pick off German officers to provoke these cruel retaliations.

But there were successes, too. Thanks to the saboteurs, no more trains were running on the two main lines that reached down from the Alps, from Grenoble to Aix and from Briançon to Livron.

'And now we're winning control of the roads,' boasted Auguste. 'The Boches are only driving in convoys now; you won't find a car venturing out singly. Neither do the motorcycle couriers roar around like they used to. Even the checkpoints are being drawn back to the outskirts of the towns where they have men stationed. The tide is turning, and they are practically prisoners where they're garrisoned.'

'You be careful. It won't be as easy as you make out,' said M Musset.

'It's true. They only go outside to get more supplies.'

'Or to effect some more reprisals.'

'When they go out, there's a fifty-fifty chance they're going to be attacked. The forces of the Maquis are being unleashed, and they're unstoppable. We're the ones who know the terrain and the back roads. Wherever they turn, there's a chance they'll be met by gunfire, hemmed in. They won't risk it now. I'm telling you, the roads are almost all ours.'

M Musset kept his counsel. His pauses and silences had always been eloquent, and now they held a restraint that gave Marthe goosebumps.

'You just be careful. Never assume. Never believe entirely what you haven't proved for yourself. We don't need dead heroes. And remember, if any one of us is caught, it will be the end for all of us.'

5

⌒

Citrus and Pine

July–August 1944

It was a Thursday, and Arlette had gone to Céreste as usual. A warm sirocco wind of the kind that sprinkled red dust like paprika and caught in the throat had strengthened throughout the afternoon. Now it sent dry leaves skittering across the ground and tugged at loose clothing.

By four the clock was already ticking ponderously. By five the faintest noise suggested Arlette's safe arrival home, and their hopes rose. Every sense was on the alert. Another *ting-ting* from the clock, the quarter-hour, made the temperature drop and stopped the heart for a few seconds. Musset's cigarette smoke.

Marthe's hands stopped moving on her book, fingertips resting on the raised patterns of the open page. She could all but feel the twitch of the minute hand on the clock. She sensed the wind stirring the valley, rolling like waves over the silence, gaining ascendancy over the hills, the almond and apricot orchards, ruffling the olive groves and meadows, over the road that should have brought the bus from Céreste.

She tried to imagine the bus on the road: Arlette in the clumsy vehicle as it climbed, watching as the plain unfurled.

I cannot see her, Marthe thought, but neither can any of us.

All those months when she had not understood why the Mussets worried so much about Arlette's trips to Céreste . . . Now, for all that the waiting for her to return was both terrible and frightening, it was shot through with a complicated, proud, painful happiness for Marthe: she was truly a part of life with the Mussets again, within the enchanted citadel where scent was the spell.

At six o'clock Arlette was still not back.

Monsieur reached for his jacket. Keys and coins jingled. 'I'm going to walk down to the village,' he said. 'Perhaps something has happened to the bus.' He kept his voice even, but a raw edge gave him away.

'You do that, my dear.'

He paused by the door to pat his pockets. Outside he whistled for the large black mongrel who usually accompanied him. His feet crunched on the gravel, and the dog's paws provided a lighter counterpoint.

'Best he goes to meet her. No use sitting around doing nothing useful,' said Mme Musset, though she too was unable to disguise the strain in her voice.

Marthe got up. 'What would you like me to do? I'll start peeling some vegetables for dinner, shall I?'

'That's the idea. They'll be bounding up the path before we've got the pans ready.'

They worked side by side, in silence.

The clock struck eight. The food, such as they could find, was ready. It waited, covered, on the stove. Mme Musset brewed a tisane. They sipped wordlessly.

When M Musset returned at almost ten, he was with Auguste.

'We're not sure what's happened—'

'She's been taken,' said Auguste.

Madame gave a cry, as if she was in pain.

'We don't know what's happened,' said Monsieur. 'There's every chance she is fine, that there's a simple explanation. We must not think the worst.'

'How? Why?' Madame was not convinced by her husband's attempt at calm.

'I'm not sure exactly what happened, but I cycled over to Pierrevert and telephoned the Woodcutter from there.'

'They have arrested Candide,' blurted out Auguste.

Monsieur lit a cigarette. 'No, we don't know for certain. It's only a rumour. Candide was in the café hunched over his newspaper as usual until five o'clock – the patron confirmed it. But Arlette wouldn't have spoken to him. That was the point. And he would never have made a mistake. They were both always careful . . .'

'Do you think she might have—'

Auguste was cut off by a knock at the door. They hadn't even heard an approach.

There was a tangible ripple of panic as they realised their conversation might have been overheard. Then Musset flung open the door.

It was their neighbour Étienne, an elderly beekeeper who lived one field down the hill. 'Have you heard anything?' He had a wheeze in his voice. He had followed them on the path up as quickly as he could.

'Hélas, no.'

'I'm going to Céreste in the morning with my honey, Victor. I will keep my eyes and ears open.'

'We would be most grateful.'

'Wouldn't have had her down as the running away sort.'

'No . . .'

An awkward moment passed, during which their neighbour would normally have been invited to take a drink and a bite to eat. Étienne hesitated, then seemed to understand that this was no time for social niceties, and bid them good night.

They waited until they were sure he had gone. 'How much does he know?' asked Madame.

'Nothing. Only that Arlette seemed to have missed the bus. I bumped into him on my way down to find Auguste. But he knew straight away from my face that something was up.'

'What now?' asked Madame.

'There's nothing we can do about Étienne.'

'I don't seriously doubt his intentions . . . but—'

'No . . . no . . . I'm sure you're right. In the morning I'm going to go down to Céreste. Until we know what exactly has happened . . . well, that's all we can do.'

Marthe lay awake on her iron bed. Only a few days earlier Arlette had come back to the distillery from a trip to Forcalquier where she had taken a large order. Marthe had added a few drops of pine-needle essence to a citrus-peel infusion, and the pervading aromatic warmth made them both nostalgic for August evenings by the sea to the south.

'Pine for hope,' said Marthe. 'And I'm going to try amber for timelessness.'

'Hope,' said Arlette. 'Our instincts are always for hope. There's something rather mysterious but wonderful about that.'

'I'm not sure it is mysterious, actually. Surely instincts are the result of noticing tiny details that the body processes quickly.'

'So quickly that it seems you were anticipating all along . . . an animal intuition . . . You're right, we do it all the time without thinking.'

'Exactly.'

Thinking about that conversation reassured Marthe a little. Arlette would be all right; she would read the signs and act accordingly. She *would*. She must not think of the other things she and Arlette had discussed. The only certainty was that others were watching.

She heard the cocks crow into an empty morning, and M Musset departing on his bicycle soon after sunrise. Her stomach contracted, but she knew she would not be able to eat.

*

Musset returned at midday. 'Cabot's finding out what he can. But Céreste stinks with informants, he says. Infested by Waffen-SS, too.'

Not all the gendarmes in Céreste were on the side of the Milice. Cabot was a living reminder of the fact that the police had once been trusted members of the community. Without a flicker of recognition, he had once pushed Auguste back onto the Digne bus just as a convoy of Waffen-SS and Milice were heard on the approach to the other side of the village. They rounded up five men that day, and only two returned.

Musset and Auguste had been to the village in the Wood-cutter's van, the most reliable transport for underground business. 'We sent word with a small boy to the Poet in the old quarter, then met him casually by the water pump. He had no information, but they're putting the word out about a young woman, about so tall, with her hair up in a blue scarf and lav-ender-print apron, an innocent bystander. The last anyone seems to have seen of her, she was walking out of the café at about the time the bus was expected.'

Musset recounted the events in a voice so flat it seemed the life had been kicked out of him: a man in a three-piece tweed suit and round tortoiseshell glasses had seemed on the point of admitting to a sighting, but then quickly took his leave when a van sped past; shutters banged shut; a grey car the size of a boat had swayed to a stop outside the Mairie, and four German officers had gone in. Then nothing.

Then, as Musset and Auguste left the café, a man walked up behind them. ' "The Milice arrested a man who was in the café the previous afternoon, a thickset man who played the drunk, pretending to read a newspaper," that's what he said. "Played the drunk", those were his exact words. Which is worrying—'

'You didn't ask him about a girl?'

'Too risky. The last thing I wanted to do was to come right out with it that they were connected – that I was connected too.'

'So you've no idea who this chap was you were talking to?' asked Madame.

'Never seen him before. He was about my age, dressed as a farmer. I didn't want to ask, and didn't want to give away more than I had to. According to him, anyway, the Milice had a busy day yesterday. They had a man held in the cells of the police station – the man who was taken from the café. That's all he knew.'

'What now?'

'There's nothing we can do. The Poet is getting a message to the Engineer, but after that, all we can do is sit tight.'

'If she's been arrested, they'll know that she's the girl from Distillerie Musset,' Marthe said.

'I expect so. All we can do is accept that she must have been taken, along with Candide – and try to find out what's going on.'

Which was exactly what the Milice would be doing, too. Everyone knew that they had their methods. Words that were not spoken.

'If they have Arlette, they will connect her to us.'

Arlette in Céreste with the deliveries. The messages in Braille wrapped around cakes of soap. The other blind girls waiting to act as translators, in Apt and Reillanne, Banon and Saint-Christol. A spider's mesh of tiny strands, only visible when the sun caught their beads of dew.

'Arlette will never break,' said Marthe. 'She wouldn't even tell me what she was doing, though I begged her to explain. She never did – it was only when she saw how I might have the answer to the problem of how to send new messages.'

'She's young and pretty – she'll charm her way out of there,' said Auguste, with a confidence that no one believed, though they wanted to so badly.

They heard nothing.

The feeling of threat intensified. If Arlette did not return, then sooner or later the Milice would come in her place. There was only a week to go before the night flight, when the Americans would be taken north over the mountains to the clandestine landing strip.

Kenton and Scotty were moved out of the barn. Marthe's room on the ground floor had a trapdoor. A small room adjoining the Mussets' contained a staircase up to the low attic, which led to another route out of the house.

Kenton was the taller and the less agile; he would find the roof space harder to pass through. And Scotty had only the most rudimentary grasp of French, so it was better he be shielded by the Mussets. Kenton would sleep on Marthe's floor, ready to spring up if anyone arrived suddenly in the night. They had practised the drill. Marthe knew exactly how to close the trapdoor and pull the bed into the right position over it.

The first night before they all retired, Marthe advanced on the two boys with a scent bottle and sprayed.

'Hey! What's this?'

'A distillation made of pepper and lavender. It puts dogs off the scent. They might bring dogs.'

The American was solicitous, only knocking on her door when she assured him she was already in her little iron-framed bed. Then he came in, shut the door quietly and lay down on a mat and a padded bedspread. She heard his breathing, but she hardly dared to speak to him. Perhaps he was already sleeping, already on his way back to a country far away.

She lay awake, her head too full. When she finally dozed off, she dreamt of waiting for the full moon. First an evening when the western sky flamed, sending great fingers of rich red light up the slopes through the trees, then the rise of the great disc that silvered the night. Then Arlette lost in a forest. The Gestapo taking Candide to Forcalquier. If he talked, they were all as good as dead. Who had betrayed them, no one knew.

She was awake again, heart pounding. Across the floor, the airman was still breathing evenly.

The Milice came on the third night.

A movement on the gravel path alerted them. For the first time she understood why the approach had been covered in tiny stones. Then their own dogs barking. She reached out wordlessly for Kenton, felt urgently for his shoulder. He started. A soft shuffling, and he had left her side. He must have sprung like an athlete into the hole.

Marthe too played her part quickly and smoothly.

Her heart was pounding as she lay back in bed, now positioned over the trapdoor.

Fear pulled her skin tight. It was a hot night, but the sheet felt cold where her sweat-soaked nightdress stuck to her back.

A whistle blew. The dogs barked loudly, and there was an eruption of harsh shouts and boots stamping outside. Blows crashed down on the wood of the front door, then the kitchen door.

M Musset shouted back at them from the bedroom window. Whatever did they want? What was so important it couldn't wait for the morning?

'Open up! Open up!'

Leather boots on the tiled floors, drawing closer. Heavy footfalls on the stairs and along the corridor to Marthe's room.

When the man came to the door, she was already waiting for him, blinking with sleep.

'What's in here? Get out of the way!'

She turned her head away from his voice and said, 'What is happening, what is going on . . . ?' A feeble voice, slightly stupid. 'Who are you?'

The first brush of his arm against her, as if he was about to push her aside. 'What does it look like is going on?' He smelled of rank garlic sausage.

Marthe put out her hands, feeling for the door frame but making an obvious, fumbling job of it.

'I'm blind . . . I don't know who you are.'

She sensed a momentary hesitation on his part. 'They keep me in here . . . they don't want me to go outside. I can't see – have you come to help me? Please help me.' She patted the fabric of his uniform. 'Are you a gendarme? A nice gendarme?'

He slapped her hand away. 'We're searching the house.'

'Well, I have seen nothing – how could I?'

Shuffling feet on the stairs. More voices. Then Musset,

demanding that they speak to Kommandant Baumann and explain why they had come bursting into the home of a trusted businessman in the middle of the night. More noise in the corridor, and then her visitor was speaking.

'She can't possibly know anything. She's a halfwit farm girl, and blind to boot.'

'I know her, anyway,' said another. 'She's a mouse who sees no one.'

They retreated down the corridor. Voices were raised in the hall.

'What about the girl you had working for you, Musset?'

'Which girl? I keep lots of girls in employment!'

'The one who makes the deliveries in Cércste.'

'Oh, her . . . Look here, we're all just going about our business. I insist that you ask the *Kommandant* . . .' Musset was still complaining, demanding that they contact Baumann. Wake him, if necessary. Telling them of all the times the Distillerie Musset had supplied the Germans with scarce products, and lamenting the lack of gratitude. The voices died away.

Then Mme Musset's arms were around Marthe, and they were trembling as one.

No further sounds until the particular footfall that told them Monsieur was coming down the passage, and he was alone. Then he was holding them both.

When he did speak, it was in a low tone. 'It's all right. We're all still here and in one piece.'

'Thank the Lord.' Madame disentangled herself.

'Just wait a while longer, my dear. Just to be sure.'

'I thought I heard a car going away down the hill.'

'So did I, but . . .'

'You think they might come back?'

'They might.'

They waited an hour before they released Kenton and Scotty from their cubbyholes.

As if he could read her thoughts, Kenton reached out and touched her hand. The Mussets had left them, urging a few hours of sleep before morning broke. But how could they sleep now? They were sitting side by side on her bed.

Marthe pulled her hand away, unsure of herself. He said nothing, and she had no way of gauging his reaction. Why had she done that? She had felt the tremor in his hand.

Very slowly, she reached out for his face. She stroked his cheek, braver now. She felt his thick hair, how it slipped straight and smoothly through her fingers. She made his brow real – real to her – then the eyes, nose and chin. Finding the lines between imagination and reality, blurring the boundaries between sight and touch. Slowly, she moved one finger to his mouth and traced his lips. They were full and soft.

'Can I get into the bed with you?'

Marthe nodded.

She felt the shape of his shoulders and chest against her side. He was wearing a rough shirt and trousers. 'I'm sorry, I can't help it – after coming so far . . . I was scared.'

She found his lips and touched his mouth with her finger. 'Put your head on my shoulder and close your eyes. Sleep here now.'

The comfort of another human body. Warm skin, limbs folding and fitting together. If he closed his eyes, there would be no difference between them.

The sun stroked the bed. Marthe was still half asleep. Then she started, realising. She had never woken up with a man before.

He was speaking to her, in a whisper, in his peculiar accent. She couldn't make out what he was saying.

'What do you look like?' asked Marthe.

'I have blond hair and blue eyes. Quite tall, quite broad. No strange distinguishing features.'

'Are you handsome?'

'I can't answer that.'

'Yes, you can. You just have. If you weren't, you would have laughed and said straight off that you weren't.'

He laughed then. 'OK. You win.'

'So do the girls call you handsome?'

'Of course.'

'Really?'

'Well, my mother does.'

'She'd be a poor mother if she didn't.'

'Very true.'

'Blond hair and blue eyes,' she repeated. 'The lavender fairy.'

'Now, hang on a minute!'

'Just *like* the lavender fairy has. There's an old story about the beautiful fairy called Lavandula who was born in the wild lavender of the Lure mountain. She grew up and began to wander farther from the mountain, looking for somewhere special to make her home. One day she came across the stony, uncultivated landscapes of Haute Provence, and the pitiful sight made her so sad she cried hot tears – hot mauve tears that fell into the ground and stained it. And that is where, ever afterwards, the lavender of her birthplace began to grow.'

'Did you ever see it?

'Not here, no. But I still remember the lavender fields near where my family lives. The fields there are much smaller, but I saw them when I was young.'

'That's awful. It's such—'

'If I hadn't lost my sight, I might never have come here, never have discovered my true vocation. I would have been just a farm girl, never knowing what I was missing, and then a farmer's wife like my mother, and set to repeat her life. Don't you see, it has opened my world, not closed it down, and I shall always be grateful for that.'

'So you haven't always been?'

'No. I could see until I was nearly eleven years old.'

'What happened?'

She liked his directness. So many people were curious but did not ask. 'It was very sudden. One day, one eye became blurred. I thought I had some dust in it, so I rubbed and blinked all day. Do you remember how simple life was at that age? I blinked and kept rubbing it, waiting for the eye to clear.'

'And it didn't.'

'No, it didn't. I told my mother, and she told me I just had

143

to wait patiently and all would be well. That was her remedy for all life's ills, and for a while I believed her. Then one day my younger brother Pierre pushed me off a windowsill where I was sitting. I can't even remember why he did it. I banged my head and sprained my wrist in the fall onto the cobblestones in the courtyard in front of the house. She took me to the doctor because she thought I might have broken my wrist, and I took my chance to tell him about my eye.'

'What did the doctor say?'

'He seemed to agree with Maman. All we could do was wait. For the next few months I concentrated hard on everything I could see with the right eye, all the while alive to the smallest variation in the left. Sometimes I seemed to make out more, but mostly I saw only fuzzy black and white, occasionally with a burst or tint of colour.'

'Then one day I went to put on my red dress and found it had changed to a dull olive green in the cupboard.'

The American stroked her hair. Even now, the memory was disturbing.

'Something strange was happening to all the colours. The sky stopped being the blue I had always known and became a stormy grey-purple on even the brightest day. The pink oleander flowers were inexplicably light blue. I couldn't understand what was going on.'

'Sounds like you'd gone colour-blind.'

'Just for a while. Then, shade by shade, they all disappeared, even the mixed-up colours. Every day the world became a darker place.'

He held her tighter. 'It must have been awful.'

'I understand now, but then . . . it was very frightening. It was always there in the cells of my body, the doctor said when I saw him again. He had to read a lot of books to find out, but when he did, it all made sense. I was born with it, so I should be pleased I saw as much of the world as I did. I was lucky in that it came on later in my childhood, and unlucky in that it was always much more likely it would happen to a boy than a girl.' Marthe sighed. 'But not in our family, it seems.'

'Do you see anything?'

'No. Though I am lucky because I have the pictures in my head. I still dream in pictures and colour, always the world of my childhood. I see the purple Judas trees at Easter lighting up the roadsides and terraces of the town. Ochre cliffs made of cinnamon powder. Autumn clouds rolling along the ground of the hills, and the patchwork of wet oak leaves on the grass. The shape of a rose petal. And my parents' faces, which will never grow any older.

'But it's strange how scent brings it all back, too. I only have to smell certain aromas, and I am back in a certain place with a certain feeling.'

The comforting past smelled of heliotrope and cherry and sweet almond biscuits: close-up smells, flowers you had to put your nose to as the sight faded from your eyes. The scents of that childhood past had already begun to slip away: Maman's apron with blotches of game stew; linen pressed with faded lavender; the sheep in the barn. The present, or what had so very recently been the present, was orange blossom infused with hope.

'I can understand that. For me, hot dogs are football games. Fairgrounds are oil and candyfloss. Paris is garlic, and Métro stations, that pungent—'

'You've been to Paris?'

'I came as a student before the war.'

'I have never been to Paris, but I'd like to. What did you study in Paris?'

'French, art . . . literature. I thought I wanted to make my mark by trying to write, and Paris is where American romantic idealists come to do that. It was a year's exchange from my college. I didn't know a thing when I arrived. I was a baby, with baby opinions and ambitions. Pitiful, really. But now? I've never been so grateful for anything in my life as I am for that year. That I learned enough of the language to get by. Without that, I'd be dead for sure by now.'

'How did you come to be in the air force?'

He gave a short, bitter laugh. 'My father had connections

. . . and they put me on a training course, and the next thing I knew I was flying in a Fortress over Europe with a full payload.'

'A long way from home.'

'Yes.'

They were quiet for a while.

'You are special,' whispered Kenton. 'In more ways than one. What you did when the German came to the door—'

'There was no time to be afraid. I did what I had to do. It's normal. And he wasn't German. He was French. That is the most dreadful thing of all.'

'Maybe that was why he went away . . .'

'Maybe, but I don't think so. We fear our own people too.'

M Musset had explained it to her when he first asked for her help. Those who helped behind the lines took the greatest risks, because there was no uniform to protect them. The greatest risk was betrayal. And if you were betrayed, you were either shot or sent to a prison camp in Germany. They said it was better to be shot.

'You are the bravest of the brave. Never forget that.'

'M Musset says we are history as it is being formed.'

'He is a fine man. But Madame is unhappy,' said Kenton. 'Or rather, she is worried. You can't see the way she looks sometimes when she thinks no one is watching.'

'But she always sounds so relaxed and encouraging.'

'It's not how things seem, it's how they are, sweetheart.'

'I know.' Marthe swallowed hard. 'What would you be doing if there wasn't a war?'

He sighed. 'I can hardly imagine any more. I would have gone back to my studies. I might have graduated and then started more studies to work at the family firm. I might have been on my way to becoming a lawyer to please my father. The Attwaters of Boston – an old family.'

'My family is old too.'

'Old rich.'

'Oh. We are old poor. Becoming a lawyer – you mean that's not what you want?'

'I don't know what I want. No, wait – I do! I want to get out of here alive. How's that for an ambition?'

'Very sensible.'

'And I'd like to come back here. It's such a beautiful place. I would love to see it again when the war is over.'

Marthe felt unaccountably pleased. 'You should. We will be better then.'

Despite what this extraordinary young man said about their bravery, it felt undeserved. So many people in this dark time were not what they should have been. Some were as closed as their shuttered houses. Too many seemed not to care about their own country. It was shaming. When the Gestapo started paying for denunciations, too many were only too happy to turn informant. Sometimes it seemed as if those who did care enough to fight back were akin to the boniest birds brought back from the shoot, the cold plucked skin that showed how very helpless they were against the hunters' guns.

Suddenly it was important to try to explain this.

'My family has lived here for as long as anyone could remember; it could be hundreds of years, because there was never any evidence that we came from anywhere else. We mark the years by vintages of walnut wine and fruit liqueurs, like the wines and olive oils of other farmsteads, and we keep our history in barrels and bottles laced with dusty cobwebs.

'If we don't stand fast now, we might be the last generation to live our lives like this.'

It was a while before he spoke.

'And when we win the war – as we will – what will become of you, sweet Marthe?'

'I shall be a creator of fabulous perfumes – and I shall go to Paris!'

She would remember that sunlit hour for the rest of her life. Like a fragile fragment of a half-forgotten dream, it would rise to the surface of an ordinary morning. Kenton opened the windows wide, and she felt the lighter air come in, the silkiness of a light breeze on her face. His touch still shimmered on her skin. There was so much to discover, so many ways to communicate.

The Milice shot Arlette later that day.

6

⁓

Lavender

August 1944

Arlette's body was dumped at midday outside the police station in Forcalquier alongside Candide's, the two of them laid like bait. It was too dangerous to claim them, and in any case a sympathetic doctor protested that corpses should not be allowed to rot in the town square and arranged for their removal to the hospital mortuary.

But they could not go to fetch her. The moon was full.

On a plateau of lavender fields shielded by mountains near Saint-Christol, British planes dropped supplies at night to the Resistance. Carts tasselled with lavender drew up by each drop zone, and men went to work releasing the precious cargo from protective containers and hiding weapons and explosives under the sheaves of flowers.

The operations were urgent now. Partisan cells received parachuted agents on rocky terrain that was really only suitable for containers. They called the long, flat field Spitfire. It had been used before to land aircraft secretly, the length of the landing strip disguised with two hundred metres of lavender. Six hundred metres of grass, then the lavender, and then it became a potato field.

Each night the Mussets had watched the waxing of the moon and waited for confirmation. A courier arrived, but only to tell them to stay where they were: the flight was delayed. Contact with the organisers had been patchy. First they were on, then the flight was delayed in Italy, stuck on the ground in thick cloud. Then, at the beginning of the second week of August, when the moon had begun to wane, the message came at last. The plane was coming in the following night. The two Americans were expected, with the Actress as guide. With no method of further communication, Caspian and his group had no option but to follow their instructions. It was not possible to tell them that the Actress would not be coming.

'I shall be the Actress,' said Marthe.

'Don't be ridiculous!'

'They are expecting a young woman with the boys. You said so yourself.'

'I can't allow that.'

'But you need a girl. They don't know about Arlette, and there's no time to tell them.'

'Even so. You're not thinking straight – none of us is, with what's happened.' Musset's voice was tight with emotion.

'I want to do it. For Arlette. You have to let me. Kenton and Scotty will lead me. I just have to play my part. And think – who will suspect a poor blind girl?'

'They would never believe we would be so stupid as to try it.'

'All I have to do is let the organisers think I am Arlette. They will be looking for a young couple and their friend wandering into the field. That is the plan, and it cannot be changed now, since we are no longer in wireless contact. If anything does not tally with the agreed plan, if we don't arrive as arranged, they will suspect we are infiltrators – it will all have been for nothing!'

'We could ask Étienne's daughter.'

'And involve someone new? You can't do that. It goes against everything you have been so careful to set up. I want to do it – and I have to do it! I'm the obvious choice. The right size and age. The boys will steer me in the right direction.'

There was a long silence.

Then Monsieur began to describe the situation she must be prepared to enter. The men in peasant clothes, the baggy serge jackets, hunting bags slung across their chests. A gun with an end like a garden hose, designed by the Czechs and dropped by parachute by the British.

'The Army of the Night,' Marthe said to Kenton. 'And I'm going to be part of it.'

'You're sure, aren't you?'

'There is no other way. Arlette . . . she would want me to do this.'

'I think – no, you're right. But—'

'Have you ever killed anyone?' she asked.

He did not answer. She was going to ask again, but before she could form the words, she decided against it. She did not need to know.

That night they slept in her room again; she in her bed, he on the floor. When they said good night, Marthe reached out and found Kenton's head, then snatched her hand away as if scalded. 'Your hair – where has it gone?'

'Shaved off. I gave myself what the army calls a number one. Too risky to travel with you, looking like an Aryan who isn't German.'

Neither of them had mentioned the time they slept in each other's arms for comfort. Courage was all now; and they had each decided, it seemed, that a need for comfort might be construed as weak. She bit her lip and tried to make no sound as hot tears rolled for Arlette.

The next evening, Madame prepared a meal they forced themselves to eat and drink. Toasts were made in cracked voices to valour and friendship. Auguste's cousin Thierry, the *garagiste*, had patched up the truck and agreed to come along in case running repairs were needed.

They would take the old roads over the mountains towards

151

the peak of La Contadour. Boxes of soaps and more boxes containing bottles of eau de toilette, antiseptic and cleaning fluid were lashed carefully to the back and sides of the truck's hold. When this was done, it was impossible to see the old wardrobe secured behind in which Kenton and Scotty were to stand.

Monsieur removed the unfilled boxes in front of the wardrobe door. It was an extraordinarily effective device. 'In you go, lads.'

Marthe felt a hand over hers briefly, then the Americans thanked Madame for all she had done before climbing up into the truck. Madame said a prayer first for the antique engine, and then for the souls it carried. 'Away with you,' she said. 'Good luck.'

The truck vibrated as Monsieur cranked the motor at the end of the bonnet. It spluttered and spat out the smell of burning charcoal from the gasogene appliance bolted on to produce the gas fuel that marked it as a non-military vehicle.

Two of the farm workers now began loading the back with implements of lavender harvesting: the bundles of twine, the ropes, the scythes, the tarpaulins. Then, more carefully, they lifted in the old alembic still that they would not miss if the expedition ended in disaster. Auguste jumped into the back and pulled down a wooden seat. It would be his job to ensure the cargo remained secure, and to provide the cover and first line of defence should they be stopped. He secured ropes around the brass belly of the still, then tapped his knife against his teeth. 'Newly sharpened,' he said. 'They say the crop's tough this year.'

Monsieur pulled Marthe up into the cab beside him; on the other side was Auguste's cousin Thierry's large, soft bulk. He was a man who spoke in bassoon tones and smelled of oil and gut-rot brandy. They rumbled off down the bumpy track.

Five minutes into the climb beyond Manosque, it was touch and go whether the old motor would keep ticking over. The jolts and wheezes became more and more pronounced. There were muffled protests from the back. Sitting shoulder to shoulder with Monsieur and Thierry, Marthe could feel the tension in their muscles as they swayed together.

There was a long wheeze and a sudden violent shudder. Then nothing. The engine stalled. Monsieur pulled sharply at the handbrake lever as they rolled backwards. His arm dug painfully into Marthe's ribs.

Before a word was said, Thierry jumped down and ran round to the crank. Not even a cough from the motor. Thierry cursed softly.

'Come on, beauty,' coaxed Monsieur, as he might to a favourite horse.

It felt like minutes before a spark caught. They were all holding their breath, willing the mechanical parts to revive. It seemed to die away, then abruptly there was a shake, and then another. Monsieur revved the engine, there were belches from the exhaust and Thierry threw himself against Marthe as the truck began to move.

They were climbing, Marthe's back pressing into the hard seat. At a stately pace, bends followed bends, the whine and grinding and rattling from the front of the vehicle rising and falling.

'We should sing a song,' said Thierry, with heavy sarcasm. No one replied.

'She was so full of life,' said Musset savagely. Arlette's death, the manner of it, was unbearable to him. Neither he nor Madame could speak of that. But they wanted to talk, to remember her as she was.

So they pushed on through the night as M Musset recounted his most vivid memories of Arlette as a child: when she had once stood on a table to sing to a family gathering, and then would not be stopped; when she put on a play using puppets she had made of paper and ribbon; the time she ate too many wild plums, unable to restrain herself because they were so delicious. 'I can't help it if I like them!' she cried, doubled over with a violent stomach ache. 'And I'd like some more as soon as I'm better!'

'You know,' confessed Marthe, 'I might once have been jealous of Arlette, when she first arrived to live with you, but as soon as I knew her better, I wasn't. Does that make sense? She was my friend, the best I ever had. She let me share her family. She never ever made me feel unwelcome, or as if I was taking too much of your attention away from her.'

'She was a truly good person. It's just so—'

'Roadblock,' said Thierry.

Musset slowed immediately, perhaps to give the men in the back time to ready themselves.

Dogs barked as they pulled up.

'Cut the engine.' The voice came from the left, through the open window. It was clearly an order.

'I'd rather not,' said Monsieur. 'It's a devil to restart, and I don't want to block the road.'

'Cut the engine.'

It shuddered and was silent. Its echoes continued to ring in Marthe's ears.

'Papers. It's after curfew. You had better have a good reason to be out.'

Monsieur reached into his jacket, jabbing his elbow into Marthe's side, and turned to hand them over.

'Where are you going?'

'To our suppliers in Sault.'

'Where have you come from?'

'Manosque.'

'Don't you have your own lavender growers over there?'

'We are in a cooperative with a few farms here. It's easier for us to take the distilling equipment there than try to transport the crop down the valley and up again. They grow lavandin here, and with our process we can extract four times the essence of traditional lavender.'

'What's in the back?'

'Deliveries. Products we made from last year's crop. That's part of the deal.'

There was a thump from the back, and renewed barking from the dogs. While one soldier was asking questions, others

154

had come round to the rear and pulled the canvas back. From the bounces, it seemed that Auguste was on his feet.

'You'll find it all in order,' said Monsieur.

'You don't make deliveries at night.'

'No, of course not. But you cut lavender by moonlight. It's the best, the traditional time to cut, when the plants are full of juices. That's how we do it here. This is the way it's always been done to extract the best-quality essences.'

The voices from the rear grew louder. It was impossible to hear what was being said.

'Papers for the vehicle. Why has it not been requisitioned?'

'It's so old no one would have it. It won't even start again for anyone who has not nursed it for thirty years or more. Perhaps not even then . . . as for papers, unfortunately those I cannot help you with. That's like asking for papers for the rusted buckets at the farm, or the birds in the trees. It has never had any papers.'

A metallic sound as if a kick had been aimed at the side of the truck was followed by a heartfelt sigh from Monsieur.

'Tell you what,' he said. 'We're running late already, thanks to this heap of tin, missing the best hours for cutting. Let me come round to the back, and I'll see what I can offer you. One farmer won't be best pleased, but that's the price you pay for keeping going in these difficult times, eh? Some eau de toilette for your girl, perhaps?'

Before the soldier had a chance to think, Monsieur swung himself out of the cab, still speaking. 'Have you any idea how important this crop is to us? I don't care a fig about politics. You can do what you want as far as I'm concerned. Ask the *Kommandant*, if you care to – he will tell you. I have nothing to hide.'

Was it too brave a speech? Had his words been unable to contain the crack of emotion? The dogs sniffed. Then one sneezed.

Musset moved off round the side of the truck. The German soldier, grumbling in a token fashion, followed.

Marthe pushed herself as far back on the bench as she

could, straining to hear what was happening. Thierry stayed quiet. They ignored each other completely.

After what seemed an hour, but must only have been minutes, the door at the back slammed. The muffled voices sounded less unfriendly. Then Monsieur hoisted himself back in the cab.

'Thierry? The crank, please,' he said.

Thierry obliged. Marthe pressed her hands together in prayer on her lap. The first and second attempts failed. The third almost ignited. The fourth was hopeless. On the fifth effort, the engine shook itself like a wet animal and then roared.

The cab rocked as Monsieur took off as fast as the old crate would go.

'Where are we?' asked Marthe.

'On the road up to Simiane. Not far now to Saint-Christol.'

Their nerves had calmed after the stop at the checkpoint, but were starting to fire again now that their destination was closer. Marthe could only imagine the discomfort in the back, in the wardrobe. So close by. Kenton and Scotty were so close they must be only a hand's width away. Her heart was a hummingbird's wings – less beating than whirring.

The closer they came, the more she drew on what she held in her head. If they had used this field before, villagers must have heard the engines of the aircraft. They must have done. Whole farming villages apparently suffering from communal deafness.

'All right, listen up,' said Musset. 'I'm going to tell you what I've been told. Marthe, you'll pass it on to the boys. The German Nineteenth Army Command has its headquarters at Avignon. There's also a detachment at Sault now. Last week some four hundred Germans carried out sporadic attacks on the road north of Apt. The Maquis took them on and sent them packing, but the Germans came back a few days ago, and this time they were too strong for the Maquis. They have control of the road from Apt to Sault, and the situation on the plateau is now more dangerous than it was before.'

'So why are we doing this?' Thierry asked.

'This plane is bringing in a large group of French military and politicians. They want to be on the ground when the Allies come ashore. It's a big plane, bigger than normal. They'll use it to get some of the escapees out.

'The landing field here is called Spitfire. The man in charge is the Engineer, also known as Xavier. He's the best of the best. You just do what he tells you.'

'How will we find him?'

'He'll be waiting under cover at the roadside edge of the field. Don't worry, he'll see you before any of you know he's there. Say nothing until you are spoken to. No names; you are the Actress.'

The truck whined and then bumped viciously as they turned. As Marthe was thrown across M Musset, she felt the wheel judder. A few more pitches, and they stopped. The engine died.

'What's wrong?'

'This is as far as we go.'

Marthe was helped down from the cab and stood, feeling disoriented. Her legs were cramped and she felt queasy, though it was hard to tell whether that was nerves or carsickness. She read the noises as the back of the truck was opened. There was a short burst of whispering and some indeterminate thumps.

The land around her was still and silent.

Then Monsieur's voice, close to her ear. 'It's this road here. Just turn left when you get to the top of the track. We'll be here, as though we've pulled in for the night, though it's so far off the main roads it would be unusual for anyone to come along. Marthe, you wait for me in the field afterwards. If it all goes wrong, then find your way to the lavender farm called Les Coulets on the road to Sault and tell them Caspian sent you to wait. Now go.'

They already knew the directions, had gone over them many times in the week since the first message came through.

Two strong arms caught hers, Kenton to the right, Scotty to the left. Whispered thanks and slaps on the back.

'Go!' urged Monsieur. He squeezed her arm to offer encouragement.

The three of them began to pick their way along the path.

'Is it easy to see?' asked Marthe.

'Moonlight,' said Kenton. 'Clear as anything. Don't you worry. We have open fields behind a hedge on each side. Then there's a tunnel of trees ahead.'

Armed with a lavender scythe, they advanced.

As they passed along the road, their footfalls were barely audible thanks to the rope-soled shoes Monsieur had insisted they wear. She thought about the way war had transformed her life. For the first time it struck her that there might be no going back, not to the blue curtain of mountains in the Luberon, nor to her family there. But she walked on, padding silently into the darkness.

The Engineer greeted them gruffly when they announced themselves as the Actress and her party. Marthe found herself bundled into a hollow under a tree and told to remain silent. It would all happen very quickly. They strained to make out the sound of the aircraft. When it finally arrived, men with torches hissed to one another to give the signal. It was returned from the plane. 'Light the red lamp on the boundary!' 'No, not there – get in line!' 'A white light – we need a white light over here!'

When the plane arrived overhead, it seemed to suck up the earth in ripples and press down the air. Marthe could feel the shadows of the great steel wings and the rush of wind. Loud vibrations shook the earth. Engines thrummed and throbbed, and then strained, changing pitch to a wail. The noise was terrifying. The immense bulk of machinery came over them so low it seemed sure to crush them. It shrank the fields and mountains. But the hoarse voices around her were telling a different story. 'Why is it not coming in?' 'What's wrong?' 'Signal, signal – have you given the right signal!'

For a moment it seemed the plane was flying on, but then the noise intensified again. 'It's wheeling round – it's coming back!'

'They've put the plane's searchlight on,' said Kenton. He was holding her arm. 'It's coming in again.'

The roar intensified.

A voice rose. 'It's still not right – the strip's not long enough, it won't stop in time . . .'

'Ssh, keep it down!'

The scream of the engines cut through the night. Surely the whole area would hear it. Marthe tasted bile in her mouth.

'It's a Dakota! Would you believe that?' Kenton's whispered jubilation was reassuring. 'It's a huge plane! I never would have believed they could get one of those in here!' He pulled her to her feet.

Gusts of air cooled them as the plane came closer. It had a presence like a living thing. The engines were still running.

Sounds of movement across the grass began immediately. There was a shout from up high, something angry she didn't understand. 'That's the pilot. He says he doesn't believe that strip is twelve hundred metres,' said Kenton. 'And what the hell was in the field at the end?'

'Potatoes,' said another voice.

Now there were more people rushing forward.

Marthe felt his arms around her and a kiss on her forehead, 'Take care, angel.' Scotty too thanked her with a kiss. Then they were gone. She wrapped her arms around herself. Now she willed the plane to go quickly. How long would it be before the Germans and the Milice arrived? They must have heard it coming down. It would surely be impossible for it to take off again without them arriving.

She wanted to ask the person standing next to her what was happening, but knew she should not alert him to her blindness. If anyone knew that she had joined the operation, they would blame Caspian for compromising it.

The plane's engines spluttered louder, and then intensified into a great roar. Now there were competing noises and pitches, some smooth, some rattling. A bumping sound, the same as the wheels of the truck going over rough ground. Then an almighty vibration seemed to shake the very earth under the tree where she clung for safety, not daring to move. A mechanical squeal rose above the spitting and growling. Marthe's ears hurt.

Something was wrong. The engines were straining too much, like gigantic animals in distress. They couldn't go on like that, surely. There would be an explosion, and the aircraft would fall from the sky in flames.

There was no one to ask what was happening. The smell of burning oil was becoming stronger. The snarling noise gave way to a whine.

'It's coming back!' she heard someone shout.

'Too heavy. They'll have to let some of them off.'

'It's a risk – every extra minute the plane's on the ground—'

More ear-piercing engine noise and a rush of wind. The ground shook again, and men were running on either side of her.

Then Kenton was back by her side.

'What happened?'

'The plane was carrying too much weight. They tried to put too many of us on it, and we snagged on the band of lavender.'

'Just you and Scotty got off?'

'Eight men – all Americans. So close and yet so far,' he said. 'Everyone's been quite good-humoured about it.'

A Frenchman cursed at him and ordered him to keep his voice down.

'What now?' she whispered.

'They're coming back tomorrow night.'

Marthe groaned. She had no idea what they would do until then. But Kenton was upbeat. 'Think of it as good news. When it comes back for us, they can maybe get some more out too. It was close, though. We almost managed to get airborne.'

Then she could hear no more against the engines. The noise intensified and moved away. Kenton tensed. 'There they go again – it's bouncing around but picking up speed. Through the strip of lavender – Jesus . . . nose-up position . . . It's not going to make it!'

All Marthe could think was that she was relieved Kenton and Scotty would not be in the crash.

'No . . . wait a minute . . . it's going through! The nose has gone up with the tail wheel still sticking in the damn potatoes – she's up!'

'Now that was a close call,' said Kenton as the engine noise grew fainter.

They had no choice but to return to Musset and the truck. Marthe's heart was beating fast as a machine gun. 'Monsieur will be coming to get me anyway,' she said. 'We'll meet him on his way here.'

They had hardly made it onto the road when shots echoed down the valley. A German patrol. More shots, closer now, and motors. Marthe was pulled into the undergrowth. 'Keep down,' hissed Kenton, shielding her head below his shoulder.

Minutes passed. 'Wait here,' said Kenton.

Marthe obeyed. She tried to orient herself by the sound of voices, but all had gone quiet. Then there was another volley of shots. They seemed to ricochet off the mountains. Then nothing but the sound of blood rushing in her ears. After a while she raised her head tentatively and listened. When she thought she heard whispering, she crawled towards the sounds.

She hit her leg against a sharp object, a rock perhaps. Involuntarily she let out the start of a cry before she managed to swallow it. Cursing her stupidity, she reached out her right hand and felt her way into the space.

Her foot struck something hard – it was the root of a tree. She followed its sinews and found a hollow. She curled herself inside and listened.

When she heard voices, they were none she recognised.

'Where's Xavier?'

'Gone already. They'll be on the road to the Armature.'

'Should we try to get there, to the area commander?'

'It's a hard mountain road—'

Marthe was about to speak, then stopped. The men were speaking French, certainly. But were they partisans or Milice?

What if the Milice knew all about Xavier? She put her head down and pulled herself tighter into the tree trunk.

'Marthe!'

It was Kenton. He pulled her up onto her feet and put his arm around her waist. 'There's a farmhouse ahead. I think we should make our way there.'

'We need to go back the way we came, back to the truck.'

'Not possible. That's the direction the Germans moved off.'

Marthe swallowed. What of M Musset and Thierry? 'Where's Scotty, is he with you?'

'No. We got separated. Perhaps he's already on his way towards the farm up there. We have to go.'

Scotty. She couldn't bear it if anything had happened to him while he was supposed to be under her protection. 'We have to stay together.'

'We'll find him,' said Kenton grimly.

They set off at an urgent pace, ready at any moment to take cover in the ditch separating the road from the field. The possibility that Scotty might be dead or wounded, and would not be coming with them, was left unspoken.

'OK, it's not far to the house. Let's hope he's ahead of us.'

They covered the ground in silence.

'Almost there,' whispered Kenton at last.

'Tell me what the farm looks like.'

'Four buildings around a yard. There's a stone drinking trough. No lights on.'

'Does it look inhabited?'

'I can't tell. They're probably asleep inside.'

'There are no animal noises or smells. Any other signs of life?'

'No vehicles. Nothing.'

'Is there a barn? We could try hiding there.'

They walked on, as quietly as they could, up to the barn. No dogs barked; all was silent. The barn was locked. There was no sign of Scotty.

'We have to risk it and go to the door. If there is anyone

there, I will speak to them,' said Marthe. The pitter-patter of water from the fountain feeding the trough matched the beat of her heart. She gripped his arm a little tighter. But this was why she had come with them in the first place. She was playing her part, as she had insisted. 'If, when they open the door, something doesn't seem right, then pinch my arm and I'll say what I can to get us out of there as quickly as we can. Do you understand?'

'Yes.'

They approached the door, braced for whatever would follow. Kenton knocked loudly. No one came. Knocked again, more urgently. Then there was scuffling inside the house.

'Who is it?'

'We were told there might be sanctuary here. We are farmers too, from Manosque.'

'Go away.'

'Please! Just for tonight—'

'Don't involve us – we don't want to be involved. I have a sick wife!'

'But we—'

'Go, just go!'

They had no choice but to walk on. They debated whether to head for the woods and wait out the night there or continue on into the village. They reached the outskirts of Saint-Christol before they decided to turn back. It would be harder to find safety in the narrow winding streets and close-packed houses, not knowing who might open the door only to denounce them. Just walking the alleys would be suspicious at this late hour.

'There's no chance of finding directions to Les Coulets tonight. We'll only draw attention to ourselves,' whispered Marthe.

They found a ditch in a wood nearby and tried to sleep for the few hours remaining until dawn.

The first warmth in the air brought Marthe round from her fretful half-slumber. She was floating in a deep black sea. The anxious feeling of being suspended in the unknown returned.

For a moment she was falling down the stairs at school, half astonished at her own daring and the anger that had propelled her forward. What would Maman say if she could see what had become of her now?

Then she felt a hand on her arm, and heard her name whispered.

'Kenton?'

'It's all right, sweetheart. It's me.'

'I couldn't remember where I was for a moment!'

'It's all right. I'm here – and, good news, so is Scotty!'

Relief flooded through her. 'Thank God. How did he find us? Did you go looking for him?'

'I wouldn't leave you, you know that. No, he followed us out of the field last night. He said he thought that if another patrol came down the road, there was less chance we'd be stopped if we looked like a couple instead of a trio. Likewise when we went to the farm, it was safer for us to knock on the door as a pair.'

'Scotty?'

'I'm here.' He rubbed her arm.

Marthe sat up. 'We need food and water. I'll have to take a chance on the nearest house,' she said. 'I'm going to get a stick to walk with – find me one that's the right length – and when you see anywhere likely, I'm going to beg for some food.'

'I'm coming with you,' said Kenton.

'Me too.'

The boys spoke together.

'No, you mustn't. Best I go alone. We're much more likely to get something.'

They waited out the following day in the woods. Marthe's begging brought in a heel of stale potato bread and some plums. Scotty wanted to try to trap for food, but they could not have built a fire to cook it. 'Better hungry and safe, than fed and give ourselves away,' said Kenton. They ate the bread and plums and drank from a stream.

'If only the plane hadn't been so heavy, or the damn field

164

had no potatoes and lavender,' said Scotty. Kenton translated.

'I know,' said Marthe gently.

Kenton retorted something in English.

'What did you say?'

'I told him you can't go through life thinking, "If only."'

'You're right,' said Marthe. 'That's what Arlette used to say.'

A terrible pause threatened to overwhelm them.

'Yet most people do,' said Kenton, forcing his voice to stay steady and not entirely succeeding. 'Even if just a little, if only regretting a very few paths not taken.'

'I don't want to live like that,' said Marthe. 'When something bad has happened, you have to use it to make yourself braver. Once you know that you will manage somehow, whatever happens, you have unlocked the secret of life.'

'I always—'

'Ssh!' said Scotty. 'Hear that?'

They listened.

A rustling noise was coming from behind them. It might have been human; it might have been some woodland creature. They froze, but the sound did not get any closer.

For the next few hours they stayed silent. The boys took turns trying to sleep. Marthe closed her eyes too, but could not rest. Her muscles twitched at the faintest sound. The scents drifting on the breeze grew stronger in the gusty heat, then faded. She told herself she had imagined it, but all day the dread rose. There were times when she was sure she could smell burning. Not the summer burning of the fields to stubble, but a vile mix of wood and fabric and perhaps worse.

She might be wrong, though she doubted it. Even so, there was always the possibility she could be wrong about the origin of the smell. The wind might have changed direction, or she might be more disoriented than she thought.

Finally the moon rose.

'How much longer do we wait?' asked Marthe.

'An hour or so. We'll let it get higher in the sky, then I'll go ahead,' said Kenton.

165

'No, we go together,' said Marthe.

'But what if—'

'We go together like last night,' she insisted. 'But before we go, there's something I think you should know.'

All movement stopped. She could feel the power her words had over them.

'What?'

'I've been smelling burning – not all the time, but on and off all day. It may not mean anything . . . but just so that you are prepared, I thought you should know.'

'Burning? You think the Dakota crashed last night?'

'No . . . that didn't occur to me. I was more worried that the Germans had come back. That they were sending us a message in response to what happened last night.'

'Why didn't you say something before?'

'I didn't see what good it would do. I'm not sure that I'm right. What was the point in worrying you when we had no choice but to stay under cover and try to conserve our energy?'

'You should have told us before now,' insisted Kenton.

'I'm sorry, I—'

'Any information – even any *intuition* is valuable! It's all we have, you must understand that. We would have had time to plan properly.'

'I'm sorry, I'm sorry! I thought I was acting for the best!' Marthe was close to tears.

When Kenton spoke it was to Scotty, in English. They seemed to be weighing up the information. All she understood was 'OK'.

Marthe chewed her fingernails. She hadn't done that since she first arrived in Manosque as a child.

'We have to go, and we have to be even more careful,' announced Kenton eventually. 'We have no choice.'

'Plane returns,' added Scotty emphatically. 'For us.'

'And Marthe?'

She nodded.

'I'm sorry too. I shouldn't have lost my temper with you.'

*

166

They walked towards Spitfire. Marthe held herself straight and stiff. Her back prickled with the anticipation of gunfire opening up on them; they were ready at any second to dive down at the side of the road and then run for their lives.

Then, a kilometre or so from the field, Marthe sniffed. 'There it is. The remains of a big fire. Still burning, I think. Can you see where it's coming from?'

There was no doubt at all that it was coming from the direction in which they were heading. The air held pockets of warm smoke and ash.

'Can't see anything yet,' said Kenton.

They walked on, hearts sinking as the smell grew stronger. Acrid fumes mingled with the sickly sweetness of still-smouldering wood.

'Farmhouse,' cried Scotty, then spoke rapidly in English.

'It's the place that turned us away last night.'

Every step was further confirmation. The reek of scorched wood and plaster.

'My God . . . it's completely destroyed! Burnt out . . . those poor people!'

'The bastards – the filthy rotten bastards!' cried Marthe. 'Those people didn't even help us!' Hot rage called tears to her eyes, but she would not cry. If she started, she feared she would never stop.

'Perhaps they had helped others before.'

'Or perhaps all they did was close their ears to the sound of the plane.'

They hurried on. The time was long past when they could have done anything to help.

There was no reception committee in the field. Marthe's hopes had soared when she heard the first whispers, but were soon shattered. A couple of other Americans pulled themselves out of the darkness to stand with them in the shadow of a tree.

'Is there no one but us here?' asked Marthe faintly.

'No.' Kenton put a protective arm around her and pulled her into him so she could speak into his ear.

'But the plane will come.'

'It might. But we only have one torch, and without the official reception on the ground, we have no idea what the code letter is to signal that this is the landing place.'

'Perhaps they are late – or we are early.'

'I hope you're right.'

They all knew it was hopeless, but they waited anyway. Conversation petered out as they sat on the ground with the two additional Americans. These escapees had spent the intervening day in a rocky cave in a cliff to the north. They too had smelled the burning. No one had any knowledge of what had happened to the missing four who should have been picked up when the plane returned.

Hours later, the big Dakota rumbled across the sky and flew on, oblivious to the distress signal flashed with the single torch by the Americans.

Low groans of frustration were countered by the possibility that the plane might be turning to come back, as it did before. They waited, listening intently.

The sound of the aircraft's engines faded into the night.

All around, the calm of loss.

Then the emptiness filled with furious voices arguing in English. Marthe could only presume what was being said. The prospect of another night in the woods and no food made her feel weak.

There was more urgent discussion, this time with someone speaking in French. Where had he come from – and the man who was replying?

'We're assuming these people can be trusted,' said the first.

'Our Americans say they're definitely Americans who were here last night.'

'Who's the girl? I don't think she's all there.'

'Simple but evidently trustworthy,' said the second. 'How else would these men have got themselves this far?'

'You never know who's playing which game these days. I trust no one. And if anyone recognises the van we'll be in trouble . . .'

'You have to help us,' said Marthe, breaking into the exchange, willing herself to sound as determined as she could. 'The van . . . is there room for the three of us in the back?'

'Oh, so you do speak . . . who are you?'

'We came with Caspian last night.'

It was clearly the best reply she could have made. 'All right. Where are you trying to get to?' replied someone.

'It's a lavender farm called Les Coulets on the Sault road. Do you know it?'

'I know it.'

'They're expecting us, if anything went wrong.'

'All right, this way. Get yourselves inside. Quickly!'

They were pushed in like animals crammed into a pen. In the back, Marthe found herself sitting on iron rods that rolled and trapped her fingers as she tried to stop herself moving with the vehicle. In the confined space they all stank of sweat and dirt.

The driver had a lead foot. They were thrown from side to side as the vehicle scaled the bends of the mountain road. When the men behind the driver cursed, he shouted at them, 'Count your blessings – you're alive, aren't you?'

'What's been going on?' asked Kenton.

'Ah – at least you speak French. They told us the Boches were marking time in Sault; that they weren't coming out of their hole. Couldn't have been more wrong, could they? They've been all through these roads, killing as they go. Want to leave their calling cards before they all get flushed out when your lot finally get here.'

'What happened to the reception committee tonight?'

'Some got it in the neck last night. Too dangerous for the rest.'

'So why did you come?'

The man gave a humourless laugh. 'Me? Perhaps I don't like being told what to do. Perhaps I thought the guy flying the Dakota might just be crazy or brave enough to keep to his word and come back.'

'You kept the two men here safe all day too.'

169

'So send me the medal when you're chief of staff.'

A high-pitched whistle was followed by a loud metal ping at the side of the van.

'Shit!' said the driver.

'Hold on tight,' shouted the other Frenchman. 'That was a bullet.'

Marthe was sent sprawling across knees and feet. The van swayed; they seemed to have veered off onto bumpy ground, still travelling at speed. She rubbed her head where it had hit something hard.

Kenton hauled her back into a sitting position, and kept hold of her. 'Are you all right?'

'Yes. What can you see?' she whispered.

'Nothing. There are no windows here in the back. I can just about see through the windscreen between the driver and his mate. It's still dark, looks like we're back in the woods.'

The van pitched onwards. Another metallic ping.

Marthe gripped Kenton's hand. She thought of her family on the Luberon farmstead, her sister Bénédicte and brother Pierre. She prayed they would be safe where they were, that there would be a way to reassure them that she had died as part of something important and honourable. She would be brave, as brave as she could be.

Without warning, an urgent change of direction slammed them all against one side of the vehicle. When they landed, the bottom of the van scraped against the ground. Then they stopped.

'Quiet!' shouted the driver. 'Listen!'

Nothing.

A light wind in some trees.

Then the choking growl of another engine. It grew louder. There was a collective shudder as it passed and then went away.

'If they're still looking for us, they'll come back,' said the driver.

'I'm not so sure,' replied the other. 'That wasn't a serious chase. Those shots were all for show. Most of them want to get out of this alive as much as we do.'

They waited in near silence for some time. All Marthe could hear was breathing. After what could have been fifteen minutes, could have been an hour, the driver started the motor again and, carefully this time, edged them out of their place of sanctuary and back onto the road.

Then they drove as if the mistral was raging behind them.

They were dropped off at the end of a track and given directions. They were shaken, thirsty. Beyond hunger. When they began to walk again, it was on blistered feet that had swollen in their shoes. Lost in the maze of foreign paths and slopes, they stumbled upwards.

Praying they were heading towards the hamlet of Les Coulets, Marthe found herself quietly singing the old shepherds' songs. Songs of the fight to survive. A vision crystallised in her mind, almost as if she were hallucinating: a carpet of caper flowers. White flowers with unearthly profusions of stamens like shooting stars. There had once been such a carpet at a property she had visited as a small child. She had seen the dust of dead stars there, or so she had thought, until she realised the glitter was broken glass and heard the flap of bird wings caught in the eaves of an empty barn. She was so tired she had to pinch herself back into the present.

'Any sign?' she asked weakly.

'There's another bend ahead.'

They trudged round it.

'Here! All OK!'

'Scotty's right . . .'

Marthe imagined the buildings huddled around a courtyard, small and modest perhaps, but generous in every way that mattered.

'It's here, outside!' Kenton swung her round suddenly.

'What?'

'The old truck. Monsieur's truck!'

They made it through an open door before her legs went out from under her. Through the relief, the sleeplessness and

171

hunger, she felt Musset's arms around her and the taste of lavender dust from his jacket as she sobbed open-mouthed against his broad chest.

7

~~

Orange Peel and Musk

August 1944

Back at Manosque, Kenton and Scotty were hidden again. The Mussets and Marthe showed them into the cellar at the factory. Wearily they climbed down and made a false wall with wooden packing crates.

Madame sat designing labels by the shop entrance in the room above. The girl behind the counter served the customers. Marthe stayed in the blending room, pretending to experiment with new fragrances. Wrapped in a large apron that concealed his loaded pistol, Auguste guarded the back of the premises: the storeroom where the cellar door was hidden, the distilling shed and the soap kitchen.

For four days and nights they hardly spoke, or even moved, except to take water to the Americans, and what little food they could find. Marthe stood at the table combining orange peel and amber resin with shaking hands, unable to process any emotion except fear.

A hammering on the back door.

She heard Auguste cross the storeroom floor and ask tersely who it was, then the creak of the door that was deliberately kept unoiled. A woman's voice, and Auguste's remonstrance.

'I need your help. I work with Xavier.' She sounded

desperate, repeating the name as if it were a password.

Instinctively responding to the exhaustion in that voice, all too familiar to her now, Marthe went through to the storeroom.

'Please help me,' said the woman. 'Do you know where Xavier is?'

'Who? I don't know who you're talking about,' said Auguste.

Marthe could smell the woman now. Fear was palpable in the sweat and dust that had dried on her clothes. This was no Milice trick. Marthe understood exactly how she could have come to be in this state.

'When did you last see this . . . Xavier?' she asked, taking her lead from Auguste. The attempt to sound as if she had never heard of Xavier rang so false she was sure the woman must know it was a lie.

'More than a week ago. When the plane came in.'

'Why have you come here?' asked Auguste.

'The only clue I had. I know about the soap packaging.'

'I don't know what you're talking about.'

Marthe put her hand on his arm. 'I think—'

'I am British, a wireless operator,' said the woman slowly, despair ingrained in every word. 'I have been working with Xavier for months, organising operations throughout the South of France. I understand that you do not want to implicate yourselves in any activity, but I must know where he has gone.'

'I wish we could help you, but we can't,' said Marthe, kindly. 'But perhaps we can help in some other way. What do you need? Fresh clothes . . .'

'Can I stay with you?'

The prospect was horrifying.

'No! Absolutely not,' said Auguste. 'You've come to the wrong place. In fact, I want you to go right now.'

'Please! I daren't go back to where I've come from! I've tried sending messages asking for assistance, but my orders are always to sit tight and take instructions from Xavier. And to make matters worse – I think the Gestapo is onto me, they've tracked one of my frequencies.'

The stink of fear intensified, an animal musk, like the civet oil used in minuscule drops to add warmth to fragrance. It rose uncontrolled, overpoweringly unpleasant. Marthe could smell ammonia, too, and the iron tinge of menstrual blood.

They had to help her, somehow. 'Maybe we could—'

'Please! I'm begging you!'

Auguste was resolute. 'You have to go,' he said.

Marthe handed the woman a scrap of cheese she had been saving and a bar of soap. It was all she had. 'We should have done more for her,' she said, after the back door clicked shut.

An odour of goat and salty dampness remained, mocking their actions.

'How could we have taken her in?' asked Auguste testily. 'If the Gestapo is tracking her, we had no choice. Every minute she was here put us in more danger. She may already have betrayed us just by coming here. And a transmitter on the premises? Are you crazy? We might as well shoot ourselves.'

Two more long days and nights passed. When she heard running feet outside, Marthe had been expecting the worst for so long she had forgotten what it felt like to react normally. She shouldn't have given the woman the new bar of soap, clearly stamped with the brand: Distillerie Musset. A stupid mistake. She had cursed herself for the implications every minute since.

The thinking part of her could only observe what the body was doing, detached and surprised. Raised voices outside the shop. A rattle of gunfire and more shouting. She tensed, primed for the attack. Could she throw the acidic liquid at the aggressors, or hurl herself at them to give Kenton and Scotty vital seconds to move?

But the sounds seemed to be coming from all directions. Shouts and running, and then – unbelievably – a cheer.

'They're coming! They're coming! The Allies have landed on the coast!'

*

By early morning of the twentieth of August, the American advance divisions streamed down from the Valensole plateau, heading for Digne. In their wake came the ragged figures that had been fighting for so long in the fields and farms and the shadows of small villages. They descended on forgotten paths from the hills and walked the streets with their heads held high.

Arlette was buried that day in Manosque. In contrast to the many partisan funerals, where only the immediate family had dared to walk behind the coffin, officers of the Gestapo and the Milice watching hawk-eyed as the town pretended never to have known the deceased, hundreds of people turned out. Arlette's heartbroken parents led the mourners, with M and Mme Musset behind them.

It was touching, how many tributes there were. Even those Manosquins who had never known her now knew of her courage. 'There was a bunch of wildflowers and lavender in almost every window in the street leading to the cemetery,' Monsieur told Marthe. 'They honoured her.'

There was more bad news, though, when he made inquiries about the woman who had come to the Distillerie Musset claiming to be a British agent working with the Engineer. If it was the same woman, she had lasted only one night in Manosque. A defensive cordon of townsfolk had watched as she left the town; the Gestapo had swooped on her as she was risking one last transmission from a field on the road up to the plateau. She was last seen being bundled into a truck. Whether or not she was still alive, no one knew. The liberators came too late for her.

'We should have shown more courage,' said Marthe.

'No,' said Musset. 'You took the only course you could. It's hard to admit, but you did right, in the circumstances.'

'I smell her still – her terror,' said Marthe.

She would never be able to forget it.

In Céreste, too, the resistants emerged. They crossed themselves as they passed Christ on the cross framed in a fifteenth-century archway, giving thanks. There were women too, wearing short socks under leather lace-up shoes, raincoats over their shoulders, holding rifles as casually as handbags, and they gathered by the Mairie. A dirty tricolour hung from the flagpole in place of the swastika.

At the café, so the Mussets were told later, a large group of villagers listened openly on a radio set to the news coming in. The US Seventh Army was rapidly gaining ground, sweeping north through the Vaucluse.

Then there was screaming. They rushed out of the café to find that a young woman had been surrounded outside in the square. A crowd had pushed her until her back was to the railings, not far from the memorial for those lost in the Great War. Men and women were shouting, shouts that quickly turned to jeers. Through a cacophony of angry voices they insisted that she had betrayed resistants – they named Candide and the Actress, and others too. They spat the accusation that she was jealous of the Actress. She denied it, of course, but it was then that they recognised her as Christine, who had once been Auguste Baumel's sweetheart.

Christine tried to escape the mob, but was jostled back, cornered. She was screaming, begging for her life. Three shots were fired. There was a look of petrified disbelief on her face as she went down. Then the swarm melted away. Afterwards, no one remembered who had wielded the pistol.

A less bloodthirsty mob might have shaved Christine Lachasse's head, or tarred and feathered her, as happened in other towns and villages after the Liberation, when summary justice was handed out to women who had betrayed resistants or slept with the enemy. Apparently the Poet had tried to dissuade the villagers from violence of any kind – the political situation between the partisan factions was too finely balanced to upset – but even he had not prevailed.

'It was Christine, then?' Marthe still could not take it in. 'Christine who was responsible for Arlette being taken by the Milice?'

'I had my doubts about her, always,' said Madame. 'You

once heard us asking if she was safe, and you thought we were talking about you, do you remember?'

Marthe did, with some shame that she had jumped to such self-centred conclusions. 'So was that why Auguste stopped seeing her?'

'Of course.'

Marthe gasped. 'She came to the farmhouse that day – when I heard Kenton and Scotty in the barn. Do you think—'

'I don't know.'

'But even so – shot in cold blood.'

'This is no time for taking high moral positions,' said Mme Musset.

The end of the fighting in Provence brought a bitter satisfaction. The settling of local scores began. The bludgeoning heat of high summer added to the unleashing of anger and resentment, which would continue for months and years. Others demanded patriotic celebrations. Kenton and Scotty made arrangements to leave.

On their last night, there was a victory dance in one of the tree-lined squares in Manosque. The townsfolk young and old linked arms and climbed the stones into the old town high above the plain, beckoned by the sound of a band whose players struggled, in their enthusiasm, to keep a coherent tempo. At the centre, the hubbub of excited talk, shrieks of laughter, drums and bass competed with the stamping of feet.

'Shall we dance?' Kenton asked Marthe as the band caught its stride. He grabbed her before she had time to reply.

And she was in Kenton's arms, letting him whirl her around. The night was still hot. Her forehead was damp around her hairline. She put her head back and felt the motion lift her. Round and round they went in time with the beat, in joy and sorrow for what had passed, and in hope for what was to come. The coloured lights would be moving around her, the other dancers, the plane trees around the square. She saw it all and more, in her imagination: the huge aircraft landing in the dark field. Kenton and Scotty walking on either side of her along the moonlit road. And Arlette, so full of life, tap-dancing across the blending room, in the café, waiting at the bus stop at Céreste.

A tear trickled down her cheek.

Kenton slowed, and then stopped dancing. He touched her face so gently, it felt like a breeze at first. Then she felt softness on her lips, then warmth and tenderness. He was kissing her, and she kissed him back.

When they arrived back at the farm, the Mussets were already asleep. Kenton took Marthe's hand and led her to her bed.

He left early the next morning.

She refused to feel sad. It was a fine lesson in love, Marthe decided. In the darkness, they had all discovered what they truly were. There were those who had flown to the light, and those who had pulled back farther into the blackest corners. They had all had to learn the architecture of darkness, just as she had once learned to read the smells and sounds and textures of constant night.

After the war, she worked harder than ever to understand the language of scent, the best marriages of disparate aromas and strengths. She used the flowers and herbs that grew all around her, blending combinations into an intimate biography of her life.

One by one, the Musset factory put the scents into production. They sold well. Buyers responded to their sincerity and their relationship with the landscape. The old steam distillery evolved into the prestigious 'Parfumeur-Distillateur Musset', and Marthe Lincel became a creator of perfumes sold throughout Provence.

'A simple scent captures a moment in time,' she once said. 'A perfume tells a story on the skin.'

The letter from Kenton came several years later.

Somewhere, somehow, he had found someone to translate his thoughts twice over: into French and into Braille. The trouble he had taken spoke as much as the words themselves.

'I have still never met anyone like you,' he wrote. 'I think of you in your blue hills with your fragrances, as I hope that you think of me too, sometimes, in my land far away, and know that we are the same, that a part of us is together.

'I wanted to tell you that I am happy, and I am getting married. I hope you are happy too. You deserve it, dearest Marthe. I shall always be grateful to you for what you did for Scotty and me. Without you, I wouldn't be here today, and I shall always love you, in my way.'

With that letter came a notice from a bank in Paris and a lawyer's letter. The Attwaters of Boston had deposited a large sum of money to be used by the Musset distillery, with the stipulation that it was to allow Marthe Lincel to continue her work as a *parfumeuse*, and in time to open a perfume emporium in Paris.

When her parfumerie opened in the place Vendôme in Paris in 1950, Marthe sent a magazine article heralding the event to Boston. The photographs showed a slim, elegant woman with a beguiling expression. She was posed in front of a counter full of scent bottles and their fashionable striped boxes, smiling. Her dark hair was cut in a short, fashionable style, and her dress was from Dior. Another captured her sitting on a gilded chair. It wasn't possible to tell from these skilful photographs that Marthe Lincel's lively eyes could not see.

The pictures she drew on were vibrant as ever, though. The crumbling stone farmstead overlooking the great Luberon valley where she was born. The blending room of the distillery in Manosque where she had experienced a kind of rebirth, beginning the transformation into the woman she was now. Scent was memory, and memory a complex blend of scent and emotion: the perfect flowers of the lavender hills, like millions of mauve butterflies fluttering on stalks; the violet; the heliotrope of home, with its heart of sweet almond and cherry vanilla. She mixed them all into her signature fragrance Lavande de Nuit, along with a breath of civet musk and a haunting trace of smoke.

BOOK III

A Shadow Life

1

Orchard Court

London, April 1943

The bath at Orchard Court was a deep black marble affair. This was unusual enough for a London flat (Iris was not the only one who looked at it longingly), but not as extraordinary as the onyx bidet by its side, the pair set off by striking black-and-white tiles. As there was nowhere else for visitors to sit as they waited, the bathroom had to serve.

Throughout March and April that year, an increasing flow of young men and women had arrived in the lobby of Orchard Court, a building on the corner of Portman Square and Orchard Street, and were shown up to this small flat, in which the sitting room and two small bedrooms were used as offices. The callers were never invited to Baker Street, but to this anonymous property a short walk away. 'Best they never set foot inside the Firm, that way there's no danger of anyone seeing or hearing something they shouldn't know,' said Miss Acton.

That day, two men and a woman were sitting on the edge of the black marble bath; another man was standing. Two partially open umbrellas were hooked over the taps, dripping.

The visitors had been greeted at the door of the second-floor flat by Iris Nightingale, newly promoted to intelligence assistant, and shown immediately into the bathroom, where they perched incongruously in their town clothes.

Colonel Tyndale had been unavoidably detained, and the reason was not good news, Iris surmised, judging from his expression a moment ago in the hall. His narrow face was not built for unnecessary argument; his brow flamed and the bags under his eyes grew pronounced whenever voices rose in anger or frustration. He had finally arrived at Orchard Court, in a hollow-cheeked fluster of raincoat and papers; he and Miss Acton were now closeted in the sitting room, where the interviews would take place.

At the door of the bathroom Iris produced a bottle of brandy and some unmatched glass tumblers. 'It won't be long now,' she said brightly. 'How about a drink?'

It really was the least she could do. Often the guests had very little idea why they had been invited to these odd gatherings. Their only qualification was that they had a French or Belgian parent, or spoke near-native French from years spent on the Continent. They came in batches after passing a selection interview in a small airless office consisting of two plain tables and some scuffed wooden chairs in the basement of the War Office, and were required to sign the Official Secrets Act.

These four were quiet ones, hardly speaking to Iris, let alone to each other. Not necessarily a bad thing. At this stage, it was merely a fact to note. Iris gave a friendly smile as she committed certain obvious traits to memory. The man she guessed was the oldest, thirty-five perhaps, in a well-cut suit, gave the briefest grimace at the mention of Miss Acton's name. He tipped his drink back in one. The man next to him wore a suit that had crinkled and was damp on the shoulders, and his blond hair was slicked back – caught out in the rain shower. He leaned back against the tiles and looked up to the ceiling. The third man was very young. He met her eye, and a nervous tic jerked beneath his own, high on the left cheekbone. The woman sat calmly, answering when she was addressed but otherwise giving the impression that she was waiting for a doctor's appointment, absorbed in private thoughts. She was in her early twenties, pretty, though her dark hair looked as if she had cut it herself. She was the only one to refuse a drink. After a while, she got out some crochet work and bent her head over it.

'Sun and showers, what a day,' ventured Iris.

'Typical bloody England,' replied the man in the smart suit. He crossed his arms in front of his chest. Defensive, despite the air of sophistication.

'Better in here than out,' said the youngest, with an eagerness to please that only underscored his nervousness.

'I expect so,' said Iris.

The woman listened, now and then looking up from the hook and yarn to watch them in the mirror by the basin. Smart cookie, thought Iris. First impressions were vital. In some situations, that was all the chance they would have.

A low buzzer sounded.

'And we're off,' said Iris, nodding towards the nervous young man and deciding to put him out of his agony by giving him the first slot. 'If you'd like to come with me . . .'

It went without saying that Iris had no idea what she was getting into, though that was true one way or another, she suspected, of everyone who enlisted, was called up, or served their country in any capacity during the war. If anyone asked, Iris made a self-effacing reference to the 'little job' at which she was still plugging away. One of the other girls told her that she used to tell her friends she worked at Marks and Spencer's London headquarters, whose building they had taken over, until the questions about the chances of obtaining good-quality clothes under the counter became too onerous. She had to pretend to leave and 'go into teaching'.

Iris had planned to join the Wrens when she left school, and might well have done so but for the intervention of her headmistress. Term was almost over when the jutting shelf of Miss Jeffery's bosom arrested any further progress down the library corridor.

'I understand you are contemplating your future in the Women's Royal Naval Service.'

'Yes, Miss Jeffery.'

'Have you considered playing to your strengths as a linguist and training as a secretary who can work in French and German? There is a bursary available, and I would be very pleased to recommend you.'

And so, because Miss Jeffery had almost always been kind and well meaning, qualities all too rare in Iris's chequered experience of school life, the advice was taken. Iris enrolled in the three-month residential secretarial course in Bedford, gratefully accepting the bursary to pay her board and lodging, and assuming throughout that the language instruction in military and naval terms was required to enable her to enter the Wrens as a secretary or wireless telegraphist. The instruction was good, and Iris, always meticulous in her work, came top of her class of twenty-five in the final exams. She emerged with a certificate in typing, shorthand and French and German translation. Her tutoring in Morse code did not seem to be certified on paper.

A few days after she'd completed the course, a letter came to her aunt's flat in Battersea from the Inter Services Research Bureau, giving no details but asking Iris to contact them to arrange an interview for a job. She telephoned the number she was given and was asked to present herself at a small hotel in Victoria the next day.

'Could you tell me a little more about the position, please?'

'Why don't you come along, and then it will be easier to explain,' said the woman's voice, clipped and authoritative, on the other end of the line.

'I will, but could you tell me please how you came to know I was looking for a job? It seems a bit—'

'You have been recommended. We'll see you tomorrow then, at ten. Goodbye.'

The next day the bus from Battersea dropped her at Victoria Station in plenty of time to walk to her appointment. October leaves had collected on the sandbags that lined the streets north of the river. The hotel was a soot-streaked commercial establishment behind Ebury Street. She was directed at the reception desk to a small room on the first floor, facing the street. She had hardly raised her knuckles from a tentative knock under the metal number 4 before a young woman wearing pearls and a grey serge suit pulled the door open. Twin beds had been pushed against opposite walls to provide seating. Between the beds, a wooden table took up most of the space.

A wide-shouldered woman with a gravelly voice stood up, held out her hand and introduced herself as Miss Allott.

'Do take a seat.'

Iris took the bed on the other side of the table.

Miss Allott stared intently at a flimsy sheet of paper for a few moments.

'Born 1922, and You've just turned nineteen.'

'Yes, that's right,' said Iris.

'Lived in Hove, but in 1931 you were sent to a boarding school in Switzerland for six years. What were the circumstances of this move?'

Iris was taken aback, but found herself answering politely as ever, the natural result of years spent under the control of Miss Jeffery and her ilk. This Miss Allott, with her carefully sculpted hair and severe expression, was undoubtedly one of them.

'My father died. My mother remarried and went to live in Berne with her new husband.'

'There follow various boarding schools in Sussex and Wiltshire . . . would you care to elaborate on the reasons?'

'My mother . . . felt she was unable to cope. She was having difficulties in her second marriage. We returned to England. She couldn't settle in Sussex, so she tried Wiltshire. I think she wanted me close by but not actually at home.'

'And where is she now?'

'She lives just outside Salisbury.'

'Other family?'

'An aunt, my mother's sister. I'm currently staying with her.'

'So . . .' Miss Allott did not pursue the investigation.

'Languages – you speak French and German well, and some Italian too?'

'I speak them well enough. French with fluency, German adequately. Some Italian, but only enough to get by.'

Miss Allott crossed her arms and leaned forward across the table. '*Que pensez-vous de la situation politique en France actuellement?*'

Iris replied that it was an impossible situation politically for the French. Was their government for or against the old France and its people; were the members of the Vichy regime motivated by political expediency or personal power? And all the while the ordinary citizens were surely only trying to get by as best they could.

After a few more questions about her unsatisfactory background, Iris was abruptly dismissed from the twin-bedded interview room. She was making for the door when Miss Allott tossed one last ball.

'Would you say you were imaginative, Miss Nightingale?'

What an odd thing to ask.

Iris hesitated. 'I don't consider that I am, particularly. I'm not a dreamer, if that's what you mean. I would say that I was rather straightforward . . . sensible. I've rather had to be, with a mother like mine.'

Miss Allott frowned. She said nothing more, and a moment later Iris was out in the corridor again. She had said too much about her personal difficulties. It seemed she had failed to satisfy her interlocutor, just as she always did her mother. But the next day a letter arrived inviting Iris to present herself for work the following Monday at 64 Baker Street.

It would be a few months before Iris realised that Mavis Acton (not Allott at all) made up her mind almost immediately as to the suitability of a candidate, and very rarely revised that opinion.

Iris signed the Official Secrets Act on her first morning at 64 Baker Street. It was an elegant light-grey stone building, six windows wide; a brass plate by the door offered the anodyne misinformation that these were the offices of the Inter Services Research Bureau. She was introduced, with perfunctory politeness, to Colonel Hugh Tyndale, head of F Section. His harassed manner implied that Iris had arrived at a tricky juncture, but it was not long before it became apparent that this was his normal demeanour. He looked down on her – he was a tall, thin man with a stoop – and blinked through round tortoiseshell glasses before nodding his dismissal and hurrying past.

It was clear too that Miss Acton was the lynchpin of the operation. She may have had a commanding manner and expectation of total obeisance, but Miss Acton carried herself in the certain knowledge that men still found her attractive despite the weight of years; she must have been in her mid-forties. Her dark hair was immaculate, waved and pinned. Her signature scent of fern whispered of Paris before the war. Her excellent legs marched in high heels. Clip-on earrings made of silver and mother-of-pearl caught the attention, as if a single butterfly wing had alighted on each earlobe. The high-necked blouses in soft fabrics were chosen to drape and flatter. Mavis Acton was calm and reserved at all times, her edicts issued in low tones that both asserted absolute authority and attested to the strength of the Senior Service cigarettes she smoked with such fervent pleasure.

It struck Iris that in many ways she had swapped a world run by schoolmistresses for an uncomfortably similar set-up run by another version of the type, lacking only the bushy eyebrows and corridor-blocking chest.

For the first few months, Iris's duties consisted of typing reports and translating from both French and German. She was part of a team gathering intelligence about all aspects of occupied France. Some of the information was very basic: the travel network, the way food coupons worked, the latest coins in the occupation currency minted by the Germans. Most of this came from newspapers provided by businessmen from neutral countries who were still permitted to travel into France, or who met their French counterparts in Lisbon or Geneva.

There were strict office rules. In the evenings, it was considered a serious breach of security to leave out any papers. Every book, every newspaper clipping, every single written word, had to be locked in steel filing cabinets.

Before they left the office in the evening, a night-duty officer would come round with one of the twenty-four-hour guard to collect all waste paper. Then they went through the room testing locks on cupboards and the steel cabinets, and checking that nothing of value was sitting in an unsecured drawer.

'A word please, Miss Nightingale.'

Iris followed Miss Acton into her office.

'You realise, don't you, that any slip-up could put the lives of our people at risk?' said Miss Acton. She did not wait for a reply. 'Blotting paper, Miss Nightingale. I am extremely displeased that you have been so careless. If you had been here longer, leaving out blotting paper would have been utterly unforgivable.'

'I'm sor—'

'It's quite possible to work out what was blotted. Do you think that we are simply playing at war here, Miss Nightingale?'

Mavis Acton raised her hand for silence as she began a tirade that rapidly increased in volume and fury: anything Iris saw or heard in the department was strictly confidential; she knew that she should speak of it to no one, should deflect any inquiries about her line of work; and yet what was the purpose of any of that if she was leaving matters of the highest national security out in full view for anyone to see?

Iris could think of nothing to say in her defence. She was sent to collect a file from the Firm's offices at Norgeby House, across the road. ('I suppose you can manage that?') In the ladies' cloakroom on the half-landing there, Iris splashed cold water on her blotchy face and tried to calm herself. She was furious to find that she was still trembling.

'It's Iris, isn't it?'

A face bobbed up behind hers in the mirror. Auburn hair and wide eyes.

Iris nodded.

'Nancy. Nancy Bateman. I'd only been here a couple of days when you arrived.'

'In the big room . . . yes, I recognise you.'

'That's right. I was moved over here a few days later. How are you finding it?'

'Well, it's certainly an interesting "little job" . . .'

'You don't want to get on the wrong side of Miss Acton, though,' said Nancy Bateman, twisting and repinning her hair in two large combs.

Iris finished washing her hands, wondering how much it was possible to say. 'Is it that obvious?'

'Let's say you're not the first to have to come in here to repair her face. What did you do?'

'I left out some blotting paper last night.' A few inky marks on which two lines of reverse writing were barely visible.

'Heinous crime.'

'I wasn't thinking. She was right. I was utterly boneheaded. But no one told me – no one says anything!' Iris looked up and met Nancy's eyes in the mirror. 'No one talks to anyone else. It's all little bits of paper with typed messages and brown envelopes and never quite explaining what's going on.'

'Talking would be far too sensible. Though of course Miss Acton is right. She's always right. But it's not the end of the world. You do know that she's known to be hardest on those she thinks have most potential?'

'Is that true? Or are you simply saying it to make me feel better?'

'Both.'

There was a firmness in Nancy's tone that made them both laugh suddenly.

'Oh, well – thank you. You *have* made me feel better.'

'Everyone's frightened of Miss Acton, even the men, though most of them have developed a manner with her that they imagine covers it up.'

Nancy was right. Iris had seen the way men stood in the

presence of that husky yet clipped voice. Madam, they called her, to her face.

'What are you doing for lunch?' asked Nancy.

They had tea and toast at the Lyon's Corner House. Nancy was twenty-one, from Lincolnshire, and had a fiancé in the RAF. She was a slip of a girl, with a determined look in those big eyes, a striking mixture of blue and green. She chatted easily about her training as a teleprinter and her previous posting to RAF Duxford near Cambridge, a Spitfire base and Fighter Command.

'When I told my mother I was off to Duxford, she kicked up a dreadful fuss. "Think of all those men!" she said, and did everything she could to persuade me not to go,' said Nancy.

'Sounds like she was right to worry.'

Nancy grinned. 'She certainly was.'

It was a great relief to make a friend. With her old school chums, even the girls she had met on the course in Bedford, Iris felt uncomfortable lying about what she was doing. Some seemed to look down on her for not joining the Wrens to do her bit. One by one they had dropped away. You were only ever completely at ease with others in the same position, and even then you needed to be certain exactly which spot on the same side they occupied.

In the capacity of a secretary at Baker Street, Iris had typed reports and kept files on the men and women who were sent undercover to France, but had never met them. Two years later at Orchard Court, she came face to face with them all, from the admired veterans to the new recruits.

As she was tall and slim with dark blond hair falling in natural waves to her shoulders, the men would invariably flirt with her; men who were confident and, if not good-looking in too striking a way, then invariably charming, with a certain allure. Miss Acton always called them 'our friends', never anything else. The 'girls', too, were lovely. Iris once overheard someone else remarking on that undeniable fact, followed by Miss Acton's response: 'Yes, because that gives them self-confidence.'

Perhaps she hoped that their charms might prove protective, and in this, as in other matters, she was often proved right.

For some who returned to Orchard Court, having passed their training at various secret northern locations, it would be the last visit to London before being sent to France. Others would never make it past initial training and assessment at Wanborough Manor near Guildford; for them, the drink in the bathroom followed by a chat with some strangers who asked personal questions would be relegated to a memory of another odd episode during the war.

When the last of the potential new agents had gone, packed off with instructions to present themselves at Wanborough, Iris took out the small notebook she always kept in her pocket and studied the scribbles she had made. At a rickety table in the minuscule kitchen, she pulled the typewriter towards her, rolled up paper and carbon and made sense of her shorthand. On separate papers for the files, she noted idiosyncrasies of speech and phrase, the cadence and tone of each recruit's words, in French and English. What she wrote now might never be needed, but in certain circumstances it could prove vital, and it was never too early to start. When the only means of communication with the agents on the ground was by coded wireless messages, there had to be safety checks in place to guarantee their authenticity.

Miss Acton put her head round the door. 'Would you type up Thérèse's debrief before you go?'

'Just about to.'

'Any thoughts?'

She meant about that afternoon's four new faces. 'The girl seemed a cool customer,' said Iris. 'I rather liked her. First man in was very young – a bit twitchy.'

Miss Acton nodded, and left her to it.

Iris made brisk work of the first job and inserted a fresh sheet of paper. After five months in France, Thérèse had brought back a substantial amount of information: details of changes to identity documents and travel permits; current living conditions; the most frequently voiced complaints; snippets of news that provoked the most comment; alterations to train timetables. Noting changes was crucial. The French magazines and newspapers she brought back would be scoured for nonsense about the latest fashions as well as the papers French citizens were expected to carry, the hours of curfew and how often ration cards were now being issued.

The first time Iris met Thérèse at Orchard Court she had put her age at about twenty. She had taken her wisp-slim figure, timid manner and perennial concern for her parents to indicate a girl way out of her depth. She was a private seamstress from the East End by trade, which seemed the perfect gentle occupation for her. Wrong on almost every count, it transpired. Thérèse (real name Lucienne Jarvis) was almost thirty and adept at self-effacement, at stepping back and observing. A Belgian mother had passed on a perfect command of the French language, and the accent had been refined by a number of years at a Parisian couture house; her father's background as a merchant seaman from the Mile End Road provided a tough resourcefulness.

She was friendly and funny, though never overplaying either quality. Not far beneath the surface was a nervousness that was considered more good than bad: the nerves would keep her alert to danger. There was no doubting her courage and determination.

Iris was not sure she could have done what Thérèse and the others did. It was suggested at one time that her name be put forward for consideration, but nothing came of it. She would have gone, thought Iris, but she wouldn't have rated her chances of coming back. She had never regretted not being chosen. Miss Acton said she was of more use where she was; she shared with her boss a sharp memory and an instinctive grasp of detail. So London was where Iris stayed, her relief the secret she kept most securely of all.

2

⁓

The Making of an Agent

London, June 1943

The self-contained girl in the bathroom made the grade at Wanborough Manor. She was sent on to the Western Highlands to learn how to handle guns and explosives and commit acts of sabotage. There, she had confounded expectations, hitting more targets with her quiet accuracy than quite a few of the men. She had emerged unscathed, apart from a sprained ankle from parachute training. She arrived back at Orchard Court in the uniform of the First Aid Nursing Yeomanry, the usual cover, newly purchased from Lillywhites department store in Piccadilly.

She was no longer Rita Williams; she had a code name now: Rose.

The physical exercise had trimmed a few pounds from her face and waist, and the hacked-about hair was greatly improved, cut short by the French hairdresser working from one of Thérèse's magazines. It was tinted a rich chestnut shade that complemented her shrewd brown eyes, and gave her an undeniably Parisian look.

'It suits you,' said Iris. '*Vraiment très chic.*'

'*Je vous remercie, mademoiselle.*'

Rose's accent was impeccable, with an easy roll of the *r*.

'You've lived in France, haven't you?' said Iris conversationally.

'Yes.'

'Whereabouts?'

'Paris. I spent time in Nice, too.'

She was a year older than Iris, and she had been a companion to a wealthy elderly woman. Not the kind of job Iris would have relished, but you never knew what circumstances dictated choice. The girl's quiet composure radiated patience. No doubt she had learned to be resourceful in attending to the whims of her employer. According to the file, Rita Williams had spent her childhood in Camberwell, south London. She had left school at sixteen and spent two years in France before the outbreak of war. Her widowed mother was killed when a bomb struck the house in Camberwell in the Blitz of 1940.

Rose sat with her hands resting on her handbag, a delicate cobweb of black crochet work.

'That's an awfully pretty little bag,' Iris persisted. 'Did you make it yourself?'

'As a matter of fact, I did.'

She didn't ask Iris how she'd guessed, though. She was friendly and polite in response to Iris's questions but did not chatter. Miss Acton rated her very highly. Self-containment and concise answers were always a plus with Miss Acton.

A click-clack of heels sounded on the polished floor of the corridor, and Rose was borne off in a waft of tobacco and steely purpose.

All the preparations seemed easier than normal with Rose.

Before the agents were sent to France, a tailor skilled in the Continental style made clothes for them: suits, jackets, skirts, appropriate to their cover story. The men's suits carried forged trade tapes, indicating in which town the clothes had been made, to fit these fictions. Shirts, underwear, socks, shoes – all these too were carefully assembled. But Rose already had a substantial and authentic French wardrobe of her own, dresses she had made herself from French fabrics and patterns, though not nearly to Thérèse's standard. The odd stretched or puckered seam gave the impression, quite usefully, of stoic vulnerability. Other authentic items of clothes had been altered and refitted from her employer's cast-offs. There would be no need to change her profession once she arrived. The backstory would be that her previous employer had only recently died; it was vague enough, and she would be kept well away from Nice to avoid any chance of being recognised. Easily confirmable facts were overlaid with fantasy, but it worked best to leave in an element of truth.

'What do you think of these specs?'

'I thought you didn't need glasses?' Iris had a jolt of panic. One of the very first criteria when the agents were recruited in London was 20/20 vision. In the rough and tumble of their work in the field, the last worry they needed was keeping their glasses safe.

'I don't – these are plain glass. But if I do this' – Rose squinted – 'I can look really quite the shrinking violet, can't I? And . . . oops, just a bit clumsy.' She caught some papers on the desk with her elbow.

'Very convincing.'

It was true. The old wire spectacles gave her a disconcertingly timid and ineffectual look, yet seemed to relax her at the same time. It made all the difference to her to play a part. She was almost ready to go to France as a wireless operator for the Swagman circuit operating between Paris and Tours. The wireless set was hidden in a small leather suitcase. False identity papers had been prepared for her, and fake German-stamped passes of various kinds, food cards and bread coupons, a Carte de Vêtements et d'Articles Textiles, all of which had to be up to date.

For weeks now she had been rehearsing her story with Miss Acton as well as Iris, immersing herself in every aspect of her fictional background until it seemed real, coming out perfectly naturally if she were challenged, however tired she was, or if taken by surprise.

'How did you meet your "fiancé"?'

'In the Parc Zoologique in Lille, where I had my first job. I was out strolling by myself, and so was Hubert. He does sound suitably boring.' Rose pulled a deadpan face and then laughed, showing pretty teeth.

As the preparations went on, she was becoming less reserved, more confident about showing a bit of personality within the Firm. Iris was pleased about that. 'The point is that it doesn't involve anyone else or any awkward details except for the layout of the park. Where is Hubert now?'

'He's working in a factory in Germany. He's a model citizen who answered the call. And if I absolutely have to give his name, it is authentic?'

'It will be there in the official files. When you get to France you will have to immerse yourself in being this character, this Rose Mielhan, originally from Paris, from the area that you know well, who worked for a time in Lille for an elderly widow who died. Her name is also in the official records, with a headstone in the cemetery there.'

'I know. I've done nothing else for the past week but memorise my dull life there with her and Hubert.'

The life expectancy of a wireless operator in a French city was put at six months. Iris was uncertain whether Colonel Tyndale or Miss Acton had passed on that information.

Iris thanked God she could talk to Nancy. Not all the time, nor about every detail, but the pressure was eased by not having to pretend when they were finally off duty. By the end of 1942, Iris and Nancy had taken a small flat together. They were putting in longer and longer hours, and if the bombing had been bad, it could take hours for the bus to cross the river and grind into town from Battersea, and Nancy's tram to come up from New Cross, where she had dismal digs. It was just too far every day, and Iris's Aunt Etty (whom, in truth, she hardly knew) had not bargained on Iris staying for longer than it took to get herself set up with a job.

Nancy and Iris sublet an attic flat off Tavistock Square from a friend of a friend. The two bedrooms were tiny, but they could walk to work. With Nancy's fiancé Phil serving abroad with his squadron, it seemed the ideal solution.

They rarely brought other friends back, not through a lack of them but because they each understood implicitly that this was their sanctuary from watching what they said outside the Firm, from speaking about cyanide pills sewn into shirt hems, and explosives, and keeping up morale. Sometimes they spent the whole weekend in companionable silence. Nancy wrote long letters to Phil, while Iris composed bland little missives to her mother in Salisbury, saddened by the realisation that they had no secret language forged in closeness.

Other times, they went out to clubs and pubs with the crowd. There were always invitations on offer to the Café Royale, to the Dorchester bar and to the shows. As the agents passed through Orchard Court and Iris got to know them, flirting a little with the men and befriending the women (though always alert to their behavioral quirks and speech patterns), some of them would be asked along. As often as not, it was a means of eating, as one of the many wealthy men who had taken what was known as 'special employment' in the secret services would settle the bill before anyone had a chance to offer to pay a share.

When they were left to their own devices, meals seemed to consist of tea and toast. They were almost always too tired to cook after work, and usually too late for the shops. Once they tried to cook a pigeon on the kitchen fire. It was not an experiment they repeated.

Iris had no shortage of admirers. There was John from the War Office, older and wiser than the others, and a full deck of servicemen: Alan, who was in the navy; Peter from the Royal Engineers; RAF pilots Jack and Rory, when they were in town. None of them was special.

'Your trouble is, you've too many to choose from,' Nancy said.

'So how did you know Phil was the one?'

'I just did.'

'No help at all! But listen, I won't be back tonight.'
Nancy raised an eyebrow.
'Nothing like that. Full moon – I'm going down to Sussex.'

3

Tangmere

Chichester, July 1943

Rose was going to France.

One afternoon, a car pulled up outside Orchard Court. Rose took a rear seat alongside Iris. Miss Acton, who usually made airfield trips, had important meetings in London. They headed south out of the embattled city, its streets made foreign by jagged grey bomb craters and ruined buildings, and into countryside that offered reassurance that life did still exist as it had before.

Cow parsley frothed from the verges of the country roads. Dog roses fluttered in a warm breeze. Birdsong and brightness imitated peacetime, if only for a few hours. Iris and Rose hardly spoke. In the green fields east of Chichester the village of Tangmere was sleepy, marked only by the shingle-clad spire on the church roof. Trees and bushes formed a green screen on either side of the road.

'Here we are,' said Iris as they drove up a short gravel pathway. 'The Cottage. The gates over there are the main entrance to the airfield.'

Rose nodded.

She looked terribly young and vulnerable, thought Iris. In the dark gabardine suit chosen to blend in to the crowd, she was so slim as to be childlike. Rose's cheekbones had become more prominent and her eyes huge. It was all too easy to believe that she was making her way in the world as best she could on her own – that part was true, after all, since the loss of her mother – while her fiancé was away. The cheap garnet ring on her finger was noticeably looser than it had been a month earlier.

'All right?' asked Iris.

'Yes.'

Rose was doing a good job covering it, but she was scared. It was only natural. Iris would have to keep a keen watch on her, perhaps make a difficult decision, when the time came.

They got out of the car. Tangmere Cottage was a low redbrick house, about a hundred years old. The brickwork was almost entirely covered with ivy, through which small-paned windows managed to assert themselves. There was one upstairs floor and a thick chimney stack on the end. The property and garden were protected from sight by a Sussex stone wall and dense hedges.

'Come on inside,' said Iris. 'They do a lovely cup of tea here.'

That got a smile. Rose gathered her bag and gloves and followed.

Inside, the cottage – a requisition, naturally – was still more domestic than military, extended over the years to produce a useful muddle of rooms, none of them very large.

'Hello, Stephen,' called Iris as they entered the back door to the kitchen.

Her cheery greeting was returned by a tall, thickset man in uniform, one of the two flight sergeants of the RAF police service who governed the Cottage.

'This is Stephen. He's cook and security all in one, which makes this the most comforting guardroom in the country. Nothing and no one gets past Stephen.'

'Hello, miss,' he said, nodding at Rose. She was not introduced, not even by her new name. 'Kettle's on, make yourselves at home.'

'Thanks! Come through to the ops room.'

Keen to keep the mood upbeat, Iris led the way into what had once been a sitting room with a simple brick fireplace, now full of heavy brown furniture. Dark wooden beams made the ceiling seem lower. On the wall hung a large map of France. A table and a selection of unmatched chairs gave the room a relaxed air. The remains of a coal fire were unlit. On a small wooden desk were a black telephone and a green telephone.

A couple of young men stood smoking by the window. Iris grinned. 'You two again! Rose, I'm delighted to be able to introduce two of our finest – Jack and Rory. One of these renegades will be taking you up tonight, and you couldn't be in better hands.'

'Unless you get Verity, of course,' said Jack, as they shook hands. He was tall and fair, with an angular frame. 'Though I fear you are indeed stuck with one of us. Heigh ho.'

He pushed back his floppy mop of blond hair. He reminded Iris of the earnest young men who worked for the BBC after graduating from Cambridge. But there the similarity ended. If he looked will-o'-the-wisp, Jack Wallace was a particularly steady pilot, a meticulous checker of everything from the wind to the instruments in the cockpit to the quality of the fuel to the political situation. He was a careful navigator, with a near-photographic memory for the routes learned from maps, and a tendency to worry masked his methodical approach and fierce determination.

'It's quite all right. We've been practising,' said Rory to Rose, who tried to smile. Rory was shorter, with a mop of dark curly hair and wide brown eyes that always reminded Iris of her childhood teddy bear. 'In fact, I'm beginning to wonder whether I wouldn't find it a shock to the system to fly in daylight now.'

'And we've been eating our carrots,' said Jack cheerfully. 'I've got the night vision of a rabbit!'

'How many of these trips have you made?' Rose asked.

'This will be my tenth sortie for Special Ops.'

Rory took a final deep drag on his cigarette and stubbed it out. 'Eight for me.'

Iris rubbed goosebumps from her bare arms, and hoped the girl hadn't noticed. All summer, agents from both F Section and the other intelligence services had been dropped into France by Lysanders, planes that were short-winged and light, able to land in restricted spaces like small fields. With so much activity, there had been many times when Miss Acton could not make the trip, and it had fallen to Iris to accompany the agents from London to the airfield during the full moon. It still seemed incredible that men like Jack Wallace and Rory Fitzgerald brought down planes deep inside enemy territory, flying by moonlight, navigating across France by picking out silvered strips of river and other memorised landmarks; when they landed it was in darkness, guided only by hand torches.

'How long do you stay on the ground?' asked Rose.

'As little time as possible. If we can turn around in less than ten minutes, that's all right. Any longer, and we risk being rumbled.'

'Well, I am very grateful indeed not to have to drop out on a parachute.'

'Any bloody fool can drop joes over France and come back without touching down, but it takes skill to land a Lizzie and take off again,' said Jack.

Rory stubbed out his cigarette and immediately lit another. 'All part of the service. Ah, tea – jolly good.'

Over tea and more cigarettes they swapped off-duty gossip: Iris telling them who had been in the crowd at the Dorchester and the 400 Club, the pilots giving the latest updates on their twin passions. In Jack's case this was an old black motorcycle he called the Beauty, which he would strip down and tend with oil cadged from the mechanics at the airfield; Rory had Sam, a collie dog he had rescued in his native Yorkshire after the death of an old hill farmer.

'We had a soppy Airedale at home, so sweet-natured,' said Rose. 'I miss her dreadfully.'

The house that was bombed out, thought Iris. It took the dog as well as her mother. She was struck yet again by the girl's composure, her ability to master her emotions. Rose would be fine, quietly resourceful and reliable.

'I was desperate to keep Sam at camp, but they wouldn't let me,' said Rory. 'It was thanks to Jack, and one of the Beauty's not infrequent breakdowns, that we found a farmer close to Tempsford who would look after her.'

'Is that near here?' Rose asked.

'Not really. But closer than Yorkshire.'

'And he writes Sam lovely letters when he's away,' teased Iris.

She did not explain that 161 Squadron (Special Ops) was based at RAF Tempsford in Bedfordshire. During the full moon they came down to Tangmere because it made for a shorter journey into the heart of France, when the range of the aircraft was crucial. From the Sussex coast they could penetrate as far as central France and return. The pilots were normally at Tangmere Cottage for a week before the full moon and a week after.

'You couldn't bring him here? Why, there's even a garden!' said Rose.

'And conditions like a cheap Turkish hotel upstairs,' said Jack. 'So many camp beds up there . . . sometimes you can't even see the landing floor. The idea of that hound howling outside all night . . . no, thank you.'

'And what about your noisy lump of metal, eh?'

'You wouldn't know it, but these two really are great friends,' said Iris. 'Except where dogs, motorcycles and women are concerned.'

'Where women are concerned, that's good-natured competition,' said Jack, sitting up straight and pretending to adjust his collar. 'Go on, Iris, You've had long enough to decide – which one of us is it to be?'

'Oh, you know I could never come between you boys. That would be treachery.'

Dusk was falling. Cooking smells drifted from the kitchen, where the mess sergeants were busy bringing a game pie to perfection: assorted meat (mainly rabbit) and vegetables (mostly carrots) under a crust of mashed potato. They had become used to rationing, but were still obsessed with food. Two trestle tables were laid for supper in the plain whitewashed dining room next door.

More young men arrived through the kitchen as the comforting aroma grew stronger. One of them cranked up a gramophone in the corner. The room grew misty with cigarette smoke, pierced by notes of exquisite pain from a saxophone. 'Give it a rest, Richie,' someone grumbled. 'Leave the torture to the Gestapo.'

The atmosphere was lively as they sat down to eat. Nervous energy was countered by banter. A young man in civilian clothes was ushered in late. He was not introduced by name, so he must have been an agent from one of the other special services. Rose remained quiet at Iris's side. She was outwardly calm, but Iris wondered how she really felt, now it was almost time to go. They were joined by squadron leader Hugh Verity, the genial, unassuming and much-respected head of Special Duties operations. Like all the pilots, he wore a mixture of uniform and civilian clothes; if he was shot down and managed to survive bailing out, he would lose or burn his battle blouse and pass for any other slightly scruffy young man.

'We had a dreadful night. The flak came at us for miles over northern France on the way back. Two joes in the back, we're well off track . . . but everyone's keeping their cool magnificently . . . then the underside takes a hit just before we cross the Channel. Somehow or other we splutter over the finishing line in low cloud and on the last gasp of fuel. We all stagger out, and the only event that provokes a reaction from the French is getting in the car on arrival and being driven off on the wrong side of the road!'

'. . . it's not stunt aerobatics, you know. Though some of them seem to think we can land on a franc coin on the edge of a cliff, some of the places they've been finding for us . . .'

'. . . remember Stamper landing in thick fog on the stumps of the Lizzie's legs? He'd taken the wheels off on a cliff, and there was telegraph wire wrapped around the tail wheel, and a hole in the undercarriage, and the supplementary fuel tank only hanging on by a couple of twisted screws . . .'

Iris felt dizzy with the effort of trying to follow as many stories as she could, but Rose was emotionless, as composed as she had been the first time Iris had met her.

After they had eaten, Hugh Verity led them back into the ops room and gave the briefing. It was a double Lysander operation. Standing in front of the map of France, he pointed out the two flight paths and shared reconnaissance photos of the landing fields. The weather forecast came in from the Met Office: mainly clear with scattered cloud. On the green telephone, fitted with a scrambler for confidential conversation, he took a call from air ops on London confirming that the BBC message had gone out, and the reception groups would be assembling on the ground in France.

Final checks were being made on the airfield. The pilots went outside to accustom their eyes to the dark. At the Cottage, Iris handed over the wireless set disguised as a small leather suitcase and went through Rose's pockets one last time to make sure no bus tickets remained, no receipts or stray coins to give away where they had been recently.

'Let me see the labels in your coat and jacket. Blouse? You've checked any labels on your underclothing – nothing British at all?'

'I've gone over everything a hundred times.'

The only sign of nerves was a slight tremble.

'Right . . . French identity card, money, food cards and bread coupons?'

They went through her handbag together.

'Photograph of the fiancé?'

'In the side pocket.'

'It's always the smallest things that give us away.'

Everything the agents took back to France with them had to be authentic. English soap, for example, lathered too well, so the poor dry stuff most widely available on the Continent had to be made specially. Imitation Gauloises cigarettes had been given up as a bad idea – the British gum used on the packets was too strong and would not disintegrate in the same way as the real ones. All the everyday items like string and matches, safety pins and hairpins, scissors, razors, pencils, had to be unmarked, with no 'Made in England' cut into them to give the game away. Best of all was to use those items that had been recently brought back by other agents.

One of Miss Acton's rules was that she would always give the agents a chance to see her alone before they went out to the plane. 'If they have any doubts, best let them confess,' she said. Iris touched Rose on the arm. 'I'm popping upstairs to the bathroom, if you want to come too,' she said.

On the landing Iris turned and asked, 'All ready? Speak now or for ever hold your peace.'

'I'm all right.'

'Completely?'

Rose took an audible breath and composed herself. 'That's a very pretty pin you have in your hair, Iris. Such a clever design.'

Iris clicked it open and took out the silver and paste clip in the shape of a rosebud. She checked it under the landing light and handed it over.

'Oh no, I didn't mean—'

'I know. But I want you to have it anyway. And—'

'Yes?'

Iris hesitated. Then she leaned forward and gave her a spontaneous hug.

'Good luck.'

When they walked downstairs, Iris had the uncomfortable feeling that she might be sending a friend to her demise.

At 10.30 p.m. a large Ford estate car arrived at the Cottage to take them to the plane waiting on the tarmac. The luggage was loaded. They stepped into the vehicle. Minutes later, they were standing underneath one of the two Lysanders flying that night.

It was stubby, with non-retractable undercarriage legs, high wings on a V-strut. The plane looked like an awkward, stunted insect, but in the right hands it was an astonishing machine, capable of landing and taking off in exceptionally small spaces. The wings were positioned at eye level either side of the pilot, who sat high in the cockpit under the greenhouse roof that allowed such good visibility.

'In case no one tells you, there's a half-bottle of whisky in front of the passenger seat,' Iris whispered to Rose.

The unnamed man arrived with an officer in another car. He and Rose climbed the ladder. Iris could see them in silhouette, stowing bags under the wooden seats. Heavier luggage, like the wireless set, was harder to manage, but they did.

Iris watched the plane move off, its wings lit silver by the moon.

Back at the Cottage, Iris gathered up any items left behind. Books and magazines in English, cigarettes, matches and sweet wrappers were the usual haul, but this time Rose and the unknown man had been completely clean on arrival. That was always a good sign. It showed they were already in character.

'Go and get some sleep upstairs, why don't you?' suggested Stephen. Her driver had already done so.

Iris shook her head. Tonight she was waiting for the return flight. She was tired, but she knew she wouldn't be able to sleep properly. Where were the planes now? Were they safely over the Channel yet? She looked at her watch. It was gone 11.30 p.m. They should be. A round trip lasted between four and six hours. Iris settled into an armchair and reached for her coat to put over her legs. Hours passed. She dozed, all the while alert for a dull engine drone overhead.

When she finally heard footsteps outside, the clock read four fifteen.

The door opened noisily. A group of men entered, Jack among them, stamping mud from their shoes, flinging off jackets and dropping bags. The drinks tray was raided and glasses clinked. Triple brandies all round. The release of tension was palpable. From the kitchen, like a well-oiled machine, came the smell of coffee and frying bacon.

'Now I know I'm in England,' said an exceptionally handsome man with a French accent and a world-weary air. He turned to Iris and winked. 'No more ersatz!'

Iris clambered to her feet, feeling dazed.

'Real coffee, mademoiselle – no more acorns and chicory, at least for now,' he said, in excellent but extravagantly accented English. He raised his glass of brandy. 'To freedom!'

'To freedom,' she replied.

He slept in the back of the car all the way up to London. A British man with him slumped against the window, staring out with bloodshot eyes while the grey light over the trees turned pale yellow with the dawn.

4

Xavier

London, July 1943

So that was Xavier Descours.

Until then, Iris had only seen his name in the files and heard accounts of his apparently fearless command of the air operations landing in France. Before the war he had been the manager of an electronics company, specializing in the manufacture and shipping of wireless components. He had been recruited in France to organise the supply of these to the British SOE and the Resistance, while still, ostensibly, running his business for the Vichy government. He was thirty-eight years old and had a reputation for being a cat with nine lives, a charmer who ran terrible risks; in the past year he had become more deeply involved in liaison missions for F Section and was now indispensable to the secret air service.

Two days later he turned up at Orchard Court. He spent a long time in the large room with Colonel Tyndale and Miss Acton. The murmur of voices rose and fell, though it was not possible to hear what was being said.

Iris served tea to two young men, undergraduate types – at least, one of them was wearing a college scarf – who were being prepped to fly into France at the next full moon. With only the six of them in the flat, there was no need to press the bathroom into service as a reception area. They drank the weak brew with little enthusiasm in the smallest bedroom office. When they were summoned into the main meeting, Iris was left alone.

She typed up some notes while they were fresh in her mind, fragments of information she had picked up while their guard was down: the Yorkshire public school and holidays in Scarborough of one of them, and his support of Leeds United football club; the admiration for the novels of Émile Zola of the other.

The atmosphere was depressing, with the dank cold, the cigarette smoke and fog rubbing up against the building like a wet dog. She stood up and moved around to try to get a little warmer, was hardly thinking when she delved into the pockets of the coats that had been thrown over the back of an armchair. It was a reflex action that brought up nothing more exciting than a book of matches, some crumpled bits of paper and a selection of bus and tube tickets that would have to be disposed of before the men went over to France.

'What are you doing?'

He had come up behind her soundlessly. She turned round and found she was looking directly into Xavier's deep brown eyes. His olive skin was smooth, and he was so close she could smell honeyed tobacco, so deliciously different from the acrid tar of Senior Service.

'Sorry, I—'

'That is my coat.'

'I get so used to doing it.'

He seemed to be weighing up the possibility that she was being disingenuous. Straight eyebrows lowered; then he pulled the coat out of her hands and folded it over his arm. He walked over to the window with a confident swagger and turned. 'We are supposed to trust each other.'

'Well, of course—'

'Do I have to prove myself to you?'

She felt herself blushing. Then the eyes crinkled, and he laughed gently at her discomfiture. He really was an extremely handsome man, she thought, well aware of his own reputation and used to getting his own way; she would do well to watch herself.

The two young men saved her from having to find an answer by emerging from the other room, visibly more relaxed as they talked cricket. Even so, she recognised the forced nonchalance of the chatter, and the shot of excitement and purpose that sharpened their features. Iris handed them their coats with a smile and showed them out. Xavier remained standing by the window.

When she returned, he sniffed in distaste at the cold remains of the tea she had still not cleared away. Then he looked up with another smile that lit up his face.

'I am going to take you out for dinner,' he said. It was not an invitation, it was a statement. 'I want to walk up past Trafalgar Square to the Coquille in St Martin's Lane with a pretty young woman.'

She ignored the compliment. 'You know it then, the Coquille?'

'I used to go there before the war.'

Iris had heard of it, but never been.

'And the Wellington pub in the Strand,' he went on, 'is that still there?'

'I think so.'

'It's short notice, I know – but do you accept my invitation?'

'I'm not sure why you're asking me.'

'Oh, come now. Don't think I haven't noticed the way you look at me!'

'But I – what—' She had to look away, fearful of giving him any more encouragement.

'No need to be embarrassed. I am flattered.'

'I'm sorry, you really have made a mistake.'

'Please, as I say, there is no need for dissembling among us here – surely?'

Iris felt herself reddening.

'So. Let us start again. Would you care to have dinner with me, mademoiselle?'

As he spoke, Miss Acton appeared behind him in the doorway. She stopped, clearly having heard.

Iris felt as if she had been caught doing something she shouldn't, but Miss Acton nodded her approval.

'All right,' said Iris. 'Give me ten minutes to tidy up here.' She scooped up the tea tray and dumped it in the kitchenette, then grabbed her bag, straightened her skirt and stockings and attended to her make-up as best she could in the black-tiled bathroom mirror.

In Trafalgar Square, the fountains were empty of water. A huge hoarding advertising 'War Savings' was wrapped around the base of Nelson's Column. It was not yet dusk, but there was already a queue outside the Duke of York's Theatre in St Martin's Lane, not long reopened after suffering bomb damage in 1940. The title of the play on the billboards was *Shadow and Substance*.

'Perhaps we should see it. It might offer us some help,' said Xavier.

'It might. I think the subject is faith – though the story is about Ireland and the Catholic Church.'

'Faith, ah – faith is what we must all keep.'

Iris, feeling unaccountably ill at ease, did not respond. She never felt like this with any of the other men she went out with. But with this man . . . she did not know quite what she was doing here with him. He was not a stranger exactly, but someone she knew only by reputation. Perhaps that was what was making her feel uncomfortable, unable to ask questions and provide the light chatter that would normally come naturally on an evening out.

Xavier, on the other hand, showed a hawk-like curiosity about the streets she took for granted, wanting to know about everything they passed: the sheet music hanging in a shop window, the words and music for 'Mexicali Rose', 'Hurry Home', 'If I Didn't Care'; the poster that read 'Let Music Lighten the Black-out'. What music did she like; did she play an instrument?

The glass in the shop window was taped into criss-cross squares. Sandbags, nine or ten deep, were propped against the walls. She was used to the sight now, like the barrage balloons that floated in the sky above central London, but what did he make of it all, this Frenchman who worked behind the lines in Nazi-occupied France?

At the Coquille they were whisked into another world of starched white linen and battalions of silver cutlery. The atmosphere was womb-like, cocooned from reality. 'It hasn't changed!' he exclaimed, visibly gratified. 'There's no need to be unsure of yourself, you know,' he said. Was it his experience living on the edge that gave him the ability to read her so accurately?

'Oh, I'm fine.'

'I hope you're hungry.'

'I'm always hungry. It's hard not to be.'

It was out of the question to discuss anything to do with work in a place where they might be overheard. Presumably, anyone who heard his French accent would infer that he was one of the numerous Free French who had pitched up in the capital. He took charge of the menu, expressing delight at the prospect of quail. A good claret was ordered after discussion of the selection on offer.

When the waiter left, he was silent for a few seconds. She was caught in another of his disconcerting stares. Sitting so close to him felt heady, even though he was doing everything to put her at her ease.

'What do you want out of life, Miss Nightingale?'

'Well . . . that's a very big question.'

It was one Iris was not sure she had ever been asked, and perhaps she had never even asked herself.

'Too big, perhaps. I understand.'

He crossed his hands on the table. Lightly tanned hands that looked strong and weathered by an outdoor life despite his elegant city clothes. He leaned forward, smiling.

'In that case, tell me about your favourite place.'

His voice was low. His full attention made her feel dull in

comparison, but she had to say something. Then she shook herself. Why shouldn't she have some enjoyment? How was this so different from being out with the pilots and chattering away to them? What was it about him that made it so much harder?

'There's a spot down by the river on the Embankment where I go to think. I should probably give you a much more exciting answer, but if you want an honest answer that's the best I can give. Now, you tell me yours.' It still wasn't a question, but she was making some progress.

He smiled, as if the thought alone of his favourite place was enough to fill him with pleasure. His teeth were straight and white, with a tiny imperfection at the front, where the bottom row had started to cross.

'When I was a boy I had a boat, just a small rowing boat, but to me it was a magic carpet. I used to take it out with my friends, and we would jump into the sea off the side and swim. But I also loved to go out by myself to a bay enclosed by rocks. I had a device my father made for me, a wooden box with a glass bottom that I could press into the water over the side of the boat and see what was under the water so sharply it was like a cinema screen. The precision of it amazed me. I would spend hours leaning over the side of the boat, my back becoming deep brown as oiled wood in the sun, just watching the shoals of fish. There are fish there that you would not believe – all painted in exotic colours, darting here and there among the rocks.'

He seemed far away as he spoke. The pictures he made were of a place teeming with vibrant life: first the fish, then the birds, against a backdrop of fruit stolen from orchards, flowers and pines and, everywhere, the sea. She had never seen anything like the scenes he described. The years she had spent abroad had been in the white mountains of Switzerland and its grim, forbidding valleys, brown and industrial. Lausanne and Montreux. The ordered grey streets of Zurich. And now the fog and grime and smoke of London, bleached of colour by the war.

The food arrived, and he told her about his boyhood wish

to become a fisherman, to spend whole days on the sea all year round.

'But alas, real life made its unreasonable demands. I had to wake from my dream. So I went to university in Lyon, and became an electronics engineer. The rest I am sure you know.'

He was serious suddenly, and checked his watch.

'Will you excuse me for a few minutes? I have to make a telephone call.'

He was gone for much longer.

She sat at the table in a happy daze, sipping the good wine. The restaurant was packed, and the hum of conversation rose. She thought of the risks he had run and shivered involuntarily.

'Did you get through?' she asked when he reappeared.

'Eventually.'

He poured some more wine, and she noticed that his hand was shaking. Whatever he had been attending to had upset his natural ebullience. She would not ask.

They ate a dessert of cheese and some apple slices while he asked her about her family and Switzerland, and her social life in London, though she sensed she had lost his full attention.

Xavier turned to gesture for the bill.

He offered her a cigarette and lit it. They smoked in silence. Mostly he looked at her, until she dropped her eyes, as if he was trying to communicate something without words that she was unable to understand.

'What is it?' she asked eventually.

'I want to ask you a favour.'

'I see.'

'You are resilient, aren't you? As resilient as you are beautiful.'

She didn't know what to say. He was making her nervous again. 'I'm wondering what you are buttering me up for.'

He hesitated, seemed about to say something, then held back. He stubbed out his cigarette in the china ashtray shaped like a shell and asked brightly, perhaps too brightly, 'So what do we do now, Miss Nightingale?'

She took a last sip of her wine. 'I believe there's a rather fascinating series of lectures on at the School of Art in the Charing Cross Road – "The Continuity of the English Town". Daily lecture, free to the public. Just the kind of improving programme we recommend to all our visitors.'

He laughed.

'Do you dance, Miss Nightingale?'

'I love to dance. But only in appropriate circumstances.'

'And where would be an appropriate place close by?'

'Well . . . the Opera House at Covent Garden is a dance hall now. They took out all the seats. It's rather spectacular, with the band up on the stage.'

'I would like to see it,' he said casually.

'It's not far to walk. I can tell you how to get there.'

'You could show me, surely.'

'I could.'

'You could then accompany me inside.'

'Just to look, with no dancing?'

'It would be a shame not to dance.'

'But would it be appropriate, given . . . our positions?'

'Perhaps not. But shall we throw caution to the wind?'

The place was thronged. He bought her gin and orange that made her light-headed and reckless after the wine. It seemed too good to be true, the light touch of his hand on the small of her back, the warmth of his hand in hers. Hard to tell if he was a good dancer or not: the place was packed with crowds as rough and temporary as the floor, the men in uniform, the giggling girls and the loudness of the band in a place designed to carry sound. They shuffled around, awkwardly, bumped into other couples.

'It's no good, I like to talk,' he said. He caught her hand as they came off the dance floor and did not let it go. 'Let's walk.'

London during the blackout was a ghostly place. At Piccadilly Circus the statue of Eros had been removed into storage. Ultraviolet headlamps from a single car picked out white dashes painted on the kerb to delineate it in the darkness. Black buildings towered unlit like a set in a dark theatre. They walked on towards Green Park.

'I have to leave London tomorrow,' he said.

She knew better than to ask where he was going.

In the park, he pulled her into the shadows. He brushed a strand of hair away from her temple. 'I wish I could stay.'

He dipped his head. His kiss was a gentle brush of her lips.

Then, when she did not pull away, he kissed her again, and this time it was electrifying, tender yet surprising, generous and impulsive.

'I will take you home.'

He found a cab outside the Ritz, and put his arm around her shoulders for the short ride. She wondered what she would do if he insisted on coming upstairs, but he said good night gallantly on the pavement of Tavistock Square.

What was she supposed to make of the evening? It was hard enough to decide what you thought of someone you had only just met, when you had only spent one evening together. But Xavier Descours? She thought of the way the women at F Section talked about him, the photographs in the file that had piqued their interest. Of all of them, he had chosen her. If they knew, they would all want to know where they had gone, what they had talked about, what it was like to be near to him, the focus of his attention. But she wouldn't tell them.

She wasn't sure she would even tell Nancy, not the important parts anyway. The light touch of his fingers on hers as he lit her cigarette. The way his eyes had seemed to soften in the low lamplight at their dinner table. His perfect height for her, not too tall, not too short. The easy gallantry with which he had helped her with her coat and guided her out of the restaurant into the darkness outside.

The experience had already assumed a dreamlike quality. It was like a date with a film star manufactured for the newspapers by the studios: one lucky woman reader will have the honour . . . She could not shake off the uneasy feeling that all was not quite as it seemed. And what was the favour he had changed his mind about asking?

5

Bignor Manor

Sussex, November 1943

It was everywhere, the sense of being trapped. Trenches dug in parks, railings uprooted, air-raid shelters and sand-bags at the end of streets – brick and concrete shelters held fifty people, with two-tiered wooden bunks crammed along the length of the walls. In tube stations, the terrible smell of people pressed so closely together without adequate ventila-tion was worse than being smothered inside the vile rubber of a gas mask. The Anderson shelters sunk in gardens were not much better: dark and cold holes where damp perme-ated the wooden benches inside and left a thin cushion of moss.

When a bomb hit the road in Balham, it left a crater like the top of a volcano into which a bus had tipped nose first, its rear upended. Tramlines twisted and hung over the hole in the ground as if the route were being diverted to the centre of the earth. Shops and houses were ripped open by the blast; papers and boxes were blown off shelves and valuable stock smashed; in private rooms, flowered wallpaper was exposed and cur-tains flapped like flags of surrender.

Grey days and months passed and were clumped together in her mind, losing any brightness and elasticity, while the memory of that one evening glowed, assuming more import, taking up ever more space, pushing all else aside. Now all she saw were the streets of grime and smoke-dirt, little improved around London Bridge from the Southwark of Charles Dickens. Prisons, and tramps, and the smut of steam trains. And in quiet streets nearby families lived in houses that no longer had glass in the windows.

For weeks afterwards, she saw the city through Xavier's eyes. She felt the soft mohair of his coat, walking by her side, one hand in his trouser pocket, hat pulled down almost to his eyes, as she walked past the queue outside the Whitehall Canteen, beside the National Gallery on Trafalgar Square, where society ladies served coffee to war workers under murals by Duncan Grant, and up St Martin's Lane to the Coquille, now imbued with a magical association. She tried to picture what he was doing in France, wondered again about the unasked favour, and relived the kiss.

In November the weather closed in. The full moon was on the wane, and so far only one Lysander had made it out of Tangmere and back. Miss Acton had spent two evenings at the airfield and gone back to London. Iris had orders to stay down at Tangmere for a few more nights on the off chance that they could make the run that month and deliver three joes as scheduled from France.

In the Cottage, a radio was tuned to a music station. Iris read and chatted to Rory and Jack and other pilots who dropped by. A ping-pong table was rigged up and in constant use for a complex knockout tournament. There were fast and frantic darts matches (behind the plywood surround that fielded stray shots was a secret cupboard containing maps of France on silk scarves and compasses). The mess sergeants gave permission for the drivers to take anyone who wanted to go to the Unicorn pub at Chichester; the landlord was particularly welcoming to the RAF, for whom he kept special bottles of claret and burgundy and never charged the full price. On the walls of the bar were pictures of pilots from the Tangmere squadrons and their aircraft, though the collection did not include a Lysander.

The fog thickened. When it was clear there would be no flights that night either, the call came through: party at Bignor.

Tucked under the rolling hills of the South Downs, Bignor Manor was less than half an hour's drive from the airfield. It was the home of Major Anthony Bertram, one of the escorting officers who met the flights at Tangmere, and his wife, Barbara. The major was attached to MI6, but down in the Sussex countryside at the sharp end of the special air operations, interservice rivalries were sensibly forgotten, or so it seemed. The couple had two young sons, and Bignor Manor was a happy family home where – or so they told any villagers who inquired – they occasionally put up convalescent French officers. The cheery and indefatigable Mrs Bertram would let the maid and the gardeners go and continue without help at night, but there was no apparent subterfuge in what she was doing.

Despite the grand name, the heavy stone and Elizabethan origins, the manor was not a particularly large house; it had only four bedrooms and was approached from a typical farm-track entrance, on which it stood discreetly, well back from the rest of the small village.

'Come on, Iris, I'll give you a lift on the back of my bike if you promise not to scream,' offered Jack.

'I'll certainly come, but not on that thing. Last time my legs were completely black with soot when I got off!'

'She's coming with me, aren't you, Iris?' interrupted Rory. 'In a nice safe car from the ministry.'

'Only if Denise is driving.'

Barbara Bertram was pretty and bright, much loved by all. She made her job seem effortless, caring for so many in conditions of great secrecy, attending to her menagerie of farm animals – the hens, rabbits and goat, the hives of bees, the dog, the cat. She was last to bed and first up in the morning, yet always had

223

time to sit and talk, to make up a four at bridge or to play darts with the party. She would cook bacon and eggs with a smile for the new arrivals at four in the morning. The young Bertram boys called the French 'Hullabaloos' on account of the strange and guttural sounds they made when speaking to each other; neither of them yet understood the language.

But always underlying the calm exterior was the strain of the danger faced by the visitors, agents working in occupied France and members of the Resistance. The anxiety often became irritability, especially if the weather reports continued to be dismal and flights were postponed. That was where Mrs Bertram's perception proved invaluable. She would call in new blood and a sense of fun to lift the mood, and 'Party at Bignor!' was always a popular shout. There would be supper, and the men might dance with the girl drivers like Denise, a popular redhead with dimples and a wide smile who knew all the latest steps. Thank God for those other girls, thought Iris; they made those evenings fun when all might have been too tense.

She got in the car with Denise, Rory and another pilot known as Stamper on account of some idiosyncrasy he had in preparation for a flight; the girls knew the nickname could apply equally to his two left feet on the dance floor. Iris had never asked his real name. They drove over in convoy, the spitting hellfire of Jack's motorcycle within constant earshot.

'Worse than ack-ack, that bike,' said Rory cheerfully. His faithful collie Sam was along for the ride too, at his feet in the back of the car next to Iris.

Everyone was in high spirits. 'Kindly remove your hand from my knee, Flight Lieutenant Fitzgerald,' said Iris.

'Spoilsport.'

Iris smiled to herself.

'Hope there's a decent feed,' said Stamper.

Rory scratched the dog's head. 'Always is at Bignor. Eh, Sam? Might even be a scrap for you.'

Mrs Bertram worked hard on a fine vegetable garden to keep all the visitors fed. No windfall from the fruit trees went uncollected, and every edible paring was judiciously used in the kitchen. Some of the French enjoyed gardening, and they would mow lawns and weed, or help to milk Caroline the goat – anything to keep active while they waited to fly. The manor's potager was a model of international cooperation.

A couple of men came through, carrying a stack of cracked plates and chipped saucers and a handful of glasses to the dining room.

'Hello, dears. As you can see, no chance of any new crockery.' Mrs Bertram sighed. 'But I'm pleased to announce that we have pheasant pie on the menu tonight – well, pheasant and rabbit.'

'Though it was only supposed to be rabbit,' interjected Tony Bertram. 'Lord Mersey expressly said rabbit only if you were to shoot on the estate.'

'But the pheasant – it flew in the way between the gun and the rabbit,' said a man with a French accent who was cheerfully laying knives and forks on the long table, his back to them.

'Oh, bad luck!' said Rory.

'Yes, awfully, wasn't it?' said Mrs Bertram brightly. 'We had to make the best of things though.' As was customary, she did not introduce the Frenchman even when he turned round.

Iris stepped back in delighted surprise. It was Xavier. The effect of his unexpected presence was electrifying. She stood, smiling stupidly, but he looked away.

'A bottle of whisky and a bottle of gin from the mess,' said Rory, reaching into his flying jacket and handing them over.

'I'll get some glasses. Why don't you go through to the sitting room? A few of our visitors are already having a drink there. The rest are still at the White Horse – there's a darts match against the village team. They did very well against them last time. As it's so important to make everything seem above board, one of the French put one arm in a sling, pretending it was his throwing arm, of course. None of the villagers could quite believe how well he played with his "wrong arm"!'

Iris was taken aback to see in the flesh the man she had spent so long building up in her imagination; it was almost an embarrassment, as if he would know, just by looking at her, what had been passing through her mind in the intervening months.

'I'll let you introduce yourselves,' said Mrs Bertram. 'I need to check on the food.'

'We have already had the pleasure of meeting,' said Iris, aware of Rory's interest as she extended her hand to Xavier.

He shook it, neutrally. '*Ma chère mademoiselle*, I am enchanted – but I think you must be mistaken.'

Jack was in the sitting room, handing round cigarettes and drinking beer. Through the open glass doors to the garden, Sam's excited barks indicated that he had found someone to play with. Iris smiled and shook hands with three men, all strangers to her.

The pilots were discussing the night the Windmill Theatre came to put on a show at the camp cinema, and the fan dancer Phyllis Dixie had delighted and amazed the men when she held both feather fans out at arm's length at the end of her act. 'The place went wild!' said Stamper. He sounded the same as ever, but Iris noticed that his eyes seemed dull and his face drawn as he told the story Iris had heard several times. He took a large glass of whisky from the tray Mrs Bertram brought round.

One of the Frenchmen, a jowly man with a moustache, watched puppy-like as Barbara Bertram turned for the kitchen. 'A wonderful woman.' He sighed. 'The first morning I arrived, she asked me to take the mud off my boots on the metal outside the back door. Madame Barbara – you know what she did? She put all this mud in a container, and she grows little salad leaves . . . yes, now I know the name, mustard and cress . . . on it, so that when I arrive last week to make my return to France, knowing that my heart is heavy, she offers the cress salad to us, the French: salad grown on French soil!'

No wonder they loved her.

Iris listened politely, her mind churning, as another man began to tell her, in French, how a darts match had been convened at Mrs Bertram's instigation when the discussion between rival political persuasions had become too lively. Darts was a perfect diffuser of tension, he averred; when the war was over, he was going to get himself a board.

Perhaps, thought Iris, she should ask for a game to calm her nerves. Xavier stood talking to a man she had never seen before, giving no indication that he was aware of her. Was it possible that he did not even remember her? She had never felt such disappointment.

They were joined by two more men and another young woman driver who knew Denise. Iris saw Xavier give the girl an appreciative glance, then continue his intense discussion.

After dinner the men all helped with the washing-up, throwing the plates from one to another, while Barbara Bertram averted her eyes. 'Do be careful, boys. Oh, I simply can't look! Have you any idea how hard it is to get enough crockery for everyone here? I didn't have nearly enough in the first place!'

Upstairs in one of the bedrooms there was a wooden mirror on the wall – no room for a dressing table with all the single camp beds for the visitors – by which the girls brushed their hair and pencilled their eyebrows. Denise applied some powder, chatting about the French. Iris rolled her hair high over the front of her head and pinned it back to show off her earrings. She was wearing her favourite dress, of thick brushed cotton with a cherry print. Normally it brought her luck, but its talismanic properties had clearly failed this evening.

The other girl introduced herself to Iris. 'I'm Aster. Two blooms together!' She was jolly in an obvious way, the kind of girl Iris was on the whole glad to have left behind at school, but it was hard not to offer some friendliness in return.

'That's a pretty lipstick shade,' said Iris.

'Thank you. A present from Paris, best not to say who from, I suppose. I say, that French joe down there . . . he's an absolute dream, isn't he?' Iris could not have failed to notice that Aster had been seated next to him at dinner. The giggles and touching of his arm had made her want to throw cold water over them.

Iris wondered whether it was worth asking which one she

meant, but it was so obvious that to say anything would only draw attention to her feelings.

'He certainly is.'

'Any idea who he is?'

'Not a clue,' said Iris.

They went downstairs to find Stamper trying to explain to Xavier in very bad French how to fly a Lysander – '*et alors vous poussez ça, et vous tirez là – et Robert est votre oncle!*'

'Are you planning on helping yourself to one of our planes, monsieur?' asked Iris neutrally.

'He used to be a pilot,' explained Stamper.

'Did he indeed?' Iris cocked her head.

'I most certainly was, mademoiselle. I fear it is no longer valid since I have been otherwise engaged these past few years, but I achieved a private pilot's licence before the war.'

She was about to ask him where he had learned to fly when Rory marched up with Aster, both of them distinctly put out to find Iris so intent on listening to the handsome Frenchman.

Stamper helped himself to more whisky and started telling another of his stories: '. . . It was a lone raider, and he didn't stand a chance against our guns – took a direct hit. Flew on for a mile, then made a terrible sound as it smacked into the ground. We jumped into a car and raced over. It was a Dornier, great big crate of a thing, broke up on impact into at least five pieces. Three bodies in the wreckage, and three live bombs. Flames shooting over the fuselage. My revolver was loaded and I was mustard keen to use it to arrest some live Germans . . . sadly, not to be.'

Music rose louder from the gramophone. The singer warbled about the spell of Paris and an April dawn. Iris, sitting on the sofa, closed her eyes and clenched her hands together to dig her fingernails deep into the flesh of her palms.

'Are you praying, mademoiselle?' asked Xavier, coming to stand in front of her. 'And if so, what for?'

She said nothing.

'*I'll be looking at the moon . . . but I'll be seeing you . . .*' sang the gramophone.

She would not ask him.

For a second she thought he was looking at her in the same way he had in the Coquille restaurant. But then Barbara Bertram passed with a tray of glasses. He caught her hand and brought it up to his lips. '*Chère* Madame Barbara,' he said fondly, taking the tray and placing it deftly on a sideboard. 'Would you do me the honour of allowing me this dance?'

His high spirits were infectious. Soon all the girls were dancing. 'He's quite something, isn't he?' whispered Aster as she finished a turn round the floor with Xavier. Her colour was high, flushed from the dancing in the too-confined space in his arms.

'Quite something,' agreed Iris, the edge of sarcasm in her voice lost as Aster was swept away again, this time by the jowly Frenchman with the moustache.

Mercurial – that was Xavier, the one all eyes were drawn to, with his olive-skinned good looks, the easy manner and appreciative story-swapping with the men, the chivalrous manners with a dash of flirtation to disarm the women. Even Sam the collie was charmed, returning again and again to his side for Xavier to rub his head and stomach until the poor creature rolled over in ecstasy.

At one point, Xavier went out through the glass doors to the garden. She half heard an argument in French outside, but Iris could not see who it involved. When he returned, his expression was closed; then, in an instant, he seemed to don a mantle of social gaiety, and the petulance lingering about his mouth was gone.

He came straight over to her. 'Is it our turn to dance at last?'

Iris accepted his hand and his arm around her. His fingertips on her back were light, barely touching the material of her dress, but she felt every connection as they began to move. In his warm hand, hers was secure. It was an odd conjunction of intimacy and awkwardness. He looked into her eyes, saying nothing. When she responded in kind, he pulled her closer. She concentrated on the present: she was in his arms again; Xavier Descours was flesh and blood. How much of our lives

229

are spent wholly immersed in the present moment? It seemed to Iris that it was not very much at all. Not nearly enough.

Was this silence a mark of their complicity – or did he really not remember her? They danced on, to all intents as strangers.

Then she was whirled away by Rory and Jack, then Stamper, and Rory again. And they drank and laughed until she felt like crying.

The following night the moon rose early like a beacon, then was smothered by clouds and rain. The operation was forced to stand down. There would be no more November flights.

Xavier's appearance at a gathering at the 400 Club on Leicester Square a few nights later was noted in the ladies' cloakroom on the half-landing at Norgeby House.

Iris listened, downcast, as a new girl from Colonel Tyndale's office described him as 'that ravishing Frenchman' who made her dance so often her feet were aching. All morning at Orchard Court Tyndale had been in a foul mood. And now Iris knew why: according to his chatty new typist (perhaps a mite too chatty?) there had been a run-in with RF Section – République Française, the Free French. Ever since General de Gaulle set up his government in exile in June 1940, they had operated their own secret-service department from a house in Duke Street. They brooked no interference from anyone, least of all the British, as they dropped their own agents and formed their own circuits in France.

With his innate sense of fair play, Colonel Tyndale could not comprehend why de Gaulle was so often hostile to his country of exile, so mistrustful. They were supposed to be working together for the greater good.

It was a trying day, and apparently endless, too. It was after nine o'clock when Iris walked round the corner of Tavistock Square, feeling for her keys in the pocket of her handbag, and almost stumbled into him in the darkness. He was leaning against the wall of the entrance portico.

'Iris?'

'Who's that?' she said, though there was only one person

who spoke like that, who would have presumed like that.

'Are you on your own?'

'How did you know where to find me?'

'I took you home in a taxi, remember?'

'I remember. I thought it was you who couldn't.'

'Can I come in?'

She left him waiting for a short while in silence before she opened the door and led the way up the winding stairs to the top floor.

The flat was cold. Iris went over to the eaves window of the main room and checked the blackout curtain before clicking on a lamp. Xavier stood at the door.

'Do you live here alone?' he asked.

'No. My friend Nancy shares with me.'

'Will she be back soon?'

Nancy had taken leave to be with Phil in Lincolnshire, but she wasn't sure he should know that. 'She might.'

Iris took a box of matches and knelt on the rug to ignite the gas fire. Xavier was so quiet that she thought for a desperate few seconds that he was not there – that he had slipped away from her again, or perhaps had never even been there at all. It was four days since he had blanked her at Bignor.

'What can I do to help you?' she asked, trying to keep her tone neutral.

He shook off his coat and dropped down at her side on the tatty rug.

'You can forgive me . . . for the other night.'

'Pretending we had never met? I'm sure you had your reasons.'

'It would not have been wise to show it,' he said.

In any other circumstances she would have asked him to explain himself. If he had been any man but Xavier Descours – if he had not been such a respected key player in the network, far senior to her. As it was, they sat and watched the sputter of the blue flames and listened to the hiss and murmur of the gas. Then, very slowly, he turned to her.

'Would you rather I left?' he asked.

231

'No.'

He seemed nervous, which surprised her. She still had no idea what he was doing here, whether it was in contravention of some official rules, whether he was here because of her job or whether it was personal.

'Is everything all right?' she asked.

'Of course it is.'

'It's just—'

'*Qui s'excuse, s'accuse.* Talk to me.'

'What about?'

'Anything. Anything that is not about the war.'

The room warmed. She found a bottle of brandy. The first glass blunted their mutual nervousness, and the second made them laugh too readily and talk nonsense. They ignored the old armchairs and the divan draped in the Moroccan blanket and remained on the floor.

'We ought to eat something,' said Iris. 'Though Lord knows what.'

'Madame Barbara is right,' he said. 'We should allow ourselves to find enjoyment where we can. Pretend to ourselves that we live only in the present, where there is no war, no inhumanity, no terror.'

Iris raised her glass. 'To the present.'

She began to talk about a play she had seen, but was disconcerted by the way he studied her, curious and alert to every movement. After a while they simply watched each other, taking in every detail. For the longest time, nothing was said.

'It's the little things that give you away,' he said.

'What do you mean by that?' she asked.

'You are clearly a dedicated follower of the rules.'

'Whereas you are not?'

'Let's say I don't dwell on the rules, the possibility of failure, of disaster. I try to find the positive wherever I can.'

His expression was serious, without a hint of a smile or the amused twist at the corner of his mouth.

There was no contact between them, but her skin was tingling. It took her by surprise; she felt naked, even through the fabric of her clothes. She wondered whether she should stop this now.

The rug seemed rougher under her hand as she shifted on its woollen ridges. 'Where are you staying?' she asked.

'I was hoping to stay here.'

Still the silence between them pressed in. He was in no hurry to break it. The gas flame hissed. A door slammed below, and footsteps receded on the stairs. A vehicle passed on the road.

She thought about the bar near the office where the men and women of F Section and other special employments mingled; the 'bedtime stories' that were common currency. There was no reason for him not to presume she was the same as all the other young women who lived fast in these uncertain times.

'I've never done this before,' she said.

A small smile reached his eyes. Was he mocking her? Anxiety rose in a wave, and then fell back as he – finally – reached out. He touched the side of her cheek very lightly with a fingertip. The gesture was so tender that she assumed it was an apology.

She pulled away. What had come over her? He was so different from other men; it was his difference and experience that she wanted.

The shapes of the room seemed to shift. The tiles on the fireplace caught the change in the light as he moved to pull her closer. She felt his warm hand on her arm, then it moved to stroke her leg, her ankle. She shifted her position, more afraid now that he would stop than she was of doing the wrong thing. Gently, he reached for one shoe and eased it off, then the other.

She felt no shame, only innocence.

She arrived at Baker Street the next morning with the warmth of his body still on her. In her bed under the eaves, he slept on. The way he felt had surprised her – so soft and yet strong, his muscles and ribs and the velvet touch of his skin; his sea and herbs scent. The gentle touches that had produced sensations she had never experienced before. The surprise that it was actually happening, the thrill of her own audacity, the impulsive wonder of it all.

It was hard to concentrate. She was light-headed, raw but elated. Don't think about what happens next, she thought, whether he will be there when I return. None of that mattered, only that she had acted on instinct and been rewarded.

He was there when she returned. In the mirror, her reflection glowed and her eyes sparkled. He stayed for the next four nights.

The only person Iris told was Nancy, when she returned from leave.

'It was pretty obvious, as soon as I walked in,' said Nancy. 'There's a look that tells the world. You're lit up from the inside.'

They were toasting crumpets she had brought back from Lincolnshire, holding them out on forks to the fire.

'Xavier Descours . . . my goodness, Iris, you *are* a dark horse.'

'Nancy, you can't breathe a word.'

'I know. You know I won't. Where is he now – am I going to meet him?'

'He's away for a few days. Tempsford, I think.'

Long afterwards, when Iris came to question her own judgement, the one thing she never questioned was the extraordinary joy of her intimate relationship with Xavier. She had wanted it as much as he had.

The troubling complexities of his character and their situation were still dormant. She did not know his real name, but she called him *chéri* – darling – rather than risk his safety by asking; it was of no importance. She knew he was capable of betrayal, though. He was married, for one thing, though he claimed it was unhappily, and there were no children. 'The worst part of marriage is the compromising. Everyone says it doesn't work without compromise, but what if that is the very death to the spirit?' She would remember that, too, long afterwards when the words were given weight by her own experience.

'Does your wife not love you?'

'She cares for me all right. That is not the problem.'

'Then what?'

'Children – I always wanted children, a family. But it has never happened.'

Even so, Iris arranged, on Nancy's earnest advice, a consultation at the Marie Stopes clinic to be fitted with a diaphragm. He was right. There could be no disappointment in the present. Who knew what might happen next week? It was war. Different standards applied.

They seized the moment, together. When he let down his guard, he was surprisingly vulnerable. 'I live my life in disguise, yet all I want is for you to know me as I really am, love me as I am – and forgive me for it,' he told her.

Love. She was amazed that he spoke so quickly of love; she had not expected that. Even in her new reckless, awakened state, she was not so lost as to be unaware that a man like Xavier Descours was used to having affairs, that he would give women only as much as he wanted. She would not press him to define his feelings; she was not even sure of her own. Was it love she felt, or exhilaration, or just plain lust?

It was not a normal relationship, and never could be. Under the eaves of the attic flat it unfolded unseen, in another secret compartment of a secret life, yet always threatening to burst the confines of this small place of safety. What was it he saw in her? Iris wondered. She held onto remarks he made unprompted but did not ask outright, fearing to break the spell.

'I have a restless spirit,' he said as they lay in bed during the second week. 'But you give me calm. You are pure spring water on a day when the sun bites.'

She took that to mean that she was uncomplicated, while he burned with nervous energy.

'But you want me, don't you?' he pressed.

'I want you, *chéri*.' More than any man she had ever met.

'I need to be wanted,' he said.

'None of the other men managed to persuade me into bed. I'm not that sort of girl, did you know that?'

'Rory told me.'

'What? Well, he shouldn't have.'

'I made him very drunk.'

'Some people would say you were not to be trusted,' she said idly, teasing.

'People say the most disagreeable things about me.'

'Do they – really?'

'I trust no one,' he said, though the implication was that he trusted her. 'Though the kindness of others touches me greatly.'

'That first evening at the Coquille. You said you were going to ask me a favour – what was it?'

'Did I?'

'You know you did.'

'I can't remember. Probably something very silly. Like iron a shirt for me. Or give me a map of London with your flat marked in red.'

It was hard to know when to take him seriously, sometimes.

He went away for several days and returned, a pattern that was repeated throughout the month. Soon it was December, and she tried not to think that he would soon be leaving.

One evening they joined a crowd at the Dorchester bar, a rumbustious mix of pilots, their girlfriends and assorted faces from the Firm. Jack Wallace was there, and Iris recognised some of the men as Free French agents she had met at Tangmere.

She spent most of her time chatting with Jack, flirting a little in the usual way, though she was uncomfortably aware that she was doing it only so no one would suspect she was with Xavier. For his part, he seemed to be exchanging terse words with one of the Free French.

'You find something you can do, and it seems to work, so you do it again,' Xavier was saying as she went past to say hello

236

to Denise, who had just arrived. Iris slowed her pace and let Denise approach.

'I work hard. It was how I was brought up, to do my best, and in doing so to help others,' she heard Xavier say, shoulders squared, chin tilted upwards.

'No question of money?'

'Not in this case.'

'You are the most cynical person I have ever met.'

'I can assure you that I am not.'

They left it there, with Xavier striding to the bar. But after that, Iris noticed, his natural vitality was held in check. He seemed remote when they got back to Tavistock Square at about ten o'clock. Nancy had taken to staying with another friend while Xavier was in town.

Iris made a pot of tea, to which he raised none of his usual objections. He said little and smoked, each cigarette lit from the previous one.

'My life has been ripped apart these past few years,' he said at last. He spoke angrily in French, as if he was thinking aloud. 'I've always refused absolutely to admit defeat. But other people are not, as I always imagined, unanimously blessed with the same dedication – or quickness of mind.'

Iris listened without comment.

'How can you understand the effort of climbing a mountain if you yourself do not climb? The greater the number of people who know anything, the greater the danger.' He dragged on his cigarette. *'Je suis entre deux feux.'*

Between a rock and a hard place.

Iris lit a cigarette for herself, was shaking the match out, when Xavier sprang up like a cat. He was halfway to the bedroom door a second later when a key rattled in the latch of the door. Nancy walked in, full of apologies for startling them – it was no go for her at Eileen's that night, as family had turned up unexpectedly.

Xavier quickly recovered his calm, pouring Nancy a cup of tea and asking about her day. If he was tense, he worked hard not to show it. A door opening – such a simple act, but he had not been expecting it. It was an insight into his life in France. He was embarrassed afterwards, tried to make a joke of it, but Iris could tell he had been truly frightened. That was the only incident she could recall when he was not in total control of his emotions.

Five days later, they were back at Tangmere.

It was another double Lysander operation: Miss Acton and Iris were seeing off the capable Thérèse, seamstress and collector of magazines, for a second mission, along with another agent, Yves; Xavier and a Free French agent were also leaving.

The BBC message had gone out, referencing Caroline, the goat at Bignor Manor: 'Caroline's milk is making very good cheese this year.' The weather was cold and cheerless, but the forecast was for a clear night.

Over dinner Xavier was in blustering good form, though. He told stories that implied his eagerness to return to his people in France: about the farmer who was told to build a haystack in the middle of a field because the Germans had realised that it was long enough for a plane to land on – he did what they wanted, but he built it on a wooden platform with wheels so that it could be moved by the reception committee and then put back into place after the plane had left.

Somewhere else, the reception committee for the incoming plane arrived to check out a landing field and discovered that a group of farm workers had been ordered to build a wall across a large field. The workers were persuaded to go very slowly, as an operation was imminent. That night they helped dismantle the wall, and build it up again the next morning as if nothing had happened.

'The hardest part is finding these fields in the beginning,' said Xavier. 'They have to be at least six hundred metres long, but you cannot go around the country pacing up and down fields to find out how long they are and how flat, and whether they flood in winter. That would surely draw attention. No, the best ones are found by our people who put on peasant clothes and go out pretending to be mushroom and truffle hunters. Or country people who know the land well, of course.'

The Free French agent and Thérèse listened attentively but said little.

Thérèse was ready. If knowing exactly what she faced on a second trip was worse than the blind optimism and courage of the first, she did not show it.

'Don't forget to send my Christmas cards next week,' she said to Iris.

'They're all in my desk drawer.'

'And here's a birthday card for Mother – January the twelfth. You do have a note, don't you?'

Iris took it. 'Don't worry. I'll take care of everything.'

'Thanks, Iris – you're a pal.'

Iris gave her a sympathetic squeeze of the hand.

Away from the others, Xavier gathered Iris into his arms for the last time. She closed her eyes and imagined they were back once again on the rug in front of the gas fire at Tavistock Square. Was it only their special circumstances, or did other love affairs run the course from delightful surprise to infatuation to commitment and cold reality in the space of a month?

'I will get a message to you,' he said.

She nodded, kissing him again rather than wasting time on words.

He released himself gently, then gathered her up again. 'I want you to know, Iris, I have never loved as I have loved you. You have been my light in this darkness.'

There was no goodbye. Minutes later the cars were taking them onto the airfield where the planes were ready. Iris watched as Jack climbed into the cockpit and gave a wave. The two F Section agents squashed themselves into the rear passenger seat, but both Yves and Thérèse were carrying two pieces of luggage, including a wireless transmitter set into the usual small suitcase for Thérèse. It was not going to work. Urgent decisions had to be made. With the weather closing in, and the missed opportunities of the previous month's moon flight, there were no other options.

'Thérèse will come with me to Châteaudun,' said Xavier. 'I can easily make new arrangements when we get there.'

She swapped with the Free French agent, and followed Xavier with her suitcases.

The smoke of last cigarettes lingered in the night air as the plane rose. For the first time Iris felt she wanted to stop the operation, to bring the passengers back to the ground. A tear prickled and slid down her cheek as she returned to the Cottage and picked up the stray belongings: an English book and a magazine, a box of Swan Vestas matches and a couple of theatre ticket stubs from a West End show she had seen with Xavier two nights before. She slipped the stubs into her pocket and put the rest in the hidden cupboard in the sitting room to await collection when the owners returned.

6

Messages

London, January 1944

They heard nothing at first from Thérèse, but Rose was doing well with her wireless transmissions from Paris. Right from the start she had proved as reliable as they had hoped. In France, the Firm's focus was moving to the north and the south. The order came from Churchill himself that the arming of the resistance fighters of the Maquis inland from the Mediterranean and the northern resistants behind the beaches of Normandy, in preparation for Allied invasion, was now the priority.

At last a message from Thérèse came through the secure teleprinter link at Baker Street.

Miss Acton handed Iris the deciphered page. 'What's your first thought?'

Iris took the paper. In the large room next door the sound of typewriters rose and fell in rolling waves of metallic clatter. Thérèse had 'a doctor's appointment on Thursday'. It was what they had been waiting to receive, confirmation that Thérèse was in Lyon, awaiting news of her contact.

'It was a "dental appointment" she was supposed to write,' said Miss Acton crossly.

'She's left out her security checks,' said Iris.

Miss Acton fiddled with her pen, the only form of agitation she allowed herself. Slapdash ways had been creeping in among the agents in France, and a new rule had been introduced: 'Adios' or 'Salut' to sign off if all was well. If the wireless was being operated under duress, then 'Love and Kisses'. And Thérèse had ignored it, giving no sign-off.

'What else?'

Iris stared hard at the message. Apart from the lack of checks, it was all as rehearsed, or almost.

Miss Acton went away and returned with Tyndale.

'Send a message back,' he said tersely. 'You have forgotten both checks.'

'But that's—' Iris didn't want to say it. How could she criticise the boss for making an elementary mistake? She looked across at Miss Acton, wanting her to be the one to contradict him.

'Silly girl,' said Miss Acton. 'I'd hoped for better from her.'

'It's very bad, this lack of attention to detail,' said Tyndale, petulance creeping into his tone. His eye bags were starting to puff and his complexion redden. 'I thought you'd drummed it into them all.'

'But Thérèse *is* careful, she always has been,' interjected Iris.

Miss Acton bristled. 'Not always, if I remember rightly. There were a couple of times when she was in Tours last time that she forgot the exact form of words we'd agreed.'

'With respect, that's not quite the same as missing the sign-off.'

'Send the message back,' instructed Tyndale. 'Get her to reply correctly. She never would concentrate properly.'

'What if she hasn't forgotten?' asked Iris.

Miss Acton's pen tapped furiously. 'Well, she has forgotten – she gives neither sign-off. She can't have been caught. She's been with Xavier Descours, and they haven't had time to do anything.'

'Please send again with security check. Be more careful,' Iris was told to signal back.

Minutes later the check was produced. 'Adios.' After that Thérèse's messages were scrupulously free from mistakes.

The next time it happened, in a message from Rose, Iris knew without doubt that something was wrong. With the first flawed radio messages it had been only a woman's instinct, and there was nothing she could say, given Tyndale's conviction that it was a simple slip-up. But in view of Rose's composure and efficiency, it seemed ever more unlikely that she had transmitted in a slapdash manner.

'The fist is right,' said Miss Acton.

Iris pulled out Rose's card from a new flip-flop wheel file system she had made of each agent's individual quirks – the spaces and natural rhythm – while sending Morse code. The 'fist' could be read like an electronic fingerprint.

It did seem right.

'But you said yourself that we should at least consider the possibility that the lack of checks was deliberate,' said Iris. 'The fist could be right because it is Rose sending the message, but under duress.'

Miss Acton hesitated.

'I know it's not my place to suggest this, but I think we should send a message back asking something personal,' Iris went on. Tyndale was out of the office, and she felt more comfortable overreaching.

'You may be right.'

But when Tyndale returned, he ignored all reason and unleashed a volley of invective, at least some of which made it across the Channel in his furious reply to Rose.

A couple of days later a Canadian F Section agent codenamed Roland sent a message in French. Tyndale sent a pithy reply: 'Why have you changed your language? Do not do this.' Roland began again in English, omitting both his bluff check and true check, again provoking fury at Baker Street.

'We agreed that he was always to transmit in English – how

are we to deal with these idiots who won't take instruction?' raged Tyndale. Miss Acton made sympathetic noises.

Iris remembered Roland from a long afternoon in Orchard Court when they had chattered for hours about the theatre. He was a big country lad from the Québécois mountains who had a talent for mimicry and liked to laugh. She had accompanied him to the Playhouse one evening to see a mindless farce, and then taken him on to meet Rory and Jack, who were in town. The evening had been a grand success, not least due to his introduction to the Bag O'Nails nightclub after Iris had left them to it.

'Tell him the bag is still full of nails,' said Iris.

When there was no personal response, just a thank you, Iris was certain. The Roland she knew would have come back with a witty retort.

'This isn't right,' she told them. She showed them the notes she had taken at Orchard Court, the quirks of his conversation and his sense of fun. 'If everything was all right, he wouldn't just have said thank you politely.'

'Signalling is dangerous. He's being sensible, keeping it to the minimum,' said Tyndale. She was trying his patience, it seemed.

Tyndale was determined to believe the agents were all safe, because any other outcome was unthinkable. He could not lose face, and Miss Acton supported him, equally unwilling to be proved wrong. Plans continued to be made over the radio. Cheerful messages were received at Christmas from Thérèse, Rose, Yves and Roland, as well as from most of the others in France.

One afternoon in the ladies' cloakroom on the half-landing at Norgeby House, Iris overheard some girls who worked for the Dutch and Belgian sections whispering in a cubicle. They were worried about anomalies in radio messages to D and B Sections too, and they didn't know what to do about it. They were scared they might lose their jobs, and if that happened, then the background knowledge they had built up would go with them, to no one's benefit.

'You heard what happened to Penelope, didn't you?' said one.

Iris strained to hear, holding her breath.

'A transmission came back saying that Anders had broken his skull on landing north of Antwerp, then there were messages about doctors' reports, and then that he had died of meningitis. Penelope kept asking questions about this. Her brother is a doctor and she asked him, and it all seemed unlikely, very unusual for a landing accident. She was certain that something wasn't right, but no one in authority would listen. Last week she was sacked for "letting sentiment override her duty".'

'But perhaps if we all—'

'Not a chance.'

Iris knew the woman was right.

She was at Waterloo Station, seeing a promising new girl off to Guildford, the night the bomb fell. Air-raid sirens had sounded, followed by distant explosions and then the all-clear. The glass roof of the station was blacked out, lamps shaded, leaving eerie silhouettes of policemen and soldiers; music played over the loudspeakers in a vain attempt to lighten the gloom. Glowing cigarette ends moving towards her. Iris and the new girl watched the clock and the empty platform. Ten minutes after the train's scheduled departure, there was no sign of it. Groups of people scurried past in earnest discussion. Announcements over the concourse loudspeaker cancelled one service after another. Iris mentally logged the way the girl's composure had quickly slipped in the confusion. That was disappointing.

The train did not arrive. It was pinned down on the track by debris when the bombs targeting Battersea Power Station failed to hit their mark. They exploded with a deafening, earth-shaking force. The wail of the sirens was too late; the streets around were filled with a hail of devastation and choking clouds of dust. One hit the mansion block where Iris's aunt Etty lived. She was pulled out of the rubble alive but badly injured.

In the weeks that followed – her aunt's fight for life; the

ruins and the smoke; the difficulties with the agents in France and intransigence in Baker Street – Iris heard nothing from Xavier. In a further devastating blow, Jack Wallace was lost, presumed dead, after a night sortie from Tempsford.

I have never loved as I have loved you. Now, when she ran the words through her head, as she did countless times every day, her joy was blunted by that invidious past tense. Attuned as she was to every shade of verbal communication, she clung to this interpretation: it was not his love for her that was in question, but the possibility of not returning.

Rose's wireless messages continued, though. She was doing exceptionally well, keeping information flowing to the network of Resistance cells in Paris. Occasionally there were anomalies in her transmissions that might have been caused by atmospheric interference, but in the circumstances that was hardly surprising; she had to try to broadcast at a certain time, no matter what.

Then, during the February moon, at past four o'clock in the morning, a Lysander arrived back at Tangmere with an unofficial extra passenger. It was Thérèse. She was thin and bruised, and spitting with anger as she stumbled through the back door of the Cottage.

'You have no idea, do you? Not the faintest clue about what's really going on in France!'

Exhausted as she clearly was, Thérèse was running on shot nerves and rage. At Orchard Court, she was debriefed by Colonel Tyndale and Miss Acton. Iris sat in, writing detailed notes.

'When we got to France, the first thing Xavier was told was that his wireless operator in Provence had been betrayed and executed by the Germans. It was all a mess. I was already dependent on him to get me down to Lyon to join up with Charles, but the heat was on there. So Xavier decided to take me with him to the south as his replacement operator. Only we didn't get that far. I was arrested, taken to Paris, and I tried to warn you, but you ignored all the signs . . . dead as mutton in London.'

'When were you arrested?' asked Tyndale, his tone cold.

'Only a few days after we landed near Châteaudun. Xavier told me to wait for him at a small commercial hotel while he attended to some business in the area.'

'What business – his legitimate business, or liaison with the Resistance?'

'He didn't say. Does it matter? He didn't show up at the hotel where he sent me, but the Gestapo did. They took me – made me bring my luggage, including the radio transmitter. The owner of the hotel was shot on the spot as we went out. They pushed me into a car and took me to some kind of SS headquarters in the town. I spent the night in a cell and was driven to Paris the next day.'

'Where in Paris?'

'The avenue Foch. A beautiful building, very luxurious – the Gestapo are enjoying themselves there, I must say. A most charming German officer by the name of Kieffer received me with great politeness,' said Thérèse. Her bitterness was palpable. 'He asked after you, Colonel Tyndale, and whether you were pleased with the progress of F Section agents.'

'Don't be ridiculous! How would any of them know my name and that of the Firm?'

'Oh, they know all right. Kieffer asked me specifically about the wireless messages: was everyone pleased with their quality?'

Iris's blood turned to ice. She glanced at Miss Acton and saw her close her eyes, as if to steady herself.

'They know everything about our activities in France. On the wall of his office, lest anyone be in any doubt how much the Gestapo knows, is what looks like a large family tree. It's us. It shows how everything links up, who knows who, when and where agents arrived. How the branches intersect.'

'Not possible,' said Tyndale, but the bluster was faltering.

'They have a number of our intelligence agents under their thumb just in avenue Foch. There's not much they don't know. They offered me a choice: either I could play along and pretend I was still at liberty by sending messages under German control, or I would be tortured and imprisoned. It was all very civilised. The whole Prosper circuit has been dismantled, and a substantial number seem to have been turned by Kieffer! I believe the SS is now in command, via our radio transmitters, of our operations in Lyon.'

Miss Acton lit a cigarette with visibly trembling fingers. Senior Service smoke, harsh and tarry, fogged the room.

'And rather obligingly,' Thérèse went on, 'the British kept sending more agents to the agreed landing fields! You do realise they now have Roland – the Canadian – and Yves? And they had Rose, too.'

It was far worse than they could have imagined.

'There was no point in lying to them – they already knew almost everything. It was there on the wall. All any of us could do was appear to cooperate while giving away nothing they didn't already know.'

Tyndale had deflated in front of them.

'But even so, I tried my best to tell you. What I cannot understand is how you repeatedly ignored my radio warnings! You put the checks in place, and then you seemed to forget they had ever been agreed! What was the point?'

What could they say? That Tyndale had taken the view that she was a silly girl who was sloppy with her checks? That the signs had been ignored because they did not sit well with their high hopes for the operation?

'And you—' She turned on Iris. 'You've always been so careful – why didn't you spot what was happening?'

'Well, actually, I did—' Iris couldn't finish. She felt deeply ashamed.

'What, you *did* realise? Then why in hell's name—'

Thérèse's contempt was clear to see. She let fly then, calling her every name under the sun, accusing them and Xavier of betrayal.

'Calm down now. You've had a rotten time, but you're out now,' said Tyndale uncomfortably.

True to form, Miss Acton was the cool head. 'What we have

to do now is work out exactly what happened, and who has been compromised.'

When it was clear that Thérèse could not or would not add to the Gestapo's understanding of F Section operations, she was beaten and transferred to the place des États-Unis. There she was held in a small room at the top of a building used as a holding pen for captives who might yet be useful to the Gestapo.

'After the avenue Foch it was much more like a prison. The rooms at the top were cell-like, and there were women on either side of me. We were not allowed to see each other, but we communicated by tapping Morse code on the water pipes. One morning, the girl on the right-hand side was replaced by someone whose situation was uncomfortably similar to mine. It was Rose.'

Iris felt sick. She kept her head down over her notepad, intent on taking down every word accurately.

'For two weeks we tapped our messages as we tried to work out what had happened and whether there was any way out. The windows did not have bars, but it was a long way down. Even so, with drainpipes and places where the carved plaster made tiny ledges, we decided it might be possible to climb down into the garden.

'We could both see a gardener in the grounds. He would stare up at us, and we would stare back. That was our first plan, but actually what happened was much simpler. Rose asked if we could take turns walking around the garden, even if only for half an hour, and the guards agreed.

'So that was what we did, very gratefully and humbly over the course of the next few weeks. When the guard saw that we were no trouble, he didn't mind when we began to walk together, Rose and I, doubling our exercise time. He started courting one of the maids, and they enjoyed a stroll themselves when she broke for lunch. One day they took themselves off under some trees.

'The gardener stopped us for a word, and then we all strolled along together. He was pushing a wheelbarrow full of leaves. We fell in step beside him. The wall of the garden was overgrown with bushes. Suddenly he pushed us both into these bushes, warning us not to make a sound. We'd no idea what was happening, it was so quick. But behind the foliage, hidden from the garden, was a small wooden door. He kicked it open and pushed us through – along with the barrow. Suddenly we were outside on a quiet street. He reached into the pile of leaves and pulled out a large bag, then told us: "Now we walk, fast, but don't run. Xavier is waiting. If we get separated, go to the Chat Noir on rue de Montreuil in the eleventh."'

Iris's heart lurched at the mention of Xavier's name.

To thick silence in the room, Thérèse went on with the account of her escape. 'We made it down one street and then another. With every step I expected someone to shout at us to stop, or to hear the screech of car tyres or gunshots. But there was nothing. When we reached a main street, we slackened our pace and walked along with all the other people on the pavement. I have never felt more grateful for city crowds.'

Xavier was waiting for them at the rear of the Chat Noir café. For a month Thérèse stayed in a safe house, and he organised her return.

'He judged you had had too much of a close shave to carry on?' asked Tyndale. 'He gave up on the plan to take you down south?'

Thérèse stared at him with something close to contempt. 'I'd had enough. My mission went wrong, right from the start. I couldn't do it – my nerves were in shreds, I'd have been a liability. In the end, it was best for me to come back and tell you in person what's going on, as you won't believe it any other way!'

'But the messages we received from you, all through last month?'

'From the avenue Foch. I had long gone.'

No one needed to mention the information that had been transmitted in return.

'Where's Rose now?' asked Miss Acton.

'She is the one who has gone south with Xavier.'

If Iris expected them to praise Xavier's actions in facilitating their almost miraculous escape, she was mistaken.

'Xavier Descours takes a lot on himself,' said Tyndale with a note of grim sarcasm.

Neither did Thérèse seem grateful. 'He was cavalier about my safety. He just left me in the hotel at Châteaudun. If you ask me, there's something not right about him.'

From their reactions, it was evident that Tyndale and Mavis Acton considered this escapade typical of Xavier, his high-handed assumption of responsibility as well as his daring. In these risky endeavours it was essential to make pragmatic decisions at crucial moments, though some would say he acted without regard for others. Iris took a deep breath and concentrated on note taking.

Two weeks later, a message was sent to London from a wireless that was now on the suspect list. Signed off '*Geheime Staatspolitzei*' – the Gestapo – it thanked them for the extremely useful information, supplies and pleasant, talkative agents. 'Some of them, most regrettably, have had to be shot, but others are being far more cooperative.'

7

What was Left

London, spring 1944

The clock at Piccadilly Circus was the centrepiece of the 'Guinness Time' advertisement. 'Guinness is good for you. Gives you strength'. Iris tried a glass, but a few sips made her feel sick.

On rainy streets the smell of wet wool and sweat-soaked uniforms of all kinds was unpleasantly overwhelming; travel by tube was unbearable. Even the air in the office at Baker Street was thick with a dusty ink-and-old-paper stench that turned Iris's stomach. It was as if her sense of smell had suddenly intensified. Was this what it was like to be a dog?

She was pregnant.

When Xavier next came to London, she would tell him. Their situation was unconventional, but even so, she knew he would be pleased. Tyndale had already sent word to France that Xavier was being recalled for an urgent update on the situation in France, and to explain himself. Though Xavier would be the one setting out certain bleak facts to Baker Street, of that Iris was certain. He was the one who knew the brutality and the hazards at the sharp end of the operation – the action, the roar of engines and rattle of gunfire – while London drowned in the quiet intensity of paper and secrecy.

'Evil is like a snake,' Xavier had told her, his bare feet rooted in the pile of her bedroom rug. 'If you flap at it or try to stamp on its tail, it will switch round and strike you. You have to aim for the head.'

She had no doubt who would prevail. But Iris's defining quality had always been determination. 'You just don't give up, do you?' her mother used to say, usually more in exasperation than wonder. She would need to draw on all her reserves for the coming months and years. She had no claim on Xavier, but that did not mean she could not hope for the future.

More immediately, she would have to think how on earth to frame the information for her mother. She would have to tell Miss Acton, too, and sooner rather than later. She dreaded doing so, but she had taken out her clothes as far as they would go. There was no longer any disguising it.

But Xavier ignored the exhortations from London and did not return to England. Since Rose's escape he had relinquished his role as air movement officer in the north and centre of France and moved south, where the Resistance was strongest.

At Tangmere the operations continued doggedly, though Iris was not often sent now. The stuffing had been knocked out of F Section – the Dutch and Belgian sections had suffered similarly at the hands of the Gestapo in what they called the Radio Game – and the traffic was predominantly MI6 intelligence and Free French.

It was one of the Free French, newly arrived by the April moon, who delivered the parcel to Orchard Court. The doorman brought up the unexpected gift with an expression of some distaste, for the paper was tatty and ripped, a Francs-Tireurs propaganda sheet on which Iris's name was scrawled.

Iris pulled off the wrapping. It was a bottle of perfume: a voluptuous lavender scent with the label 'Distillerie Musset, Manosque'.

'Was there a message?' she asked, desperately trying to damp down her hopes.

'No card, miss. But the gentleman who brought it did say something.'

'Yes?'

'This is from Xavier.'

'Nothing else?'

'No, miss.'

He had not forgotten her. She ran her hands over the bottle.

'Careful, miss.'

'I'm sorry?'

The doorman bent over and picked something up from the floor. 'This fell out of the packaging. You didn't even notice.'

It was soft, an envelope of black velvet two inches long, hand-stitched. No wonder she hadn't heard it fall.

'Thank you,' she said.

Iris returned to her desk before opening the flap of the velvet pouch. She pulled out a necklace: a single pearl on a fragile gold chain. She sat transfixed by the lustre of the tiny globe. Through her tears, it glowed against the velvet like a miniature moon in the night sky.

She undid the clasp and put it on.

After that, nothing.

At the end of May 1944, rockets charged with high explosive thrummed across the London sky before their engines cut out. In the ominous silence as they began their descent, the souls on the ground could only pray to avoid a direct hit, that the device would remain airborne for a few seconds longer. On impact, houses caved in like matchwood. As if to defy the destruction, allotments sprang up everywhere on the cleared spaces between smoke-streaked buildings, but there was no security or certainty anywhere.

Iris was let go from F Section. She would not – could not – wish the baby away, though she wondered how on earth she would manage. Then she stopped herself. How many other women were in the same position? How many were young widows? She would only be one of many. It wouldn't be easy, of course, but she would manage. What else could she do? A letter to her mother resulted in four pages of disappointment and invective by return post, leaving it clear that she could expect no support from that quarter.

'I know there's no hope of marrying Xavier, or any kind of relationship in all probability,' she told Nancy, 'but I do want to tell him.'

So much death – what else to do but balance it with life where it took hold?

'Is there really no chance of a relationship?' asked Nancy.

Iris touched the pearl at her throat for reassurance. 'I have no idea – but who knows? Who knows anything any more?'

When France was liberated that August, and with the baby due any day, Iris steeled herself and telephoned Miss Acton to ask for news but was given short shrift by one of the secretaries who had always previously been polite. Iris felt the moral superiority down the line; she was told she could leave a message, but she should be aware it was unlikely to elicit a response.

The child was born at the beginning of September, and named Suzanne. Iris and Nancy moved into the bottom half of a bomb-damaged house in Chester Row, near Sloane Square. The house was solid enough, but the wooden fittings had skewed with the force of a nearby explosion, so that the stairs mounted at a disconcerting angle and few of the doors closed properly. They didn't mind; the rent was cheap in consequence, and they would never otherwise have been able to afford such a pleasant location.

An early visitor was Rory Fitzgerald. Iris was well aware that her situation had been much discussed among her former colleagues: most were surprised, to say the least; almost all felt quietly sorry that she had ruined her chances of a decent marriage; several publicly expressed the view that she was an utter fool. Not Rory. He arrived with a bunch of red dahlias from Yorkshire, a teddy bear for Suzanne and a soppy grin on his face. She was so delighted to see him that she almost accepted impetuously when he asked her to marry him; but then reason prevailed, and she let him down as gently as she could. He was too bound up in the events that had brought her into Xavier's world, and she knew she would never be able to dissociate the man she loved from the man she would have to make herself love.

She tried again to contact Mavis Acton, with no more luck than before. She wrote her a letter, addressed to Baker Street and marked 'Private', reiterating her wish to help in any way she could and giving her new address. She received no reply.

Iris cradled the warm, plump weight of the child, feeling the slub of her daughter's flannel nightdress and the softness of her feet. She cupped the shrimp toes in her hand, and the child moved and settled deeper into her arms with a small breath of contentment.

Sometimes it seemed the baby was the only part of her life that was still in colour, while the rest had receded into the monochrome of her wartime memories and present losses. All she had left of Xavier.

Now that it was over, the great, momentous events of the war seemed insignificant compared to the powerful, painful, small personal experiences that had given her this new life. The first kiss in the blackout at Green Park occupied more space than the repetitive work at Baker Street; their nights under the eaves at Tavistock Square glowed more brightly than the flames above bomb-blasted London. Her mind lacked all sense of perspective. The birth of their child was made bearable by the liberation of France and the hope that Xavier would return.

Loud knocks on the door made them jump.

It was the week before Christmas. They were not expecting visitors.

'I'll go,' said Nancy. 'You look far too comfortable to move.'

'Another pack of carol singers, I expect,' said Iris. 'Not that you can blame the poor children for trying anything to earn pennies.' But even as she said it, she could hear there was no feeble rendition of 'Away in a Manger'.

Nancy returned with Mavis Acton.

Iris got to her feet with the baby.

Miss Acton glanced at Suzanne, made no acknowledgement and spoke as if Iris had never left Baker Street. 'I got your letter. It's not good news, I'm afraid,' she said.

Iris swallowed, feeling grateful for the matter-of-factness. The less emotion, the better. She could deal with Mavis Acton's brand of compassion.

Her former boss accepted a cup of tea, and Nancy slipped away to make it.

She took off her elegant coat and sat by the fire, getting straight to the point.

'In September, Colonel Tyndale and I went to Paris to set up a meeting point at the Hotel Cecil where our people could come in. We had about a hundred F Section agents still missing, sixteen of them women. At first there was a steady stream of returning agents. Over the following months almost half did turn up, most of them with harrowing tales to tell.

'We did a tour of the F Section circuits, gathering information and offering congratulations, rather in defiance of General de Gaulle, who is now railing against the presence of any British intelligence in the country, denigrating any part we played. He seems determined to peddle the myth that the French people rose up and liberated themselves without help from anyone. It's shameless, it really is.'

Iris had the disloyal thought that perhaps Tyndale had gone to make sure all traces of F Section's failure in London were covered over.

'Gradually the trickle of new arrivals in Paris dried up. We began issuing the names of our missing to all the agencies that were piling in, especially the Red Cross. Captured German officers and agents were being interrogated by the Allied military. We started going through the transcripts of these interviews, checking their versions of events with what we knew from our own sources, looking for clues, trying to build up the picture.'

Miss Acton looked at the baby, still unable to bring herself to speak of the child's connection to the story.

'Most of the men involved – in MI6, the SIS, the Foreign

Office – are convinced that those agents who have still not made it will get home at some stage. I think otherwise. My responsibility is to remain in place until all are accounted for, especially the women agents. There is some . . . disparagement of my continuing efforts.'

Her use of the pronoun *my* was telling. Tyndale had slid from the scene. Iris understood immediately the opportunity she was being offered.

'You will need some help,' said Iris.

'I have informed the War Office, such as it remains, that I require an office and an assistant until further notice.'

'I accept.'

'How will you manage?' Miss Acton, nodding towards Suzanne.

'I don't know yet, but I will.'

Nancy stepped in. Not for the first time, Iris realised she would never have been able to do what she did without her friend. It was the best chance she had to find out about Xavier, and they both knew it. And Rose, who had gone south with him. Rose was also among the missing.

Good intentions had gone wrong, mistakes had been made. Mavis Acton was big enough to admit as much, which was more than some of the men would do. There was an embarrassed lack of will to go in search of those who had not returned. It was as though they knew they ought to do it, but would or could not. But they could save face by permitting the women to follow their sentimental instincts, even while they disparaged their efforts. To her immense credit, Miss Acton carried on, past caring who thought her unconventional.

That winter, the atmosphere turned as dark as the days. Accusations of treachery and collaboration were made. Information was hard to assess. The French security police took control of German records and limited British access. They were told repeatedly to keep away, to stop requesting records pertaining to the actions of years past. The more obstacles thrown in their path, the more dogged their search became. Only now had the

Firm begun to be referred to as SOE, the Special Operations Executive, as conceived by Churchill himself.

Iris left Suzanne with Nancy and went to Paris, where she and Miss Acton (there had been no invitation to call her Mavis) went with a former SIS agent to 3a, place des États-Unis, the building used as a Gestapo prison, where Rose and Thérèse had been held and from where they had escaped. They were shown blood on the walls, some from SOE agents who were last seen alive there.

The SIS agent survived thanks to being held back at 3a place des Etats-Unis for further interrogation. He managed to escape by befriending the guards, and made a run for it through the same garden gate. One of the guards, a Russian conscripted from Georgia on the Eastern Front, had been bribed to leave it unlocked. The agent had remained in hiding in Paris until the city was liberated.

The Poles had most of the up-to-date information. It was through colleagues in the Polish Section that they first heard of Ravensbrück. 'Before, I thought the worst thing I ever had to do was to sew a tablet of poison into the shirt cuffs of men who knew they would be tortured if captured. Now I know that was a mercy,' Iris told Nancy on her return.

It was becoming clearer what had happened to the prisoners held as spies. More and more reports were emerging that many of these missing men and women had been 'transferred to Germany'. They had been taken to the concentration camps.

In Paris, more than four hundred people linked to the Prosper network built up by SOE had been killed – and leads to Xavier abounded, though the information was often contradictory.

One overcast afternoon, in a private room above a nondescript café close to the Gare du Nord, Miss Acton and Iris interviewed a former resistant from the Swagman circuit based in Tours. He was an elderly gentleman, a watchmaker by trade who often had business in Paris. His white hair, round cheeks and veined nose gave him a harmless, avuncular look.

He had last seen Rose in the summer of 1943, shortly after she arrived in France; he had known Xavier too.

'Descours appeared just at the time when the secret air operations were beginning in 1942. The landing grounds in France, chosen by Resistance members who were not pilots, were most unsatisfactory. But Descours had been a private pilot, and he knew what was required. He said he would arrange it, and he did. He was impressive.

'There had always been rumours that he had certain links to the Gestapo. But we looked at his record in France. All we saw was that the fellow did more good than harm. More than a hundred agents transported with no losses. Yes, he was . . . what you call, a chancer, but at that stage we took a line of pragmatism. To operate successfully, it was part of the thin line one walked.

'But he was quite an operator.'

The watchmaker lit his pipe.

'Some people didn't like him. They wondered if he could be trusted.'

'Why was that?' asked Miss Acton evenly.

'The Gestapo in Paris knew too much. There must have been a double agent somewhere. Someone who knew exactly when and where the agents were meeting.'

'Do you have any theories about who that was?'

'Personally, no.'

'But some people were suspicious that it might be Descours?'

The old man spread his neat, steady hands. 'Circumstantially, it could have looked that way. They asked themselves how aircraft could fly secretly over an occupied country without incident – how was it that there were so few shot down? They deduced that it was because the Germans knew all along, and allowed the planes to land.'

'Suppose that was the case,' said Iris. 'If they had stopped to think properly, they would have seen that any contact with the German authorities was a necessary evil. Perhaps the Germans were the ones being used.'

'That's true. We all knew about a high-ranking German

officer here who smuggled gold back to Germany every leave. He had it welded behind his teeth by a French dentist. The dentist had had no choice but to give him this gold service treatment, but he was no collaborator. The German thought so highly of him that he was often invited to dine at the officers' mess, where he was privy to all kinds of information, which he naturally passed on to our network.'

Iris nodded, heart pounding. Xavier had told her that very story. 'Where did this gold come from?' she asked, remembering her lover's disgust at the presumed source, the molten remains of jewellery stolen from Jewish deportees.

'Better not to ask,' said the watchmaker. 'But then, perhaps there was a bigger game.'

'What do you mean?'

'Only that. There were rumours that Xavier Descours was seen at the avenue Foch, and he was no prisoner of the Gestapo. On the contrary, he was on very good terms with the SS man there, Kieffer.'

Once a person had a first twinge of suspicion, there could be no recovery of complete trust. When Iris thought back to the times she'd spent with Xavier, and examined what happened in the light of what she knew to be true, she was forced to admit that there was plenty of cause for suspicion. The more she found out, the harder it was to see the man she thought she knew; he was as evasive in absence as he had been ruthless in action.

But then she remembered his self-reliance and energy, his ability to withstand pressure. The secretive nature of all that they did. His underlying sadness, too: the way he would not speak of his family; the tightly closed emotions whenever he spoke of home, wherever that was.

Iris always thought Xavier loved the danger every bit as much as he loved her. He was an egocentric, a marauder, a diehard. Perhaps that was exactly what had attracted her.

'*Qui s'excuse, s'accuse*,' he once told her. Whoever makes excuses accuses himself.

And also: 'People say the most disagreeable things about me.'

Back in London, they were thanked for their efforts and advised to confine themselves to 'welfare work'. The head of the security directorate had asked for the F Section files, a hand-over that Miss Acton staunchly resisted. Time was running out to find what they needed.

'Rules will have to be broken,' Miss Acton decreed.

The rules had been broken in the first place to get the SOE agents, especially the women, to France. The women were issued with First Aid Nursing Yeomanry suits as a cover story while in Britain, but they had none of the internationally agreed protection conferred by a uniform; in France they wore civilian clothes, which meant they were spies and likely to be executed if caught.

It was a fight every step of the way. It took six months before the Security Directorate sanctioned the names of SOE agents being published in prisoner-of-war casualty lists. While they waited for any news, they worked their way through the thousands upon thousands of pages of testimony that was spilling out of commissions in Germany and territories that had been under Nazi control.

Unspoken was the mutual agreement between Miss Acton and Iris that they would not countenance these agents remaining in limbo with 'Missing Presumed Dead' stamped on their files; they would uncover their fates, no matter how terrible. Meanwhile, they parcelled personal effects that had been brought back from the Cottage at Tangmere and sent them back to the families of the agents with a brief note: 'Unfortunately we are still without further news.' Knowing that the Baker Street office was likely to be closed at any time, they gave out the address of the Special Forces Club, with a polite request that all inquiries should be made through F Section and no other agency, so as not to complicate matters.

Iris worked on the files, checking and cross-referencing in the sitting room of the house she still shared with Nancy, as Suzanne slept or watched her from the rug on the floor. A telephone was installed (negotiated by Mavis Acton to facilitate the suggested welfare work) that enabled their investigations to continue.

Among the last letters forwarded to 64 Baker Street was one from 'Fabienne Descours' asking if the SOE had any news of her husband, using his code name so there could be no misunderstanding. Iris knew then, in her bones, that he was not coming back.

Over the months, pieces of the picture began to fit together. Iris was physically sick the first time she read part of a concentration-camp file: there had been nothing to prepare her.

The British were finally allowed to interrogate the French collaborators who had worked in these death camps, testimonies taken before the collaborators were executed. Some of them recalled agents by description, men and women of British and many other nationalities, including French. The trail led to other camps where the staff who had given useful witness statements, and might have been able to provide further clues, had already been executed, confessions unheard.

By the summer of 1945 there was additional pressure on the search. Relations were deteriorating fast between the Allies and the Russians, and if they wanted access to camps in the east, there was little time to waste.

The public was not even supposed to know that women had been sent into occupied Europe as spies. Even after the war, when so many were telling their astonishing stories publicly for the first time, as many others were seeking to cover their traces. The father of Violette Szabo, the SOE agent executed at Ravensbrück and later to receive a posthumous George Cross for her heroism behind the lines, was making waves as the War Office dithered about admitting what was considered an unpalatable truth.

Quietly, it came to be generally accepted that anyone in Europe who had not returned home by August 1945 was not coming back.

Never one to give up, Mavis Acton travelled to Germany in January 1946 with a list of fifty-two SOE agents who were still missing, twelve of whom were women.

In London, Iris read the newspapers avidly. Miss Acton telephoned with descriptions of the destruction in Berlin: the jagged walls of bombed buildings, the dust and desolation. Long queues snaked from water pumps in rubble-strewn streets. And the quietness. Defeat manifested as a heavy, silent state of shock.

From Berlin, Miss Acton travelled to Bad Oeynhausen, headquarters of the British zone, having been promoted to the rank of squadron officer both to facilitate access to the documents she needed to see and, more importantly, to interview key German personnel awaiting trial for war crimes. In particular she wanted to speak to the camp *Kommandants* of Sachenhausen and Ravensbrück, where she knew several of her 'girls' had been transported.

She compiled a roller index of card files, of names and places where they were last seen alive.

'Colette and Francine were in Dachau by November 1943, executed two months later,' she said, businesslike. 'However, not all our girls were sent over the German border. There was another camp, in the Alsace, tucked into the Vosges mountains: Natzweiler. A small camp. Not many people knew about it. That was how it was supposed to be. It was for resistants, spies and political dissidents, where they were to vanish without trace. *"Nacht und Nebel"*, they called it, Night and Fog, into which prisoners would disappear. Very few records, no hard evidence of who lived or died there.

'There are reports that at least one British woman was taken there. Two Frenchwomen and one Englishwoman arrived at the camp in June 1944.'

Iris braced herself.

'According to the evidence I've seen, that woman was Rose. We can't be absolutely certain. We are reliant on witness testimony and description, some from surviving prisoners.'

'What points to Rose?'

'The description fits – height and build, hair, all corres-
pond. A fellow prisoner saw her arrive. He particularly remembered her calm bearing, was astonished by it, in fact. The
most important account comes from a German who worked at
the camp' – Miss Acton hesitated uncharacteristically – 'as a
stoker in the newly built crematorium. He has stated that these
three women were given injections, gassed and then burned.
There were no remains.'

'But Rose went south with Xavier . . . how did she end up
in Alsace?'

'The women were held first in a prison in Karlsruhe. They
could have been sent there from anywhere in France. One of
the Frenchwomen left a message scratched on an enamel cup
there, of their three names and the date they were moved out.
Two names mean nothing to us, but the third was Rosa Williams. Rose's real name—'

'—was Rita Williams.'

Iris took the news like a blow to the chest. She should have
acted more decisively on her instincts when the agents' wireless messages came in with their embedded warnings. She
should have made Tyndale take her seriously. As it was, the
story was growing that the British had known exactly what
was going on but decided to play the game themselves, though
it involved the sacrifice of their own people. As a face-saving
story, it was not convincing in the slightest, thought Iris.

But it seemed Miss Acton had not discounted the possibility of truth in the watchmaker's reference to a bigger game. As
far as she was concerned now, Xavier Descours was a traitor, a
double agent embroiled with the SS in Paris.

Could that have been the case? He had been recruited in
France, and so had never passed through the F Section training and vetting. His cover story was that he worked closely
with the Vichy government, and by extension, the Germans,
providing electronics equipment, at least in the beginning.
Was that a blind to his true loyalty? After most of the members
of his circuit were betrayed, he insisted on going back to find
out what had happened and to alert other cells to the disaster

– or was he returning to betray more himself?

He had still not been traced.

The office in Baker Street closed. Iris continued to work from home and to speak on the telephone with Mavis Acton. Over tea at Fortnum and Mason, Miss Acton's preferred venue to meet face to face, Iris tried one last time.

'If Xavier was in contact with the Gestapo, you could say that he was playing them for all he was worth – far from betraying his circuit when he disappeared, leaving Thérèse at Châteaudun, he was trying to protect her. Don't forget he organised the escape for her and Rose.'

'In the end, he was not one of ours,' said Miss Acton.

'But we were all in it together, weren't we?'

'That's a rather *romantic* view of things, wouldn't you say?'

There was no doubting her meaning. She closed the subject, with an imperious wave to the waiter.

Mavis Acton was now convinced of Xavier's guilt, and there was no persuading her otherwise. In the long weeks afterwards Iris felt as if she might have been used – it was just possible Miss Acton had been keeping an eye on her all the time they had been working together, waiting to see whether she was still in contact with Xavier.

But no contact was ever made, and somehow Iris had to live with the ambiguity of their intimacy and promises, and the knowledge that he and she had been complicit in at least one betrayal – that of his wife.

On the strength of a fine reference from Miss Acton – she was always fair, which made her conclusions about Xavier that much harder to take – Iris secured a part-time secretarial job at the Home Office. Her minuscule salary went almost entirely into the pot at Chester Row, where the top two storeys of the bomb-damaged house had become available.

Iris lived here with Suzanne and a young mother's help called Jane, who had lost her family and all her possessions in the Luftwaffe's firestorms over the capital. Nancy and Phil, who had married as soon as Phil came home from the Far East, had the lower maisonette. When Nancy and Phil's first child was born ten months after the wedding, Jane worked for them all. She came to be treated as part of the extended family, and the arrangement proved a boon all round.

8

Never Give Up

Provence, May 1948

After the war, Xavier was sometimes mentioned in the many books about SOE that began to appear. But a man who is no longer there cannot defend his reputation. He was a convenient scapegoat. Many years later, when more authoritative histories were written with the benefit of newly opened archive material, there were still more questions than answers about Xavier Descours.

Those who knew him and worked with him always expressed surprise that he was the one who had betrayed them. He was a good man, a moral man, they said. If he had been in cahoots with the Germans, he must have been doing so for the greater good. How had so many of his people escaped capture? How had his flights never been intercepted? During the moon periods, the Luftwaffe was active all along the north coast of France, and although other flights had been intercepted or shot down, the Descours flights had achieved an astonishing record of success. Had he been blamed for others' failures? Did he take German money? Many claimed he did. But the truth was harder to call.

It transpired that he had indeed been to the avenue Foch, on more than one occasion. The first time he was called in to be interviewed by the Gestapo's Kieffer, but he walked free afterwards. Had Xavier managed to persuade the Germans that he should be allowed to go about his business, while keeping them informed? Did he, like the German officer's dentist, intend to get more out of the arrangement than the Nazis did?

His fury when he realised how inept London had been in handling messages from the captured radios was real enough. The Germans had everything, from the codes to the timetables when the signals were due. Some ventured that he was so angry, he didn't care any more, because to him it was clear that he had been working for idiots. Others remained convinced that the setback had spurred him to work ever harder, but more independently from the British, away from his dangerous game with the Gestapo in Paris.

Was he dead – or had he begun a new life far away from all the complexities of his wartime tightrope? '*Heureux sont ceux qui ont beaucoup peché, il leur sera beaucoup pardonné*' – Happy are those who have sinned greatly, for a great deal will be forgiven them – he had once told her. For years she had pulled that aphorism apart, wondering if it held an answer.

As the years went by, it was not hope of finding Xavier alive that drove Iris, but the desire to know what to tell Suzanne about her father.

Time and again, Iris came back to the last known sighting of him.

On the night of 10 August, 1944, Xavier Descours was the flight liaison officer for a joint British-American operation in Provence. The RAF flew a Dakota in from Cecina in northern Italy to a secret landing strip known as Spitfire, close to Saint-Christol in the Sault lavender area. The mission that night was not a complete success. On board were fifteen men, including returning French politicians and agents, and seven hundred and fifty kilos of freight. The disembarking French and the freight – mainly weapons and explosives – vanished into the night without incident. But the turnabout and take-off with a total of thirty men, most of whom were escaping

US Fortress aircrew, was more problematic. The Dakota – the largest aircraft to set down at Spitfire – ran out of runway at the end of the field, snagging on a band of lavender growing across the strip to disguise its length from the Germans. The only solution was to let down eight of the US escapees to lighten the load, with promises to return for them the next night. Even then, the plane struggled to get airborne again, though it eventually lifted off at the very limit of its capacity, thanks to the skill and nerve of the pilot.

But by then the repeated bursts of aircraft noise had alerted a German patrol – or had the Germans been expecting the operation? As the reception committee and their charges scattered, shots were fired. Reprisals were swift and cruel.

After that, nothing. Had Xavier been killed, or captured, then executed? Or had he melted away into a night and fog of his own devising, having played a double game all along, as some were convinced?

Through the Libre Résistance, a society formed by what was left of the old networks, Iris was put in touch with some of the old *maquisards* in the south. They exchanged letters, and she used her fortnight's leave in the late spring of 1948 to go to France. She crossed the Channel and travelled by train to Paris, on to Avignon and then Sault. She was met at the railway station by Gaston Durand and his young wife Émilie.

Gaston took her suitcase and led her to a van that looked like corrugated cardboard on wheels. 'We'll go to Saint-Christol, but before I show you the field, we'll all have lunch,' he said.

The van lurched through a rocky landscape of twisty roads and fields. In the village of Saint-Christol they parked in a narrow street of cracked houses. A cold wind gusted, and a clock struck twelve with a thin, tinny sound. Chickens scurried across their path as M and Mme Durand led her into a café that was surprisingly full, and over to a table where a man was already seated.

'May I introduce Thierry LeChêne? He was there at Spitfire that night.'

He rose to shake her hand.

'So you want to know about the last Spitfire operation?' he opened directly. He had a broad Provençal accent that took a moment or two to understand.

'Yes – and one participant in particular,' said Iris.

'We will do what we can to help you, but as I'm sure you know, these things were complicated.'

'I realise that. I'm very grateful—'

Gaston Durand waved that away. 'We are the ones who are grateful. We won't forget what was done here by the RAF.'

Iris smiled. 'That's . . . rather refreshing to hear. General de Gaulle has not been so generous-spirited since the end of the war.'

It was undoubtedly for the best that any further discussion of the president's aggressive nationalism was interrupted by the arrival of a waitress bringing plates of pâté and salad.

'The centre for our cell was Céreste,' said Thierry. 'Each person in the group knew only the participants closest to themselves, and everyone else by a pseudonym only. A knock at the wrong door might be a death sentence. You were never sure of other people's loyalties, even those you had known all your life.'

'We knew of Xavier Descours, but only by his first name. More often he was referred to as the Engineer,' explained Gaston.

'And he was . . . well respected?'

'Very well respected. He was one of the best.'

'What do you think happened to him?'

They exchanged glances and shrugged expressively. 'You have to understand. Xavier was not a local. He came in like the British and the Americans came in, and then he left. We never saw him afterwards, and he didn't turn up for any of the honours ceremonies, but there could be many reasons for that.'

'Do you have any reason to think that . . . he didn't make it to the end?'

He shook his head. 'We have been putting the word out, as you asked. But no one has come up with any new information.'

'What about a young woman code-named Rose, his wireless operator? Was she there that night?'

Again, they looked blankly at each other.

'You never came across her at all?'

'No. But that was as it should be. There had been problems keeping our wireless operators safe. The first one was shot. Maybe too many people knew what he was doing. If the Engineer was doing his job right, he would have kept his operator well out of it.'

As they ate, Thierry showed her photographs: grainy pictures of men in peasant clothes, posing in groups in the fields. Some carried a gun with a rose at the end like a garden hose.

'Dropped by parachute by the RAF, those,' said Thierry.

'Designed by the Czechs,' added Iris acerbically.

Afterwards, at the field they called Spitfire, they stood in contemplation.

'Is that the strip of lavender that proved such a hazard to the plane?' she asked Thierry.

'More has been planted since then. There wasn't that much during the war, but we had to disguise the length of the fields somehow.'

'The people living on the farms out here must have heard the engines,' said Iris.

'They knew,' said Émilie.

'They say now,' said Gaston, 'that five per cent of the French population actively collaborated with the Germans, five per cent were active in the Resistance and ninety per cent did nothing. But here, one has to revise that to take account of all the small acts of resistance. The farmers who gave their land to allow the planes to come down and the drops of equipment to be made, which meant that at a time of hunger they couldn't use it to grow crops, and also implicated themselves and their families. They had to count on the loyalty of villages close to the landing fields – all the people who closed their eyes and ears to what was going on. It was a complicity of the many.'

They looked out at the lavender field, its neat corduroy rows and the plants still in the process of waking from grey to purple. Hills rose on three sides.

'Hell of a place to land a plane as big as a Dakota,' said Thierry.

'How did you get here that night?' Iris asked him. She was trying to picture it: the full moon, the night noises, shadows moving.

'I came in the lavender van with the man they called the Philosopher – Victor Musset. He ran a soap and scent factory at Manosque. My cousin Auguste was a committed resistant, but in his other life he was a lavender farmer, a big supplier to Musset's. That was how the connection was made.'

The bottle of scent.

'Musset . . . is he still alive?'

'Certainly.'

'Might it be possible for me to meet him?'

The Durands put her up on their farmstead in the hills above the town of Apt. Émilie told her how she had been the network's courier, usually on her bicycle.

Two days later Iris was shown into a bar in the medieval heart of the town by the cathedral. It was a dark and undistinguished room with a vaulted ceiling, made to seem lower by Victor Musset's height. He was a large man; judging by his girth, he enjoyed his food. He did not generally talk about the war, he told her. Too many bad memories.

M Musset had a small glass of cloudy pastis in front of him, from which he hardly drank.

'It is a long time past,' he said, in a kind voice, sadness in his spaniel eyes. 'People change their stories. Sometimes they don't even know they are doing it. They hear more of the background in later years and assume they knew those facts at the time. But they did not. None of us could see the whole picture, or foresee the outcome. All I know is what I saw, but even then I cannot be certain I am not overlaying that with knowledge acquired subsequently.

273

'What you must never forget is that the Resistance was diverse, made up of all kinds of people with all kinds of allegiances. We wanted to emerge from the war into a different country from before, a different political landscape. By August 1944 an active member of the Resistance had a life expectancy of three months, yet many young men felt it was worth the risk.'

'According to the RAF records,' said Iris, 'the Dakota did return the next night for the Americans stranded near Spitfire, but there were no lights on the ground at the coordinates.'

'The reception committee decided it was too dangerous to try again.'

'Were the Germans watching the field?'

'They might well have been. The morning after the Dakota landed, they shot an elderly couple who worked the nearest farm, no doubt after torturing them for whatever information they had, and burned the farmhouse to the ground. Terrible, simply terrible – and so pointless, you know? The war was nearly over – why did they have to do that?'

Iris shook her head.

'That was the first time one of Xavier's operations had gone wrong,' he said. 'They used to say he was the best of the best.'

'Is he still alive?'

'Who can say? Many people grabbed what they could at the end of the war, especially those who had been striving for a new France, a better France. It was a time when scores were settled, and sometimes not everything was as it seemed. He may be someone else now, or he may be the person he was before the war that we never knew. From what we now understand, it was not just the South of France that he covered, but right up to Paris. He was a wealthy man, we knew that. He could have come from anywhere, and returned anywhere. Or his body might be in a mass grave.'

'He was a successful businessman, I can tell you that. Before the war, and during it, he ran an electronics company. We made inquiries all over France, but he is not involved now in any similar business,' said Iris.

'He was usually known to our cells as the Engineer. That makes sense.'

'What do you think happened to him, monsieur?'

'In the absence of any further information, if you ask me what I believe, then I have to tell you that he is probably dead.'

'But there is no evidence of that?'

'None that I know of.'

Iris nodded slowly, not willing to speak.

'I have made some inquiries,' Musset went on, 'but no one here knows what happened to him after the night the Dakota landed. I remember there was an incident at the time because not even his wireless operator knew where he'd gone. I've even asked the Poet.'

'The Poet?'

'The leader of our cell. A man who would never have been passed fit for any army – too shambling, too apparently disorganised. He had two safe houses in Céreste, each with two exits, just like the fields we used. It was quiet in this region, but strategically important, between Lyon – a hotbed of intrigue, denunciations and Gestapo terror – and the coast.

'Tough decisions had to be made. When we heard that a woman who worked at the pharmacy here in Apt where messages were dropped had threatened to denounce the network, one of us had to take action. Our man was on a bicycle. He shot her while she was outside the station, did it very quietly, and cycled back to Céreste.'

'Was that one of the stories that had to be changed?' Iris said.

'Maybe. Ah – you can rouge the corpse, but it remains dead,' said the Philosopher. 'There were times when grave sacrifices had to be made. The Poet had a protégé, a young man of twenty-two who was as courageous as he was talented as a writer. The Poet himself had supplied his false papers – and one terrible afternoon, not very far from a village, he saw this young man taken by the Germans.

'The Poet could have saved him; he was out of view; he had the Germans in his gunsight; he could have squeezed the

275

trigger, but he did not. He had to make the decision not to fire, to save the village from the ferocious reprisals this would have unleashed. Afterwards he wrote the most moving words I have ever read; he called it "an ordinary village, an extraordinary place". It was a time that marked us for life.'

'I understand that,' said Iris.

Musset gave her a sad smile. 'Yes, I think you do, mademoiselle.'

9

Almost Happy

Sussex, 1950 onwards

Miles Corbin was a good man, apparently without a secret life. For many years after she met him Iris was almost happy. A civil servant like Iris, he rose to a senior position in Customs and Excise; he was as scrupulously honest at home as he was at work. He once told Iris that he had never cheated at golf, though he was once sorely tempted at Sandwich and never quite forgave himself. It might have been that confession that persuaded her to marry him.

If not quite handsome, with his wispy sandy hair and hollowed cheeks, Miles had a certain dash. During the war he had served as a navigator in the RAF's Coastal Command, from which he developed a serious interest in marine cartography; he also had a passionate interest in Greece, its history and poetry. He clearly adored her, was amusing and kind to Suzanne, and he loved to travel – though it went without saying that not even the smallest bottle of cognac or perfume from Paris went undeclared at Dover on their return.

When Iris fell pregnant with their daughter Betsy, she gave up work and became a full-time housewife. When Suzanne was old enough to understand, she was told that her father had died in the war, like so many brave men.

Iris could not easily forget Xavier. At the smallest provocation he insinuated himself into her thoughts. In Paris in the 1950s, she smelled a distinctive lavender fragrance on a woman who passed her in the street. She almost ran after her to ask what it was, but then held herself in check. The familiar scent lingered in the air, leaving a musky trail and an inexplicable sense of danger. She stood in the rue Saint-Honoré, feeling both trapped and euphoric – or had the perfume only triggered these sensations in her brain?

It wasn't quite the same fragrance. This was a deeper, warmer, more complex distillation than the scent she knew so well: the perfume he had sent her, eked out drop by careful drop; the scent of hope that had diminished by the day, month, year. She still wore the pearl he sent her, symbol of the moons that brought them together and took him away. What a fool she was.

Sporadically over the years, Iris was approached – usually by letter – by the writers and researchers of various books on the clandestine operations of the Second World War. Invariably she turned down their respectful requests to meet. Some of those who had been involved, especially the agents who had faced the greatest dangers, were eager to tell their stories and enjoyed the recognition. Others, like Thérèse, preferred to remain in the shadows. Iris never heard a word from Thérèse after her last furious outburst at Orchard Court, and respected her all the more for it.

When she succeeded in banishing him from her waking hours, Xavier shook Iris awake from dreams that began with the night sky, clumps of cloud, moonlight. The small plane waiting.

He was there, even if she could not see him. She only had to glimpse the silvered darkness to know what would happen. Sometimes she was in the seat next to him, so close she could feel the wool of his coat and the brush of his hand.

For so many years, Iris found him in transcendent dreams; he lived with her, still speaking and dancing and tangling in absurdities with her as she slept. In endless variations of the same dream, Xavier climbed into planes and flew into the night, nights so vivid she felt what he felt: the rush and lift of the headwind under the wings; the chill of the glass beyond which gleamed the moon. Ahead, storm citadels and skies planted with forests of electric trees. High in a sea of cloud, the small aircraft hardly moved across gusting waves, hanging like a spider on a thread.

Always the same ending: the sky convulsing, throwing up ridges and folds that might be walls of cloud, or hills, or rising waves. Sea or sky? No difference; no place of safety. The pilot knows when his plane passes the point of no return. The crash is imminent. The black night is still beautiful, clouds lit by moonlight. Time slows. It is all so simple now. No more decisions. What to say? What to do? There are only minutes left, only seconds. There is no time left, only the beginning of time.

The plane is carried onwards, blown by the wind into emptiness.

Long, long after he slid up into the night sky away from her, Iris held him in her sights.

After Miles died in 1990, Iris embraced widowhood. She moved to The Beeches, an ample Edwardian cottage on the edge of a village near Chichester, happily relinquishing along the way the slavery of the lunch and dinner service, the boredom of making conversation with a decent man with whom she had no spiritual connection. Not that she was heartless, far from it: she had made an honest mistake in imagining she could make a successful marriage to a man she had once respected but never loved. It had always been a contract of companionship, and she thought he knew that. Did that make her a bad woman, or simply a pragmatic one? It was all she was able to be. After the war and its aftermath, there were too many damaged souls; she was yet another. For all those years she had been the perfect wife and mother to Suzie and Betsy while Miles commuted up to London from their home in Surrey, to his government desk; Miles with his ever more solid demeanour,

279

his golfing friends, his increasing dependence on whisky, his outbursts of frustration.

Iris did not tell him that in one of the thick folders she kept in a bedroom trunk was the note she had scribbled the night she had seen Tyndale on *Panorama*, admitting that he knew there were double agents, and intimating that London had sanctioned them, though without telling any of the other agents. The sacrifices, in other words. There were other notes and references. One, a photocopied page from Hansard, answered the questions in Parliament that arose after the first books had appeared, with their notions of conspiracy: 'Penetration (by German agents) was deliberately concealed.'

The only person she ever spoke about the war with was Nancy. They both enjoyed their long exchanges by letter and occasionally on the telephone when any genuinely new information surfaced. It had become a touchstone of their long friendship, more than an expectation of a final resolution.

10

⁓

Vapour Trail

Sussex, September 2013

The telephone rang. Iris moved so slowly in the early mornings – frustratingly slowly, as if she were no longer in complete command of her own limbs – that she was sure whoever it was would give up long before she arrived in the hall to pick it up. If it was yet another cold call about solar panels, she would tell them that no meant no, and if they bothered her again she would report them for harassment.

'Hello, is it possible to speak to Iris Corbin, please?'

'Speaking.'

'Mrs Corbin, this is Anna Lester from the *Daily Telegraph*. I'm not sure whether you remember, but I wrote a piece a couple of years ago about the National Memorial Arboretum in Staffordshire and the Mavis Acton memorial, and you very kindly gave me some background details.'

Iris sat down carefully on the chair next to the telephone table.

'I remember.' The one time she had relented and agreed to speak, and then only to make sure the facts were correct.

'Do you think I could come and see you? I'm working on a related story, and sometimes it's easier face to face.'

'I'm very sorry, but I'm not sure I can help you.'

'The thing is—'

'The answer's no, I'm afraid. I – I am not myself at the moment, a family bereavement.'

'I am sincerely sorry for your loss, Mrs Corbin. But you see, the – the way – sorry, I—' Anna Lester was struggling to find the right words, 'There's no easy way to say this. I had no idea that Ellie Brooke was your granddaughter until I started researching an in-depth piece about . . . about her death. And I've found something . . . that I think you would want to know about.'

'When would you want to come?'

'As soon as possible, whenever suits you best.'

Waiting was always so much worse than facing news head-on. 'Come this afternoon, then,' said Iris.

Through the open kitchen window, the pumping of a tractor engine from a field below echoed Iris's heartbeat. Here on the outskirts of the village, it was quiet and secluded. Cars passed on the road, but not too many. The hedge was kept high on that side. From the rear of the property were sweeping views of the Sussex countryside and farmland beyond a sloping lawn.

'Shall we go for our walk, Marion?'

The housekeeper glanced at her watch. 'Right now? It's early. Might be a bit dewy – why not give it an hour?'

Marion had been at The Beeches so long, she was a vital fixture of the house, like the stairs or the roof. Every elderly person should have a Marion, and it was a crying shame that most couldn't.

'I just have the feeling I have to get on,' said Iris. 'Silly, really.'

'Well, all right. We'll go now if you like, Mrs C.'

The trick of it was never to stop. Walking, in this case, but the same dictum might apply equally to anything in life, thought Iris. Never stop, no matter how much you might want to give in. She worked on the principle that if a person walked every day, there would never come a day when she couldn't. It was stopping that would cause the muscles to weaken and the joints to complain.

Marion dried her hands as she slotted the last breakfast plate in the drainer. She was a large, motherly woman with a soft voice. Her hair had turned grey over the past year, which had saddened Iris. For so long, Marion had been the young woman who 'did', the young pair of legs up and down the stairs.

'Not necessary to go far, but necessary to go,' said Iris.

Marion smiled. 'Quite right. Breath of fresh air never hurt anyone, neither.'

The only concession Iris had made to her daily walking routine was to allow Marion to accompany her. A fall, at her age, would put her out of action for too long.

('Slippery slope,' said Iris. 'In all senses.')

A bridlepath led down one side of The Beeches, meandering to a large pond and a cluster of agricultural buildings and a holiday let. It was a gentle English landscape, of flowing fields and winding paths under trees. The kind of landscape that made one feel safe – that was what he had once told her, wasn't it?

A lively wind threaded grass into silver patterns. A chintz of cow parsley danced on the breeze, and a vapour trail smoked high in a blue sky.

'You're very quiet, Mrs C.'

'Just thinking.'

'There hasn't been any more news . . . from the island, has there?'

They made a slow but steady footfall on the stony path. In a wooded hollow, the pond water was a dusty antique mirror, reflecting oak and beech.

'I may be about to find out.'

The death of Suzie's daughter Ellie on the island of Porquerolles had been a loss more terrible than any other. The random nature of the tragedy, the circumstances so unforeseen; that was what had been so shocking.

When Ellie did not turn up to take the return flight she had booked from Hyères to London Stansted, there had been days of worry. Her partner in the garden design business, Sarah, raised the alarm when Ellie failed to contact her. It was three agonising days before the body was found washed up on the south-western rocks of the island. From the start, it was deemed most likely to be a dreadful accident, or perhaps what was termed inconclusively 'misadventure'. Various sightings of Ellie the day before her flight put her close to the Fort de l'Alycastre, the harbour and the hotel where she was staying – then nothing. It was suggested that she had gone swimming alone and run into difficulties when the weather changed. The sea had done its worst to the body. She was identified by a ring on her finger and the necklace she always wore.

That was the salt in the wound for Iris: the necklace. Ellie had been wearing the wartime 'moon' pearl, Iris's one superstition, and it had failed to protect her. It had been given to Suzanne when she was eighteen, and she had passed it on to Ellie. The pearl pendant had come back to them, but Ellie had not.

The accounts carried by the newspapers had been respectful, by and large, but still painfully speculative. But it was a poignant story: the young woman making a name for herself as a designer of gardens, the evocative Mediterranean location, the dream job and the tragic outcome. Iris and her daughters understood why some of the journalists had made much of the details, but could not forgive them for the intrusion on their grief.

Even now, Iris had difficulty in accepting what had happened. It had been bad enough when Ellie had lost her young man in Afghanistan, an act of war that had brought granddaughter and grandmother closer than ever. But for Ellie to be taken in this way still seemed perverse.

All the young men and women she knew who had died young had died in war. They had signed up to carry out acts of exceptional bravery; all of them were daring, motivated and reckless and knew the risks. Some of them had themselves killed.

Different times.

It hardly mattered. Ellie was dead.

Anna Lester was slightly older than her voice on the telephone had intimated, with dark shoulder-length hair and clever brown eyes. A pleasant smile reached her eyes, and her handshake was firm. She wore minimal make-up, if indeed any, and her short linen jacket and trousers seemed to wrinkle more with every movement, an outfit that gave the impression more of a harassed off-duty schoolteacher than a cut-throat reporter on a national broadsheet. There was a resolutely self-deprecating air about her that did not fool Iris for a second: she had been extremely well informed the last time they had spoken, her questions informed by a genuine interest in wartime history.

'Do you mind?' A small recording device came out of a large bag.

Iris shook her head.

'I find it easier. I make notes too, but . . .' She pressed a button and set it on the side table by Iris; then, perched on the edge of her seat with a notebook, she stared around the sitting room. Duck-egg-blue walls, hung with fine prints and watercolours. A walnut display cabinet. A magnifying glass poised on a side table on top of the morning newspapers, the *Times* and the *Daily Telegraph*.

Marion brought in tea, served in the decent porcelain cups, then left them to it.

'Best get straight to the point,' said Iris. She smoothed down her skirt and swallowed hard.

'Last week I went to Porquerolles,' said Anna Lester. 'We had a tip-off that the police had taken Ellie's client Laurent de Fayols in for further questioning. By the time I got there, he had been released without charge. I was hoping I might get an interview with him, but – understandably, I suppose – he refused to meet me. I decided to retrace your granddaughter's journey and visit the locations where she was known to have been, trying to build up a fuller picture of what happened, looking for details, descriptions that went beyond the police reports. I'm sorry, this must be hard for you to hear.'

'Go on.'

'I stayed at the hotel where she stayed, and spoke about her with the assistant manager. He was friendly and helpful, and remembered her very well. She had arrived looking distressed but said nothing about the suicide on the ferry that delayed her – it was only later he found out why her trip to the island had started so badly.

'She went out every day and often seemed distracted when she returned in the evenings. Though there was one night when she did not come back.'

'Is that significant?'

'Possibly.'

The journalist opened a notepad at a marked page and ran a finger down a column of writing mixed with shorthand squiggles. 'I gather Ellie's client sent someone over to collect her luggage in order that she could stay over at the Domaine de Fayols. But the next day she was back at the hotel. On the Friday evening, the last night she was booked to stay at the hotel, she came back much happier. Jean-Luc Martin – the assistant manager – passed on a couple of messages, and she went out again, using a bicycle he lent her. But before she went, she gave him something to put in the hotel safe. Jean-Luc had forgotten about it until I came along, asking questions.'

'What was it?'

'A notebook containing sketches, ideas and plans for the garden she'd been working on.'

'He must have remembered to show it to the police, surely?'

'Of course. He said he did show it to them in the days after she died, but they looked through it and dismissed it as unimportant. After that, well, I think the truth is that it got lost for a while when it didn't go back into the safe. The Oustaou des Palmiers is a charming little hotel, but the reception and office are extremely cramped and, frankly, a bit of a mess.'

Anna Lester cleared her throat and flushed. 'I'm afraid I have a confession to make. I may have let him believe I was rather better acquainted with the family than our conversation a couple of years ago would warrant. But as it turned out—'

'A very old reporter's trick. Spare me the justification.'

'Well, you may not be entirely displeased when I tell you that' – she bent over the capacious leather bag at the side of her chair and fished out a black book – 'I have the notebook here. Jean-Luc let me have it, on condition that I handed it over to Ellie's family.'

She held it out.

'I think he was pleased to have it taken back to its rightful owners. They hadn't known quite what to do with it. It wasn't much of a gamble that I would bring it to you. I was upfront about being a journalist, and he was astute enough to realise that I would get a better story by handing it over in person.'

Iris took the bulging, stained book. Minutes passed as she flipped through the pages filled with drawings and notes, measurements and perspectives.

She looked up. 'You have read it right through, haven't you?'

'Yes.'

'I thought so. There must be more than planting schemes and topiary designs to bring you here with it. What is it?'

The journalist indicated the book. 'May I?'

Iris handed it back. Anna Lester turned the pages carefully. 'Here. Can you read this?'

'I'll need my glasses . . . where did I put them? Read it aloud for now.'

'It says: "A message for Iris." Your name is underlined twice. Then it reads: "Thy word is a lantern unto my feet: and a light unto my path."'

Iris composed herself, determined not to react. 'Anything else?'

'Yes. There's an account of a Second World War operation involving a French Resistance agent and the lighthouse on Porquerolles.'

'Read it.'

The journalist did so.

Iris tipped her head back on the high-winged chair and closed her eyes to listen. Trembling, she was actually trembling.

In August 1944, a plan was made to disable the lighthouse beam in order to confuse the German night defences as the Allies landed at Saint-Tropez in August 1944. British and Americans working with the Resistance in southern France had originally wanted to bomb the lighthouse, but Xavier (a French liaison agent) refused to sanction the destruction of the Porquerolles lighthouse, arguing that it could be more effectively and subtly disabled. He was born on the island – he had known Rousset the lighthouse keeper since he was a boy. How could he allow him to be killed in an explosion? He volunteered to go to Porquerolles himself.

The island was ringed with barbed wire and mines. Xavier was a native of the island, knew every rock and cove, but realised it would be impossible to come by sea. Time was not on his side. He was already running late after waiting an extra day for a repeat landing on the Saint-Christol plateau that had been called off. He begged the use of a Firefly aircraft hidden near Rians in Provence, and piloted the plane himself on the night of August the thirteenth, the last possible night. Allied bombardment prior to invasion was due to start on the fourteenth.

Landing on flat ground by the cliffs at the Domaine de Fayols, he ran to the lighthouse. The lighthouse keeper Rousset was astonished to see him but agreed to what Xavier asked. He would disable the beam on the night of August the fourteenth – and claim there was a mechanical fault.

It was highly dangerous for Xavier to be on the ground. He ran back to the plane and took off as quickly as possible from a field on the cliff where the wind lifted the wings. The take-off was risky, but he made it. Then the German guns opened. The plane was hit but flew on. Halfway to Marseille, it began its final descent into the sea.

'There are a few notes at the end,' said Anna. ' "Are there any records in London regarding that night? Any records at all of Xavier? Why has the wreck of the plane never been found before now on the seabed? (This must be G's big discovery . . .)" Are you all right, Mrs Corbin? This obviously means something to you.'

'Yes.'

'Can I ask what that is?'

Iris pulled herself together. 'Is it possible that this has a bearing on . . . what happened to Ellie?'

'I honestly don't know.'

'Can we verify this story – can it be true? Where would Ellie have found this account?'

'Iris? What on earth are you doing?'

Iris, on her knees in front of the old travelling trunk in her bedroom, started at Marion's admonishment but was relieved to see her. She wasn't entirely sure she would be able to get up again. The lid of the trunk was open. Piles of photograph albums and papers were banked around her.

'I'm looking for something.'

'I can see that,' said Marion, indulgently. She was a big woman, tall and strong; she nearly filled the doorway. 'You said you were having a rest once your visitor had gone.'

'It must be here . . .'

'What? What are you after? If you tell me, perhaps I could help.'

Iris raised her head, straightening painfully. 'You can help me up, in a minute.'

Marion nodded. They had come to an understanding, many years ago. Marion never mentioned age or its limitations.

It had been so long since Iris had last seen what she was searching for. Could it somehow have disappeared? How could it not be there? But it was. Among the most private papers, letters, and mementos was the file marked with his name and enclosing the pitifully few photographs. The papers too sensitive to have a place in the bulging filing cabinet she kept in her, admittedly, rather untidy study downstairs. The cabinet had been exclusively her domain for decades, ever since Miles passed away, but even so she had these items under separate guard. This trunk, leather-bound, scuffed and dented, was the cradle of her older, frailer possessions.

Iris reached farther into the trunk, finally exhuming a small parcel of tissue paper. She peeled back the crackling layers. Inside was a glass bottle, five inches tall. The perfume it had once held was nothing more than a brown stain on the base. She fumbled with the stopper, twisting it off with some effort; it seemed to have stuck. Or was it the shaking in her fingers? She put her nose to the lip of the glass and inhaled. She sat and waited for a moment, concentrating before she took another breath. But it was no good. The scent had finally evaporated. There had been times when she had seemed able to catch a remnant of it, but now nothing came. If she smelled anything, it was the dust and cold hard glass of the present.

Downstairs, in Ellie's notebook, lay what might be the final chapter of the story, and yet it was impossible. How could Ellie have heard it, or stumbled across it? She knew she should contact Suzie, but she felt too exhausted. If Nancy had still been alive, she could have picked up the phone right then. She missed her, too.

A week later the telephone rang. It was around the time Suzie or Betsy usually called, and Iris picked up the phone in full expectation that it was one of her daughters.

'Mrs Corbin, this is Anna Lester.'

'Anna.'

'Look, I know we agreed you would call me when you were ready, but something has happened. Trust me, you will want to know about this. Laurent de Fayols has told the police that he has some more information, but he wants to meet you first.'

11

⁓

Le Train Bleu

Paris, September 2013

Naturally, Suzie and Betsy had counselled against travelling, ridiculously overprotective as they were. Betsy, in particular. Slighter, blonder, more cerebral than her sister, she was her father's daughter: risk-averse to a fault. Iris had rather enjoyed the heated exchange that ensued, in which her daughters' opinion that she was too old to charge off to Paris had been countered by Anna Lester's reassurances that she would send a car to bring her up to London and remain at her side every minute of the first-class rail journey on the Eurostar. A five-star hotel would be booked for the night, and the meeting over lunch would take place the next day. Even Marion had been drawn into the argument, finally asserting that Iris really was not your average ninety-one-year-old lady, had never been average at any age and still had plenty of the old get-up-and-go.

Whatever anyone else thought, it was immaterial. Iris was resolute. If Laurent de Fayols had asked to see her, with Anna there as part of the deal, nothing was going to stop her from granting his request that she join them.

'Why can't he come to London?' asked Suzie.

'I don't know. We didn't ask.'

'I want to come with you. I should be there.'

Iris put her hand on her daughter's shoulder, almost the same height as her own. The calm determination on Suzie's face reminded her of Xavier every time she saw that expression. 'I know. I did ask, but he specifically said he wanted to speak to me alone – if I could do it without Anna, I would.'

'It's very odd.'

'It will be fine. You want me to find out what he has to say, don't you?'

The high-speed train across northern France seemed to fly over fields stretched wide and flat under white skies. It was mid-morning, and the carriage was quiet except for a middle-aged couple at the other end and a group of businessmen intent on their own discussion, conducted over four open computers. Even so, they kept their voices down.

'Has he intimated anything about what he has to tell us?' asked Iris.

'No. I got the impression he was not going to say anything until you were there.'

'I see.'

'The police have spoken to him several times, which is as you would expect. He was the reason Ellie went to the island, and she . . . her body . . . was found quite close to his estate. He didn't want to speak to me when I was there, but I left my card in case he changed his mind.'

Iris put her chin on one hand. 'You asked when you came to see me whether the message and the story in Ellie's notebook could be connected to her death. It seems incredible that it could be.'

'But not impossible?'

She had decided that there was no point in obfuscating any longer. 'If it is, then it is a long and complex story, and one that – I have to warn you – I have never managed to unravel myself. Frankly, I had come to terms with not knowing.'

'Either Laurent de Fayols has something to confess – or he too needs to understand something that only you can explain.'

'We'll find out soon enough. It's a question of trust, Miss Lester, isn't it?'

'Please call me Anna. So . . . if this story goes back to the war, it must include your days with SOE. There is currently a great deal of interest in those operations. More and more information is becoming available—'

'With every obituary published in the newspapers.'

'Also being released from archive files.'

'This story may not *be* in the archive files, despite the notes that indicate Ellie's intention to try to find some corroboration there,' said Iris. 'It may involve the unthinkable, perhaps for me, perhaps even for you.'

'I don't understand.'

'How cynical are you, Anna?'

'Not much surprises me.'

'About people, their passions and self-interest, about political movements and government agencies?'

'Very cynical.'

'Good.' Iris reached out and picked up the recording device. 'Condition one. I may be old, but I am still wary. Please turn this off. Now put it where I can see that the red light has gone. You may make notes, of course. Condition two is that you publish nothing without my approval. Is that agreed?'

'That's exactly how I would want to do it.'

'All right. Now I will do everything I can to help you.'

'The story about Xavier in Ellie's notes,' said Anna. 'Am I right in thinking that this must refer to Xavier Descours?'

'I think you must be.'

'You knew him, I take it?'

'Yes,' said Iris. 'I knew him. Clearly, you are familiar with Xavier Descours from the many accounts of the SOE in France. Some of those accounts are admirably perceptive; others bear no relation to reality. There again, elements of them seemed like complete fantasy, until I found out later they were true.' She smiled. 'I was in love with him – but even at the time I only knew a part of him. I accepted that. It was necessary to what we were doing that only certain aspects of one's life were known. But later on, of course, the deceptions and disguises we had used made it doubly hard to discover the truth.'

Anna nodded, made some rapid notes.

'After the war, Xavier did not turn up in Paris with the other agents who survived. Neither did he surface in the south. It had to be assumed that he had either been captured or killed. I did my best to trace him, without success.'

'Surely others were searching for him too?'

'If they were, they kept me in the dark. But you're right, other people were looking for him, and I should imagine some were mightily relieved when he would not be found.'

'Explain exactly who you mean.'

Iris sighed. 'The intelligence services, all of them: British, French and what remained of the German. I'm not sure how much you know about the wider picture of the intelligence services, the petty internecine spats between them, what was really going on.'

Anna nodded. 'I've read enough to know that SOE was considered a liability by other services, SIS and MI6. There was little sharing of information. It was possible they were undermined from within the establishment.'

'We all deal in lies – that is the only truth.' That was what he had told her. Perhaps the time had come to put it all on the record.

'I think now,' said Iris carefully, 'that Xavier was not only working for SOE as air movements officer – but that he was working for the British Secret Intelligence Service, and that his real boss was there. I once ran into him unexpectedly, at a Tangmere fog party over at Bignor. He pretended we had never met, and I couldn't understand at the time. But it was clear he knew Bignor Manor and the Bertrams well. The Bertrams were MI6, not SOE.'

She cleared her throat.

'This sounds outrageous, but it is just possible that the whole of F Section was being used as a blind while the real intelligence work went on at SIS or MI6 – and that the decision to sacrifice the Paris agents and the Prosper network was made at the highest level.'

Anna stopped writing. 'I've heard that theory, of course, but consigned it to the conspiracy file.'

'I said, "just possible". SIS ran a network of deniable agents – expatriate businessmen, mostly, who had been operating on the Continent for years before the war. Xavier's profile – the wireless component company, the international contacts – it all fits much better with SIS than SOE.'

'Where does that leave you?'

'A very good question,' said Iris. 'If it's true, then he was probably using me to keep tabs on what was going on inside SOE.'

It was not a happy thought, and the first time she had ever admitted it to anyone but Nancy.

'Don't imagine I was completely naive,' said Iris. 'I was young, but I had become involved in matters of national security – I was pragmatic. I thought his interest in me was probably motivated by some . . . favour I could do for him. Either that or the simple fact that it was easier for him to be with me than to find another woman who might complicate further an already complex life. Apart from everything else, he was a married man.'

'But you did try to find out the truth about him, after the war.'

'The powers that were didn't take me seriously,' said Iris. 'Miss Acton thought that because I was in love with him, my judgement was impaired. Why was it so hard for them to accept that I needed to know the end of the story, precisely because I had been in love with him? I wanted to know the truth, not to bend it, as those who were covering their backs were doing. And I had to be so careful, not only out of consideration for Miles, but for Xavier's wife as well. He would never have wanted me to upset her, nor would I have wanted to. That would have been cruel, and I never intended to be unkind. I was very lonely, for a long time.'

*

Laurent de Fayols was waiting for them at Le Train Bleu. How had he known it was one restaurant in Paris that always reminded her of the war and its networks? Above the jostling concourse of the Gare de Lyon, it was a time capsule, pure belle époque: all gilded mirrors, brass fittings and white linen, a vast cathedral to the glories of rail travel and dining a hundred years ago; above were the wall and ceiling paintings of Mediterranean destinations depicted in sun-drenched, flower-strewn whimsy: Toulon, Marseille, Nice, Montpellier, Perpignan, Cassis, Hyères.

Iris thought of all those meetings with Mavis Acton and their French contacts after the war, the leads that seemed to promise solutions, then went nowhere. All those names, all those places.

Laurent was a dapper little man, dressed in a dark suit and tie; his hair was suspiciously brown for a man in his sixties, and the tan could not disguise the shadows under his eyes. A bottle of white burgundy was cooling in a silver bucket on the table.

Introductions over (gracious but awkward), orders efficiently taken (memorised, not written down, by the waiter), Laurent de Fayols seemed nervous as he turned his attention fully to Iris. 'I understand you knew Xavier Descours, madame?'

'I did.'

'How much did you know about his background?' It could have sounded like a brutal question, but his voice was low and sympathetic.

Iris attempted a wry laugh. 'Only what he told me – what he told any of us. That he ran a company making radio and electric components.'

'That's true,' said Laurent. 'It was in Toulon. He made a lot of money out of it before the war. He was known as the Engineer by the Resistance in the south, even though that was not quite right. As for the rest, it seems he did an admirable job of covering his tracks.' He turned to Iris. 'Did you ever know his real name?' he asked gently.

'I did not. If he had been recruited by F Section, I would have known, but not otherwise. We never asked. You have to understand—'

'You could never have asked. I do understand.'

There was a long pause.

'His name was Gabriel de Fayols.'

Iris brought her hand up to her face.

'He was the son of the doctor on Porquerolles. My father's cousin.'

The island boyhood, the deep blue waters he had described to her. It was all falling into place.

'Gabriel?' Anna pulled out a pencil sketch from inside her notepad. 'Is this him?'

Laurent narrowed his eyes, too vain perhaps to find his reading glasses. Iris took the paper from him.

'That's Xavier . . . as I knew him,' said Iris, her glasses already in place. She traced his lovely face with a finger that, like her unreliable legs, no longer seemed to belong to her but to the elderly stranger who had usurped her body. 'Where did you get this?' she asked the journalist, irritated that this was the first time she was seeing it.

'It's a photocopy,' said Anna. 'The original is in Ellie's notebook. Didn't you see it?'

Iris had not.

'The sketch was in there,' said Anna. 'In the blank pages at the back, as if she opened the book at random and made the drawing. She wrote the name Gabriel underneath and dated it June the seventh.'

'I don't understand.'

Anna was sharp, you had to credit her. 'It implies that Ellie found out about Xavier – and exactly who he was – only three days before . . . she was found dead. The last day she was seen alive, the seventh of June,' she said, turning to Laurent. 'Remind me where Ellie was that day – in the garden on your estate?'

'No, she wasn't there – that is, not during the day. She came to the Domaine in the early evening.'

'So how did she find out about Xavier?' cut in Iris.

Laurent looked distinctly uncomfortable. For the first time the suave exterior cracked. 'It must have been from my mother. I believe you knew her too, a long time ago, Mrs Corbin.'

The waiter brought tiny rounds of foie gras with quince jelly and thin curls of toast. Iris was not sure she would be able to eat any of it.

'Your mother? Who is your mother, monsieur?'

'*Was* my mother—' He checked himself. 'I regret to say she died two weeks ago.'

None of them seemed able to eat. Anna seemed flushed with excitement at the unravelling tale, though perhaps it was the wine; Iris was uneasy, sensing that more was about to be revealed. Anna had brought her notepad to the dining table, a lack of manners that Iris overlooked in the interests of accuracy. Her mind seemed incapable of concentration, sliding dangerously between the present and past fears.

Laurent de Fayols was intent on establishing certain events.

'Mrs Corbin, I understand that you worked for SOE during the war,' he said. 'And that a woman called Mavis Acton was ruthlessly protective of the young women sent secretly to France.'

'Many people admired her,' said Iris, gauging from his tone that he was not one of them.

'My mother despised her.'

'Mavis Acton was not universally liked,' said Iris. 'She recruited women into the SOE as agents in France, when no women had ever been to war in quite this way before. She coordinated their missions and worked tirelessly after the war to trace the final movements of those who did not return. She pursued this with great determination – against much opposition from those who were equally determined to wrap the recent past in convenient silence.'

The speech came out pat; she had used it before. There was much to admire about Miss Acton, and Iris would always defend her if she was asked her opinion of her former boss, having learned to keep her real thoughts to herself. 'Strong meat, that was Miss Acton,' she would say. 'A powerful personality. Well, one had to be, didn't one?' Mavis Acton could have done no more; after the war she traced all her girls; it was a great pity that Iris never managed to persuade her to keep going on the men.

'You kept in touch with her when the war was over, though?'

'Yes. I was her assistant.'

'You were good friends?'

'I wouldn't go that far. We worked well together.'

Iris had seen Miss Acton only once more after their tea at Fortnum and Mason. The occasion was Colonel Tyndale's funeral in London. It wasn't so much respects Iris was paying as hoping to run into one last chance, among the assembled signatories of the Official Secrets Act, of finishing what she had started all those years before. But Miss Acton appraised her beadily, as she always did, and made it clear that her inquiries had met a dead end a long time ago. She lit one of her strong cigarettes and dismissed her with the same hand that tossed the match.

That had angered Iris. If anyone should have understood how she felt, it should have been Mavis Acton, but the woman displayed a perplexing lack of empathy. She showed no heart, though clearly she had one.

'I have not been successful in finding many declassified papers about the SOE women,' Laurent was saying.

'I gather there are very few actual SOE papers that survive,' said Anna. 'They were due to be handed over to the Foreign Office, but there was a fire.'

'A most convenient fire.'

He straightened his cutlery, smoothed his napkin. This was a man who would have loved to light up a cigarette as he always used to in restaurants, thought Iris. He caught her gaze.

'How did you feel when you first found out that the real agents were being held and manipulated by the Gestapo, and that SOE was unknowingly making arrangements directly with the Nazis?' he asked Iris.

How do we feel? Always the same question, so lazily emotive. It was invariably asked on the radio and television, when it was facts that were required. It wasn't possible to begin to express how they felt, and certainly not for public consumption. Iris pushed away the hundred thoughts that threatened to engulf her. Had she made a mistake in coming? But she of all people knew that if you never took the risk, you might never find what you were seeking.

'I was furious. It was the first time I realised that those in charge were not taking women like me seriously.'

They had known – or rather some of them had known. The women who would gather to gossip in the ladies' cloakroom on the half-landing at Norgeby House knew, but they spoke only among themselves and said nothing to their superiors, because they were not supposed to know.

'It seems astonishing, but the position of women in society has changed so radically from those times that it barely seems possible now,' said Iris. 'But back then, that was the way it was.'

'And it was left to two women to track down what had happened to the SOE women who never returned.'

'That's right. It was important to know what happened, for the families of those who never came back, even if the conclusion of the story was harrowing . . . For some it was many years spent not knowing, and in some ways that was worse . . .'

'But you were satisfied that you managed to find out exactly what happened to each of them?' asked Laurent.

'Yes.'

Anna said nothing, but listened intently.

'Does the name Rose mean anything to you?'

Iris straightened her back and gave up the pretence of eating. She put down her knife and fork. 'It was a code name.'

'What happened to Rose after you sent her over here?'

'She was arrested while working as a wireless operator in Paris. She spent some months being held by the Gestapo, before being helped to escape, along with another woman agent.'

It was strange, thought Iris, how readily these facts came

300

to her, when the details of other, far more recent memories remained frustratingly elusive. 'The other woman, Thérèse, was flown back to London. Rose went south with Xavier. It was he who had organised the escape. We had only sporadic contact with her after that.'

'Why was that?'

'By 1944 the RAF and the American Air Force had bases in North Africa, Corsica and Italy – most of the Resistance communications from the South of France would have been to those bases. It seems that she was arrested again. There is circumstantial evidence, unproven, that she was sent to Natzweiler, a concentration camp in Alsace. She died there, executed as a spy.'

They were silent for a few moments.

'No,' said Laurent. 'Rose didn't die in a concentration camp.'

Iris frowned. 'What are you saying – that you knew her?'

'Rose was my mother.'

Laurent summoned the waiter to pour more wine, and said, 'Rose was still working as a wireless operator for the man known as Xavier Descours in August 1944. He was the man who habitually took enormous risks . . . and she kept pace with him. But he abandoned her, left her to fend for herself after a big air operation upcountry in Provence went wrong. She was told to lie low and wait for him, but Xavier never came.

'She was arrested by the Gestapo as she was making for the plateau above Manosque where the lavender grows. She had a transmitter – she would have been shot as a spy immediately at any other time – but the Germans knew the tide was turning. It was only days before the Liberation began. They took her north to Digne, threatened her, trying to get as much information as they could, but they didn't kill her. That night, a young German officer helped her get away. Maybe he just wanted to save his own skin at the end, but he saved her too.'

'Why did she never make contact with us in London?' asked Iris. Too many disconcerting thoughts were chasing themselves. Too many questions.

'She felt she had been badly let down. Perhaps she had no reason to go back. She took the chance to make another life for herself here.'

'Many people did, after the war. For a long time, I thought that was what Xavier must have done.'

'It always comes back to Xavier. Do you know, Mrs Corbin, that it was because of Xavier that my mother met my father? Charles de Fayols – code name Maurice – was one of those who had helped her escape the first time in Paris.

'Rose met Charles again sometime after she fled Digne. She must have gone south, possibly still looking for Xavier. Anyway, she married Charles in 1946 and became chatelaine of the Domaine de Fayols. I was born two years later. She kept the name Rose, by the way – she liked it. Rose was who she had become.'

Iris pressed her fingers into the linen tablecloth. Her ears buzzed, and too many competing memories derailed her train of thought. Rose and her neat crochet work in the bathroom at Orchard Court, her silence and self-possession, the history that was still being rewritten.

'She must have told Ellie the story in the notebook,' said Iris eventually. 'But . . . how did Rose know who Ellie was, her connection to me?'

'A newspaper article, I gather.'

'It would explain the "message for Iris",' pointed out Anna.

'I suppose so.'

Iris tried to stay calm. Too many different strands of thought still coiled in her head. When had Xavier given Rose the message intended for her? Just before he had disappeared? She had never conveyed it to Iris, so was it possible that she had only recently passed it on via Ellie? It seemed absurd, but it was the only logical explanation.

Laurent twisted the stem of his wineglass. 'It was my mother who persuaded me to try an English designer for the memorial garden – one designer in particular. Ellie Brooke. She was most insistent. I thought it was a good idea, something that would make her happy. She was not well, had not been well for

302

many years . . . she was unpredictable . . . there were episodes of mania . . .'

Unexpectedly, Laurent reached over the table for Iris's hand. 'I will tell you now what I think happened to your granddaughter – including what I did not tell the police while Rose was still alive.'

Time slipped as she looked into his eyes, so like Xavier's brown eyes.

'On that last evening, my mother was very unwell. All day she had been in the grip of a manic episode. She was convinced that she was seeing Xavier, that he had come for her at last. She was screaming and shouting that she was in greater danger than before, and that Jeanne and I were the ones who had to help her now.

'She was so disturbed, gibbering about evil spirits, cowering in her chair and crying that we did as she demanded, and called a priest who agreed to come and bless the house. Whether it was a real exorcism or not, the incense and the chanting calmed her for a while. She slept that afternoon, a relief to all of us.

'Not long after six o'clock, Ellie arrived to collect her phone. I'm sorry to say that my mother had picked it up and kept it when Ellie left it in the library where she had been working on plans for the garden. We were having an aperitif, Ellie and I, when Rose appeared. She seemed improved at first, but then her mood reverted. She pulled out an old pistol. I had no idea she possessed such a weapon. Perhaps it had been my father's. Even when she took it out, I thought it was not real, that it could not possibly be loaded, or even if she pulled the trigger, it would never fire. But it did. I was moving carefully behind her, intending to take it from her, but then the gun went off. She fired twice. One bullet hit the floor and the other hit a case of butterfly specimens. The glass shattered, but no real damage was done. Ellie ran. Not just for cover, but out the doors and down the terrace steps into the garden.

'I have to tell you, she was nervous, agitated that evening. Different from the confident young woman I first met. I tried to go after her, to reassure her that she was in no danger. My mother dropped the gun as soon as it went off – she was in shock, and Jeanne was calming her.

'But Ellie – she ran fast. A storm was breaking. It was raining. It is steep on the path down to the *calanque*, and slippery underfoot. You can trip over stones. It's hard enough to walk down in daylight, but on a wet night . . . to fall . . .'

Iris stared up at the murals of coastal scenes set high on the walls, at the painted ceiling, hearing the noise of the lunch service and the conversations over white-clad tables, holding her emotions in check. Carefully, she brought her eyes back to Laurent. It was only then that she became aware of the men sitting at the next table. She recognised the way they held themselves as they sat, alert and quietly powerful. Laurent de Fayols had not come alone to tell her; he had been escorted by the police.

'There is one last thing you need to know. As I say, Rose was aggressive as well as unbalanced, and it was difficult. It was only after she died that we found out why. The myrtle liqueur she drank was contaminated with datura – a spectacular but highly toxic plant. The effects can be hallucinogenic. Perhaps her illness as well as her behaviour that night can be partly attributed to her regular consumption of it.

'It was analysed after she died, and was found to contain an alarming quantity of datura poison. I don't believe she added it deliberately, or at least, I don't want to believe that. That part of the garden had been neglected over the years, and the datura had spread in an extraordinary way alongside the myrtle hedge, threading itself through the place where she always picked the berries. The liqueur killed her, in the end. I'm sorry to say that it's possible that Ellie drank some too.'

Laurent looked ashamed. 'I am so very sorry. Until my mother told me exactly who Ellie was, I knew nothing of these old connections. Rose was hardly making sense by the end, but when she was lucid, it was all about the past. When she was dying, she kept repeating the name Xavier, and that I should tell you she was sorry. I gave her my word.'

There was a long pause, then he turned to the men at the next table. 'Lieutenant Meunier? Thank you. It is done.'

Suzie was waiting when the Eurostar came in at Ebbsfleet. Nearly seventy years old now – unbelievable! – but she looked younger. The family resemblance was strong, particularly the height and the dark blond hair, now artificially ash blond, but she had her father's perceptive brown eyes and olive skin. Even now, her face was not lined as deeply as that of most English women her age, but Ellie's death had snatched away the natural exuberance and self-confidence.

She drove Iris home, concentrating on the road, changing lanes in her usual deft manner, asking no questions, aware of the undercurrents as ever; waiting until the time was right, insisting that Iris rest for a few hours when they arrived back at The Beeches.

Late in the afternoon they shared a pot of tea in companionable silence, Iris both marvelling at her daughter's composure and concerned by it.

'Come with me,' said Iris. 'Let's take a turn round the garden.'

They went on patrol among the leaves and petals, dealing with any unwanted developments, the sooner the better. In the kitchen garden a few tomatoes had ripened, and Iris pulled them off the vine for Marion to serve with supper. Waste not, want not.

Iris told Suzie all she could, choosing her words carefully, about Rose de Fayols, and how Ellie had died. How Laurent and his loyal housekeeper had initially covered up his mother's part in the story that night, reasoning that the firing of the gun could have been construed as attempted murder, that nothing could have been changed by the admission except for further deterioration of her mental state. After the old lady died, how the pathology examination had led to an investigation of the chemical content of the liqueur she had always made.

'Datura can have dangerous effects. Anna did some research on her computer while we were waiting for the train.

305

It can be a soporific as well as a hallucinogen. In certain circumstances, it can induce drug trips that recur for as long as a week after taking it. Sometimes it's enough to smell it, or even to think about it, to prompt the brain to return to an altered state. It's not the physical effects like a racing heart that can kill, it's the illusion that a path goes straight ahead – or that the sea is a garden where you can lie down for a little sleep . . .'

They sat on a bench by the apple tree, noticing the dry leaves and the first copper curls on the grass. They would never know exactly what had happened to Ellie on that last night. So they talked of her vitality and the enormity of the space she had left; her drive and determination.

'What she wrote about Xavier in her notebook,' said Suzie. Too late now to call him by any other name. 'Do you think that could have been what happened to him – that his plane went down over the sea?'

So many years, so many variations of the dream: the aircraft beating through the dark, the climb into the night sky. The seas of cloud, the controls that did not respond, the start of the strangest journey the pilot has ever made. The horror that habitually jolted her awake: the plane rushing onwards into the emptiness; no time left, only the beginning of time; then, afterwards, the closeness she felt to him as she lay there in the dark. Once, she felt a tender kiss on her cheek that was so warm and real she felt his presence there at her bedside. A long time ago, but vividly recalled despite having convinced herself that she must still have been on the cusp of dreaming and waking.

'I have the feeling it is.'

'And the sketch of Gabriel – what was that, a copy of a photograph?'

'Laurent swore he'd never seen one like that, and there was nothing even similar in his mother's effects.'

'From a book, maybe.'

'The policeman Meunier said something odd,' said Iris. 'Ellie had consistently claimed there was another witness to the suicide on the ferry, but this man could not be traced. The sketch matched the description she gave of him.'

'Perhaps she was trying to be helpful, getting it down on paper the way she knew best.'

'She wrote the name Gabriel underneath,' persisted Iris.

Suzie stared out over the fields. 'You understood the message, didn't you?'

'I understood.'

'Will you tell me what it means?'

Iris considered. *Thy word is a lantern unto my feet: and a light unto my path.* She could not explain the miracle by which the message had been delivered, nor the picture; it was no stranger than the dreams but equally unthinkable to articulate. *I have never loved as I have loved you. You have been my light in this darkness.* Those were Xavier's words in their final seconds together before he flew back to France. She had never been sure, and now she was.

'He did love me,' said Iris to their daughter. 'And he would have loved you, too.'

Epilogue

In the early hours of 4 November, 2013, a small fishing boat working the waters south-east of Marseille caught a twisted piece of metal the size and shape of a shark. The boat pitched in heavy rain and darkness as the two fishermen cursed the rips in the net caused by the object's sharp teeth, and were about to cast it overboard when one of them noticed a flash of silver as he eased away the torn netting and removed knots of weed.

Closer inspection revealed a band of steel imprinted with a serial number. They took a GPS reading of the exact location. The metal shark returned to the harbour with the catch of *rascasse*, *girelle* and snapper.

The barnacled metal was identified as part of the engine casing of a Caudron C270 Luciole, a light aircraft built in the 1930s and known as a Firefly. The remains of the plane were recovered by marine archaeologists from a deep shelf in the seabed between the Golden Isles and Marseille, where it had landed, presumably sometime during the Second World War, to judge from the explosive damage to the undercarriage.

Author's Note

The area of Provence I know well was a stronghold of the French Resistance during the Second World War. It's the kind of country place where people are proud of their past and stories are passed down in everyday conversation. The Resistance years are spoken about – to British, American and Canadian visitors in particular – with considerable pride and a sense of shared history.

I have long been intrigued by the stories of clandestine wartime airdrops of arms and agents by the RAF, and the secret landings of planes while France was under Nazi occupation. When I began research into these air operations, I discovered a poignant detail in the memoir *We Landed by Moonlight* written by one of the RAF's finest Special Operations pilots, Group Captain Hugh Verity. On the makeshift landing strip known as 'Spitfire', close to the great lavender fields of Sault, a Dakota was flown in carrying key French personnel just before the Allied landings on the south coast in August 1944. The plan was to land, drop the passengers and collect a group of escaping American airmen who had been on the run. But the Dakota was too heavy, and the makeshift runway too short. On the run-up to take-off, the undercarriage snagged on a wide strip of lavender that had been planted to disguise the length of the field from the ever-vigilant occupying authorities. Before another attempt could be made, some of the US airmen had to disembark. Promises were made to come back for them the following night, but it was too late. The botched operation had taken too long, the Nazis and their Vichy enforcers, the Milice, were now aware of it and took brutal reprisals. The next night, the Dakota returned but there was no Resistance reception team waiting to signal it down.

That strip of lavender was the spark behind *The Lavender Field*, the first section to be written. It features the blind perfume maker Marthe Lincel, who appears in *The Lantern*, and tells the story of what really happened to her during the war when she began her apprenticeship with the perfume factory in Manosque. I should say here that the main characters and stories in my book are all fictional, even if they are underpinned by real events.

For the historical aspects of the book, visits to the Musée de la Résistance at Fontaine de Vaucluse, the Musée de la Lavande, Coustellet and the working lavender distilleries at Les Coulets in Rustrel and Les Agnels at Buoux were invaluable.

More insights came from the work of the French poet René Char. In his secret wartime life, Char was a highly respected and successful Resistance leader, code-named Alexandre, based in the village of Céreste at the eastern end of the Luberon valley. The account by his friend Georges-Louis Roux, *La Nuit d'Alexandre*, is full of local detail. It might have seemed, to eagle-eyed readers who notice these things, that my mention of the trustworthy local policeman Cabot in the story was another thank you to my literary agent Stephanie Cabot (as indeed it was), but the good gendarme Cabot did exist in real life; he was instrumental in recovering some jewels which had been stolen on their way to being sold to buy food supplies, not only for Char and his host family, but for the army of resistants hiding out in the hills for whom 'Capitaine Alexandre' was responsible.

In *A Shadow Life*, another young woman experiences a different aspect of the war. In bomb-blasted, monochrome London, Iris Nightingale works for the SOE, Churchill's Special Operations Executive, formed to sabotage and disrupt behind the lines in occupied France. Iris works behind the scenes, recruiting and preparing the agents for their missions in France, and evaluating their wireless messages from enemy territory.

The starting point for this story was the real-life figure of Vera Atkins, the senior woman officer at SOE's French Section in London (Mavis Acton in this novel). A strong woman who provoked strong reactions, Vera Atkins proved her mettle by her resolute determination to discover what had happened to those SOE agents who did not return after the end of the war, especially the women she had personally recruited. In this, I am indebted to Sarah Helm's brilliant and gripping book, *A Life in Secrets: The Story of Vera Atkins and the Lost Agents of SOE*.

The character of Xavier Descours was suggested by the real Henri Déricourt, a pilot (in civilian life) and wartime flight liaison officer between the RAF and the French Resistance. After the war, there were many questions about his true motives, and whether he was a double agent for the Nazis, or triple agent working for the Allies. It is a question that remains unresolved.

Quite by chance, I acquired another source of information and background when I was asked to join a charity fundraiser, Authors for Autistica, an auction in which authors pledge to include the name of the winning bidder in a new book – or a name of the winner's choice. I was invited to talk about the auction on BBC Radio Kent, which I duly did, mentioning that I was researching the RAF/SOE 'Moondrop' flights taking special agents into France. I didn't give any details or character names. I had only just begun writing, though the synopsis was complete at that stage. I already had a character called Nancy, a young woman who was working for the RAF. How strange, then, that the request of the winning bidder was to give a character the name of Nancy Bateman, his mother, who was ninety-one and had worked in the wartime RAF . . . I spoke with the family, and was sent a photo of their Nancy. I have woven some of her experiences into the novel.

The air museum at what was once RAF Tangmere in Sussex was a fascinating source of information. The clandestine flights carrying passengers into and out of occupied France operated from this airfield, and there is a large collection of artefacts from the era. The curator David Coxon and his staff took evident pleasure in telling me of ghostly sightings at quiet times, especially around the doomed Battle of Britain plane that has been reassembled from fragments dug out of its crash site. They also told me a tale of the disembodied arm clad in wartime RAF uniform that politely opens doors for the cleaners early in the morning ...

The late Barbara Bertram is another real-life character, the indefatigable hostess at Bignor Manor. I have not changed her name, and drew on many of the details in her memoir, *French Resistance in Sussex*.

The island of Porquerolles, off the southern French coast, is the setting for the first story, *The Sea Garden*. Early in the summer season, before the main crowds have arrived, the diving by the cliffs and *calanques* is spectacular, and there are shipwrecks on the seabed that are now home to fish and corals.

Some of the wrecks date from the Second World War, when the island was occupied first by the Italians and then by the Germans. The only Frenchmen allowed to remain were the lighthouse keeper, Monsieur Pellegrino, and his assistant. In 1944, Pellegrino saved the lighthouse from destruction by the Germans, an act of heroism for which he earned the French Cross of the Legion of Honour. Although I proceeded to take liberties with the historical facts in this story, this was the starting point for this section.

What links these stories is the theme of communication, or the lack of it: coded wireless messages; torch signals; lighthouse beams; Braille; the human senses, especially that of smell; information withheld; misinformation; differences in language; symbols. The novel's structure mirrors the oblique connections between underground cells, where security is paramount and the best defence is limited knowledge of the activities of others in the organisation.

Of the very many books I read while researching this one, these are the ones I found most illuminating, and recommend without hesitation to anyone who would like to know more about the true stories that lie behind the fiction.

We Landed by Moonlight, Hugh Verity (revised edition, Crécy Publishing, 2000)

Wartime Writings 1939–1944, Antoine de Saint-Exupéry (translation: Harcourt, 1986)

The Resistance, Matthew Cobb (Pocket Books, 2009)

A Life in Secrets: The Story of Vera Atkins and the Lost Agents of SOE, Sarah Helm (Little, Brown, 2005)

Déricourt, The Chequered Spy, Jean Overton Fuller (Michael Russell, 1989)

French Resistance in Sussex, Barbara Bertram (Barnworks Publishing, 1995)

Black Lysander, John Nesbitt-Dufort (Whydown Books, 2002)

Moondrop to Gascony, Anne-Marie Walters (revised edition, Moho Books, 2009)

Résistance et Occupation (1940–44), Midi Rouge, ombres et lumières.3, Robert Mencherini, (Éditions Syllepse, 2011)

The Death of Jean Moulin, Biography of a Ghost, Patrick Marnham (John Murray, 2000)

La nuit d'Alexandre: René Char, l'Ami et le résistant, Georges-Louis Roux (Grasset, 2003)

Feuillets d'Hypnos, René Char (Folioplus, 2007)

René Char, Selected Poems, edited by Mary Ann Caws and Tina Jolas (New Directions, 1992)

Acknowledgements

My sincere thanks go to my literary agent Araminta Whitley, assisted by Sophie Hughes at Lucas Alexander Whitley in London, and the dream Orion team of Kate Mills, Susan Lamb and Juliet Ewers, along with Candace Blakely, Rachel Eley, Gaby Young, Alex Young and cover artist Sarah Perkins; my US literary agent Stephanie Cabot, and Will Roberts, Rebecca Gardner, Anna Worrall and Ellen Goodson at The Gernert Company in New York; and to my wonderful editor Jennifer Barth, David Watson, Miranda Ottewell and Katherine Beitner at HarperCollins, New York.

Louise Cummins, garden designer at the award-winning Garden Makers in London and Surrey, generously gave me the inside track on design and landscaping projects for a private client and the Chelsea Flower Show.

Peter Coxon, curator of Tangmere military aircraft museum, and the magnificent group of enthusiasts there could not have been more helpful. I would also like to thank Philippa Stannard and Authors for Autistica for the introduction to her mother, Nancy Bateman, and the use of her name along with some of her RAF memories.

My own mother, Joy Lawrenson, was, as ever, my valued first reader, along with Robert Rees.

Gardens of Delight

KT-376-719

Also by Erica James

A Breath of Fresh Air
Time for a Change
Airs and Graces
A Sense of Belonging
Act of Faith
The Holiday
Precious Time
Hidden Talents
Paradise House
Love and Devotion

Gardens of Delight

ERICA JAMES

ORION

Copyright © Erica James 2005

The moral right of Erica James to be identified as
the author of this work has been asserted by her in accordance
with the Copyright, Designs and Patents Act, 1988.

All rights reserved. No part of this publication may be
reproduced, stored in a retrieval system, or transmitted, in any
form or by any means, electronic, mechanical, photocopying,
recording or otherwise, without the prior permission of the
copyright owner.

First published in Great Britain in 2005 by Orion Books,
an imprint of the Orion Publishing Group,
5 Upper St Martin's Lane, London WC2H 9EA

1 3 5 7 9 10 8 6 4 2

All characters in this publication are fictitious
and any resemblance to real persons, living or dead,
is purely coincidental.

A CIP catalogue record for this book is
available from the British Library.

ISBN (hardback) 0 75285 639 1
ISBN (trade paperback) 0 75286 897 7

Typeset by Deltatype Ltd, Birkenhead, Merseyside
Printed and bound in Great Britain by
Clays Ltd, St Ives plc

ROTHERHAM LIBRARY &
INFORMATION SERVICES

AF

B52038636X

GIFT

www.orionbooks.co.uk

To Edward and Samuel,
the best things I ever grew!

Acknowledgements

Once again I am indebted to the Morris family for their help and expertise. Thank you, Lis, for your time and know-how.

I'm enormously grateful to my two wonderful Italian guides – Monica Luraschi and Rita Annunziata – who gave me an invaluable insight into the area of Lake Como, in particular, Villa Balbienello, Villa Carlotta and Bellagio. *Tante grazie!*

Thanks too, to the staff – especially Francesco and his excellent team – at the Grand Hotel Villa Serbelloni, who made my stay so enjoyable.

And though I must be her worst student, *ever*, thank Elian Toye Southerden for trying to teach me to speak Italian. *Grazie mille!*

A very special thank you to Bev Hadwen for being so intuitive and patient, and providing me with my very own garden of delight.

Many thanks to John and Lesley Jenkins at Wollerton Old Hall Garden in Shropshire for providing the ideal setting for a scene in my book and for being such an inspiration to so many.

As always, a rousing cheer of thanks to everyone at Orion. Mr Keates should be singled out (if only for his taste in shirts and appalling jokes!), and so should Mr Taylor for hitting forty (ah, ah!). Thanks of course, to Kate Mills, Genevieve Pegg, Jon Wood, Jo Carpenter, Ian Diment, Jo Dawson, Emma Noble, Debbie in the art department, (great job, Debbie, on the new jackets!) and last but not least, Susan, who cracks the whip so efficiently. It's been a spectacular year!

A garden is a delight to the eye,
and a solace to the soil;
it soothes angry passions,
and produces that pleasure which
is a foretaste of Paradise

SA'DI (1184–1291)

SWANMERE

Chapter One

Lucy's last job of the day was to water the plants. It was something she always enjoyed doing, not only because it brought out her nurturing instinct, but also because of the sense of power it gave her. Wielding a hose was a bit like holding a loaded gun – nobody, if they knew what was good for them, was going to argue with her.

This sense of power first came to her at the age of fifteen, when she was put in charge of the ramshackle greenhouse at school while their biology teacher, a nervous, stammering man who had been in the middle of explaining seed germination, was called to the telephone in the secretary's office. His parting words, as he scurried away – his pregnant wife was two weeks beyond her due date – were 'D-d-d-don't touch anything while I'm g-g-gone.' He might just as well have said, 'F-f-f-feel free to t-t-t-trash the place.' The first act of subordination came in the form of a group of Lucy's classmates unbuttoning their shirts, tying them to expose their midriffs and going outside to lie on the sun-parched grass whilst sharing a cigarette. That left Lucy and the rest of the class looking for some way to amuse themselves. Having already spied the neatly coiled hose and tap, it was only a short leap to a masterstroke of an idea. Within minutes she had everyone positioning the empty plastic and clay flowerpots on the bench at the furthest end of the greenhouse into a makeshift coconut shy and was taking aim with the hose. The first clay pot to take a direct hit from the blast of water fell to the floor with a clattering smash. Another followed suit, then another. *Aha! Take that!* Shouts of encouragement urged her on and she turned up the power on the hose and gave the plastic pots a real beating, sending them flying in all directions: they ricocheted off the glass panes like enormous bullets. Most spectacular of all was the clay pot that shot straight through a pane of glass in an explosion that would have passed

3

muster as an action movie stunt. Way to go! She hadn't had so much fun in ages.

The girls who had been lying on the grass sunning themselves now came to see what all the noise was about. Their snooty, superior expressions brought out the worst in Lucy and without a thought for the consequences she turned the hose on the gang of girls whom she had never liked because they were always going on about their fathers and their generous wallets and how awful it must be for Lucy because her father didn't care about her any more. Not true. It was she who didn't care about him any more! The powerful jet of water soon took the sneering look off their faces; as they staggered backwards and everyone around Lucy let out awed gasps, Lucy felt an exhilarating surge of triumph. She was invincible! She was all-powerful! She was the business!

She was also up to her neck in trouble. The teacher who had been hastily despatched to replace Mr Forbes appeared in the doorway of the greenhouse to find a scene of what she later described to the headmistress – somewhat over-dramatically in Lucy's opinion – as Armageddon.

'Mrs Gray,' the headmistress had said, her face as prim as a tightly shut pine cone, when Lucy's mother was summoned the following day to account for her daughter's behaviour, 'this sort of hooliganism is simply not tolerated at our school. I'm afraid, as of now, I'm going to suspend Lucy for the rest of this term in the hope that it will give her time to consider what she's done and, more importantly, give her time to consider her future.'

'Her future?' Lucy's mother had repeated. 'What do you mean by that exactly?'

'I'm suggesting you might want to consider the possibility that the environment we foster here at Fair Lawns is not best suited to Lucy.'

The message was loud and clear. Lucy Gray, with her sloppy attitude to lessons, her insolence, her general indifference to authority and her unique approach to truth and honesty – '*Do I have to remind you, Mrs Gray, about that incident with the forged exeat note?*' – wasn't welcome to return to Fair Lawns.

'I absolutely do not know why I bother,' Fiona Gray had said when they were driving away with Lucy's hastily packed trunk wedged into the boot of the car. 'Why do you keep doing this to me?'

After leaning out of the window and waving goodbye to her

friends, who had gathered at the end of the chestnut-tree-lined drive, Lucy settled back into her seat and toed off her gruesome school shoes. No need for those any more. With a quickness of hand her mother didn't notice, she dropped them out of the window. Her equally hideous grey socks met the same fate. She put her bare feet up on the dashboard. 'Enlighten me, Mum: what do I keep doing to you?'

'Embarrassing me. Shaming me. As though your father hasn't put me through enough. What did I ever do wrong? What did I do to deserve such treatment? And where on earth will I find a school that will take you on when they discover what you're like?'

'You could always take time out of your frantic round of shopping and social engagements and home-school me.' The look of horror on her mother's face was priceless. 'Face it, Mum. I'm a problem child.'

'You're a feral child, more like it. The wonder is that you lasted as long as you did at Fair Lawns. It's all your father's fault. But who gets the blame? Yes, that's right. Me! It's me who's accused of being a bad parent, when all I've done is my best. Do put your feet down. Try and act like a lady even if you can't actually be one.' She sighed heavily. 'People have no idea how hard it is to be a good mother to a difficult child.'

It was a rant with which Lucy was all too familiar. Poor old Mum; she took everything so personally, as if every disaster in the world was a way to get at her and sully her good name.

Fourteen years on, and her mother still occasionally acted as if Lucy's every waking moment was spent trying to invent some new way to vex and annoy her. No matter that Lucy was all grown up now, that she had celebrated her twenty-ninth birthday last week and was the epitome of good behaviour. To her long-suffering mother, she was the same obnoxious teenager who had made her life a living hell. Maturity had taught her that she probably had given her mother an unnecessarily hard time in the aftermath of her parents' divorce, and while she had more or less made her peace with Fiona, she had not done the same with her father. As far as she was concerned, he no longer existed. Nothing he could say or do would put right the harm he'd done to their family.

Although relations between Lucy and her mother were much improved these days, they had their differences, namely that Lucy *still* didn't have a proper job. Working in a garden centre did not, according to the Fiona Gray Career Handbook, constitute a proper career path. A going-nowhere garden path was what it was. As if her mother had ever had a career! Following hot on the heels of this complaint was another old standby: 'Why, oh why, do you *still* insist on dressing so unimaginatively? People will mistake you for an asylum seeker. It's such a crime not to make the most of yourself, darling. You're not a lesbian, are you?' But Fiona's biggest concern was that Lucy showed not the slightest inclination to settle down and marry. 'If you leave it too late all the best men will have been taken and you'll be left to scrape the marriage barrel and end up with a dud.'

Whenever this topic was raised, Lucy wanted to point out that marrying young hadn't saved Fiona from acquiring a dud husband – a man who had strayed into the arms of an Italian woman many years his junior – but she knew better than to stir up her mother on the legendary subject of Marcus Gray. As it was, his presence, or rather his absence, had carved out a top-billing, all-starring role in their lives without giving him extra house room.

Ironically, despite her urgings for Lucy to find herself 'a nice young man,' Fiona hadn't been in any hurry to rush to the altar for a second time herself. But then twelve months ago along came Charles Carrington, a warm-hearted, kindly soul, and a one-time confirmed bachelor. He was possibly the bravest man alive, having the guts to take on Lucy's mother. Or maybe he just had the thickest skin. In a whirlwind romance, he whisked Fiona away from the village of Swanmere in south Cheshire to his splendid country house in Northamptonshire, leaving Lucy all alone. 'You don't mind, do you, Lucy?' her mother had asked when she was showing off the antique diamond ring Charles had given her and was explaining how their lives were going to change. As though it wasn't obvious.

'Mum, I'm a big girl now. You go and have fun. You've earned it.'

'Why don't you come and live with us? I'm sure Charles wouldn't object.'

'The last thing Charles needs is a step-daughter mooching about the place. Besides, my job and friends are all here.'

This, not surprisingly, elicited a dismissive click of the tongue. The extent of Fiona's disapproval for Lucy's job at Meadowlands Garden Centre was matched by her dislike of Lucy's friend Orlando. She held him personally responsible for holding her daughter back.

Orlando Fielding was Lucy's best friend and for five months now he'd been her lodger. He was a year younger than her and was her boss's son. They'd met when she was sixteen and had applied for a job working weekends and school holidays at his dad's garden centre. Orlando, who had been working part-time for his father since he was old enough to lift bags of compost and use a hose responsibly, had been instructed to show her the ropes, and they'd soon struck up a firm friendship. People often mistook them for brother and sister, they got on so well.

Much to his father's disappointment, Orlando had turned his back on the family business and with a degree in botany already under his belt, he then did a one-year diploma course in garden design and recently started his own business as a garden designer. But money was tight and rather than see Orlando suffer the ignominy of having to move back home with his parents, Lucy said he could move in with her now that her mother wasn't around.

By the time she'd finished watering, nearly everyone else had gone home and the place felt deserted. She tidied away the hose, checked with Hugh there wasn't anything else he needed her to do, hoisted her small rucksack onto her back and climbed onto her bike. As she pedalled home in the evening sun, she wondered if she dare risk wearing shorts for work tomorrow. The weather forecast had given warm and sunny; as it would be the first day of May, and a bank holiday weekend to boot, she knew she would be rushed off her feet and warning customers till she was blue in the face that it was too early to put bedding plants out yet, that there was still a danger of ground frost. There was just no telling some people.

Before long she was freewheeling downhill towards the village of Swanmere, her long blonde hair streaming like ribbons behind her, her skin tingling from the wind on her cheeks. For the sheer hell of it, she stuck out her legs either side of the bike and relished the moment, basking in the delicious feeling that all was right in the world. After months of wind, rain and gloomy skies, spring was finally here. The hawthorn hedgerows were vibrant with unfurling leaves of lettuce-green freshness, and the fields of rape over to her right, where the sun was slowly dropping in the sky, were in full glorious bloom, the dazzling yellow flowers so bright they were almost luminous.

Hearing a car bearing down on her from behind, Lucy put her feet back on the pedals and steered closer to the grassy verge that was peppered with daisies and dandelions. In a matter of days, there would be cow parsley springing up too. The car – a large black Mercedes with a personalized number plate – swept smoothly past her. They were two a penny round here. Swanmere was one of Cheshire's wealthiest hotspots, where old money mixed with new.

She and her mother had moved here from London when she was sixteen – when her parents' divorce had finally been settled. Before everything had gone wrong, Lucy's father had run his own advertising agency. They'd lived in Fulham and the way Lucy remembered it, it had been a perfect life. But then he'd ruined everything by having an affair. Stinging with hurt and fury, Fiona had employed the smartest divorce lawyer she could get her hands on and fought hard. She got the house and a considerable chunk of the business that Marcus decided to sell so that he could go and live in Italy with the Tiramisu Tart, as Lucy had always referred to his mistress. Fiona had grown up in Cheshire – her parents still lived there at the time, though they were both dead now – and she had sold the house in Fulham and bought Church View, a beautiful Grade II listed Queen Anne townhouse in the heart of the historic village of Swanmere, where pretty black-and-white half-timbered cottages abounded. Often it felt like they lived on a film set. Some years ago, the village had actually been used in a costume drama for the BBC. Everyone had wanted to get in on the act and be an extra.

Lucy couldn't think of anywhere she would rather live. When Charlie Carrington had appeared on the scene she had known a moment of dread and panic – would this mean she would have to move out of Church View? Would her mother want to sell it and expect Lucy to find a place of her own? She was, after all, at an age when she should at the very least be thinking about leaving home. Her fears were blessedly short-lived. Fiona had no intention of selling Church View, and amazingly went as far as to say that it was home to Lucy for as long as she wanted it to be. Being in love had turned Fiona into a magnanimous woman Lucy hardly knew. She even grudgingly agreed that Orlando could move in.

Orlando had proved to be the perfect housemate – he was clean, tidy and an excellent cook. What's more he wasn't one of those ghastly men who hogged the remote control then hid it down the back of the sofa when there was something girly on that she wanted to watch. In fact, the only thing they ever disagreed about was gardening, in particular the amount of time devoted to makeover gardening on the television. She was as big a purist as the next RHS member, but whereas she was prepared to let people have the choice of wrecking their gardens with decking and faddy ornamentation, Orlando was not. He held Alan Titchmarsh personally responsible for everything that was cheap and tacky in suburban gardens throughout the land. Orlando said that gardening was like porn: it was best left to professionals.

She pedalled along the main street of the village, passing the shops that, with the exception of Clayton's upmarket wine shop, were all closed for the day. Noticing Mac Truman coming out of Clayton's with a wrapped bottle tucked under his arm, she rang her bell and gave him a wave. He smiled and waved back at her. She liked Mac. And his nephew. Conrad Truman was officially the most eligible and hottest bachelor in the village. It was the combination of being drop dead gorgeous and a widower that did it. Nothing sexier than a heartbroken good-looking man, was the general consensus of opinion.

She pedalled on, passing the chemist, the newsagent and post office, and then just opposite the church she turned left into a cobbled lane scarcely more than a car's width. She jumped off her bike, pushed open a wrought iron gate and stepped into the calming oasis of a small courtyard garden. Home sweet home.

She let herself in at the back door and after calling out to Orlando and getting no response – she could hear the shower running upstairs – she checked the mail that he'd left in a tidy pile on the kitchen table. Humming happily to herself, she flicked through the pile to see if there was anything of interest and stopped when she saw an envelope with an airmail sticker on it. Closer inspection revealed an Italian stamp and postmark. Judging from the thickness of it, and the timing of its arrival, it was a late birthday card from her father.

She dropped it into the bin without a second thought.

Chapter Two

Helen wondered if the haughty, bucket-faced woman sitting opposite her would ever leave.

With her fearsomely bracing outdoorsy manner and sturdy old-moneyed vowels, Olivia Marchwood, sixty-something-spinster-of-this-parish, was just the kind of woman Helen usually took pains to avoid. And as the woman ground her not inconsiderable behind into the cream sofa, she gave off an air of permanency that made Helen want to fetch a crowbar and lever her off. The disagreeable guest had called on the off chance that Mrs Madison-Tyler might be at home (not 'in' but 'at home'), more than an hour ago and was showing absolutely no sign of bringing her visit to an end. She was clearly one of those insensitive, high-handed women who, even if Helen threw open the front door, wouldn't take the hint that it was time to leave.

The thrust of her visit was clearly to suss out the new owners of the Old Rectory – 'Two weeks have passed since you moved in and I thought it high time I personally welcomed you to Swanmere' – and to bring to Helen's attention the variety of good works, societies, clubs and groups on offer in the village. All of which Helen made a mental note to steer well clear of, especially the ones (underscored and in upper case) for which her visitor was on the committee. She had never been one of those hearty join-ing-in kind of people, preferring always to be on the periphery of what was going on. Experience had taught her it was the best way to keep out of trouble. Hunter said it was why she'd put off marriage for as long as she had. It was one of her husband's more perceptive observations. They had been married for six months now, the wedding coming a week after her forty-fifth birthday, and following seven months of determined pursuit on Hunter's part. 'I'm not a man who changes his mind or makes compromises,' he'd told her five weeks after they'd met, 'so you might just as well get on and choose yourself a wedding dress.'

'Mm ... a man who doesn't change his mind, eh?' she'd mused. 'How do you account for the two ex-wives?'

'Ouch,' he'd said, 'that's a little below the belt, don't you think?'

'Not really. After all, I ought to know what I'm getting into.' Although she had a pretty good idea exactly what she was getting into. 'Would it be anything to do with you being unfaithful to them?'

'Yes,' he'd said baldly. 'Are you sure this is a subject you want to pursue?'

Rightly or wrongly, Helen never did, and she married Hunter – sixteen years her senior – committed to the belief that the future was more important than the past.

She'd met him at a charity fundraising lunch for the local hospice in Crantsford. As one of its main sponsors, he'd given a brief but entertaining speech and it didn't slip Helen's notice that he was the focus of much attention from the predominantly female audience in the hotel dining room. Not overly tall, he was nonetheless a good-looking, charismatic man and Helen didn't doubt for a second that he knew the effect he had on people. He reminded her a little of one of her favourite actors, Michael Kitchen. When he'd stepped down from the podium and resumed his seat at a nearby table, Helen's friend Annabel, who had invited her to the lunch and was a patron of the hospice, had whispered in her ear, 'I'm going to introduce you when the gabbing's all over.'

'And why would you do that?'

'Because,' Annabel tilted her head meaningfully in Hunter's direction and lowered her voice yet further, 'he asked me to.'

'When?'

'When you went to the cloakroom. He came over and asked very specifically who you were.'

But Annabel hadn't needed to play the role of mediator; just as soon as the lunch was officially over, Hunter introduced himself and insisted on buying Helen a drink at the bar, forcibly leading her away from her friend. 'I suppose you find this masterful approach usually gets you what you want,' she'd said, bristling with furious indignation.

'Never fails. What would you like to drink?'

'Nothing. I'm not thirsty.'

'Me neither. Let's go somewhere we can talk.'

When she refused, he said, 'Please don't be churlish.' Once more, and against her will, she was being propelled across the crowded room. Outside in the hotel gardens he said, 'Will you have dinner with me?'

'No thank you.' She started to walk away. What a revoltingly arrogant man he was.

'Please,' he called out, but not moving to follow her. 'Have dinner with me so I can prove to you I'm being serious.'

She stopped and turned to face him. 'Serious about what?'

'About you.'

'I think you must be confusing me with someone else. A figment of your imagination, perhaps.' And with that, she did walk away. And kept on walking until she was in the hotel car park and getting into her car. She was just putting the key into the ignition when her mobile trilled. Ever since her grandmother had suffered a fall and broken a hip eighteen months ago, an accident from which the old lady had never fully recovered, Helen was permanently on tenterhooks in case it was more bad news. She put the mobile to her ear and heard a voice say, 'If not dinner, how about lunch?'

'What the ... ? How on earth did you know my number?' She looked up and saw him standing on the steps of the hotel; he was staring straight at her.

'Don't be cross but I made your friend Annabel give it to me. I told her it was a matter of life or death.'

'It'll be your death if you carry on hounding me like this.'

He laughed. An easy, assured laugh. 'You don't mean that. Come on, how much would it cost you to spend an hour or two with me over lunch?'

'I don't *do* lunch.'

'You did today.'

'That was a favour to Annabel.'

'Then how about doing me a favour? Maybe you'd feel happier just having a drink. Surely that wouldn't hurt too much.'

Thinking it would be easier to give in and let him have his own way, she agreed to meet him for a drink the following week. Chances were, he was one of those men for whom once the chase was over, boredom kicked in and he'd leave her alone. But she'd misjudged him and from then on, he romanced her hard. He bombarded her with gifts and flowers and even a new car after she'd turned up late for dinner one night because her ageing Peugeot had refused to start and she'd had to call out a taxi. Six months after that charity lunch, whilst on holiday in Egypt and flying over the Nile in a specially arranged hot-air-balloon flight, he presented her with a glass of champagne and an emerald ring, just as dawn was breaking. 'Helen Madison,' he'd said, 'I've pursued you every way I know how; will you stop prevaricating and agree to marry me?' Glancing at the two young Egyptians who were piloting the balloon and trying to pretend they weren't present at so intimate a moment, she said, 'How can I refuse when you put it so romantically?'

The marriage took place in a private chapel in the grounds of a country hotel in north Yorkshire. The only guests present were Annabel and her husband, and Hunter's oldest and closest friend, Frank Maguire. The one person Helen had wanted to be present couldn't make it – her only living relative: her precious grandmother, Emma Madison.

With a jolt, Helen realized that Olivia Marchwood had interrupted the tortuous flow of her monologue with a question. She was asking Helen if she knew what she was going to do with the garden at the Old Rectory. 'It shouldn't be neglected for much longer,' Olivia Marchwood was saying. 'A shame poor old Alice couldn't take it with her. Are you a gardener, Mrs Madison-Tyler? I'd advise against too much change too soon. You should live with a garden for a couple of seasons before pulling anything up.'

Seized with the urge to say she fully intended to rip out every single shrub and bush and then torch what was left, Helen said, 'Please, call me Helen. And regrettably I'm not much of a gardener. What with work, and ...' she cast her eyes round the drawing room at the carpet and fabric samples she had been sorting through before being interrupted, 'still having so much to do on the house, the garden will have to wait a little while, I'm afraid.'

'I'd be more than willing to offer you any help and advice. As I mentioned earlier, I am the chairwoman of the Garden Club. Perhaps you ought to think of joining us. We meet once a month and have always been extremely lucky with our visiting speakers. Last month we had a talk about—'

'Goodness, is that the time?' interrupted Helen as the clock on the mantelpiece conveniently chimed the hour – it was seven o'clock. Time for decisive action. 'I'm dreadfully sorry, but I have a couple of important phone calls I really must make.' She got to her feet.

Thankfully – *oh, miraculously!* – the other woman rose from the sofa and before she could embark on another lengthy discourse, Helen was steering her towards the drawing-room door, the hall, and finally the front door. Olivia Marchwood's parting words were: 'Remember what I said about getting stuck into the social scene here in Swanmere. Do you think your husband would be interested in putting himself forward for the PCC? I've just resigned after many years of service, so there is a vacancy. I told the vicar that I'd had enough, and that he could jolly well do without me from now on. I dread to think how he will cope.'

Trusting that the vicar would be quietly celebrating this stroke of good fortune, Helen waved her guest off and closed the door. She shook her head at the thought of Hunter being on the Parish Church Council and went through to the kitchen.

Like most of the rooms at the Old Rectory, this had been gutted and thoroughly brought up to date. The messiest of the work, at Hunter's insistence, had been carried out before they'd moved in; there were just two bedrooms and one bathroom left to decorate. The kitchen, when they first saw it, had been a cramped, poky affair and had boasted little more than the absolute basics, probably installed during the seventies. There had been a rusting free-standing cooker, cracked linoleum tiles, a stainless steel sink, a couple of cupboards and marble-effect Formica worktops that were burned and scarred. Now, after some judicious knocking through, it was a much larger and lighter room with cream-painted cupboards, granite work surfaces, a deep ceramic sink and the biggest Aga Helen had ever set eyes on. She had wanted a range-style cooker, but Hunter had said it was an Aga or nothing. 'But they're so expensive,' she'd argued. 'They cost nearly as much as a small house.'

'How many times do I have to tell you, Helen, money isn't a problem?'

She unlocked the French windows and stepped outside. Standing against the stone balustrade she took several deep breaths as if cleansing herself of Olivia Marchwood. It was a glorious evening. Bathed in a golden light from the dipping sun, the garden, even in its bedraggled state, filled Helen with immense joy. How she loved it! The lawns were more like meadows with dandelions and daisies sprinkled throughout. There were rhododendrons on the cusp of flowering, their blushing buds ready to burst. Unpruned bushes sagged wearily out of the borders. Bluebells shimmered beneath shiny-leafed magnolias. Beyond all this, beyond the copse of silver birch and hawthorn trees and a sweep of chestnuts she could see the clock tower of the Norman church in the distance. She had discovered since moving in that Tuesday was bell-ringing practice night. She imagined balmy summer nights when the air would resonate with the sound of bells. She hadn't had time yet to explore, but she knew there was a twisting path that led down to the church from a gate at the bottom of the garden.

Despite what she'd told Olivia Marchwood, she wasn't as inept a gardener as she'd implied. Her enthusiasm outweighed any real skill, but she knew enough to know that this garden was going to need a lot of tender loving care to bring it back to its former glory. She would have to find a gardener; it was too large to manage on her own. She had no idea how much gardeners charged, never having employed one before, but Hunter had told her to pay whatever it took. 'No bean counting,' he'd teased her. 'Just get the best man for the job.'

Her 'bean counting' as Hunter called it was a habit she was trying to kick, but it wasn't easy. Scrimping and saving came as naturally to her as breathing. For the last six years she had run her own travel company, specializing in cultural tours of the British Isles and Europe. Whilst it had adequately kept the wolf from the door, it had never been a big money spinner, and with a dependent grandmother to take care of, her finances were always stretched. To make matters worse, 9/11 had hit her badly. A large percentage of her business had been aimed at American tourists and when they stopped travelling, money became tighter still.

Then, to top it all, it became all too apparent that her grandmother needed more care. Helen had done her best to look after her, but they both knew that a nursing home was the only realistic solution. Emma's modest house was sold and the money invested so that the interest would pay for the kind of nursing home Helen felt confident would look after her grandmother. But the nursing home turned out to be a disaster and Emma's mental and physical health deteriorated fast. Seeing the sadness – and fear – in Emma's face when she left her after each visit tore at Helen's heart. If this wasn't enough, the investment Helen had made with the proceeds from her grandmother's house sale wasn't the sound proposition she'd been led to believe it would be and given the current climate of poor returns, she was losing money faster than water leaking from a sieve. It was a catastrophe. All she had left was her home, a modest three-bedroom terraced house with a tiny sheltered garden. And then, out of the blue, along came Hunter and her life was changed.

Only once they were seriously involved did Helen grasp the extent of his wealth. The arrival of a brand new Mercedes coupé outside her house with a pink ribbon tied to the bonnet gave her cause to review matters. Before then, having listened to Annabel's tales and seen him in the society pages of *Cheshire Life*, as well as an article about him being North West Businessman of the Year, she'd thought that he was what one would call 'reasonably well-off'. When she realized she'd wildly underestimated his bank balance, she refused to see him any more. When he pressed her for a reason, she admitted that she didn't feel comfortable with the disparity in their financial situation. 'People will think I'm only involved with you because of your money,' she told him.

'And people will say I'm involved with you because you're young and look bloody good on my arm. Come on, Helen, sod what anyone else thinks. So what if I'm a millionaire many times over; I want to share my success with you. Is that so wrong? Should I be penalized for knowing my arse from my elbow?'

Knowing his arse from his elbow had given him the ability to set up his own warehousing and storage business in his twenties, offering fully secure storage for domestic and office use, and then to go on expanding it until it became the largest storage company in the UK. Meanwhile, with his son Clancy doing the everyday running of the business, he'd moved into the overseas property market, in particular holiday apartments and second homes in the Caribbean, Florida, Spain, and more recently Dubai. He was quoted in the business pages of *The Times* recently as saying, "I don't believe in the meek inheriting the earth. If it was left to the meek, the world would be in an untenable sorry state."

It was a typically brash no-nonsense comment from Hunter. But there was the other side to him, too: the abundantly generous side. Without his financial support, the hospice in Crantsford would undoubtedly close down. His engagement present to Helen, along with the emerald ring he'd surprised her with in the hot-air balloon, and which she always wore slightly self-consciously, was something that meant more to Helen than anything else. He paid for Emma to be moved to the best private nursing home money could buy. It meant she didn't have to sell her little house in Crantsford. Hunter had told her to get rid of it, saying that she didn't need it any more. But reluctant to part with her old home, she'd rented it out to a young professional couple.

Helen knew that she would spend the rest of her life thanking Hunter for what he'd done. Nothing she ever did would come close to repaying the debt she felt she owed him.

It didn't take her long to realize that this was exactly how Hunter liked things to be.

Chapter Three

More than a week had passed since Orlando had poked around in the kitchen bin and retrieved the card that Lucy's father had sent. It was now hidden in the chest of drawers in his bedroom; he was waiting for the right moment to give it to Lucy. He was going to insist that just once, she open a piece of correspondence from Marcus Gray.

Having known Lucy for as long as he had, Orlando knew the reasons why she refused to have anything to do with her father, and even though he'd never met the man, he couldn't help feeling slightly sorry for him; every birthday, every Christmas, without fail, he would send Lucy a card and it always ended up in the bin. It was anybody's guess what else was inside the envelope – a letter, or a cheque perhaps – but Lucy's reaction was always the same: she flatly refused to have anything to do with it. She said her father only kept up the charade out of a sense of guilt and duty. For all Orlando knew, she might be right, but he had inherited his own father's view on life, and that was always to try and give people the benefit of the doubt.

In all other respects, Lucy was one of the most positive and forgiving people he knew, and the most fun to be around, but get her on the subject of her parents' divorce and she became a different person. It was as if a huge shutter came crashing down whenever her father was referred to. Orlando blamed Fiona Gray. Or Fiona Carrington as she was now. She was the exception to his rule about cutting people a bit of slack; he just couldn't do it with her. A more selfish and shallow woman he had never met, but then he was completely biased. Lucy's mother defined everyone and everything as either 'suitable' or 'thoroughly unsuitable'. As a 'mere gardener', he was definitely in the latter category. According to Lucy, in the months that followed her father's departure her mother fell apart and at the age of fourteen it was down to Lucy to hold things together. She rarely spoke of that time, but odds on that was when the die was cast and Lucy learned to hate her father.

It was getting late. Orlando drained the mug of tea his prospective client had made for him and rallied his thoughts to the job in hand – a small, brand new (the builders of the development were still on site), un-turfed plot of garden that the owners wanted him to turn into something they'd seen on the television. He hoped to convince them that the concept of hard geometric lines and a raised decking area with bright blue pots of ornamental grasses was totally passé. Very last century, in fact. What he was going to propose was gentle curving lines, beds that were naturalistic in shape and form rather than stiff and ornamental. For the sake of getting the job, he would have to compromise, but only so far; he had his integrity to think of. Lucy said his integrity was all very well, but if it meant he starved to death, then what was the point? 'The point, Luce,' he would say, 'is that I'm serious about what I do. I want the gardens I design to mean something. To be something lasting.'

For all her teasing, he knew that Lucy understood him. And the fact that she charged him next to nothing in rent was something for which he would be for ever grateful. When he'd first moved in with her and occasionally had trouble finding the rent because the amount of work he was getting was so pitiful, she'd told him it didn't matter. Occasionally, when he couldn't get the manpower he needed to get a job done, she would pitch in on her days off. Just recently the design work had picked up, especially the kind he was currently doing – the easy bread-and-butter work. A new development of houses was being built on the edge of the village of Swanmere, and after dropping leaflets through the letterboxes of the newly occupied properties, he'd garnered himself a steady flow of business. A healthy number of people were keen to pay him to create something individual for them, rather than leave it to an unimaginative job-lot outfit chosen by the builder. The challenge was to steer customers away from the fads they saw on their television screens which often encouraged inappropriate planting. Gardens were a living and breathing entity; they had to be treated with reverence and intelligence.

Reeling in his tape measure, then adding the final measurement to the rough plan he would draw to scale later, he packed away his gear. After promising the prospective client that he'd be in touch in the next day or two, he drove home. He thought again about the birthday card he'd retrieved from the bin and wondered how to go about making Lucy open it. It had crossed his mind to open it himself, to see what sort of message her father had written – if it was nothing more than 'Happy Birthday Lucy,' then he'd chuck it away. If the guy couldn't be bothered to write more than that, then he deserved to be blanked. But what if Marcus Gray was ill? Or dying? Could Lucy live with herself knowing that she'd denied him a last and vital wish to be reconciled? He had no idea if Lucy's mother ever heard from her ex-husband, but if she knew he was ill, keeping it from her daughter was just the kind of thing she'd do.

He was probably letting his imagination get the better of him, and really it was none of his business, as Lucy would be quick to tell him. He could picture her clearly with hands on hips, giving him one of her don't-mess-with-me looks.

The first time he'd laid eyes on her she'd been wearing an expression just like that. With her stripy dyed hair tied up on her head so that she resembled a multi-coloured pineapple, her clumpy shoes and skinny legs, he'd wondered why on earth his father had given her a job, especially when she seemed a bit on the accident-prone side, knocking things over or bumping into people. He was glad Dad had, though, because she was like a breath of fresh air about the place. In those days, just about everyone else who worked at Meadowlands was a million years old.

'I reckon she's just going through a phase,' his father had said when Orlando had asked him about the new part-time member of staff. 'I thought I'd give her the benefit of the doubt. She seems bright enough.' It was a classic example of the Hugh Fielding way of doing things. Before long his father was proved right: Lucy turned out to be a quick and enthusiastic learner, and when she announced that she was quitting school halfway through her A-levels, Orlando's father offered her full-time work and the chance to do a day-release course in horticulture at the nearby college.

It was six-thirty when Orlando let himself in at Church View. A note on the kitchen table told him that Lucy had gone to the allotment. If he didn't have so much work to do, he'd go there himself and see if she needed a hand, or just fancied some company.

Lucy loved being at the allotments. Situated on the brow of a gently sloping hill – the highest point in the village – the views, stretching for miles around of the surrounding countryside, were beautiful. It wasn't only the scenery she liked, or the sense of purpose she always had when she came here, it was the camaraderie of the other allotment users that she enjoyed. Her mother thought it was the most appalling thing she had ever done when Lucy told her she'd applied for and had been granted a plot. Fiona associated it with the working classes, with the cloth-cap-wearing folk whose threadbare trousers were held in place by a piece of string. It was no place for a well brought up daughter of hers. How wrong could she be! There were two teachers, a doctor, and a magistrate who had plots up here, all of them women.

As she opened the gate and walked along the well-kept path to the area of land that was owned by the Church of England and leased for a peppercorn rent, Lucy breathed in the sweet-smelling fragrance of freshly mown grass. The creamy-white flowers in the hawthorn added to the sweetness in the air. Once she'd emerged from the path she could see that the usual suspects were out in force and making the most of the warm, dry weather. Tending their immaculate vegetable plots were the Old Boys as Lucy called them: Joe, Bill and Dan. They were always there waiting to ambush her. Bill was the youngest of the trio at a mere seventy-four years old, and was the first to notice her. He called to the others. 'Here she is, lads, our very own Queen of the May.'

Joe and Dan came over. 'Where's lover-boy, then?' asked Joe, who was a bristly chinned, sprightly seventy-eight-year-old.

It was a long standing joke between the Old Boys that Lucy and Orlando were an item. No matter how vociferously she denied their fantasies, they refused to believe her.

'He wasn't back from work when I left the house,' she said, playing along with them, 'but I left him a note, so don't get any ideas about coming onto me like you normally do because he could appear any moment and sort you out.'

Joe laughed. 'I always thought he looked the nasty jealous sort.'

Dan, the quietest member of their gang, and the most senior at the age of eighty-one, smiled at Lucy. 'Need a hand with anything?' he asked.

'Thanks, Dan, I'll let you know.' Dan was her favourite of the bunch. He was the first friend she made when she moved to Swanmere. She'd been skiving off school one afternoon and for somewhere to go she had wandered up to the allotments. He'd got talking to her and before she knew what she was doing, she had a spade in her hand and was helping him to dig in some foul-smelling manure. When they'd finished the job he showed her how to peg down strawberry runners to create new plants and to check for grey mould on the fruit. He explained why he put straw under the plants – to keep plenty of air moving around them so the fungus wouldn't spread – and invited her to come back in a few days' time when the strawberries would be perfect for eating. It was Dan who'd got her hooked on gardening. And it was Dan, with no family of his own, and in his quiet unassuming way, who took her under his wing and kept her from going off the rails.

Leaving the Old Boys to get back to their digging and hoeing, Lucy walked further along the path, following it round to the right, until she came to her plot. She walked round it for a moment to scrutinize it for uninvited guests. On the face of it, the precautionary measures she'd taken were working – the solution of water and washing-up liquid she'd sprayed onto the surrounding areas had got rid of the aphids; the canes with bottles on top that rattled in the wind were doing an excellent job of frightening the rabbits away, and the circles of stone chippings, together with the dishes of beer, had kept the slimy enemies away from their juicy targets. Nature was a wonderful thing, but it certainly benefited from a helping hand now and then.

Unlocking the small wooden shed that Orlando had helped her build, she frowned at the uncomfortable reminder her words had given her. How many times had her mother said much the same thing to her? 'If only you'd make more of yourself, darling,' she used to say. On one occasion she'd said, 'Nature has given you a pretty enough face, but with a little more effort on your part, you could be beautiful.'

'But I don't want to be beautiful!' Lucy had shouted back at her. 'Not ever!'

'Nonsense. Of course you do. Every girl wants to be beautiful.'

'Well, I don't! I hate the thought of it. And I hate you.'

'No you don't.'

'Stop telling me what I do and don't think. I hate, hate, hate you!'

It was one of those awful arguments that grew out of nothing but kept on spiralling until Lucy had finally exploded. 'What's more I wish I didn't have to live with you,' she'd screamed. 'I wish I could live with Dad!'

Lucy had often seen her mother angry – her tantrums easily matched her own – but what happened next took her by surprise. Fiona slapped her face. Not once, but twice. Crack. Crack. When she came at her again a third time, Lucy dodged out of her way, but Fiona wasn't finished. 'Go and live with him, then!' she screeched. 'If he's so bloody marvellous, pack your bags and go to him. That's if he wants you. Which, of course, he doesn't!'

The memory was so sharp and so painful, Lucy could feel the stinging hurt of it rise up within her. Sometimes it was difficult to know who had caused her more pain, her father or her mother.

Chapter Four

Conrad Truman was trying to work. But it was one of those days that seemed destined to be peppered with petty disturbances guaranteed to break his concentration. It was the downside of working from home.

His first interruption had been in the form of his cleaner, Evie, coming over to his office to tell him the vacuum cleaner wasn't working properly. 'You really should invest in a Dyson, Mr Truman,' she'd told him and had then gone into elaborate detail about the merits of such a device. From there she went on to remind him that she wouldn't be in next week. 'I'm off to Llandudno to stay with my sister in her guest house. Beautiful, it is. Right down by the esplanade. Lovely views of the sea. Just what I need after the time I've had lately.' Much as he depended on Evie Hawkins to keep the house running smoothly for him and his uncle, he often wondered if the effort expended on listening to her updates was worth it. Every week there was always some new drama to recount to him – last week it had been her husband's refusal to let her have their bedroom decorated pink, and the week before that it was her trip to the dentist which had resulted in an allergic reaction to the anaesthetic injection. Whilst he had every sympathy when it came to visits to the dentist – he was the biggest coward going when it came to the high-pitched whirr of a drill – he wished she'd get the hint that he had work to do.

When she had eventually returned to the house to pour yet more scorn and loathing on his humble domestic appliances, it had been the constant ringing of the telephone that interrupted him. Then Mac had come stomping up the stairs to his office, demanding to know what the hell was going on with the post: why hadn't it been delivered yet? When his uncle was in one of his cantankerous moods – 'Where are my glasses? Who's moved my book? Has that bloody awful woman been tidying my room again?' – all

Conrad could do was bury his head in his work.

At the sound of barking he took off his glasses and went to look out of the open window. Down in the garden Mac's faithful old dachshund, Fritz, was chasing a squawking blackbird across the lawn. Mac then came into view with a roll of netting in one hand and a bunch of canes in the other. 'Shut up, Fritz!' he roared. 'Any more of that racket from you and I'll toss you into a bin bag and take you to the tip.'

This isn't how my life was supposed to be, Conrad thought.

It was, of late, an increasingly regular thought. How had he ended up in this state – forty-nine years old and living with his curmudgeonly uncle and a German sausage dog? This was definitely not how he'd imagined his life.

When Mac had suffered a stroke three years ago, Conrad hadn't thought twice about offering his home for Mac to recuperate in when his stay in hospital came to an end. It took a while, but fortunately his uncle had made a good recovery, and his only remaining problem – apart from controlling his temper – was with his balance. But it was the knowledge that the chances of Mac suffering a second stroke were so worryingly high that had Conrad suggesting his uncle sell his house in Cobham and live permanently with him in Cheshire. 'It's the most sensible thing to do,' he'd told Mac, who was then seventy-five. 'I have plenty of space here, so it's not as if we'd be living on top of each other.' Conrad didn't underestimate the wrench Mac suffered in selling his rambling old cottage in Surrey – after years of globetrotting, it had been his home for nearly twenty years – and he endeavoured to make the transition as easy as possible for his uncle.

But for all the grumbling and disagreements, Conrad didn't regret the decision he'd made. His sister Susan, who lived in Hertfordshire, said he was a saint for what he was doing, but Conrad didn't think so. The way he saw it, Mac had played an enormously important role in his life – from childhood through to adulthood – and this was his way of thanking him. Mac had become an active member of the community in Swanmere, frequently sticking his oar in to whatever cause or event took his fancy. He was a keen gardener and Conrad had to admit he enjoyed the fruits of his uncle's efforts. With help from Orlando when it came to the heavy digging work, he'd transformed what had been an ordinary bushy, grassy kind of garden (that was the extent of Conrad's horticultural know-how) into something really quite pleasant. The herbaceous borders were Mac's pride and joy, as were the fruit and vegetable plots that provided them with a good supply of beans, broccoli, courgettes, cabbages, potatoes and carrots. Conrad was conscious, though, that his uncle took longer to do things these days. He was also easily distracted; he'd start one job then move onto another without finishing the first. Frustration usually fuelled Mac's temper and Conrad could appreciate how infuriating it must be for his uncle that his once hugely alert brain was slowing down and diminishing the man he'd been. But there was something else affecting Mac. Ever since Alice Wykeham had died last Christmas he had been morose and out of sorts. Alice had been a true one-off and her death had left a large hole in Mac's daily routine. Rarely had there been a day when he hadn't been up at the Old Rectory with Alice or she'd been here instructing him on how best to germinate, prune or feed some plant or other. It had been Alice who had piqued Mac's interest in gardening, almost to the point of obsession. He now spent so many hours in the garden, Conrad worried that it was only a matter of time before he found his uncle lying face down on the lawn. There were worse ways to go, he mused. Much worse. He instantly regretted the direction of his thoughts.

Time for a coffee break.

At the far end of his office, behind a partition wall, was a small kitchen. Through a door beyond this was a shower room and what had originally been a bedroom when the outbuildings across the courtyard from the main part of the house had been converted into an annexe by the previous owners. Conrad had never used it for this purpose; instead he had turned it into a mini gym. He had a rowing machine, a treadmill and a going-nowhere bike. By no means was he a fitness fanatic, but sitting at his desk day in, day out, he knew he'd soon pile on the pounds if he didn't take regular exercise. He played tennis now and then, but that was more of a social thing. As Mac frequently pointed out, it was actually the only sociable thing he got up to.

He made himself a cup of filter coffee and went back to his desk. He was halfway through translating a shipping contract from Japanese into English. It was standard stuff, nothing he hadn't seen before, but what with all the interruptions it was taking him longer than normal. He didn't seem able to knuckle down. Perhaps it was the warm spring weather that was distracting him. May was his favourite month of the year. He might not know the first thing about gardening, but he could appreciate the changes going on around him. Trees were suddenly in full leaf, the blossom and bluebells were out, the verges and hedgerows were bursting with growth, and that tree by the back door – the one he could never remember the name of – was the most amazingly vibrant shade of electric blue.

May had been a favourite month for him when he lived in Japan. Whenever he saw cherry blossom he was always reminded of his stay there. The first time he'd seen for himself one of Japan's most enduring symbols – the sakura – had been during his second year at university when he'd been studying contract law in Tokyo. It wasn't his first visit; at the age of sixteen he'd spent a summer in Osaka with his uncle, whose two-year stint with an American bank was coming to an end. Before then Mac had been in Hong Kong, and before that, Frankfurt. During that stay with his uncle, Conrad had been so captivated by the country and by its people, he decided that he would study law with Japanese. This he did and on graduation he landed a job with a law firm in Tokyo. He spent nine very happy years there until made redundant in a corporate bloodbath, forcing him reluctantly back to England where he found a job in London as a legal translator. The work was interesting enough, but life seemed dull in comparison. He missed the richness of his life in Tokyo. Clichéd as it was, he missed the efficiency of everything, from trains that actually arrived on time to the exacting way business was carried out. He missed his friends – the zany fruitcakes with their bizarre sense of humour who dragged him round smoky, ear-splitting *pachinko* parlours, then on to drink in the *Akasaka* district. He missed the painfully courteous elderly couple who lived in the flat above him and taught him to play *shogi* and regularly supplied him with homemade *gyozato* – fried dumplings of minced meat and vegetables – because they didn't think he ate enough. He missed the extraordinary number of festivals that went on; the country's two main religions, Shinto and Buddhism, both got a fair crack of the celebratory whip, and there was always something incomprehensibly weird and wonderful to observe or take part in.

Tempting as it was to jack in London and return to Japan, he stuck it out. Then when he was least expecting it, a week before his thirty-sixth birthday, he fell in love.

He'd never fallen for anyone the way he did for Samantha. Like him she was a legal translator, except her language of choice was

Russian. They met at a legal translators' conference. She was the smart-arse near the front of the morning lecture who kept putting up her hand to ask questions. To everyone's amusement, she was actually asked to leave if she couldn't keep quiet. It was when she walked past Conrad, her head lowered but an unmistakable smirk of amusement on her face, that he noticed her legs. They were perfectly streamlined with exquisitely fine-boned ankles. But what struck him most was that they were completely at odds with the scholarly face – the glasses, the hair loosely tied back, the lack of make-up, and the slightly ill-fitting skirt and boxy jacket. Every inch of her said she didn't give a damn.

During the buffet lunch he found himself seeking her out in the dining hall of the conference centre. Curious, he wanted to know more about her. Which law firm did she work for? Or rather, which law firm was brave enough to employ her? But there was no sign of her. He asked around, did anyone know who the Know-it-All was? His question was met with, 'Oh, God, what a pain she was!' And, 'There's always one, isn't there?'

Lunch came to an end and there was still no sign of Miss Legs. Back in the conference hall, he checked her seat. It was empty. Disappointed he hadn't been able to satisfy his curiosity, he took out his pen, turned to a new page of his notepad and waited for the next speaker to get to his feet.

It was then, when a rippling murmur went around the hall, that he realized that Miss Legs was actually on the stage and adjusting her clip-on microphone. Good God, she was the next speaker. He checked the running order of lecturers. Her name was Dr Samantha Tempest and she ran an international translation firm. He sat back in his seat and waited to see what she had to say.

Plenty, it turned out. She knew her stuff. She was eloquent and erudite and he could quite understand her lack of tolerance towards the earlier speaker, who by contrast had been excruciatingly long-winded and inaccurate on several points. It wasn't long, though, before his concentration wandered and instead of listening he became far more interested in the woman herself. The boxy jacket had been removed, revealing a close-fitting white blouse through which he could make out a pair of surprisingly full breasts and a small waist.

Two hours and another speaker later, during a coffee break, he once again scanned the room for Miss Legs. This time he found her. She was having trouble trying to hold her cup of coffee without spilling it as she repositioned her bag on her shoulder; there was a briefcase on the floor between her feet. 'Do you need a hand?' he asked. Up close he could see why she didn't bother with any make-up. She didn't need to. The bone structure was perfect. So was her complexion.

She looked at him – a questioning, full up and down appraising scan – as though he'd just exposed himself to her. Which in a way, he had. Because from then on, his heart and soul were vulnerably open to her.

Once more his thoughts were disturbed by barking, followed shortly by the sound of Mac's voice. He went to the window.

'I'm going to Norrey's,' Mac called up from the garden. 'I've run out of netting. If I don't cover these seedlings the bloody birds will have the lot. Anything we need while I'm out?'

'You could call in at the delicatessen and get some of their fresh spaghetti for supper tonight if you like.'

'Right you are. And to leave you in peace, I'll take Fritz with me.'

Relieved that his uncle's bad mood had been relatively short-lived, Conrad went back to his desk. Glasses on, he resumed work.

What with all the competition from the out of town DIY stores, it was good to know that there were still hardware stores like Norrey's in business. You could buy anything here: stainless steel teapots, washing lines, sandpaper, varnish, electrical flex, gardening gloves, light bulbs, paint, bird seed, barbecues, hand towels, every conceivable size of screw, coving, padlocks, carpet gripper rods, rat poison, enamel saucepans, cup hooks, draught excluders, and all manner of bits of wood and tools, powered or otherwise. It was the eclectic mix that appealed to Mac, and as he waited his turn to be served, he picked over the basket of cut-price bargains on the counter. A light-up keyring caught his eye. Now how the dickens had he lived to be seventy-eight without needing one of these before? he thought ruefully.

'Yes, Mr Truman, what can I get you?'

That was another plus: the personal touch. Would some spotty, grunting youth in a crudely worded T-shirt know his name? 'I'd like some more of that netting I bought from you yesterday.'

'Certainly, Mr Truman. How much this time?'

'Six yards should do it.' That was another thing he liked about Norrey's; they were still prepared to sell you stuff in imperial measurements.

Ten minutes later he was untying Fritz from the post outside and making his way further up the street to the delicatessen, attached to which was a coffee shop where they sold the best cup of Puerto Rican this side of the Atlantic. If he wasn't in such a hurry to thwart those scavenging birds, he'd buy a paper and while away an hour or two. Perhaps he'd treat himself to a decent cup of coffee tomorrow. With a bit of luck the latest edition of the *English Garden* would arrive in the morning's post. It should have come today by rights, but then what else would you expect from a postal service that was on its last legs?

Everyone had expected him to hate retirement; they'd all been convinced that he wouldn't know what to do with so much free time. He'd soon proved them wrong. Since he'd left the bank he'd had time to indulge himself in all sorts of interesting new hobbies – photography, art appreciation, wine tasting holidays, and watercolour painting. Now it was gardening to which he devoted his time and energy.

For most of his working life he'd rarely lived anywhere longer than three years. He'd led a nomadic existence right up until the final stages of his career, when he'd been moved from Paris to be put in charge of the London office. He'd bought a flat in Hammersmith and a weekend retreat out in the country, and for the first time he'd felt as though he was putting down roots. He'd never married, although he'd wanted to. Oh, yes, he'd have done anything to marry the love of his life, yet it wasn't to be.

But that was all in the past. Which, on some days, seemed to be all he had.

It had been decent of Conrad to take care of him after his stroke, but when Conrad had suggested that he move to Swanmere permanently, he'd been horrified. His whole being had been called into question. To be considered too frail to live on his own was anathema.

'I don't want your charity, Conrad,' he'd told him. 'I'm not a decrepit, dribbling, incontinent old man in need of a handout.'

'Nobody's suggesting you are,' Conrad had replied. 'But look at it from my point of view. If anything happens to you, I want to be first on the scene to get a look at your will.'

'Aha! Now we're getting to it. It always comes down to money.'

'You know me so well.'

And that was the point. Mac did know Conrad well, and that was partially why he'd gone along with him and moved in permanently. Nothing was ever said – they tiptoed around the subject as though it were a sleeping tiger – but he suspected that the boy was lonely. The death of his wife had knocked him for six. He'd all but shut down.

Given that he'd never lived with anyone before, Mac had to admit that the arrangement worked well enough. What he couldn't come to terms with was how badly the stroke had affected him. Waking up in that hospital with a catheter sticking out of him and being told what had happened had been terrifying. His fear could be summed up in one word: old. He was old and he didn't like it one little bit. He did his best to keep alert – use it or lose it – but he knew there were days when he was more absent-minded than others. There were days too when he had trouble remembering the simplest of things. His greatest fear was that he might end up with Alzheimer's and start wandering around Swanmere in his slippers and pyjamas.

To stop his brain from slowly atrophying, he knew it was essential to keep active. The day he gave in to slothfulness he'd be scuppered. He had to keep a routine going, make sure there was always a shape to his day. It was a far cry from how he used to be, the globetrotting, go-getter young blood who, in his time, had managed more people and more money than some governments ever did. Who was this doddery old fool who kept mislaying things, who tore Conrad's head off each time he showed him any kindness?

Oh, God! It was the kindness he couldn't bear! That was why he was always trying to rub the boy up the wrong way. He'd rather spar with him than be treated as a halfwit and have his feebleness magnified. When Conrad showed him an excess of patience, or went the extra mile to accommodate him, it was tantamount to looking him in the eye and saying, 'Just remember, old man; it can only get worse.'

The sad fact was, there was no escaping this ineffable truth. Ever since he'd suffered that bloody stroke he'd been on the slippery slope. He'd never admit it, but when he came out of hospital he'd undergone such a loss of nerve that he'd been only too glad of Conrad's invitation to come and stay. He'd been warned that his confidence would be affected, but he hadn't bargained on losing it altogether.

His friendship with Alice Wykeham had been an important factor in his decision to stay at Conrad's. She'd been a game old thing who'd done more to get him properly back on his feet than any medicine or doctor could have. He missed her terribly. She was the only person with whom he could be honest.

He was almost home when, just as he was rearranging the bundle of netting under his arm, Fritz's lead dropped out of his hand. For some unaccountable reason, the stupid dog took it into his head to make a dash across the road.

Just as a car going much to fast was approaching.

Chapter Five

Back from visiting her grandmother, Helen could hear raised voices coming from the library. That, coupled with the badly parked Porsche on the drive, made her wish she'd stayed out longer. She wasn't in the mood for an encounter with Hunter's second wife, Marcia, and his thoroughly spoiled twenty-year-old daughter, Savannah. She stood for a moment to listen to what they were discussing so heatedly – forewarned was forearmed. From what she could hear, Savannah, in her customary offhand way, was saying that there wasn't anything she could have done, and what did it matter anyway? Nobody was hurt.

'That's the problem with you, you little madam,' muttered Helen under her breath. 'Nothing has any value to you.' She was reminded of the time Savannah smashed an antique perfume bottle that Emma had given Helen when she was eighteen and claimed it wouldn't be a big deal to replace.

With two failed marriages behind him it was only to be expected that Hunter came with an above-average number of complications, namely his ex-wives and his three children. Kim and Clancy (thirty-five and thirty-seven respectively) were from his first marriage to Corinne. All three children had been thoroughly indulged and as a result tended to treat everything as disposable. Clancy was perhaps the least offensive of the bunch. He at least had the same work ethic as his father, and that was something Helen could respect. Idleness she could not. And as far as she could see, Savannah had no intention of ever getting a job, just as her step-sister Kim hadn't. They played at life, expecting every good fortune to fall in their lap. When it didn't, especially in Savannah's case, all hell would break lose.

In contrast, from a very early age all Helen had ever wanted was to be self-sufficient. Her grandmother used to say that she had an iron will, that if she set her mind on a particular course

33

then nothing would deter her from her objective. Travel was her big thing when she was a teenager. She didn't care how she did it, just so long as she could spread her wings and explore. Her most prized possession as a child had been a globe. She had spent hours and hours studying it, slowly turning it, imagining the trips she would one day take. At the age Savannah was now, Helen had been working her way round France picking grapes and waitressing. She hadn't been twiddling her thumbs waiting for Daddy to top up an already obscenely generous monthly allowance.

Hunter's family was the reason they were living at the Old Rectory. Helen had suggested it might be healthier not to live on the doorstep of his ex-wives (whom he fully supported financially) and his children, who all lived in and around Crantsford. 'Fine,' Hunter had said. 'Choose an area you'd like to live in and trawl the estate agents.'

'Just like that?'

'Sure. How else should we go about it?'

That was what she liked about Hunter: his no-nonsense pragmatism. She had expected him to resist the idea. After all, he liked nothing better than to have his family around him, and here she was trying to prise him apart from it. She had felt horribly uncomfortable doing the rounds of the estate agents and asking for properties in the price range Hunter had settled on, but the moment she saw the Old Rectory and its enchanting garden, her heart overruled any squeamish guilt she had been experiencing. Besides, she knew Hunter would love the house. Especially when she told him it had a library.

Still listening in to the conversation going on inside the library, Helen heard Marcia saying that if it was anybody's fault it was that fool of a man who couldn't control his dog. 'What else does he expect if he can't keep the wretched thing on its leash? I've a good mind to sue him. We could have been killed.'

Hunter's voice came next: 'But you're both all right? Savvie, you didn't suffer any whiplash, did you?'

'Nah. I'm okay. Anyone mind if I go and help myself to something to eat? I'm starving.'

Knowing that any second Savannah would fling wide the library door and find her lurking the other side of it, Helen quickly made herself scarce. She timed the banging shut of the front door perfectly with Savannah's appearance in the black-and-white tiled hallway. 'Oh, it's you,' her step-daughter said, as though Helen had no right to be there.

'Hi,' she said as cheerfully as she could. 'How's things?'

A stroppy shrug was all she got for an answer. That and a glinty wink from the sparkly stone hooked through Savannah's navel. She had the smallest, flattest waist Helen had ever seen and it was permanently on display, no matter what the weather. She was an attractive girl with a slight frame and beautifully long straight hair the colour of honey, but like so many girls her age, she wore too much make-up. She hadn't yet learned that less was more, and that a smile would do more for her looks than anything bought over the counter.

Helen watched her slouch off down the hall towards the kitchen, her baggy trousers hanging off her hips and dragging on the floor as she went. It was then that Helen noticed two large suitcases and a ghetto blaster at the foot of the stairs. Wondering what was going on, Helen decided it was time to brave the library. She opened the door and stepped inside.

'Ah, Helen, I thought I heard you.'

Hunter rose from his chair and came round his desk to meet her. He gave her a kiss. Another man would have made do with a discreet peck on the cheek, given that Wife Number Two was looking on with daggers in her eyes, but Hunter wasn't like other men. He kissed her full on the mouth, at the same time hooking his arm through hers and forcing her further into the room.

Marcia, who was nearing her fiftieth birthday but dressed more like a twenty-five year-old, was today sporting a pair of drop-waisted DKNY white jeans with a T-shirt that looked like it might have been designed for a ten-year-old it was so small. It was slashed at the front and revealed a glimpse of cleavage. Her white-blonde hair was cut short and heavily styled with goodness knows how much mousse. Diamante-encrusted sunglasses were perched on the top of her head and icy blue eyes stared back at Helen from an overly tanned face.

'Hello, Marcia,' Helen said, trying to sound friendly and slipping her arm out of Hunter's. She didn't think she would ever get the hang of being comfortable around Hunter's ex-wives. Whilst Marcia seemed to be Corinne's bosom buddy, she felt sure she would never be a member of their gang.

'Helen.' Marcia's tone was chilly. Almost as arctic as her gaze. She reached for her handbag, which had been resting on a pile of papers on Hunter's desk. The papers became dislodged but she ignored the mess she'd made. Instead she said, 'I'll get out of your way now, Hunter. I'll give you a ring when I arrive.'

Out in the kitchen, Savannah was eating a slice of toast with peanut butter. Sitting on the work surface, she was banging her bare feet against the cupboard door, in a foul mood. And not just because her mother was dumping her here with Dad while the decorators moved in at home and she went off to the States to see some old school friend. No, what was really bugging her was that old man and his dog. The way he'd carried on you'd think she'd done it deliberately. She hadn't. It was his fault. Any fool could see that. Even a learner driver like her. He should have held onto that bloody lead properly. When he'd started to cry, everything had got seriously weird and too embarrassing for words. He'd shouted at her. At Mum, too. That was when she'd put her foot to the floor and got the hell out of it. No way was she going to stick around for any more of that.

Realizing she wasn't as hungry as she'd thought she was, she threw the remains of the uneaten toast into the sink, slipped down from the work surface and went to the fridge. She took out an opened carton of orange juice and drank from it, tilting her head back, closing her eyes. An image of the old man cradling his whimpering dog came into her mind. She mistimed a swallow and spluttered juice down her front and onto the floor. 'Oh, sod it!'

While Savannah was upstairs unpacking, Helen and Hunter were having a drink out on the terrace. It was a lovely evening, but Helen was feeling peevishly irritable. It was the extraordinary cavalier attitude with which Savannah's visit had been foisted on her that rankled. Did she have no say in who could stay with them? Okay, the wretched girl was Hunter's daughter, but couldn't he have discussed the matter with her? When she'd put this to him, after he'd taken Savannah's cases upstairs, he'd said, 'I didn't think there was anything to discuss. Would you have said no?'

'Of course not.'

'Then what's all the fuss about?'

And that was an end to the matter. She would have appeared petty to say that a simple act of courtesy on his part might have been appropriate.

Now, as she watched him swirl the ice cubes round in his gin and tonic, she remembered what she'd overheard. 'Were Savannah and Marcia involved in some kind of accident?' she asked. 'I thought I heard you asking them earlier if they were both all right.'

He pulled out the slice of lemon from his gin and tonic and tossed it into the shrubbery. He was a man of habit – he always added a slice of lemon to his drink, and always removed it half-way through drinking it. 'Oh, that. Some man's dog ran out in front of the car while Savannah was driving through the village.'

'Did she hit it?'

'No, thank God.'

'Whose was it?'

'They didn't know. Just said there was an old man on the scene who got upset.'

'What kind of dog was it?'

He frowned. 'How should I know? Is it important?'

'We live here, Hunter. Of course it matters. The owner of the dog must be a neighbour of ours.'

He seemed to consider this. At length he said, 'Marcia mentioned something about it being one of those neither use nor ornament types. Long body scraping the ground, hardly any legs.'

'A corgi?'

'No. Smaller still.'

'A dachshund?'

'Yes, that's it! Clever you.'

Helen took a sip of her wine. 'Do you think it was wise of Marcia to let Savannah drive her car? She's only been learning for a short while. I noticed there weren't any L plates on it, either.'

Hunter swirled the ice round in his glass. 'It's not like you to be so openly critical of Marcia. What's brought this on?'

Helen had promised herself she would never ever criticize or disparage the two women who had gone before her, but in this instance it was nigh-on impossible not to. 'A Porsche with a young, inexperienced driver behind the wheel strikes me as a recipe for disaster. Whoever the parent.'

He swirled the cubes of ice again. 'Fair point. Perhaps I'll buy her a more sensible car. What do you suggest? Or better still, if you're not working tomorrow, why don't you go out with Savvie and choose one together?'

Oh, great! Next time, Helen Madison, keep your big mouth shut!

Madison-Tyler, she corrected herself.

37

In bed that night, after turning out the light, Helen turned onto her side. Hunter took it as an invitation to kiss the back of her neck and to pull her closer. She looked at the luminous hands on the alarm clock: half past midnight. 'Don't you have an early start in the morning?' she said.

'And since when has an early start stopped me?' His hands began to massage her thighs, then moved round to her front, fingers exploring and caressing. She tensed and then relaxed. But fifteen minutes later, after Hunter had cursed and disappeared to the bathroom, she lay in the darkness wondering what she should do. Go to him and risk provoking yet more anger, as had happened the other night, or let him work through it on his own? It's only the third time it's happened, she told herself. It doesn't mean anything. He's probably tired. Having Savannah in the house while they were making love might also be a problem for him.

He eventually reappeared. 'I'm sorry,' was all he said as he pulled the duvet over him, his back to her.

'There's no need to apologize,' she murmured, rolling over to his side of the bed where he lay isolated and rigid with humiliation.

His response was to shift away from her.

Long after he'd fallen asleep, Helen lay watching the curtains swaying at the open window. Tired but too on edge to sleep, she thought of her afternoon; she'd managed to finish work early and had gone to spend a couple of hours at the nursing home with her grandmother. Emma had had the radio on and was sitting at a table by the window overlooking a small patio area and a patch of grass – most of the 'guests', as the patients were called, had their own private space within the grounds of the nursing home. She was methodically cutting out money-off coupons from the selection of magazines Helen had taken in for her last week. 'This one's for soya milk,' she explained to Helen. 'I can't remember; do you like soya milk?'

'Not particularly.'

'Well, I'll cut it out for you anyway. You never know, it might come in handy. It's fifty pence off, so not to be sneezed at. And look, there's one here for tinned salmon. We could have that for our tea tomorrow when you get back from school. I'll make us some sandwiches and cut off the crusts the way you like.'

Helen hated seeing her grandmother in what the medical staff called her 'happily confused' state. With infinite care, she tried to lasso the old lady's brain and drag it back to the here and now. 'Grandma,' she said softly, 'why don't you have a break from those coupons and let me take you for a walk? It's a lovely day. Then later I could show you some photographs of the new house.'

'Oh, no dear, I don't have time. Your grandfather will be home from work soon and I need to tidy the place up.'

There was no rearranging of the time zones and Helen did the only thing she could do: she went with it. Some days it was worse and Emma mistook Helen for her daughter, Daisy. Daisy had been her grandparents' only child, and Helen's mother.

Helen had never known her mother and everything she knew about her had been pieced together through what she'd been told or photographs she'd been shown. The image she had of Daisy was that she'd been sensitive and fragile, a wisp of a girl prone to self-doubt and mood swings. She had been exceptionally bright, but lacking in the kind of social skills that would equip her for everyday life. As a result she had been bullied at school, and it was no surprise that when the first man to pay her any real attention came along, she fell under his spell. She gave up on her plan to go to university, dropped out of school and moved in with him, much to Emma and Gerald's horror; they viewed him as a waster and the very worst influence on their daughter. Because their disapproval was so obvious, Daisy refused to have anything more to do with them. But then, out of the blue, she turned up on their doorstep in tears. She was pregnant and homeless; her boyfriend had kicked her out. Could she come home? Emma and Gerald didn't hesitate. They welcomed her home with open arms. The baby – Helen – was born exactly on time and without complication, but Daisy couldn't connect with it. Every time she looked at the baby in the cot beside her, she cried and cried. Post-natal depression would have been diagnosed these days, but then the condition was ascribed to Daisy's normally anxious and fragile state. 'She'll soon buck up,' was the considered medical opinion. But she didn't. Five months later, after taking their granddaughter for a walk in the park, Emma and Gerald wheeled the pram home and discovered Daisy dead in the bath, her wrists slashed with one of Gerald's razors.

The next morning Hunter went to work without saying goodbye. Silence wasn't the answer, Helen thought as she watched him drive away. They needed to talk. Maybe they needed help.

Downstairs in the kitchen Helen could hear the thump of loud music coming from Savannah's bedroom. She decided it was time to teach her step-daughter a lesson – a lesson in How To Be A Better Person. They would find out whose dog it was Savannah had very nearly run over and then Savannah would apologize. Evie Hawkins would be arriving in a couple of hours, and seeing as she knew everything that went on in the village, Helen would ask her who the man was and where he lived.

Chapter Six

After shutting Fritz in the kitchen, Mac went to answer the door. He stared at the two faces before him and wondered if he should recognize them. The younger of the two women looked vaguely familiar, but who did he know who went to such lengths to look so miserable? It was difficult to imagine how a body that size could cram so much hostility within it. Perhaps they were Jehovah's Witnesses; they usually went round in pairs. Hostility wasn't usually part of their double act; peace and joy was what they peddled.

'Yes,' he said to the woman who had addressed him by his name. She was very attractive. In fact, she was a bit of all right. Mid-forties, he reckoned. Auburn-haired. Peachy skin. Nice long legs. And a stonking great emerald ring on her wedding finger. She was much too poised and elegant for the God Squad. And how did she know his name? 'What do you want?' he demanded.

'I'm Helen Madison-Tyler and this is Savannah, my step-daughter.'

Madison-Tyler. The name rang a bell. 'Be quiet, Fritz!' he yelled over his shoulder towards the kitchen door where he could hear the dog barking and scratching at the paintwork. Conrad would go mad if he caused any more damage. 'Are you collecting for something?' he asked, turning back to the cause of Fritz's excitement. 'Some sponsored event in the village? Fritz! I told you to be quiet!'

'May we come in, Mr Truman? Perhaps your dog might calm down then.'

The cheek of the woman! But hang on, maybe they were professional thieves who talked their way into your house, distracted you by asking for a glass of water and while your back was turned ransacked the place. 'What did you say your name was?' he asked.

'It's about your dog,' the surly young creature said.

He caught the bored impatience in her voice. 'What about my dog?'

'I'm ...' She broke off and looked away. 'I'm sorry I nearly ran it over yesterday,' she muttered. She then twisted round to the auburn-haired woman. 'Satisfied? Can I go now?'

Mac felt the colour rush to his face as recognition dawned and he relived that terrifying moment when Fritz had narrowly missed being killed by this ... by this graceless teenage savage who didn't look like she had a whit of intelligence let alone any manners. He was incensed that she could show up here and pretend she was sorry when clearly she didn't give a damn. If she'd really cared, she would have got out of the car yesterday. But no, she'd just sat there and waited for him to retrieve his bundle of netting that he'd dropped when he'd chased after Fritz. Unbelievably, she'd then roared off down the road.

'Savannah!' the other woman hissed. 'We're not leaving until you show Mr Truman the courtesy of apologizing properly.'

Now this he had to see! But ten out of ten to the step-mother. At least she had a shred of decency to her. But then he remembered there'd been a woman in the car with this brat. Had it been her? He went on the attack. 'And what the hell did you think you were doing letting her drive such a powerful vehicle and at such a ridiculous speed? Eh?'

This seemed to amuse the diminutive savage. But the Madison-Tyler woman came back with a stiff retort. 'If it had been me in that car, Mr Truman, I assure you this whole situation would never have arisen.' Then in a softer voice, she said, 'Is your dog really all right? And how about you? It must have been a terrible shock for you.'

'I'm fine,' he said, slightly mollified. 'So is Fritz.'

'I'm glad. I know it's no real compensation for what you've been through, but I wanted to give you this.' From a carrier bag, which Mac hadn't noticed before, she drew out a bottle of claret. 'It's from my husband's wine cellar. I'm not an expert, but apparently it's quite good.'

Never one to look a gift horse in the mouth, he took the bottle and looked at its label. Quite good was an understatement. This was sixty quid's worth, give or take. It would be remarkably fine. 'But I still want a proper apology from you.' He glared at the savage and took pleasure in seeing her flinch. To really embarrass her, he stepped away from the door and said, 'You might just as well come inside and say sorry to Fritz while you're about it.'

It seemed to Helen that Mr Mac Truman was intent on making Savannah squirm. She didn't blame him. She sensed a kindred spirit as they stood in the kitchen waiting for Savannah to say her piece, while Fritz circled them. Judging from the girl's scowling face, an apology looked as forthcoming as a meteorite dropping through the roof of this charming house. Evie had told her the Trumans lived in the converted chapel on New Street; it was a property Helen had often admired since moving to Swanmere. She would have loved the opportunity to snoop further than the hall and kitchen, which was all she'd glimpsed so far. Evie had said you wouldn't catch her living in it. 'Not with the main sitting area being such a big old draughty place,' she'd said. 'It must cost Conrad a fortune to heat it. Though, from what I understand, he's not short of money.' In true Evie fashion, the moment Helen had made her a pre-getting-down-to-work cup of coffee and asked who in the village owned a dachshund, the floodgates had been opened and she'd been regaled with an in-depth history of Mac and Conrad Truman. 'Mac can be a bit of a pain at times,' she'd told Helen, 'but that's just his way. I ignore him when he tries it on with me. To be honest, he's got worse since he lost his closest friend here in Swanmere. He and Alice Wykeham were as thick as thieves. Who knows, if they'd met when they were younger, they might have been more than friends. If you know what I mean '

'Come on, girl, get on with it. I haven't got all day.' At the sound of Mac's stentorian voice, the little sausage dog barked and pattered over to sniff Savannah's ankles. To Helen's surprise, Savannah bent down to the dog. She would have been less surprised if the girl had taken a boot to the animal and sent it flying. From her crouching position, Savannah glanced up at Mac. 'I meant it earlier when I said I was sorry. You just didn't hear me right.'

He narrowed his eyes. 'Is that it? Is that the best you can do?'

She shrugged. 'Take it or leave it.'

'In that case, apology accepted young lady. But I suggest you drive a lot slower in the future. Exactly how old are you?'

'Mind your own business.'

'Savannah!'

The girl stood up. 'Look, I've done what you wanted me to do. Now I'm going.' She pushed past Helen, stomped off the way they'd come and banged the front door shut after her, eliciting yet another bark from Fritz.

'She's a regular charmer, isn't she?' Mac Truman said. 'A real barrelful of fun.'

Furious, Helen said, 'I'm sorry. I thought if I made her come and see you it would teach her that she has to start taking responsibility for her actions. Clearly I was being naïve.'

'Is she your responsibility?'

'No. Thank goodness. She's staying with her father and me while her mother's away in America.'

'How long for?'

'A month.'

'Sounds like four weeks too long. I'd appreciate you keeping her out of my way.'

'With any luck she'll stay in her room the whole time she's with us.'

Still holding the bottle she'd given him, Mac said, 'Thanks for the wine, by the way; I admire your husband's taste when it comes to claret, if not his children. He's patently a man who doesn't stint. I shall think of you when I'm sampling it tonight.' He went over to the table in front of a pair of French windows that looked out onto a flagstoned area of garden. It looked like a perfect sun trap: lavender – almost on the point of flowering – along with lady's mantle, alliums and catmint filled the raised beds and reminded Helen of some of the areas of the garden at the Old Rectory. It was the way the plants seemed to be interwoven, producing a natural tapestry of texture and colour. She watched him put the bottle on the table next to a large open notebook – the pages were covered in handwritten notes interspersed with intricately drawn sketches of plants. 'Are you a keen gardener, Mr Truman?' she asked.

He caught her eyes on the book and snapped it shut. 'Yes. Are you?'

'I'd like to be. But please don't tell Olivia Marchwood that; she'll have me press-ganged into her Garden Club faster than you can say—' She stopped abruptly. For all she knew, Mac Truman might be a fan of the dreadful woman. Her anxiety was short-lived. He pushed back his shoulders and said, 'Olivia Marchwood may think the Garden Club belongs to her, but it doesn't.'

'Are you a member?'

'Yes.'

'Is it worth me considering joining?'

'You'd certainly help to bring the average age down.'

She smiled and sensed a thaw in the conversation. It gave her the courage to say, 'I don't suppose you could recommend anyone to help me with my garden? Evie Hawkins has suggested I get in touch with Orlando Fielding. Do you know him?'

'He's an excellent gardener. Helps out here now and then. He does the heavier stuff my nephew thinks I'm too doddery to manage. But I don't think he's looking for maintenance work so much these days; it's the design stuff he's more interested in now. No harm in trying him, though. Where do you live? Do you have a large garden?'

'I'm up at the Old Rectory. Evie told me you knew the previous owner, that Alice Wykeham was a friend of—'

'Of course,' he interrupted, none too politely. 'I should have realized who you were. I thought the name rang a bell. So you've made the acquaintance of that dreadful gossip Evie Hawkins, have you?'

'I couldn't manage the house without her.'

'Alice did.'

Helen flinched at the unequivocal put-down. She'd never before employed the services of a cleaner and she was still getting used to it. She thought of the state of the Old Rectory when she and Hunter had first viewed it. Even the estate agent had apologized for the smell. 'The house has been shut up for some weeks,' he'd explained. 'A few days with the windows open and it'll be fine.'

'It'll take more than a bit of fresh air to sort this place out,' Hunter had said. 'Apart from the obvious signs of damp and decay, and the dated fixtures and fittings, it's filthy.' This wasn't strictly true – the dust and grime was superficial – but Helen knew that each of Hunter's negative comments was aimed at bringing down the value of the house.

'The house is a little tired,' the agent had admitted.

'Tired?' Hunter had repeated. 'It's bloody knackered!'

'Miss Wykeham was ill for some months before she died,' the agent went on. 'Sadly, everything, including the garden, was left to fend for itself.'

The estate agent's words had created a poignantly sad image of a dying woman who no longer had the strength to look after her home and garden. For Helen, it was all too reminiscent of her grandmother. It also reminded her of the many people she met through her work. She and her friend Annabel ran Companion

Care, an enterprise they'd dreamt up together. They offered a personalised service for the elderly, assisting them with all manner of tasks, such as filling out forms, tracking down a plumber, helping with the shopping, ferrying clients to the dentist, chiropodist or hospital, or just taking time to have a chat over a cup of tea. The service was proving popular and kept Helen busier than she'd imagined it would. Hence the need for Evie. Rallying to defend herself in front of this antagonistic man, she said, 'If I'm not mistaken, Mr Truman, you use Evie here.'

'That's my nephew's decision,' he said sharply. 'It's his house; he makes the rules. If I had my way, we'd manage perfectly well without her. I can never find anything after she's paid us a visit.'

From what Helen knew of the previous owner of the Old Rectory – her main source being Evie – Alice Wykeham hadn't been one to stand on ceremony or suffer fools gladly. Helen could understand why this irascible man and Alice Wykeham had been such good friends. But mindful of the closeness between them – she had no wish to antagonize Mac Truman any further – she found herself wanting to get to know him better so that she could make a connection with the woman who had lavished so much love and attention on the garden now in her care. 'This may sound strange,' she said, 'but I feel a real weight of responsibility taking on the garden at the Old Rectory, as though I've been given the job of custodian. I believe, through your friendship with Alice Wykeham, that you know it well. If you have the time, I'd appreciate any advice you could give me. I'd hate to spoil it.'

For a moment he didn't reply. Perhaps he was thinking how best to get rid of her. When he did speak, it was to say, 'I suppose I could do that. Just now and then. But why don't you come along to the Garden Club? We have a meeting this Friday evening. I could introduce you to some of the more interesting members of the group if you want.' He was smiling now – mischievously so. 'I could also keep you safe from La Marchwood, stop her from dragging you off to her lair.'

As she walked home, taking the winding path that connected the church to the Old Rectory, enjoying the tunnel-like effect created by the thick hedgerow and the overhanging branches of the chestnut trees, Helen realized she had just made her first friend in Swanmere. Perhaps now she would finally start to feel at home. Since marrying Hunter, she had felt rootless.

Chapter Seven

Lucy wasn't feeling well. With a hot water bottle in place and her head resting against Orlando's shoulder, she lay on the sofa watching television, trying to take her mind off the cramping pains in her stomach. But it wasn't working. 'Is it time for some more Ibuprofen?' she asked.

'No,' he said firmly. 'You have another hour and a half to go.'

'You're such a fascist when it comes to drugs.'

'You can sweet-talk me all you like but you're not overdosing on painkillers while I'm around.'

'I'm dying.'

'Still nothing doing.'

'You'd hate it if I did die.'

He squeezed her shoulder affectionately. 'As far as I know, there isn't any medical evidence suggesting you can die from period pains.'

'Maybe I'll be a test case, the first in medical history. Then you'll be sorry.'

'True. But in the meantime, how about I redo your hot water bottle?'

When he came back from the kitchen ten minutes later, she said, 'I know what would make me feel better; why don't we watch a film?'

He handed her the bottle and groaned. 'Let me guess. Something cheesy and totally passé?'

She smiled. '*Love Actually* it is, then.'

Another ten minutes and the coffee table in front of them was laden with snacks and drinks and Orlando was pointing the remote control at the television. 'Let's see if you can at least get through the opening credits without crying,' he said.

But already Lucy was reaching for a tissue and wiping away a tear. 'You know this bit in the airport always gets to me,' she

sniffed. 'It's their faces. They all look so happy to see each other.'
He put his arm around her. 'I thought this was supposed to make you feel better.'

'It is. Now *ssh*!' She rested her head against his shoulder and sighed. It was evenings like this that made her realize just how incredibly lucky she was. Orlando was the best friend ever. She had never known any man comfort her the way he did when she had a bad period, let alone watch a Richard Curtis movie with her. They had never once argued or fallen out. The nearest they'd got to doing that was when she'd dated a garden furniture salesman a few years back. Orlando had been convinced from the start that there was something iffy about the man, but she'd refused to believe him. She'd even accused him of being jealous, but then she'd discovered the two-timing cheat was married with a baby son. She was devastated that she'd been so stupid, but Orlando had been wonderful. He didn't utter a single 'told you so' word of recrimination. He'd hugged her when she cried, and joined in when she called the cheating bastard every name under the sun. Given her background, any man who cheated on a wife and family was the lowest of the low. Ever since that error of judgement on her part, she'd been wary of getting involved with anyone, preferring the risk-free reliability of her close friendship with Orlando to the perilous journey of falling in love.

Their friends couldn't understand why she and Orlando had never got it together. Some of her friends were particularly vocal on this point, but then that was because most of them were madly in love with Orlando and thought he was to die for. 'How can you live with him and be immune to that gorgeously fit body of his?' they frequently asked Lucy. Angie at work would often say that she could gaze all day long into Orlando's sexy blue eyes. She even admitted to fantasizing about running her hands over his broad chest and shoulders and then down to his narrow waist. All in all, he clocked a pretty high score on her friends' shagometer, but to Lucy he was just good old Orlando. He'd kissed her once, a long time ago, and she'd rather enjoyed it, but she had known from his embarrassed reaction afterwards that he'd realized he'd made a mistake, that he'd crossed a line. There was an unspoken agreement between them that if they were to get romantically involved with each other, it would spoil everything. Because if it all went wrong, as just about every relationship seemed to, what then? They probably wouldn't even have their friendship left. She'd seen it happen before amongst their friends and she had no intention of jeopardizing what she had with Orlando. They were perfect as they were. What's more, he was someone she could always depend on; she trusted him implicitly. There wasn't anything she wouldn't do for him, and of all the people she knew, he was the one whose good opinion really mattered to her. Lying here with him, as one of his hands played absently with her hair, she couldn't think of a better way to spend an evening.

They were just getting to the bit in the film when Emma Thompson discovers her stupid husband is being taken in by the office tart, when the phone rang. 'I'll go,' Orlando said.

'Shall I pause the film?'

He hauled himself out of the sofa. 'No need.'

He picked the phone up in the kitchen and automatically reached for the handy pad of paper and a pen, expecting the call to be work related. He was wrong. It was Olivia Marchwood.

'I shan't keep you long, Orlando,' she bellowed at him. 'I just wanted to let you know there's been a change of plan for Friday evening. I'm afraid the speaker's let us down. But all is not lost; I've found a replacement, a woman who's a guide for a specialist holiday firm.'

'What kind of holiday firm?' Orlando asked. He had a sudden image of a Saga Holiday rep coming to talk to the Garden Club to drum up trade.

'One that specializes in garden tours in this country and Italy. She's the author of several books and is in great demand. We're jolly lucky to get hold of her. I certainly hope everyone appreciates the trouble I've gone to.'

Orlando's interest rose. The Saga rep was at once replaced with an image of grandiose gardens against a background of splendid neoclassical architecture, of perfectly clipped box hedges, of elegant cypress trees, of parterres and terraces, and Baroque statues and over-the-top fountains. 'What's the subject of her talk?'

'The gardens of the Italian lakes. It should be a fascinating talk.'

Orlando couldn't agree more. He suspected Lucy might not be so enthusiastic. She wasn't a member of the club but occasionally, if the talk was of interest to her, she would come along as his guest. However, in this instance he'd bet a week's wages that just a whispered murmur of Italy would incite a hammer-blow of resistance.

He still hadn't got around to giving Lucy the card he'd retrieved from the bin and the longer his dithering went on, the more difficult it was going to be to give it to her.

At Chapel House later that evening, Mac was delighted with the news that there had been a change in speaker for Friday evening. He'd been wondering how he was going to feign interest in an hour-long talk about bonsai trees. The month before it had been 'Natural Healing from Plants', which had been exceptionally good. Before that it had been 'Biological Pest Control'. But bonsai – good God, even Conrad, that lover of all things Japanese, wasn't interested in stunted trees as gnarled and knobbly as a witch's bum.

He made a note to ring Helen Madison-Tyler in the morning to let her know about the change. He didn't think she'd care one way or the other, but the courtesy call would give him the opportunity to further establish his interest in helping her with the garden at the Old Rectory. He'd thought a lot about her unexpected visit that afternoon, and in particular her request. He'd come to the conclusion that he owed it to Alice to keep an eye on her garden for her: it was, he'd decided, a matter of duty. For those in the know, the Old Rectory garden had been a landmark on the gardening calendar; people had travelled from miles around to see it during June and July when Alice opened it to the public to raise money for charity. He'd first seen it for himself several months after he'd come here to convalesce – when he still believed his stay would be temporary. Conrad had driven him the short distance to St John's and with the aid of a walking stick he'd managed to make it to the back of the church for morning worship. It was after he'd insisted there was no need for Conrad to stay that he'd met Alice. She had joined him in the pew where he sat alone, and as she made herself comfortable – depositing a bulging, grubby PVC shopping bag on top of a faded needlepoint kneeler depicting a cross and a dove – she had said, 'You're new, aren't you? I'll warn you now; I don't participate in the giving of the peace. If you want hugs and kisses and an evangelical grope, I suggest you sit in another pew.'

Amused, he'd said, 'I'm all for maintaining an air of decorum, so I think I'll stay where I am if you don't object.'

No one else joined them in the pew and throughout the service his companion, whose weathered face with its sharp bright eyes reminded him of a raisin, sang not a word from any of the hymns, nor did she join in with any of the responses. When it came to receiving communion, he rose unsteadily to his feet, stood for a moment to gather himself together while putting his weight on his walking stick, but then lost his nerve. What if his legs gave out halfway up the aisle? What if he took a flyer and went arse over tit? As if sensing his predicament, his companion said briskly, 'Here, lean on me.'

Humiliated that this small woman – only when she was standing did he realize how little there was of her: she was all presence – he said with defiant pride, 'No fear. If I lay so much as a finger on you, you'll accuse me of groping you.' And with that, he set off up the aisle. Everything was going according to plan until he tried to stand after kneeling at the altar rail. His knees had locked: he was stuck. A firm hand appeared at his left side and he found himself being hauled to his feet by the raisin-faced woman. 'I hope you were praying to be rid of your stubbornness,' she said when they were seated once more. 'What's wrong with your legs?'

'I had a stroke last year.'

'A bad one?'

'No. Thank God.'

When the service was over and he was waiting for Conrad to come and fetch him home, Mac decided he ought to introduce himself.

'Ah, so you're Conrad's uncle,' she said. 'I should have guessed.'

'You know my nephew?'

'Every woman in the village knows him. He's the focus of far too much attention. Although, to his credit, I doubt he notices it. How long are you staying in Swanmere?'

'Just a few months. Until I can convince Conrad I'm well enough to cope on my own.'

'Well, if you find yourself at a loose end, you're welcome to pay me a visit.'

'Where would I find you?'

She was already walking away from him now, taking the gravel path that led in an easterly direction away from the church. 'At the Old Rectory,' she called back to him. 'Ask Conrad; he'll know.'

'But I don't even know your name.'

'Alice. Alice Wykeham.'

He later learned just how few invitations of this sort Alice Wykeham gave out. Other than opening her garden to the public, she rarely invited anyone to step over her threshold. Five days later he took her up on her invitation and asked Conrad to drive him to the Old Rectory. Feeling like a teenager being dropped off for a first date by his father, he'd knocked on the door while Conrad waited in the car just in case no one was at home. But the door was opened and he was admitted. 'I'll have him home in time for his bath and tea,' she told Conrad with a wicked smile.

'You wretch,' he told her when Conrad had left them. 'You did that deliberately to make me feel worse than I do already.'

'Oh, do stop whingeing. Anyone would think you had an incurable disease.'

'I have. It's called old age.'

'Mmm ... self-pitying as well as stubborn. I can see I've got my work cut out with you. What you need is a large vodka martini. I invariably have one at this time of day. It sets me up nicely.'

'Thank you. I'll have mine dry with a twist of lemon.'

She raised an eyebrow. 'Is there any other way? Now go and sit in the garden while I do the honours. There's a copy of *The Times* on the bench. See if you can help me with eight down. It's been driving me mad.'

Their friendship was sealed from that day on, as was his passion for gardening. Alice enthused him in a way no one had in a long, long time.

The Euston to Crewe train was packed, and sitting cheek by jowl in a first-class carriage Conrad was surrounded by an army of fidgety men in shirtsleeves tapping at their laptops, shuffling through files of papers or speaking volubly into their mobiles. Perhaps they didn't have workplaces, just spent their days using the railway network as a mobile office. Before he got too carried away with this idea and started calculating the cost of office space versus a round-the-country lifetime first-class season ticket, he switched his thoughts to his own day's work. It wasn't often he was asked to present himself down in London for the law firm he freelanced for, but just occasionally, if the contract was an important one or if the Japanese company involved wanted a more personal approach, he would be expected to make an appearance. Hence the suit and tie. He didn't object to slipping into this role now and again, but he much preferred his usual routine of working at home and playing the part of happy slob. Samantha had never shared his love of working from home; he'd told her that was because she derived an unhealthy pleasure from being the boss of her own company. 'Don't deny it,' he'd said to her when he first took her out for dinner. 'You clearly get a hell of a buzz from having twenty-plus people working for you.'

'Anything wrong in that?' she'd asked.

'Only if it starts going to your head.'

'And how would that manifest itself?'

'Oh, you know, the usual thing; you'd try bossing me about.'

'The result being?'

'I'd have to take firm steps.'

'Such as?'

'Are you trying to have the last word?'

'No, I'm flirting with you. You're just too stupid to catch on.'

She was as sassy as she was ambitious. From the moment he'd met her, he'd had it bad for her. He was no dumb jackass himself, but compared to her fierce intellect, he'd scarcely evolved beyond the amoeba stage. Not only was she fluent in Russian and knew all about Russian trade law and the unglamorous world of machine tools, milling equipment, cable- and wire-making machinery, all of which were the core industries that made up her translating work – but she could speak passable French, Spanish and Italian and a smattering of Greek. When they became seriously involved and he took her to Japan for a holiday she surprised him on their arrival at their hotel in Kyoto by checking what time breakfast would be with the girl behind the desk – in Japanese. 'How the hell did you do that?' he'd asked.

'I've been learning secretly,' she'd admitted with a smile.

'But now there's nothing I'm better at than you.'

She had linked her arm through his and guiding him towards the lift, she'd said, 'I can think of several things you're much better at than me. Let's go to bed.' He didn't need asking twice, and they practically had their clothes off before they'd made it to their room.

It was when he saw her record collection and realized she was a massive Nick Drake fan that he knew he had to marry her. 'Nothing else for it,' he said, putting on his favourite album – *Five Leaves Left* – you have to marry me. It's the law.'

She'd responded by saying, 'I'm sorry, but I'm going to have to think about that.'

She did. For all of a split second.

Their backgrounds were very different, but it never got in the way of their relationship. Whereas he came from a strapped-for-cash, middle-class family – his father had been an unambitious vicar – Samantha's family was a well-heeled, close-knit outfit. Not long after he met her, she inherited a 'regular bundle' as she'd called the hefty sum of money a great aunt had left her. 'You'd better watch it, buster,' she'd told him. 'If you're interested in me because of my money, think again. My family will kill you before they let you get away with anything so sneaky.'

Her parents were both dead now, but there was a brother and a sister who were both married with grown-up children. Samantha had been much younger than her siblings – a surprise baby for her parents in their mid-forties. Conrad still got together with them occasionally, usually around Christmas. Family time.

There wasn't much left of his own family. His mother had died of cancer a year before he met Samantha and his father had died of an embolism almost a year to the day later. Apart from his sister, Susan, whom he seldom saw, mostly because he couldn't abide her badly behaved children or her po-faced husband, Mac was all he had.

Samantha and Mac had got on famously. She'd called him her Big Mac and would regularly race him over the phone to see who could be the first to complete the crossword in *The Times*. When Conrad had had to telephone his uncle with the news that Samantha was dead, Mac had been devastated. 'She was like a real daughter to me,' he'd said, his voice ripped apart with emotion. 'She was the best. The absolute best.' Then: 'Oh my God, Conrad, how will you manage? How will you ever get over it?'

'I won't,' he'd said simply.

Chapter Eight

What Helen most enjoyed about Companion Care was the variety of work it offered and that every day was different. In theory Thursday and Friday were the only full days she worked, with Monday and Tuesday being mornings only, but in practice her schedule was very much a moveable feast. However, with the way things were going with Savannah lolling about at home and looking for every opportunity to stir up trouble, Helen was contemplating working full time.

It was Friday morning and with the prospect of being away from the Old Rectory for a whole eight hours, Helen couldn't be happier. She had about an hour's worth of paperwork to do and then she'd be on the road. Her first client of the day was Isobel Jenkins who needed taking to the doctor, followed by the chemist to pick up the prescriptions and then on to the library. Her afternoon was to be spent with Mr Haddon who had an appointment at the hospital for a blood test and an x-ray. It was anybody's guess how long it would take, but she would stay with Mr Haddon until the job was done and would doubtless be treated to more graphic accounts of the countless illnesses he'd suffered as well as the many operations he'd undergone. She often joked with him that she was more intimate with his prostate than was decent.

Yet this was the whole point of Companion Care; they were more than just a taxi service for the elderly. Most of their clients lived alone with no family on hand to turn to. Quite a few were too proud to accept what social services could offer, preferring instead to pay for a tailor-made service, thereby keeping the arrangement on a respectable business footing. In many ways it was a face-saving exercise; it provided people with the means to accept help whilst at the same time hanging onto their pride.

And pride was something everyone fell prey to, including herself. When it was obvious her own business was going to the wall she had hated the thought of losing her independence. She had got used to being her own boss and didn't relish working for someone else again. But then marrying Hunter had changed everything. 'You don't need to toil away to keep the wolf from the door now,' he'd said, 'so why not do something to help others?' She suspected that he was old-fashioned enough to prefer a wife of his not to go out to work – neither Corinne nor Marcia had done so – but charity work of some sort was quite acceptable, to be encouraged even. Within weeks, she and Annabel had come up with the idea of Companion Care, had found some office space and with a modest loan from Hunter at their disposal, they were open for business. It was never their intention to make a profit – what they charged their clients just covered their overheads. They currently had four other part-time members of staff, but they were sufficiently busy now to think about expanding the team.

Leaving Annabel to open the mail, Helen put the kettle on for their first coffee of the day. Situated above a bathroom showroom in Crantsford, their premises comprised one reasonable-sized office, a narrow landing with a kitchenette off it, and a toilet with a flush loud enough to wake the dead.

As she poured boiling water into two mugs, Helen thought of Mac Truman. She had no doubt that he was as proud a man as any and that his gruff manner concealed a very real fear of growing old. She and Annabel saw it all the time. It was a trait especially prevalent amongst their gentlemen clients. She could fully sympathise. So many of them had fought in the Second World War; they had saved a nation – if not the world; they had come home, married and fathered children and got the country back on its feet. They had been a driving force, only to be thought of now as a spent force. No wonder they kicked against the unfairness of it.

Based on what Evie had told her about Mac Truman – that he'd been 'something big in the world of banking' before retiring – Helen could understand his reluctance to go quietly. She had been delighted when he telephoned yesterday morning to say that he was available any time she wanted his advice or assistance. He'd also given her Orlando Fielding's number, which she'd immediately rung. She'd explained to Orlando that for now all she wanted was for someone to cut the grass regularly and maybe do some hacking back. He'd pointed out that general maintenance work wasn't what he was looking for, as Mac Truman had told her, but seeing as it was Alice's old garden and that he knew it well, he'd take a look at it as soon as he could. She'd then asked him about the Garden Club. 'Mr Truman said you were a member. It's not too highbrow, is it? A novice like me won't stick out too much, will I?'

He'd laughed. 'I'm afraid you'll stick out like the proverbial sore thumb. But don't worry; anyone new gets the same treatment. It'll be the full-on interrogation, I'm afraid. Especially as you live at the Old Rectory. Your garden has a reputation all of its own.'

'Did you used to work on it?'

'Yes. It was a great inspiration to me. As was Alice. She taught me more about gardening and design than any textbook or college lecturer ever did. She was a genuine plantswoman. Really knew her subject.'

'She sounds a regular Gertrude Jekyll.'

He laughed. 'And some!'

The telephone rang just as Helen put Annabel's mug of coffee on her desk. Annabel answered it, then immediately handed the receiver over to Helen. 'Your lord and master,' she said with a grin.

Helen rolled her eyes and tutted. 'I don't have one of those.'

'What don't you have?' Hunter asked when she said hello.

'Nothing,' she replied, turning her back on Annabel. 'So what can I do for you?'

'How do you fancy lunch at Juno's?'

Helen thought of Isobel Jenkins. To make time for lunch with Hunter she'd have to put off Isobel's trip to the library. She knew this would disappoint the old lady. 'I'd love to, only I have—'

'Excellent. I'll book us a table.'

'No, Hunter, listen. I can't. I've got—'

'Nonsense. You can spare an hour for your husband. Get Annabel to cover for you. I'll meet you at Juno's at one o'clock. Don't be late; I've got a hectic afternoon ahead of me.'

Helen put the phone down with exaggerated care.

Savannah had lost track of how long she had been standing at her bedroom window wearing nothing but a towel. The object of her fascination was a fit-looking guy down in the garden. He was dressed in jeans and a dark-blue T-shirt that clung to the kind of chunky, muscular build that she strongly approved of. He was certainly worth the effort of getting some clothes on and going down to see what he was doing here. She raised her arms above her head and let the towel drop to the floor. She stayed where she was for several seconds, hoping he'd look up at the house and notice her. But he didn't. She quickly pulled on a pair of jeans and a halter-neck top and went to check him out before he disappeared.

'And who might you be?' she asked after she'd crept up behind him. With his hands on his hips, he seemed to be giving a lot of thought to a massive bush covered in purple flowers.

He turned at her voice. 'I'm sorry; I didn't think anyone would be here.'

She was glad to see that he was even better-looking close up. With his thick, sun-bleached hair, tanned face and blue eyes, he was a top buzz. 'Why? Were you hoping to burgle the place?'

He smiled. 'I've already cased the joint. I didn't find anything worth taking.'

'You should have looked upstairs where I was.'

The smile slipped from his face and he turned away to look at the purple-flowered bush again. Narked by his being more interested in a stupid bush than her, she said, 'You haven't answered my question. Who are you and what are you doing here?'

'I'm Orlando Fielding and I'm figuring out how much work there is for me to do here.'

'Work?'

'Garden work. I'm a gardener.'

'You don't look like a gardener.'

He hooked his thumbs through the belt loops of his jeans and gave her his attention once more. 'I assure you I am.'

Seeing as he was the first decent thing she'd come across since being dumped in the land of the dead, she decided to go for it. 'Would you like me to make you a cup of coffee?'

'No thanks. If I don't get a move on I'll be late for my next job.'

'But you'll be coming back?'

'I expect so. It depends when your mother wants me to start work.' He looked at his watch. 'In fact, I'd better get going now. See you again some time.'

Disappointed to see him go so soon, she watched him walk back up towards the house, then round to the front. Good legs, she noted. And decent arse into the bargain. But then it registered what he'd said and anger flared. That stuck-up bitch Helen was not her mother.

She didn't think she would ever forgive Helen for making her go and apologize to that decrepit, freaky old man. The worst bit was that she'd somehow got Dad to take her side. 'Helen did the right thing,' he'd said when he came home from work in the evening and she'd told him what Helen had made her do. She'd expected him to tell Helen not to mess with stuff that had nothing to do with her, but he hadn't. Instead, he'd said, 'With a bit of luck your apology will have smoothed the waters. After all, we don't want to get off on the wrong foot with our new neighbours.' And since when did Dad ever care about what other people thought of him? There was a satisfying moment, though, when he twigged Helen had given away an expensive bottle of his favourite wine. 'Didn't you look at the label, Helen?' he'd said.

'I did, but it didn't really mean a lot to me.'

'But you know that particular wine is a favourite of mine.'

'Let's hope it's a favourite of Mr Truman's, then,' Helen had fired back. 'After what Savannah did, I think it's the least we can do.'

'Technically Savannah didn't do anything,' her father had said, looking at Savannah. 'You just happened to be driving by when the dog ran out – isn't that right, Savvie?'

'Yes, Dad. There wasn't anything I could have done.'

But Bitch Queen Helen couldn't let it rest and had chipped in with, 'Mr Truman thinks otherwise. He said that Savannah was going much too fast.'

Mum described Helen as a shallow opportunist, a woman who'd seen her chance and grabbed it. 'And now she's bloody lady of the manor she thinks she can lord it over the rest of us,' Mum said. Her parting words to Savannah when she'd driven off the other day were, 'Don't let that snooty, double-barrelled piece of work push you around.'

Annoyingly, Savannah had allowed that to happen on day one of her stay by giving in to Helen and apologizing to Mr Truman. Well, it wouldn't happen again. And anyway, she'd only gone along with it because she wanted to know that the dog was okay. When she was little she'd pestered Mum and Dad endlessly about having a dog as a pet. She wanted a dog more than anything in the world. But they wouldn't let her have one.

*

Isobel Jenkins always took her time when it came to choosing her library books. She would methodically cruise the shelves of romance, historical and crime novels at a steady, unhurried pace. Today was no exception. Observing her from the seated area where she was pinning a flyer for Companion Care on the library notice board, Helen was in two minds what to do – should she discreetly hurry the old lady, or let her take as long as she wanted? She was still furious that Hunter had railroaded her on the telephone earlier and was tempted to stand him up for lunch. How dare he treat her, and her job, so dismissively, as though what she did didn't really matter. As though her job was little more than a hobby that she could pick up and put down at his convenience. He may well have treated his previous wives that way, but he was in for a nasty shock if he thought he could do the same with her.

'I'm ready now.'

Helen turned. At less than five feet tall, and clutching her nylon string bag of books and dressed in a navy blue raincoat, Isobel Jenkins looked like a small wrinkled child anxiously waiting to be taken home after a long day at school.

'You're sure you've got everything you wanted?' Helen asked her. She was almost willing Isobel to go back for another book.

Which had been petty of her, she thought when later she had dropped Isobel off at her neat-as-a-pin Victorian semi and was driving on to Crantsford. A glance at her watch told her she'd be at least ten minutes late for Hunter. Good. It served him right. She was doubly annoyed with him now because Isobel had been so obviously disappointed when Helen had had to refuse her offer of a cup of tea and a slice of homemade cake. 'Another time,' she'd had to say. 'I've got a lot on today.'

The old lady had smiled and hugged her bag of books. 'Silly me. I keep forgetting how busy you are.'

'I'll see you next week for your chiropodist's appointment.'

'I'll make another cake, shall I?'

'That would be lovely. But only if you have the time.'

'It gives me something to do.'

Annabel was better at keeping clients and their problems at an emotionally safe distance, but Helen wasn't so adept. Isobel Jenkins was a sweet, lonely old lady whom Helen couldn't shrug off the moment their allotted time together was over.

She had just pulled into the car park at the back of Juno's when her mobile rang. Assuming it was Hunter wanting to know where she was, she flicked it open and said, 'I'll be there any minute. I'm just parking the car.'

There was a slight pause and then: 'Is that Mrs Madison-Tyler?'

Not recognizing the voice, she said a lot less sharply, 'Yes, it is.'

'Oh, hi, this is Orlando Fielding. Is it a bad time? I could call back later if you'd rather.'

'No, now is fine. Is it about the garden?'

'Yes. I had a look at it this morning. You're right about the pruning work that needs doing. The lawns are in pretty bad shape, too. It's amazing how quickly nature takes over when it's given the chance. If you want, I could get things tidied up for you straight away and then we can discuss what other more regular help you need.'

'That sounds perfect. When can you start?'

'I could come on Monday afternoon.'

'That's excellent.'

'We haven't discussed money yet, but I usually charge—'

'Don't worry about that now; we'll discuss money on Monday.'

'Okay. I'll see you tonight, then.'

'Tonight?'

'The Garden Club?'

'Of course. I'd forgotten all about that. Thanks for jogging my memory.'

After she'd rung off, Helen took a moment to check her appearance in the mirror. She never used to worry too much about how she looked, but Hunter was always so well turned out she felt she had to make an effort to try and keep up with him. Reapplying her lipstick, she wondered if he'd invited her for lunch so that they could chat without any risk of Savannah eavesdropping on the conversation. If that was the case, then maybe he was finally going to open up and talk about what was going on between them in bed. Or more to the point, what wasn't going on. So far he hadn't said a word about it.

When she entered the restaurant, Hunter rose from his chair. 'What kept you?' he asked after he'd kissed her cheek.

His question rattled her, but all she said was, 'I've had a busy morning.' She then explained about Orlando's call and that she'd be out that evening.

'Are you sure you really want to get involved? Won't it be a bit jam and Jerusalem?'

'I won't know unless I try. Do you want to come with me?'

He laughed and shook his head. 'Thanks, but no. Come on, let's order. I haven't got much time.'

'Nor have I,' she said pointedly.

It was when the waitress had taken their order that Helen understood Hunter hadn't arranged to meet her here so they could discuss anything of an intimate nature. No, it was a set-up, pure and simple. 'I have to go to Barbados tomorrow,' he said. 'There's a development of apartments being built that I want to check out. I would ask you to come with me,' he added, 'only there's Savannah to keep an eye on.'

After she'd counted to ten, Helen said, 'Isn't she old enough to keep an eye on herself?'

'I promised Marcia that I'd look after her.'

'Then why don't you take Savannah with you?'

'I could, but I'd rather not.'

Their food arrived, but Helen had lost her appetite.

Chapter Nine

Conrad switched off his computer. It had been one of those days that had been and gone without him noticing; one minute it was eight-thirty and he was starting work and the next it was seven in the evening. There had been a time when he would have gone on working right through the night. Anything rather than be alone with his thoughts.

After locking his office, he crossed the cobbled courtyard to the main part of the house. There was no sign of Mac downstairs, but seeing the empty soup bowl on the kitchen table, along with the hacked-about loaf of bread, an unwrapped wedge of cheddar cheese and an opened jar of olives, he remembered that it was Friday – Mac's Garden Club night. Having made himself an early supper, he was probably upstairs now getting ready to go out. His uncle was always complaining what a useless bunch of people made up the club these days now that Alice was no longer around, but he never missed a meeting. Conrad often teased him that it was the attention of the female members of the club that piqued his interest. Conrad had never attended one of the meetings, but he could picture what went on down at the village hall – all those good ladies of Swanmere fussing over Mac as they vied for his attention. One only had to flick through the old family photo albums to see what a good-looking young man Mac had been. Even now, slightly stooped and slow of gait, there was a distinguished air about him. He possessed an ease of manner and authority that Conrad's father had never owned.

The two brothers could not have been more different. Edwin Truman had believed in an ideal world where all had a roof over their heads and something to eat in their hands. This in itself was no bad thing, but to Conrad, when he was growing up, it always seemed that he and Susan had to be the ones to go without to provide for The Poor. And not just The Poor on their own doorstep in their father's parish. This was The Poor in some faraway place where the sun scorched the earth to arid dust and every night little black children went to bed hungry. He and Susan were frequently encouraged to put all their pocket money in the tin kept on the mantelpiece – an old Brooke Bond tin that without fail was always shaken whenever a visitor made the mistake of calling. They were expected to part with a sizable proportion of their birthday and Christmas money, too, most of which came from Mac. 'A sacrifice here, a sacrifice there,' their father would tell them, 'is all it takes to make the world a better place for everyone.' Once, when Conrad dared to challenge this and asked why no one thought to improve the quality of his own life, he was sent to his room without any tea and told to reflect on his selfishness.

As a child, Conrad hadn't realized the extent of the hostility between the two brothers, Mac and Edwin. All he'd been aware of at the time was that whenever Mac came to visit – whether it was to the depressing seventies flat-roofed vicarage on the edge of a council estate, or the draughty old Victorian manse that was burgled on a regular basis, even though they had nothing worth taking – the house seemed to come alive, the walls practically vibrating with his colourful dynamism. He would do magic tricks for Conrad and Susan; coins would disappear before their eyes, then reappear behind their ears or from under their chins. He would have swordfights with Conrad, the two of them running around in the garden pretending to be crusading knights or swashbuckling, one-eyed pirates. He would brighten their lives with wonderfully imaginative books and toys, and there would be gifts, too, for their parents: silk ties and scarves, cashmere sweaters, bottles of whisky and delicious chocolates. They were all things Edwin Truman could never afford on his meagre vicar's salary. On one of his visits, Mac gave Edwin an expensive camera for his birthday and several months afterwards, when Conrad found the camera still in its box at the back of the china cupboard in the dining room, he'd asked his father why he hadn't used it yet. Edwin, normally so mildly spoken, a man who rarely raised his voice, never mind his hand, had told him sharply to mind his own business and didn't he have some homework he should be doing instead of poking around in cupboards that had nothing to do with him?

It was only when Conrad was older that he noticed how frequently, on the pretext of writing that week's sermon, his father would retreat to the quiet of his study when Mac was around.

Conrad was older still when he understood just how diminished his father became when he was in his brother's presence.

Slow, emphatic footsteps on the stairs had Conrad turning towards the door. Seconds later Mac appeared in the kitchen with Fritz close on his heels. Mac usually went to the trouble of smartening himself up when he went out of an evening, but tonight Conrad could discern an extra snap, crackle and pop to his uncle's attire. In place of his customary tweed jacket and corduroys was the blazer and grey flannel trousers he wore for church or occasional drinks parties. His suede lace-ups had been replaced with his best loafers. He was also freshly shaved and doused in something citrusy.

Conrad whistled. 'Look at you. Who are you out to impress tonight?'

'Don't be ridiculous. I just fancied a change, that's all.'

'Whoever she is, she won't appreciate the grumpy act from you. Better do something about that before you meet her.'

Mac tutted. 'Now you're just irritating me.'

'At last the tables are turned!'

The doorbell rang. 'That'll be for me,' Mac said, already moving to answer it. 'I'll see you later.'

One of the many unspoken rules they lived by was that they had to respect each other's privacy, which meant they had a no-questions-asked policy. However, fully fired up with curiosity, and relying on his uncle's hearing not being quite what it used to be, Conrad quietly followed Mac to the front door. Something was going on and he sure as hell wanted to know for whom Mac had gone to so much trouble. Not since Alice had become such a close friend to Mac had Conrad seen his uncle so nattily dressed.

Expecting to see an ageing lovely from the village, he was taken aback by the sight of an attractive woman who had to be half his uncle's age. The old dog!

'I hope I'm not too early,' she said. She was softly spoken with an instantly engaging smile. Hair the colour and sheen of a glossy chestnut framed a pale face.

'Not at all,' Mac answered. 'I would ask you in, but my nephew has the manners of a barbarian.'

Over Mac's shoulder, the woman's eyes flickered imperceptibly towards Conrad where he stood half hidden behind the balustrade, then back to Mac. 'Really? In what way?'

'In every way. Shall we?'

65

Mac stepped outside and banged the door shut, not before Conrad caught a glimpse of a bemused smile from the woman as she looked at him again. She had clearly sussed who he was – the barbarian nephew. But who the hell was she? And just what had his uncle been up to while his back was turned?

The village hall was much busier than Helen had expected. There were as many men present as women, so bang went Hunter's theory about it being an extension of the WI. Mac explained that some of the people present weren't actually members of the Garden Club. 'They're gatecrashers,' he informed her. 'If they like the sound of the speaker, people show up uninvited. We charge them, of course.'

'Are they all here expecting the talk on bonsai trees?'

He chuckled. 'I doubt that very much.'

'But you only knew about the change in speaker the other day.'

'Word travels fast here in Swanmere. I'd have thought you would have learned that by now.'

'Oh dear, does that mean everyone knows my ghastly step-daughter nearly killed your poor dog?'

'More or less. But don't let it worry you. I'm rather hoping that my bringing you here this evening will get them all gossiping about us. By breakfast tomorrow morning we'll be the talk of the village.'

Helen laughed. She was enjoying Mac's wicked sense of humour. Earlier, she'd had the feeling that he'd known perfectly well that his nephew was within earshot of his comment about him. He certainly didn't look like he had the manners of a barbarian. He was much too handsome for that.

Mac Truman was now beckoning a young couple to come over and join them. When they had, he said to the pretty blonde girl, 'We're honoured to see you, Lucy. This is a rare treat. Let me introduce you to someone who's here for the first time.' He turned to Helen. 'Helen Madison-Tyler, say hello to my favourite people, Lucy Gray and Orlando Fielding.'

Helen shook hands with them both. They made a strikingly attractive couple, both blonde and blue-eyed with a fresh, natural look about them. Lucy had exactly the kind of long, wavy hair that Helen had been desperate for as a child. 'It's good to meet you at last,' she said to Orlando, suddenly feeling all of her forty-five years. 'I believe you met my step-daughter this morning.'

Before he had a chance to reply, a booming voice cut through the conversation. It was Olivia Marchwood bringing them to order. 'Looks like we'd better sit down,' he said.

'Are you sure you want to hang out with us?' Lucy said as they looked for a free row of seats. 'We're considered the bad set, you know. You'll be tainted by association and become a social pariah.'

Thinking she was in with exactly the right set, despite the age gap, Helen settled back in her seat. If Mac was happy to be friends with the enviably youthful Lucy and Orlando, then so was she.

Olivia Marchwood cleared her throat and declared the meeting open. The next ten minutes were given over to reading the minutes from the group's last meeting – Helen could hear Lucy shuffling restlessly in her seat – along with a list of suggested outings to various gardens in the coming months. 'For those interested, I shall be taking names at the end of this meeting,' Olivia Marchwood told them. 'As always, numbers will be limited, so places will be offered on a first come first served basis.'

Helen leaned into Mac. 'What do you reckon? Shall we go on a trip together and really give Swanmere something to talk about?'

His mouth twitched with a smile. 'I'm game if you are,' he whispered back.

'And now we come to the highlight of the evening,' continued Olivia, flicking over a page of her notepad. 'We've been most fortunate—' Her voice broke off abruptly at the sound of a mobile phone trilling from somewhere in the audience. As her eyes searched the rows for the guilty offender, Helen thought her glare was one of the most formidable she had ever seen. Then to her horror it settled on Helen herself, prompting the realization it was her mobile. She hastily bent down to her bag to deal with it, and registering that it was Hunter calling her, she switched off the phone. Whatever it was he wanted to say, it could wait. She still hadn't forgiven him for offloading Savannah onto her while he went waltzing off to Barbados. There had been no blazing row between them, which with hindsight was a pity. It might have cleared the air to have a damn good yell at each other. As it was she could feel her anger and resentment gently simmering.

The commotion over, Olivia was now introducing the speaker: Philippa Hutton from the Gardens of Delight tour company.

Lucy was hardly listening to what the speaker was saying. Jumpy and on edge, each time a new image appeared on the screen, Lucy half expected to see her father's face staring back at her.

She blamed Orlando. He'd told her the talk was going to be about the Lake District. She'd been really looking forward to hearing about the gardens in the Cumbrian Lake District – those at Levens Hall, Holker Hall, Holehird, and Muncaster Castle. Instead, she was being forced to listen to a woman waxing lyrical about Lake Como, where her father lived. Orlando had whispered an apology to her when the talk had got underway, muttering something about having got hold of the wrong end of the stick from Olivia. Mistake or not, she still held him responsible for putting her through this ordeal.

The last time she had seen her father, she'd been fourteen years old. He had taken time off from work to take her out after school for something to eat. He said he had something important to tell her, something he'd already discussed with her mother that morning. He told her he couldn't live with her mother any more, that it just wasn't working between them. Her first thought, and what she actually said to him was, if she could live with her annoying mother, then why couldn't he? 'It's not as straightforward as that, Lucy,' he'd said. 'I've fallen in love with someone else.'

'But you can't. You're married to Mum.'

'I'm sorry. Truly I am.'

For several minutes she had just sat there shredding the paper napkin on her lap, the hurt and anger growing inside her.

'I'm sorry, Lucy,' he repeated. 'You must believe me; I never intended for this to happen.'

'Then why don't you stop it?'

'I ... I can't. I have to be with the woman I love. One day you'll understand what I'm saying.'

'No I won't! I'll never ever understand how you could do this. Who is she and where does she live?'

'Her name's Francesca and she lives in Italy.'

'*Italy!* You mean you're going to live in another country? But that means I'll *never* see you.'

'Of course you'll see me. You'll come and spend the holidays with me. It'll be fun. There'll be lots of new places for us to explore together. Just the two of us.'

'But I don't want to spend the holidays *exploring* with you. I want it to be like it is now.' She'd started to cry then. Loud wailing sobs that made people stare at them. He came round to her side of the table. He tried to put his arm around her, but she shrugged him off. 'Don't touch me! I hate you! I just can't believe you would do this.' Pushing him away, she jumped up from her seat, sending her chair flying, and ran out of the café.

Blinded by her tears she didn't see the black cab coming as she blundered across the busy street. A squeal of brakes followed by a car horn and a man shouting didn't stop her, though. She ran on and on until she reached home. Letting herself in, she called to her mother. There was no reply. The house felt eerily quiet. No radio on. No music playing. It was as if she'd walked through the wrong front door. She found her mother upstairs lying on her bed, staring at the ceiling. An empty bottle of champagne lay beside her. For a heart-stopping moment, Lucy thought she was dead, that she'd killed herself. 'Mum?' she whispered. 'Are you all right?' She moved slowly towards the bed, aware that to the left of her, the wardrobe doors were open. A row of empty hangers told her that some of her father's clothes were gone.

Her mother stirred. 'He's told you, then?'

'Yes. But we have to stop him. We have to make him understand he's made a mistake. We can't let him go.' What she meant was: I can't do this. I can't be on my own with you.

Fiona shook her head. 'It's too late for that, Lucy. It's just you and me now.'

Lucy blinked hard. The memory of that day was so clear in her mind it might just as well have been part of the slideshow they were watching. With the passing of so many years it shouldn't hurt, but it did. If he had loved her, as he said he did, he wouldn't have turned his back on her and left her. He hadn't been the man she thought he was. He was nothing but a selfish bastard.

It was still light when they left the village hall and having accepted Lucy and Orlando's invitation for him and Helen to join them for a drink at the Swan Inn, Mac was leaning against the bar waiting to be served. He knew that Orlando had wanted to pay for the drinks, but he also knew that the boy had precious little money to chuck about.

The drinks paid for, he made his way slowly over to their table, carrying the tray of glasses carefully and willing his hands not to shake. Sometimes they did, sometimes they didn't.

'You're looking mighty sharp tonight, Mac,' Lucy said to him when he sat down and had passed round the glasses. 'What's with the blazer? Hoping to pull tonight, were you?'

Glad to see a smile back on Lucy's face, and suspecting what had caused her to look so unhappy earlier, he said, 'Hush your mouth, wee girl. And who's to say I haven't pulled already?' He threw a glance in Helen's direction, hoping she'd play along.

She did. 'Didn't you know, Lucy? Mac and I are having a bit of a fling. It was love at first sight.'

He laughed, and remembering their first meeting, he said, 'Actually, I think I was jolly rude to you.'

Lucy put down her glass with a bang, spilling some of her wine. 'My God, Mac, that's the first time I've ever heard you admit to being rude.'

'But quite understandable,' Helen said. 'After what my stepdaughter did, he had every right to be as rude as he wanted.'

'Don't encourage him, Helen,' Orlando said. 'It's taken us for ever to make him half civilized. Don't undo all our hard work.'

Lucy reached for her glass again. 'I think we should officially welcome Helen as a new member of our exclusive gang. After her mobile phone went off like that, she deserves nothing less. All those in agreement, raise your glass.'

They were still in the pub an hour later. Helen had made half-hearted noises about going home; Hunter would be in bed early to be up at the crack of dawn to catch his flight for Barbados, but she was enjoying herself too much to leave the party. She was touched by the way Lucy and Orlando teased and humoured Mac. He was clearly very fond of them, and they of him. How different he was from the irascible old man she'd met at Chapel House the other day. She wondered why he had been so rude about his nephew earlier. Had they just had an argument, perhaps?

As intrigued as she was by Mac and his nephew, she was curious too about the relationship between Lucy and Orlando. She couldn't work out why there wasn't more than friendship between them. She'd earlier made the mistake of assuming they were an item and they'd been quick to put her right. On the face of it they seemed perfect for each other. They were about the same age – late twenties, she guessed – and were clearly in tune with each other. Like a couple who'd been together for ever and a day, the rapport between then was so strong they had a habit of occasionally finishing each other's sentence. But perhaps Orlando was gay.

Weren't all the best men gay these days? Or for that matter, maybe Lucy was gay. She was just thinking how complicated relationships were, and knew from personal experience how true this was, when she heard Mac say, 'So, what do we think of La Marchwood's suggested trips this summer? Any takers?'

Lucy shook her head. 'The dates suggested are all Saturdays when I'll be working.' She wagged a finger at Mac. 'Some of us have jobs to hold down.'

'The same for me, I'm afraid,' Orlando added. 'I'm working six days a week now.'

'That's too bad.'

'What about the proposed trip to Lake Como?' Helen said, taking out the Gardens of Delight brochure from her handbag.

An awkward hush fell on the group. No one spoke, until Lucy said, 'Well, you can count me out on that. I'm not going anywhere near Lake bloody Como.'

Chapter Ten

Over the following days Helen saw a lot more of Mac. He came to the Old Rectory at the weekend to take a look at the garden, then again on Tuesday, the day after Orlando had been to mow the lawns. On both occasions he brought Fritz with him and they'd had the house and garden to themselves – Savannah had been who knew where and Hunter was thousands of miles away in the Caribbean. Helen was amused and entertained by Mac. He was a man of unpredictable mood swings, though. One minute he could be witty and jolly, the next grumbling and complaining over the slightest thing.

He was here now, Wednesday evening, minus Fritz and in the kitchen with Helen. He was grousing about the length of time it had taken for him to see his GP that afternoon. His whingeing had gone on for fifteen minutes and had covered every aspect of his visit to the surgery, from the attitude of the discourteous receptionist to the ineptitude of the young locum he'd finally seen.

'Okay, Mac,' Helen said, deciding she'd heard enough. She had covered for Annabel today and had endured much the same gripes from one of her clients and she wasn't prepared to put up with it at home as well. 'What's it going to take to make you button it?'

He raised his glance from the carrier bag he'd been rustling on his lap. He looked furious: brows drawn, lips pursed.

'Well?' she said when he didn't say anything and the silence reverberated to the thumping sound of music coming from Savannah's room upstairs. 'What's it to be? Because I'll tell you this, I've had a day of it and one stroppy madam in the house is quite enough for me.'

'Is that how you speak to the old folk you take care of?'

'No. I put them against a wall and shoot them if they don't behave. How about a glass of wine? Will that improve your mood?'

He let out a boisterous laugh, sending his bushy eyebrows back into place. 'I'm beginning to see a new side to you. There was I thinking you were a sweet little thing who wouldn't say boo to a goose, and all the time you were a despot in disguise. And thank you, a glass of something from your husband's excellent wine cellar would be most welcome. Any news yet when he'll be coming home and I'll have to curtail my visits?'

Uncorking a bottle of Pouilly Fumé that she'd put in the fridge in readiness for Mac's visit, Helen said, 'It looks like he might be extending his trip. He's thinking of going on to Antigua. Or perhaps it was Tobago. I forget. Anyway, net result is, I'll be stuck on my own with the beast from the deep for longer than ever.' She tilted her head toward the ceiling.

'The girl needs a lesson in manners and to know when she's well off, that's all.'

Helen handed him his glass. 'You're not wrong there. Last night she didn't come home until nearly three in the morning. I have no idea where she'd been, but she was as sick as a dog. I've left the mess in her bathroom for her to clean up. I don't see why I should have to do it. It's not as if she's a child.'

He shuddered. 'I consider myself a lucky man indeed that I haven't had the misfortune to raise any children. Cheers.'

Helen took a sip of her wine, and pushing Savannah from her mind, said, 'So what's in the bag, Mac? The way you're clutching it anyone would think you had the crown jewels there.'

He put down his glass. 'I ... I wondered if you'd like to have a look at these.' He opened the bag and pulled out a bundle of notebooks. Some were old and worn around the edges, while others looked to be in pristine condition. 'They belonged to Alice,' he said. 'They're her gardening journals. She gave them to me shortly before she died.' He carefully offered them across the table with an air of reverence. 'They might help you to understand what Alice's garden meant to her. And maybe what it could mean to you.'

Helen took the books from him. She opened one and saw that it was very like the notebook she'd seen on the kitchen table that day at Chapel House when she'd first met Mac. She remembered how he had snapped it shut when he'd caught her looking at it. Now she knew why. These books meant more to him than a mere record; they were a precious bond with a woman he'd been immensely fond of. 'Are you sure you want to lend them to me?'

He took a long swallow of his wine. 'I trust you to take good care of them. Besides, they're of more practical use to you right now than lying about at Chapel House. Just as Alice taught me, her notes will teach you to understand plants, where they're from and how they survive in their natural habitat.'

'Have you read them all?'

'No. I started to, but hearing Alice's voice speaking from the page wasn't the comfort I thought it would be.'

Helen was touched that he was prepared to go to such lengths to help her. She said, 'I know this may sound borderline crazy, and I know we've only known one another a short while, but I feel like we were always meant to be friends.'

For a moment he looked baffled by her words, but then, to her consternation, tears welled in his eyes. 'I know exactly what you mean,' he murmured. 'That's how it was with Alice.'

Helen went over to the larder cupboard to give him a minute to compose himself. He wasn't the only one who needed time out. She didn't know if it was because Hunter was away, but she'd started to feel lonely here at the Old Rectory. Lonelier than she'd ever been in her life. Which was stupid and completely unlike her. She'd always been so happily self-contained. She put it down to being an only child and having been brought up by grandparents who didn't have the energy younger parents did.

But if it was Hunter's absence that was making her feel lonely, why, when he'd been away countless times before, had it not bothered her then? And why did she feel so emotionally close to this man in her kitchen? What was the connection?

She selected a bag of sweet chilli flavoured crisps from the middle shelf, poured them into a dish and thought how this bluff man certainly had his soft, vulnerable underbelly. She'd seen it on Saturday morning when he'd visited for the first time. She'd heard the knock at the door just as she was tidying away the mess Hunter had made in his dressing room when he'd been packing for his trip. 'I thought I'd give our passionate affair more credence by calling on you the moment your husband was out of town on business,' he'd said when she let him in. He'd given her a loosely thrown together arrangement of flowers from the garden at Chapel House – sprigs of flowering rosemary, creamy-white May blossom and sweetly scented lily-of-the-valley. It had struck her that Mac might like to wander round the garden on his own, so she'd invited him to go outside and enjoy the sunshine while she made them some coffee. When she'd found him sitting on the stone bench in the sheltered bower of the rhododendrons and azaleas and staring at the sunken fish pond – the carp had long since been taken by the herons – there had been no mistaking the look of sadness on his face. How many times had he sat there with Alice? she'd wondered.

Closing the larder door, she put the dish of crisps on the table.

'I'm sorry,' he said gruffly, putting away a handkerchief. 'I'm becoming a sentimental old fool. It's just that I miss her. We understood each other, you see. We were extraordinarily compatible.' He swallowed noisily. 'Come on, let's talk about something else.'

Helen thought fast, and said, 'Perhaps you can help me with something. The other night at the pub, I clearly said something that annoyed Lucy. What was it? What did I inadvertently put my foot into?'

'Ah ...' he said ponderously. 'Yes, that was a tricky moment, wasn't it?'

'Tricky doesn't come close. It was a real conversation stopper. I felt awful.'

'We all have our raw spots, and unfortunately you prodded at Lucy's. Her father left her and her mother when she was fourteen and she's refused to have anything to do with him since.'

'But what's that got to do with going to see some gardens in Italy?'

'Marcus Gray lives on Lake Como.'

Now it was Helen's turn to say, 'Ah.'

'Any chance of a top-up?' Mac held out his near-empty glass.

She fetched the bottle from the fridge. 'Do you think I ought to apologize?'

'No. Lucy isn't the sort of person to hold a grudge.'

'It sounds like she does with her father.'

'True. But then we're on the outside looking in and don't know the full story. I've always believed that there is nothing so complicated as a family, especially if there's been an altercation amongst its members.'

'So what do you think about Olivia Marchwood's suggestion that the Garden Club should go on a trip to Lake Como?'

'It has its appeal.'

'And?'

He winked mischievously. 'As I've said before I'm game if you are. But if your husband wants to join us, I'd have to draw the line. I'm far too full of myself to play the gooseberry.'

She laughed. 'I think there's about as much chance of Hunter wanting to join the group as there is of Savannah wanting to come with us.'

At that exact moment, the girl herself appeared in the kitchen. Call it paranoia, but Helen had the feeling that she'd been listening at the door. Her trousers noisily dragging on the floor as she went over to the fridge, Savannah said, 'Talking about me again, Step-ma?'

The atmosphere in the kitchen instantly grew super-chilled. 'I'd better be making a move,' Mac said. 'It's bad form to overstay one's welcome.'

Up on the worktop now, her bare feet swinging as she chewed on a chicken drumstick, Savannah said, 'How's your dog, Mr Truman?'

'He's fine. But then he's not been dodging badly driven cars of late.'

Savannah smiled and pointed at him with the drumstick. 'Better tell him to watch out; my new car's being delivered tomorrow.'

This was news to Helen. Having told Hunter she was too busy to go shopping for a car with Savannah, she'd assumed the matter had been dropped for the time being. 'When was that arranged?' she asked.

'Dad called me this morning while you were at work. He arranged it as a surprise, said the garage was just waiting for the tax disc to be sorted.' The drumstick was now being waved at Helen. 'So guess what, you get to take me for driving lessons now.'

Out in the hall, Mac said, 'Fate cast you a difficult card with that girl. Still, it won't be for ever.'

'Knowing my luck, it might be.'

'Perhaps she's just bored. Find her something to do. Something worthwhile that shows her how lucky she is. Why don't you take her to work with you?'

'Are you mad?'

'It could do her good to see how others less fortunate than her have to cope with life.'

'Our clients aren't the great unwashed, Mac. Anyway, what have they ever done to deserve her? How would you feel if she turned up on your doorstep?'

He gave her a peck on the cheek. 'She did. And amazingly, I survived.'

*

Conrad had finished work more than an hour ago. But instead of locking up and going across to the house to make some supper, he'd put Nick Drake's *Five Leaves Left* on the CD player and started flicking through the pages of a photo album. It was a bittersweet process. Some might say he was a masochist, and maybe he was, but he was beyond caring what anyone thought of him. He'd long since accepted that he'd become emotionally and sexually dysfunctional in the eyes of his friends, who, he knew, all thought five years was a hell of a long time to grieve for a person. Some had hinted that it was self-indulgent. Yet to him there were still days when it felt like yesterday that Samantha had died. One of the senior partners of the law firm he freelanced for in London had lost his wife to cancer some years back and he'd confided in Conrad that his wife's actual death hadn't hit him as hard as people thought it had. 'The bereavement started the moment we got the diagnosis that she had terminal cancer,' he admitted. 'It meant I was prepared.'

Conrad had had no such preparation. Sam's death had come from left field. It had caught him right in the solar plexus and damn near killed him, too. A year to the day following her death, when the raw ache of loss and loneliness was too much to bear, he meticulously planned his own suicide. With the kind of thoroughness Sam would have described as being so typical of him – she used to joke that he had an anal retentive disorder – he put his financial affairs in order, changing his will so that everything would go to Mac and his sister, Susan. He'd then rigged up the necessary hose-piping to his car in the garage, turned the key in the ignition, closed his eyes and calmly waited, hoping that the end would be quick. He knew what to expect, that the lethally poisonous, colourless and odourless gas would combine with the oxygen-carrying molecule haemoglobin in his red blood cells and stop it from doing its job: when sufficient tissues had been starved of oxygen, asphyxiation would kick in.

But it had been a mistake to close his eyes, for at once all he could think of was Sam. He thought of her as she was the day he met her – how awesome she'd seemed. He relived the first time he'd kissed her properly and managed to catch one of his fingers in her necklace. He remembered the day they bought their first flat together and found a pair of knickers behind the radiator – they'd hurled them out of the bedroom window only to see them sailing down into their neighbours' garden where a barbecue party was in full swing. But when he pictured the two of them on their wedding day – Sam coming towards him in the church, the confident smile on her face, the wink she'd given him, and the knowledge that this really was the first day of the rest of their lives together – he had snapped his eyes open. Sam had been one of the most fearless people he knew; what would she think of his cowardly way out? 'Suicide?' he heard her saying with contempt, as clearly as if she were beside him. 'I'd have expected better of you, Conrad. Do you think that's the kind of man I'd have married?'

In the days that followed he'd almost believed that Sam had been in the car with him, that her spirit, ghost, call it what you will, had saved him, because with tears streaming down his face, he'd fumbled to turn off the engine, and dragging himself from the car, he'd thrown open the garage door that led to the garden and collapsed onto the sodden grass. With the rain beating down, he'd lain there racked with gut-wrenching sobs and vomiting like an animal. Hearing the noise, his neighbours, Tim and Ann, had found him and taken him inside. It didn't take them long to realize what he'd tried to do. Their suspicions were further aroused when they saw an envelope on his bedside table addressed to his uncle. Tim had then rushed back downstairs and checked the garage. Being a doctor, he'd jumped into full professional mode and made Conrad sit by the open window, breathing in the wet night air. He'd wanted to take him to hospital, but Conrad had begged him not to. 'I'm okay, Tim,' he'd said. 'Check me over if you want, but please, no hospital. Anything but the degradation of everyone knowing how flaked out I've become.'

A deal was struck. Tim insisted on staying the night with him as well as extracting a promise that Conrad would see a grief counsellor. He never did, though.

Chapter Eleven

It was as quiet as the grave at Meadowlands Garden Centre. The weather had taken a turn for the worse, a chilly wind had sprung up and the temperature had plummeted. It was not a day for wearing shorts; Lucy was dressed in jeans, a T-shirt, an old woollen sweater of Orlando's and her green fleece with the Meadowlands logo. With so few customers to deal with, she was able to get on with unloading that morning's delivery. A lot of what they sold came from local nurseries, but the weekly delivery of plants from Holland was an integral part of their stock. The plants had a tendency to be a bit 'soft', having been overly mollycoddled in the massive Dutch greenhouses, and they always required extra care initially. After loading up a trolley of verbascums and astilbes, she pushed it to the covered area and transferred the pots to the awaiting tables. Sheltering the plants here for a few days would acclimatise them to the cooler temperatures – not having experienced the rigours of the real world yet, they had little resistance to the wind.

It was beginning to rain now. Lucy thought of Orlando; he was starting work on a new garden today. If the rain turned into a continuous downpour, he'd be sloshing around in a mudbath. Part of her thought he deserved it. After putting her through that talk at the village hall on Friday evening – honestly, how could he have made such a mistake! – he'd presented her with an envelope when they were at home. 'Either you open this and read it, or I do,' he'd said.

'Where's that come from?' she'd asked him, recognizing at once the handwriting and Italian stamp.

'I got it out of the bin.'

'Why? Why the hell would you do that?'

But instead of answering her, he'd said, 'Open it, Luce. Come on, what harm can it do?'

'No harm to me,' she'd said, 'but I can't vouch for what I might inflict on you.'

'That's a risk I'm prepared to take.'

When she realized that he wasn't going to give up, she'd snatched it out of his hands. 'Oh, give it here.'

Except she hadn't opened it there and then, she'd taken it upstairs to her bedroom, promising Orlando she would read it. In her own time.

It was now Thursday and she still hadn't got around to it. She could have thrown the wretched thing away again, but there was something in Orlando's face every time he asked if she'd read it yet that stopped her. Today was the day, she'd decided. She'd brought it with her in her rucksack and was going to read it during her lunch break. She had asked Orlando why he had chosen now to start taking such an active interest in her nonexistent relationship with her father and he'd shrugged and said, 'Just do it for me, Luce. Do it to humour me.'

At one o'clock she stopped for lunch. Behind the display of conservatory furniture was a cafe. On days when it wasn't too busy, members of staff were allowed to use it. Otherwise they used what had once been a store room and had recently been converted into a staff room. It contained a couple of long bench tables with chairs, a sink, a fridge, a kettle and a microwave. It was here Lucy chose to eat her lunch – cheese and pickle sandwiches she'd made that morning, along with a banana and a piece of fruit cake. She was alone, just as she'd hoped she would be – everyone else on this lunch shift having gone to the empty cafe. She held the envelope in her hands for a few moments, wondering why she was doing this. Why had she let Orlando bully her this way?

Unable to come up with an answer, other than that she didn't want to appear petty in Orlando's eyes, she slid her finger under the sealed edge. Sure enough, just as she'd expected, there was a card. Without bothering to take in the picture on the front, and with her heart stupidly beating faster, she opened it.

Dear Lucy,

Knowing how atrocious the Italian postal service is, I'm sure (despite sending this card in good time) it will still arrive hopelessly late. Nonetheless, I wish you love and happiness on your birthday.

As always, I would give anything to see you. Please, won't you have a change of heart? Why not come and visit us? Or let me come and see you. It would mean so much to me.
   With all my love,
   Marcus.

Not *Dad.* Not even, *your father.* But *Marcus.* It seemed to magnify the enormous gulf between them, as though he wasn't her father at all. What else should she have expected from him? The knot of rejection tightened deep within her.

'All alone, Lucy? What's going on? Have the others sent you to Coventry?'

She stuffed the card back into her rucksack and turned round to see her boss standing in the doorway. Hugh Fielding was a tall, solidly built man with thick wiry hair; the only resemblance to Orlando was his blue eyes. 'I fancied a bit of peace and quiet,' she said.

'Oh, well I'm sorry to have disturbed you.'

'Was there something you wanted?' Her tone was sharper than she meant it to be.

He came into the room and pulled out a chair. 'You okay? You don't seem yourself.'

She slumped back into her seat. If ever proof were needed that she was better off pretending she didn't have a father, it was right there in her rucksack. Just that one reading of his card and her mood had gone from nought to sixty in the blink of an eye. 'I'm sorry,' she said. 'I'm just a bit out of it at the moment.'

It was on days like this that Lucy regretted never having learned to drive. By the time she'd battled home on her bike in the buffeting wind and the lashing rain that evening, her tetchy mood had escalated into a full-blown cyclone of bad-temperedness. And it was aimed directly at Orlando. If he hadn't poked his nose into matters that had nothing to do with him, she wouldn't have spent the afternoon getting so steamed up. Dumping her bike against the wall and letting herself in at the back door, she stripped off her wet outer clothes in the laundry room. She was just removing her boots when she cocked her ear. Voices: Orlando's she's recognized, but not the girl's. Company was the last thing she wanted. She pushed open the kitchen door.

'Oh hi, Luce,' Orlando greeted her, mid-laugh and swinging

back on his chair. 'I didn't hear you come in. God, you're drenched. Let me get you a towel.'

But as welcome as a towel was, Lucy was much more interested in the stranger who was sitting at the kitchen table drinking from her Winnie the Pooh mug. Orlando knew jolly well that no one but she was allowed to use that mug. What was this? Party Central all of a sudden?

Orlando had had enough of tiptoeing round Lucy's foul mood. Ever since Savannah had gone, he'd been treated to some top-whack dirty looks. 'Okay,' he said after they'd sat in grim silence for most of supper. 'If you've got something to say, Luce, just spit it out.'

'I don't know what you mean.'

'Not much you don't. Are you still angry at me for—'

'I'm not angry at anyone,' she snapped. 'Just leave me alone, will you?' She got up abruptly and began clattering the plates and cutlery. He watched her practically hurl them into the dishwasher.

'Have you opened that letter from your father yet?' he asked, not caring that she might well turn and take a knife to him.

A moment passed and then she swung round, eyes blazing. 'It wasn't a letter, if you must know.'

'Oh, so you've finally opened it? What was it?'

'It was a card. Just as we both knew it would be.'

'Did he write anything?'

She rolled her eyes. 'Happy birthday, blah, blah, blah. What else would he write?'

'He didn't suggest that you meet, for instance?'

She narrowed her eyes. 'Sounds to me like you already know what the card says. You didn't by any chance steam it open before giving it to me?'

'No!' More calmly, he said, 'So he says he wants to see you, does he?'

When she didn't reply, he said, 'Why don't you, Luce? Haven't you paid him back enough?'

'This isn't about paying anyone back. It's about being true to myself. It's about self-respect. It's—'

'It's not about you wanting to hurt him?' he interrupted her. 'To teach him a lesson for walking out on you and your mum?'

She looked at him, stunned.

He could hardly believe what he'd just said either. What had got into him? Why did he feel so strongly about Lucy making her peace with her father? What did any of it have to do with him? 'I'm sorry,' he said. 'Forget I said anything. It's really none of my business.'

'And that's the first thing you've said in a long while that I can actually agree with!'

That was it. He'd had enough. He scraped back his chair and stalked out of the kitchen. Upstairs in his room, furious that he'd handled things so badly, he stared down on to the rain-soaked garden. The last of the cherry blossom from the tree in next door's garden had been blown by the wind into theirs, littering it with pale-pink petals. He hoped the weather would improve tomorrow. This afternoon had been a washout and he'd had to come home early. He'd been in the house only a few minutes, just long enough to change into some dry clothes, when there'd been a ring at the doorbell. Helen's step-daughter, Savannah, was the last person he'd expected to see on the doorstep.

'Hiya!' she said, 'Can I come in? It's peeing down out here and I'm getting drenched.'

Taking in the bedraggled state of her – hair plastered to her head, make-up smudged and running, clothes soaked through – he'd ushered her in. 'Haven't you heard of that amazing little device known as an umbrella? Or that other handy thing, a coat?'

She laughed. 'I got caught out. Hey, nice place you got here. Shame I'm dripping all over the carpet. Any chance of a drink while I wait for the worst of the rain to pass over?'

Amused at her directness, he said, 'I expect we can manage that.' Knowing that Lucy worried about keeping the house as pristine as her mother had left it, he took Savannah through to the kitchen where her wet things wouldn't cause too much harm. 'Tea or coffee? Or do you want a cold drink?'

'Coffee would be great. Cheers.'

He busied himself with the kettle and coffee. When he turned round, she was standing behind him squeezing her long wet hair into the sink. 'Do you need a towel?' he asked.

'I'll survive. We Tylers are pretty tough, you know.'

Somehow he didn't doubt it.

He'd barely made her drink and invited her to sit at the table when Lucy had arrived home from work. One look at her face told him she hadn't had a good day. It was a shame Savannah had been so slow to pick up on the bad vibes Lucy was giving off – he'd never known anyone to take so long over one cup of coffee – but eventually, after Lucy, having changed her clothes, had started to cook their supper, she left. He'd seen her to the door and given her an umbrella; the rain hadn't stopped.

'I'll drop it off tomorrow, shall I?' she asked.

'It's okay, I'll pick it up the next time I'm up at the Old Rectory.'

She'd smiled goodbye and as she sauntered off, all cocky and jaunty, throwing him one last wave, he'd been struck by how much she reminded him of Lucy when he'd first got to know her.

A tap at his bedroom door made him swing round from the window. It was Lucy.

'Can I come in?'

'Only if you promise to declare what weapons of mass destruction you're carrying.'

She came in and joined him at the window. 'I'm sorry,' she said. 'I was a real bitch down there, wasn't I?'

'I'd say you were doing a fair impersonation of one.'

'It's just ... Oh, I don't know, it's impossible to explain. But any connection with my father hurts. And I hate him for that. I hate the fact that he still has this ability to hurt me. I wish I could just forget all about him.'

'Face it, Luce, that's never going to happen. But what you could do is take control of the situation. Why not agree to meet him and finally have it out? Confronting him might not make you best buddies, but ...' he hesitated and smiled, 'it might make you easier to live with.'

She gave him a tentative smile back. 'I'll think about it.'

He put his arms around her and pulled her to him. With his chin resting on the top of her head, he decided now was the perfect time to say what had been on his mind ever since Friday night. 'You know what we should do? We should go on this trip to Italy with the Garden Club. You could take time out from the tour to meet your father, safe in the knowledge that you'd have a posse of back-up, should you need it.'

She leaned away from him. 'You've put a lot of thought into this, haven't you? Why?'

It was a question he'd asked himself several times this last week. He still didn't really know why he'd lied to Lucy about the talk on Friday, then made out he must have misheard Olivia Marchwood on the phone, but for some weird reason he'd got it into his head that she should be there in the village hall that evening. Just as he'd picked that night to give her her father's card. Perhaps it had been a full moon or something.

'Orlando?'

He looked into her face, saw that she was waiting for an answer. 'Because, you idiot,' he said, 'you're my best friend and I care about you. Why else?'

Chapter Twelve

Savannah couldn't believe this was happening to her. How had she wound up hanging around a hospital with her step-mother and this wrinkly, midget woman with a string shopping bag? And if that pervy bloke in the anorak opposite them stared at her any more, she'd bloody well give him something to stare at. With any luck, it would give him a heart attack and finish him off.

She pushed her legs out in front of her, tilted her head back and stared up at the fluorescent strip lighting. How much longer would they be kept waiting before this old woman would be called for her physio appointment? Or maybe this was how the NHS saved money; they kept people waiting long enough so that they died before any time or money was wasted on them. Thank God Dad had private medical care for the family.

Next to her, Helen and the old crone were wittering on about how hot it was in here. Savannah yawned. Could her life be any more tedious? Knowing Helen, this was probably the high point of the day. If she'd known the Bitch Queen was going to pull this stunt on her she would never have asked her for some driving practice. Next thing she knew, she was being told that in exchange for this she had to come to work with Helen. She'd had a rough idea of the sort of stuff she did – Dad had told her about it and Mum had said how smart Helen had been to scam Dad for the start-up money – but she'd had no idea just how dreary it was. Why did Helen do it? Mum had never worked; she'd always said she didn't have time. What was the point, anyhow? Dad earned stacks of money. Why rob some other person of a job they'd need more than she did? It was just selfishness on Helen's part.

She supposed that some time soon she'd have to start thinking about getting a job herself. Although her step-sister, Kim, never had. She just took the easy route and got married. Trouble was, Savannah didn't want to do that, any more than she wanted to work for her father, like Clancy. There again, she wouldn't say no to driving a forklift truck in one of Dad's warehouses. That would be all right. A laugh, too. Most of her friends from school had gone to university, but having screwed up her A-levels, she'd thrown that option away. She blamed the school. Mum and Dad should never have made her go to that twatty all-girl school; she'd hated every day of being there. It could have been worse. Originally they'd wanted her to go to the same boarding school Kim had gone to, but she'd said if they forced her to do that, she'd burn the place down. 'I'd sooner go to prison,' she'd told them. The look on their faces when she'd said this still made her smile.

Which was more than her night out in Manchester earlier in the week had done. She'd been invited to celebrate Tasha Morgan's twentieth birthday. She hadn't wanted to go, but what else did she have to do, stuck in dullsville Swanmere?

Tasha was the daughter of one of Mum's friends, and Savannah had had an on-off friendship with her for several years. Because their mothers got on it was assumed they would, too. But they had bugger-all in common – Tasha worked as a beauty therapist and she was always on about finding herself a rich husband. She had chosen the club they'd ended up in because she knew it was where a couple of footballers had started to hang out. 'I'm gonna find myself a rising Man-U star,' Tasha had told them all when the bouncers had waved them inside.

Within no time Savannah was bored of dancing and had found herself a seat at the bar where she planned to get quietly off her head. Anything was better than watching Tasha and her coked-up friends make fools of themselves in front of a crowd of potato-faced blokes they didn't know from Adam. She didn't touch coke these days; she'd had a scary episode once, blacked out in a club and woken up on the floor of a loo, her bag missing. Now she just stuck to alcohol. To ensure a good night, the trick was to drink until she was sick, and then when she'd thoroughly emptied her stomach and cleared her system, it was back to the bar for another tequila shot. Only once had she got it wrong; she'd ended up in hospital. Having her stomach pumped hadn't been as bad as she'd thought. Her parents never knew anything about it – Mum had been at some ball or other and Dad had been away. Clancy had been called to the hospital instead. He'd given her a bit of a lecture, but afterwards, when he was driving her back to his place, he'd agreed that if she promised not to do it again, he wouldn't tell Dad.

'Dad'll ground you until you're collecting your pension if he knows what you've been up to,' he said.

'Did you never get drunk when you were my age?'

'Sure. All the time. But I'm of the male species. You're of the other kind. The kind Dad expects to be sweet and well behaved. Stomach pumps don't enter the equation.'

'That sucks.'

'Life does. Better get used to it. Why did you do it?'

'Do what?'

'Get so drunk?'

'Because I wanted to.'

'I'm expecting a bit more of an explanation than that. Is it to do with Dad and your mum getting divorced?'

'Hey, what is this? Are you training to be a social worker or something?'

He hadn't pushed it, which was just as well. Another question from him and she might have told him the truth.

Watching Tasha on the dance floor that night in Manchester, grinding her crotch into the face of some bloke kneeling at her feet, Savannah had decided she'd had enough, and had got herself a taxi home. The cab driver hadn't been too pleased when she'd told him how far away he'd have to take her, but after she'd assured him she could pay in cash, he'd agreed and said the fare would come to sixty quid. 'Whatever,' she'd shrugged. If there was one thing Dad had drilled into her, it was that she should never go anywhere on her own without plenty of cash in her pocket.

It must have been the cab driver's awful driving down all those country lanes, but by the time he'd pulled into the circular drive of the Old Rectory, she'd felt her stomach heaving. She'd stuffed three twenty-pound notes into the driver's hand, let herself into the house and staggered upstairs to be sick. She knew Helen had heard her because a light had switched on as she'd taken the final run up the stairs. She didn't make it in time to the loo in her en suite bathroom, but she didn't care. Dad had a cleaner to see to that. Except there'd been no sign of the cleaner the next day – apparently she only came once a week – and the Bitch Queen had thrust a bucket of cleaning stuff at her and told her to deal with it herself.

She shuddered at the memory of the puky mess all over the

bathroom floor. The Bitch Queen was probably keeping a score of how many times she got the better of Savannah. Well, she'd better look out; two could play at that game.

She yawned again. Helen and the Old Crone were still at it, yacking on and on. God, what wouldn't she give to be somewhere else? She closed her eyes and thought of Orlando. Gorgeous, sexy Orlando. It had been a score of an idea yesterday to call on him. She'd been sitting in the cafe at the deli waiting for the rain to ease up when she'd seen him driving by in his van. Home early, she'd thought. Maybe she'd brave the rain after all and take a little wander down the main street of the village. She knew exactly which door to knock on because she'd casually asked Helen where he lived. Deliberately leaving her jacket and umbrella behind at the cafe – if they weren't there when she went back for them she could always buy some new gear – she'd ventured out into the rain. She'd arrived at Orlando's in exactly the drenched state she knew would have him welcoming her inside.

Everything was going just fine until that girl he lived with had shown up. Talk about cutting the atmosphere with a knife the minute she joined them. Now if ever there was a girl who needed to chill, it was dear old Lucy! Enjoying the fact that she was causing such an obvious stir, she'd taken for ever to drink her coffee. It always amused her to make people feel uncomfortable.

She wasn't entirely sure just how old Orlando was – she was just about to ask him when Lucy had burst in – but it didn't really matter. He was fit and cool and would go a long way to keeping her occupied while she was stuck in Swanmere. And based on that look he'd given her when she'd said goodbye in the rain, there was every chance he might be interested in her.

She sensed movement beside her and opened her eyes. At last the Old Crone was being led away for her physio appointment. The pervy bloke opposite had gone too.

'Would you like a cup of coffee?' This was from Helen.

'What's the catch?'

The Bitch Queen frowned. 'Why would there be a catch?'

'There always is with you. I asked you to take me out in the car and look where I ended up: Planet Catatonic.'

'I'm sorry you see it that way.'

'Yeah, well, just so as you know, don't make the mistake of thinking I'm stupid.'

'I've thought many things of you, Savannah, but stupid isn't one of them. I promise you this, the coffee comes without any strings or conditions.'

'Milk, two sugars, in that case.'

As Savannah watched her step-mother disappear round the corner in search of a vending machine, her thoughts returned to Orlando. If things took off in that direction, maybe she'd want to extend her stay in Swanmere. Question was: who would that annoy most?

Helen?

Or Lucy?

She smiled. Bring it on!

Chapter Thirteen

Spoilt. Devious. Undisciplined. Self-indulgent. Reckless. Mouthy. Manipulative. Sly.

These were just a few of the more polite adjectives Helen could use to describe her world-class brat of a step-daughter. She had been stuck with Savannah for over a week now and each day had brought her closer to losing her temper, something she'd sworn she wouldn't be reduced to. However, yesterday she'd very nearly lost it. She'd found Savannah rummaging through her jewellery box. 'Why don't you just ask me for what it is you want and I'll give it to you,' she'd said from the open bedroom door. The girl hadn't even jumped, just stood there staring insolently back at her, a pair of tear-drop diamond earrings in her hand.

'That's not like you, Savannah,' Helen had said, stepping into the room. 'Stuck for words. This must be a first.'

'If you must know, I was working out how much Dad's spent on you.'

'That's easy. He's spent far too much. None of which I've asked for.'

'You wouldn't need to.'

'Meaning?'

Savannah dropped the earrings back into the jewellery box. 'That Dad's got a heart of gold. What else could I possibly mean?'

With gritted teeth and clenched fists, Helen had left it at that. She'd known perfectly well what Savannah had been getting at: that she had worked a number on Hunter and was milking him for all she could get.

Hunter was due home tomorrow and the second he set foot over the threshold Helen was determined to wash her hands of his daughter. She knew she would never be able to convince him that his darling girl was the spawn of Satan, but for the remainder of Savannah's stay, he needed to know that she was all his responsibility. As far as Helen was concerned, she had done more than her bit; she had gone way beyond the call of duty. Bloody hell, she was teaching the girl to drive! Would any other woman in her place do that? And what thanks did she get? None. Absolutely none. Let it not be said she hadn't done her damnedest to keep the peace, for the sake of her marriage.

They were in the car now, Savannah cursing and swearing as she crashed through the gears of her brand-new 1 Series BMW. When Helen had suggested Hunter buy a sensible car for his daughter, a 1.6 litre engine, 16" alloy wheels, heated leather seats and air-con was not what she'd had in mind. When she'd been Savannah's age, she'd been the proud owner of a rusting, third-hand Ford Escort. So bad was the rust she could see daylight through the floor. Her feet used to get soaked on rainy days.

'Brake! I said *B R A K E !*'

The car screeched to a tyre-burning halt, just inches from the rear of the truck they'd been following along the dual carriageway to Crantsford. Roadworks had brought the traffic to a standstill.

'Didn't you see the truck's brake lights?' Helen demanded, when the seatbelt jamming mechanism had released itself and she was able to turn and face Savannah.

Savannah shrugged. 'I guess I didn't.'

'You need to pay more attention to what's going on around you.'

'I was.'

'Obviously not enough.'

Savannah drummed her fingers on the steering wheel. 'I have a question,' she said after a brief silence. 'Are you going to keep freaking out?'

'I'll keep freaking out as long as you keep scaring the hell out of me.'

To Helen's annoyance, the girl actually smirked. She was probably thinking she'd like nothing more than to keep scaring her. To death if needs be. Calm. Calm. Calm. A car hooting angrily from behind had her saying, 'You'd better drive on.'

'Oh, really?' Savannah said sarcastically. 'That hadn't occurred to me.' But, in the wrong gear, she stalled the engine. 'Shit!'

'Try first.'

'Oh, like I wasn't doing that already.'

'If you had been we wouldn't have stalled.'

'Stupid buggering thing won't go in! It's stuck.' Helen could see the girl was getting rattled.

The driver of the car behind hooted again.

Helen silently chanted to herself: Calm. Calm. Calm. 'How about putting the clutch pedal down?' she suggested.

'I am! It's—'

They suddenly lurched forwards and stalled once more. Immediately this elicited a long and disagreeable honk from the electric-blue Subaru behind them. Helen had had enough. The red mist was down. She flung off her seatbelt and leapt from the car. She marched round to the rear and approached the Subaru driver who had formed such a close and meaningful relationship with his horn. His shirtsleeves rolled up, he was now banging his hands on the steering wheel and watching in wild-eyed despair as the queue of traffic to his right moved steadily by. She knocked on his window. It slid down. 'So what's your problem?' she said, bending down to the open window. 'Have you forgotten what a nightmare it is learning to drive? Or maybe you didn't bother with lessons. The same way you skipped classes on manners.' On the man's lap was a half-eaten packet of sandwiches. A can of Coke rested in the specially made holder, and a road atlas lay on the passenger seat.

'Are you crazy, or what?' he yelled back at her. 'Can't you see you're holding up the traffic?'

'And I shall continue to do so until you've apologized.'

He goggled at her. 'What?'

'You heard. Out of the car. *Now!*'

'Not on your life. And if you don't get away from me, I shall call the police.' He reached for his mobile.

'And tell them what?' she demanded. 'That there's a madwoman holding you hostage on the A556?'

'You said it!'

'Helen, what the bastard hell are you doing?'

It was Savannah, looking murderous. How very fortunate.

'Ah, just the girl we need,' Helen said, her tone falsely cheery. 'Right, how easy can we make this for you, Mister? Just say the sweet words, "I am very sorry for being such a dickhead; it will never happen again," and we'll be on our way.'

Whether or not it was the fear of what she might be capable of doing next, or he'd simply accepted his fate, the man muttered something that came close to resembling an apology.

'I'm sorry,' Helen said, at the same time cupping her ear

exaggeratedly. 'I don't think we caught that, did we, Savannah?'

'Are you deaf as well as off your trolley?' he shouted. 'I said I was sorry! Now let me go. I'm late for a meeting.'

Back in the BMW – the Subaru driver having driven off in a blaze of fist-waving and screaming engine – Helen said in a serenely calm voice, 'Right then, mirror, signal, and ... manoeuvre.'

They'd been driving for several minutes when Savannah said, 'What was that all about?'

'I can't abide bad manners,' Helen said.

'You don't say?'

'There was no need for what he did. He could see the L-plate on the back of the car. He should have made allowances.'

Savannah didn't know what to say. She felt confused. She was convinced Helen hated her. So why had she stuck up for her like that? Mum would never have done that. From the safety of the passenger seat, Mum would have called the man every name under the sun, but she wouldn't have got out and confronted him. Savannah couldn't decide whether the Bitch Queen had earned her respect, or whether she should consider her one hundred per cent fruity-loop material.

She drove on, trying to concentrate on the road as well as the mirrors, the gears and her speed. Friggin' hell, there was so much to remember! She'd be glad when she was back at home and could have proper driving lessons again with her instructor. While she was staying with her father, they'd been put on hold. She'd only had two lessons so far, but with a bit of luck she wouldn't need too many more. Especially if she could convince Helen to keep taking her out like this. Except, of course, Helen was continuing to apply strings. The only reason she was getting some driving practice today was because Helen had said she could drive her to Crantsford to visit her grandmother. God, you'd think she had enough of old people, working with them all week.

'My grandmother can appear a little vague at times,' Helen said to Savannah as they walked the length of a royal-blue carpeted hallway.

Savannah couldn't care less how vague the old woman was; she had no intention of sticking around for long. She'd clocked a garden at the back of the nursing home – the expensive nursing home that Dad had to be paying for, according to Mum – and after she'd satisfied her curiosity by having a squint at Helen's grandmother, she was going to go and sit outside in the sun.

For some reason she was cutting up the pages of a newspaper when they opened the door of her room. The old lady put down her scissors, and as if not even noticing Helen, she stared long and hard at Savannah. Savannah cringed. What was it with old people? Didn't they know it was rude to stare? But when an enormous smile covered the wrinkled old face, she took a step backwards. Scary or what? 'Daisy!' the woman exclaimed suddenly. 'Where on earth have you been? We've been worried sick about you.'

Savannah edged closer to Helen. 'What's she on about?'

Before Helen could reply, the dotty old woman was saying, 'Come and sit with me, dear. I want to hear everything you've been up to. Helen, why don't you make us a drink? You'd like that wouldn't you, Daisy? A nice drink. What about a piece of cake? I bet you're starving. Goodness, this is a surprise! Wait till I tell Gerald.'

In a lowered voice, Helen said, 'Could you play along with her, please?'

'You're kidding?'

'Please, Savannah.'

Savannah sighed and gave in. What the heck? She could use this to her advantage. 'I just want you to know that this is seriously weird, okay? You owe me big time. And who the hell is Daisy?'

'She was my mother.'

'Your *what?*'

'What are you two whispering about over there? Come on, Daisy. Sit with me.'

Reluctantly Savannah crossed the room. As she dropped into the offered chair, she was suddenly enveloped in a bony hug that smelled of vanilla custard. She tried to wriggle out of the woman's grasp, but couldn't. She'd heard that crazy people are always stronger than they look. Now she knew it was true. 'Make her stop,' she hissed at Helen.

Helen came over. 'Like I said, just play along with her,' she whispered. 'It'll only be for a few minutes. Then she'll forget.'

'What will she forget?'

'That we're here. I'll go and make us some tea.'

That evening, after posting some letters, Helen decided not to go straight home. She needed time to think and cool off. She would go for a walk.

Whilst driving back to Swanmere after leaving Emma dozing in front of the television, Savannah had raised the subject of euthanasia. Up until this moment in the car, relations between them had been bordering on the cordial. Grateful for Savannah's performance at the nursing home, Helen had tried to put her animosity aside and make an extra effort to be nice to her step-daughter, to keep her instructions about her driving to a minimum, and to suggest they picked up a DVD to watch that evening. But all that had been forgotten when Savannah said, 'God, if I ever get to be like your grandmother I hope someone would do the decent thing and slip something into my cocoa. How can you bear to visit her when she scarcely knows you? I mean, what's the point?'

'She did know me,' Helen had said quietly.

'She sure as hell didn't grasp who I was. So what do you think about euthanasia?'

'I think it's abhorrent.'

Turning to look at her, Savannah had said, 'It'll soon be a fact of life.'

'Eyes on the road! And don't you mean death? A fact of death?'

'You're only saying that because you're over forty and starting to get squeamish about not living for ever.'

'Oh, that's right; it's only the young who can see the world objectively. Mental note to self: I must stop being so subjective.'

'Hey, chill with the attitude, why don't you? There's no need to be sarcastic. I'm only trying to have a proper conversation with you about something important.'

'No you're not!' Helen's voice had risen. 'You're saying you think the person who means the most to me should be put out of her misery to suit your convenience.'

'Actually, I was thinking of your convenience. Because let's face it, you only visit her out of a sense of duty, don't you? And anyway, shouldn't it be Dad who means the most to you?'

They completed the rest of the journey home in pin-drop silence.

It was a lovely, balmy evening. The sky was a beguiling soft shade of blue; insects had gathered in gauzy clouds in the still, warm air. After days of rain, everything had taken on a vigorous spurt of growth. Helen was following the footpath that started between the post office and the bank and skirted a row of attractive houses, their neat front gardens colourful with flowering laburnums, ceanothus bushes and wisteria. But instead of following the fork in the path that would lead her home to the gate at the bottom of the garden, she continued straight on. Either side of her were hedges of hawthorn covered in creamy-white flowers giving off a sweet appley smell; bees hovered lazily from flower to flower, their droning hum already replacing the sound of traffic from the main road. As she ventured further along the verdant path, the overhanging leafy branches of the lime trees filtered out the evening sunshine; it was like entering a magical tunnel of emerald luminescence. At the end of the path, she could see a stile and daylight. It was an omen, she told herself. As of tomorrow, when Hunter came home, everything would settle down again. He would take Savannah off her hands, and the gloomy mood she'd been suffering this last week would go.

But what if it didn't? What if the feelings that had been building during his absence didn't go away?

And anyway, shouldn't it be Dad who means the most to you?

How had she made such a slip? Hunter was her husband; of course he should mean the world to her. But the truth was he didn't. How could he? How could he be more important to her than Emma? She had known him for so little time in comparison. But then he wasn't the first man in her life who had been denied full access to her heart. 'Has any man ever been allowed to get close to you?' a disgruntled boyfriend once asked her after she'd politely finished with him over dinner when he'd suggested they move in together. Another relationship ended similarly and on this occasion she was accused of maintaining an unnecessarily high level of security around herself. The words Ice Queen were mentioned. It was meant to be a hurtful criticism, but it merely endorsed her view that she was better off on her own. And what was wrong with self-preservation, anyway?

She stood for a moment and peered through a small gap in the hawthorn hedge, breathing in the smell of damp earth. Cow parsley fringed the meadow of long grass that was sprinkled with dandelions. In the distance she could see the church tower just peeping over the trees and rooftops, one of which belonged to Lucy and Orlando. She wondered how they were. And Mac. She hadn't heard from him since he'd given her Alice's journals. If

Savannah wasn't at home, she'd give him a ring and invite him up for a drink. How would he have reacted to Savannah's views on euthanasia, she mused? Now that she was calmer, Helen could see that the girl's comments were made because Savannah was incapable of feeling anything for anyone but herself. For this, the girl had to be pitied.

She climbed over the stile and pressed on towards the pool, where those with fishing permits came to sit and while away the hours on the wooden jetties dotted around the water's edge. There was nobody about this evening. She was just nearing the still, reflecting pool of water and enjoying the scent of wild garlic on the air when she heard the sound of something cracking underfoot. Her heartbeat instantly went into overdrive and she looked around her, but couldn't see a soul. A series of gruesome images flashed through her head – being chased, her cries going unheard, a hand reaching out, her throat being—

Another crackle of breaking twigs had her spinning round. Emerging from a screen of chestnut trees was a man with a small dog. She recognized them at once. It was Mac's nephew: Conrad the Barbarian, and Fritz.

Chapter Fourteen

With Fritz suddenly charging at full steam through the long grass and bluebells, his ears flapping, Conrad had no choice but to follow. When he'd caught up with the dog, Fritz was lying on his back having his tummy scratched by the woman Mac had been seeing so much of recently. His first and very brief sighting of Helen Madison-Tyler had left him with the impression of an attractive woman, a woman he could quite understand his uncle wanting to spend time with: she would be a very pleasant balm to Mac's fractious temperament. But he now revised his opinion of her. She was beautiful. Composed and cool-looking, but definitely beautiful.

'I'm afraid that like his owner, that dog is a terrible tart,' he said when he was looking down at a head of glossy auburn hair. She stood up, a slow, elegant movement. The dying sun was behind her, making her hair glow with a golden intensity. She was taller than he remembered. Friendly eyes the colour of brandy stared back at him.

'It seems odd that we haven't met properly before now,' she said, her hand outstretched. 'I've heard so much about you from Mac, an introduction seems superfluous.' Her grasp was firm.

'I can only guess at what my uncle has told you about me. None of it good, I'm sure. How do you like living here in Swanmere?'

'I like it,' she said simply.

'You don't find its inhabitants a bit too intrusive?'

'No worse than anywhere else I've lived. Why, do you?'

'Yes.' He immediately regretted his response. Now she'd want to know why. But there again, in view of her friendship with Mac, she probably knew everything about him anyway. Keen to deflect any further interest in him, he said, 'Mac's not been well. That's why I'm walking Fritz.'

'I wondered why I hadn't heard from him. It's nothing serious, is it?'

'No. Just a cold. He makes a terrible patient.'

She smiled. 'Show me a man who doesn't.'

Still lying on his back and waving his paws in the air, Fritz let out a bark as if to say, 'Hey, remember me down here?' They both bent to him at the same time, their heads bumping. Apologizing and backing off awkwardly, Conrad said, 'That dog's very nearly as demanding as Mac.'

'Is your uncle well enough for a visitor? I could come and read him the riot act. If it would help,' she added with what he took to be a smile of collusion. It was the same smile he'd seen that evening when she'd looked at him through the gap in the doorway at Chapel House. Knowing that she clearly had the measure of his uncle, he couldn't help but warm to her. It had been the same with Alice Wykeham. She had sized Mac up in no time and the two of them had formed an alliance, a convergence of minds that had held the 'miserable old bugger' – Alice's description – in check.

'Do you have time?' he asked. From the little he'd winkled out of Mac, he knew that she ran some kind of charity helping the elderly. 'Hence the interest in you,' he'd teased his uncle. To which Mac had responded, 'That wouldn't be the stirring of jealousy I can hear, would it?'

'I could come now, if you like,' she said. 'I don't have anything planned for the evening.'

'Now?' he'd repeated, taken aback.

'Yes, why don't we surprise him? Or did you want to be out longer with Fritz?'

Perhaps this was what his uncle liked about her, Conrad thought, her spontaneity. As they climbed over the stile – he stopped to offer Helen his hand – he wondered vaguely how untidy the house was and if it was entirely suitable for a visitor, but then he remembered Evie had been that morning. Evie he could count on; his uncle, on the other hand, was an entirely different matter. It was anybody's guess how he would react to a visitor in his current state.

Chapter Fifteen

June was upon them. Summer was here. And so was Savannah.

Helen could hardly believe her bad luck. Marcia had phoned from the States to say that she was going to extend her visit, and was it all right for Savannah to stay with them for the rest of the summer? Expecting Savannah to embrace this news with her usual propensity to fly off the handle and blame everyone around her for forcing such a miserable time on her, and maybe, with a bit of luck, stomp off in a huff back to Crantsford, Helen had been astounded to hear her say, 'Is that okay with you, Dad? You're sure I wouldn't be in the way? I could go home – the decorators have finished now.'

His reply had been, 'Of course you won't be in the way. It'll be a pleasure to have you here. Isn't that right, Helen?'

In danger of cracking a tooth by gritting her teeth so hard, Helen had nodded and disappeared to the kitchen where she had vented her frustration by bashing the living daylights out of a piece of pork tenderloin for supper.

Two weeks on, Helen and Hunter were enjoying a rare evening sitting in the garden – Savannah had gone out. Helen watched her husband absently swirl his drink round in his glass whilst reading a document that had been faxed through for his immediate attention. As if sensing her gaze on him, he glanced up from his papers. 'You look tired, Helen,' he said. 'Are you sure you're not overdoing it?'

In an effort to avoid spending any time with Savannah, Helen had been working longer and longer hours at Companion Care, but this was hardly something she could admit to Hunter. 'That's rich coming from you,' she said lightly.

He smiled. 'Two of a kind, aren't we?' He went back to reading his document.

Annabel had also commented on the extra hours she was

working, but whereas Helen had to be carefully evasive with her husband she could at least be honest with her friend. 'I know it sounds like I'm paranoid,' she explained to Annabel, 'but it's as if there's this negative forcefield around Savannah and everything she touches suffers. I don't understand why Hunter doesn't see it himself.'

'Is it serious? Is she undermining your relationship?' Annabel had asked.

'Oh, I don't think it will come to that,' she'd replied glibly, although this was exactly what she was worried about.

'Well, you've got to remember that Hunter's between a rock and a hard place, trying to please both you and his daughter. What you can't get away from is that Savannah is his pride and joy and he expects you to share that view.' Helen was surprised how much Annabel's advice annoyed her. It was as if her friend was taking Hunter's side, which in turn felt like a criticism of Helen's behaviour. And since when did childless Annabel know so much about children or step-families?

But it wasn't just Savannah that was causing difficulties for them. There was a far greater problem. Since Hunter's return from the Caribbean, they had made only one attempt to make love. As before, it had ended badly.

Like cancer, impotence was one of those words you weren't supposed to say out loud. The subject had become a no-go area and Helen was at a loss to know how they were ever going to resolve the problem if Hunter wouldn't discuss it with her. Each time she tried to get near it – to get closer to Hunter – he backed off. What hurt him most, she suspected, was the slur it cast on him. He had reached an age when physically things were going to start developing glitches; perhaps he was worried that there was something more seriously wrong, but was too scared – and too vain – to do anything about it. That was the trouble with men like Hunter; they believed themselves to be invincible and couldn't be seen to be anything but on top of their game.

Mac was the same. When Helen had visited him, he had been mortified that she should see him so ill-disposed. Sitting up in bed, unshaven and pyjama-clad, the pages of *The Times* scattered across the duvet, his face had been a picture of discomfort. He'd given Conrad a fierce scowl of reproach, but Conrad had ignored him and simply walked away, not before giving Helen a smile. He'd reappeared with two cups of coffee minutes later, then left them alone. Through the open window in Mac's bedroom she'd watched him cross the courtyard. Shortly afterwards a desk lamp was switched on in an upstairs room. She could see Conrad sitting in front of a computer, putting on a pair of reading glasses. More than once, before she got down to work at the Old Rectory, Evie had extolled the merits of her employer at Chapel House to Helen, calling him 'a smasher' and 'a dreamboat'. Whilst Helen might not go so far as to use these outmoded expressions herself, she couldn't help but agree with Evie. He was tall and well built, and there was a measured and decisive quality about him that she approved of. His light-brown hair was cut short and pleasantly shot through with a smattering of grey at the temples. His brow was broad and strong and gave him an intelligent, scholarly air. An air of sincerity, too. All this she had secretly noted while they were walking through the village to surprise Mac at Chapel House. Still staring at him across the courtyard, she'd wondered if he was aware of his appeal. Following her gaze, Mac had interrupted her thoughts by saying, 'He does nothing but work, that boy. It's a wonder I get anything to eat or drink round here being stuck in bed. I could be dead and he'd still be in that bloody office of his.'

'Perhaps if you were a better-behaved patient, he'd want to spend more time with you,' she'd scolded him. 'Stop feeling so sorry for yourself. You're not at death's door yet.'

'It's only a matter of time.'

It was dark when she'd left Mac, and seeing the light still on in Conrad's office, she had been tempted to go and thank him for the coffee, but decided against it, he probably wouldn't welcome the intrusion.

Why, she wondered now, as she listened to the faraway sound of a woodpecker, could she be utterly frank with Mac, but couldn't be anywhere near as honest with her own husband? Why was she so afraid of upsetting Hunter?

Talk to him, she told herself. Right now, whilst you're alone. 'Hunter,' she said.

'Mm ...' he said without looking up, a pencil pressed against his lips.

'Can we talk?'

He tapped the pencil against his teeth and glanced at her.

'I'm worried about you,' she murmured, her nerve only just holding out.

He frowned, then his gaze turned steely. 'I've told you before; I don't want to talk about it.'

Pretend he's anyone but Hunter, she told herself. What's the worst that could happen? 'Why not?' she asked.

His expression darkened. 'Ever thought that the fault might be yours? After all, it's never happened to me before – with other women.'

Ouch! But then in his eyes she'd probably asked for that. 'It's not about fault, Hunter,' she said. 'If it helps, why don't we see a doctor together?'

'What use would that be?'

'You're an intelligent man; please don't be obtuse.'

He flung the pencil and partially read document onto the table and reached for his gin and tonic. He downed it in one, but didn't say anything.

'Look,' she said more gently. 'I know this is difficult for you. No man likes to admit—'

'And how would you know how it feels to be a man?' he interrupted.

'I don't. But maybe if you opened up to me more, I'd have a better understanding of how to cope with what's happening.'

'Forget it. I'm not in the mood for some half-baked psychobabble you've read in a magazine. And I'm certainly not going near any doctor.'

'But Hunter—'

'Enough!' He rose abruptly, knocking the table as he did so and sending his empty glass flying. He marched off across the terrace and went inside the house through the drawing-room French windows.

Unaccountably near to tears, Helen chewed on her lip. So much for talking to him. How would they ever sort this out if he refused point blank to admit they had a problem? Staring down at the mess of broken glass, she got to her feet. She'd better fetch a dustpan and brush.

She took the route into the house that Hunter had taken and to her surprise found him in the drawing room standing in front of a small table. He had his back to her, but she could see that he was holding a framed photograph of the two of them on their wedding day. Oh, God, she thought, he's wondering why he married me. It was as if he was weighing up her worth and deciding their future. Never had she felt so judged. She wanted to slip away unnoticed, but she wasn't fast enough, or quiet enough. He turned at the sound of her shoe on the step. He looked awful. Older. Tired. Betrayed.

A wave of compassion swept over her. She knew instinctively that they'd reached a crisis point. Do the wrong thing now and it would all be over. 'I'm sorry,' she said, 'I shouldn't have said anything. Forgive me, please.'

Very slowly, he replaced the photograph on the table and then just as slowly, he held his arms out to her. She went to him. He crushed her to him, then pushing her head back, he kissed her throat, her neck, and then her mouth. He kept on kissing her, desperately, demandingly, his body iron-hard against hers, as though he'd never let her go. His breath was coming faster and suddenly his hands were pulling at her clothes, almost ripping them. His need for her was so powerful she was sure this time they'd be all right. Maybe it had been getting too samey and lacking in spontaneity upstairs in their bedroom. He stumbled with her over to the sofa, manoeuvred her down onto it and unzipping his trousers, he knelt before her. For a wildly inappropriate moment, almost laughing out loud, she remembered that this was where Olivia Marchwood had sat on that day she'd come calling. But the thought was short-lived. Hunter was thrusting deep inside her. She stifled a gasp, not wanting anything to distract him.

Chapter Sixteen

Up at the allotments Lucy was spitting bricks. 'Bloody stupid Orlando!' she panted. 'Can't he see what she's up to? Anyone with half a brain cell could figure out that girl's trouble.'

'You know what they say about people who talk to themselves?'

She looked up from where she was preparing the soil for the first of three wigwams of runner beans. Dan was leaning on his hoe and staring at her with that benign expression of his, the one that always made her want to hug him. Despite the warmth of the evening, he was dressed as always in a shirt and pullover and his tatty old tweed jacket with its frayed cuffs and abstract artwork of stains down the front. 'How long have you been there?' she asked, pushing her hair out of her eyes and breathing hard.

'Long enough to know that you've got one on you this evening. You're digging away like a pile-driver. What's got you into such a lather?'

'I'm not in a lather.'

'Come on,' he said. 'Come and sit with me for a while.'

She pushed the spade deep into the soft earth. Dan meant well, but she was nowhere near ready yet to be derailed from her anger. 'I can't,' she said. 'I've got too much to do. Orlando said he'd help and he's buggered off for the night.'

'Ten minutes won't harm. I've got raspberries. First pick of my canes. I'll make us a brew and you can tell me all about it.'

She wilted under the onslaught of his kindness. That was the thing about Dan; he was always able to disarm her. 'Oh, go on, then.'

Dan's plot was easily the neatest and most well cared for of all the allotments. It was also one of the biggest and on its farthest corner stood a shed half-hidden in honeysuckle: the warm evening air was thick with its rich, sweet scent. While Dan fiddled around inside the shed, boiling a small aluminium kettle on a Calor Gaz burner, Lucy snapped open two lightweight deckchairs. When she'd done that she sat and observed the activity going on around her. June was always the busiest month at the allotments; it was when everyone really made an effort. The place was buzzing with the sounds of summer: cheerful voices as people compared their crops (the first of the new potatoes were being pulled and admired); and hedge trimmers and strimmers whirring. For a nominal amount of money, their electricity was supplied by Ronnie Tadget, whose house and garden backed onto the allotments.

'There you are; one cup of tea, just as you like it.'

She took the chipped mug from Dan's knobbly hand. 'Thanks, Dan. You're a star.'

'And you're in a terrible mood. What's Orlando done to upset you?'

'So you *were* listening to me?'

'I should think everyone heard you cursing the boy. What's he been doing?'

She had never been very good at confiding in other people, and much as she liked and trusted Dan, she didn't want to open up to him. 'Where are those raspberries you promised?' she asked.

He clicked his tongue and handed her his mug. While he was gone, she thought how best to distract him. The truth was, she didn't want to be honest with Dan in case he got the wrong end of the stick and suggested she was jealous of Savannah. But it wasn't jealousy that made her dislike the girl. It was the sure knowledge that she was a devious and manipulative piece of work. Lucy had come across any number of Savannah Tylers at school, and had never made the mistake of underestimating the power they wielded. Annoyingly, Orlando seemed blind to the obvious, that Savannah was seriously bad news. But then that was Orlando all over. He was just too nice; he always wanted to see the best in people. 'I'm just giving her a chance,' he'd said after Lucy had come home and found Savannah sitting at their kitchen table yet again. That was three times in the last week.

'What do you mean you're giving her a chance?' Lucy had asked, when Savannah had cleared off and she was wiping up the mess from the table where empty packets of crisps and chocolate bars lay strewn.

'It just strikes me that she's used to people giving her a hard time,' he'd said.

'Maybe that's because she deserves it,' Lucy had argued.

'Well, it's a good thing my dad didn't do that to you when you came to him for a job,' he'd muttered, pouring the remains of his coffee down the sink.

That had hurt. How could Orlando compare her with that spoilt little rich kid who probably hadn't done a day's work in her life? She'd brought the subject up again at breakfast this morning and that was when Orlando admitted that Savannah had asked him if she could work for him.

'What? But you scarcely earn enough money to support yourself, never mind pay her as well.'

'I didn't say I was going to pay her.'

'She wants to work for you for free?'

'She says she wants to learn from me.'

'I bet she does.'

'And what's that supposed to mean?'

'Oh, please, Orlando. She's winding you round her little finger. That's what girls like her do. And what kind of work does she think she's going to be doing with you? I can't see her being any help at all, only a hindrance. She's no more interested in gardening than I am in nuclear physics.'

When he hadn't responded, just concentrated on pouring milk on his cereal, she'd said, 'So are you going to take her on?'

'I haven't decided. I'm meeting her for a drink tonight to give her my answer.'

'Tonight? But I thought we were going up to the allotment. We've got all the runner beans and sweet potatoes to put in. If we leave it any longer, it'll be too late.'

He'd looked at her then, his normally open and engaging face clouded with awkwardness. 'I forgot all about that,' he said. 'I'll give Savannah a ring and put her off until tomorrow. I'm sure she won't mind.'

'Oh, not on my account, please. I can manage on my own. I always have.' She'd buttered her toast so vigorously it had shattered. She'd thrown the mess into the bin and slammed the lid down hard.

'You don't think you're overreacting and being just a touch unreasonable?' he'd said quietly.

Unreasonable? Her? No way! She'd left him to his bowl of Cheerios and cycled to work in record time. She tried to focus her anger on Savannah, not on Orlando, but it made her feel worse.

She could imagine all too well what a prize Orlando would be to a girl like Savannah. Gorgeous men like him didn't grow on trees. He wasn't just a good-looking man; he was kind and endlessly generous. He didn't have a mean bone in him. Perhaps that's why his hunkability, as Angie referred to it, had never been important to Lucy. It had always been his personality that counted. But the thought of Savannah getting her hands on Orlando – and not just metaphorically – filled Lucy with hatred for her. He deserved someone so much better. Her thoughts took an unexpected turn and she recalled all the times she'd seen Orlando practically naked, when he'd emerged from the bathroom in a cloud of steam with just a towel wrapped around his waist, his wet hair slicked back and dripping water down his broad shoulders and smooth, hairless chest. She pedalled even faster. No way should Savannah ever be allowed to get her grasping little mitts on Orlando! Her legs were aching so much when she got to the garden centre she had to sit down and wait for them to stop shaking. Angie asked if she was okay, but had quickly made herself invisible. Half expecting Orlando to call her on her mobile and apologize, Lucy had spent the day nursing her disappointment in him. But he didn't call, and when she got home and found a note saying he hadn't cancelled his evening with Savannah after all, she'd pulled on her boots and marched off up to the allotment.

Dan was back. 'Sorry I was so long,' he said, exchanging a small plastic bowl of raspberries for his mug of tea. 'I was picking off the greenfly for you, knowing what a classy girl you are.'

'You're too much, Dan.'

'Aye, it's been said many a time. Now tell me what the trouble is. It's nothing to do with that trip to Italy, is it? What with you and your Dad, like.'

As convenient as the ready-made diversion was, Lucy approached it warily. 'Yes and no,' she said. She popped a raspberry into her mouth. It was perfectly firm, yet perfectly ripe. Perfectly delicious, too. Home-grown raspberries, especially Dan's, were a breed apart from the mangy efforts supermarkets sold.

The Garden Club's proposed trip to Lake Como was gaining momentum and proving to be the talk of the village. People had been quick to sign up for a place. Orlando had put his name down, and Mac said he was considering going, too. He'd told her this when she'd called round to see him after hearing on the grapevine that he was unwell. When Conrad had shown her through to the sitting room, she'd found him stretched out on the sofa, covered in a blanket and chatting to Helen. 'Hey Mr Popular,' she'd said, noticing Conrad discreetly removing himself from the room, 'how's it going?'

'All the better for seeing you. Have you brought me a present?'

'I have, as a matter of fact.' She'd passed him the box of Turkish Delight she had bought at the deli, knowing it was his favourite.

It was then that he'd raised the subject of the trip to Italy, saying that he fancied going because it would probably be his swan song, his final holiday abroad before popping his clogs. She'd given him a thwack on the shoulder for being such a misery. 'You used to be fun,' she told him. 'Now you're getting maudlin.'

'Correction, my girl; I'm getting ready to die.'

'Any more talk like that and we'll help you on your way,' Helen had said, giving his other shoulder a light thwack.

Helen had also said she'd be interested in the trip, but she would have to see how it would fit in with work. 'There's always the chance that Hunter might like to go,' she'd added, 'but to be honest, I doubt he'll have the time or inclination.' It was funny, but Lucy was so used to seeing Helen on her own, it was difficult at times to remember that she was married. Her husband was a bit of an enigma.

But one absolute dead cert and up for no negotiation of any kind, as she'd told Helen and Mac, was that Lucy Gray would not be going on the trip. No amount of wheedling on anyone's part, in particular Orlando's, would budge her from her decision.

'What do you think of the raspberries?' Dan asked, bringing her out of her thoughts. 'Are they as good as last year's?'

'They're heavenly. I really must grow some myself. I don't know why I haven't got around to it before.'

'That's because you're what my dear old mother used to call a Maybe Queen. One day this, one day that. Some time soon, you'll realize you can't keep putting things off.'

'Is that really how you see me?'

'It's not a criticism.'

'It feels like it.'

'Then I'm sorry. So, will you be going to Italy?'

She suddenly smiled. 'I'll go if you come with me.'

He laughed and clumsily ruffled her hair with his big hand. 'I'm not even a member of the club.'

'Nor am I.'

'And what would a simple fellow like me do in fancy old Italy? I've never been further afield than Worcester, and that was when I were a lad. No, I'm quite happy to hear all about it when you get back. Besides, someone'll have to stay behind and keep an eye on things here.'

She put another raspberry into her mouth. 'There won't be any need for you to do that; I'm not going.'

He looked at her fondly. 'We'll see, my little Maybe Queen.' He sipped his tea with noisy relish.

As he sat in the garden of The Swan, waiting for Savannah to reappear, Orlando was feeling bad about Lucy. Just lately they seemed to be disagreeing with each other more and more. The atmosphere between them had become strained and edgy and it troubled him. It was possible that living together hadn't been such a smart idea. Too much of a good thing, perhaps? But did he really want to move back in with his parents? If it saved his friendship with Lucy, then it was something he should think about seriously. One thing was sure, on his current earnings, he'd never find anything remotely affordable to buy in Swanmere; it was an expensive place to live. He'd have to look elsewhere, somewhere cheaper.

The design work was beginning to take off, but it would be a while before he felt confident enough to make any serious financial commitments, such as taking on a mortgage. As a favour to Helen, but still getting paid for it, he was working regularly at the Old Rectory – Helen had decided that she had hugely underestimated the amount of work needed to keep on top of the garden. He could have told her that at the outset, but that would have been rude and patronizing. With such low overheads, thanks to Lucy, he was saving hard as well as managing to set aside some money each week for the trip to Italy in September. He smiled to himself; who knows? He might be able to claim the trip as a tax deductible expense – after all, research had to be a vital part of his work as a garden designer, didn't it?

'That's what I like to see: a bloke smiling when he sets eyes on me.'

Back from the loo, grinning broadly, Savannah plonked herself on the bench next to him and resumed drinking her glass of lager. He noted the fresh blast of perfume that had been applied, along with a new coating of lip-gloss. Doubtless Lucy would claim that these were all crafty tactics on Savannah's part to ensnare him.

No matter that every girl he'd ever been out with always touched up her make-up when she made a trip to the loo. But there was no telling Lucy that right now. What annoyed him most was that she felt he was so stupid he'd fall for any tricks Savannah, or any girl, might try on him. All the poor girl wanted was a friend here in Swanmere. He had absolutely no intention of getting involved with her. She was too young for his taste.

'So come on, then,' she said, 'have you decided if I can work with you?'

'You're sure you really want to do it? There'll be no money involved. I can't afford to pay you.'

'I'm not doing it for the money. I told you before, I want something to do while I'm here. I'm bored out of my skull. And anyway, I want to learn. I've even been reading some of Helen's gardening books. How's that for commitment?'

He laughed. 'We'll talk about commitment when I see you up to your behind in mud and covered in nettle stings.'

'So is that a yes? Am I officially your partner?'

'My apprentice, more like.'

'Cool. When do I start?'

That same evening Mac and Conrad were sitting in the garden at Chapel House. Back from his weekly game of tennis, Conrad was relaxing with a beer. Mac, while despatching *The Times* crossword with snorts of derision, and with loyal old Fritz at his feet, was onto his second gin and tonic. Now that his uncle had finally shaken off the cold that had confined him to bed for several days, his company, like his health, was vastly improved. However, he still hadn't forgiven Conrad for bringing Helen back that evening when she'd first visited him. 'Damn and blast you, Conrad,' he'd said after Helen had left and Conrad had cooked them their supper. 'You could have warned me she was coming.'

'How? Telepathy?'

'Didn't you have your mobile phone with you?'

'I was out walking Fritz. Why would I take my mobile with me?'

'What if I'd needed you?'

Mac hadn't made a remark like this since recovering from his stroke. Conrad didn't want to read too much into it, yet at the same time he couldn't ignore what it might mean: that his uncle, whilst being confined to bed, albeit briefly, had undergone another loss of confidence.

'Conrad?'

He raised his gaze from his glass of beer. 'Yes?'

'There's something I want to ask you.'

'I'm listening.'

'The thing is, you know Olivia is organizing a trip to Lake Como for the Garden Club? Well—'

'You want to go? I think that's a brilliant idea.'

Mac sat up straighter in his chair. 'I wasn't asking for your permission,' he said sharply.

'I wasn't giving it,' Conrad replied evenly. 'I was merely commenting on what a good idea it was. You'll enjoy it, I'm sure.'

'Don't patronize me, boy!'

'Then don't call me boy. I'm forty-nine years old, in case it's slipped your memory.'

Mac gave him a baleful look. 'There's nothing wrong with my memory.'

Conrad clenched his jaw. How did they do it? How did they always manage to bring out the absolute worst in each other? To his certain knowledge, Mac never treated anyone else the way he treated him. He knew the old adage about familiarity breeding contempt, but Mac's contempt for him was getting beyond a joke. He'd once asked Alice why this was the case, and she'd said that everyone needed a punchbag in their life. 'Sorry, Conrad, but it looks like you're Mac's. He needs to take out his frustration on someone, and you're the one person he can do that to with total impunity. He'd be like a rhyme without a tune if he didn't have you.'

With Alice's words echoing inside his head, Conrad took hold of his own frustration and said, 'I'm sorry, Mac, I interrupted you. What was it you wanted to say?'

'It doesn't matter. It was probably the stupidest idea I've ever come up with.'

'Please. Just say it. Whatever it is.'

Mac cleared his throat noisily. 'It's the trip to Italy. I want you to come with me.'

'You're kidding.'

'Do I look like I am?'

'But I'm not even interested in gardening. You know that.'

'The break would do you good. And ... I'd like your company. What's more, you'd keep those old biddies off my back. You know how they're always looking for the slightest chance to turn me into a lap dog.'

Conrad smiled. 'I hardly see you as a poodle, Mac. More of a Rottweiler.'

'You know what I mean. Will you come?'

'I'll think about it.'

'You'd better think fast; Olivia needs definite names asap.'

'I said I'd think about it.'

Chapter Seventeen

The expression 'master bedroom' had always jarred with Helen. She couldn't imagine Alice Wykeham looking too favourably on those two simple words either. On the other hand, Hunter, who was standing in front of the full-length mirror and fixing his tie, at the same time whistling something tunelessly cheerful, would have their bedroom at the Old Rectory described in no other terms. He was definitely a man who considered himself a master. A master of all he surveyed. A master of his destiny. A master in bed too, so it now seemed.

A week had passed since they'd successfully made love downstairs in the drawing room and the difference it had made to Hunter was as extraordinary as it was understandable. Light-hearted, attentive and full of energy, he was a man reborn. She was relieved that The Problem had gone away, but she wasn't so sure about the new side to her husband she was seeing. Now when they made love, she felt locked out. There was no tenderness to the act, only a rough expediency. It caused her to wonder what was going through his mind when he took her so forcibly. Perhaps it was nothing more than staking his territory, reasserting himself after those previous disastrous moments. It'll pass, she told herself as she finished applying her lipstick and sprayed her neck and wrists with perfume. 'Ready?' she asked.

Hunter pulled on his blazer, straightened the cuffs of his shirt, checked his cufflinks, and came towards her. The colour of his shirt matched his piercing blue eyes, and, still tanned from his trip away, he looked particularly handsome. He came and stood next to her in front of the mirror. 'I am now,' he said. 'Mm ... you smell gorgeous.' He kissed her cheek, then lifted her hair so that he could nuzzle the back of her ear. 'It's a shame we have to go downstairs.'

'It was your idea to throw a house warming party.'

'A man's allowed to change his mind.' He pulled her closer to him.

'You once said you weren't a man who changed his mind,' she murmured.

'I lied.' He circled her waist with his hands and kissed her on the mouth, his teeth grazing hers, his tongue working deep into her mouth.

She kissed him back, but knowing that any minute the doorbell would start ringing, she pulled away. 'Now you've gone and ruined my lipstick,' she said good-humouredly.

He smiled and kissed her again, a hand sliding between her legs.

'Hunter, we can't,' she said. 'Our guests will be arriving any minute. '

'So what? Let 'em wait. I can't.' He took her against the bedroom wall, her skirt hitched up around her waist, her mouth crushed beneath his. He climaxed almost immediately, his groan of pleasure so loud it sounded like a cry of triumph. They'd just rearranged their clothing when they heard a car on the gravel drive below. 'I'll leave you to redo your make-up,' he said with a wink, checking the zip on his trousers.

Alone in the bathroom, Helen stared at her reflection. Her face was flushed, her lipstick smeared. On closer inspection, she saw that her lower lip was swollen. She ran her tongue over the swelling inside her mouth and tasted blood. The back of her head, where Hunter had banged it against the wall, felt tender too. A wave of self-disgust surged through her. She felt soiled.

Conrad didn't know why he'd bothered to come; most people here were strangers. Mac had told him that the majority of the guests would be friends and family of their hosts. It was the first time he'd met Helen's husband and although he hardly knew Helen, they seemed an unlikely pairing. Everything about Hunter's overtly self-assured manner suggested he was a man of excess and Conrad found himself wondering how faithful he was. Men like Hunter seldom were. They always had something to prove. Some years back he'd done some translation work for a guy who had two mistresses, both of whom his wife knew about. Apparently she turned a blind eye to his philandering because it meant he left her alone and she was able to enjoy the lifestyle his success brought them. Perhaps Helen was the same.

Bored with hovering like a spare part on the crowded terrace – he had no idea where Mac was – he took the steps down to the next level of the garden. It was vastly improved since he'd last seen it when Alice was dying. He knew from Mac that Orlando had worked hard on re-establishing the borders and reinstating the original design and its effect. He'd done an amazing job; the drifts of flowers with their softly muted colours looked good even to Conrad's uneducated eye. He almost wished he knew more about the plants and flowers he was looking at. He could pick out the obvious ones – roses, lupins, lavender, catmint and foxgloves – but the rest were unknown to him. Alice used to joke that it was a shame he was such a knuckleheaded Philistine. She also used to say that it was a shame he was so unsociable. He felt that now. He was only here because Mac had insisted it would be rude to decline Helen's invitation. Mac had also said that he needed Conrad to give him a lift, that his legs were feeling a bit shaky. 'I want you there just in case I keel over,' he'd said. It had sounded as though it was supposed to be a joke, but Conrad had his doubts.

He spotted an unoccupied stone bench and claimed it before anyone else did. It overlooked an oblong pond, its still surface as smooth and reflective as a mirror. He tilted his head back and enjoying the bright summer sunshine on his face, he closed his eyes. He'd been sitting there for no more than a few minutes when his peaceful solitude was disturbed by the sound of voices. He flicked his eyes open,

'What a lovely spot,' a woman said to him. 'Mind if we join you?' She was accompanied by a man – her husband, presumably. They introduced themselves as Annabel and Simon, friends of Helen. 'It's a bit like attending a wedding, isn't it?' the woman said. 'Trying to find out which side of the church to sit on. Which camp do you belong in, bride or groom?'

'I'm a neighbour. So that puts me slap bang in the middle, I guess. Please, have the bench, I was just going.'

He left them to it, not caring if they thought he was rude. He wasn't in the mood for small talk. But then he never was. He went in search of another bolthole and hadn't gone far when he saw Helen coming towards him. 'Hello,' she said. 'All alone?'

'I'm afraid I'm a bit of a bore at parties,' he said.

'Why did you come, then?'

He frowned. 'Because you invited me.'

'And do you do everything asked of you?'

'Not always. Tell me, do you interrogate all your guests this way?'

She frowned. 'I'm sorry, that was appallingly rude of me. Perhaps, like you, I'm not in the mood for this.' She cast her gaze back towards the house and terrace where everyone else seemed to be thoroughly enjoying themselves.

'If it would help, I could kidnap you from your own party.'

She returned her gaze to him. 'What an excellent idea. Where will you hide me?'

'Anywhere you like. But first we'd better write a ransom note. How much do you think your husband will be prepared to pay up for you?' He was smiling now, but when he realized that she wasn't smiling with him, he said, 'You okay?'

She looked away, as though embarrassed. He noticed then that there was something wrong with her lip. For some inexplicable reason, it suddenly mattered to him to make her smile. He held out his arm. 'Come on, consider yourself officially kidnapped.'

Their destination was an area of walled garden that was approached through a pretty arched gate built into a hornbeam hedge. Conrad knew that originally it had been the kitchen garden but with only herself to grow vegetables for, Alice had turned it into what she'd called her secret garden. A brick path ran the narrow length of it, with borders of cottage-style plants either side. At the end was an arbour draped in pink roses.

'I see Orlando has been busy here,' he said. 'The last time I saw this part of the garden it looked very sorry for itself. Or is it your green fingers that have been at work here?' he added as an afterthought.

'I'll take a small amount of the credit, but really it's Orlando's efforts you should be appreciating. I don't know what I was thinking when I assumed I'd be able to take the place on myself. Alice must have been Superwoman.'

'It was what she lived for. She spent her every waking moment out here.'

'Some days I wish I could too. It's so lovely.'

They were settled on the wrought-iron seat now. The air was thick with the sweet old-fashioned smell of summer – roses, pinks, honeysuckle. On a nearby bush of buddleia, butterflies quivered on the sun-washed purple spikes. Choosing his words with care, Conrad said, 'Presumably you could if you wanted to. According to village gossip your husband is richer than Midas and there's no need for you to work.'

'I work because I always have. It's what I want.' Her tone was sharp and defensive. Seconds passed. 'I heard a rumour that you don't need to work either,' she said, then less acerbically, 'Is it true?'

'Who did you hear that from? Mac?'

'I'm not saying.'

'Whoever your source was, they're half right. When my wife died the payout on her life insurance policy meant that I would be financially secure for the rest of my life, but the truth is, I work because I enjoy it. No doubt your source will have also informed you of my mental state, that I'm practically unhinged with grief.'

'You mean I've allowed myself to be kidnapped by a madman?' she said, giving him a sideways glance.

Her comment was so unexpected he laughed out loud. 'Bloody hell! That'll teach me to go looking for sympathy.'

'Was that what you were doing?'

This time he didn't laugh. Nor did he answer her. 'Mac's asked me to go with him on that trip to Lake Como.'

'Yes, he mentioned that to me. He said you weren't keen. Why do you think he wants you with him?'

'Probably to get me back for some imagined slight.'

She smiled. 'You have a strange relationship with each other, don't you?'

'It never used to be so complicated. As a child I idolized him; even as an adult I was in awe of him, but now ...' His voice trailed off. He couldn't bring himself to say the words. It was too disloyal.

'But now you feel sorry for him,' she said quietly. 'And I'll bet you any money you like, he knows that.'

He let out his breath. 'You're good, aren't you?'

'No, it was just a guess. Based on my own feelings for my grandmother.'

'But I'll wager you don't keep mentally pushing and shoving each other the way Mac and I do.'

'No, we don't. Although who knows how we would behave if her mental faculties weren't so frail.'

'Mac told me she's in a nursing home. Was that a difficult decision on your part?'

'Why, worried you'll have to make that same decision for Mac one day?'

'Are you always so brutally frank?'

'Frank, yes. But I didn't think I was being brutal. Anyway, you don't have to answer any of my questions.'

'And be branded a wimp for it? No fear. You're right, though; of course I'm worried about Mac. But I've promised myself a home will be a last resort. I'll do all I can for him. Right to the end.'

'See if you still think that when he starts wetting the bed several times a night.' Her voice was flat.

There was nothing he could say to this, other than apologize for his blunder. 'I'm sorry. I wasn't suggesting for one minute that I'd manage any better than you.'

She seemed to rouse herself and turned to look at him. 'No. It's me who should be sorry. I don't know what's got into me.'

'Too much of a good thing perhaps,' he said, suddenly aware how arresting her eyes were. He'd remembered them being the colour of brandy; now he could see they were lightened with tiny flecks of gold.

'What?'

'Too much party food,' he said with a smile. 'Sugary cakes and pop – never a good combination.'

They sat in silence, then through the mellifluous trill of birdsong came a raucous burst of voices from somewhere the other side of the walled garden. 'Sounds like the party's going well,' he said. 'Thank you for inviting me, by the way.'

'I was told you wouldn't come.'

'Who by?'

'Oh, Evie, Lucy, Orlando. And Mac.'

'It's good to travel through life with such a ringing endorsement,' he said dryly.

More raised voices and laughter drifted over the wall. 'I really ought to be getting back,' Helen said. 'Hunter will be wondering where I am.'

'Yes, I suppose I have rather monopolized you. As husbands go, is he the jealous kind?'

'I have no idea. The situation's never arisen.'

'Mac will be disappointed to hear that. I think he's been working hard at being the other man in your life.'

She smiled and rose from the seat. 'I enjoy your uncle's company,' she said simply. 'He makes me laugh.'

'Your arrival here has given him something else to think about,' he said. 'Alice's death hit him badly.'

'I know,' was all she said.

It was when Conrad was holding open the gate for Helen that he thought to ask if she was going on the Lake Como trip – she hadn't mentioned earlier if she was or not. It had just occurred to him that the holiday might be almost bearable if she was there too.

'Any idea where Dad is, Savannah?'

Savannah swallowed a mouthful of beer and turned at Clancy's question. 'I don't know, the last time I saw him he was talking to some woman.'

Clancy laughed. 'Yeah, that sounds like Dad. Wouldn't you agree, Mum?'

Corinne rolled her eyes. 'He'll never change.' She looked about her distractedly. 'Oh, there's Frank. Excuse me while I go and see how he is. It's ages since I've seen him.'

When they were alone, Clancy lowered his voice and said, 'Poor old Mum, she can't lie to save her life.'

'How do you mean?'

He inclined his head to where Corinne was now chatting with Dad's oldest friend and business partner. 'They're seeing each other. Have been for weeks. They've kept it quiet because they're worried what Dad will say.'

Savannah was surprised. Not that Corinne was seeing Frank, but because her father's first wife was seeing anyone at all. Although she was actually a year younger than Dad, Corinne appeared much older. She took no interest in her appearance whatsoever and wore clothes that were years, if not decades, out of date. Savannah had seen photographs of her when she was young and she'd been quite attractive then, but now she had no figure to speak of and it was a joke within the family that she cut her own hair. She spent most of her time with her dogs and horses, saying you always knew where you stood with a four-legged friend. She couldn't be more different from Savannah's mum, but somehow they got on with each other. Maybe because they were so different. It didn't take a genius to reach the conclusion that Corinne and Marcia had come out of divorce well. Especially Corinne, who according to Clancy had helped Dad with the running of the business when he was starting out and was entitled to a decent whack of the profits. Neither woman had to work and despite giving them both one-off settlements, Savannah knew that Dad still regularly bunged them money when the mood took him. To her knowledge they hadn't ever shown a desire to remarry and Savannah supposed it was because they liked the security of having a man like Dad still taking care of them. But now here was Corinne secretly seeing Frank.

'I wouldn't have thought Dad would care less who your mum goes out with,' she said to Clancy. 'She's free to see whoever she wants.'

'They've got it into their heads that Dad will think Frank's stepped out of line. You know Dad – he expects us all to stick to the script. As devised by him. Anyway, how are the driving lessons going? I hear Helen's been helping you.'

'Not now she isn't. Dad's taken over. Well, he's taken me once. Trouble is; he's hardly around and when he is, teaching me to drive isn't high on his priorities.'

Out of the corner of her eye, Savannah saw Orlando come into view. She watched him walk across the lawn, then on to the area around the pond where Mac Truman was sitting on a bench with the frostily uptight Lucy. He was wearing a pair of faded, ripped jeans and a white T-shirt that showed off his tan. God, he looked amazing! Her plan to see more of him had worked brilliantly. A shame she had to pretend she enjoyed gardening. That was a real drag. But it was a mark of how great he was – and how keen he had to be on her – that even when she pulled up a load of small plants thinking they were weeds, he didn't shout at her. He was trying to teach her the names of plants and had given her one of his books to study. There was only thing she wanted to study and that was his sexy, hot body!

'I hear you've taken up gardening,' Clancy said.

She turned and saw where the direction of her step-brother's gaze lay. Nothing ever got past Clancy. 'You could say that,' she said.

'How old is he?'

'Twenty-eight.'

'What does Dad say?'

She shrugged and took a long swig from the bottle of Budweiser in her hand. 'He's way too busy to worry about what I'm getting up to,' she said. 'If it's not work with him, it's Helen.'

She thought of the disgusting noises she'd heard coming from his and Helen's bedroom earlier and cringed. Was there anything worse than hearing your own father at it?

Chapter Eighteen

Helen could see that Hunter was thoroughly pleased with himself. Surrounded by his family – Savannah, Clancy and his wife Paula, Kim and her husband Terry, Corinne and Frank Maguire, who was as good as family – he could not have looked happier. For the first time Helen realized that she envied him this simple pleasure. For all his love of the good things in life, it was his family that really provided him with the most satisfaction. Particularly when he was at the centre of it.

It was nearly ten o'clock, the rest of their guests having left some hours ago. Inside the house, the caterers were packing up the last of the crates of glasses and crockery. Just as soon as they were gone, Helen would go in and make coffee for those who wanted it. Hunter, Clancy and Terry would probably move onto brandy or whisky. Frank would stick to wine. He usually did. With so many different conversations going on around her, Helen stared up at the sky that wasn't yet fully dark. Dramatic brush strokes of pink, violet and deep indigo gave it a theatrical unworldliness. She longed to leave the table and walk around the garden, to breathe in the sweet smells of the flowers and plants, to kick off her shoes and feel the cool grass beneath her toes. Maybe when everyone was gone, she'd do exactly that. She would go down to Alice's secret garden, shut the gate behind her and pretend it was her entire world. That nothing else existed beyond those walls and hedge. It was a magical place, somewhere she'd come to feel most at ease. She loved the sense of containment it gave her. It had been Conrad's suggestion that they go and hide there this afternoon. On any other day she might have enjoyed his company, but her mood had not been a happy one for the duration of the party. Annabel had remarked upon this earlier when she was saying goodbye.

'Everything all right, Helen?' her friend had asked. 'You seem a bit down.' She had used tiredness as an excuse. What else could she have said? Certainly not the truth: that she felt as if she had woken from a dream and was living some other woman's life. Who, she wanted to know, was this man to whom she was married? And what kind of woman was she who allowed herself to be treated the way she was?

Suddenly sensing that the tone of the conversation around her had changed – everyone was clearly delighted with what had just been said – Helen forced herself to focus. Hunter and Clancy were on their feet and embracing each other. Now Hunter was kissing his daughter-in-law and congratulating her. From Paula, he went to Clancy's mother, Corinne, and with his hands resting on her shoulders as he stood behind her, he kissed the top of her head affectionately. 'How about that, Corinne? We're going to be grandparents!'

Corinne laughed and covered one of Hunter's hands with her own. 'And not before time,' she said with a happy smile directed at Clancy.

Kim and Savannah were next to be singled out. 'Just think; you two are going to be aunts! What a thought!' Hunter beamed.

Then, as though he'd only just remembered she was there, still with his hands resting on Corinne's shoulders, Hunter looked over to Helen. 'Isn't this great news, Helen?' Everyone turned to look at her where she sat isolated and excluded at the end of the table. Never had she felt such an obvious outsider.

Hours later, seeking refuge in the garden, she blamed herself for feeling this way. Hadn't she always deliberately kept life at a safe distance because it was the surest way to avoid being hurt? She'd witnessed the pain her grandparents had suffered at the loss of their only child, had seen how their lives had been blighted through no fault of their own, and had vowed she would never put herself at risk in the same way. Not ever. Her philosophy had been that it was better to tiptoe through life under the cover of darkness, hoping no one would pay her too much notice.

So it stood to reason, she thought now as she moved barefoot across the dewy grass in the moonlight, that having kept Hunter at an emotionally safe distance, she would end up feeling isolated from him. Perhaps he'd been right and The Problem had been her fault. Had she inadvertently been cold and unresponsive towards him? If so, no wonder he was treating her the way he was. Following the adage that you reaped what you sowed, then she had brought this on herself.

When she reached the gate in the hornbeam hedge she raised the catch carefully, not wanting to disturb the beautiful peace of the night. It was three in the morning, and unable to sleep she had crept downstairs to make herself a drink, but the sight of the garden, lit by a full moon and a clear starlit sky, had been too much of a lure to ignore and so she'd slipped on her gardening fleece over her nightdress and unlocked the back door.

She made herself comfortable on the seat where she and Conrad had sat that afternoon. With her knees drawn close to her chest, she stared up at the moon; it was high and unfeasibly bright. The air was still and around her the shadows were motionless. Continuing to stare into the infinity of the night sky, she wondered how to save herself from the most dangerous and destructive person she knew: herself.

Somehow she had to make this new life of hers work. But how?

There was so much to admire in Hunter – his commitment and pride in his family; his strong work ethic and all that he had achieved through it; his generosity, public and private; and his powerful dynamism. It added up to an immensely attractive persona. But sometimes she glimpsed a vulnerability in him, a need that she doubted he would ever express. It was this perhaps that had won her over when he'd proposed in Egypt. She had convinced herself that out of her respect and gratitude, love would slowly grow. Or if not exactly love, then something profoundly good and enriching. She would be the person she suspected Hunter needed in his life. Someone strong and loyal. A worthy companion.

The only time she had hesitated over marrying him after agreeing to do so, was when she was being asked during the marriage service if she wanted to take this man, Hunter Kyle Fraser Irving Tyler, to be her lawfully wedded husband. *Kyle Fraser Irving*? He'd never said. Never told her he had all those other Christian names. What else hadn't he told her? She must have answered in the affirmative because the next thing she knew the deal was done, the knot was tied and Hunter was kissing her and then they were laughing and hugging and being applauded by the few friends they'd invited to the service.

She closed her eyes wanting – needing – to relive that moment, to remember the happiness of the day. But she couldn't do it. She could picture the scene – the delighted expression on Hunter's face, the piercing blue of his eyes, the whiteness of his shirt – but she couldn't summon the actual sensation of being happy.

It was gone.

Chapter Nineteen

Ever since the weekend of Helen's party, the weather had been awful. Every morning that Lucy drew back the curtains and was greeted with yet another overcast sky and the threat of rain, she felt her spirits plummet. The rain might be good for the gardens, but it was disastrous for business. There was nothing like a steady downpour to keep the punters away. 'If it goes on like this for much longer,' Hugh had complained, 'we might just as well start getting the Christmas stock out.'

Today, the last Friday of June, the rain was a fine, misty drizzle. It was sneaky rain, the sort that soaked you to the skin while your back was turned. For once, Lucy was glad to be working in the dry. She was tidying the racks of seed packets. So far she'd found half a dozen packets that had been got at by mice. These particular mice either had magical powers or circus skills by the looks of things. For the life of her, Lucy couldn't figure out how the little devils were getting at the packets, given that they were three feet off the ground. She wasn't keen on the idea, but she knew the simplest solution was to put down traps at night. It was a pity they couldn't do the same for the people who pinched the seeds during the day. It never failed to surprise her the amount of seeds that were stolen on a daily basis. The worst offenders were the pensioners who seemed to think that they were perfectly entitled to help themselves. One man they'd caught stuffing his pockets full had the cheek to say, 'What difference does a few packets of seeds make to anyone?' Hugh had told him to push off and never come back. 'If I see you again I'll call the police,' he'd added.

'You'd do that for a few measly seeds?' the man had responded incredulously.

'It's my livelihood you're depriving me of. So sod off!'

It was never a good idea to rile Hugh Fielding.

Or Orlando, Lucy was learning. Like father, like son, she

thought, as she went to fetch a dustpan and brush to sweep up the trail of mouse droppings. She had always known that Orlando had a strong streak of stubbornness, but his refusal to see what a girl like Savannah was capable of was just plain dumb. She hadn't thought there would ever come a time when she would actually agree with her mother, but Fiona had been bang on the money when she used to say that a man couldn't see beyond the end of his nose once a woman was involved. Now wasn't that the truth!

Orlando had told Lucy several times that she was reading too much into the situation, that there was nothing going on between him and Savannah. 'But she's practically superglued to you,' Lucy had said. 'It's obvious to anyone that she's got more than gardening on her mind when she's around you.'

'If I didn't know better I'd say you were jealous, Lucy.'

Two days later Orlando had told her that Savannah was going on the Gardens of Delight trip to Italy. Lucy hadn't trusted herself to say anything. Instead, feeling as if she was being slowly dipped in icy cold water, she'd listened to Orlando saying, 'Apparently her father is over the moon that she's found herself something to do, something she's really enjoying. Savannah says I'm very much the flavour of the month with her dad.'

'Is that so?' Lucy had managed to mutter.

Orlando had then gone on to raise the subject of whether or not Lucy was going to join them on the trip. 'There aren't many places left, so if you're going to go, Luce, you'd better get a move on. Mac's a definite now, as is Conrad.'

'Already ahead of you,' she'd said, forcing herself to sound upbeat. 'I've put my name down.'

'You have?' He'd seemed both surprised and pleased. 'That's brilliant.'

She'd been lying, of course. She hadn't done any such thing. But in that split second, she'd pictured Savannah throwing herself at Orlando while wandering around some garden by Lake Como, and had made up her mind to go. Someone would have to keep an eye on Savannah and it might as well be her. The second Orlando had gone out and she'd had the house to herself, she'd phoned Olivia Marchwood. 'You've left it a bit late,' the irritating dragon had said, 'but you're in luck; there are still a couple of places available. I'll need a deposit of a hundred and fifty pounds from you by the end of the week. Am I right in thinking that your father lives on Lake Como?'

'I'll drop the cheque off to you tomorrow,' Lucy had told the nosy old witch. This had nothing to do with Marcus Gray and everything to do with protecting Orlando.

The mouse droppings dealt with, Lucy was putting the dustpan and brush away when she heard the counter bell being rung. Not once, not twice, but three loud, long, insistent rings. She hurried over to see who needed serving and immediately wished she'd left it to someone else.

'Hiya, Luce,' Savannah said. 'Orlando's given me a list of stuff I need to get for him.' She waved a piece of paper in the air. 'I haven't a clue what any of it is; could you give me a hand?'

'Sure.' Although I'm surprised you need my help, thought Lucy, you've helped yourself to just about everything else. 'Where's Orlando?'

'Outside looking for his dad.'

Lucy took the list from Savannah. It was standard stuff: bone meal, organic liquid seaweed, chicken manure pellets, twine, bamboo canes, peat-free compost. 'We'll need a trolley,' she told Savannah. She pointed towards the trolleys the other side of the automatic sliding doors, where it was still raining. Fetching and carrying for Savannah only went so far. But at least the girl looked as if she was more appropriately dressed for the part of assistant gardener. On her first day she'd worn a pair of minuscule shorts that even Kylie's famously pert bum would have struggled to squeeze into. Today she was decked out in baggy combat trousers with a black puffa jacket and a woolly hat pulled down over her ears. 'Right,' Lucy said when Savannah had returned. 'Follow me.'

They were halfway through the list when Savannah said, 'You don't like me very much, do you, Luce?'

Adding a ball of twine to the trolley, Lucy said, 'Do you mind not calling me Luce?'

'Orlando calls you that all the time.'

'Yeah, well, he's the only one who gets away with it.'

'Why's that?'

'We've known each other for so long, I suppose.'

'Are you in love with him?'

Lucy stopped what she was doing. 'Better make that three bottles of organic liquid seaweed. It's on special offer; three for the price of two.'

'So are you in love with him?'

Anger coiled inside Lucy. 'No, I'm not. And why would you think I was?'

Savannah shrugged. 'Because you see me as a threat and hate me for it.' Her voice was all sweetness, but the jut to Savannah's chin unnerved Lucy. No way was she going to let this girl with her cheeky gob outmanoeuvre her.

'I don't hate you,' she lied, her voice equally sweet.

'Yes, you do. You took a major dislike to me the moment we met.'

Ten out of ten for observation, thought Lucy. 'That's rubbish,' she lied again. 'I don't hate anyone. It's a highly counterproductive emotion.'

'Orlando says you hate your father.'

Her hand resting on a box of bone meal, Lucy struggled to keep her composure. 'Does he now?' she said tightly.

'Orlando also said that you haven't seen him since you were fourteen. My dad can be a complete pain when he wants to be, but I can't imagine not seeing him in all that time.'

Lucy swallowed. She almost threw the heavy box of bone meal onto the trolley. It was either that or throw it in Savannah's smug, pixie-like face. Did she have any idea just how offensive and insensitive she was being? Or was it deliberate? What really rankled was that this young girl, nearly ten years her junior, could annoy and unnerve her so easily. What was it about her that set her teeth on edge? Why did even the thought of Savannah bloody Tyler remind her of nails being dragged across a blackboard?

'It must be tough if you love someone and they don't love you back.'

Bloody hell, the gobby little pixie was off again! 'I told you, I don't love Orlando.'

'I wasn't talking about him; I was talking about your father.'

'Shit,' muttered Lucy.

'You what?'

'Chicken shit. Over here. Six drums of chicken manure pellets.'

They loaded the drums onto the trolley.

'Can't we at least be friends?'

Her eyes firmly on the list in her hands, checking she hadn't missed anything, Lucy said, 'I don't think so, do you?' And with that, she took hold of the trolley and wheeled it over to the checkout area. She rang up the items, subtracted the usual discount Hugh gave Orlando, and presented Savannah with the bill. The girl pulled out a wad of ten- and twenty-pound notes Orlando must have given her. The transaction was almost finalized when Orlando appeared with his father. *Traitor!* Lucy wanted to hiss. How could you tell Savannah all those things about me? *I thought you were my friend!*

'Aha! So this is the protégée I've been hearing so much about,' said Hugh. 'You look very young; are you sure you're old enough to be working?'

Orlando rolled his eyes. 'Savannah, this is my father. Do your best to humour him. Hello, Luce. I bet you're glad you're working inside today. It's miserable out there.'

Not half as miserable as I am, she thought bitterly.

She spent the rest of the day going over what Savannah had said. Each time she completed a circuit of the conversation, she came to the same conclusion: the girl had been talking total chicken manure.

Chapter Twenty

It was the first week of July and Mac was restless and bored. He needed something to occupy him. There was plenty of work to do in the garden now that the rain had finally stopped and the sun was making a guest appearance, but he wasn't in the mood for feeding, weeding or staking. He assuaged his guilt by remembering something Alice had told him, that some carefully considered neglect never did a garden any harm, in fact it was positively beneficial. 'To constrain nature with a fist of iron,' she used to say, 'is the worst crime a gardener can commit. You have to give Mother Nature her wings now and then.'

With a sigh of irritation, he abandoned the crossword – nine across had him stumped – and tossed the paper onto the ground in disgust. Fritz gave a startled yelp. Mac hauled himself out of his garden chair, an expensive teak steamer affair that Conrad had bought for him, and straightened his back. He felt stiff all over. His knuckles were sore and his knees ached. All of which did nothing to improve his mood. He hated to admit it, but he was lonely. He briefly considered going across the courtyard for a chat with Conrad, but damn the boy, he'd be far too absorbed in what he was doing and would welcome the interruption with his customary grace. Sometimes he admired Conrad for the way he stayed so focused on his work. Other times it infuriated him. There was more to life than work.

With Fritz close on his heels, he went inside the house and while making himself some coffee, he listened to Evie banging about upstairs with the vacuum cleaner. He wondered if Helen was at home and whether she'd like a visitor. He would have to ring her first. Unlike Alice, who had always been reliably 'in', Helen was a busy woman who worked unpredictable hours. There was also her husband to consider. Mac didn't want the man to view him as a nuisance, the kind of pathetic individual who was always loitering on the doorstep. But given that it was a weekday and that Hunter was probably at work, Mac decided to make the call. When he heard Helen's voice at the other end of the line, his spirits rose. 'Helen, my dear, it's Mac.'

A cacophony of background music and what sounded like a scraping noise came down the line at him. 'Can you hang on a second, Mac? I'll have to go downstairs and use the phone in the kitchen.' Less than a minute later he was listening to her voice again. 'That's better. I've got the decorators in and I'm trying to keep an eye on them and work at the same time, but it's hopeless. I can't concentrate.'

'You're doing more to the house? I thought you'd done it all.'

'We're almost there now. Thank goodness.'

Disappointment crept up on him. 'With so much going on, I suppose a visitor would be the last thing you'd want. Are you too busy to come out and play?'

'Absolutely not. Hunter's away again so I could do with the company. What are you suggesting?'

'Come and entertain me. I'm withering on the vine with boredom. I need amusing.'

The sound of her laughter was like the sun breaking through the clouds for him. 'What time do you want me there?' she asked.

'Now! It's an emergency.'

'I'll be there in fifteen minutes. Get the kettle on.'

'I've a better idea; I'll make us a vodka martini.'

It was nine in the evening in Kyoto and with the receiver pressed to his ear, Conrad could hear the rain beating down all those thousands of miles away. He was talking to his old friend Tsubasa Itani, a professor of Japanese Poetry and Literature. The two men had a tradition of ringing each other on their birthdays – it was Tsubasa's fiftieth.

'Did that make you feel homesick?' Tsubasa asked him, when he came back on the line. He had momentarily put his phone just outside the window of his apartment so that Conrad could fully appreciate the rainy season that hadn't yet come to an end. The city of Kyoto was like a vast bowl and the rain poured into it for longer than it did in Tokyo or Osaka. And yes, he admitted to Tsubasa, the sound of the rain beating down on the roof of the apartment did make Conrad miss his days in Japan. It also gave him a twinge of regret that it was two years since he'd last seen his friend and his wife, Shinobu.

'So when are you coming to see us again? Shinobu is always asking after you.'

'I'd love to come over, but you know how it is. Work keeps me pretty busy these days.'

'Yes. Yes, I can see that work would keep you busy, and that it would leave you no time for your old friends.'

'Tsubasa, stop it.'

'Stop what?'

'You know very well.'

'I know all too well. But it won't stop me from wishing you happiness one day.'

'I'm happy enough as I am.'

'*Uso!*'

Conrad was taken aback. For the excruciatingly polite Tsubasa to call him a liar was the equivalent of the Queen telling the Archbishop of Canterbury to go screw himself. 'Hey, why are you having a go at me all of a sudden?'

'It's time to move on, Conrad. Time to leave Sam behind. Sure, you loved her. Sure, you still love her. But she is in the past. She is no more. Only a memory. The next time we speak you will be fifty. And what will you have achieved? Fifty and still living alone with only your work to comfort you late at night. Is that what you want?'

'You're forgetting my uncle.'

'Ah, so I was. But he too will soon be a memory.'

'If you carry on much longer like this, I'll be over to Kyoto on the next available flight and it'll be you who's nothing but a memory!'

Tsubasa laughed. And then it was as if his laughter was coming at Conrad in stereo. Craning his neck to look out of the window, he saw that his uncle was in the garden and that he had company: Helen. The two of them were sitting at the table in the shade of the apple tree, a cocktail glass apiece. Fritz was lying on his back in front of Helen, and she was absently tickling the dog's tummy with a bare foot. Lucky old Fritz, he found himself thinking. She had nice feet, he observed. Nice ankles, too. He craned his neck further still and nearly fell out of his chair.

'Conrad? Are you still there?'

'Sorry, what did you say?'

'I was asking if there is genuinely no hope of you coming to see us this year. Or if indeed there is any chance of you allowing yourself some time off.'

'Actually, I am going on holiday later this summer.'

'Oh?'

'To Italy.'

'Alone?'

He was all set to explain about the Gardens of Delight trip when he changed his mind. 'I'm going with a friend,' he said. 'Her name's Helen.'

Inevitably his words left him wide open to the most intense interrogation. 'You're not getting another word out of me,' Conrad said when he'd grown tired of repeating, 'No comment.' 'Now get on with enjoying your birthday. And say hi to Shinobu from me.'

When he'd hung up, he sat staring at the phone wondering what he'd just done. What had got into him? *I'm going with a friend. Her name's Helen.* Where had that come from? Okay, he'd finally given in to Mac's cajoling because he was worried about him and had signed up for the trip, but why put the spin on it that he had? He switched his gaze from the telephone to the woman who had caused this mental aberration. The bare foot was no longer rubbing Fritz's tummy, it was tapping the air as though in time with a piece of music only she could hear. Conrad watched her face as she chatted to Mac – as she sipped her drink, as she pushed her hair behind an ear, as she readjusted her sunglasses – and came to the only conclusion he could reach: he was attracted to her.

But why? And why, after living like a monk all these years, did he find himself attracted to a married woman? What was that all about? Was it a clever trick on the part of his subconscious to make him want something that was strictly out of bounds and therefore unattainable? A safe fantasy, in other words – one to which he would never have to seriously commit. He shook his head in disbelief. What a crackpot supposition.

As far as work was concerned, his concentration was done for. He might just as well stop for lunch. And maybe have some company whilst he was about it.

'Not interrupting, am I?' he asked as he approached Mac and Helen in the garden.

'Good Lord!' exclaimed Mac, making an irritating play of looking at his watch. 'What brings you out here at this time of day?'

Conrad shrugged. 'I needed a break. Can I get anyone another drink?'

'Evie was mucking out the kitchen a minute ago. So unless you want to brave a verbal avalanche from her, I'd wait until the coast is clear.'

Helen laughed. 'I don't believe it. Two grown men afraid of Evie Hawkins. You should be ashamed of yourselves.'

Conrad took the chair next to his uncle so that he could take advantage of the view across the table towards Helen. 'She likes to boss us around,' he said. 'She thinks we can't manage on our own.'

'And can you?'

Mac snorted. 'Of course we can!'

'It's easier with Evie around,' Conrad said more reasonably. 'Neither of us is motivated to do half the things she does for us.'

Another snort from Mac suggested Conrad knew where he could stick his motivation. The old man got to his feet. 'Just to prove I'm not scared of her, I shall go inside and mix us another drink. Same again, Helen?'

'I shouldn't really. I'll have trouble finding my way home if I'm not careful.'

'Oh, go on,' urged Mac. 'If needs be, Conrad can drive you home. Conrad, what about you?'

With several hours of work still to get through, he said, 'No offence, but I'll play safe and eschew one of your super-strength cocktails in favour of a beer.'

'Didn't I tell you he wasn't any fun, Helen?'

When they were alone, Conrad said, 'Once again my deficiencies and inadequacies are brought squarely to your attention.'

She smiled. 'He tells me you work too hard. Do you?'

'I do whatever needs doing.'

'Approximately how many hours a week do you put in?'

'I haven't a clue.' He sat back in his chair and crossed one leg over the other, wishing as he did so that Helen would take off her sunglasses so he could get a better look at her. 'I hear from Mac that your step-daughter is working with Orlando.'

'And how surprised were you by that?'

'Totally surprised. I don't know the girl, but from what Mac says, she doesn't seem the green-fingered sort.'

'I've a feeling it's less to do with what colour her fingers are and more to do with Orlando being drop-dead gorgeous. She's even going on the trip to Lake Como. I couldn't believe it when she asked her father if she could go.'

'And will your husband be joining us?' He was deliberately fishing. The last he'd heard from Mac was that Helen's name had been added to the list but Hunter still hadn't decided if he'd be free.

'No, he won't be coming.'

Now why did he suddenly want to cheer out loud?

'What swayed you in the end?' she asked.

'The fear of never hearing the last of it if I didn't.'

'And the real reason?'

He looked over his shoulder, to make sure there was no danger of being overheard. 'I'm worried about my uncle.'

'Really?'

'He doesn't seem himself. He hasn't said anything to you, has he?'

She shook her head. 'Not a word. But then I'd hardly have expected him to. It's not like I'm an old and trusted friend.'

'Maybe not an old friend, but I suspect he trusts you. Which, take it from me, means a lot.'

She smiled. 'Perhaps he just needs cheering up. He was telling me earlier about a garden over in Shropshire he and Alice used to visit together. Do you think he'd like it if I took him there?'

'I think he'd love it.' Part of Conrad thought he might love it too, and before he knew what he was doing, he was saying, 'Perhaps it would be a good idea if I came along too. You know, just in case anything happened to Mac. It wouldn't be fair for you to be lumbered in any way.'

She removed her sunglasses and leaned forward, an anxious frown on her face. 'Are you that concerned about Mac?'

Perhaps he had laid it on a bit thick. If his remarks ever reached Mac's ears, he'd be a dead man. Back-pedalling slightly, he said, 'Not really. It's just better to be safe than sorry. Or would I be in the way?' He deliberately fastened his gaze on hers, then wished he hadn't. God, those eyes! It took all his willpower to look away. For something to do he bent down to Fritz and scratched him behind the ears.

'Of course you wouldn't be in the way,' she said. 'When's a convenient day for you?'

He straightened up and risked another direct glance. To his relief and disappointment the sunglasses were back in place. 'How about tomorrow?'

She hesitated. 'It's my day to see my grandmother. I was going to take her out for the afternoon.'

'Why not bring her with us?' What was he doing? Why the eagerness? Why was he pressing her so hard?

Mac was in the kitchen, cocktail shaker in hand. Had Helen been there, he would have made more of a performance of it; as it was, only Evie was observing him. She was standing on a chair, theoretically cleaning the top of the wall units. In his opinion, she did a lot of theoretical cleaning – a cursory wipe of a duster here, a dab of polish there.

'You can make me one of those while you're about it,' she said.

'Not on your life. You're sloppy enough as it is without any alcohol inside you.'

'Cheeky sod!'

'Foul-mouthed harpy.'

She shook out her duster. 'That's rich coming from you.'

With his back to her, he smiled. He rather enjoyed his tussles with Evie. He was just adding a twist of lemon to the glasses when suddenly the worktop moved. It rose up towards him and he felt the room shift on its axis. The blood seemed to rush out of him. He felt suspended in time, separated from his body. He took several deep, panicky breaths, convinced that this was it. Goodbye life! He reached for the worktop to steady himself, trying to stop the kitchen from spinning. He held on tight. He didn't want to die. Not yet. He wasn't ready. He still had so much to do. Then, as suddenly as it had started, it stopped and the room was perfectly still. He could hear a voice. It was Evie's. She was standing next to him and asking if he was all right.

'I'm fine,' he snapped. But he wasn't. He was bloody terrified.

Chapter Twenty-one

The next day Helen woke to a glorious morning. It had rained during the night, just a light fall that she'd heard pattering against the windowpane, but with brilliant sunlight streaming into the bedroom now the day promised to be warm and sunny. It also held the promise of some fun. She was looking forward to driving over to Shropshire to see Wollerton Old Hall Garden.

When she and Conrad had told Mac what they had in mind, he'd been oddly lukewarm about the suggestion. Eventually he'd come round to the idea, but Helen had been left to ponder on what Conrad had said, that his uncle didn't seem himself. When Mac had brought their drinks out, he'd certainly seemed distracted. Quite unlike the man who'd gone inside to make their vodka martinis. What could have caused the sudden downturn in his mood?

She stood at the window for a moment to enjoy the view of her own garden. It was a delight. The blades of grass in the immaculately cut lawn (care of Orlando) and the plants and flowers in the borders glistened with jewel-bright droplets of water. Her eyes ran over the white delphiniums and pearly pink hollyhocks, the towering verbascums with their grey-white stems and leaves and pale yellow flowers, the creamy lilies and delicate mauve campanulas, and the hummocks of santolina, their vivid yellow flowers adding a sharp crispness to the overall effect. Even at this distance, she could see that the edging of lavender was attracting the early-morning bees. The sight of the gently curving border near the summer house, which she'd weeded after coming back from Chapel House yesterday afternoon, gave her a happy sense of satisfaction; its freshly dug soil looked rich and wholesome. With Hunter away in Dubai, she hadn't felt any guilt about staying out in the garden until the church bell struck ten, when only the fading light forced her inside. She hoped that Alice was smiling down with approval. She also hoped that Alice wouldn't disapprove of the changes she thought she might make in the walled garden. Orlando had pointed out to her that a fair number of the plants were nearing the end of their life and that they should be replaced. This was another reason why she was looking forward to visiting Wollerton Old Hall Garden. Mac said it was one of the most inspirational gardens he knew, a favourite of Alice's, as well.

Once she had showered and dressed, she went downstairs. Savannah was sitting at the table with a plate of toast and a glass of orange juice.

'You're up early,' Helen remarked. The atmosphere between them these days was a lot less spiky. She had a feeling that ever since the incident with the man in the Subaru, Savannah had viewed her differently, was maybe even harbouring some grudging respect for her. It wasn't often Helen lost her temper, and when she did it was usually over something quite trivial. The really important issues she kept firmly under lock and key.

'Orlando's got a lot on today,' Savannah answered her.

Helen smiled to herself. Orlando this, Orlando that. She filled the kettle, lifted up the lid of the hotplate on the Aga and was met with a blast of heat. With the kettle in place, she opened a window. She didn't think she'd ever see the sense in having a cooker that produced so much heat when you didn't need it. 'So where's the first job of the day for you and Orlando?' she asked Savannah.

'One of those poxy estate houses. He's designed a new garden for the woman who lives in it.'

Helen refrained from reminding Savannah that just because a house was on an estate it didn't necessarily mean it was poxy, and said, 'You're really enjoying working with Orlando, aren't you?'

Savannah chewed on her toast and nodded. 'Well, yeah. Why wouldn't I?'

Helen knew her step-daughter well enough now to recognize that the question was rhetorical and so kept to herself the list of reasons why this change in Savannah was such a surprise. What surprised Helen more was Hunter's reaction to this turn of events. She had expected him to come down hard on Savannah, saying that this was not a suitable occupation for a daughter of his. To Hunter's credit, he applauded Orlando's sponsorship of his daughter, joking that the lad didn't know what he was taking on. It was possible he viewed it in the same way that he did Helen's work – something worthwhile but not to be taken too seriously.

'What are you doing today, then?' Savannah asked. 'You don't look like you're dressed for work.'

Helen felt Savannah's critical eye taking in her cropped jeans, strappy top and silk overshirt. 'I'm going out for the day with Mac and Conrad,' she replied. She explained about the garden they were going to see and that she was taking her grandmother with them.

'Sounds deadly.'

She set off to the nursing home, having called ahead to check that Emma was well enough for the outing. She was parking the car when her mobile rang. It was Annabel at the office. 'Don't panic, I'm not going to hassle you on your day off. I just wanted to see if you could cover for me next week.'

'I don't see why not. When were you thinking?'

'I've been invited away for one of those dreadful girl-only weekends where we sit around getting drunker by the minute and moan about our awful husbands. Okay if I play hooky until Wednesday?'

After they'd ended the call, Helen reflected on how few girl-only weekends she'd been on. It was a deliberate choice on her part; she had never been fond of women en masse.

Emma was ready and waiting for her, sitting on the edge of her bed in her thickest overcoat, her handbag gripped tightly on her lap. 'I've told her it's going to be a scorcher today and that she won't need such a thick coat,' the auxiliary nurse told Helen, 'but there's no prising her out of it.'

'Not to worry; we can always dispense with it if needs be.' Then addressing Emma directly, Helen said, 'How about we take your much lighter raincoat as well, just in case it rains?'

Emma looked worried. 'If it's going to rain, we'd better take an umbrella.' There was no arguing with her logic.

It took for ever for her grandmother to get settled in the car. It wasn't always like this. Most days when Helen took her out, she drifted happily along on the tide of Helen's instructions. But today the seat was too far forward. The seatbelt was cutting into her neck. The car was too warm. Then it was too cold. 'Where's that draught coming from?' she wanted to know.

'It's the air con, Grandma.'

'Air what?'

'Air conditioning.'

'Well, it's too cold. I knew I was right to wear my winter coat. It's like the Arctic. What does this button do?'

The radio burst into life and mercifully, as if Emma was a fractious child, the no-nonsense tone of Jenni Murray's voice lulled her into a more relaxed state and she sat back. But when the next subject to be discussed started, Helen wondered if some music might not be more appropriate.

'I was listening to that,' Emma said, smacking Helen's hand as she reached out to change the radio station.

'Sorry.'

'What we have to remember,' said the so-called expert who was promoting her latest book, a sex manual for the over forties, 'is that sex is the glue that holds a relationship together. Whilst carrying out extensive research for my book I interviewed hundreds of mid-life couples who all said the same thing: if the sex was no good, the marriage was doomed.'

Out of the corner of her eye, Helen could see that Emma was nodding her head vigorously. 'Your grandfather and I used to have sex in the afternoon when you were at school.'

Helen gripped the wheel. This she did not need to hear.

'He liked doing it from behind.'

No-oo!

The expert on the radio was now giving her top tips for a healthy sex life. They included using plenty of baby oil, having an armoury of sex toys – apparently you couldn't have enough of those – and always, *always* – the expert couldn't stress this enough – one had to keep experimenting with new positions and any number of fantasies, no matter how silly they might sound. Also, and this was Rule Number One – use it or lose it!

Heavens! When had things changed so dramatically? When had it become practically de rigueur for everyone to be discussing sex in such detail? It was ten thirty-five in the morning and they were now being told that for some women the only way to climax was through oral sex.

'That was something your grandfather was good at,' Emma said sagely. 'What's your husband like in bed?'

The conversation was so surreal: for a start Emma had remembered that Helen was married, but also they had never *ever* discussed sex. Helen was tempted to speak the truth and open her heart to her grandmother, safe in the knowledge that Emma would not recall her confession. She was suddenly curious to know how it would feel to hear the words out loud, that Hunter was bloody awful in bed. That his every touch seemed fuelled by a powerful need to possess and dominate. And how every time he climaxed, it was as if he'd scored a winning goal. She badly wanted to talk to him about it, to hint that he might like to try a more gentle and loving approach, but coward that she was, she was concerned he would take it as a criticism. An attack on his technique could well trigger off a reappearance of The Problem.

Instead of answering her scarily uninhibited grandmother, she said, 'Are you warm enough now?'

Confusion registered in Emma's face, as though she was sure she'd asked a question but couldn't remember what.

Back in radio-land, the expert was explaining to Jenni that sometimes an affair could make a tired, worn-out marriage shift up a gear. 'Affairs aren't always the bad thing people think they are,' she expounded.

Oh, go ahead, why don't you? Helen wanted to shout at the stupid woman. Give everyone carte blanche to lie and cheat on each other!

Honestly, where did they get these people?

The last time Mac had come here he'd been with Alice. It had been a muggy, overcast day with thunder crashing around in the distance, but that hadn't spoiled it for them. It had been late in the season and they'd had the place almost to themselves. Today, despite it being a hot July afternoon, the garden still wasn't busy. He could see that Helen was clearly impressed and even Conrad looked to be showing some interest. Mac still hadn't got over Conrad willingly taking time off work and spending it this way. Perhaps it had been Helen who had persuaded him to do it. He was damned sure that if he had asked Conrad to come, the answer would have been no.

Helen had insisted on driving them here and her grandmother – the poor old girl – had slept for most of the journey. She'd woken up just as they turned off the main road and pulled into the field that was used as the car park. There had then been an awkward couple of minutes when Emma had got upset because she was disorientated – 'Where am I? ... Who are these people?' – and then she'd suddenly wanted to make a bolt from the car. It transpired, after some furtive whispering, that she needed the loo. And in a hurry. Once this had been accomplished, she'd calmed down and was happy to be guided round the garden. Much to Mac's amusement she kept referring to Conrad as Helen's husband. 'I'm sorry,' she'd said at one point, 'but you're going to have to remind me what your name is. Helen did tell me, but it's gone.' Give Conrad his due; he was damned patient with her. Better than him. This was just the kind of madness Mac was terrified of being reduced to: the twilight zone of senility. Although if he experienced another episode like the one he'd had in the kitchen yesterday, the end might come sooner than he'd bargained for and he'd be spared the humiliating ordeal of slowly going ga-ga. He knew he ought to go and see the quack, but the fear of being given rock-solid, irrefutable confirmation that he was on the slippery slope in a greased toboggan heading towards life's great exit filled him with horror.

Wollerton Old Hall Garden wasn't in the least bit grandiose or pretentious like some places Helen had visited. It was seductively exquisite, a gem of design and plantsmanship. The use of colour was key, as were the structural elements, and the overall ambience was intoxicatingly tranquil. Every corner they turned brought them to somewhere as enchanting and interesting as the area they'd just left. She liked the way the three-acre space was divided into gardens within a garden. Each was individually named – there was even one called Alice's Garden – and there always seemed to be a strategically placed bench so that one could stop and admire the view.

'I think we may have taken a wrong turning,' Conrad said, looking up from the map in his hands. 'If I'm not mistaken we're back in the Daisy Borders.'

'So we are,' agreed Helen, recognizing the sundial and colourful borders of hollyhocks and delphiniums and stunning roses. Spotting a summer house as well as a bench, and thinking that Mac and her grandmother might benefit from a rest, she said, 'Why don't we sit down for a while?'

'We're not going home now, are we?' Emma's voice was papery thin with disappointment. She shot Helen an anxious glance.

Helen took her by the hand and led her to the seat. 'We're having a break from all the walking round in this heat, Grandma. Here, sit down. Do you want to take off your coat?' Emma seemed to think about this, and then began to fumble with the buttons. Helen reached out to help but Emma pushed her hands away. 'Leave me alone. I want him to help me.' She was pointing at Conrad.

'Conrad's busy, Grandma.'

Emma looked at her as if she were crazy. 'Busy doing what? He's just standing there.'

'It's okay, Helen. I'll do it if she wants me to.'

Moving aside, Helen watched Conrad bend down so that he was eye to eye with Emma. When he'd undone the first button, her grandmother looked at him shyly, a hand pressed to her lips. She then giggled like a teenager. 'Has anyone ever told you that you're very handsome?' she said.

Behind her Mac said, 'Mind if I break ranks and have a snoop round the summer house? They used to have a display of "before and after" photographs of the garden in there.'

Helen watched Mac disappear inside the summer house, then turned back to see Emma shuffling along the bench to make room for Conrad. He's so patient with her, she thought, as he took the offered seat. With no space left, Helen sat on the grass in front of them. From behind her sunglasses she observed her grandmother, who was bright-eyed and smiling radiantly. Helen suspected that it had a lot to do with being paid so much attention by an attractive man. She hoped Conrad wouldn't mind that Emma kept muddling him up with Hunter. She was doing it again now. 'I hope you're a good husband to Helen,' Emma said.

Helen tensed. She hoped the conversation wasn't going where she thought it was.

Conrad parried the question effortlessly. 'Did you have a good husband yourself?'

The question elicited a coy grin and a wink. 'He was a real man,' she said. 'In every sense of the word.' She dug Conrad in the ribs and gave off a laugh that would have served Sid James well.

What had got into her grandmother? Ten minutes with Jenni Murray and she'd become a saucy caricature of a woman obsessed with sex.

'I remember the first time we did it,' Emma said wistfully. She lowered her eyes and pleated the fabric of her skirt with shaking hands. 'It was in a wood. It was early in the morning and we'd been mushroom-picking. It was too cold to take all our clothes off but we lay on a soft bed of leaves and moss, with the sound of birds all around us.' She stared into the distance. 'I can still smell the moss. And the mushrooms.' She slowly turned and looked at

Conrad. There were tears in her eyes. 'I can remember that day so well. I'd never been happier.' She frowned. 'What did you say your name was?'

In a gesture that was so solicitous, so unbearably kind that it made Helen's throat tighten, Conrad put his arm around Emma.

Chapter Twenty-two

Half an hour later Emma announced that she was hungry. They slowly made their way back towards the house and the tea room. It was self-service, and after reading the blackboard menu Helen had to explain everything at least three times for Emma's benefit, then answer her questions, which were so loud the young girls behind the counter were trying not to laugh – 'Salmon and broccoli quiche – will I like that? Lentil soup, does it have bits in? Does the ploughman's salad come with pickled onions? Pickled onions give me wind.' Finally they chose their meals. Helen steered her grandmother towards a table in an area where nobody else was sitting. She felt a twinge of guilt as she did this – was she so embarrassed by her grandmother that she wanted to keep her away from other people? Did she really care what others thought?

To her shame she had actually thought twice about bringing Emma today; she had been worried how Mac and Conrad would cope with her diminishing faculties. It wasn't everyone who could Hunter couldn't. It was why Helen had only taken Emma home to the Old Rectory on one occasion. Hunter had been hopelessly at sea with the situation. Going with the flow of Emma's erratic behaviour was beyond him; he just wouldn't allow himself to get caught up in the tangle of her thoughts. As if picking up on this, Emma had become fidgety and clumsy. After knocking over a small table and smashing a cup and saucer, she had locked herself in the downstairs loo, saying she wasn't coming out until the horrible man had gone.

In contrast, Conrad seemed infinitely patient. Compassionate, too. Helen didn't think she would ever forget the way he'd put his arm around Emma. What he'd done had been as poignant as the story Emma had just told them. Whilst it seemed all wrong hearing the intimate details of her grandparents' relationship, it had occurred to Helen that she would never have the same tale to tell. She had never loved anyone the way her grandparents had clearly loved each other. There had been plenty of boyfriends over the years, along with numerous moments of sexual rapture, but she doubted the memories would still be with her when she was in her eighties. Other than the bond she'd had with her grandparents, there had been nothing lasting in her life.

When they'd finished lunch, they ventured back into the garden for a final look around. Helen was keen to revisit the Yew Walk, the Rose Garden and the Cottage Garden, as well as the Main Herbaceous Border. She wanted to take some photographs and make some notes.

They had just walked through the pretty arched doorway into the Yew Walk – Helen had her camera poised – when Emma came and stood in front of her. 'We've been here before, haven't we?' she said.

'That's right, Grandma.' Helen stepped away from her so that she could take the photograph, but the moment she raised her camera to her eye again, she saw Emma staring back at her through the lens.

'I want to see the pond again,' the old lady said. More uncertainly, she added, 'There is a pond, isn't there?'

Conrad intervened. 'Why don't we show Emma round the garden and leave you free to take your pictures, Helen?'

Thinking that Conrad had done more than his share of babysitting her grandmother, Helen said, 'There's no need; I'll be quick.'

However, Emma now seemed to think it was an amusing game to keep standing in front of the camera.

'Come on, Emma,' Mac said, 'Let's go and find that fish pond, shall we?'

Half expecting Emma to shrug off Mac's hand, Helen watched her grandmother happily led away. She was surprised to see Conrad still standing next to her. She must have guessed right: that he did feel he'd done his bit.

'Would you rather I left you alone?' he asked.

'No, that's okay. So long as you're not bored. It must have been a tedious day for you so far. Mac says you hate gardens.'

'Correction, I hate *gardening*. I can't see the point in continuously slogging one's guts away, day in day out, just to keep on top of something.'

'Not even when the result is as beautiful as this?' She cast her gaze round the Yew Walk.

He smiled. 'Okay, I admit it; I'm being disingenuous, covering up the fact that I'm just a lazy slob.'

'You're hardly that.' She fiddled with the camera, momentarily awkward. She wanted what she said next to come out right. 'You were very good with my grandmother earlier,' she said. 'You made what could have been an excruciating moment something I'll always remember. I just wanted you to know that. It meant a lot to me. It's not everyone who would have treated a rambling old lady with such kindness.'

'Only someone with ice in their veins could have been unmoved by what she said.'

He was suddenly looking at her oddly. Very intently, as though there was something else he wanted to say. As though he ... She swallowed. No, she told herself. She was being fanciful. The warmth of the day was getting to her. But still he went on staring at her. His eyes, she noted for the first time, were blue. But not the piercing shade of Hunter's eyes. His were the softest of blues and reflected the paleness of the sky above them.

She swallowed again and tore her gaze away from his. She snapped her first picture of the borders with the immaculately clipped pyramids of taxus, then took some close-up pictures: a metal frame covered in a clematis the colour of pink marshmallow and surrounded by roses; and a climbing hydrangea that framed the arch through which they'd just come. Still peering through the lens of the camera, she panned round checking for anything else that was worth recording. She did a double take when Conrad came into view; he was leaning into the border to smell one of the roses. She zoomed in closer until his sideways profile filled the frame. The intensity of seeing him so near, coupled with the memory of that look in his eyes, did something extraordinary to her. She wanted to reach out and touch his face, to run a finger along his jaw, then kiss—

She pressed down on the shutter release button.

He swung round at the sound.

'You looked so thoughtful,' she said, by way of explanation.

He came over. 'Seems only fair that I should get my own back and snap you in return.'

She held onto the camera tightly. 'No way.'

'Don't be a spoilsport. Hand it over.'

'Would you like my husband to take a picture of you and your wife?'

They both turned, neither having noticed that a couple in matching beany hats had joined them in the Yew Walk. Helen was about to explain that there was no need, when Conrad whisked the camera out of her hands and passed it to the man. 'Thank you. We'd really appreciate it.'

The man briefly familiarised himself with the camera, then held it to his eye. 'That's it, get nice and close now. You call that close?'

'Better make it two,' Conrad told the man, when he'd released the shutter. 'Just in case.'

Helen glanced up at him. 'Just in case of what?' she murmured.

'In case the first one isn't any good,' Conrad said. He then dipped his head and kissed her lightly on the cheek. It was a whisper of a kiss. A delicate touch that was over in a flash.

But it left Helen in no doubt that she hadn't imagined that look Conrad had given her.

Chapter Twenty-three

Mac was glad to get home that evening. He felt drained. He'd spent the day fighting off a barrage of maudlin thoughts, most of which had been related to Alice. He'd felt her presence so strongly at Wollerton. Perhaps it was because they had enjoyed themselves so much there. It was where he'd first kissed her. They'd been alone in the summer house near the Daisy Border, looking at the display of photographs, when all of a sudden he'd been seized with the need to let her know how fond he was of her. Up until then they hadn't so much as held hands. At their age, it hadn't seemed necessary, he supposed. But in the cool shade of the summer house, with no one around to see, a kiss had seemed an absolute necessity. 'Well,' she'd said, when he released her, 'I'd been wondering when you'd get around to that.'

'I wasn't sure how it would be received,' he'd said.

'Worried I might slap you, eh?'

'Something like that, yes.'

She'd laughed so heartily the years had stripped away from her lined and weathered face and he'd caught a glimpse of what she might have looked like as a young girl. How different his life might have been had he met her when he was just starting out.

But there was another reason she had been on his mind today: she was the one person in whom he would have been happy to confide. He'd had another dizzy episode. It had happened when he'd been on his own in the summer house. Suddenly the walls had begun to spin and he'd fallen back against a table and nearly lost his footing. Luckily he'd managed to keep himself upright. For the rest of the day he'd been on red alert, anticipating the worst. He was paying the price now. By keeping his muscles permanently tense in the irrational belief that he could fend off an attack by being on his guard, his body ached all over. He was exhausted.

He made himself a gin and tonic, then went and stood on the

terrace. A gentle breeze was stirring and he could smell lavender. He sat down heavily and once more considered the day. He had spent most of it wrapped in his own thoughts, but even so he'd sensed that something else wasn't quite right. During the journey home when he'd been sitting in the back of the car with Emma, there had been a palpable tension between Helen and Conrad in the front. They exchanged no more than a couple of words the whole time and not once did they turn and look at each other. Had Conrad upset Helen in some way? But how? Conrad might have his faults but he didn't go round annoying other people – only him – and Helen was very easy-going. Even when she'd finished taking her photographs and reappeared with Conrad to find Emma sitting on the edge of the fish pond dangling her stockinged feet into the water, she hadn't been cross. 'I tried to stop her,' Mac had explained to Helen, 'but she wasn't having it. He'd been concerned that he would be blamed for not keeping an eye on the old girl properly, that she could have come to harm while in his care. Yet all Helen had done was to nod and take a picture of her grandmother as she wiggled her toes in the water and beamed like a happy child. Passers-by had smiled too and in a funny way, her benign happiness had spilled out to them. A small boy had tried to struggle free from his pushchair to join in the fun and his parents had had a hard job convincing him it wasn't really allowed. But not as hard a job as Helen had had in persuading her grandmother that it was time to go. Using paper napkins that Conrad fetched from the tea room, they'd dried Emma's feet and eventually steered her – forcibly at times – in the direction of the car.

As he now recalled the strained expression on Helen's face as she'd taken the napkins from Conrad, Mac wondered if he'd been mistaken in his earlier belief that Conrad had had something to do with the tension in the car. It was more likely that Emma's behaviour was what had caused Helen to be so quiet while she drove them home. It had to be a wretched and painful process watching a loved one deteriorate like that.

He set his glass down on the arm of his chair and looked at his watch. It was nearly six-thirty. The evening stretched before him. Perhaps he'd suggest to Conrad that they nip across to the Swan for a bar snack later on. He certainly couldn't be bothered to cook. He yawned hugely, then his eyes slowly closed and he gave in to sleep.

*

Conrad was in his office checking his emails. He scanned the messages for anything urgent, decided that it could all wait until the morning, hit the disconnect button and then leant back in his chair, feet up on the desk. It was now time to explain himself.

He'd made a pass at a married woman. Oh, nice going! Let the record show just how badly he'd lost the ability to think straight!

Even in his darkest moments, when he was scarcely able to rise above the swell of his grief and had thought he could screw Sam out of his system with any woman he chanced upon, he had avoided married women. There were certain decencies to uphold, if nothing else.

That dark and furious period in his life was not something he ever spoke about. It was hardly his finest moment, and the series of one-night stands and disastrous relationships had culminated in his pathetic attempt to commit suicide. He had hated himself for betraying Sam that way, but the self-loathing he had to live with was nothing compared to the devastating loneliness. He'd come to believe that the intense bereavement he'd gone through meant that the world had been split in two; there were those who knew what he was going through because they too had experienced the death of a loved one, and there were those who didn't have a clue what he was experiencing because their lives hadn't been touched by anything more troublesome than a broken fingernail.

Ironically, until Sam's death he had been jogging along quite happily in the broken fingernail camp. But then the horror of holding Sam's dead body in his arms changed his perspective for ever.

They had only recently moved to Cheshire when it happened. The move had been at Sam's request and was a direct result of her becoming pregnant – she wanted to get out of London and be nearer her old home and her parents. 'I don't want our child to grow up as a cockney baby,' she joked. He'd dragged his feet over parenthood, believing their life was perfect as it was, but had gone for it in the end because Sam said at her age she couldn't put it off for much longer. She had it all worked out. 'Once you have impregnated me with your seed,' she told him in bed one night after he'd had a good go at doing exactly that, 'I'm going to sell the business.'

'But I thought it meant everything to you.'

'Wrong,' she said, 'you mean everything to me. Besides, I want to have some fun. I want to start wearing aprons and keep chickens.'

'There won't be any wringing of necks, will there?'

'Only yours if you don't get a move on and fertilize one of my eggs.'

Eight weeks later they discovered he'd obliged in this department and a month on, a rival firm of legal translators made a lucrative offer for TransLex Ltd. They moved to Cheshire soon after, having bought a delightful black-and-white half-timbered cottage with two acres of land, part of which was already given over to a well-established fruit and vegetable plot. While he was shut away in his office banging out shipping contracts, Sam was in her wellies getting in touch with her earth mother side. He used to tease her that he'd give her a year before she'd want to be back in the work place.

She was seven and a half months pregnant when he was told by the law firm he was then freelancing for that they wanted him to go to Japan to meet a client. He was torn. He wanted to go, but didn't want to leave Sam on her own so late into her pregnancy. 'Oh, don't be such a pain in the butt,' she told him. 'Pack your case and get going. I'll be fine. Just make sure you bring me back plenty of wasabi peas.'

She drove him to the airport, but still he wasn't happy about leaving her. 'Why don't you go and stay with your parents while I'm away?' he urged her.

'Now you're just annoying me. Boris and I will be just fine.' Despite not knowing what sex their baby was, Boris was the nickname they'd given it.

He kissed her goodbye, never once imagining that it would be the last time he would do so.

He phoned her every day from his hotel in Tokyo, and she laughed at him for being a sentimental devil when he told her he'd spent over an hour in the department store Seibu in Ikebukuro, choosing some baby clothes and toys. 'Yeah, but that's why you love me. Look, I've got to run; I have one last meeting, then I'm on my way to the airport. And don't worry about coming to meet me, I'll get a taxi.'

'Forget it, I'll be there.'

Secretly he was pleased. There was nothing like being met at the airport by someone you loved.

He was one of those irritatingly smug people who can sleep for most of a long-haul flight, especially in business class. What he always liked about flying with predominantly Japanese passengers was the quietness of the flight: Japanese travellers were the quietest in the world, he reckoned. Twelve hours later he was joining the stream of people filing through to the arrivals hall. On one occasion when Sam came to meet him she'd greeted him with a placard she'd made: 'Miss Capulet for Mr Montague'. When the tables were turned not long after and he was meeting her following a trip she'd made to Moscow, he'd been waiting for her with a sign that said, 'Vronsky for A. Karenina.'

He scanned the crowd for her face and maybe a placard. But there was no sign of Sam. He hung around for ten minutes then tried her on her mobile; she'd probably got stuck in traffic. Getting no response – her mobile was switched off – he tried home. Again there was no response. Don't panic, he told himself. If she's gone into labour, she'll have got her family involved. They'll all be there with her at the hospital. So why hadn't someone left a message on his mobile?

He kicked his heels for a further thirty minutes, trying both numbers repeatedly and telling himself that she'd probably lost track of the time, had rushed out of the house and forgotten to switch on the answer machine. And forgotten her mobile? When another ten minutes had passed, he gave up and grabbed a taxi. In the back of the cab he called Sam's parents. Her father answered and it sounded like they had company; Conrad could hear voices and music tinkling away in the background. Maybe it was an impromptu Tempest get-together and Sam was there being pampered by her mum and dad, something she always denied enjoying, but which Conrad knew she secretly loved. It took all of ten seconds for this cosy, reassuring picture to be shattered by Phil saying, 'Hi Conrad, how's my darling girl doing?'

It was dark when the cab driver swung into the drive. The first thing Conrad noticed was that Sam's recently bought Chrysler Jeep was parked alongside his Beamer. There were no lights on and two bottles of milk stood on the doorstep. Every fibre of Conrad's being screamed at him that something was wrong.

He inserted his key into the lock, but when he tried to push open the door, he couldn't get it further than a couple of inches: the safety chain was across. He went round to the back of the house. The door into the utility room was locked. By now his heart was threatening to burst out of his ribcage. He smashed a pane of glass in the kitchen and opened the window. With difficulty he climbed through it and stepped over the broken glass. He called out to

Sam, but his voice echoed eerily in the hush.

Switching on lights as he went, he found her in the hall, at the foot of the stairs. Nausea lurched from the pit of his stomach, sweat broke out all over him, and he knew with heart-stopping certainty that Sam was dead, and that this moment would stay with him for the rest of his days. She was wearing her night clothes, and his towelling bathrobe ... the one she always liked to wear because ... because it trailed the floor and kept her warmer than her own. The dark pool of blood on the carpet from the congealed gash on her head told him she'd been there for some time. He sank to the floor and cradled her in his arms. His tears splashed down onto her pale face, but when he brushed them away and felt the terrible coldness of her skin he cried out in anguish. *Dead! Why? Why had she been taken from him?*

He was still crying when his mobile went off in his jacket pocket. He tried to ignore it, but it kept on ringing. And ringing. Eventually he answered it. It was Phil. He was just checking in with Conrad to see what news he had.

He rubbed his face and wondered how long he'd been trawling the past. A glance at his watch told him half an hour had disappeared. He lowered his feet to the floor and switched his thoughts back to where he'd started.

Helen.

She was the first woman he had met since Sam's death who genuinely interested him. In the aftermath of his aborted suicide attempt, he'd vowed not to look at another woman. He told himself that he owed it to Sam to stay loyal to her. Celibacy wasn't the big deal people made it out to be. It was manageable, he'd come to know, so long as he kept himself permanently busy. Moreover, from listening to other men moaning in the changing rooms at the tennis club, he reckoned that there were plenty of men out there who despite being married had long since given up on a sex life. 'It's okay for you, Conrad,' they often said, 'you're a single man; you can have a different woman every week.'

Yeah, that's right. That's exactly how it works.

But now he'd met Helen. He pictured her face, that wonderfully calm expression. Those beautifully arched eyebrows, and those eyes. Oh, those eyes. They drew him in and left him floundering like a fool. Which was how he'd behaved when he'd kissed her. Okay, it was no more than a peck on the cheek, but was it appropriate behaviour? he asked himself, given that she was married.

And given that once his lips had brushed against her skin, and he'd realized that he'd wanted to kiss her ever since that evening down at the pool, where exactly did that leave him?

It left him precisely where he was before: alone. He could long for her all he wanted, but there was damned all chance of it ever coming to anything. She was married. That silence in the car on the way home had told him everything he needed to know. Back off, it had said. Back off now!

Chapter Twenty-four

From her second-row seat in the village hall, Lucy had far too good a view of the visiting speaker, a beardy, sandal-wearing man with the ugliest, boniest white feet and thickest yellowing toenails she had ever seen. His talk on bonsai trees could not have been less interesting. She'd always regarded this so-called art as cruel, like bandaging little girls' feet to stunt their growth. To top it all, the speaker had one of those irritating voices that made you want to kick the owner up the backside. His hesitant, stop-start delivery was like the feeble whistle of a kettle that can't decide if it's boiling or not.

If it hadn't been for that gobby pixie, Savannah-bloody-Tyler, Lucy would be up at the allotment enjoying herself. But instead here she was, for the sake of keeping an eye on Orlando, having her brains turned to mush. Except, and here was what really galled her, Savannah hadn't bothered to show her face. Just as they'd been taking their seats along with Mac, Orlando had received a text from Savannah saying she'd changed her mind and would skip the Garden Club talk and see him afterwards at the Swan where they were going for a drink. The girl was smarter than Lucy had given her credit for.

Since that conversation they'd had at the garden centre, when Savannah had slyly gone on about them being friends, Lucy had decided to keep a closer eye on the girl, to catch her out as much as anything. Lucy was convinced that Savannah was only pretending to be interested in gardening so that she could be with Orlando. Had she been the right girl for Orlando, Lucy would forgive her the subterfuge; she might even admire her for the lengths she was going to. But she knew in her heart that Savannah was totally wrong for him. He deserved someone so much better. More his own age would be a good start.

Orlando still refused to accept the obvious, that Savannah

wanted a lot more than just friendship from him and Lucy had given up trying to make him see sense. She was worried now that he might start getting the wrong idea if she pushed the matter any further, especially if Savannah was filling his head with the kind of stuff she'd spouted at Lucy – '*Are you in love with him?*' What nonsense! The only reason she was so concerned about Orlando was because he was her best friend. Hadn't he said exactly that when he'd tried to warn her about that married man she'd been involved with? 'You're my best friend; I don't want to see you get hurt,' he'd told her.

Although, after he'd gone behind her back and gossiped to Savannah about Lucy and her father, it had been a close-run thing as to whether she still considered him her best friend. What had got into him? And how dare that girl think she had the right to comment on Lucy's father, much less make that extraordinarily inaccurate assumption that Lucy must love him. She had intended to have it out with Orlando, to make him apologize, but she knew it would only make her look petty. Better to pretend it was neither here nor there. She was determined to treat the trip to Lake Como in the same way. She didn't want anyone thinking it was a big deal. So what if she was visiting a place where her father lived? What of it? Maybe if she had the time she'd look him up. Or maybe she wouldn't. It was no one's business but her own. Marcus Gray was completely incidental to the reason she was going to Italy. Orlando was her number one concern. She was sure that that was when Savannah would make her move and manoeuvre him into something he would regret.

A sudden burst of clapping brought her out of her thoughts. Thank goodness for that; old beardy had finished his talk. Olivia Marchwood was now on her feet, notebook in hand. 'I think I can speak for everyone,' she said when the applause ran dry – it was noticeably short-lived – 'that we've all learned something here this evening. I for one had no idea that the world of bonsai could be so fascinating. Thank you, Mr Brown; you've spurred us on to give it a go ourselves.' She encouraged everyone into giving another round of applause and then announced that there would be an interval during which tea and coffee would be served. 'If you could then return to your seats,' she instructed, 'I have the latest news on our trip to Lake Como. The Gardens of Delight people have sent me a brochure of the hotel we shall be staying in. I've run off copies for everyone.'

'A shame Helen couldn't make it this evening,' Mac said when they were in the queue for a drink.

'Did she say why?' Orlando asked.

'Yes. She was collecting her husband from the airport.'

'Does she mind him being away so much?' Lucy joined in.

'She's never said anything, but who knows?'

They were at the front of the queue now and after putting a handful of coins into the small basket and passing round their cups of coffee and biscuits, Lucy said, 'Anyone know if Hunter is coming on the trip with us?'

'I believe not,' Mac said.

Orlando added – a little too quickly for Lucy's liking – 'According to Savannah he's much too busy.'

It had rained on and off for nearly two hours when Orlando said, 'Come on, let's give this up as a bad job and make a move for home.'

Despite being wet through – the last shower had been so heavy they'd got wet through before making it to the van – Savannah tried not to show how disappointed she was. She'd been enjoying being in the cab of Orlando's van sheltering from the rain. The woman whose garden they were supposed to be working on had brought them out mugs of tea and chocolate mini rolls and with the radio on it was all right sitting here, just the two of them. She'd never talked to anyone as much as she talked to Orlando. He was great; he listened to her properly. He never did that bored glazed-eye thing that Mum and Dad did when they pretended to listen to her.

If she had a complaint about Orlando it was that he didn't seem to catch on to how much she fancied him. At the pub last night, despite the looks Lucy kept giving her, or maybe because of the looks the stuck-up bitch was giving her, she'd really made an effort to let him know that she was interested in him. She put it down to wariness on his part. He probably thought he was too old for her. What else could it be? Unless Lucy was quietly brainwashing him and warning him off her. If that was the case, then there was nothing else for it. She'd have to up her game. It was laughable really, what dumb old Lucy was playing at. Just because she couldn't have Orlando, she didn't want anyone else to, either. Watch and learn, girl!

'Why don't we give it another ten minutes?' she said to Orlando. 'The rain doesn't seem so heavy now.'

He laughed. 'I didn't realize you were such a misplaced optimist.'

'There's lots you don't know about me,' she said with what she hoped was just the right amount of flirtatiousness to her smile.

'One thing I do know is that I could do with a shower and a change of clothes.' He reached across for her empty mug from the dashboard, clanked it against his and opened the door. 'I'll be back in a minute; I'll tell the others, and Mrs Moreton, that we're going home.'

Savannah observed Orlando talking to the two gormless lads in the van in front of them. Thick as shit, they were. How he put up with them she didn't know. Craig, the one from Stoke with the silver nipple ring and tattoo round his neck, who thought he was Robbie Williams, had tried it on with her and she'd told him exactly where he could shove it!

Orlando was now sprinting through the downpour towards the front door of the house. He was soaked, his hair plastered to his head. She suddenly pictured him in the shower, and an idea came to her.

They were almost back in Swanmere when she slapped her hand against her forehead. 'Durr! How stupid am I? I've just remembered that there won't be anyone at home. Both Dad and Helen will be at work.'

'Don't you have a key?' Orlando asked.

She shook head. 'I forgot today.'

'Not to worry. You'll just have to come back with me. You can have a shower and we'll see if we can get your clothes dry in the tumble dryer.'

Savannah smiled. 'You're sure I won't be in the way?'

'Of course you won't. Besides, Lucy won't be back yet.'

Better and better, she thought.

Orlando let them in at the back door. They kicked off their muddy boots along with their socks and jackets, which he hung on the clothes airer in the laundry room. In the kitchen, he called out Lucy's name. There was still an hour to go before she was due home, but even so it seemed a wise precaution. He knew how poorly she viewed his friendship with Savannah. It was a mystery to him why she was so against the poor girl, but he'd long since accepted that they would never be friends.

He sometimes got the feeling that Savannah was coming on to him, but he put it down to nothing more than her mischievous nature. He reckoned that most things she did or said were done to provoke a reaction. He also reckoned that her home life – despite the fact that she'd been given everything money could buy – hadn't been much cop, and that all she wanted was for people to take notice of her. He'd have thought Lucy, of all people, would have picked up on this and empathized.

He found a clean towel for Savannah, pointed her in the direction of the main bathroom, and went to use Lucy's en suite bathroom. He hoped Lucy wouldn't mind too much. He stripped off his jeans and T-shirt and stepped into the shower. As tempting as it was, he didn't linger for too long. He dried himself off, then after wrapping the towel around his waist, he padded back down the landing towards his bedroom for some clean clothes. He closed the door after him, dropped the towel to the floor, turned round and got the shock of his life.

Savannah was sitting up in his bed. All he could see of her was her head and bare shoulders above the duvet, but odds on she wasn't wearing anything underneath it. Before he could say anything, or bend down for his towel, he heard a voice calling out.

It was Lucy.

Chapter Twenty-five

As Lucy dragged herself up the stairs she had only one thing on her mind, and that was knocking back some super-strength cold remedy, or any other pain-numbing substances they had in the house, and getting into bed. The thick woolly head she had woken up with that morning had developed into the mother of stinking colds. Luckily the weather was so bad there had been hardly any customers and Hugh had let her go early. 'Go home now and take your rotten germs with you!' he'd ordered.

The ride home on her bike in the pouring rain had very nearly killed her, and the moment she'd let herself in she'd thrown her stuff onto the floor – for once not caring about the mess – and made for the stairs. She knew Orlando was back because she'd seen his van parked on the street at the side of the house and she was glad. A little bit of TLC from him would go a long way to making her feel better.

'Orlando,' she called out again.

No response. Perhaps he was in the shower. At the top of the stairs, the bathroom was empty: splashes of water on the floor suggested he'd been in there recently. Wanting to see him, to tell him she wasn't feeling well, she crossed the landing and knocked on his bedroom door. Her hand was poised to turn the handle when she heard a noise that made her hesitate. It was the unmistakable sound of giggling. She snatched her hand away as if she'd just received a massive electric shock.

Savannah!

Who else could it be?

She backed away from the door, desperate to put as much distance between her and Orlando's room. The last thing she needed was for him to respond to her knocking.

But she wasn't fast enough. The door opened a couple of inches. It was Orlando, and he was dressed only in a towel tied around his waist. She had seen him in exactly this state of undress countless times before, but now it seemed altogether different. It was as if he was a stranger. She averted her eyes, embarrassed. He stepped towards her and closed the door behind him, but not before another giggle had slithered through the gap. 'It's not what you think,' he said, his voice low. 'I thought she was—'

Lucy took another step back and raised her hands. 'Hey, it's none of my business. You don't need to tell me anything.'

'But Luce, you've got it all wrong. There's nothing to tell. I ... she—'

'No really, I don't want to know. And if you could keep the noise down, I'd be grateful. I'm going to bed. I'm not feeling very well. It's why I came home early.'

She made her exit as dignified as she could, even managing to ignore the pain when she stubbed her toe on the wooden chest by the airing cupboard. But when she closed her bedroom door, she lost what was left of her composure and threw herself on the bed. For no reason she could think of, she buried her face into the duvet and sobbed. 'How could he?' she croaked. 'And with *her?*

Chapter Twenty-six

Nearly a week had passed since Hunter had returned from his trip to Dubai. But it was only today – Sunday – that Helen felt he was truly home. He'd been so busy following up on all the potential deals he'd set in place during his time away, which had included the acquisition of a lease on some office space, that she had hardly seen him. Every morning he went to work early and came home late at night. 'Don't bother about making me anything to eat,' he'd say on his mobile from the car, 'I sent out for a sandwich earlier.' His absence left her feeling disappointed and anxious. Vulnerable, too. Never before had she so badly needed to know that he cared for her. She wanted to be close to him, to be protected by his larger-than-life presence.

And why? Oh, that was easy. To stop herself dwelling on the memory of what had happened at Wollerton with Conrad. All during the drive home that day, unable to meet his gaze or speak to him, she had told herself it meant nothing, that kiss. Or that look. But she couldn't stop herself from replaying the gentleness of his lips against her cheek. Oh, such gentleness. Later, her stomach had skittered like that of a love-struck teenager whenever she thought of Conrad.

Since then she had kept herself busy with work and made her excuses whenever Mac called. It was important that, whilst the memory of that day was still fresh in her mind, her path didn't cross with Conrad's.

She looked at Hunter now, across the table where they were having breakfast in the garden. She willed him to look up and make some kind of connection with her. Why couldn't he realize that she needed him? She started counting in her head, telling herself that when she reached ten, he would put down the report he was reading and look at her.

Amazingly, he did.

His face was very tanned from his time away, making his blue eyes seem brighter and sharper. He looked well. Just the kind of man any number of women would look at twice. 'I've been thinking of joining a gym,' he said.

'Really?' She was genuinely taken aback. He had always been so vociferous in his belief that a healthy body was a body that was worked hard and fuelled sensibly.

'I used the gym at the hotel in Dubai and found I quite liked it,' he said.

'You'll be telling me next you played golf there and want to take that up.'

He shrugged. 'Who knows? I might do just that. If I do as much business there as I intend to, the golf club is the 'in' club to join. You wouldn't believe how much business is conducted whilst out on the greens. Pass the orange juice, will you?'

She handed him the glass jug, conscious that it was the first real conversation they'd had since he'd come home. 'So what was Dubai like? You haven't really told me much about it.' She knew exactly what Dubai was like. It was one of those ghastly places she had never wanted to visit; it was overly manufactured, a lavish Disney world for the wealthy who no longer wanted to live in the real world.

'It was forty degrees and swarming with property developers,' Hunter replied. 'It's an enormous building site. There are currently more construction cranes in Dubai than anywhere else in the world.'

That much she also knew. Along with the disgusting fact that there were construction workers there being paid as little as forty-six pence an hour. 'Is that it?' she asked.

One hand still holding the report, he filled his glass with the other. 'There's not much to tell. Another five years and the place might be finished. By then the Russians, Eastern Europeans and Chinese will have joined the party and made a killing.'

She suddenly felt angry, as if he was patronizing her. The fact that he was still holding that report added to her annoyance. Was she worth such a scant amount of his attention? 'What kind of properties are you buying?' she pressed.

He took a long, slow sip of his orange juice. 'This is a strange phenomenon. You've never been interested in my business activities before. What's brought this on?'

She hesitated. Why was she doing this? Why was she so desperate to push him into engaging with her when he clearly didn't want to? Did she really trust herself so little? Obstinately, she said, 'Are you saying I've disappointed you by not showing more interest before now?'

Confusion – or was it irritation? – flickered across his face. 'Question after question, Helen. Do you feel neglected? Is that it?'

'Yes,' she said, suddenly deciding that maybe this was the easiest way to stop what she'd started. And wasn't being neglected part of the problem? If he was around more, perhaps their marriage wouldn't seem so … so ambiguous. 'Yes,' she repeated. 'I do feel neglected.'

Hunter's face softened. He put down his report and reached out to her. 'Why didn't you say? You should come with me when I go back to Dubai. I'd like your opinion on the Arabian ranch properties I'm buying. Maybe we could choose a place for us there.'

'To live there, you mean?'

He laughed. 'Don't be daft, I couldn't leave my family. No, what I meant was we could buy a holiday home for ourselves.'

'Well—'

'Excellent. That's settled, then. I should have thought about taking you in the first place. Am I forgiven?'

'Nothing to forgive,' she said faintly.

He went back to his work and she felt as if she'd been dismissed.

Five minutes later his mobile buzzed with a text message. Leaving him to deal with it, she gathered up some of the crockery and went inside the house. All was quiet. Presumably Savannah was still asleep upstairs. Feeling more unsettled than ever, she pulled down one of Alice's journals from the shelf on the dresser and went back outside. Not to where she'd been sitting with Hunter, but down to what she now always thought of as Alice's secret garden.

Disappointingly she hadn't got around to implementing any of the changes she wanted to in this area. Time had been a factor, but more importantly the inspiration for the project was still curled up inside her camera. She hadn't had the nerve to have the film developed yet.

She should never have taken that picture of Conrad. It was what had started all the trouble. She had as good as flirted with him when she'd zoomed in on his profile and pressed down on the shutter release. She would have to watch her behaviour in the future. There could be no more slip-ups.

Closing the arched wooden door behind her, she wandered slowly along the central brick path with its pretty herringbone pattern: immediately she felt at peace in the calming solitude and uplifted by the deliciously heady scent of the Gallica and Alba roses. The planting Alice had carried out in this area had created an atmosphere of timeless serenity and Helen knew that when she came to add her own personal touch she would have to take care not to spoil what Alice had achieved. She had tried to share her ideas with Hunter but he was no more than politely interested. He seldom ventured down here; he said it was because he couldn't get a signal on his mobile this far from the house. As a consequence, Helen liked knowing that it was her very own special place.

Where she had once sat with Conrad.

There! It had happened again. He had sneaked his way into her thoughts. It was happening too often. The harder she tried to keep him out, the more persistent his presence became. Only the other day she had found herself remembering the first time she'd met him. Back from her long weekend away, Annabel had caught her staring out of the window. She must have had a strange expression on her face because Annabel had laughed and said, 'That looks more than a penny's worth of thought. Care to share it with me?'

To deflect her friend, she'd said, 'Tell me about your girls' weekend. Did you get very drunk and verbally trash your husbands into the ground?'

Annabel had groaned. 'You don't want to know. We behaved worse than a hen party in Tallin. I don't think we slept at all.'

From the exhausted look of her, Helen could believe it.

She settled herself on the wrought-iron seat and opened Alice's journal. Here, at least, in the place that had belonged to Alice, was a world free of turmoil and disappointment.

If we are passionate about our gardens, we can't help but look to the future, Alice had written. *We can't help but be cock-eyed optimists. If we weren't, we would surely go mad.*

Chapter Twenty-seven

Over the coming days, Lucy's cold got a lot worse. As did relations between her and Orlando. The atmosphere in the house was spiralling out of control. They seemed to be on at each other the whole time, even rowing over something as trivial as forgetting to put out the wheelie bin.

If only he would be honest with her then she might be able to respect him. But no, he kept denying that there was something going on between him and Savannah. Did he take her for a complete idiot? Hadn't she seen for herself what he'd been up to? How could he even think of insulting her by saying that he'd had no idea Savannah was playing at Goldilocks in his bed? 'Look, I came back from using your shower and there she was,' he had said. He was about as convincing as Bill Clinton claiming he'd never had sex with Monica Lewinsky. She'd told him as much. 'Oh, what the hell, Lucy!' he'd suddenly shouted. 'If you don't believe me, that's your problem. Go ahead and call me a liar. I don't see why I have to explain myself to you, anyway.'

'Problem!' she'd croaked as loudly as her painfully sore throat would allow. 'I don't give a damn who you go to bed with. You can sleep with the entire female population of Swanmere for all I care. I just thought you had more intelligence than to waste yourself on a girl like Savannah.'

'You know what the real problem is, don't you?' he'd said, his voice loaded with coldness. 'You're turning into your mother. I've never known you to be so irrational or so bitter and twisted. And for reasons beyond my understanding, you're blinded with jealousy. All I'm doing is giving Savannah the same chance my father and plenty of others gave you when you were—'

She hadn't heard the rest of what he had to say; she'd been too busy barging past him to go to the bathroom. Once she'd locked herself in and had heard his footsteps thumping downstairs, she'd slumped to the floor and wept. As she'd crouched with her back against the bath panel, her chin resting on her knees, she'd felt as if her heart was ready to break. But why? Why did any of this matter to her so much?

That was when she began to wonder if her feelings for Orlando were more complicated than she'd ever considered. Was it possible that she loved him? The enormity of this question provoked a fresh wave of sobbing. But worse was to come when she made the mistake of imagining Orlando making love to Savannah. She'd clenched her fists, driving them against her eyes. Why had that bloody awful girl come into their lives?

Oh, what wouldn't she give for things to be the way they'd been only a few months ago, when she and Orlando didn't argue, when they spent nearly all their free time together, talking, laughing and being the best of friends? It was as though they'd been made for each other. Everything was so easy between them. When she really thought about it, they'd been as good as married for years.

Her greatest fear, if things got any worse, was that Orlando would move out. Just like her father had walked out on her and her mother.

Now, two days later, as if things couldn't get any worse, Lucy's mother was on the phone. Within seconds it was clear that her only purpose for calling was to sound off about Charles, who must have committed some unspeakably vile crime towards Fiona.

Dragging herself around the kitchen in her slippers and dressing gown whilst opening a can of tomato soup, Lucy held the cordless phone away from her ear, just occasionally bringing it nearer so that she could keep the gist of the one-sided conversation within her grasp.

At last her mother paused for breath and said, 'Are you listening to me, Lucy, or am I wasting my breath?'

'Sorry, Mum,' she said hoarsely, 'I'm not feeling well. I've been off work the last few days with a horrible cold. Now tell me about you and Charles. What's he done? Stopped your pedicure allowance?'

Fiona tutted. 'You know what I've always said about sarcasm.'

'Yes, that it's best left to moronic halfwits. Which is exactly how I feel at the moment, so spare me the prevarication. Just tell me what the problem is.'

'I don't want to discuss it.'

'Then why did you ring me?'

'I thought you'd be interested. But obviously you're too wrapped up in yourself to worry about me. How's that young man of yours? Treating you better than Charles is treating me, I hope.'

'Which young man would that be?' Lucy knew exactly to whom her mother was referring, but she'd rather push hot needles through her eyeballs than admit it to Fiona.

'I'm talking about Orlando, as well you know.'

Lucy switched on the gas to heat up her soup. 'Firstly, he's not my young man, and secondly, I haven't a clue how he is. I hardly see him these days. He's out most of the time.'

Fiona's tone audibly brightened. 'Oh? Have you had a quarrel? If so, I'm not going to beat about the bush and lie to you. Frankly, I'm delighted. I always said you were too good for him, that he had no real prospects. It wouldn't have been so bad if he'd stuck with his father's business. At least then he would have had some kind of security to offer you.'

Lucy had heard her mother express this view on many occasions in the past, but it was poignantly painful hearing it now. 'We've only ever been friends, Mum,' she said tiredly. 'It's never been a matter of what he can offer me.'

'Oh, don't give me that. He's been after you for years. Take it from me, this will be a good opportunity for you to meet a decent chap. I just wish it had happened a long time ago.'

Too weak and emotionally drained to argue with Fiona, Lucy stirred the pan of soup. She wished, just once, that her mother would act like a mother and notice all was not well with her daughter. But no. It was always about Fiona. And accordingly, Lucy would always be the one to bolster up Fiona's confidence and convince her that everything would be all right. Turning the gas down beneath the bubbling pan, she thought of all the times when, in an attempt to lift her mother's deflated spirits, she had uttered the rallying war cry of, 'Sod Marcus Gray! Who needs him anyway?' How many times had she been the child masquerading as the adult, the one to lock up and turn out the lights, then check that her mother hadn't fallen asleep with a lighted cigarette in her hand? It was a burden that had eventually driven her to fight tooth and nail to be free of it. To be rid of her mother's suffocating neediness by defying her every way she could.

With the greatest effort she said, 'Come on, Mum, let's get back to you and Charles. You know he loves you to bits.'

*

It was nine o'clock and Orlando and Savannah were just finishing a bread and butter job he had promised the clients would be completed by tomorrow, in readiness for a party they were throwing to celebrate their thirtieth wedding anniversary. He switched off the petrol powered mower, and as he tipped the last of the grass cuttings into the refuse sack, he watched Savannah sweeping the terrace and repositioning the pots of pale-pink nemesia and white petunias, having dead-headed and watered them as he'd instructed. She was proving to be a good worker. Particularly so since that crazy stunt of hers. 'What the bloody hell do you think you're doing?' he'd demanded, after Lucy had knocked on his bedroom door, put a whopping great two and two together and gone off in a monumental huff. 'No, don't even bother to explain. I don't want to hear it. Just get dressed and go, Savannah.'

Doing as he'd instructed, she'd slipped out of his bed and crossed the room to the bundle of clothes on the floor. The sight of her completely naked should have had him turning away, but his eyes swept over her slim, perfect body, lingering for longer than was decent on her breasts, which were full and high. His face must have betrayed him for she'd stepped towards him, her hands on her hips, and said, 'Tell me you're not tempted.'

He swallowed. 'I'm nine years older than you, Savannah.'

'That's not answering my question.'

The confidence of the girl was extraordinary. And a massive turn-on. Trying to ignore what was going on under his towel, he'd said, 'Please, just get dressed.' With more resolve than he thought himself capable of, he'd grabbed a pair of clean jeans, some boxers and a T-shirt, and left her to get dressed. Outside on the landing, his heart was pounding and his mouth was dry. Shocked that she'd had such an effect on him, he'd gone into the bathroom and splashed cold water onto his face. Hurriedly throwing on his clothes, he'd waited for her to reappear. No way was he going to risk going downstairs leaving her up here alone with Lucy on the warpath.

She'd emerged within seconds, dressed in her wet work clothes, and to his surprise he saw that her face was suddenly without a shred of guile. She looked so young, almost fragile. 'Does this mean I'm sacked?' she'd asked. Gone was the brazen act he'd witnessed just moments ago and in its place was a look of pure misery. He'd felt a stab of regret that he'd rejected her so cruelly. In an effort to soften her humiliation, he'd smiled. 'Hey, sexual harassment goes on in the workplace all the time. Just don't let it happen again. Okay?'

She'd raised her chin from where it had been tucked into the v-neck of her top and very nearly looked him in the eye. 'You mean that? Really? You're not going to dump me?'

The pleading tone in her voice had caused something to shift inside him. He'd felt like taking her in his arms. 'Why don't we pretend it never happened?' he'd said.

A faint flush had stolen over her face and she'd chewed on her lower lip. 'I'm ... I'm not sure I can.'

He'd put a hand on her shoulder. 'Come on, let's go downstairs and I'll see you out. I'll pick you up for work at eight-thirty sharp tomorrow morning. We've got Mrs Moreton's garden to finish off. It'll be just you and me; Richie and Joel are starting another job.'

The next day the sun had shone in a clear blue sky. Savannah had hardly said a word all morning. It wasn't until lunchtime that Orlando decided to do something about the embarrassing silence between them. He missed the old Savannah, the lippy, self-assured girl who had an answer for everything. Knowing that Mrs Moreton was out for the day, he'd suggested they eat their lunch on the patio. He had watched her unscrew a bottle of Pepsi and was just thinking what to say to put her at ease when she tilted her head back to take a long, thirsty swig from the bottle. The sight of her smooth neck fully exposed stopped him dead. Still drinking, she'd turned and caught him looking at her. 'Want some?' she'd said, lowering the bottle and offering it to him.

He had shaken his head. Nine years older, he'd reminded himself. But the seeds of desire had been sown. He wanted her. He wanted her badly.

'I suppose you're wondering why I did what I did yesterday,' she'd said in the silence, at the same time kicking off her boots and removing her socks. Mesmerized, he'd watched her stretch her legs out in front of her and wriggle her toes in the sun. On her right foot, she wore a silver toe ring.

'It had crossed my mind,' he'd replied.

'Yeah, well, I'm sorry. It was pretty stupid of me. It's just that I'm used to getting my own way, I guess. I get it from my Dad.' Leaning back into the chair, she had rolled up her vest top to sun her already tanned midriff. He'd had a sudden urge to lean over and kiss the taut flatness of her stomach and that cute little twinkling gemstone that was catching the sunlight.

173

He'd cleared his throat. 'What exactly was it you were hoping to get your own way with?' he'd asked. Yeah, like you don't know, he'd said to himself.

Without turning her head or even opening her eyes, she'd said, 'I've fancied you from the first moment I saw you and decided it was time to get things moving.' She'd opened her eyes, but hadn't turned to look at him. Replacing the cap on the bottle of Pepsi, she had rested it on her crotch. 'It's okay. I can handle knowing that you don't fancy me. It's a shame, but I'll get over it.' She'd turned then and looked at him. 'Is that okay with you? I mean, I really enjoy working for you and would hate to think you had a problem with me.'

That should have been the moment when he'd done the sensible thing and said it would be better if she did stop working for him. But he hadn't. Instead he'd torn his gaze away from the provocatively placed bottle and went to great lengths to deny that he had, or ever would have, any kind of a problem working with her.

Since then he'd come to realize that his problems had only just begun. By day he was continuously distracted by thoughts of Savannah and by night he was subjected to countless moods and sarcastic comments from Lucy.

Lucy's behaviour was astonishing. He had never known her to behave so irrationally. It didn't matter how many times he tried to deny he'd slept with Savannah, Lucy refused to believe him. In the end he simply thought, what the hell? Let her believe what she wanted. And anyway, he had a right to sleep with whomever he wanted. Just because he and Lucy had been friends since for ever, it didn't mean he was answerable to her.

It annoyed and saddened him that things had deteriorated so badly with Lucy, but as far as he was concerned he'd done nothing wrong. He certainly had no intention of apologizing. If anything, it was she who needed to apologize to him for all those barbed comments she'd made. Perhaps when she'd got over her cold, she'd start thinking more reasonably.

'Orlando, I'm finished here; shall I start putting the stuff on the van?'

Savannah's voice broke into his thoughts and he pushed the mower up to where she was waiting for him on the terrace. He checked that she'd done everything he'd asked her to and said, 'Yes, go ahead. I'll just have a word with Mr and Mrs Meade.' He paused. Then: 'Seeing as I've kept you so late, how do you fancy a drink and a bite to eat at the Swan before I drop you off?'

She looked at him steadily with her almond-shaped eyes. 'You're not worried I might try and jump you in the bar?'

He laughed. 'Just try it.'

And with something of her old swagger, she said, 'Who knows, play your cards right and I might just do that.'

Chapter Twenty-eight

It was only Wednesday, yet for the third time that week, Helen was destined to spend the evening alone. Hunter had told her at breakfast that he and Clancy were getting together after work to go over some papers with the company's finance director and that he wouldn't be home until late. 'No need to wait up for me,' he'd said. 'Clancy and I will probably go for a meal and a drink afterwards. If it's a really late session I might even stop the night with him and Paula. You don't mind, do you?' He'd kissed her cheek and left, not even waiting for her reply. Not long after, just as Helen was gathering her things together to go to work herself, Savannah had appeared in the kitchen and announced that she wouldn't be home until late either. No explanation was forthcoming.

Now, as Helen shut the front door behind her and picked up the mail, the house seemed to resonate with an unwelcoming emptiness. Leaving her briefcase in the hall, she went through to the kitchen. The remains of Savannah's breakfast – crusts of toast, an orange juice carton and a half-eaten apple – lay strewn across several work surfaces. The girl was easier to be around these days, but she was still an unthinking madam who expected others to clean up behind her.

Helen held Orlando entirely responsible for the slightly improved Savannah. When she'd bumped into Mac outside the newsagent just recently, he'd implied that Orlando's championing of her step-daughter was putting a strain on his friendship with Lucy. Helen couldn't understand why he would want to jeopardize what he had with Lucy for the sake of continuing his interest in Savannah. Unless, of course, there was more to the situation than met the eye. Once or twice Hunter had teased Savannah, saying that he hoped it was only gardening she and Orlando were getting up to. 'That's strictly none of your business, Dad,' Savannah had laughed. There was something to that laugh – it was more girlish than one usually heard from Savannah – that suggested she was quite taken with Orlando. And what right-thinking girl wouldn't be? Orlando Fielding was cuter than cute.

Helen had asked Mac, seeing as he was so in the know, if he thought there was something going on between Orlando and Savannah. For once Mac had to admit ignorance. After he'd remarked on how little he'd seen of Helen lately, and she'd brushed him off by saying work was frantic just now, he'd then told her he was on his way home to listen to an Italian language cassette in preparation for their trip. 'I hate sounding like an ignorant oik in a foreign country. Always better to have a few pleasantries under one's belt, in my opinion.'

Knowing that Conrad was a fluent Japanese speaker, and wondering what other languages he knew, Helen had said, 'Does Conrad speak Italian?'

'Oh, he's one of those clever dicks who can pick up the basics through a process of osmosis. His wife, Sam – now she was a real linguist.'

This was the first direct reference Helen could recall Mac making about Conrad's dead wife. It gave her the courage to ask how the love of Conrad's life had died. The answer was far worse than she could have expected. 'It was an appalling out-of-the-blue accident,' Mac told her. 'Conrad came home after a business trip to Japan and found her dead at the bottom of the stairs. She must have tripped. It was as simple as that. One mis-footing and she was no more. Their unborn baby dead, too. The boy's been to hell and back since then.'

Helen could believe it. She knew how devastated her grand-parents' lives had been by the death of her mother, Daisy. The horror had never truly left them. Especially for her grandfather, who had discovered the body. How could anyone not be changed for ever after an ordeal like that? Sometimes Helen was grateful that Emma now lived in such a state of confusion; it meant that she was probably no longer haunted by those awful memories. Small mercies.

Helen also considered it a small mercy that she had managed to put that day at Wollerton Hall behind her. Whatever had been going through Conrad's mind at the time was his business, not hers. Since then, she'd pulled herself together. Other than the occasional two-second sighting of him in the village, either in his Saab or walking along the main street, she hadn't seen him to speak to.

However, as effective as she'd been at casting him from her mind, every so often, when she was least expecting it, there would be a frisson of recall. It was the compassionate tenderness of the man that still crept into her thoughts. With a new awareness, she could see that Hunter, for all his grand gestures, his altruistic giving to charity and generous all-round benevolence, was not a tender-hearted man. She suspected that he would argue that practical help was of far greater worth than tears and sympathy. He would no more stop to breathe in the perfume of a fragrant rose than he would cry at the opera.

But he was a good man, she reminded herself. Look how he'd responded when she'd told him she'd been feeling neglected. And there wasn't anything he wouldn't do for his family. Okay, he wasn't able to give Savannah as much time as she would probably like – his half-hearted attempt to teach her to drive had fallen by the wayside and Savannah's new car stood unused on the drive like an abandoned toy – but then time was a precious commodity to him. He needed most of it for his business interests – they were his whole raison d'être. Anything else had to fend for itself. He was out all hours and when he was home, he was on the phone. She worried sometimes that he was pushing himself too hard. Especially as he'd gone ahead and joined the gym he'd spoken about. He was surely a classic case of a middle-aged man putting himself in the direct line of fire of a heart attack.

There was also his recent sudden lack of interest in sex. Wasn't this another sign that he was suffering from exhaustion? She knew better than to air this thought – an alpha male like Hunter would deny such a weakness to his dying breath. After the way things had been, though, his lack of interest came as a relief.

Slipping the rubber band off the bundle of post and separating it into the appropriate piles – most of it was for Hunter – she came across a pale-mauve envelope addressed to her in a spidery hand. She opened it and pulled out a thank-you card from Isobel Jenkins. It had been Isobel's birthday last week and Helen had sent her a present, a copy of Maeve Binchy's latest novel. With a happy smile she put the card on the dresser and returned to sorting out the rest of the post. There were two more large buff-coloured envelopes for Hunter and then … a package for her: it was her photographs back from the developers.

She had deliberately not taken the film anywhere local to be developed for fear of setting tongues wagging, and had very nearly thrown it away at one stage. But she hadn't. She had wanted to see if the camera had recorded what she'd felt that day.

Despite being alone in the house, she found herself looking over her shoulder before opening the package. She slid the glossy prints across the work surface, her heart picking up pace as she waited for Conrad's image to appear.

And there it was, the picture she'd taken when he wasn't looking. She stood for a moment just staring at his handsome, intelligent face, taking in the set of his jaw, the line of his nose, the colour of his light-brown hair, made even lighter by the brilliant sunshine. How pensive he seemed. Almost melancholic. She moved on to the other pictures. The one of them together – Conrad's arm around her, his expression anything but melancholic – and then the one with Conrad's lips skimming her cheek. She put her hand to where he'd kissed her. How easy it was to imagine him doing it again. Right now. This very minute.

Wrong! She told herself. *Absolutely wrong!*

The ringing of the telephone less than two feet away made her start. She reached out to it. 'Yes?' she said, expecting it to be Hunter. With her free hand she guiltily covered up the photographs.

'Helen, it's Mac. How are you?'

'Oh, not too bad. I'm just wondering what to do with myself this evening; Hunter's not home until late.'

'In that case, why don't you come and help me out. Conrad's cooking one of his curries and I can't face it alone. What do you say? Can I tempt you to take pity on a desperate man?'

Don't even think about it, she told herself. Say no. Say no thank you and hang up.

'I'd love to, Mac. What time shall I come?'

'Soon as you can.'

You're playing with fire, she warned herself when she'd hidden the photographs and was changing.

I don't care, she answered herself back. I'm bored and lonely. Why not spend the evening with Mac and Conrad?

Because bored and lonely equals dangerously vulnerable. It's an equation every neglected wife knows.

Mac looked at Conrad and wondered what the hell was wrong with him. 'I don't understand,' he said, 'I thought you'd be pleased to have someone more interesting than dull old me sitting round the table.'

'Did you stop to think whether I was in the mood for social-izing?' Conrad snapped back at him.

'But it's Helen I've invited, not some passing stranger.'

'All I'm saying is that it might have been nice to ask me what I thought.'

'And what do you think?'

'I think that was the doorbell I just heard. You'd better go and answer it.'

Unable to fathom Conrad's reaction to his inviting Helen to join them for supper, Mac went out to the hall. 'That was quick,' he said when he opened the front door and saw her standing there. 'Come on in. But a word to the wise, keep away from Conrad.'

She frowned and looked alarmed. 'Any reason why?'

'He's having one of his little tantrums. Apparently he's not in a sociable frame of mind.'

'Would it be better if we took a rain check?'

'Certainly not. I'm sure he'll buck up once he sees you. Look-ing as lovely as you are, I guarantee you'll be able to disarm the grumpiest of sore-headed bears.'

'I think that might be stretching a compliment just a tad too far, Mac.'

He laughed and took her by the arm. 'Nonsense. You're exactly what this house needs; a breath of fresh air. Come and work your magic.'

After several glasses of wine in rapid succession, Conrad was fi-nally relaxing and had forgiven his uncle. In fact he'd go so far as to say he was enjoying himself. The awkwardness he'd expected to feel while in Helen's company – and which he'd hoped to avoid at all costs – hadn't been as bad as he'd thought. Initially he'd been conscious that they were both trying to avoid any direct eye contact, which led him to suspect that she'd been equally unsure about coming here this evening. He was glad now that Mac had invited her, and more importantly that she'd accepted the invi-tation. He only wished he could get her alone so that he could apologize for that moment of madness at Wollerton and put her at ease. Trouble was, he knew that if he did get her alone, he'd want to kiss her again. And kiss her properly.

He looked at her across the table while she listened to Mac showing off his recently learned Italian phrases. They were eating in the kitchen – he and Mac rarely used the dining room; it was too much bother – music was playing, and the urge to reach across and touch Helen's cheek where he'd kissed her was so strong he had to force himself to think about something else. She didn't make it easy, though; the cream top she was wearing hugged her body as close as he'd like to. His pulse quickened at the thought. Then suddenly she'd turned her brandy-coloured eyes on him and was asking how much Italian he could speak. '*Parlo italiano un po*',' he replied. He held up his fingers to show just how little.

She smiled. 'I don't believe you. I think you're being modest.'

He returned the smile and gave her a 'Who, me?' shrug. 'And how about you?'

'I'm a little rusty but I used to be able to speak enough to get a tour group round the main sites in Italy without too much difficulty.'

'Will it feel strange for you, the boot being on the other foot, so to speak? Poacher turned gamekeeper?'

'No. I shall relish every minute of not being the tour leader, knowing that it isn't my responsibility to get everyone from A to B.'

'Good for you,' said Mac. 'And seeing as your husband won't be joining us, it will be our pleasure to take care of you in his place. We shall be your official chaperons. How does that sound to you, Conrad?'

Conrad nodded. 'That's fine by me,' he said casually. 'But we mustn't assume Helen wants chaperoning. How about some coffee?' he added.

'Or a liqueur?' Mac suggested.

Helen folded her napkin and placed it carefully by the side of her cheese plate. It was another thing about her that Conrad liked – how measured and precise she was. There was no rush to her. 'No thank you,' she said. 'I really ought to go. But before I do, can I help with the washing up?'

'Absolutely not,' Mac said. 'Conrad's a dab hand in that department.'

'Actually,' Conrad said, suddenly seeing an opportunity the size of the Atlantic appear before him, 'I was going to put forward the idea, Mac, that while you tidy up here, I'll see Helen home.'

While Helen didn't refuse his offer he noticed that her perfectly pale complexion blushed faintly.

It was a beautifully clear night as they set off down the main street.

It was just gone midnight, and the village was deserted. Above them the stars shone brilliantly and a silvery husk of moon hung in the sky. Putting a hand to the small of her back, he guided her across the road. He then took a deep breath. 'Helen,' he said.

'No. Don't say anything.'

Her words brought him up short. She knows, he thought. She knows how I feel about her. Even so, he said, 'But you don't know what it is I was going to say.'

'I think I do.'

'And you don't think I should just say it anyway?'

She slowed her pace. 'I'm married, Conrad.'

'I wish you weren't.'

'Don't say that.'

'I wish you weren't,' he repeated. 'I wish you were single and I could—'

'Please don't.'

'Then why did you agree to let me walk you home?'

'Because ... because it would have been rude to refuse.'

'So it's better to be polite than speak the truth?'

She turned and looked at him, her eyes as dark as the sky above them. She looked so troubled, almost as if she was scared of him.

'I'm sorry,' he said, shocked. 'From now on I'll keep my big mouth shut.'

And he did. He made no attempt to kiss her goodnight, as he'd planned to, just stood on the doorstep at the Old Rectory and watched her go inside. He listened to an owl hoot, then he turned and walked away, his footsteps crunching on the gravelled drive.

He wanted to believe that if he turned and looked back, he would see her standing at one of the windows, her face full of longing for him.

He didn't look back, though. He was too busy looking to the future, to the trip to Lake Como.

Chapter Twenty-nine

For some inexplicable and annoying reason, so it seemed to Lucy, everyone suddenly fancied themselves an expert and wanted to give her the benefit of their worldly wisdom. First it had been her mother offering advice, then Mac, then Dan, then Angie, and now Hugh was pitching in. Her mother, with her all-weather downer on Orlando, had said it was about time Lucy woke up to the truth about him, and everyone else was saying their bust-up was nothing but a storm in a teacup. Some storm, she'd thought. What pained her most was remembering those cruel things he'd said about her: that she was becoming just like her mother.

Irrational.

Bitter.

Jealous.

If he'd ever cared for her how could he have said what he did, knowing how deeply it would hurt her?

She'd been back at work for a week now – her cold finally making a timely exit – and having deliberately and successfully gone out of her way to avoid being alone with Hugh, her luck had now run dry. He'd cornered her while she'd been making a start on tidying the bedding plant section, which after the weekend onslaught looked like it had been trampled on by a herd of charging elephants. He was staring at her now with what he probably thought was his caring I'm-not-just-your-boss-I'm-your-friend look.

'How's it going then, Lucy?' he asked, while clicking a biro in one hand and fiddling with the walkie-talkie clipped onto his belt with the other.

'Busy,' she said. Couldn't he see that? She gave the ground a vicious swipe with the broom.

'Too busy for a chat?'

Head down with the broom, she said, 'I can spare you five

minutes. I'm expecting a delivery any minute and I've got this lot to sort out before—'

He cut her short as she knew he would. 'I'm aware what time the delivery's arriving, Lucy, and it's not till after lunch, so do yourself a favour and hear what I've got to say.'

'I don't have to, you know.'

He clicked the biro. 'You don't have to, but just for once I'm calling the shots round here. So put that broom down and come and have a coffee with me in my office.' Without waiting for her response, he signalled to where Angie was chatting to one of the vacation workers. 'Hold the fort, will you, Angie? I need Lucy for a few minutes.'

Hugh's office was the untidiest area in the entire garden centre. Squalor was its close cousin. Whenever Lucy stepped over its threshold she longed to roll up her sleeves and carry out a cull of the ancient catalogues, brochures, files, seed packets, newspapers, crushed cardboard boxes, and chipped china mugs – most of which had mould growing inside them. There was even a broken lopsided chair that had been there for as long as Lucy could remember; the padded seat had been chewed away by a family of nesting mice. 'I'd prefer to stand,' she said, when Hugh placed their mugs of coffee on what little area of his desk would safely accommodate them and invited her to sit down. 'This place is a health hazard,' she pointed out to him. 'You really should do something about it.'

He laughed. 'Not a chance. It's my sure-fire method of getting rid of pushy sales reps. They can't get away soon enough.'

'I wouldn't be surprised if one showed up dead and decomposing under the clutter some day. It would explain the awful smell.' She wrinkled her nose. 'Doesn't it ever get to you?'

'No. But what does get to me is knowing my son's upset you. What's he done?'

Damn! She'd handed him the perfect opening, right on a plate. 'Haven't you asked Orlando?'

'I tried but he went all non-committal and tight-lipped on me. Is it something to do with that girl who's working for him?'

Lucy picked up her coffee mug and took a cautious sip – not because there was a danger of it being scalding hot, but because Hugh's coffee-making ability was on a par with his housekeeping skills. A domestic engineer he was not. She winced at its bitter strength and said, 'Savannah doesn't even figure on my radar.'

Hugh raised one of his bushy eyebrows. 'Judging from your tone I'd have to dispute that.'

Feeling she was being backed against the wall, she said, 'Look, Hugh, I'd hate to get above myself but really this is none of your business.'

'Wrong! You're very much my business. Why, you're practically family. Like a daughter to me.'

His words whittled away at her resolve. She cleared her throat, suddenly overcome. 'I had no idea you could use such persuasive rhetoric,' she said with a rallying attempt to bluff her way through the conversation. *Keep the defences up and you'll soon be out of here unscathed.*

'Oh, come on, love, you can do better than that. Stop stonewalling me. If the lad's stepped out of line, I want to know about it.'

'We've had a disagreement, that's all.' *First defence down.*

'It must have been a hefty one for him to be spending more time back at home all of a sudden. I get the feeling from him that the two of you are hardly speaking to each other.'

She took another diverting sip of coffee and instantly regretted it. 'We said stuff,' she said. 'Things got heated.'

'And the *stuff*? Did it have anything to do with that girl, Savannah?'

'Why do you keep going on about her?'

'Because you and Orlando have been inseparable since you met and shortly after she comes along the two of you aren't speaking to each other. Is there something going on between Orlando and Savannah? Is that the problem?'

'Hugh, be fair; if Orlando was going out with a suspected serial killer it still wouldn't be my place to tell you about it. Can I get back to work now?'

'So you think she's on a par with a serial killer, do you? You dislike her that much?'

Damn! 'I didn't say that.'

'No, you didn't need to. It was written all over your face that day you served her here. I know men are famed for being a bit slow on the uptake, but does Orlando know how you feel about him?'

Lucy froze. 'What do you mean?'

'Now you're just insulting me. Have you told him how you feel? Or have you just let him go off to make a fool of himself with this young girl who's flattered his ego so effectively?'

She stood staring at Hugh, unable to speak.

'If I were in your shoes,' he went on, 'I'd consider putting up a bit of a fight for him. Some men have to be bludgeoned over the head and dragged back to the cave by their hair. It's what my wife had to do with me. So if it runs in the family, you'd better find yourself a large blunt instrument.'

Lucy's head was telling her to battle on, to keep up the pretence and convince Hugh that he'd allowed his overactive imagination to run away with itself, but her heart was telling her to be honest with him. And herself. To say that yes, there was the strongest of possibilities that she did love Orlando, that she had loved him all these years but had never realized it. And now she had pushed him out of her life and into the arms of another. Finally she said, 'It's too late, Hugh. Orlando has made it very clear to me that there's only ever been friendship between us.'

'Are you sure?'

Just like your mother ... irrational ... bitter ... jealous. She swallowed. 'Oh, yes. He couldn't have stated his feelings more plainly.'

'Things are often said in the heat of the moment. I've never been the kind of father to interfere, but how would it be if I spoke to him? Really pinned him down and made him see sense. After all, this thing with Savannah has to be nothing more than a passing fancy.'

She was nearly crying now, knowing that Hugh cared so much that he was prepared to intervene on her behalf. She shook her head and mumbled something about getting back to work.

But he wasn't finished with her yet. 'You won't go and do anything stupid, will you?'

'Such as?'

'Such as pulling out of the trip to Italy.'

Astonished at his intuitiveness – several times already she had come within a whisker of calling Olivia Marchwood and cancelling – she said, 'Have you taken up mindreading on the quiet?'

'I thought as much.' He came round from his side of the desk, stepping over a block of crumbling polystyrene. 'That would be the coward's way, and you're no coward, Lucy. You get on that plane to Lake Como, you strut your stuff there and you bloody well enjoy yourself while that fool of a son of mine is getting that girl out of his system. And more importantly, you meet your father and say whatever needs saying. It strikes me that now might be the perfect time to be reconciled with him. Hey there, don't go all wobbly on me and cry. I'm just your average boring, middle-aged bloke; you know I can't handle displays of emotion.'

'I'm not crying,' she sniffed. 'It's this bloody awful coffee. It's making my eyes water.'

Chapter Thirty

Savannah was having lunch with her mother. They were eating in one of Marcia's favourite restaurants in Manchester, a trendy, minimalist, wooden-floored establishment where the waiters were all so snooty and up themselves that Savannah longed to hurl, or at least belch very loudly.

Back from her visit to the States, Marcia was dressed in a pair of skin-tight powder-blue hipster jeans with a diamante belt and a plunging white top. Even to Savannah's critical eyes, her mother looked amazing – years younger than when she'd last seen her. She was used to feeling overshadowed by her mother, but today she felt totally eclipsed. She hated knowing that all around them heads were turning, not to look at her, but to get a better eyeful of Marcia. And as her mother batted her eyelashes at the waiter who was pouring out their wine, Savannah had a sudden thought. She stared harder at her mother's face – her mother's perfectly smooth face – particularly around the eyes and forehead. Then her chin. And then her ... *Bastard hell!* That was why she'd been away in the States so long. She'd had a friggin' face lift and a boob job while she was there. She must have stayed there until the bruising and swelling had gone down and she could come home looking a million dollars with no one the wiser.

And how typical of Mum not to tell her own daughter what she was up to. No change there, then. That was what she hated about her parents: they couldn't even be arsed to give her the time of day. They never confided in her. Never asked how she felt about something. They just expected her to fit in with their plans.

In contrast Orlando always had time for her. He had to be the most patient guy she'd ever known. And easily the fittest and coolest. But she'd nearly blown it with him. She hadn't bargained on him being so different from the rest of the guys she knew. His rejection of her that day in his bedroom, when she'd laid it on a plate for him, had been one of the most humiliating moments in her life. She'd made herself look cheap, and decent blokes didn't do cheap. Everyone knew that.

But he'd been so nice to her about it. He'd even made a joke of it. She'd felt even worse then and had come embarrassingly close to bursting into tears. And that was something she never did. She had *never*, in the whole of her life, cried in front of a bloke. No bastard way was she going to let some guy see her fall apart. Somehow she'd kept herself together and the next day she'd decided to be completely honest with Orlando. She reckoned she had nothing to lose by this stage. As it worked out, it was the best thing she could have done. Since then they'd got on fine. Well, actually, a lot more than fine. And with Lucy and her great big yapper out of the picture now, things were really looking up.

It was kind of weird, but Orlando's enthusiasm for his work was infectious and she'd found that she was almost enjoying learning all that plant stuff he knew so much about. Then yesterday he did something that took her by surprise. He kissed her. He'd just got the news that he'd been given the job of designing a garden for some bloke off the telly who lived in Nantwich, and he'd been so pleased he'd put his arms around her and hugged her. He'd lifted her off the ground and swung her round. 'You've brought me luck,' he'd said. 'This is going to be such an important job for me.' And then he'd kissed her – a direct hit on the mouth. Not exactly a snog, but a taster of what might be. He'd then asked her to have dinner with him to celebrate his good news.

'So what have you been up to whilst I've been away?'

Savannah snapped out of her thoughts and regarded her mother. Her freakily fresh-faced, unlined, high-boobed mother. She suddenly felt the need to compete with Marcia, to show her which one of them was the real deal. And so she told her all about Orlando.

'And exactly how old is this gardener fellow?' Marcia asked, after a waiter had cleared their table and copped a good look down her front.

'He's eight years older than me. But the age difference doesn't matter. He's the first man who's ever treated me—'

'And your father's allowed this?' Marcia interrupted.

Savannah's hackles began to rise. 'I'm old enough to go out with whoever I want.'

'But a gardener! And you working for him. You. Gardening.' Marcia shuddered. Savannah supposed that had her mother's newly stretched skin allowed it, there would have been an expression of horror and outrage covering her face. 'It's hardly what your father and I imagined you'd end up doing when we sent you to that expensive school,' Marcia added sniffily.

'The school and the cost of it were entirely your choice, not mine. But it's my choice what I do with my life.'

Marcia dabbed at the corners of her mouth with her napkin. 'I notice you didn't answer my question about your father. Does he know you're involved with this older man?'

'Bloody hell, Mum, you make Orlando sound like he's as ancient as you.'

'There's no need to be rude. Needless to say, your father's probably so preoccupied with work and Helen he hasn't a clue that you've been running around with the hired help and making a fool of yourself into the bargain.'

Savannah had had enough. Describing Orlando as the hired help was just so typical of her mother. She went in for the kill. 'If you must know, Dad and Helen have been great about me working with Orlando. Maybe you should have got your prejudices checked out whilst you were having your face and boobs done, Mum.'

For a moment Marcia said nothing. She just stared at Savannah. 'And since when has *Helen*'s opinion meant anything to you?'

Good question, thought Savannah, when minutes later her mother had excused herself to go to the loo, probably to look in the mirror to see what had given her away. Helen might have her faults, Savannah pondered, but she'd never once made a single disparaging comment about Orlando. The memory of her tearing that Subaru driver apart still made Savannah smile.

They were outside on the pavement when her mother said, 'So, darling, when are you coming home?'

It was a question Savannah had been expecting. 'The thing is, Mum, I'd kind of like to stay on at Dad's.'

'You're joking, right?'

'If I come home I can't carry on working for Orlando.'

'Oh, I might have known he'd be at the bottom of this!'

'And one more thing, Mum. I'm going to Italy in a couple of weeks' time, with Orlando.'

'The two of you alone?'

She explained about the trip.

'Well, it looks like you've got it all sorted. I'm just glad you could spare me the time for lunch today.'

'Now you know what it feels like, Mum.'

Orlando was nervous. He was picking Savannah up from the Old Rectory, and apart from wondering if her father would be there, and what he might have to say about his daughter going on a regular date with him, he was still in two minds as to whether he was doing the right thing. By asking Savannah out, he'd given her an unequivocal message: he was interested in her. But she must have reached that conclusion when he'd kissed her. It had been such a spontaneous act on his part – he hadn't thought twice about it at the time – and it was only later that doubts had crept in. Just what was he getting himself into?

In the past if he'd had something on his mind he would have turned to Lucy for advice. She'd always been there for him in times of uncertainty. It had been Lucy, along with Alice, who had urged him to do the garden design course. He'd been wary of upsetting his father at the time, knowing how keen he was for him to take over the business one day, but Lucy had encouraged him to follow his own dream and had even talked to his father.

As he parked his van on the drive at the front of the Old Rectory, he made a promise to himself. He'd apologize and make it up to Lucy. He'd said some awful things and he knew he'd hurt her. He hadn't meant to, but his temper had got the better of him. It rarely happened, and in this instance he regretted it deeply. He hoped Lucy would forgive him.

He rang the doorbell. It was answered immediately by Savannah, and the moment he set eyes on her, Lucy and any doubts he'd had flew from his mind. 'You look fantastic,' he said as Savannah closed the door behind her and stepped towards him. He was so used to seeing her in her work clothes, the sight of her slim body wrapped in a figure-hugging black dress that finished just short of her cute little bum made his mouth go dry. She was wearing a pair of strappy, high-heeled shoes – the kind to make a bloke sit up and take notice – and the transformation was unbelievable. He felt like one of those ridiculous cartoon characters; if he opened his mouth, his tongue would roll out and dangle somewhere on a level with his knees.

'Thank you,' she said. 'You don't look so bad yourself.'

He couldn't help thinking that they made a striking entrance when, later, he pushed open the door of the Italian restaurant. There wasn't a man who didn't look at Savannah's legs when she sashayed past. Dream on, he thought proudly. She's all mine!

It was a feeling that stayed with him throughout the evening, and any reservations he'd had about what he was getting into were long gone by the time he was seeing her home and was once again standing outside the front door of the Old Rectory.

'I've had a great evening,' she said, her hands clasped behind her back, her breasts jutting out towards him.

'So have I. Do you think you'd like to repeat it?'

'What do you think?'

'I think I'd like to kiss you.'

'Any reason why you shouldn't?'

'I'm worried that if I so much as touch you it will set off an alarm causing security lights to flash on and your father to come rushing out here.'

She smiled and positioned herself on a higher step so that she was eye to eye with him. 'Shall we put it to the test and see what happens?'

They did.

There was nothing like the stir of a proper first kiss. The excitement. The promise. Then the clamouring hunger for more than a kiss. He pressed her slender body close, his mouth open wide over hers, her tongue darting over his.

'There,' she said, when they finally drew apart, 'no alarms, no lights, and no angry father.'

'You might not have seen any flashing lights,' he joked, 'but I did.'

She smiled, kissed him one more time, lightly on the lips, and said, 'See you tomorrow, then.' She turned and disappeared inside the house. She was gone so quickly, it was as if she and the whole evening had been a figment of his imagination.

Chapter Thirty-one

Oh, this was bad. Worse than bad. It was potentially disastrous. How had she, Helen Madison-Tyler, normally so level-headed and rational, allowed it to happen? How could she have given Conrad all those mixed messages? She should never have agreed to let him walk her home. She might just as well have given him a written statement that she was miserable in her marriage and looking for a distraction. Better still, why not set herself up in a brightly painted booth as a fairground attraction – Roll up! Roll up! See the lonely, disenchanted married woman!

This was not a description she ever thought she would apply to herself, but she *was* lonely, and she *was*, although it pained her to admit it, disenchanted with marriage to Hunter. But an affair wasn't the answer. Not with Conrad. Not with anyone. She had her principles and she wasn't about to throw them out of the window along with her self-worth.

'You've missed one.'

She looked up into the faded eyes of her grandmother. 'What's that, Gran?'

'You've missed a coupon. Look.'

'So I have. Sorry. I was miles away.' She snipped away at the magazine, then added the coupon for a box of dog biscuits to the pile of money-off vouchers Emma would never use. The poignant futility of the exercise made Helen want to scream. Why did it have to be this way? Why was life so bloody unfair? She suddenly needed to get out of here. The smell of death was too much. No matter how elegant and refined the furnishings were in this place, it was all around them; the very structure of the building was permeated with the sour, unpalatable odour of death and decay. There was no mistaking that it was the holding bay for meeting one's end.

How could a life as bittersweet as Emma's had been, be reduced to this? Hadn't she suffered enough? A rush of fierce love for Emma caused tears to spring to Helen's eyes and she thought of everything her grandmother – and her grandfather – had done for her. Had it not been for them, what would have happened to her when her mother killed herself? As a young child she had developed a heart-stopping fear of being left behind somewhere. A trip to the local shops became a terrifying ordeal. What if her grandmother let go of her hand? What if her grandmother disappeared into the crowd of people and Helen couldn't find her? What if she couldn't find her way home? Then, through sheer determined willpower she decided she would have to learn to fend for herself. She committed to memory the number of the bus they used, the road names they passed, and the shop names. She became obsessed with landmarks: that was the row of terraced houses where they'd once seen an ambulance parked on the kerb, its lights flashing; that was the butcher's shop where they always put sawdust on the floor and the men wore funny straw hats; and that was the zebra crossing where the nasty woman had smacked the little boy because he'd dropped his ice-cream. It was an exhausting process initially but it soon became second nature and her confidence grew. But what she couldn't cope with were the looks of sympathy. She hated that, hated knowing that people knew she was different. She even hated her dead mother for a while. How could Daisy have been so selfish? To kill herself and not care what happened to her child or what it would do to her parents? She vowed she would never be as weak. She would be so strong that nothing, and more importantly no one, would cause her to falter. Independence was the key, she discovered. So long as she had that, she would be all right.

'Why don't we go for a walk?' she said, getting up from the table and going over to her bag for a tissue.

Emma put down her scissors, her face instantly bright with a smile. 'Can we go to that garden again? The one we went to yesterday?'

Pleased that her grandmother had some recall of that day at Wollerton – even if it did feel like yesterday to her – but saddened there wasn't time to drive all that way, Helen said, 'We'll go there another time. For now let's just go for a walk in the gardens here.'

The smile vanished from Emma's face as quickly as it had appeared. 'I don't want to. I have too much to do.' The scissors were back in her hands.

In need of something more constructive than the relentless task of chopping up more copies of *Chat* and *Good Housekeeping*, Helen offered to make them a cup of tea. Minutes later she was back in Emma's room with a tray of tea things and a plate of shortbread she'd brought with her.

'You don't look happy,' Emma said when she'd helped herself to a biscuit and had crumbled some of it down her front within seconds.

The statement was so unexpected, Helen just opened her mouth and said, 'I'm not.'

Emma's expression grew serious and she drew her whispery white eyebrows together. 'Oh, that's so sad, Daisy. Why aren't you happy?'

Daisy. Helen. What did it matter? 'My marriage is a disappointment to me,' she said simply.

The frown deepened into an intense look of concentration. 'I can't remember; have I met your husband?'

'Yes.'

'Did I like him?'

Recalling the smashed cup and saucer and the locked cloakroom door, Helen said, 'People generally like Hunter, Gran. He's charismatic, the sort of man who stands out in a crowd.' She passed her grandmother another biscuit and surreptitiously brushed the crumbs off Emma's cardigan.

'Stop fussing over me,' Emma said, taking a swipe at her hand. 'Just talk to me.'

Why not? Helen thought, if that was what her grandmother wanted. 'The thing is,' she said, 'I've met someone. He's everything Hunter isn't. He's quiet, thoughtful, and very kind. You met him that day at the garden in Wollerton. Ever since then I haven't been able to get him out of my mind. He's touched my heart in a way Hunter never has. I don't know why, but he's made it clear he's interested in me, and I know I shouldn't react to anything he says or does, but I can't help myself.' She paused to reign herself in as much as for the need to draw breath. 'What do you think I should do, Gran?'

Emma, who had been gazing up at the ceiling with a faraway look in her eye, suddenly gripped the arms of her chair anxiously. 'I need the lavatory,' she said.

It seemed no coincidence at all, when Helen drove home, stopping off at the delicatessen, to find that the only other customer was Conrad. With a baguette sticking out of the top of a carrier bag, he was just leaving. And, of course, it was only natural that when he asked how she was, she told him that she was fine. He was fine, too, he told her. Good, they both concluded. It was good that they were both fine. All out of sparkling repartee, they then danced an awkward two-step around each other as they tried to get past, and by the time he'd shut the door after him and Helen was standing at the counter, she'd forgotten what she'd come in for. She made a random choice of some stuffed olives and a piece of stilton and left in an embarrassed hurry.

Conrad was waiting for her outside.

Chapter Thirty-two

'Did you forget something?' she asked.

Conrad blinked, as though it would help him to summon up the necessary courage. To push him where he ought not to go. 'Yes,' he said. 'I forgot to ask if you'd—' He broke off.

Her achingly beautiful eyes stared back at him, but she didn't say anything.

He cleared his throat and tried again. 'The thing is, I can't stop thinking about you.'

Her gaze slid away, down to her shoes. 'But you must,' she said faintly.

'Maybe I don't want to. Let me walk you home.'

She looked up again, as startled as if he'd fired a gun.

'I only want to walk with you,' he pressed.

He could see the hesitation in her face, but then she nodded. They waited for a break in the traffic and when the last car had gone by with Olivia Marchwood at the wheel – she gave them an imperious wave – they stepped across the road. 'We'll go the long way,' Helen said, 'through the churchyard.'

His first thought was that his luck was in, that she wanted to prolong the length of time they could be together. His second thought was that maybe she thought the consecrated ground of St John's would keep her safe from him. This thought was given extra credence by the speed at which she set off, as if she was running for cover. However, once they'd passed through the lychgate, and were within the dappled shade of the ancient yew tree, she slowed her pace. They followed the gravel path, then, catching sight of the bench he used to sit on whilst waiting for Mac when he had to be ferried to and from church, he said, 'Why don't we sit here for a while?'

Again she nodded her agreement. It was impossible to know what she was thinking. Was she merely humouring him?

Once they were settled, he said, 'I meant what I said earlier, that I can't stop thinking about you. I keep trying to put you out of my mind, but you won't budge.' He turned his head. 'It's ... it's a long time since anyone's had this effect on me. Just my luck you have to be married.'

'I've never cheated on anyone in my life,' she murmured.

'Neither have I.'

'I've always believed that people who behaved that way had no self control. That they were selfish and lacked a sense of right and wrong. And I'm well aware that that sounds prim and holier than thou in this day of winner takes all.'

'Not at all. I used to think people who were going through some kind of crisis or other had only to pull themselves together to get over it. Sam's death taught me otherwise. Life isn't the orderly black-and-white business we'd prefer it to be. It's messy and complicated and horribly blurred around the edges. All we can ever do is make the best of it. And maybe grab at those fleeting chances of happiness.'

'But never at the expense of anyone else's happiness.'

'Meaning your husband's happiness?'

'Yes. Hunter may not be the perfect husband, but he deserves my loyalty.'

'He's a lucky man.'

'No. I'm the one who's lucky.'

There was so much he could say in response to this wholly inaccurate remark but Conrad held his tongue. Instead he listened to the sound of a blackbird chirruping, of pigeons cooing, and the distant thrum of a lawnmower. But all the while he was consumed with the need to bridge the two-inch gap between them as they sat on the bench. He wanted to touch Helen. To hold her. To kiss her. It was so long since he'd felt this way, it was all he could do to stare straight ahead in the hope that she wouldn't guess at the strength of his feelings for her.

At last he couldn't take the silence any longer. 'I just want to spend time with you,' he said. 'I want to get to know you better.' He risked a sideways glance. 'Would that be so very awful?'

She turned and finally looked at him. His heart lurched. There was an expression of such sadness in her face, he caught his breath. I'm responsible for this, he thought with shame. I can't do this to her. If I really care about this woman, I have to leave her alone. Abruptly he got to his feet. 'I'm sorry,' he said, already moving away. 'I have no right to pester you like this.' He was some distance from her when he stopped and glanced back. 'Forget I ever said anything,' he called to her. 'You were right and I was wrong.'

For what seemed for ever, Conrad stood firm in his resolve to cast Helen from his mind, but three days later he couldn't fool himself any longer and he decided to accompany his uncle to the last Garden Club meeting before the trip to Lake Como. It was a sure way of spending a legitimate evening with Helen without causing an unnecessary stir.

Except it did cause a stir in one particular quarter: Mac. 'You're coming to the meeting?' his uncle asked him incredulously. 'What on earth for?'

'It was you who wanted me to go on the wretched trip in the first place,' he countered. 'I just thought it was time I showed some interest in what I've signed up for.'

'You'll be bored stiff. I'd give it a miss if I were you.'

'It's okay. I've come this far, I might just as well go the whole hog.'

They were having lunch, one of those rare occurrences when Conrad had been lured away from his office by the appeal of sitting in the garden in the hot August sun for an hour. That and the need to quiz his uncle about Helen. He knew that yesterday Mac had spent an afternoon at a local nursery with her, helping to choose some plants for the garden at the Old Rectory.

'So how was Helen yesterday?' he asked. By talking about Helen, he felt closer to her. Closer was good. Closer meant he could kid himself that one day she would look at him with something other than sadness in her eyes.

Helping himself to another bread roll, Mac said, 'Funny you should ask. I thought she seemed quieter than usual.'

'How quiet?'

'Perhaps preoccupied would be a more apt description. Several times I had to repeat what I'd said because she hadn't heard me. She's usually more attentive than that.'

'Perhaps you were boring her?'

Mac scowled. 'Thanks a bunch. Pass the butter.'

'Or do you think she was upset about something?'

Mac shot him a look. 'Such as?'

Conrad shrugged. It was time to stop fishing, but he couldn't.

199

'I don't know; I get the impression all is not as it could be in that marriage of hers. Her husband's hardly ever around.'

'It's never wise to speculate on other people's marriages. The bond that holds most relationships together is often incomprehensible to the outside eye. You only have to think of your own parents' marriage to know the truth of that.'

Not wanting to be sidetracked, certainly not by his parents' nebulous relationship, Conrad said, 'But what do you make of Hunter?'

'I hardly know the chap.'

'And since when has that ever stopped you from forming an opinion of someone?'

Mac narrowed his eyes. 'What's going on, Conrad?'

'I don't know what you mean. We're sitting here in the garden having a chat.'

'I make that two unprovoked insults in the space of as many minutes. Even by your standards, that's going some. And more to the point, why the sudden interest in Helen? What could she have possibly done to deserve your under-the-microscope scrutiny?'

Something in Conrad's face must have given him away. Either that or the effect of Mac hearing his own question out loud clearly had him wondering. Seconds passed. 'Conrad, is there something you're not telling me? You and Helen ... you're not ...' His voice trailed off. 'Dear God! What have you done?'

Conrad saw no point in lying. 'Nothing much. But not for the want of trying.' He added.

'Don't talk in riddles. Are you or are you not having an affair with Helen?'

'An affair isn't what I want. And to Helen's credit, neither is it what she wants.'

Mac looked ready to explode. 'So what the hell is going on between the two of you?'

'Let's just say if her circumstances were otherwise, things could be very different.'

'But she is married!' roared Mac. 'I won't let you hurt Helen this way.'

Whatever reaction Conrad had expected from his uncle, it wasn't this vociferous outburst of protectiveness. 'Hurting Helen is the last thing I want to do,' he said.

'Well, I want nothing to do with it.'

'Good! Because guess what, I wasn't looking for a threesome.'

Mac bristled. 'How can you be so flippant about this? A marriage is at stake here.'

'No it isn't. Helen's being eminently sensible and loyal. She hasn't done anything, and won't do anything, to jeopardize her marriage.'

'And what about you? If you keep sniffing around her, she'll—'

'Look,' Conrad interrupted his uncle, 'this isn't easy for me. Do you think for one minute I deliberately went looking for a situation as complicated as this? I can't explain or justify it. It just happened. It's how it is. She makes my heart soar. She makes me feel like I used to. Can that be so very wrong?'

To Conrad's surprise, all the fight suddenly went out of his uncle. The old man leaned back in his chair heavily. He looked weary. 'It may not feel wrong to you,' he said almost inaudibly, 'but trust me, Hunter will view the matter very differently. A cuckolded husband is a dangerous unknown quantity. Especially a man like Hunter. And I'll wager you any sum you care to mention that he's a volatile man.'

'There's nothing for Hunter to find out about. And I meant it when I said the last thing I want to do is hurt Helen.'

The village hall was stuffy and airless that evening. Every window was open but it made no difference; there wasn't the slightest breeze of cooling air to be had. Whilst waiting for the meeting to get underway, people were fanning themselves with whatever they had to hand and complaining about the sweltering heat. There were mutterings of the humid days that were apparently ahead of them and even more mutterings of the threat of fungal disease in the garden, of mildew and rust and leaf spot.

Mac wasn't listening. He was in a state of shock. He'd had no idea about Conrad and Helen. How the devil had he missed that? He felt betrayed. Had Helen only been sociable with him to spend time with Conrad? Could she really have been so devious? He didn't want to believe that. He liked Helen. He liked her a lot. Truth be known, he was even a little jealous. Helen had been his friend.

He leant forward slightly and looked to where she was sitting, just the other side of Conrad. Conrad had sworn blind that nothing had happened between them, yet it didn't make Mac feel any easier. The intent was there, if only on Conrad's part. All the situation needed was the right spark and then where would they be?

He sighed inwardly. It was all too familiar. Another time. Another two lives.

Chapter Thirty-three

Lucy was trying hard to sound as though this conversation with Orlando wasn't causing her anguish. For the sake of their friendship she had to appear upbeat and magnanimous. Above all else, she had to convince Orlando that she was totally okay that he and Savannah had become Swanmere's latest hot couple.

It was eight o'clock in the evening and they were at the allotments. Getting Orlando to meet her here was the only way she could be sure of talking to him without the Gobby Pixie in tow.

He'd turned up exactly on time – punctuality had always been a strong suit of his – and initially they'd kept the talk on a strictly safe level, about the sweetcorn that was perfectly ripe now and the bumper crop of tomatoes she'd earlier been showing off to Bill and Joe. When at last there was nothing left to divert them, she said, 'Shall I make us a drink and we can talk about what really matters?'

And now while she fiddled around with the Calor Gas burner inside the shed, which was hotter than the Sahara desert having had the sun on it all day, she told herself that everything would be all right. They'd apologize and be best mates again.

But was best mates what she wanted?

It's all that's on offer, she reminded herself. So you can forget about anything else!

They sat side by side on the two rickety collapsible stools Dan had given Lucy about a million years ago, and stared into their mugs – Orlando into his black coffee and Lucy into her peppermint tea. She was getting through a lot of peppermint tea these days; it was supposed to keep her calm and settle her stomach. In times of worry it was always her stomach that was the first casualty.

As it turned out, they both apologized simultaneously and in perfect unison.

'I'm sorry for all the things I said, Lucy.'

'I'm sorry for the way I behaved, Orlando.'

They smiled tentatively at each other.

'I was way, way out of order,' Lucy said. 'Completely off the chart.'

'So was I. I still can't believe what a jerk I've been. Do you forgive me?'

'Only if you forgive me.'

'Already done.'

They put their mugs down and hugged each other.

'I've missed you so much, Lucy,' he said. 'Don't let's ever argue like that again.'

'Trust me; You're my oldest and closest friend, I won't do anything to jeopardize that.'

He kissed the top of her forehead. 'Ditto for me.'

'So come on,' she said, once they'd let go of one another and were sipping their drinks. They could hear Bill and Joe singing – for some strange reason – 'You'll Never Walk Alone' at the top of their voices. 'How's it going with you and Savannah?'

She sensed him tense, could see he was reluctant to talk about the girl. It was sweet of him to want to spare her feelings, but she was having none of it. She had to know the worst. 'It's okay, Orlando. I'm over all that nonsense.'

Before long she was regretting her encouragement. She could see that he was enjoying talking about Savannah, that just saying her name out loud made him smile. His obvious happiness caused Lucy's throat to constrict and her heart to feel as heavy as a stone. She wanted to tear it out of her chest and hurl it as far away as she could. Maybe then it wouldn't hurt her any more.

She made herself smile back at him, to give him the chance to share his feelings. If she really cared about him she would want him to be happy, she kept telling herself.

'It sounds serious, Orlando,' she said.

He shrugged. But that sickening smile was still radiating out from him.

She nudged him playfully with her foot. 'Go on, you can tell me: do you love her?'

'It's far too soon for that, Luce.'

'And since when has time had anything to do with it?'

'But love, that's—'

'Oh, don't give me all that. I can see it in your eyes, Orlando. You're crazy about her.'

The colour rose to his face. 'You always did know me so well. I don't know how it happened. She just kind of crept up on me.'

'That's love for you.' And didn't Lucy know the truth of that. All these years she'd regarded Orlando as a friend, then suddenly out of nowhere her heart gives a breaking newsflash that he means so much more to her.

He put his arm around her. 'I can't tell you how pleased and relieved I am that we're okay again,' he said.

'Me, too.'

He squeezed her shoulder. 'You're the best, Luce.'

Yes, aren't I just, she thought wretchedly.

Later, when he'd gone and only a few people were still pottering in the fading light, Lucy stood alone in her shed. She was crying as silently as she could, her head in her hands. She was so racked with misery she didn't hear the sound of footsteps approaching.

'Lucy? Are you all right?'

Dan was framed in the doorway. The look of concern on his weatherbeaten old face was too much and she cried all the more. He stepped inside the shed and wrapped her in his arms. She rested her head against his chest, finding comfort in the rich, earthy smell of his tatty old jacket. 'Oh, Dan,' she said, 'I think I'm falling apart.'

'Oh, lass, whatever it is, it can't be that bad.'

'It is. It's worse than anything you could ever imagine.'

The 9.10 Virgin West Coast train out of Euston was twenty minutes late. London had been stinking hot and the temperature inside the first-class carriage where Conrad was sitting wasn't much better. With his laptop open on the table in front of him, he prepared to kill the next two hours by doing some work. All in all it had been a good day. He'd come away the blue-eyed boy because he'd spotted a dodgy clause in the contract that the Japanese lawyers had slipped in at the last minute, a clause which would have cost his clients dearly in the long run. Arses had been whipped!

The train hadn't been moving for long when somebody further up the carriage answered the ring of his mobile phone. The man's voice carried well. A little too well. The young woman opposite Conrad looked up from her copy of the *Evening Standard* and rolled her eyes at him. Conrad gave her a small nod of collusive understanding. Five minutes later and the annoying man was still giving everyone the benefit of his one-sided conversation. 'I'm telling you, the Dubai vision is going great guns,' he told the caller. 'You'd be a fool not to get on board; it's the business centre of the Middle East. There are properties there that are just soaring in value, some of them by as much as a hundred per cent. Yes, through the stratosphere. But I'd advise you to get a move on. Everyone's wanting a slice of the Palm Projects action.'

Unable to resist getting a look at the know-it-all big-mouth, Conrad leaned to his left to peer through the gap in the seats opposite. What he saw had him pressing himself back against the window. It was Helen's husband, Hunter. He felt foolish for not recognizing his voice, but there again he'd only met him the once and had barely spoken to him. Still, the coincidence felt bloody weird. Or was it just a guilty conscience that was responsible for that?

Hunter may not be the perfect husband, but he deserves my loyalty.

It wasn't the first time those words of Helen's had played inside his head. What did she see in him? What bound her to him? Did she, as he'd speculated before, simply enjoy the lifestyle her marriage gave her? It was not a thought he wanted to dwell on because it cast Helen in a less than favourable light.

But whatever her reasons for making that remark, he was convinced love wasn't a factor.

It was possible, of course, that he was being overly simplistic. By using the benchmark of his own marriage, was he jumping to the conclusion that all relationships were as straightforward, or as deeply rooted in love and compatibility?

He risked another surreptitious glance through the gap in the seats. Helen's husband was winding down his phone conversation now. 'No problem. I'll get my secretary to email you the details. Cheers!' He snapped his mobile shut and turned to his left, winked and then moved out of Conrad's eye line.

The wink suggested Hunter wasn't travelling alone. Was Helen with him? Conrad strained a little further to his left – causing the man sitting next to him to back away with a disgruntled look – and caught a glimpse of Hunter's companion.

Except, frustratingly, he couldn't quite see enough. All he was sure of was that the blonde woman Hunter was now kissing was most certainly not Helen. His secretary, perhaps?

Anger surged through Conrad. How dare Hunter cheat on

Helen! How dare he abuse her trust! What kind of a man was he?

But then the irony of the situation caught up with his self-righteousness and he pulled the plug on his anger and condemnation. As the train pulled into Watford Gap, Conrad speculated on what this discovery might mean to Helen. Would it make her feel less guilty about embarking on an affair with him? Or would it make her leave Hunter? If so, and if he was being purely selfish, wouldn't it be in his interest to tell her about this other woman? But should he? Could he really be that brutally selfish?

He deserves my loyalty.

As misplaced as this sentiment now seemed, wouldn't the knowledge that her husband was cheating on her upset Helen?

No. He couldn't do it. He didn't want to be the one to cause her a moment's unhappiness.

That was when he knew for sure that he'd fallen in love with her.

BELLAGIO

Chapter Thirty-four

Maybe it was a sign of him getting older but Marcus didn't like it when Francesca was away from him for too long. He could have gone with her to Milan, as he'd suggested, but she'd been unusually insistent. 'You'd hardly see anything of me,' she'd told him, 'I'm going to be busy with my friends the whole time I'm there.'

The invitation to get together with her old university friends had materialized out of the blue and whilst he didn't begrudge his wife spending time reminiscing with them, he did have an uneasy feeling about her absence. It was an uneasiness that had been following him round these last few weeks, maybe even longer. It wasn't anything he could really put his finger on, more a sense that Francesca had become vague and distracted. She felt distant from him, something he'd never before experienced. He'd tried talking to her, slipping in a subtle question here and there in the hope that she'd take the bait and open up to him. She hadn't.

They had always been so intensely close that he couldn't help but be sensitive to the merest hint of a change between them. He was convinced he wasn't imagining the shift in Francesca. Moreover, he was sure she was hiding something from him. His greatest fear was that she was unhappy – with their marriage and with him.

Until now he hadn't dared articulate this thought, not even to himself. So saddened was he by it, he flung aside his glasses, switched off his laptop and decided to go for a walk. He'd go to Bellagio. He needed to call in at the bank anyway. Then he might pay a visit to Anna. If anyone knew what was going on with Francesca, Anna would be the one.

It was mid-afternoon and the hot August sun was high in the sky, but the quiet, narrow streets of Pescallo were cool and shady. When Francesca had first shown him the small fishing village, he had taken to it at once and asked her – hoping she'd say yes – if this was where she would like to live. She'd been delighted with his reaction and when the right villa became available, they snapped it up. That was a little over twelve years ago. The intention had been for it to be a family house with a couple of children running about the place, but it had never happened. After several miscarriages and seeking countless medical opinions, Francesca was told that it was highly unlikely she would ever carry a child to full term. It had been heart-wrenching disappointment, and her loss was compounded by the ease with which the rest of her family were able to conceive and give birth. So overwhelmed initially was she by the starkness of this diagnosis that Marcus had been genuinely concerned he might lose her. He'd had the same sinking feeling then that he was experiencing now.

But with the resilience that he so admired in her, Francesca emerged from her sadness and settled for being her many nephews' and nieces' favourite aunt. They called her zia Cica and adored her as much as she adored them. Yet he knew this role could never fill the vacuum of her need to be a mother. He'd have given anything for it to be otherwise.

He loved her as deeply as the day he'd fallen in love with her all those years ago when, as they'd always later joked, he had literally swept her off her feet. Their meeting had been one of those extraordinary events that one just doesn't see coming. Literally. During a moment's loss of concentration when he'd been reflecting on yet another row he'd just had with Fiona, he'd knocked her off her bike as she was pulling out of a side street. Fortunately the worst of the damage had been inflicted on the bike. Picking herself up from the ground, she'd shrugged off his attempts to help her and began hurling abuse. Even though she was ranting at him in Italian, it was clear to him and to those who had stopped to offer assistance, or in some cases to gawp openly, that he was on the receiving end of some pretty explosive stuff. It wasn't long, though, before the tirade became English and he felt the full force of her anger. Shocked that in a second of carelessness he could have killed her, all he could do was keep repeating how sorry he was and offer to pay for the damage to her bicycle. He'd then insisted on taking her to the nearest A and E department to make sure she really was all right. Throughout the short drive, she'd sat in the front passenger seat with her arms folded across her chest, berating him for his negligence. When he could squeeze in a word to the vociferous outpouring, which had reverted back to Italian, she just stared at him. And though he was genuinely concerned that he might have injured her, he tempered his anxiety by reminding himself that Italians were drama- and crisis-rich and liked nothing better than having something at which they could gnash their teeth.

They spent the best part of two hours in casualty, by which time he was beginning to think how attractive she was and what an amazingly sexy voice she had – her English was near-perfect but beautifully accented with her native tongue. In answer to his questions, she told him she was studying English at Milan University and was in London to do an English Literature dissertation. He'd been impressed. His recollection of being forced to read Shakespeare, the great poets and Chaucer was that it had been an overwhelming chore, but here was this young Italian girl writing a dissertation on Emily Bronte's *Wuthering Heights*. How on earth she could wade through all that dialect he didn't know. But at least they seemed to have found themselves on safer ground. Her animosity towards him had melted away and she was talking about a trip to Yorkshire she was hoping to make, to see where the Bronte sisters had lived. From nowhere he suddenly heard himself saying, 'I'm going up to Yorkshire on business next week; why don't I give you a lift?'

She looked at him with her impossibly dark eyes. 'Why? Why would you want to drive me all that way?'

'I just said I was going there anyway.'

She pursed her lips. Then: 'I think I would have to be crazy to get in a car with such a bad driver.'

'You chanced it to get here to the hospital,' he pointed out.

'Only because I was in shock. Maybe I am still in shock. Maybe I have concussion and I am going to die from a brain haemorrhage.'

He smiled. 'You're studying medicine as well as English literature, are you?'

'Which is more than you have ever done! Have you had any driving lessons at all?'

Amused at her sharp retort, he bowed his head. 'First game to you,' he said.

He did take her to Yorkshire and with each mile he drove he grew more aware of the danger he was deliberately getting himself into. Except it didn't feel dangerous. It felt good. Better than good.

This young Italian girl with her animated face, flashing dark eyes and amazingly long lashes was good to be around. By the time they arrived in Haworth and he was dropping her off at the bed and breakfast she'd booked herself into, he didn't want to leave her, not for a single second. He arranged to come back for her two days later, even though it meant extending his stay for longer than he'd originally planned. When he pulled up outside the stone-built farmhouse he almost hoped that she'd appear in the doorway and he'd feel nothing for her, that whatever he'd experienced had been a crazy flight of fancy. But no. He took one look at her as she came towards the car with her rucksack bouncing off her shoulder and a smile lighting up her face, and his heart swerved.

They were on the M1 with London only a short distance away when she said, 'I know you're married,' – he'd told her this during the drive up – 'but I'd like to see you again. Would that be possible?'

'I'd like to see you again too,' he'd replied, taking his eyes off the road for a split second to look at her. 'So yes, it would be possible.'

She didn't say anything else, but she placed a hand on his leg and kept it there for the rest of the journey. From that day on he saw her or spoke to her on the telephone, on a daily basis. When she'd finished her dissertation and it was time for her to return to Italy, he knew he couldn't let her go. He offered her a job at his advertising agency, which she turned down with tears in her eyes. 'I'm sorry, *caro*,' she said, 'but I have to go home to my family. Bellagio is my home, not London.'

He pleaded with her not to leave him. 'I can't stay,' she said. 'It's selfish of me, I know, but I can't carry on as we are. I want the whole of you or nothing.'

He knew what she was asking of him, but could he do it? If it weren't for Lucy, then yes, he'd go without a second thought. His daughter ... he loved her so much. But he loved Francesca, too. In the end, he forced himself to believe that love would conquer all, that Lucy would find it in her heart to forgive him. One day.

He was still waiting for that day. Perhaps it was futile to think that she would ever understand what he'd done. A year after he'd left England there had been a brief period when he'd stopped writing to Lucy – the agonizing silence that followed each card, letter and present that he sent was too painful. Permanently living with the hope that she would answer one of his letters became intolerable and he told Francesca that he'd come to the conclusion it would be better if he tried to pretend he'd never had a daughter. She was furious with him and said she'd leave him if he ever did that. With hindsight he knew she'd been right. It was better to live in hope. But why, after all these years, could Lucy not accept that this was something he'd had no say in? He just had to be with Francesca. He would have thought that by now she would have discovered for herself that love – the real thing – was a law unto itself. It wasn't the rational process everyone wanted to believe it was.

For some years he had tried to ignore the obvious: that his marriage was over. For his daughter's sake, he'd done his best to hold things together; it had never occurred to him to go looking for anyone else. He just threw himself into his work instead. This in turn provided more grounds for disapproval – 'You're never here,' Fiona would complain. Was it any wonder? he wanted to fire back at her. But he didn't. He hated confrontation. As a small boy he'd witnessed too many arguments between his own parents when their marriage broke up and he couldn't bring himself to enter the arena of snipe and fire. Even when the arguments with Fiona had escalated to the point where she seemed to be goading him for the sake of it – she would argue that he spent too much time with Lucy, or too little time – he couldn't bring himself to fight with her. Perhaps that had been his mistake. If he'd been more forceful and stood his ground maybe things might have been different. As it was, whatever he did was wrong.

It was no wonder, when Francesca came along, that he should find her company so enriching and diverting. He could have stopped right at the outset, had it not been love. If it had been some shabby infatuation, then yes, he'd have had some power over what he was getting into. He'd been telling himself this ever since, because as happy as he was with Francesca, he still felt the weight of guilt for what he'd done to Lucy.

He stood for a moment to catch his breath. He'd been so lost in his thoughts that he hadn't paced himself for the steep climb up the cobbled steps towards Bellagio. He turned and looked back to the lake: the Lecco arm of Lake Como. The water was perfectly still. He wondered what Francesca was doing now. Was she with her old university friends? Or was she with someone else?

A man ...

He shivered, despite the early September heat. If Francesca left him, not only would his life be over, then the colossal sacrifice he'd made would have been for nothing. He couldn't let that happen. He would have to talk to Francesca, give her the opportunity to tell him what was wrong. It was possible that he had been neglecting her recently. With the expansion of his office in Milan, work had been busier than ever these last couple of months. Not once had she complained, and often, if her own work as a freelance writer and tour guide permitted, she would stay with him at their apartment in Milan.

But if she did feel as though she was being treated as second best he would have to take steps to rectify the situation. He had a perfectly good team working for him, so in theory delegation shouldn't be a problem. He knew, however, that it would be a challenge. He had never been good at delegating. When he'd left England, he'd had visions of leaving behind the rat race that had been his life up until that point. But he soon discovered he wasn't cut out for idling along in the slow lane. He needed the buzz of the next deal, the next account. Advertising was in his blood. Once he'd mastered Italian and felt confident enough to do business in a foreign language, he was soon competing with the best of them. He found that Italy had so much to get excited about. Forget about the crazy bureaucracy and the barely disguised corruption and xenophobia, Italy, in particular Milan, was a hotbed of opportunity. With so much industry based in Northern Italy, his agency had never been short of clients. As to be expected, it had taken him a while to become established. To begin with, he'd rented a small office in Bellagio, where he and Francesca were then living and which just so happened to be within walking distance of nearly every member of her immediate family. He had then taken his favourite sister-in-law's advice and got involved with several local businesses. On the face of it, the only industry going on in Bellagio was tourism, but behind the scenes there was an established plant nursery industry and a glass-making factory specializing in ornaments and Christmas decorations. These intricately handcrafted, high-quality glass baubles were now exported on a satisfyingly large scale to the States – a staggering ninety per cent of what they produced ended up in America – and Marcus was pleased to have been a part of the company's still growing success.

Enrico Mosto, the owner of the largest nursery in the area, was one of Marcus's closest friends and a week rarely went by without the two of them getting together for a drink or a meal. He was meeting Enrico at the Serbelloni that evening. The restaurant at the Grand Hotel Villa Serbelloni – one of the finest on Lake Como – was Enrico's favourite place to eat and he always insisted on taking Marcus and Francesca there for dinner at least once a month. Tonight, for the first time ever, it would be just the two of them: Francesca was driving back from Milan that evening and Enrico's wife had died earlier this year. The poor man was still in deep mourning for her.

His breathing back under control now, Marcus pushed on. Then blessedly the steep climb was over and from here on it was downhill all the way to Bellagio.

The densely packed town often reminded Marcus of Venice, so crammed was it with narrow passageways, most of which were cobbled, and, so Francesca claimed, a pain to walk on in high heels. When he'd first arrived here it had taken him some days to navigate around the small town, especially at night.

At the bottom of Salita Genazzini he passed the Hotel Splendide and made for the bank. Ten minutes later he was back out onto the tourist-filled street. Across the road, cars were queuing for the ferry; one had just pulled into the terminal and a slow-moving crowd of yet more tourists were being disgorged into the busy lakeside resort. Another two months, he thought, and all would be quiet. Come the first week of November, the whole town would grind to a shuddering halt. The hotels would close their doors, most of the shops and restaurants too, with only a handful staying open to service the needs of the three thousand or so locals and the Milanese who visited at the weekends. The sense of relief that descended on Bellagio in November was as tangible as the snow that would later appear on the surrounding mountaintops.

From the bank he turned right and continued along the main street; all around him he could hear the sound of English-speaking voices, whether they were Australian, American or from the south east of England. Visitors tended to be of the older variety, bringing with them the ever growing power of the grey pound and dollar. He waved at the waiters at the San Remo Bar and for a split second he was tempted to stop for a beer, but seeing that all the tables were taken, he carried on towards his destination.

Chapter Thirty-five

It was only when they were thirty-five thousand feet up that Helen felt she was calm enough to speak. 'I still don't understand why you had to do this,' she said. 'It was so unnecessary.'

But Hunter was deaf to her. He was too busy accepting a minuscule bag of pretzels and a gin and tonic from the pretty, smiling stewardess, a young, dark-haired Italian girl with the whitest teeth Helen had ever seen. Out of the corner of her eye she watched the exchange between her husband and the girl. As ever, Hunter was doing what he did best, charming the stewardess and singling himself out. Impeccably dressed in his open-necked, pale-blue shirt, classic blazer, and cream chinos – the only piece of jewellery he was wearing was a gold Rolex watch (three times married, and he had never worn a wedding ring) – everything about him gave off an air of confidence and affluence. What young girl wouldn't think he was worth an extra smile? Or an extra bag of pretzels? Question was; was Hunter tempted? Had he ever been tempted since they'd been married?

'Signora?'

The smile and sparkling teeth were now pointing her way. 'White wine, please,' she said, mustering what little politeness she was still in possession of. It wasn't the stewardess's fault that Hunter attracted attention wherever he went. Or that he had acted with scant regard for anyone else's feelings, riding roughshod over the rest of the group and upgrading his and Helen's flight tickets. Never had Helen felt so embarrassed or been so appalled as she had when they'd all met up at the Alitalia check-in desk, as per Olivia's instructions, and Hunter had announced that his days of slumming it in coach class were long since gone and that he'd upgraded their tickets. As he'd pushed her towards the business class check-in desk, she'd felt everyone's eyes on them and wished that he hadn't changed his mind at the last minute and decided to join her on the trip. Apparently he'd been under pressure from Marcia to keep an eye on Savannah and Orlando. Helen had nearly laughed out loud when she'd heard this. She'd always thought Marcia was stupid, but now she knew the woman was completely mad. Who did she think Savannah was – a fourteen-year-old innocent?

What irked her more was that when she had asked Hunter to come to Italy with her, he had said he was much too busy. Then Marcia had snapped her fingers and he'd moved heaven and earth to do as she wanted.

Helen was wrong about Hunter not hearing her. Having ripped open his bag of pretzels, tipped them out onto his napkin and put one in his mouth, he said, 'I don't know what all the fuss is about. You've never objected to travelling business or first class before.'

'This is different,' she said. 'And you know it is. We're travelling with a group of friends and neighbours, which means we should all travel together. You'll be telling me next that you've gone behind my back and upgraded our hotel in Bellagio.'

He chewed on another pretzel. 'I'll warn you now, if the hotel doesn't come up to standard, it'll be the first thing I do. I'm not staying somewhere I don't feel comfortable. And I don't see any reason to apologize for that.'

How tempting it was to say, 'And I won't apologize for staying exactly where I want to.' But she kept quiet and turned to look out of the window, squinting slightly at the brightness of the snow-white clouds and brilliant blue sky. She wondered what was being said of her behind the curtain, ten rows back. And in particular, what Conrad must think of her.

A couple of days after the evening at the village hall, when Conrad had turned up unexpectedly for the meeting, she'd heard from Mac that Conrad had flown to Tokyo on business. She'd been both relieved and disappointed that there would be no risk of bumping into him in the village for the next few days. It was a bewildering time; she seemed to be nothing but a jittery mass of contradictions – wanting to see Conrad, but terrified of what she might do if she did.

That day in the churchyard, when he'd talked so candidly about the effect she had on him, she had come perilously close to giving in to temptation. Just one little touch from him would have been enough to tear away her defences. But then suddenly he was on his feet and telling her to forget he'd ever said anything.

She'd sat there a while longer on her own, confused and shocked

– shocked that she could have been overcome with such longing for him, and confused by his erratic behaviour. What had she said or done to cause him to run off like that?

When he'd sat next to her during the Garden Club meeting, she'd hoped he might offer an explanation for what had happened, if only to put her mind at rest that she hadn't offended him in some way, but other than exchanging a few pleasantries with her, he'd said nothing.

She knew he didn't rate Hunter too highly, and after today's debacle, her husband could only sink lower in Conrad's estimation. She hated the thought of being tarnished by association and hoped the others – Mac, Lucy and Orlando – would understand that she'd had nothing to do with Hunter's offhand decision.

To her surprise, Savannah had not been included in the up-grade. Helen had a feeling that the girl would have told her father exactly where he could stick his business-class seat if it meant she was going to be separated from Orlando. As things stood, only a nuclear explosion would be capable of separating those two.

Hearing the sound of food being served, Helen closed her eyes and pretended to be asleep. She wasn't hungry. Her appetite seemed to have disappeared completely this last week. Annabel had commented on it only the other day. 'Have you lost weight?' she'd asked.

'Just a little,' Helen had admitted.

'I didn't know you were on a diet. I mean, it's not like you need to.'

Part of her had wanted to confide in her old friend, to tell her that she couldn't eat or sleep properly because of Conrad. But she hadn't. Annabel would never understand the situation, not when she thought Hunter was the perfect catch. Instead, she'd again poured out her feelings in a one-sided conversation with her grandmother whilst taking her for a visit to a nearby garden centre. The only response from Emma had been to ask if she could have an ice-cream.

Strangely, she had very nearly confided in dear old Isobel Jenkins during one of their mornings together. After taking her shopping for a new coat, Helen had been helping her to complete an insurance form when Isobel had remarked how tired Helen looked. It had taken all of her professionalism not to blurt out that her life was in turmoil, that she had met a man who tapped into a place deep inside her, a place that no one else had ever discovered.

Her head resting against the window, Helen let her thoughts roam. How had this happened? How had she allowed Conrad to get under her skin to the extent that people were aware of a change in her?

Had Hunter sensed anything different about her? she wondered. Probably not. He hardly seemed to notice her these days. This wasn't a pathetic ah-poor-little-me thought; it was a fact, plain and simple. She'd always been good at dealing with facts. It was uncertainty she wasn't so good with.

Mac was agitated. No matter how many times he shifted his position he couldn't get comfortable. There was bugger-all leg room and he felt hot and light-headed. He'd had another of those dizzy incidents last night when he was doing his packing, having gone for days without a problem. But it wasn't that that was really bothering him. Deep in his guts, he had a bad feeling about the coming days. All around him there were people getting themselves into situations that at best could only end in tears.

First off there was poor Lucy trying to put a brave face on an impossible situation. He'd always liked and respected Orlando, but the wretched boy seemed to have lost every ounce of his common sense. Surely he couldn't be serious about Savannah. Everyone knew that he and Lucy were ideally suited in every way and the assumption had been practically carved in stone that it was just a matter of time before they got it together officially. Mac was convinced that either Orlando would eventually come to his senses or Savannah would get bored and leave Swanmere. She didn't seem the sort to have any staying power. She was a natural drifter in his opinion, but then maybe that was just her age. For the young, nothing was for ever, everything was for the moment. All life's pleasures were there to be taken in great greedy gulps of capricious and impatient thrill-seeking need, with not a thought for the consequences.

The consequences here were that when Savannah decided the itch had been satisfied and slunk away in search of the next cheap thrill – and it was a matter of when, not if, Mac was sure on this point – Orlando would do what any man in his position would do: he'd turn to Lucy for solace. And Lucy, who adored him, would feel ... what? Used? Betrayed? Maybe even glad that he'd got his fingers burned. It was anybody's guess. But in the meantime, one thing he was certain of was that Lucy was going through hell, and Orlando was ignorant of it. The three of them were sitting directly in front of Mac and Conrad – the two girls side by side with Orlando in the aisle seat. Being so tall, Mac was able to see over the seat backs and could clearly observe what was going on. Savannah was resting her head against Orlando's shoulder and making a big thing of cosying up to him. Every now and then there would be a loud, irritating giggle from her. All of which must be sickening for Lucy. Mac's heart went out to her. As if she didn't have enough on her mind, what with being on the verge of maybe meeting her father for the first time in years.

Mac had spoken only briefly to Lucy about this, wanting her to know that whilst they were away, she could turn to him, should the need arise. He hadn't been fooled by the cheerful response she'd given him. 'Oh, Mac, that's so sweet of you, but I'll be fine. Probably all that's going to happen is that I'll knock on his door and find he's away on holiday. It would be just my luck. And who knows, maybe it would be for the best.' He admired her for making light of the situation, but he knew her well enough to see through her brave words. He'd bumped into Dan in the Swan one night and Dan had asked him to take care of Lucy for him while they were away.

'The lass isn't herself at the moment,' Dan had said. 'And it's hardly surprising what with that Orlando carrying on the way he is. He's breaking her heart.'

Orlando probably wasn't aware of it, but he wasn't too popular in certain quarters. Even Olivia Marchwood, not known for having anything to say when it came to matters of the heart, had added her voice to the mutterings of disapproval. 'Men!' she'd been heard to exclaim in the paper shop. 'They're all the same.'

And if Orlando was in blissful ignorance of his fall from grace, Mac hoped Lucy was equally unaware of the sympathy that had been circulating the village for her. She'd hate to be the object of anyone's pity.

He sighed and feeling his right leg beginning to stiffen, he tried to stretch it by sticking it out into the aisle and giving his knee a rub.

'You okay?' asked Conrad.

'I will be when we land. Perhaps we should have done the smart thing like Helen's husband and upgraded.'

Conrad carefully refolded his paper napkin and added it to the remains of his lunch tray. His only comment was: 'Do you want to get up and have a wander round to get the blood circulating in your legs?'

'Worried I might conk out with DVT?'

'More to the point, are you?'

'Not a bit. I'm determined to inflict myself upon you for a good while yet.'

'I'm glad to hear it. Are you going to eat any of your lunch?'

'And you can drop the care-in-the-community routine right there!'

'Suit yourself. I'm going to grab some sleep.'

Mac watched Conrad push his seat back. Knowing that he was still jet-lagged from his trip to Japan, he wasn't surprised when, almost straight away, Conrad was fast asleep, his head tilted to one side. And you're the second reason I have a bad feeling about this trip, Mac thought.

He turned and looked down the aisle to where Helen and Hunter were hidden out of sight behind two flimsy pieces of segregating curtain. No one knew better than Mac that loving another man's wife was no picnic. Oh, it felt wonderful for a time, but when it finally hit you that the woman you loved wouldn't leave her husband, that she was bound to him by something you could never comprehend or compete with, well, that was when the pain began. When you understood you were destined not to be together, that your love just wasn't quite enough to win the whole of her heart, then that was when your life ceased to have any meaning. He wouldn't wish that misery on his worst enemy, let alone Conrad.

Feeling sleepy himself now, Mac closed his eyes. He thought of the strain that both Conrad and Lucy must be under, and how well they were hiding their feelings. But then he too was doing much the same. He still hadn't told anyone about the dizzy episodes. He ought to have said something to Conrad, but he didn't want to worry the boy. He had worries enough of his own right now.

His last conscious thought before the blurred edges of a foggy sleep claimed him was that it felt like they were heading towards Lake Como with a bomb strapped to them. Who or what would make it go off, he didn't know.

Chapter Thirty-six

Marcus's destination was the Hotel Villa Rosa; it had been in the Fontana family for nearly fifty years. Francesca's father – Rinaldo Fontana – had bought the four-storey dilapidated property as an ambitious young man and turned it into a traditional albergo and restaurant. Since Rinaldo's death the running of the hotel had been handed over to Francesca's brothers – *i Fratelli Fontano* – and their wives. It was still very much a family affair.

The first-time Francesca had introduced Marcus to her family they had regarded him with unconcealed dislike and suspicion. Francesca was Rinaldo and Rosa's only daughter, and their youngest child to boot, and to say they had their doubts about his suitability was a colossal understatement. Perhaps only a convicted mass murderer might have received such a chilly welcome. Their suspicions were not unfounded. After all, who was this man who was so much older than their precious daughter? What kind of man was he to abandon his family in England and take up with Francesca? And would he do the same to her one day?

The first eighteen months were the worst of his life. The Fontanas' politeness towards him was so thin as to be transparent. The following Christmas, Francesca took matters into her own hands and made an announcement. She told the entire family over dinner that now that his divorce was finalized, they were going to be married, with or without the family's approval. 'There is no shame in what I am doing, marrying a man who is divorced,' she told them, 'or that he isn't a Catholic. The only shame I feel is the shame my very own family is inflicting on us. Surely you can find it in your hearts to give the man I love a second chance?'

Marcus had been unutterably proud of Francesca, but reaching for her hand as she sat down, he didn't hold out any hope for a thaw within the Fontana clan. He was wrong. Rinaldo rose slowly to his feet and with tears in his eyes he raised a glass in Marcus's direction. 'To my prospective son-in-law,' he said. He even managed to smile. Then one by one everyone else followed suit, and the ice was finally broken. He was in. Accepted.

The marriage took place three months later, in March, a couple of weeks before the season started up again. It was conducted in the local *biblioteca* – and was the first time there had been a civil wedding in the Fontana family. Afterwards Francesca warned him that very likely some of the older members of the family would never consider them truly married. 'My grandmothers are very conservative,' she explained. 'Tradition and religion is everything to them.'

And all the while he had been trying to prove to Francesca's father that he was worthy of his prized daughter, he'd been ostracized from his own daughter. Not a letter or a phone call did he receive from Lucy. He suspected at times that the letters he sent didn't actually reach her, that Fiona was intercepting them. He knew that Fiona was still angry and bitter and that he had to accept he had no control when it came to her influence over Lucy.

Taking the next turning to the right, Marcus once again climbed upwards; the cobbled passageway was so narrow he could almost touch the buildings either side of him. In an elevated position, just back from the main street of shops and other hotels, Hotel Villa Rosa was quietly situated with excellent views of the lake. On a clear day, Cadenabbia and Tremezzo could be clearly seen across the water, but today the view was blurred by a purplish haze of humid heat. He pushed open the glass door and stepped into the welcome cool of the hotel's air conditioning. Antonia – Francesca's oldest niece – was on the telephone behind the marble reception desk; she gave Marcus a flutter of her fingers and mouthed *Ciao!* at him. He went to look for her mother, Anna.

He found her on the first floor, outside in the shade of the terrace garden. She was watering her precious collection of terracotta pots and antique urns which were home to a spectacular display of pink roses, creamy white hydrangeas, and stunning bushes of vermilion oleander. The hotel was smaller than most of the others in Bellagio; it didn't boast a swimming pool, a spa, or a gym, yet these days there was rarely an empty room. Most of the guests were American, followed by Brits and a smattering of French and German visitors. What they all appreciated about the Hotel Villa Rosa was the uncompromising quality of the service they received, as well as the excellent standard of cuisine. They also raved about the lovely terrace garden that Francesca had helped Anna to create. During the summer months, this was where breakfast was served.

Anna put down her watering can when she saw Marcus. Wiping her hands on her broad hips, she came over and kissed him on both cheeks. '*Ciao! Come stai?*'

'*Sto bene*,' he replied warmly. He'd always liked Anna, but then she'd been his only ally when the rest of the family had all but shunned him. Married to Franco – the oldest of the Fontana brothers – Anna might well have been yet another determined force to drive him and Francesca apart, but she hadn't. Instead, she'd quietly supported and encouraged their relationship, telling Marcus to be patient, that it was merely a matter of time before their love would win out. Only two years older than her, he'd always felt particularly close to Anna. She was also exceptionally close to Francesca, and since Rosa's death three years ago, she had been something of a replacement mother figure to her.

'You look like you could do with a beer,' Anna said.

He pulled a face. 'I look that bad, do I?'

She smiled. 'A little hot, perhaps.'

While Anna went to fetch him his drink, he made himself comfortable in one of the cane chairs at the far end of the terrace. In the shade of the vine-covered pergola, he listened to the clanging chime of San Giacomo's bell striking the hour – it was three o'clock – and then to a couple of guests as they studied their guidebook and map of the lake. They were American, smartly dressed and from Chicago, judging by their accent. They were exactly the sort of guests Marcus had urged the Fontana brothers to target when he'd advised them to give the hotel a major refurbishment two winters ago. Business had begun to slide and in Marcus's view it was easy to see why: the Hotel Villa Rosa had seen better days. As tactfully as he could, he'd explained to the family that Italian Shabby, as he called it – worn-out rustic plumbing, faded décor, threadbare rugs and dusty, tarnished gilt – was no longer appropriate for the twenty-first century traveller. He'd encouraged them to dramatically update the hotel, to give it a smart, pared-back look. He introduced them to a pair of young interior designers from Milan, who took one look at the time-warp décor and furnishings and threw their hands up in horror. Once the theatricals were over, the two men convinced the Fontana brothers that they needed to make their hotel stand out from all the others in Bellagio. To their credit, Franco and his brothers approached the bank and took the plunge. The result was that the Hotel Villa Rosa now had a growing reputation as a chic, class act of a hotel offering simple yet up-to-the-minute stylish accommodation and the kind of efficient service that the more sophisticated and discerning traveller had come to expect. It had been regularly featured in several magazines since its reopening and the upgraded restaurant was gaining in reputation as well.

'Sorry I was so long,' Anna said, when she appeared with his beer and an espresso for herself. The Americans had gathered up their things and left, leaving them alone in the quiet. 'I was caught by the telephone,' she explained. 'It was Alessio. The good news is that he's agreed to my proposition and is arriving here later this afternoon.'

'And since when has anyone not agreed to do anything you've asked of them?'

Anna smiled. 'I'm just persuasive, that's all. Like you, Marcus.'

Marcus took a long, thirsty swig of his beer. Alessio was Anna's nephew – her only sister's son – and a classically trained pianist. He was a member of the orchestra at the Conservatorio di Musica in Milan and had always been fêted within the family as a child prodigy. He was a devil for the girls, too. Which, of course, only enhanced his status within the family. At the age of thirty he was an arrogantly handsome young man with the fragile temperament of a skittish thoroughbred. Apparently, so Marcus was frequently told by Anna and Francesca, it made for a devastating combination. Privately, Marcus pitied the poor girl who ever thought of marrying Alessio in the belief she would be the one to settle him. But there was talk that he had changed. He'd contracted meningitis in the spring and had very nearly died. Many candles were lit for him and his recovery, which the doctors said was nothing short of a miracle. He was still recuperating. 'So how is Alessio?' Marcus asked.

'Still not a hundred per cent. Everyone at the Conservatorio is being very considerate towards him and has said that only when he feels he's ready should he return to playing full time.'

'They'd be crazy to treat him any other way. He's a gifted player; it would be a crime to rush him when he's not ready.' Whatever Marcus thought of Alessio's private life, his talent as a musician was never in doubt. 'So he's agreed to come and play for you here in the restaurant, has he? He won't feel that's a bit of comedown for him?'

Anna shook her head. 'It's too bad if he does. His mother and I have decided the change of scene will do him good.'

'He'll certainly provide an extra draw. The restaurant will be packed every night – mostly with women weak at the knees and disgruntled husbands grinding their teeth.'

Anna laughed and tipped a sachet of sugar into her espresso. 'By the way, we have another of those gardening groups arriving today. It was a good idea of Francesca's for us to target the English and American speciality tour groups. We're getting a lot of business that way now.'

'You'll be taking up my suggestion of cookery holidays next.'

'Oh, that's all very well for the Tuscany set, but I'm not sure it's for us here in Bellagio.'

'I seem to recall you saying something similar about the garden tour groups.'

She waved his comment aside. In the background a phone began to ring. Anna cocked her head, as if ready to go and answer it, but it was picked up almost immediately. Marcus took the brief lull in the conversation as his cue to probe for anything Anna might know about Francesca.

Twenty minutes later he was on his way back home to Pescallo. Disappointingly, he was none the wiser. When he let himself in, he went straight out to the garden with its beautiful view over the lake. The garden was Francesca's pride and joy and she had lavished so much love on it. It would be horribly simplistic to say that each and every plant she'd used to fill the garden was a child substitute, but as he stared out across the water to the villages of Lierna, and further to the north, Varenna, Marcus hoped that maybe it was true. If it was, there was a small chance that the garden – if nothing else – might stop her from walking away from him.

Chapter Thirty-seven

The bus that had come to meet them at the airport hurtled along the busy motorway, where all the other drivers seemed to be driving bumper to bumper and at a terrifying breakneck speed. Lucy felt ill.

It wasn't travel sickness she was suffering from, but a nasty case of being overexposed to the sight of Savannah slobbering and pawing over Orlando. The fear of what lay ahead was also causing her stomach to flip and wobble. Would she or would she not meet her father whilst she was here in Italy? Did she have the bottle to go through with it? Dan had said she was more than equal to the task. Hugh had said much the same thing. And, of course, Orlando had been the one to set the ball rolling in the first place. Three men telling her it was time to put the past behind her. Was it easier for men to do that? Did women find it harder to forgive? Did the hurt go deeper for women? So deep inside it was impossible to mend or cure it?

She kept having imaginary conversations with her father, all of which ended in exactly the same way: her telling him just what she thought of him and then walking away, never to see him again. She'd imagined the encounter so many times now she was word-perfect. It wasn't what was expected of her, she knew. Nobody had come right out and said it, but the expectation was that she would undergo some kind of miraculous conversion. As if one minute in her father's company would be all it took to sweep the past aside and have her falling into his arms crying, Daddy! Daddy!

At the front of the bus their tour guide for the next five days, Philippa Hutton – the woman who had come to Swanmere and given her talk to the Garden Club – was telling them with the aid of a crackling microphone that they would be arriving in Bellagio in approximately an hour, depending on the traffic. Battling on with the faulty microphone, Philippa was now explaining about the rest of the members of the tour group who had flown in that morning on the Gatwick flight. 'Aha! The north-south divide,' muttered Mac, who was sitting next to Lucy. 'I trust we'll be put on different floors. We don't want any cross-pollination.'

'You're a southerner yourself, Mac,' Lucy said. 'Just as I am.'

'Yes, but a bit of tribal argy-bargy on holiday is too good an opportunity to pass up.'

'I'll take your word for that. Me, I've got all the aggro I need.'

She stared out of the bus window. Why was she here? Why was she putting herself through this double whammy of misery, playing gooseberry to Orlando and Savannah, and maybe meeting her father? She recalled Dan's pet name for her – his Maybe Queen. Well, this was definitely a Maybe Situation. Maybe she would go through with it, maybe she wouldn't.

She closed her eyes briefly, and when she opened them they were off the motorway and passing through a town of some sort. She gave their surroundings more of her concentration. Then suddenly they turned a corner and there was water before them. The lake.

'This is the town of Como,' Philippa informed them from the front of the bus. 'It was founded by the Romans in 196 BC. The town's population today is sixty-five thousand. Over to your left, if you look quickly, is the Duomo—'

'I wish she'd shut up,' Mac said under his breath. 'If she's going to be like this the whole trip I'll have to invest in some earplugs.'

'You want to get yourself one of these,' Lucy said. She rummaged in her bag and pulled out her iPod. 'No offence, Mac, but I think I'll listen to some music for the rest of the journey.'

'None taken, my dear.'

With Muse's *Absolution* blasting her eardrums, Lucy watched the landscape unfurl before her. Narrow and winding in places, the road ran parallel with the lake. Everywhere looked lush and green. Tall, elegant cypress trees rose up like church spires towards a pearly blue sky. Pink and scarlet geraniums tumbled from window boxes, blushing hydrangeas swelled in the sun, and bushes of oleander punctuated every twist and turn in the road. It was prettier than she'd thought it would be. And the lake was certainly larger than she'd expected. She had bought a guidebook but hadn't as yet got around to reading it. She'd have plenty of time to do that in bed at night. She just hoped that when they arrived at the hotel she wasn't put in a room anywhere near Orlando or Savannah. If she was next door to either of them and could hear the sound of bed springs, she wouldn't be responsible for her actions. She had no idea if they'd been to bed together yet; goodness knows what went on whilst she was out of the house, but she knew for a fact that Savannah hadn't stayed the night. She supposed it would only be a matter of time before she was forced to endure her presence at the breakfast table. She knew that separate rooms had been booked in their names, but only a fool would think they wouldn't spend the night in the one bed. Not even Savannah's father could think they'd do otherwise.

She blinked hard to keep back the tears. Why, oh why, had she realized too late what she felt for Orlando?

She quickly switched her thoughts to what she intended to do once they had arrived in Bellagio. She had her father's address and just as soon as she had unpacked, she planned to check out where he lived by getting hold of a map. She had no idea how big the town was, and was slightly concerned that if it was very small she would be tripping over him at every street corner. She was in no hurry to track him down, but what she wanted to guard against was accidentally bumping into him and not being in control of the situation. Chances were he didn't live right in the town centre anyway.

One thing she didn't doubt was that she would know him instantly. But would he recognize her?

'If I was your husband, I wouldn't be sitting at the bar and ignoring you.'

'He's not ignoring me.'

'Isn't he?'

When Helen didn't say anything, but turned to gaze out at the night sky and the lake where a ferry, its lights reflected with a magical brightness, was crossing the inky-black water, Conrad said, 'I'm sorry. That was cruel of me.' They were standing at the furthest end of the terrace garden of the Hotel Villa Rosa, waiting for dinner, and it was the first time he'd managed to get Helen alone all day.

'Yes, it was cruel of you. What made you say it?'

Conrad shrugged. Ever since he'd witnessed Hunter kissing that woman on the train he had wanted to let Helen know what kind of a man she was married to. But he'd promised himself he wouldn't. He didn't want Helen to have an affair with him to get back at Hunter, which is what he knew would happen. It was human nature – you hurt me, I'll hurt you. No. He needed Helen to want him the same way he wanted her. Having spent so many hours on his own this last week travelling to and from Tokyo, he'd had a lot of time to think about Helen. He'd tried to talk himself out of his feelings, but it hadn't worked. If anything, he felt even more strongly about her.

'I have a theory,' she said, turning to look back at him, 'based on all the years I worked as a tour guide.'

'Go on.'

'When people are away on holiday they behave differently; they do and say things they wouldn't dream of doing at home.'

'Point taken and I'm sorry again for my rudeness. Put it down to tiredness. I'm still on Japanese time.'

'The thing is,' she said softly, as though he hadn't spoken, 'I've never been able to decide if they're acting out of character when they're away from home, or being their true selves. What do you think?'

He stepped a little closer to her. So close his shoulder was touching hers. 'I think—' But he got no further.

'And what are you two whispering about all alone here?' It was Olivia Marchwood and she was decked out in what was clearly her idea of holiday wear – a sleeveless, lime green dress with an elasticated waist. Around her shoulders was a shawl the colour of English mustard and it couldn't have clashed more with the dress. Conrad had never seen the woman in anything so tasteless before. Talk about acting out of character.

'We were just enjoying the view,' he said in answer to her question, conscious that beside him Helen was managing to look as guilty as sin, as though they'd just been caught having oral sex right there on the terrace. 'How's your room, Olivia?' he added for something else to say.

'As billets go, it's perfectly adequate. All I need is a firm mattress and a hot shower. I'm not like some of these other travellers who expect countless frills thrown in. I heard a dreadful woman complaining earlier that her bathroom wasn't big enough. Have you spoken to the Gatwick contingent yet?'

The inference was crystal clear. 'No, not yet. I've only just come downstairs. I was chatting with Helen whilst waiting for Mac to put in an appearance.'

Having recovered her composure now, Helen said, 'It's a lovely spot here, isn't it? Much quieter than I thought it would be.'

'Philippa told me we'd approve of her choice of hotel,' Olivia responded. 'Apparently she uses it all the time for her tour groups to this area.' She glanced at her watch. 'Dinner's in five minutes; Mac had better get his skates on or he'll be late. No sign of Lucy, either, I notice. I do hope people won't become too disorderly. In my experience, if people start breaking rank the whole thing disintegrates.'

'Oh, I expect Philippa will be able to handle us all,' Helen said.

'Of course, I was forgetting you used to do this kind of work, didn't you? Before you married Mr Tyler.'

There was something in the woman's tone that Conrad didn't care for. Changing the subject, he said, 'How about an aperitif, Helen? You too, Olivia, what can I get you from the bar?' *Something as tart and sour as that tongue of yours, perhaps.*

Without answering him, she said, 'Ah, there's Philippa! Do excuse me, I need to ask her something about the itinerary for tomorrow.'

'Was that offer of a drink genuine?' Helen asked when they were alone again. 'Because if so, I'd like a vodka tonic. And make it a double measure of vodka.'

'What rattled you most?' he replied, 'her comment, or her finding us talking?'

'Oh, definitely the latter. I couldn't give a stuff about her thinking I married Hunter to feather my nest.'

'And did you?'

'What do you think?'

Her voice had taken on a sharp, chilling quality he'd never heard from her before. For some reason, it made him unable to meet her eye. 'I'll get those drinks,' he said.

Lucy didn't think she could face eating anything. But when Mac knocked on her door, she knew he wouldn't take no for an answer. 'Not changed for dinner, then?' he said.

'I thought I'd give it a miss, Mac. I'm really not very hungry.'

He looked at her sternly. 'I'll give you five minutes.'

'Really, Mac. I don't want—'

'Five minutes and counting. I'll be outside waiting for you. By the lift.'

She gave in, swapped her jeans for a pair of white linen trousers – the only smart pair she'd brought with her – and slipped on a white strappy top and a pair of suede, mint-green flip-flops she'd picked up for next to nothing in the summer sales. As a token gesture, she slapped some lip gloss on and ran a brush through her hair, but then decided to tie it up with a scrunchy the same colour as her flip-flops. It would have to do, she decided.

Her room was directly next to the lift and staircase and she found Mac waiting there for her. 'You look lovely, my dear,' he said. 'Quite the ravishing beauty. You'll do an old man's ego a power of good when we enter the dining room together.'

'Any more talk like that and I'll feed you alive to La Marchwood and her coven of hotties.'

He laughed and summoned the lift. The doors sprang open immediately and they stepped inside the mirror-lined cubicle. They had only just begun to descend to the first floor when all of a sudden Mac seemed to lose his footing. Lucy grabbed hold of him. 'You okay, Mac?'

He swallowed and his eyes wavered, as though he couldn't focus properly. It was a while before he spoke. 'Just a bit of vertigo,' he said. 'Had it for years. Nothing to worry about. Lifts often have this effect on me.'

'You look very pale. Are you sure you're all right?'

'It's the mirrors and lights in here. They bleach a person out.'

Lucy wasn't convinced. They came to a stop and the lift doors opened. Stepping onto the white-tiled floor, she said, 'You won't go overdoing it here, will you?'

'Don't you start! I get enough of that from Conrad. Now where's that arm for my dramatic entrance? I want all eyes on us. Is that understood?'

She did as he said but couldn't summon up the smile she knew was expected of her.

An area of the restaurant had been put aside for the tour group. Lucy's heart sank when she saw that there were two long tables with place cards awaiting them. Philippa, looking flushed and clutching a clipboard, explained that they would be having a set meal and that she'd mixed them all up for the evening. 'It'll give everyone the chance to get to know one another,' she said as she started to herd people about.

'I hope there's not going to be too much of this jollying along nonsense,' Mac growled at Lucy's side. 'Or too many set menus. I won't be told what to eat.'

As luck would have it, Lucy ended up sitting at one end of a table with Mac on her left, but opposite Olivia Marchwood. Their nearest neighbours were three grey unknowns. It was funny; she never thought of Mac as being old, but these people – part of the Gatwick contingent – looked depressingly dull and ancient. The squat, chubby-faced man the other side of Olivia reminded her of a Toby jug. And while Olivia launched into an enthusiastic round of introductions, Lucy looked further down the table to where Orlando was wedged in between two other unknowns but facing Vi Abbott and Barbara Slattery – they were Olivia's closest buddies on the committee for the Garden Club, being treasurer and secretary respectively. Orlando didn't look too happy as he stared over at Savannah, who was sitting on the other table with Helen, Hunter and Pat and Colin Campbell, who when they weren't gardening were avid bird watchers. Lucy couldn't bear to see the disappointment on Orlando's face. 'Pass the wine,' Lucy whispered to Mac. 'I think it's the only way I'm going to survive this.'

She was right. Within minutes Olivia and the others had found their level and taken the conversation to the mind-blowingly dizzy heights of their eating habits. Top of their collective menu was a bowl of homemade carrot and coriander soup for supper with a yoghurt to follow. Maybe an apple thrown in for a special treat. Their pious self-righteousness had Lucy wanting to say that she regularly stuffed a dozen Big Macs down her throat with a fistful of king-size Mars bars for afters. She gulped back her wine, then suddenly registering that she was actually hungry now – starving, in fact – she looked around her at the other tables and occupants, wondering what the food would be like. She was just eyeing up a mouth-watering dish of seafood risotto and a plate of mozzarella salad when she noticed a tall, angular man enter the room. Dressed in black jeans and a white shirt open at the neck he crossed the marble tiled floor and came to a stop in front of a piano that until now Lucy hadn't noticed. He sat down, lifted up the lid of the piano, shuffled about on the seat, repositioned it, repositioned it again, ran his hands through his sleek, jet-black collar-length hair, fiddled with his shirt cuffs, then placed his long slender fingers on the keys. Way too good looking, Lucy thought. And knows it. All that fidgeting around was nothing more than a ploy to attract attention. He'd succeeded. Over on the other table Savannah, along with most of the other women, had stopped what she was doing to take a look. Interest in him was certainly intensified once he started to play. Lucy had no idea what the piece of music was but it had the instant effect of mellowing the atmosphere. It was as if someone had turned out the lights and illuminated the dining room with candles.

'Smooth, wouldn't you say?' Mac murmured in her ear. 'A chap destined to play the rascal, if ever I saw one.'

'Couldn't have put it better myself,' she replied.

'You wouldn't be tempted then?'

Lucy laughed out loud, causing people to glance their way. Including the pianist. He looked straight at her. And continued to stare at her, right until the end of the piece of music he was playing. She only knew this because Mac told her that that was what he'd done – the second his gaze had settled on her she'd turned away embarrassed. 'He's got you in his sights,' Mac said when the room was filled with the sound of applause. 'Mark my words, he'll be coming on to you, my girl.'

'Yeah, and I can smell him from here. He reeks of pride and vanity. Not to mention sexual conquest.'

'Best smile on, Lucy; he's looking your way again.'

Unable to stop herself, Lucy twisted her head round to see if Mac was speaking the truth. The arrogant devil smiled and winked at her.

Chapter Thirty-eight

Francesca had scarcely had time to unpack after arriving home from Milan when the telephone rang. Now, and with a slow and careful hand, she replaced the receiver and thought about what Anna had told her. Was it really possible? After all these years, could this moment have finally arrived? Something told her it was exactly as it was meant to be. The timing of it was too perfect to discount that fate – or God – wasn't at work in their lives. She crossed herself as she always had as a child. It was a habit she had only recently readopted. For most of her adult life she had cut herself off from the Catholic faith of her upbringing, had turned her back on what she'd seen as a means to brainwash and control. Her family had been as shocked by this rejection as they had been over her relationship with Marcus. And it was only natural that they should hold him accountable. In their eyes he had led her astray in every way and forced her to live in a permanent state of sin. It had upset and angered her in the beginning, but then, because she genuinely loved her parents and knew that they loved her, she had tried her hardest not to overreact, to keep in mind that they really did have her best interests at heart.

Hearing the sound of Marcus's key in the door – he was back from his dinner with Enrico – she considered how best to break the news to him. He had waited so long for this. But what if Anna was mistaken and had leapt to a conclusion that would get his hopes up, only to have them instantly dashed? Poor Marcus, he didn't deserve that kind of pain. Not when Francesca knew that in the coming days, weeks and months, she was going to put him through the very worst kind of heartbreak.

Marcus drove the short journey from Pescallo to Bellagio – the way he'd just come – in record time. He parked his car and hurried across the road without looking, almost colliding with a scooter.

Recovering himself, he took the cobbled steps up to the Hotel Villa Rosa, his mouth dry, his heart hammering in his chest. He didn't really know what he was going to do when he got there, but at the back of his mind he thought the sensible thing to do would be to observe Lucy discreetly before making himself known to her. He was frightened of blundering in and making a fool of himself – and in his current state there was a real danger he would do exactly that.

He had absolutely no doubt that it was Lucy staying at the hotel. Anna had read out the details at the back of her passport and everything fitted – the name, the dates, and the place of birth. It was all too much of a coincidence for it not to be his daughter. Besides, the address on the checking-in form was Swanmere, Cheshire. He would for ever be grateful to Anna for making the connection when she'd been sorting through the passports of the guests who had checked in that day. Lucy Gray wasn't that unusual a name, but as Anna had just said on the phone to him, 'It caught my eye for obvious reasons.'

The reception area was empty when he pushed open the heavy glass door. He paused to catch his breath and to straighten himself out in front of a mirror-lined wall. He didn't want Lucy's first sighting of him to be that of a dishevelled, breathless, red-faced man.

The second Francesca had told him about Anna's telephone call he'd kept asking himself the same question: why was Lucy here? Was it a coincidence? Or had she come to Bellagio to seek him out? Please God, he thought as he summoned the lift, let it be the latter. Let her be here because she wants a reconciliation.

The lift doors opened. 'Marcus!'

It was Franco. He stepped out of the lift. 'I'm so sorry, Marcus,' he said, 'but she's gone.'

'Gone where?'

Marcus's brother in law, a square-shouldered, square-jawed man, shrugged. 'I don't know. One minute she was in the dining room and the next she had disappeared.'

'To her room?'

'We don't think so. Anna tried knocking on her door, pretending she was housekeeping, but there was no answer. Anna thinks she may have gone for a walk.'

The disappointment of not being able even to catch the merest glance of his daughter when he was this close, hit Marcus hard.

'Show me her passport,' he said. 'At least then I'll know for sure that it's Lucy.' And then I'll wait here until she comes back, he thought. He'd made a promise to Lucy, all those years ago – a stupid promise he should never have made – that he would never spring a surprise meeting on her, but this was different. This, he was convinced, was a cautious attempt on her part to reach out to him.

Or was that just wishful thinking on his part?

It was nearly one o'clock in the morning, yet the streets weren't entirely deserted. A few arm-in-arm couples were strolling along the main street that bordered the lake. Save for the sound of water lapping gently against the shore and some nocturnal ducks quacking, all was quiet. This was Lucy's first wander round Bellagio and much to her surprise she felt quite at home. Following the curve in the road, she passed the ferry point and continued on along a gravelled promenade that was lined on one side with attractive street lamps and on the other with neatly clipped trees of oleander. There were raised beds of brightly coloured flowers, and benches placed every few yards. Looking back the way she had just come, she paused to take in the view. Spilling out from the waterfront of hotels and bars, light poured across the water in long drizzled, reflected lines of softly diffused pink and liquid gold. She decided to sit down and review the evening.

Dinner had been nothing short of extraordinary. Once that piano player had embarked on whatever game he was up to – as if she didn't know what that was! – the tone of the evening had changed completely. It certainly hadn't been the tedious torment she'd imagined. He'd played a mixture of popular classics and foot-tapping show tunes and people had soon got in on the act and started making requests. He clearly revelled in the attention, almost as much as he seemed to enjoy making her blush from head to toe. If she was to be entirely honest, she couldn't say the experience had been altogether unpleasant. All those over-the-top smiles and come-on glances had given her an oddly warm glow. Compared to how she'd been feeling before, the change was a vast improvement. Cruel as it might sound, the icing on the cake was seeing the expression on Orlando's face. He'd looked like thunder, as though he could have slammed the piano lid down on the pianist's hands. She was just smiling to herself and wondering if a bit of old-fashioned jealousy would bring Orlando to his senses, when she heard the sound of footsteps crunching on the gravel.

Suddenly conscious that she was all alone in a strange place, she turned nervously. When she saw who was coming towards her, the smile was instantly wiped from her face.

Chapter Thirty-nine

He seemed to have appeared out of the shadows from nowhere, his presence all at once dominating the space around him, just as it had earlier at the hotel. How did he do that? And what was he doing here? Had he followed her?

'*Ciao!*' the piano-playing smoothie said as he covered the last few steps and stood looking down at her. 'You are English? Yes?'

She got to her feet, feeling that if there was to be any conversation between them it should be conducted as formally as possible. 'Yes,' she replied. 'And so that you know, I don't speak a word of Italian.'

He smiled. It was a strong, carefree smile. 'Not a word? Not a single word? How disappointing. Italian is a very beautiful language.'

Go on, she thought, tell me it's the language of *lurve*.

'But please, sit down.' He gestured to the bench. 'Perhaps you will allow me to join you?'

'Actually, I was just leaving.'

'I don't think you were.' And before she could stop him, he'd taken hold of her arm and they were both sitting on the bench together.

'I'll warn you now,' she said, 'this heavy-handed approach of yours won't get you anywhere. I didn't appreciate being made to look stupid throughout dinner and I certainly don't like being forced to sit here against my will.'

He gave her a baffled look. '*Che?*'

Oh, hell, so his English was as superficial as he was. 'I said—'

The megawatt grin was back in place. 'It's okay,' he said, 'I understand perfectly what you are saying. My English is more than adequate. I lived in London for a year. In Wimbledon. Perhaps you know it? But tell me, when did I make you look stupid? From where I was sitting, you appeared flattered by my attention during dinner. Your face turned a lovely shade of pink. It made you look very pretty. And that is why I continued to smile at you. So really, it is all your fault that you find yourself sitting here with me. How could I possibly resist you?'

Lucy's mouth opened to protest in the strongest terms at the absurdity of this arrogant man, but no words came out. Never in her life had she heard such a stream of unadulterated rubbish. She tried to think where to start in putting him right, but something suddenly bubbled up inside her. For the first time in weeks, she laughed. Once she started, she couldn't stop. She went and leant against the railing and tried to concentrate on the lake, as if picking out the spangling lights dancing across the water would somehow stop the madness. Because that was what it felt like. Pure madness. What did this man think he was doing by prattling on at her this way? Did he really think she'd be taken in?

He was standing next to her now. 'Did I say something amusing?' He asked. He looked quite pleased with himself.

She used the backs of her hands to wipe her eyes. 'I'm sorry,' she said, 'but you sounded so ridiculous.' She mimicked his smooth but heavily accented words: '"How could I possibly resist you?"'

He raised an eyebrow. 'You find that funny?'

'Hilarious!'

'But why? It is the truth.'

The solemnity of his manner set her off again. 'Look,' she said when she'd got herself under control again. 'This is just a word of advice, but you might like to turn down your charm level. At the moment it's cranked up much too high. You'll never get anywhere with English girls like that.'

'Cranked? *Che cosa?*'

'It means you're trying too hard with the charm. Ease off a bit.'

'Ease? So many English words you speak that I do not know.'

'Forget it. I'm just trying to point out to you that you shouldn't try so hard.'

'Ah! *Ho capito!* You think that would help to give me the leg up?'

'Mm ... you could put it that way.'

'In that case, please, sit down again and I will try to ease off the crank in order to get the leg up. Or do I mean the leg over?'

She realized then that he had been playing with her. Instead of making her cross, it made her laugh again.

'You have a lovely laugh,' he said, when once more he had manoeuvred her back onto the bench. 'I'm glad you find me amusing. Tell me your name.'

'It's Lucy.'

'*Tanto piacere!* And I am Alessio.' He held out his hand. 'It is very good to meet you, Lucy. How long are you staying here in Bellagio?'

'I'm here for five days. I leave on Saturday.'

'That is not long. Not nearly long enough. I will have to tempt you to make a return trip.'

She wagged her finger at him. 'Oh no you don't. Remember what I said about the charm?'

He wagged his finger back at her. 'That was not charm; that was a fact. Now tell me, what are you doing staying at the Hotel Villa Rosa with all those old people?'

'They're not all old. My friend Orlando is my age.'

'Was he the one during dinner who looked as though he might like to kill me?'

Oh, so he was more perceptive than she'd thought. Interesting.

'He loves you, eh?'

She shook her head. 'No.'

'*Davvéro?* Are you sure?'

'I'm very sure. He's an old friend and he probably thought you were behaving badly towards me.'

'He is the protective kind?'

'Maybe. He's also madly in love with a girl called Savannah. I expect you noticed her during dinner. You seem to have observed just about everything else.'

'She was the young girl with too much eye make-up and the lips closed too tightly? She looked very cross with life.'

Lucy didn't know how it had happened, but this man with his abundance of self-assurance had totally disarmed her and she felt a comfortable affinity towards him. Or maybe it was just because he'd criticized her number one sworn enemy. She looked at him properly for the first time, trying to see the person behind the dark-chocolate eyes and the dazzling smile. He had an angular face with wide-set eyes and his black, collar-length hair was swept back from a broad forehead. His nose was long and straight and his eyebrows arched, giving him a permanent expression of amusement. For all his arrogance and industrial-strength charm, he was probably fun to be around.

'The stars are very pretty tonight,' he said as though they were old friends and waiting for a bus. 'They seem brighter than usual.' He tilted his head back and she found herself doing the same. How strange, she thought, the stars did indeed seem brighter. It suddenly occurred to her what a beautiful night it was. And how different this discovery made her feel.

'Will you have lunch with me tomorrow?' he asked.

She sat up straight. 'I'm sorry but I can't; I'm going on a tour of some gardens tomorrow. That's why we're all here, to see the gardens.'

'Then I shall see you in the evening.'

'You'll be playing in the dining room again?'

'*Sì*. Every night.'

'You play very well.'

'I know.'

'And you're much too modest.'

He frowned. 'I am being honest. I am an excellent pianist. Everyone says so.'

'And is this what you do, play in hotels for a living?'

'No. I am here only for the rest of the season in Bellagio. I live in Milan. I play for the Conservatorio.'

'Why are you here, then?'

'I'm recovering from an illness. Meningitis. I very nearly died.'

He said this so matter of factly, she wondered if he was exaggerating. 'Really? How do you feel now?'

'Sitting here with you, I feel wonderful!'

She rolled her eyes. 'You're hopeless.'

'*Davvéro!* I am speaking the truth. I took one look at you in the restaurant this evening and thought you would be the perfect medicine for me.'

'No. You took one look at me and thought, aha, someone new to flirt with.'

'And is that so very wrong?'

Perhaps not, she thought when ten minutes later he was walking her back to the hotel. She went to bed that night not once thinking of Orlando. Or worrying about her father.

It was gone four in the morning but Marcus wasn't in bed. He couldn't sleep. But then he'd known he wouldn't be able to. He was sitting in his study, and in the soft pool of light cast from the desk lamp, he had his most treasured possession in front of him:

a photograph album. It contained all the pictures he had of Lucy, from baby photos to the last adolescent pictures he'd snapped of her. His favourite photograph was one he'd taken in the Lake District. Set against a backdrop of Coniston Water, the light just fading, the water like milky glass, she was staring straight into the camera, a woolly hat pulled down to her eyebrows, her hair sticking out comically. Lucy had hated the picture when she'd seen it and had made him promise not to have it framed and on show. It was another of his promises he'd made for her. He'd always tried to put her feelings before his own. Except that one time, when he'd fallen in love with Francesca.

Comparing the images he knew by heart with the one he'd seen in Lucy's passport tonight, it amazed him just how little she had changed. It both delighted and pained him that he could have so effortlessly picked her out as his daughter in a crowd. He had waited for more than an hour with Anna and Franco for Lucy to reappear but eventually he'd accepted the folly of his actions. 'Go home,' Anna had said. 'Get some sleep and come back in the morning.'

He'd come home to find Francesca waiting for him, but seeing how tired she was, he'd insisted she went to bed. 'I'll be up soon,' he'd told her. 'I just need some time to unwind.' She had always been good at gauging his mood and she'd left him to sit in the semi-darkness of his study. To be this close to Lucy was unbearable. Knowing that in a matter of hours he might see her, maybe speak to her, made him want to rush back to the Hotel Villa Rosa and camp outside her room. The morning couldn't come soon enough.

Chapter Forty

Helen was awake early the next morning. Having slipped out of bed and dressed without disturbing Hunter, she was standing on the small balcony of their room. With the doors closed behind her, she was taking in the enchanting view. The light was sublime, serenely muted with a gossamer mist. Across the perfectly still water, the mountains were almost lost in a blurry, blue haze. Presumably, once the sun had made its impact, the mist would lift and the tops of the mountains would be revealed. The sky for now was delicately pale and pearly.

She was reminded of countless other trips to Italy; all those mornings as a tour guide when she'd deliberately risen early so that she could enjoy an hour or so on her own before the day would be given over to the demands of her charges. There had been a time when she had thought she could make Italy her home, find herself a little apartment tucked away in some pretty town or city. Somewhere like Padua. Padua held a special place in her heart. It was where she'd met Giovanni. A quietly spoken, flawlessly mannered academic, he'd worked at the university. Their paths had crossed early one morning when she'd gone for a walk on her own. Dawn had just broken and the only other people around were street cleaners and sleepy-eyed students shuffling home to their beds after an exhausting night out. Much to her embarrassment the heel on her shoe had snapped off and he'd come to her rescue by insisting that she come back to his apartment where he could repair it for her. Not knowing him from Adam she had declined his offer, but in perfect English he had told her to stay where she was and he would return within minutes with a tube of superglue. Ten minutes later he reappeared in the Piazza Cavour with not only some glue but a bag of warm, sweet-smelling brioche. From then on, whenever she took a tour group to Padua, she would meet up with Giovanni. A year later they became lovers. But then

Emma's health deteriorated and Helen had to forget all about Italy – and Giovanni.

Those days seemed a lifetime away, yet she wasn't bitter. She would do anything for her grandmother.

Just being away from Emma for a few short days gave Helen cause for concern. The medical staff had assured her that everything would be fine, that Emma would be well taken care of during her absence. But what if they were wrong? What if something terrible happened to Emma and Helen couldn't make it home in time? Memories of the last nursing home Emma was in came back to Helen and she felt a surge of guilt-fuelled anger. She remembered the fear on Emma's face, the trembling hands that held onto her, the whispered words: 'Don't leave me. Please. Please don't leave me here.' But she had left Emma. And she would always regret that.

You had no choice, she reminded herself before her guilt could do its worst. You did what you thought was right. Forget the past. What's important now is that Emma is safe and happy. Be grateful for that.

Making a mental note to ring the nursing home after breakfast to check on her grandmother, Helen's attention was caught by a pigeon flying by, its wings flapping half-heartedly as if it didn't want to disturb the peace of the morning. Directly beneath Helen and all around the hotel was a delightful jumble of terracotta rooftops. TV aerials and chimney pots of differing sizes added haphazardly to the chaotic charm of the little community. Sitting at the base of one of the chimneys was another pigeon; it was fat and round and looked like a slightly squashed cushion. The sound of shutters opening had Helen looking to her right. An elderly woman in slippers came into view on a neighbouring balcony. She began pegging out a basket of washing consisting of several large pairs of what could only be described as comedy bloomers, a vest and a row of socks. At home Helen would never have dreamt of watching someone perform such an intimate task, but, just as she'd said to Conrad last night, less than twenty-four hours into the holiday she was already behaving differently.

Her theory about people acting out of character on holiday was something she'd thought about when she'd been in bed waiting for Hunter to come up from the bar, where he'd been chatting with one of the other guests, a Russian who'd lived in California for the last eighteen years. It was, she'd decided, to do with being a stranger in town; it gave one a shield of anonymity. A licence to be different.

When Hunter had finally come to bed she'd pretended to be asleep. She'd listened to him moving about the room as he'd undressed. When he was in the bathroom, she'd heard him drop something and then curse loudly. He hated the hotel; it was much too small for his taste. When they'd been shown into their room, he'd made no attempt to conceal his disgust. 'It's a budget-priced holiday,' she'd told him in defence of the room, which in her opinion was chic and simple with a lakeside view, more than adequate for their stay.

He'd replied tetchily, 'I would have thought you'd know by now that I don't do budget-priced anything, Helen.' More good-humouredly, he'd added, 'Why don't I check out the Grand Hotel Villa Serbelloni first thing in the morning? We could have a suite there and be much more comfortable.'

'I'm perfectly comfortable here,' she'd said.

'But I'm not.' His voice had adopted that steely edge she'd heard him use on the phone so often when he was conducting business. Simmering with resentment, she'd dropped the subject and started her unpacking. She felt that if she argued the point any further they would go on doing so for ever.

The woman who had moments earlier pegged out her washing was now watering the window boxes of begonias and petunias that lined her balcony. Helen looked at the scarlet geraniums that tumbled from the boxes fixed to the wrought-iron balustrade of the balcony she was standing on. Although it was the first week of September, the flowers showed no sign of coming to the end of their life. Unlike some of the bedding plants back at home which had already taken on that faded, do-I-still-have-to-perform look that pre-empted the beginning of autumn. Here in Bellagio it was still summer and the day was glorious. Nothing was going to spoil it for her. If Hunter started up his nonsense about switching hotels, she was going to stand firm.

To her left, two balconies along, another pair of shutters swung open and Conrad appeared. His feet were bare but the rest of him was covered in jeans and a T-shirt. He placed both hands on the wrought-iron railing and leant forward as though embracing the day. She held her breath as she so often did when she saw him, or even thought of him.

She recalled the weird conversation they'd had before dinner last night. She'd been in a strange mood. Still cross with Hunter for upgrading their seats on the flight, but concerned that her morality was fast reaching a deeply questionable level, she'd been scratchily defensive and on edge. Especially when Olivia Marchwood had made her patronizing comment. She brought to mind the uneasy look on Conrad's face when she'd been unnecessarily sharp with him after he'd asked if she had married Hunter to feather her nest. Even if he'd been joking, it had been too close to the truth. Perhaps, in a perverse way, she had been trying to frighten him off by deliberately giving him a reason to view her with contempt. There were definitely times when she despised herself, so why wouldn't he feel the same?

A pair of pigeons landed on a nearby chimney pot; it was to the right of Conrad's vision and as Helen watched him turn to look at the birds, she knew she would also come within his line of vision. 'You're up early,' he said when he saw her.

'So are you,' she said self-consciously. He'd probably guessed that she'd been secretly staring at him.

He said something else but his words were lost in the clamour of bells. Helen glanced at her watch: seven-thirty. The mellow clanging sound continued and whilst Helen thought it was the perfect accompaniment to the start of such a beautiful day, she knew that Hunter would not be so captivated. Anything that disturbed his sleep would be given short shrift.

Breakfast on the terrace was a simple buffet affair – croissants, bread rolls, jam, cheese, ham, fruit juice, and tea and coffee. Helen had just poured a second cup of coffee for Hunter when his mobile rang. 'I'll take this back upstairs in the room,' he said when he'd checked who the caller was. 'It could go on for a while.' As he hurried away, the phone pressed to his ear, Mac, Conrad and Lucy materialised. Mac waved over to Helen. She returned the gesture and watched Mac pull out a chair for Lucy. She was glad Mac was making such a fuss of the poor girl. The last few weeks hadn't been kind to her. There was no sign yet of either Orlando or Savannah, Helen noted as she tore off a corner of her croissant and dabbed it into a dollop of cherry jam. Odds on they had spent the night together and were probably enjoying room service. Hunter could kid himself all he liked, but his presence in Bellagio would have little effect on what his daughter chose to do.

She looked up from her breakfast plate to see Conrad standing over her. 'We wondered if you'd like to join us on our table,' he said, 'seeing as you've been abandoned.'

She could have said no, that she hadn't been abandoned, that Hunter would be back any minute, but she didn't. She gathered her things together and followed behind Conrad as he wove his way round the other tables.

'Hi, Helen,' Lucy greeted her. 'Are you looking forward to our first tour this morning? There's no sign of Philippa yet. I half-expected her to be here jollying us along like she was yesterday.'

Lucy's chirpiness surprised Helen. She hadn't seen her looking so animated in a long while. 'Maybe she's having breakfast in her room,' Helen suggested. She'd never met a tour group leader who didn't hide herself away in her room if she could get away with it. She herself had done it many times. Taking care of a disparate group of travellers was exhausting work, especially if one of the members was lonely and wanted to be the tour guide's best friend. Helen had a wealth of experience of this, with both men and women. There was a man once, during a trip to Venice, who had never left her side. He'd badgered her night and day, asking her to help him with a hundred and one things – finding a lost key, checking to see if the butter at breakfast was salted, putting a telephone call through to England. His last cry for help was to ask her to find his underpants, which he'd washed and put out to dry on the window ledge of his hotel room only to find that they'd disappeared overnight. How she'd kept a straight face – he'd gone on to explain that the situation was serious because they were his only pair – she didn't know. Her solution was to go out and buy him a new pair of Y-fronts.

She hoped Philippa would have an easier time with this particular group.

As soon as Lucy had finished her breakfast she excused herself from the table. 'I want to go and explore for a few minutes before Philippa rounds us up for the day,' she said.

'I thought you did that last night,' Mac said.

'I did, but it was dark. Permission to wander about in broad daylight?'

'Permission granted,' Mac said with a crisp salute. 'We'll see you in the lobby at the appointed time. Nine forty-five, wasn't it?'

They all agreed that that was the itinerary and Lucy went upstairs to her room. It hadn't slipped her notice that neither Orlando nor Savannah had made it for breakfast, but she'd accepted that that was inevitable.

Her teeth brushed and her small leather rucksack packed for the day – sunglasses, money, bottle of water, sun cream and camera – she shut the door behind her and took the stairs down to the lobby. She was pulling open the glass door when the woman behind the reception desk called out her name.

'*Signorina Gray*, I have your passport. Would you like to take it now or shall I keep it for you until later?'

'Oh, that's all right, I'll take it now. Thanks.' As an afterthought, and with Alessio's accent ringing in her ears, she added, '*Grazie*.'

The woman smiled back at her. '*Prego*.'

Lucy slipped the passport into her bag and was just about to go when she remembered the map she wanted. 'Do you have a street map of Bellagio?' she asked.

The woman reached down behind the counter, then laid out a small map for Lucy to look at. With a pen she pointed to a street and said, 'This is the Hotel Villa Rosa. As you can see, we're very central.'

'Thank you,' Lucy said. She took the map to study later and stepped outside into the narrow passageway. The last thing on her mind was that she might bump into her father. But that was exactly what she did.

Chapter Forty-one

Lucy recognized her father instantly. Admittedly he was older, but he barely seemed to have changed at all.

'You knew I was here,' she said, matter of factly, although she had never felt less matter of fact in the whole of her life. She felt that any second her legs would work of their own accord and she'd start to run. She would run as fast as she could, all the way back to Swanmere. But somehow she stood firm, resolute in the face of this unwanted pre-emptive strike by her father. A pre-emptive strike that had taken away her control of the situation – something she had badly wanted to keep.

'Yes,' he said. 'I knew you were here. And that you arrived yesterday.'

'How?'

'I ... I know the people who own the hotel. They made a connection with the name and—'

'And tipped you off?'

He nodded.

The narrow alley where they were standing was suddenly crowded with tourists trying to get around them. 'Can I take you for a coffee?' he asked.

'So that we can have a nice little chat?' She knew she sounded belligerent, that she wasn't doing anything to help this watershed moment. But why should she? She was the hurt party. It was down to him to make good the damage he'd inflicted.

'Something like that,' he said.

'I'm sorry,' she said, 'but I'm busy right now.' Why should she make it so easy for him?

'Later, then?'

Relieved that she was now back in the driving seat, she said, 'Give me your phone number and I'll call you.'

He took out his wallet and handed her a card. 'Ring me

any time you want, Lucy. Please. My mobile is always switched on.'

She pocketed the card and without another word set off down the steep, cobbled steps as casually as she could. Yes. That was more like it. That had showed him. She had covered no more than half a dozen steps when she felt compelled to look over her shoulder. He was still standing in the same spot. But now his face was hidden behind his hands.

She told herself to turn and walk away. Whatever he was feeling was entirely his affair. But to her disgust she was inexplicably filled with pity for him. No! She was not ever supposed to feel sorry for him. She cast her mind back to how it had felt that day in the café when she'd been fourteen years old, when he'd told her of his plans to leave her to live another life. A life that could never include her. Her throat tightened. Hold that thought, she told herself. Don't let it go. Not ever.

Yet the memories, as painful as they were, couldn't compete with the here and now. The sight of her father's desolate figure as she watched him slump against the wall opposite the hotel, his head lowered and unaware that she was watching him, or that passers-by were staring at him oddly, bludgeoned her resolve.

Very slowly she retraced her steps until she was standing next to him. She put a hand on his arm. Startled, he looked up. His eyes were wet with tears. 'Do you still want to go for that coffee?' she asked.

Marcus ordered their drinks. When the waiter had gone, he clenched his hands into tight fists under the table; it was the only way he could stop them from shaking. He was in shock and fighting hard to resist throwing his arms around Lucy and telling her what a beautiful young woman she'd grown into, that he couldn't be more proud of her, that he'd missed her more than he could ever put into words. There was so much he wanted to say and ask, but where to start?

Instead they were being, as Francesca would say, so very English and hiding behind a murmured exchange of small talk – yes, she liked what she'd seen of Bellagio so far … did she like the hotel? Who were the people she was with? It was better than he could have hoped for. What he'd done to her could never be brushed aside with a simple kiss and apology. He had years of hurt and resentment to overcome.

Their coffees arrived. As did the moment to say something that mattered. 'Lucy,' he began.

She looked straight at him. 'Yes?'

On the receiving end of such a direct stare he was poignantly reminded of that day he'd held her as a newborn baby and had experienced that first bolt of fierce love for her by simply looking into that fragile, unfocused, ash-blue gaze. Self-conscious nerves took away his courage to say what he wanted to say. He pushed the bowl of sachets towards her. 'Sugar?'

'No thanks. I don't take sugar in my drinks.'

He winced. Was that a pointed remark on her part? See, had you been a better father – a father who hadn't walked out on his family – you would have known this. He watched her carefully scoop off the froth from her cappuccino and lick the spoon clean. Compared to him she seemed utterly composed. He took a very deep, slow breath and tried again. 'Why are you here in Bellagio, Lucy?'

'I'm on holiday.'

'So it's coincidence, then, that you're here where I live?'

She put down her spoon and gave him a look that was hard to read. 'No. Not exactly.'

When she didn't expand on this, he said, 'Were you planning on getting in touch with me during your stay?'

'Yes. But when I was ready. When I'd decided the time was right.'

'I'm sorry I forced your hand. I just couldn't wait any longer.' He explained about Anna's telephone call last night and his visit to the hotel only to find she wasn't there.

She seemed genuinely surprised by this. 'You came straight away?'

'Of course. I wanted to see if it really was you.'

'I'd gone for a walk,' she said.

'It was late to be out on your own.'

She raised an eyebrow. 'Not as late as you thinking you can play the heavy father with me. And anyway, Bellagio strikes me as being about as dangerous as a marshmallow.'

'I'm sorry,' he said softly. 'If it makes you feel better, it's the kind of well-meaning, sexist thing I'd say to Francesca.'

There was a deathly awkward pause. That was clumsy of him. He shouldn't have brought up Francesca's name so soon.

'So how is Francesca?' Lucy asked after the awkward pause had made its mark.

'She's well. But don't worry, I'm not about to say you must meet her. I won't do that to you.'

'Good.'

He did his best to hide his disappointment. He was sure that if Lucy gave Francesca a chance they would take to each other. He'd always believed that Francesca might actually help Lucy to accept the past, that she could be part of the reconciliation he so badly wanted. 'How's your mother?' he asked. 'I heard on the grapevine that she's remarried. Hopefully second time around is suiting her better than our disastrous attempt—'

She cut him off at the pass. 'Yes,' she interrupted. 'Charles makes Mum blissfully happy.'

Rather unkindly he thought that blissful happiness was not a state Fiona was capable of ever knowing. However he sensed Lucy's words were meant as another stinging reproof rather than an accurate description of Fiona's current situation. 'I'm glad,' he said. 'Glad that someone has succeeded with your mother where I failed.'

There was another strained pause while they both drank their coffee. They were then blessedly distracted by a glamorous couple settling themselves at a nearby table: from their sleek clothes and languid bodies, Marcus put money on them being from Milan. But it wasn't the man and woman themselves that were worthy of attention; it was the dog they were making an enormous fuss of that was the star turn. Or more particularly, it was the extraordinary lead the raven-haired woman was holding that Marcus couldn't take his eyes off. He had come across many a pampered Italian pooch since living in Bellagio but never one that came on the end of a dog lead that had been designed to look like a string of sausages. He caught Lucy's eye and they both smiled. It completely made his day.

And then the moment was gone. Lucy glanced at her watch and leapt to her feet, the starched white tablecloth caught up in her movements. He was reminded of her as a young child, always in a hurry, always knocking things over. 'I have to meet the others back at the hotel,' she said. 'I'm booked to go on a tour.'

He knew better than to say, but isn't our sitting here more important? He straightened the cloth and said, 'I'll walk with you. If that's all right?'

She shrugged.

He chucked some Euros on the table and led the way back

to the Hotel Villa Rosa. They hadn't discussed anything of real importance – how could they in only twenty minutes? – but that smile just now, that one single shared smile, spelled hope for him. It was all he needed.

As they boarded the *traghetto* to cross the lake for Villa Carlotta, it was obvious to them all that Philippa, their guide, was not going to make it through the day. She was putting a brave face on it, but she was fooling no one. Her eyes were bloodshot, her complexion was flushed and her voice was so painfully Rod Stewart croaky it made Helen want to keep clearing her own throat. Whilst they all offered the poor woman sympathy – at the same time keeping a healthy distance from her – there were other mutterings in the camp. Namely: 'What was the point in having a guide who was losing her voice?' Someone – an irritating man from Epsom whom it was impossible to take seriously because he was wearing open-toed sandals with socks and a shirt tucked into a pair of trousers with a drawstring waist – had very helpfully said he was going to complain to Gardens of Delight and demand a refund if they were to be without their guide. He had the air of a man who could waffle on until the end of time if given the opportunity. He also had the full backing of his po-faced wife, who peered out from beneath her sunhat, which was tied in a childishly large bow under her chin, to say, 'We're here to learn; it's not just a holiday for us.'

Guarding against coughs and sniffles had always been a priority for Helen when she'd been a tour guide. Only once had she come close to thinking she would have to let a group down. But for all her years of experience, she had never worked for an outfit who could provide protection against problem travellers like this uncharitable couple, who could so easily infect an entire group with their poisonously divisive comments.

'Cap'n, I sense storm clouds gathering and mutiny a-brewing,' Mac said. He was sitting on Helen's right with Conrad and Lucy the other side of him. Hunter was at the back of the boat talking to someone on his mobile. To Helen's knowledge, it was his fourth call of the morning already.

'How about we throw the troublemakers overboard?' Conrad suggested.

'A lovely thought,' Helen replied. 'But I suspect the combination of the ringleader's inflated ego and his hugely puffed up self-importance will act as a very superior buoyancy aid.'

Mac laughed. 'You're on form this morning, Helen.'

'Unlike Philippa,' said Conrad. 'What do you think will happen if she has to take to her bed?'

'Personally,' Mac said, 'and no offence meant, but if we are left to our own devices, I shan't mind a bit.'

'She'll probably organize a local guide for us,' Helen said. 'It's what I would do in her shoes.'

They were in the middle of the lake now and the delicate light of early morning had given way to a sky of eggshell blue, and the mountains had emerged from their lacy shroud of mist. It was captivatingly beautiful. Wondering if Conrad thought so too, she risked a glance in his direction, only to crash headlong into his gaze, which must have been on her while her head had been turned.

A shadow fell across her and she looked up to see Hunter standing over her. 'Bad news, Helen,' he said. The expression on his face didn't look like he had bad news to deliver. Anything but, in fact.

'What is it, Hunter? Nothing serious I hope.'

'I have to go to Dubai. A problem's developed with the lease on the office premises I was hoping to acquire. They're trying to screw me.'

'Can't someone else handle it?'

The exact same question had been on Helen's lips, but it had been voiced by Mac.

'I don't like to toot my own horn too loudly,' Mac went on, 'but when I worked for the bank, I always ensured that I had a team behind me who could step in when needed. It's the sign of good work practice, being able to delegate with confidence.'

Hunter smiled thinly. 'It's a bit different when the company's your own.'

'When do you have to leave?' Helen asked. She knew there was no point in trying to dissuade Hunter. She could see his mind was made up. Part of her was willing him to go right away. Oh, the relief! But oh, the guilt!

'Judith's checking the flight availability as we speak,' he answered her.

Good old reliable Judith, thought Helen dryly. She'd only met Hunter's murderously loyal PA a couple of times but knew that the fifty-something spinster was utterly devoted to him. She also knew that Judith disliked Helen for having the audacity to be Wife Number Three, and that she would get her beloved boss on the next available flight out of Italy if only to get him away from Helen's evil clutches. 'You'd better go and break the news to Savannah,' Helen said. 'I'm sure she'll be disappointed that you're leaving.'

Hunter snorted. 'I doubt that somehow. Now she'll be able to carry on as badly as she wants to with that Orlando of hers.'

On the end of the row of seats, Lucy suddenly got up and walked away.

The *traghetto* pulled into Tremezzo and everyone disembarked. At the top of the gangplank, Philippa counted them off. Her voice croakier than ever, she instructed them to cross the busy road and to wait for her at the entrance to Villa Carlotta. They weren't the only ones heading towards the famous house and garden; nearly half of the people who'd been on the boat surged across the road and brought the traffic to a halt.

'You're very quiet,' Mac said when he found himself walking alongside Lucy. Conrad was trailing behind. Bad enough that Hunter was always on his mobile, now Conrad was at it too. 'Everything okay?' he asked.

'Any reason why I wouldn't be?'

'That idiot husband of Helen's could have been more tactful for a start.'

Lucy looked at him sharply. It was the first time he'd so much as hinted that he knew all was not well between her and Orlando, and that the cause of the problem was Savannah. He wondered if he'd overstepped the mark. When she didn't say anything, he said, 'Have you done anything about meeting your father?'

'Actually, I've met him already.'

Ahead of them Philippa was struggling valiantly to instruct the group on what would happen next. 'I'll tell you more later,' Lucy whispered.

'No! You can't leave me dangling like that. Was it all right? How did it go? How did he—?'

The man in the drawstring trousers turned briefly and told Mac to *ss-sshh*!

'Oh bugger off, you ghastly jumped-up little prat!' Mac mouthed at his back.

'A shame you weren't brave enough to say it to his face,' Lucy sniggered when the group moved on.

'Give it time,' Mac said. 'Now tell me all about it. How did you feel when you saw your father?'

*

Savannah was in a foul mood and as a consequence Orlando didn't seem able to say or do anything right. He'd decided to keep his head down and his mouth shut, trying to make the most of the garden they were visiting. But even that was as good as a red rag to a bull.

'You could at least talk to me,' Savannah had sniped at him only moments ago when he'd stopped to take a photograph of a tulip tree he'd never seen before and write down its name.

'What's the point?' he'd retaliated, thoroughly pissed off now by her behaviour. 'The minute I open my mouth you just bite my head off.'

She'd glared at him and then marched off.

I should go after her, he thought as he put his notebook back into his pocket. But he couldn't be bothered. Why put himself through the hassle?

It had all started to go wrong when they went up to his room after dinner last night. He'd made the mistake of asking her what she'd thought of the piano player. 'Yeah, he was hot,' she'd said. 'And he certainly looked like he had his eye on Lucy, didn't he?'

'You thought that too, did you?'

She'd laughed. 'Come off it, Orlando, everyone in the room could see what was going on. Why do you ask? You're not jealous, are you?'

'Of course not.'

'Good. Because I'll tell you this for nothing: I'm not competing with Lucy. Now get yourself over here on the bed and kiss me. This is our first whole night together and I want it to be perfect.'

He'd made an effort to oblige, but sex was the last thing he'd had on his mind. He had a thumping headache and embarrassingly all he really wanted to do was turn out the light and go to sleep.

'No way,' she said when he'd explained the situation. 'I know just what will cure you of that.' She started to undo the zip on his trousers.

'Trust me, it won't,' he said, gently pushing her hand away and hardly believing he was passing up the opportunity.

That was when she'd turned nasty. 'I don't frigging well believe it!' she said. 'The first night we're properly alone and you go all flaky on me!'

He tried to laugh it off and reassure her that tomorrow she'd better look out as he'd be firing on all cylinders.

'That means naff all to me right now,' she snapped, jumping off the bed. 'I'm feeling horny now!'

It struck him that a more understanding girlfriend might have offered to massage his neck and shoulders. He went to the bathroom to find the packet of Paracetamol he'd brought with him. Minutes later when he came out of the bathroom she was pulling on her jacket. 'I'm going to my room,' she said. 'I know when I'm not wanted. I hope you sleep well.'

'Shall I knock on your door for breakfast?' he'd asked. He had no intention of stopping her from going. If she was choosing to take it personally, then there was sod-all he could do to convince her otherwise.

'Oh, do what you want.'

But he'd slept so heavily that he'd overslept and missed breakfast. This was his first faux pas of the day. Things had gone steadily downhill from there.

Still, at least his first love wasn't disappointing him. The garden at Villa Carlotta was a horticulturist's dream. He hoped Lucy was enjoying it as much as he was.

Chapter Forty-two

The garden at Villa Carlotta was the first of the tour and frankly Conrad didn't think it was all that it was cracked up to be. But then he was no botanist or horticulturist. Not even a gardener. However, the rest of the group seemed suitably impressed by the many different varieties of plants and trees on offer in the English-style landscaped garden that dominated this area of hillside on the western shore of the lake. Under Philippa's strained tutelage, he had had pointed out to him the biggest magnolia grandifloras he'd ever seen, a Chinese camphor tree, azaleas that were a hundred and fifty years old, swathes of rhododendrons (apparently these had to be seen in the spring to be believed), a bamboo garden, japonicas, exotic succulents, palms, hedges of camellias, ferns, an arbour of citrus trees, sequoias, myrtles, roses, and countless other specimens. None of which he could claim had any great interest for him.

Everyone else was now exploring the garden on their own, including Mac, who'd gone off with Lucy. Conrad had had more than enough for one morning. He followed a cool, shady path until he found himself back where the wrought-iron gazebo was located. The view across the lake towards Bellagio was quite something. Best of all, sitting in the jasmine-covered structure, he was entirely alone. It was good to escape some of the other members of the group. Just as Helen had her theory about people behaving out of character on holiday, he had a theory about gardeners. With a few exceptions, female gardeners were either beanpole thin, as Alice Wykeham had been, or built like butternut squashes. Olivia Marchwood, along with nearly every other woman on the tour, was definitely in the butternut squash category. And about as interesting.

Thank God Helen was here and was capable of talking about something other than gardening.

Since that slightly odd conversation before dinner last night they hadn't spent any more time alone. But now it looked as though that might change. With Hunter conveniently out of the picture, who knew how things would shake down? By rights he should be smiling and rubbing his hands in glee, but he wasn't. Instead he was angry. Hunter was playing dirty. He was blatantly lying to Helen and cheating on her. Okay, Conrad's own moral compass wasn't a perfect paradigm these days, but he hated the idea that Hunter was abusing Helen's trust.

Helen might not have suspected Hunter of lying earlier, but Conrad had. Which was why he'd got straight on to his mobile and checked the available flights to Dubai. If Hunter came up with a flight time that didn't fit with what he'd been told, then he'd know for sure that the man was lying. He wouldn't do anything with the information – he certainly had no intention of telling Helen – but he'd always considered it wise to know one's enemy. And Hunter was his enemy. Conrad disliked him intensely. He was arrogant and far too sure of himself. He was the kind of man who considered himself to be at the top of the food chain and enjoyed looking down on everyone else. There was a cruel streak to him, too. Conrad had no evidence to support this suspicion, but every time he looked at Hunter he imagined him capable of wantonly inflicting pain on another person. As far as Conrad was concerned, there wasn't one redeemable facet to the man's character. What had possessed Helen to marry him?

'Looks like you're doing the sensible thing. Mind if I join you?'

Who else but the man himself!

Conrad shifted along the seat to make room for Hunter. 'Any news on your travel arrangements?' he asked.

'It's fixed. I've got a car organized to take me to Milan at three o'clock this afternoon.'

Go on, thought Conrad, make my day. 'What time's your flight?' he asked.

'Six thirty-five. I was lucky to get a seat at such short notice.'

'A direct flight?'

'Yup.'

Conrad clocked the lie. Without having to refer to the slip of paper in his pocket – on which he'd written down the only two possible direct flights – he knew the time didn't tally.

'I bet you wish you were coming with me.'

Conrad glanced up at Hunter. 'Why do you say that?'

'I'd put money on it that this is hardly your scene. I keep asking myself why you're here.'

Conrad tensed. Had he underestimated Hunter? Was it possible that he'd got wind of his feelings for Helen? 'I'm here because my uncle wanted me to accompany him,' he said. 'His health isn't what it could be. He suffered a stroke a couple of years ago.'

'So you're a nursemaid, are you?'

'Mac wouldn't thank you for saying that.'

'I dare say he wouldn't. Not when he likes to give the impression of being as strong as a cart horse. No, I think you're here for an entirely different reason.'

Keeping his tone level, Conrad said, 'Really? And what would that be?'

Like a burst of gunfire going off, Hunter let out a loud, cheerless laugh. 'It's got to be for the women, hasn't it? I mean, where else would you get such a fine-looking bunch? But listen, if you're not too busy chasing the fat-arsed beauties, I'd appreciate you taking care of Helen for me when I'm gone.'

'Sure, that's what friends are for.'

'So they say.' Hunter flicked at a tiny leaf that had drifted down from above their heads and landed on his leg. 'Back at home, my wife spends a lot of time at your place, doesn't she?' he said.

Again Conrad tensed. 'I have it on good authority that she and Mac are as thick as thieves,' he said lightly.

Hunter let off another short bark of a laugh. 'Yes, I'd noticed that. I reckon if your uncle was a younger man I'd have cause to be worried.'

It seemed to Conrad that every word that came out of Hunter's mouth was loaded with accusation and menace. Or was he being paranoid? The symptom of a guilty conscience? Best thing to do was to go on the attack. 'Let's hope your trip to Dubai is a success, then,' he said. 'No chance that you can get the problem wrapped up in double-quick time and rejoin us before the end of the holiday? It would be a nice surprise for Helen, wouldn't it?'

'It would. But sadly, I don't see that as being very likely. I'll catch up with you all back in Swanmere.'

'Yes, and then we'll bore you rigid with our holiday snaps. Show you what you missed out on.'

'That sounds like a threat to me.'

Conrad was about to reply when he heard voices. With Pat and Colin Campbell, and Vi Abbott and Barbara Slattery in her wake,

Olivia Marchwood approached the gazebo. 'Ah, excellent!' she declared. 'Another two rounded up. Philippa says we're to meet her at the back of the villa by the camellia hedge; she's booked us a guide to take us inside.'

'If it's all right with you good folk, I'll pass,' Hunter said.

Not wanting to spend another minute in Hunter's company, Conrad got to his feet. 'I'm sure the house is worth a look.'

The young Italian girl who was their guide for the tour round the villa was as enthusiastic as she was knowledgeable and twenty minutes into her stride, Conrad was getting the feeling that by the end of the tour, no stone of Villa Carlotta's history would have gone unturned. She'd started with its late seventeenth-century roots and its creation at the hands of the Marquis Giorgio Clerici, a wealthy merchant from the area, had moved on to 1795 when the Sommariva family became its owners, and she was now giving a detailed account of its purchase by the wife of Albert of Prussia, Princess Marianna of Nassau, who bought it as a wedding gift for her daughter Carlotta. Some wedding present!

Finally, as the young Italian drew breath, she ushered them into the next room. It was the Central Parlour, otherwise known as the Statue Room. The first thing she pointed out to them was the ornate vaulted ceiling with its fake stuccowork of stars, coffers and rosettes. Next to be brought to their attention was the Carrara marble high-relief frieze that ran the perimeter of the room and which depicted the Entrance of Alexander the Great in Babylonia. 'It is the jewel in the crown of the Sommariva art collection,' the guide explained, 'and is made up of thirty-three panels.' But Conrad's eye had caught on something else. At the far end of the room was a marble statue; there was something vaguely familiar about it. He peeled away from the group and went over to take a closer look at the two figures that made up the piece. Within seconds he knew why it was familiar to him. The last time he'd seen it, he'd been with Sam in the Hermitage Museum in St Petersburg. 'Don't you think it's just about the most erotic statue you've ever seen?' Sam had asked him. Had he not been with her and had the statue brought to his attention, he probably wouldn't have even noticed it.

'What's it called?' he'd asked after he'd decided she was right. There really was something profoundly erotic about the couple and their embrace.

'Amore and Psyche Reclining,' she'd told him. 'Don't you just love the tender way he's holding her and the way she's giving herself up to him?'

'And what's the story behind it?'

'In a nutshell; jealousy and the power of love.'

'And?'

'Do you really want to know, or are you just humouring me?'

'No, I want to know. Really.'

'Well, Psyche was such a stunner, Venus's nose was well and truly put out of joint. In a fit of jealousy and envy, Venus instructed Amore, also known as Cupid to his mates, to make Psyche fall in love with the ugliest specimen he could come up with. As is the way of these things, Cupid fell for Psyche himself and was forced to hide his identity to her. But when urged by her sisters to discover who it is she's been making secret whoopy with, Psyche goes and spoils everything and Cupid hops off sharpish. Venus then puts Psyche to some hard labour, which of course should by rights have finished off the poor girl, but because Cupid still loves her, he's sneakily helping her to survive. Being the heroine of the story, Psyche finally overcomes Venus's hatred and jealousy, becomes immortal and at long last, she's united with Cupid for ever. A charming crowd-pleaser of a tale, don't you think?'

'And the moral of the story?' he'd asked.

'Oh, that's simple. We have to go through hell before we reach heaven. Whatever that might be.'

Conrad swallowed. It was as if Sam was here telling him the story all over again.

'Ah, I see that you are admiring the beautiful work of Adamo Tadolini, who was Canova's most prized pupil.'

Conrad swung round to see that the guide and the rest of the group had now joined him to look at the statue.

'This is one of the most loved exhibits at Villa Carlotta,' the guide went on, 'but I have to tell you, it is a copy. The original is in the Hermitage Museum in St Petersburg.'

Conrad edged away from the group. He needed air. And space.

Outside in the garden, he wandered over to the terrace that was lined with pots of vibrantly red hibiscus plants. From there he looked down onto the arched citrus walk. The sun was high in the sky now and he could feel it on his neck and face. After the cool interior of the house, and the chill of the past wrapping its ghostly fingers around him, it felt good. He stared out at the lake, its rippling surface twinkling and shimmering in the sunlight. He tried to make sense of his reaction just now inside the villa. It wasn't the actual memory of Sam that had shaken him, he decided, it was her words. Words he hadn't thought of since that day. *We have to go through hell before we reach heaven. Whatever that might be.*

He for one had been to hell and back since Sam's death. Did that mean he was in for something better any time soon?

He was just raising a hand to shield his eyes from the glare of the sun as he continued to stare out at Bellagio on the other side of the lake, when he heard a flinty bark of laughter. It was coming from below him, from the citrus walk. He stayed where he was until, as he knew would happen, Hunter emerged at the end of the archway nearest Conrad. Hunter was oblivious to his presence and it wasn't difficult for Conrad to hear him say into his mobile phone: 'I'll see you later, then. And make sure you have the champagne on ice. And your knickers off!'

Gotcha! thought Conrad. Not that he'd needed any more evidence to confirm that Hunter was cheating on Helen. How tempting it was to show himself and let the lying, cheating bastard know that he'd been overheard. But what good would that do? Would it stop a man like Hunter Tyler? He very much doubted it. And did he really want to stop him? Wasn't it in his own interests to let Hunter go right ahead and pull the pin and detonate his marriage?

Chapter Forty-three

According to the itinerary, as Philippa was hoarsely pointing out, now they were back in Bellagio, the group had the next two hours to themselves and were free to explore and have lunch wherever they fancied 'I'll meet you all in the foyer of the hotel at two-thirty,' she croaked. Privately, Mac thought they'd be better off if she took to her bed and kept her germs to herself. The last thing he wanted was to go down with some dreaded lurgy. Since his stroke, he'd developed a strong sense of self-preservation. He hated being ill. He simply couldn't abide that feeling of being at someone else's mercy, of someone else making decisions for him. It was so humiliating.

He caught up with the conversation going on around him. To his annoyance, Helen's husband had somehow taken charge and was insisting on taking some of them for lunch, seeing as he was leaving that afternoon. 'Conrad and Mac, you'll join us, won't you? Savannah, you and Orlando must make up the party. And don't look like that, Savvie; you'll have plenty of time to eat lunch alone with your fella when I'm gone. What about you, Lucy? We can't leave you out, can we? No, no. I absolutely insist. You *must* join us.'

'This should be fun,' Mac muttered as he fell in step beside Conrad and followed some yards behind Hunter. The man's overly bonhomie manner was getting right up his nose. 'Where's he taking us?'

'Where else but to the Serbelloni?' Conrad replied. 'And do try to behave, won't you? For Helen's sake if nothing else.'

'Oh, don't you go worrying about me. I'll be the model of good behaviour. But spare a thought for poor Lucy. We've seen just how sensitive and subtle that bloody man can be.'

'She could have said no.'

'Yes, just as the rest of us could have opted out. Only we're all too polite to tell him where to stick his lunch.'

Conrad smiled. 'I had no idea you'd taken such a violent dislike to Hunter.'

'I've never had to suffer his presence so much as I am now. Years ago I knew a chap like him out in Hong Kong. He was enormously wealthy and an arrogant bully, always used to getting his own way. Worst thing was, no matter how close to the wind he sailed, nothing ever stuck to him.'

'Go on, tell me there's a happy ending to this story. He died a lonely, grisly death, broke and broken-hearted.'

'Far from it. He got wealthier and wealthier and his wives got younger and more beautiful. We called him Teflon Terry.'

'Now you're just depressing me.'

'What I'm trying to tell you, Conrad, is that men like Hunter always win out. They're not like us. They operate differently.' He slowed his step and put a hand on Conrad's forearm. 'If Hunter discovers you've got a thing for Helen, heaven help you.'

'That's not going to happen.'

Mac removed his hand and picked up the pace again as they dodged the crowds of tourists. 'Listen to me, Conrad; I've seen the way you look at her. And I can't be the only one to see it.'

'Okay, I admit I've looked, but I haven't touched.'

'Not yet you haven't. But tell me what happens the moment Hunter disappears this afternoon to Dubai?'

'I don't know what you mean.'

Mac rolled his eyes, but left it at that. They were now approaching the revolving door of the hotel where Hunter was treating them to lunch. Bloody show-off, Mac thought when he saw the splendid opulence of the hotel. He'd stayed in plenty of top-quality hotels in his time, some of the best in the world, but never had he rammed his good fortune down anyone else's throat the way Hunter enjoyed doing. It was so distasteful. He could see from Helen's silence that she thought so, too. He'd noticed that about her – that whenever Hunter was around she hardly opened her mouth, that she became almost invisible.

She reminded him of another woman from a long time ago. His beautiful Hannah. The only woman he'd truly loved. She had been such a wonderfully animated presence when they'd been alone together, but the minute her husband was around, she reverted to the quiet, unassuming wife and mother he had turned her into. For years Mac had urged her to leave her husband, to become the woman she was meant to be, but she wouldn't. It broke his heart.

He stood back to let Conrad go on ahead and waited for Lucy. Frustratingly they hadn't had a chance to talk properly about how it had gone between her and her father. Every time she had started to say something, someone had popped out from behind some bush or other.

'If I'm extra nice to you, will you promise to sit next to me during lunch?' he asked her when they were inside the hotel and Hunter was talking to the concierge.

'I'd prefer you to be your usual grumpy self, Mac.'

He smiled. 'It can be arranged.'

Lunch at the Grand Hotel Villa Serbelloni was served on the terrace overlooking the swimming pool and beyond that, the lake. They were shown to a table in the shade of a large awning and their waiter's deferential manner, as he handed them their menus, suggested that nothing would be too much trouble for him. Lucy listened to Hunter ordering some champagne. 'That's just for starters,' he said, when the waiter left them alone, 'until we've decided what wine we want to drink.' He picked up his menu. 'Now then, let's see what they've got to offer us.'

'I hope they do pizza,' Savannah said without bothering to look at her menu and fiddling with her hair – she was wearing it in two large bunches either side of her head; dangling from her ears were large hooped earrings. She couldn't have looked more churlish or more out of place. 'Cos that's what I was planning on having before you—'

'I'm sure they'll cook you whatever you want, Savvie,' Hunter interrupted her smoothly.

'They better had.'

Lucy gritted her teeth. Was she the only one here who wanted to slap Savannah? Glancing round the table, she saw Helen's face and knew she wasn't alone. On the other hand, you had to hand it to the ungracious spoiled brat; she was the only one brave enough to say what she thought. It was blatantly obvious that most of them were sitting here against their will. Lucy had tried to say no to Hunter when he'd said she must join them, but some kind of sick, masochistic need to observe Orlando and Savannah at close quarters had kicked in. She'd noticed earlier at Villa Carlotta that Orlando had spent most of the tour round the garden on his own. She'd also overheard Savannah arguing with him, something about him ignoring her. Was it so very wrong to feel a ripple of pleasure at this?

'My, this is grand,' she whispered to Mac.

'Yes,' he whispered back, 'but don't worry, I'm already under orders from Conrad to behave myself. Now tell me about your father.'

'Let's order first.'

Ten minutes later their waiter had taken their order – the chef couldn't do a pizza for Savannah, and she sulkily said she'd make do with bruschetta with tomatoes, followed by the Parma-wrapped chicken – and Mac was holding Lucy to their bargain. 'Spill the beans,' he said.

It was difficult to know where to start. Initially she'd tried to block out all thoughts of her father. She'd wanted to put everything on hold, to let the shock of their meeting pass so that her reaction could slowly unfold and reveal itself. But that hadn't happened yet. She was still reeling from the suddenness of it all.

'So?' prompted Mac.

'I had a coffee with him,' she said, her voice low so no one else could hear them. 'We talked. It was ... it was weird.'

'But not too awful? Not too confrontational?'

'I didn't let rip at him, if that's what you're asking.'

'If you had, would it have mattered?'

She thought about this and remembered her father's beaten look when she'd turned on the steps outside their hotel. Yes, she thought with a sadness she hadn't known she was capable of. Yes, it would have mattered. In that instance he hadn't deserved her animosity. And yet ... that hurt and anger she'd carried around with her all those years was still there. It still needed to be vented somehow. Some time. He needed to know what it had been like for her. And for her mother. There's a price to be paid, she thought, her heart hardening just a little. When you inflict that much pain on another person you have to face the consequences.

'Lucy?'

She looked up and saw that Mac was waiting for her to say something. 'I'm sorry,' she said, 'I got lost in my thoughts for a moment.'

'I'm not surprised. This is proving to be a momentous day for you.' He squeezed her hand. 'And for your father, I suspect.'

At this, another voice said, 'What's that about your father, Lucy?'

Once again Lucy's hand itched to slap Savannah. Or maybe yank on those ridiculously large hooped earrings she was wearing. How dare the Gobby Pixie barge into a private conversation! 'Nothing,' she muttered and was glad when two waiters appeared at Hunter's side, each carrying an ice bucket and a bottle of champagne. It was the perfect distraction.

Or so she thought.

'Did you know Lucy's father lives here, Dad?' Savannah said, her voice even louder than usual. 'He buggered off with some Italian tart when Lucy was fourteen and she's refused to see him ever since. If you'd dumped me like that, I'd have killed you and the woman you'd gone off with.'

Lucy froze. Irrationally she felt a surge of anger towards Orlando. Why couldn't he control his girlfriend's enormous mouth? Everyone, except for Savannah and her father, was looking awkwardly down at their place settings. They knew. They all *knew* that this was something Lucy would never want to discuss so openly. She wished Orlando had the guts to look her in the eye. But he didn't. And she found herself despising him for it.

In the process of tasting the champagne – 'Yes, it's fine, go ahead and pour it,' – Hunter said, 'I'm no saint, but I'm not the sort of man who could abandon his kids. But then we're all different. He must have really loved the woman he went off with.' He looked straight at Lucy. 'I suppose that's what hurt most, isn't it, thinking that your father loved someone else more than you?'

'Perhaps this isn't something Lucy wants to discuss.'

Lucy looked gratefully at Conrad across the table.

'Yes,' agreed Helen. 'Savannah, I think you might be more tactful. This is an extremely difficult time for Lucy.'

Savannah sat back in her chair and laughed. 'Hey, lighten up everyone! You're fine with this, aren't you Luce? You wouldn't be here if you weren't.'

'Savannah—'

'Oh, not you as well, Orlando! Honestly, what's got into you all? Anyone would think Lucy was made of glass; one little bump and she'll break. You're made of stronger stuff than that, aren't you, Luce? You better had be or you'll never get anywhere.'

Lucy had had enough. Oh, she'd had more than enough from this stupid, self-obsessed, ignorant piece of trash. She pushed her chair back and stood up, making the china and cutlery on the table rattle. 'For once, Savannah, you're dead right. I am made of strong stuff. And you know what? The sooner I see the back of you, the better. You're nothing but a foul-mouthed, empty-headed rich kid, who can't even manage joined-up thinking. I don't know what the hell Orlando sees in you. But get this, because it's my final word on the subject. Please don't call me Luce, ever again!'

As dramatic exits went, it was right up there with the best. She stormed out of the hotel and marched down towards the crowded main street. Her heart was clattering in her chest, and her head was thrumming, but boy, did she feel bloody proud of herself!

'*Ciao!* Lucy!'

She looked across the busy road and saw a fantastically good-looking man waving to her. Who on earth did she know here? It was only when he pushed his glasses up on to the top of his head that she recognized him. It was the piano player from last night: Alessio. He waited for a gap in the traffic and came over. 'I was just going for a drink. Do you have time to join me?'

Why not? she thought. 'Okay,' she said. 'Where do you suggest?'

He put a hand to the small of her back and led her further down the street.

Orlando was furious. Furious with Savannah, but more so with himself. He should have stopped her from goading Lucy like that. But he hadn't, he'd just sat there like an idiot hoping the moment would pass.

He'd finally roused himself when, seconds after Lucy had left them, Hunter had said, 'Well, there's a girl who needs to learn some manners.'

With just about everyone in the restaurant staring at them, including the waiters, he rose from his chair. 'I'd better go and see if she's all right.'

'Yes, that's right,' he heard Savannah hiss at him. 'Go and see if the frigid bitch needs any oxygen up there on her high horse. Don't worry about how hacked off I feel!'

The hotel was now behind him, and he was scanning the busy street for Lucy. She couldn't have got far. And then he saw her, but she wasn't alone. That piano player from last night was with her. He had his hand on her waist and looked much too bloody cosy for Orlando's liking. What the hell was Lucy up to? Couldn't she see what kind of a bloke he was?

Chapter Forty-four

To keep herself occupied, Francesca was in the garden deadheading her favourite richly scented Alba shrub rose that Marcus had given her when they'd moved here to Pescallo. Many years ago on a trip to England with Marcus she had visited Sissinghurst Castle Garden in Kent, the home of Vita Sackville-West and Harold Nicolson, and had been so enthralled and inspired by the famous White Garden, with its formal box hedge parterre and serene colour scheme, that when she and Marcus returned home she had promised herself she would create her own scaled-down version. Even now, with such a black cloud hanging over their lives, her modest homage to Sissinghurst still filled her with joyful satisfaction. As well as being a welcome balm on a hot day, it had long since become a place of sanctuary for her. Never more so than now. She hoped that maybe it would come to mean as much to Marcus and would bring him a degree of consolation.

The ring of her mobile sounded in the still, warm air. She put down her secateurs and walked quickly up the length of lawn to where she'd left the phone so that she wouldn't miss the all-important call she was waiting for. She crossed herself, took a deep, bracing breath, and flipped open the mobile. When she saw that the caller wasn't who she was expecting, she relaxed.

But not for long.

Fate seemed to be pushing them in one unavoidable and inevitable direction, she thought minutes later when she'd rung off. She could have said no to Claudia at the agency; after all, she was planning on resigning in the next couple of weeks, so that she could concentrate on her magazine work whilst they still wanted her. But she hadn't. She'd said yes because a part of her wanted to believe that nothing was going to change.

It wasn't unusual for her to stand in at the last minute for a tour guide who was sick, but the group she would be leading this afternoon was no ordinary group – it was the British party of garden enthusiasts staying at the Villa Rosa Hotel, one of whom was Marcus's daughter, Lucy. She didn't know how Marcus would react – he was inside the house working in his study – but she had no intention of seeking his approval.

She didn't fool herself that overnight Lucy would want to be best friends with her, but what really mattered was the hope that at long last, the girl might be capable of forgiving her father. Maybe Francesca as well. So, this afternoon they would meet for the very first time. There was a risk that Lucy, once she realized who their guide was, might become upset, but it was a risk Francesca was prepared to take. She would introduce herself to the group simply as Francesca, making no mention of her surname, and if Lucy became suspicious and hostile as a result, she would deal with whatever situation arose. She didn't think this would happen, though. Her hope, if Lucy did work out who she was, was that Lucy would use the opportunity to observe her and perhaps come to the conclusion that she wasn't the so bad after all.

Marcus would probably say that she was forcing Lucy's hand too soon, but Francesca had kept her counsel for long enough. It was perhaps the only thing she had ever shown any patience over. Hot-headed impulsiveness came more naturally to her than cautious restraint, as her family would be the first to say. Hadn't it been her crazy impulsiveness that had got her involved with Marcus in the first place?

But now it was time to bring matters to their rightful conclusion. She wasn't afraid to confront whatever needed confronting.

Lucy was having lunch with Alessio. The small fishing village he'd brought her to was charming and had seemingly appeared out of nowhere. Back on the busy main street of Bellagio, he had told her it was a short walk away and using his mobile he'd phoned ahead to book them a table at the one and only restaurant. It had taken them no more than ten minutes to get here but the sun had been high and hot and the winding path they'd followed had been both steep and cobbled. Once they had dropped down onto flatter ground and were in the cool shade of a narrow wall-lined path, they were passing pretty houses of dusky pink, terracotta and caramel. Some were draped in lush green ivy, some had balconies of scarlet geraniums and purple salvias, and some were partially hidden behind towering cypress trees, wrought-iron gates or high walls covered in yet more ivy.

When they had arrived at the pink-walled Pergola Ristorante, Alessio was greeted warmly by an attractive, olive-skinned girl who clearly knew him. Lucy had stood to one side, letting them get on with the protracted greeting. She had decided that very likely there wasn't a girl in the area whom Alessio didn't know – intimately or otherwise.

They were shown to a table out on the terrace in the shade of a well-established vine that sprawled the full width and length of the pergola. Beneath them was the pebbly shore of the lake, littered with a row of beached fishing boats, their hulls cluttered with nets, spare oars and buckets. Moored further out were sailing boats of various sizes and colours, their masts swaying to the subtle rhythm of the water. It was as picturesque as it was peaceful.

They were now on to their main course, having already polished off two plates of king prawns in olive oil and garlic. Had Lucy been on a date, she would never have eaten garlic, but this was no date: this was lunch with the local Lothario who wasn't going to get so much as a peck on the cheek from her.

Although – and she would never admit this out loud – she could think of worse men to kiss. He was a stunner, no two ways about it. But she'd sooner undergo colonic irrigation on national television than let him know she thought this. All the same, he was excellent company and, unusually for a man, wasn't bursting to talk about himself the whole time. He'd listened to her telling him about putting Savannah in her place up at the Serbelloni – though she'd kept the bones of the disagreement to herself – and he'd asked her about her job back in England, all the while hardly revealing anything about himself. Perhaps he'd learned that listening was the best way to a girl's heart.

'Lucy, why are you staring at me?' he suddenly asked.

Damn! Caught in the act. How did that happen? 'I wasn't staring at you,' she lied.

'*Sì*. You were studying my face most intently. What were you thinking?'

Oh, no you don't. You're not reeling me in that easily. 'I was thinking about colonic irrigation,' she said.

'Eh?'

She laughed. 'Forget it. How's your pasta?'

'*Perfetta*. And yours?'

'*Perfetta*,' she repeated.

'Ah, so you are learning Italian now. *Brava!* Would you like me to be your *professore*? Your teacher?'

'I don't suppose you'd have time, what with entertaining all the girls you know here in Bellagio.'

'Correction. We're not in Bellagio, we're in Pescallo, where I know only a few girls.'

'Wherever we are, you wouldn't have time—' Her voice broke off. An alarm bell was ringing. 'Where did you say we were?'

'Pescallo. Did I not mention that earlier?'

She felt the colour rise to her face. Pescallo ... wasn't that part of her father's address? She looked anxiously around the terrace. 'No, you didn't,' she said. 'I would have remembered if you had.'

He shrugged. 'More wine?' He held out the bottle.

'Yes,' she muttered. 'More wine is just what I need.' How had she ended up in a restaurant right on her father's doorstep? Once again she glanced around her, half expecting to see him sitting at one of the tables. Which was stupid of her. She had survived this morning's unexpected meeting – she had his telephone number in her bag; she'd even promised she would call him later today – so why the fear and dread? Because it was all happening so fast. For what felt like for ever she had wrapped herself in a protective shell of reproach, and she knew now, having met him this morning, that without that protection she would be left feeling vulnerably exposed.

Alessio looked at her and frowned. 'What is wrong? Have I said something to upset you?'

'Nothing's wrong.'

'Yes, it is. I can see it in your eyes. You are upset with me for bringing you here? Why?'

'I ...' Oh, what the hell! Why not tell him? What harm could it do? She took a gulp of her wine. 'My father lives here in Pescallo.'

'Your father? Here? *Davvéro*? Why didn't you say anything?'

'For a start I didn't know where you were bringing me, and secondly, it's complicated. We've been ...' She tried to think of a suitable word. 'My father and I have been estranged for many years,' she said.

Once more Alessio frowned and she suddenly found herself thinking how sexy it made him look. Inappropriate behaviour, she reminded herself. Get a grip!

He put his elbows on the table and leaned forward, his handsome face even more attractive with the intensely solemn expression he'd adopted. 'Lucy,' he said, 'tell me, what is your surname?'

'It's Gray. Why?'

He snapped back in his seat and banged the flat of his hand down on the table. '*Dio mio! Non ci credo! Non è possibile!*'

'Hey, stick to English, please.'

'Lucy, this is amazing. We are practically related. Now let me see if I can get this right. *Sì, capisco!* Francesca *è la tua matrigna! Mia zia*, Anna – my aunt – is married to Franco, the brother of your step-mother.'

'I don't have a step-mother.'

'*Sì. Sì.* Francesca Gray is married to your father. Your father is Marcus Gray, is he not?'

'Yes, but ... I've never considered her my stepmother.' Even to her own ears, Lucy knew she sounded stubbornly obtuse in the face of legitimate fact.

Alessio picked up his glass of wine and regarded her thoughtfully. 'I've heard a lot about you over the years. I have often wondered what you were like.'

She tilted her chin up. 'Well, now you know. I'm the daughter who could never forgive her father for what he did.'

'For falling in love with a beautiful woman?'

'For leaving me.'

'You had a choice. You could have come to him any time you wanted.'

Her chin dropped. She suddenly felt like she was scaling the sheer face of a mountain, desperately fumbling for a toe-hold. Anything to keep herself from falling backwards, arms and legs flailing, as she contemplated the inconceivable: that she might have been wrong all these years. 'You make it sound so reasonable,' she murmured, 'but I had a mother who wasn't coping. She needed me.'

He sighed. 'I know nothing about your mother, but this I do know; your father needed you too.'

'Then he should have thought about that before taking a hike.' Yes! That was more like it. She was back on firmer ground now. There was no arguing with that!

'A hike? *Che cosa?* I don't understand.'

It was clear that Alessio had a very one-sided view of things and Lucy didn't see any point in pursuing the subject further. 'It doesn't matter,' she said tetchily, at the same time dabbing viciously at some breadcrumbs on the table with her finger.

'No!' Alessio said firmly. 'That is not true. I can see it matters a lot to you. Talk to me, Lucy. Tell me how it has been for you.' His voice was raised and people around them were looking their way.

'Not here,' she said.

'Later, then. When we have finished our lunch, we will go for a walk and you will talk and I will listen.' He leaned forward and covered her hand with his. 'Will you do that?'

She met his gaze – his dark penetrating gaze – and suddenly found it difficult to say anything. Shocked, she looked away. Don't let him see how vulnerable you are right now, she warned herself. Don't make it that easy for him.

Sometimes Helen wondered if Hunter deliberately made it easy for her to pick an argument with him.

Savannah's behaviour at lunch had been atrocious. How Mac and Conrad had forced themselves to endure the meal, she didn't know. She wouldn't have blamed them if they'd made their apologies and slipped away. It had all been so thoroughly embarrassing. Within seconds of Orlando disappearing, Savannah had turned on the waterworks, saying she wasn't feeling well and that it was Lucy's fault for overreacting to what she'd said and that it was so humiliating for her to have Orlando taking Lucy's side. Hunter, of course, had been full of sympathy for her and told her not to worry. 'It'll blow over, Savvie,' he'd said. 'Have something to eat and you'll soon feel a lot better.'

'But he should have backed me up, Dad!'

'I agree, but because Lucy's the one who provides a roof over his head, he's probably just keeping his bread buttered side up. Isn't that right, Helen?'

Helen had stared in amazement at Hunter. Why couldn't he just tear a strip off his daughter for once? She'd been appallingly rude to Lucy. Why did he continually pander to her? Deciding not to make an even bigger scene in public – they'd done enough to appeal to the voyeur in their fellow diners – she said, 'I'd like to think that Orlando was more sincere than that.'

'Don't get me wrong,' Hunter laughed expansively, 'I'm not making him out to be a devious sod, but in my experience one doesn't look a gift horse in the mouth. What do you think, Conrad?'

'I think it's none of my business.' Conrad's tone was measured.

'You must have an opinion, though?'

'I do, but I'd prefer to keep it to myself.'

Their food had arrived then in a flourish of activity but afterwards they'd sat in a prickly atmosphere for the duration of the meal.

Now, back at their hotel, whilst Helen was freshening up before that afternoon's tour and Hunter was packing for Dubai, she decided to say something. 'Have you ever told Savannah off?' she asked him.

He finished folding the last of his shirts and laid it carefully on top of the case. 'You've never been a parent, Helen, so please don't question the way I've brought up my family.'

'Does that mean it's a no-go area for discussion?'

'It is if you're going to criticize the way I handle Savannah.' A coldness had crept into his voice. 'And seeing as you've brought the matter up, it wouldn't have killed you to have shown Savannah some support when Lucy got her claws into her. Anyone would think Lucy meant more to you than my Savvie.'

Helen ignored his rebuke. 'Didn't it cross your mind that Savannah was deliberately stirring things up for Lucy, trying to make her look petty in front of everyone?'

'I think you'll find Lucy did a fair job of that all on her own. Frankly, anyone who's harboured a grudge for that long needs to look very closely at themselves.'

'That sounds overly simplistic to me. Especially as you hardly know Lucy.'

She saw his jaw tighten.

'I haven't got the time or the inclination to listen to this. And if you really want to know what I think, I'm proud of Savannah. She should be applauded for calling a spade a spade. A bit of plain speaking never hurt anyone. Perhaps that's what's been missing from Lucy's life. Maybe she wouldn't be in the mess she is if someone had given her a damn good talking to a long time ago.'

And maybe a damned good shaking while that well-meaning person was about it, thought Helen as she stood in the bathroom and brushed her hair with hard, punishing strokes.

I can't keep doing this, she thought as she looked in the mirror and saw the angry frustration in her face. If I bite my tongue any more I'll bite it clean off. I can't keep bending to his will.

Tears of cruel regret threatened to spill over. No! She told herself. No tears. No feeling sorry for yourself. You knew it wouldn't be easy. 'But I hadn't bargained on hating myself so much,' she whispered bitterly.

Still staring at her reflection, she thought of Hunter's words about Orlando wanting to keep his bread buttered side up. A chill ran through her. Had he been reminding her of her own position?

Chapter Forty-five

Her fingers drumming on the railing of her balcony, Savannah decided that she'd had enough of sulking. For the first time in her life she was getting the feeling that it wasn't going to get her what she wanted. And seeing as Orlando was very much what she wanted, she was going to have to perform a pretty spectacular u-turn to get things how they'd been. If she left things as they were, Lucy would sneak back into the picture and pinch Orlando from right under her nose.

She watched a hydrofoil crossing to the other side of the lake, churning up the smooth water, and thought of the moment it had all started to go wrong. It was at dinner last night, when that piano player had started giving Lucy the come-on. Typical foreign bloke for you. All eyes and no subtlety.

Orlando's reaction had hardly been subtle either. He'd been as mad as hell. Which in turn had pissed Savannah off. Then on top of that, when they'd been alone in his room, he'd come up with some twatty lie about having a headache. If he didn't want to have sex with her, why didn't he just come out and say so?

In the morning everything had suddenly seemed wrong about her being here. What the bastard hell was she doing on a holiday like this with a bunch of aged whiskeries? She should be in Ibiza getting off her head! Except ... then she wouldn't be with Orlando.

She didn't know what it was about him that did it for her, but back in Swanmere she'd always felt better when she was with him. He seemed to enjoy life so much, to be genuinely happy with what he had. He loved his job and rarely had a negative word to say about anything or anyone. It sounded stupid, but he made her want to be the same.

She had tried to tell herself that the only reason he'd gone chasing off after Lucy during lunch was because he was naturally considerate towards other people, that he cared for Lucy as anyone would for an old friend. But somehow, given what a disaster the morning had been, she couldn't quite convince herself that this was all it was. So what was she going to do about it? That was the bastard question.

With hindsight, having a go at Lucy at lunch hadn't been the smartest of moves. But she just couldn't hack Lucy's presence at the table. There she was, chatting, all pally like, with Mac and suddenly Savannah felt hatred for the girl. Trouble was, once she'd started having a go at Lucy, she couldn't stop. She could hear herself making it worse, but instead of keeping quiet she'd blundered on, trying to turn the whole thing into a big joke.

But it hadn't been a joke. Something about the whole scene had reminded her of a day she still hated to think about. It was the day Mum and Dad had told her they were getting a divorce. They'd sprung their news on her during lunch on holiday in the Maldives. One minute they'd been ordering their food and the next Dad was saying, 'We've got something to tell you, Savvie.' Apparently they'd decided to tell her while they were on holiday in the mistaken belief that their surroundings would soften the blow, that it would make the whole thing less upsetting. Their announcement shouldn't have surprised her, not with all the arguments she'd overheard, but it had still been a shock. Divorce was going on around her all the time – any number of her friends' parents were splitting up – but somehow she'd never thought it would happen to her own parents. She'd stupidly believed that she was the one thing holding them together. Hadn't Dad always said that there wasn't anything he wouldn't do for her? No amount of palm tree fringed beaches or rum punch was going to take the sting out of their selfishness. She'd listened to them explaining how very little was going to change for her – she and Mum would stay in the house in Crantsford but Dad would be moving out. But, and this was important: wherever he lived, it would be Savannah's home too. She could even help him find a new house. Yeah right, she'd thought, like she had any say in what was going on. And then she'd burst into tears and refused to speak to them for the following two days. She'd holed herself up in her room realizing that grown-ups only ever thought of themselves. That they didn't give a toss how screwed up their actions made their children feel. She could still remember thinking how she'd teach them a lesson, that she'd make them miserable for doing this to her. But here was the thing: nothing she did bothered them. They hardly seemed aware of her at times. That was when she'd started staying out all hours in Manchester getting drunk. Anything was better than being stuck at home on her own. Mum was always out with some bloke or other and Dad – well, Dad was doing what he always did, pulling off some deal somewhere.

So when Lucy was sitting across the table from her with everyone rushing to protect her, it had made Savannah want to yell, 'Oh, give it a rest, why don't you? We've all been there, all done it and all got over it! What makes you think you're any different from the rest of us?'

Why Dad had insisted on Lucy joining them for lunch, Savannah didn't know. But that was her father all over – generous to a fault but completely blind to anyone else's feelings.

And now he'd gone off to Dubai again, but not before she'd managed to get some money out of him. He'd handed over a stack of Euros and said, 'Treat yourself to something nice while I'm gone. Something to put the smile back on your face.'

There was only one thing that would put a smile on her face and that was if she could get things with Orlando back to how they'd been before last night. And probably the only way to do that was to apologize to him. She'd sooner he made the first move and said he was sorry for taking Lucy's side, but she figured an apology from her would have the desired effect.

With ten minutes to go until they were supposed to be meeting Philippa downstairs in the foyer, Savannah went to knock on Orlando's door.

He didn't look too pleased to see her, but she didn't doubt that she could win him round. Hadn't she had years of experience of wrapping her father around her little finger? A shame Lucy hadn't learned the same trick. She'd be less of a pain if she'd discovered how easy it was to play the guilt-trick game – playing one parent off another and getting what you wanted, whenever you wanted it.

Conrad was worried about Mac. This afternoon's tour of the park at Villa Serbelloni – not the hotel, but a conference and study centre owned by the Rockefeller Foundation – had so far involved a lot of strenuous uphill walking. The sun was even more intense than it had been in the morning and Mac had forgotten his hat. Conrad could deal with a crotchety Mac, but a dehydrated Mac suffering from heatstroke and exhaustion was something he could do without. Each time their replacement guide, an attractive Italian woman called Francesca, had something to tell them about the park and the surrounding area, Conrad tried to manoeuvre his uncle into the shade. 'Don't fuss over me,' Mac, red-faced and panting, would growl. It would be so easy for Conrad to give up on the old fool, but he knew he'd never forgive himself if he did that. Like an ancient married couple, they were joined at the hip, whether they liked it or not. All he could do was keep a surreptitious eye on his uncle and hope for the best.

He was also keeping a discreet eye on Helen, conscious that ever since they'd set off from the hotel with their new guide she had kept her distance from him. Unluckily for her, Swanmere's Holy Trinity – Olivia, Vi and Barbara – had taken it upon themselves to add her to their number. 'We can't have you all on your lonesome,' Conrad had overheard Vi saying to Helen.

Another steep climb ahead of them, Conrad slowed his pace to match Mac's. 'You're not fooling me,' Mac said. 'I know what you're up to.'

'Good. So let me get on with it in peace.'

'I wish Lucy were here. She never fusses over me. Where do you suppose she is?'

'Seeing her father again, maybe.'

'I'm sure she would have said something at lunch if she'd made plans to do that.'

'Perhaps Savannah's performance brought on a change of plan?'

'You could be right.' Mac paused to wipe the perspiration from his forehead with a handkerchief. 'All in all, that was quite a lunch, wasn't it?'

'Excruciatingly awful is how I'd describe it. Why are we always so damned polite? We should have both walked away.'

'Oh, come on, Conrad, you were as curious as I was to see how much worse things could get. I wouldn't have missed it for the world.'

'You sick bastard!'

They both laughed in a rare moment of accord. Before long, though, Conrad became immersed again in his own thoughts.

Hunter.

Helen.

What was he doing involving himself in their lives? Did he really want to risk getting on the wrong side of a man like Hunter? Or was it too late? Was he already on the wrong side of him? Judging by some of the comments Hunter had made today, it was quite possible that he was on to Conrad. Why else had he pressed him the way he had at lunch? And why else had he made those comments about not looking a gift horse in the mouth and keeping one's bread buttered side up? They were warning shots, directed not at him, but at Helen. He was sure of it.

Aware that Mac, along with everyone else, had stopped to take advantage of a photo opportunity, Conrad took in the view. Set against a backdrop of azure blue water was a hillside of lush vegetation and cypress trees. In the distance was a small, isolated village. Disorientated for a moment, he tried to work out which side of the promontory they were now on. He wasn't the only one to be wondering this – a clamour of voices rose as everyone started examining their maps, turning them round and pointing. Conrad noticed their guide was smiling.

'The village you can see is called Pescallo,' she said. 'It's a delightful fishing village and I would strongly recommend you visit it. There's also a wonderful restaurant there.'

'Is it easy to get to?' asked the mealy-mouthed troublemaker in the drawstring trousers.

'It's a relatively short walk, but as is typical of this area, the path is quite steep in parts. Now, if everyone has taken their pictures, shall we move on?'

'Just one more?'

This was from Savannah, who was telling Orlando to smile. Despite her encouragement, he didn't look like he wanted to. He looked embarrassingly uncomfortable, especially now that everyone was staring at him.

Mac sidled over to Conrad. 'So what did you make of that pretty little apology Savannah made to us earlier whilst we were waiting for our guide to appear?'

'I thought I was going to be sick.'

'Me too. She's quite a performer, isn't she? Oscar-winning material.'

'You don't think she meant it, then?'

'I wouldn't be at all surprised if Helen told her to do it as a lesson in good manners. Just as she did when the wretched girl nearly ran over Fritz.'

'You're wrong.'

They both turned to see Helen standing behind them. Her expression was so fierce, Conrad almost jumped back.

'I can assure you I had absolutely nothing to do with that girl's apology,' she said. 'More likely it was Orlando who twisted her arm.'

'Oh. Well. I'm glad we've got that sorted,' Conrad said nervously. He could feel an anger as hot as the sun coming off Helen. 'How do you like the garden here?' *Atta-boy! If in doubt, reach for your lexicon of small talk!*

'The views are good,' she said flatly, 'but the garden itself is disappointing.'

'I agree,' said Mac. 'It's too much like a municipal park.'

'That's it, exactly.'

'And there was me thinking I was missing something,' said Conrad. 'Now I don't feel such a lowbrow. Come on, we'd better catch up with the group.'

With Mac playing piggy in the middle, the three of them fell in step. They walked along the gravelled path in silence until Helen said, 'I suppose I should apologize for lunch. It was quite horrendous, wasn't it? I'm so sorry.'

'No argument there, my dear,' Mac said. 'But we don't hold you personally responsible. The conversation may have been a little hard going, but at least the food was delicious.'

'I could cheerfully wring Savannah's neck. And then her father's.'

'Presumably he got off okay?' Conrad said, giving himself the pleasure of mentally helping Helen to throttle her husband.

'I assume so. I left him waiting for his taxi so he could go off to play the big tycoon.'

'Sorry to be a pedant, but he is a big tycoon, Helen.'

'I know, Mac, but sometimes it would be nice to think I was married to a normal man.'

'No such thing, my dear. We men are all shallow, egotistical beasts.'

'Speak for yourself,' said Conrad.

Helen smiled and Conrad sensed her anger beginning to cool. She hadn't risked a direct look at him, though, he noted.

Ahead of them their guide was saying that it was all downhill from now on and they should take extra care on the path where the ground was loose and stony in places.

'She's very good, our new guide, isn't she?' Mac said. 'Very easy on the eye. Philippa was all right, but she was a little lacking in the looks department. This one's definitely an improvement.'

Helen gave him a playful flick with her hand. 'You sexist pig! I'm glad I never had you in one of my tour groups.'

'Nonsense. You would have loved the attention. I might even have swept you off your feet.'

'In your dreams!'

They turned a corner and entered a refreshingly cool tunnel of trees and rhododendron bushes. 'That's better,' Mac said with a sigh. 'I had no idea it would be so hot.'

'You should have brought a hat,' Helen told him.

'Not you as well. I've had enough of that from Conrad. Oh, look,' he said, stooping to peer into the undergrowth on the edge of the path. 'Cyclamen. I've never been able to grow them successfully. I swear Fritz sniffs out the corms, digs them up and eats them.'

Helen smiled. 'Have you spoken to Evie today?'

'Yes, I phoned home this morning. She said Fritz is as big a pain as his owner. The cheeky bint. I don't know what possessed me to think it would be a good idea to ask her to dog-sit for me.'

'What tosh! The pair of you are devoted to each other.'

Mac laughed. 'That'll be the day. And what about you? Have you phoned home to check on your grandmother?'

'Yes. I did it after breakfast. All's well, apparently.'

'That's excellent.'

As he so often did when Mac was dominating the conversation with Helen, Conrad let his uncle get on with it. Mac always seemed to know the right thing to say to cheer her up. It made Conrad think that in his younger day, Mac's pulling power must have been quite something. It was a shame that he himself didn't have the same relaxing effect on Helen.

'Do you know where Lucy is?' he heard Helen asking Mac.

'No, we were discussing that earlier. Conrad thinks she might have gone to see her father.'

Helen turned to Conrad. Her gaze, like a skittish butterfly, finally came to rest on his.

'It was only a guess,' he said, managing a weak smile. 'For all I know she could be happily sunning herself somewhere with a glass of wine in her hand. Something I wouldn't mind doing right now.'

'Me too,' Helen said quietly. Her face, which earlier had looked hard and ready for battle, was now soft and beguiling.

He swallowed. 'Then let's do it when we're finished here.'
Mac cleared his throat noisily, presumably as a warning.
Too late for that, thought Conrad. Much too late.

Chapter Forty-six

With her head tipped back and her eyes closed, Lucy was sunning herself on the pebbly shore of the lake at Pescallo. She couldn't remember the last time she'd felt this good, or this deliciously lazy. The amount of wine she and Alessio had put away during lunch might well be responsible, but hey, she was on holiday and could do as she wanted. Which included behaving badly.

Opting out from the group's action-packed itinerary this afternoon was her first act of rebellion and she didn't care. She wasn't even that bothered that she was less than five minutes away from her father's house. Alessio had offered to show her where he lived, but she'd said it could wait. For now she was happy to sit here with the sun on her face and forget all her troubles.

It was funny; she had known Alessio for less than twenty-four hours, yet she felt extraordinarily connected to him. She had told him everything that really mattered to her. She had shared things with him that she hadn't even told Orlando. How, when she'd tried to support her mother through the really bad times, she had helped Fiona destroy anything that reminded her of Marcus Gray. Together they'd smashed, ripped and burned anything that he had left behind. They systematically took apart the photograph albums, removing pictures, or slicing them up, so every last trace of the man was eradicated from their lives. 'He's never coming back to us, Lucy,' her mother had told her as they stood by the bonfire they'd made in the garden, watching the flames lick and curl around his hateful image, 'so what's the point in keeping anything of him?' Her mother had found her crying in bed that night; clutched in Lucy's hand was a photograph she'd kept of her father. When Fiona saw it, she snatched it away from her and ripped it up, letting the pieces drop to the floor. In the morning, Lucy flushed the pieces down the toilet. One small fragment stubbornly remained. It took four more flushes to get rid of it.

If Alessio was shocked by what she told him, he didn't show it. He simply listened and never once lost eye contact with her. He was so focused. She'd found it unnerving at first, but gradually she grew used to it. He in turn had told her about his family – the family her father had married into. He spoke of the happy, carefree childhood he'd experienced, how special his parents and relatives had made him feel whilst growing up, and their encouragement to pursue his love of music. 'You're telling me you were a spoilt child by the sounds of it,' she'd teased him.

'I like to think so,' he'd smiled.

And then he'd said something that surprised her: that his family was her family too. Now that was a strange thought – suddenly discovering that there were all these people who knew of her existence, but whom she knew nothing about. It certainly made her wonder.

Almost as much as she wondered about her reaction to Alessio himself. She alternated between feeling perfectly relaxed in his company when they were talking, but the moment they fell quiet she was suddenly aware of the attraction she felt for him. It was quite disconcerting.

Now, as she sat next to him, she was conscious that Orlando was a long way from her thoughts. She decided this was a good thing. Right now, she was happier and more relaxed than she'd been in months.

Nearby a group of young children – Italian children – were playing at the water's edge. Two were fishing with makeshift rods of sticks and string, while another, the smallest, with a mop of black curly hair, was peering into a plastic bucket. His navy-blue shorts and stripy T-shirt were much too big for him and with his huge dark eyes and long lashes, he looked adorable. Lucy wondered if Alessio had been as sweet at that age. Probably yes. A heartbreaker then, just as he was now.

She wanted to turn and study his face, but didn't dare. She wanted to analyse that beautifully shaped mouth of his, and the way his eyebrows arched when she said something he didn't understand. She liked the way his eyes had danced with amusement earlier, when he'd told her that from now on he was going to call her by her Italian name, Lucia. Instead, she kept it safe and sneaked a glance at his hands. They were not the work-roughened hands of a gardener, unlike hers. Or Orlando's. Smooth with long, slender fingers, they were sensual, yet gave the impression of being immensely strong. She watched him playing with a stone, switching it from one smooth palm to the other. She wondered what it would be like to be touched by those hands.

'Lucia?'

She turned her head to look at Alessio and fell headlong into his amazing eyes. Her stomach lurched and she felt like she'd just fallen off a cliff. *What was it about him*? 'Yes,' she managed to say.

'I'm glad that you are Marcus's daughter; it means that you will have to come back again.' He smiled. 'And, even better, I will get to see you again.'

'That all rather depends on how things turn out with my father,' she said.

He reached for her hand just as he had in the restaurant during lunch. 'I think it depends on you, Lucia. Your father loves you, that much I know. All you have to do is find it in your heart to forgive him.'

Oh, here we go again. Why did everyone assume that her father loved her? Where was the evidence? But how could she expect Alessio to understand when she could scarcely put her feelings into words herself? She tried to slip her hand out from his, but he kept hold of it. She said, 'Unless you've experienced the same situation, you can't possibly understand how complicated it is.'

'I agree. But maybe it is better if you try to simplify things. It is what I do.'

I bet you do, she thought.

He went on: 'I have the Italian soul. I am romantic by nature, but always pragmatic. That is how I keep things simple. I am often told I love too easily.'

'And do you?'

'Love is a search, I've come to believe. One keeps going until one has found what one is looking for. And you, Lucia. Do you love easily?'

She paused to think about this. 'No,' she said at length. 'I don't believe I do.'

He stroked her hand. 'As I thought. You don't love enough. That is a pity. *Allora*. Why don't we play a game?'

'What sort of game?' she asked guardedly, still pondering over what he'd said and not liking the picture it painted of her.

He pulled her to her feet. '*Andiamo!*' He led her to the water's edge.

'You're not going to push me in, are you?'

'Would you like me to?'

'Don't even think about it.'

He bent down to pick up a stone and passed it to her. It was flat and warmed by the sun. 'You have played this before, I am sure,' he said as he selected a stone for himself.

'Many times,' she answered.

'But we will play it differently. If I am the winner, my reward is a kiss from you. How does that sound?'

'But what if I'm the winner?'

He flashed her one of his super-megawatt smiles. 'I don't think that will happen. I am very good at this game.'

It was all the encouragement she needed to bring out the arch competitor in her and give him a thorough thrashing.

'Watch and learn,' she said, getting into position and flexing her arm.

Chapter Forty-seven

At last they were alone. Or as alone as the San Remo bar with its lakeside view allowed them to be. The open-air bar was crowded with tourists; all around him, Conrad could hear a plethora of languages being spoken – German, Swedish, Dutch, American, Russian, and even Italian.

In contrast, he and Helen had hardly uttered a word and the tension between them was so palpable he longed simply to take her in his arms and convince her everything would be all right. He didn't have a clue what his definition of 'all right' was, but he'd do anything to take that strained look off her face and make her relax in his company. He didn't think he'd ever seen her look so miserable. As before, it pained him to think that he might be responsible. To assuage his guilt he told himself that it wasn't him who was the root of her problems, it was that bloody awful husband of hers.

A breeze was blowing across the lake, skimming the surface, making the water ripple and glint in the late afternoon sunshine. Over in Tremezzo, where they'd been that morning, the white façade of Villa Carlotta stood out, along with the orangey-red awnings of the Hotel Tremezzo. Nearer to where they were sitting, a small boat jam-packed with tourists was disembarking at the nearby pontoon. The boat didn't look large enough for the number of middle-aged passengers clambering out of it, all of whom were laughing and shrieking at the top of their voices. They were unmistakably British. 'Our country's finest ambassadors,' Conrad muttered under his breath.

'You sound like Mac.'

Conrad groaned. 'Oh, please, I can take any kind of criticism you care to level at me, but don't ever liken me to Mac.'

'You don't really mean that.'

'Don't I?'

'I think you're far closer to Mac than you allow yourself to admit.'

'And why wouldn't I admit to being close to him?'

'Because he knows you better than anyone else alive. He's been there for the best times of your life and the worst. It can't always be easy for you.'

This wasn't the conversation he'd expected them to have and he shifted in his seat, feeling the spotlight was just a little too focused on him. 'You've given this a good deal of thought.'

She took a sip of her wine. 'And you haven't?'

'When you've had a really big life-changing moment, you learn to accept whatever comes your way. You don't reason it out, ad infinitum.'

'I don't believe you. I don't think you do anything without putting a lot of thought into the matter. Isn't that why we're here?'

'Are you saying I've manipulated you? Forced or tricked you here against your will?'

Her face softened with a small smile. 'You can be very persuasive.'

'Only because—' He stopped himself short and shifted again in his seat.

'Only because of what?'

'I was going to say something crass. Something along the lines of you being so tempting.'

Now her face coloured. 'I'm glad you didn't. It would only have embarrassed me.'

'Me, too. How's your wine?'

'Fine. And your beer?'

'It's fine.'

'Good.'

He risked a smile. 'So much for the small talk.'

'Is that what we were doing?'

'It's what we always do. It stops us from saying anything we might regret.'

'That has to be a good thing, doesn't it?'

'Except it could lead us going round in ever-decreasing circles.'

'Which, by definition would imply we'd eventually—' Now it was her turn to stop short.

'Yes,' he said. 'We'd eventually meet up somewhere in the middle. Together.'

She looked away, distracted by Britain's Finest Ambassadors

who had made their raucous way up the pontoon and were now scanning the bar for somewhere they could all sit. One of them declared the obvious, that there was no room at this particular inn, and they moved on to the next bar.

'We're going to have to talk properly some time, Helen; why not give it a go now?' He watched her draw a line in the condensation that had formed on her wine glass.

'You know I won't do anything to jeopardize my marriage.'

He'd heard her say as much before but he sensed there was less conviction behind her words this time. 'Are you happy?' he asked.

'Are you?'

'I'm happy sitting here with you. And I think you could be if only you'd let yourself.'

She swallowed nervously and chewed on her lip. 'But you don't understand,' she murmured, 'there's so much at stake.'

He watched her closely, sensing that it was a make or break moment. One more push and whatever it was that was holding her back – that was stopping her from being honest with him – would be no more. He noticed she was fiddling with the gruesome emerald ring on her finger. 'Go on,' he pressed, 'tell me exactly what's at stake. And while you're about it, tell me what could be more important than your happiness. Because from where I'm standing, I've never seen you happy in your husband's company.'

She whipped her head round and looked him squarely in the eye. So squarely he knew with crystalline certainty he was going to regret pushing her. 'Okay,' she said, her voice as firm as the strength of her gaze, 'I'll tell you what's more important to me than my own happiness. My grandmother's. That's what means the world to me. My grandmother being happy.'

Now he was confused. 'Your grandmother? What does she have to do with it?'

'How do you think I can afford to keep her in such an expensive nursing home? I sold myself, Conrad. I sold myself to Hunter to make sure Emma would never have to suffer at the hands of some sadistic nurse who would leave her to freeze in a cold bath. I married him to keep Emma safe from some perverse freak who thought old people were fair game for a bit of slap and tickle, who claimed that the bruises I found on Emma were a result of her falling out of bed.'

Conrad listened in horror, then all at once the strength went out of Helen and she started to cry. 'I'm so sorry,' he said. 'I had no idea.' He reached out to put his arm around her, but she put her hand up to stop him.

'No! There's nothing you can say.' She rummaged in her bag, and thinking that she was looking for a tissue, he found one from his trouser pocket for her. Once again she shrugged his help away and threw some Euros onto the table. 'Don't let it ever be said that I tried to sponge off you as well.' She then jumped to her feet and threaded her way through the closely packed tables.

He went after her. 'Helen, please. I don't give a damn why you married Hunter. I love you.' He tried to grab hold of her but she wrenched herself free from his grasp.

'No, you don't! After what I've done, I don't deserve to be loved by anyone. Certainly not by anyone as kind and as genuine as you.'

'Don't ever say that about yourself. Anyone would have done what you did.'

'Would you?'

'Yes. I'd do anything for the person I loved. *Anything.*'

Fresh tears spilled from her eyes and he put his arms around her. 'Come on,' he said, the roar of traffic almost drowning out his voice, 'let's find somewhere quieter to talk.'

They'd almost reached the end of the flower-filled promenade before they found a free bench. They sat down, but still Conrad didn't take his arm away from her. He'd kept it round her shoulder the whole time they'd been walking. It felt good. Just as the silence had. Yet now Helen knew she would have to talk. She wasn't sure she could manage it. Hearing herself confessing aloud that she had sold herself for her grandmother's sake had been so very painful. The truth was like that – hard to swallow but harder still to live with.

'I'm sorry I pushed you the way I did,' Conrad said.

'Please don't keep apologizing,' she replied. 'It's me who's to blame.'

He took his arm away from her shoulder and turned her to face him. 'What exactly are you to blame for?'

'For not being fairer to you. For letting you think there was any chance of us being more than friends.'

He frowned. 'You never encouraged me, Helen. Far from it. And for the record, we were more than friends the moment we met. I looked into your eyes and knew that you would always be in my future.'

'I didn't ever mean for that to happen.'

'That's what falling in love is about. It's not something you have any control over.' He took her hands in his and held them tightly. 'Listen to me, Helen; you deserve a second chance. You can change your life. It's not too late.'

'But you don't understand. I care about Hunter. You don't know him the way I do. Also, I'm … I'm obligated. I have a duty to be the best possible wife I can be to Hunter.'

'Obligated. Duty. Listen to yourself, Helen! These aren't the words of an intelligent forty-five-year-old woman living in the twenty-first century. What the hell's he turned you into?'

She snatched her hands away from his. 'It's what *I've* turned myself into.'

'Rubbish! He's manipulated you, Helen. He knows full well what's going on inside your head and he turns the screw every now and then just to keep you in your place. What he said about Orlando wanting to keep his bread buttered side up had nothing to do with Orlando; it was a message to you. He shores up his massive ego by making others dependent upon him. He's a shrewd and clever man, Helen, make no mistake, but he's going to trip himself up sooner or later. I guarantee.'

Surprised at the vehemence of Conrad's words, Helen said, 'You make him out to be some kind of monster.'

Conrad's jaw was set firm. 'In my eyes, he is.'

'But don't forget what he's doing for Emma.'

'Yes. And that will always be his trump card. As he well knows. Does he ever visit her? Does he ever suggest you should have her to stay? Or offer to take her places with you?'

'He's a busy man. He's—'

'You're making excuses for him. I'm a busy man too, but I'd still make time for you and the person who means the most to you.'

Helen remembered their day at Wollerton Old Hall Garden and Conrad's sensitivity towards her grandmother. It was the day that had changed everything for her, when she'd understood just what she'd done and how trapped she was. She blinked back the threat of another bout of tears. 'None of what you say changes anything, Conrad,' she said. 'I'm married to the man who pays the bills for Emma. And that's an end to it.'

'But you needn't be. You have a choice. There must be other

nursing homes, cheaper ones that could take care of Emma. They can't all be as awful as the one she was in before.'

'She's had enough changes. She's happy where she is. I'm not prepared to take the risk. She means too much to me. If it was Mac, would you want to inflict yet more unnecessary upheaval on him?'

'Mac wouldn't want me to give up everything for him. That much I know.'

'Emma is beyond understanding what I've done for her, but I know that she's settled where she is and is extremely well cared for. It's peace of mind for me. You don't know how awful the guilt was, and still is, knowing that I was responsible for putting her in that dreadful place and leaving her there. I didn't believe her when she said she was frightened whenever I left her. I thought it was her mind going. That she was acting like a child.'

'You couldn't have known.'

She lowered her head, letting her hair flop down in front of her face so that he couldn't see her expression. 'But that's the worst bit,' she said quietly. 'I knew. Or rather I suspected. But I didn't know what else to do.'

'Didn't you confront the staff?'

'I tried, but they closed ranks. You have no idea how much abuse goes on when it comes to the elderly. Child abuse is talked about all the time now, but shameful neglect or downright cruelty inflicted on a defenceless old man or woman is still conveniently ignored in certain quarters.'

In the painful silence that followed, she felt a hand lightly touch her cheek. She looked up and allowed Conrad to gently push her hair away from her face. The tender love in his eyes was too much to bear and she tried to turn away. He wouldn't let her.

'You should divorce him, Helen,' he said. 'Take the settlement you'd be entitled to and use it for Emma's benefit.'

'And just how would I live with myself if I did that on top of everything else?'

'Then let me take care of you.'

Chapter Forty-eight

It had been a long day for Marcus. He'd tried to concentrate on work but it had been a lost cause. Whenever his mobile rang his heart jolted and he caught his breath. Each time he answered it, though, he had to endure a thump of disappointment. None of the callers had been Lucy and he'd rudely hurried the conversations along so that the line wouldn't be engaged when she did call. Perhaps it had happened several times already and she'd given up trying.

He swivelled his chair and looked out at the garden and the view of the lake that he'd derived such pleasure from ever since moving here. Often when he was unable to concentrate on work, or he had some problem to deal with, he would go for a row in the dinghy Francesca had bought for him. He would row and row until the last vestiges of whatever it was that was troubling him had been seen off. He doubted it would work today, but he decided the distraction might be worth a try. Slipping his mobile into his pocket, he went to find Francesca, then remembered she'd had a last-minute request from the agency to escort a tour group somewhere.

That was what she'd told him.

He groaned. His suspicious mind was getting worse. He had to stop it. More importantly, he had to talk to Francesca. Just as soon as he knew where he stood with Lucy, he would find out where he stood with his wife.

At the bottom of the garden, he unlocked the boathouse he'd built with the help of his brothers-in-law, and hauled the boat down onto the shingle and the water's edge. He pulled off his socks and shoes, rolled up his jeans and pushed the dinghy further into the lake. He winced at the coldness of the water as it lapped around his shins and then stepped into the wooden hull. With a strong, rhythmic stroke, he powered away from the shore, and with little boating traffic to worry about, unlike the Bellagio side of the lake, he was able to row without having constantly to glance over his shoulder. He passed the promontory that separated their villa from their nearest neighbours – a Swiss couple who owned a chain of restaurants and who spent their summers here and their winters in St Moritz.

The sun was dropping in the sky, making him squint. He was hot and sweating from all the exertion. But at least he was doing something positive, which had to be better than sitting in his study waiting for Lucy to get in touch. All day he'd wondered where she was and what she was doing. Was she thinking of him? And if she was, *what* was she thinking? He'd never felt so vulnerable in all his life. As Lucy's silence continued, he knew that he was being judged – did she or did she not want to see him again? – and there wasn't a damned thing he could do about it, except wait for what was beginning to feel like the Sword of Damocles to fall on him.

He pulled on the oars, harder and faster, and when at last he'd gone as far as he wanted, he began rowing towards the shore. Needing to catch his breath, he drifted for a while, then knowing that he was within range of the Pergola Ristorante, where there was always more boating activity going on, he turned to check for other boats. Save for an elderly man fishing, his passage was clear. Seconds later, the sound of laughter followed by a high-pitched scream had him turning to look again. In the distance, at the water's edge, he could see a young couple larking about on the beach. The man had the girl over his shoulder and was threatening to drop her into the water while she was laughing and pummelling his back with her fists. Marcus stopped rowing and smiled at their antics. After the day he'd had it was good to see people enjoying themselves. It occurred to him that it was a while since he and Francesca had laughed together. He tried to think when that had started – the uneasy quiet between them – but couldn't come up with anything specific, other than it was weeks rather than months.

Another loud shriek had him looking at the couple once more. Watched by three young children, the man had carried out his threat and the girl was soaked from the waist down. Her language was pretty colourful. And was English, Marcus registered with a delayed reaction. 'Alessio, just you wait!' she screamed, her voice carrying clearly across the water. She then went after him. But he was too fast for her and had already made a run for it up the beach.

Marcus could hardly take in what he was seeing. But there was no mistaking what he was watching. He thought about rowing flat out to the shore, jumping from the boat and grabbing hold of Alessio by the throat, asking him what the hell he thought he was doing with Lucy. For pity's sake, she'd only been here twenty-four hours and the dog had made a move on her! No wonder he hadn't heard from her all day!

But do that and he'd lose what little stock he had with his daughter. If he had any at all. Moreover, they would probably be long gone before he made it to the beach. So instead he dipped an oar into the water and manoeuvred the boat so that he didn't have to twist round to see what else Alessio was up to with Lucy. With the water lapping against the hull, shielding his eyes from the sun, he suddenly wished he was anywhere but here. Alessio had taken Lucy in his arms and was kissing her.

Marcus gripped the oars so tightly his shoulders shook. Just about every man that was connected to Francesca's family thought Alessio was the epitome of what a red-blooded Italian male should be. They were proud of his prodigious track record of having bedded more girls than the rest of them put together. His legendary promiscuity was a sign of heightened manhood to them, and they seemed to live off it vicariously. The women were equally enamoured with Alessio, always charmed by his attention, and always given to spoiling him. Francesca said that he'd been the same when he was a small boy, a child who could get away with murder because he was so adorable, as well as being a precocious talent at the piano when he was only six years old.

But how would any of them feel if it was their daughter who was about to be added to Alessio's list of conquests then tossed aside when he'd finished with her?

By the time he'd rowed home, had dragged the boat up the shingle and into the boathouse, Marcus had worked himself into such a state he could scarcely think. A fury like no other he'd experienced was boiling within him.

Francesca had returned from wherever she'd been and was in the garden picking tomatoes for supper that evening. She took one look at him and said, 'What on earth's happened to you? You look dreadful.'

'I'll tell you after I've had a very large drink.'

She followed him into the house and to the drinks cabinet in the dining room, where he poured himself a generous Scotch. 'Is it Lucy?' she asked. 'Have you had a row? Has she—'

'It's not Lucy,' he snapped. 'It's that spoiled sod Alessio! I tell you, when I get my hands on him he'll be lucky to play the fool, never mind the piano!' He knocked back half the drink in one go, then added some more to the glass.

'Alessio? What could he possibly have done to upset you like this?'

Marcus's throat was burning nicely now. So was his temper. 'I've just seen him and Lucy together. He was ... he was doing what he always does. Trying out one of his little numbers on her. God, he makes me sick!'

The surprise showed on Francesca's face. 'But he doesn't even know Lucy!' she said. 'He's never met her.'

'Yes, he has. God knows how or when, but I've just seen him kissing her.'

'Where?'

'On the mouth, where else!'

She frowned. 'I didn't mean that. I meant where did you see them?'

'I couldn't concentrate on work so I went for a row.' He took another long, angry slug of Scotch. 'I saw them on the beach here in Pescallo. At first they were just mucking about, but then he kissed her. And please don't suggest that I mistook what I saw.'

'Did Lucy look like she was resisting him?'

'Oh, for goodness sake, what kind of a question is that? How should I know!' He downed the rest of his drink and banged the glass down on the sideboard.

Francesca came towards him. 'Marcus, she's a grown woman. If she didn't want to be kissed by Alessio, or any man for that matter, she wouldn't go along with it. And who knows, for all we—'

He raised his hand to interrupt her. 'If you're going to say that for all I know she might have been the one to instigate things, then don't bother. We both know what a sexual predator Alessio is. He's only ever after one thing.'

Francesca stared steadily back at him. 'What annoys you most, Marcus? That Alessio was kissing your daughter, or that she was with him and not you?'

'I would have thought it was perfectly obvious what I'm concerned about. And that's Lucy getting hurt.'

Francesca let out her breath. 'I can see there's no point in discussing this with you any further. When you've calmed down, then we'll talk again. For what it's worth, I think you're over-reacting.'

She left him standing alone with only his impotent anger for company. He wasn't overreacting. He was trying to protect his daughter. Was that so very wrong? But then he should have known better than to think a member of the Fontana family would criticize the wonderful Alessio.

He was just putting the top back on the bottle of Scotch when his mobile went off inside his pocket. He hoped to God it wasn't another client. That was all he needed.

But it wasn't a client; it was Lucy.

Spurred on by Alessio and maybe the effect of an excess of alcohol still sloshing around inside her system, Lucy had decided it was time to speak to her father. Alessio had convinced her that she'd put things off for long enough. 'You do not strike me as being a coward, Lucia, so why will you not speak to him?'

'Don't ever accuse me of being a coward,' she'd told him fiercely.

'Then stop acting like one.'

That was when she'd tried shoving him into the lake at Pescallo, except he'd grabbed hold of her and suddenly before she knew where she was, she was hanging off his shoulder and he was dangling her over the water. 'You're only doing this because I beat you at skimming stones!' she'd taunted him.

'I'm doing it because you need someone to put you in your place. Which is right here ... in the lake!'

'No Alessio! Don't you dare! *No!*'

As great a shock to the system as her soaking had been, it was nothing compared to the moment his lips had touched hers. She'd known that he would try it before the day was over, but when he did move in to kiss her, when his hands had circled her waist and drawn her closer to him, she hadn't been prepared for how it would make her feel. As his immaculate white shirt and black jeans touched her, she remembered thinking, good, he'll get wet too, but then her mind seemed to go blank and it was just his mouth on hers. The warmth and lightness of his lips mirrored what her body was feeling. She was floating, set free, like a balloon sailing away on a warm current of air. She could feel the heat of him against her cold, wet body and it made her skin tingle and her head spin.

With enormous willpower, she'd pulled away from him and said, 'And now that you have that out of your system, perhaps you'll start behaving yourself. Besides, didn't you say we're practically related?'

He hadn't switched on his usual dazzling smile at this quip of hers. Instead, he'd said, 'We're not related by blood. Will you have a drink with me after I've finished work this evening?'

'I think I've had enough to drink for one day.'

'Are you always so difficult to romance?'

'I'm sorry, is that what you were doing?'

He placed a hand on her neck and kissed her firmly on the mouth. 'Meet me tonight, please.'

'I'm not going to bed with you, if that's what you think will happen. I don't believe in sleeping with anyone on a first date.'

'I agree. It is much better to wait until the second date. One knows the other person so much better by then.'

She'd laughed and said, 'I want to go back to the hotel now. I need a shower and a change of clothes.'

They were almost at the Hotel Villa Rosa when Alessio took hold of her hand and said, 'I have enjoyed today, Lucia. You are a very special girl. Your father will be the happiest man in Bellagio when you are reconciled with him.'

In spite of herself, she blushed at his compliment. 'You're very sure about my father, aren't you?'

'Some years ago, I was at his house for a party. There was a framed photograph of you when you were about thirteen years old. I picked up the picture to study it more closely – even then I was curious to know more about this missing person from our family. Your father came over to see what I was doing and took the picture out of my hands. He held it closely to him and then put it carefully back on the table where it had been. I have never forgotten the expression in his eyes. The poor man looked like he was in mourning for you. I really think you should give him the chance to say how sorry he is.'

With slightly trembling hands, Lucy put the telephone receiver to her ear. When the unfamiliar dialling code sounded, she took a deep breath. Then it ended and she could hear her father's voice. She swallowed. He sounded just as he had in that other life they'd once lived.

'It's me,' she said. 'Lucy. I don't know if you're free this evening, but if you are, would you like to take me for dinner?'

Chapter Forty-nine

There was a very different atmosphere in the restaurant at the Hotel Villa Rosa that evening. Much to Mac's relief and approval, the Gardens of Delight tour group weren't being forced to eat en masse at two long tables. There was no sign of Philippa – the word was that under doctor's orders she was consigned to bed with glandular fever – and in her absence, in true whilst-the-cat's-away-the-mice-will-play spirit, the group had asked the hotel to set the tables out as normal and they would organize themselves accordingly. Having spent most of the day in one another's company, friendships had formed and jolly little foursomes had sprung up like weeds around the dining room. Lively conversation and cheerfulness abounded.

Philippa wasn't the only absentee from tonight's dinner. Orlando and Savannah had opted to eat out – presumably Savannah wanted to find a place where the average age was nearer her own immature level. And, of course, Lucy wasn't joining them because she was spending the evening with her father.

Mac had been resting on his bed with a drink before getting ready for dinner when Lucy had knocked on his door. 'Guess what,' she'd said, when he'd let her in.

'You were abducted by aliens and that's why we didn't see you this afternoon.'

She'd laughed. 'You're closer than you might think. Try an Italian alien!'

Raising his eyebrows, he'd offered her something from the minibar. 'A tipple to oil the wheels of your news? Although it doesn't look like you need anything to help you along. I swear there's a radiance about you that wasn't there this morning.'

She'd laughed again, leaving Mac in no doubt that she'd had a better afternoon than the one originally planned for her on the Gardens of Delight itinerary. 'Do you have any vodka?' she'd asked.

'Help yourself. I'll fetch you a glass from the bathroom and then we'll withdraw to the balcony and you can fill me in on everything.'

Across the lake, the mountains were disappearing in the lilac dusk of twilight; the air was cool and soft. From a nearby apartment came the tantalizing smell of garlic and onions frying. 'Right then,' Mac had said when they were both settled. 'I'm all ears.'

'Where would you like me to start?'

'Oh, I think you should dive in at the beginning. Where did you go after that appalling scene at lunch? I thought you handled yourself marvellously, by the way. That was some exit you made. I was so proud of you.'

'I felt quite proud of it myself,' she said with a smile. 'But I'm sure my name will be absolute mud from now on with some people.'

'I wouldn't waste any time worrying what Hunter or his silly daughter think of you. Did you know that Orlando went rushing off after you?'

'Really?'

'Yes. He told us later that he couldn't find you. He didn't say as much, but we could all see he was very annoyed with Savannah.'

'Really?'

'You're repeating yourself, my dear. And looking much too happy at what I've just said.'

She feigned a look of innocence.

'You'll have to do better than that. It's written all over your face that you'd like nothing better than for Orlando to come to his senses and see that Savannah is merely a distraction from the main event, which is you.'

She blushed but didn't comment on what he'd said. A faint breeze stirred and she took a long sip of her drink. 'Did Orlando and Savannah have a full-blown barney?' she asked.

'Not to my knowledge, but things did seem strained between them during the afternoon. I think it's only a matter of time before it dawns on him that he's made a mistake. Just be patient is my advice.'

Lucy shrugged. But still she didn't respond.

'Anyway, enough of Orlando and Savannah. Tell me what you got up to whilst we were being shown round the Serbelloni Park by a lovely new Italian guide. But I'll bring you up to speed on her later.'

He'd then listened to Lucy filling him in on her afternoon spent with Alessio, and how he'd encouraged her to ring her father. 'What a busy girl you've been,' Mac had said when she'd finished. 'This Alessio sounds quite a chap. Anything about him you're not telling me? Anything I should know about?'

The smirk on her lovely face was enough to let him know that there was plenty she'd omitted but he wasn't going to push her. She deserved some fun. She'd had precious little of it recently. 'You'll be careful, won't you, Lucy? These Italian men have a reputation to uphold. Playing the rascal is a matter of honour to them.'

'I keep telling you not to worry about me, Mac. I can handle the likes of Alessio.'

'In that case, I shall leave it at that. Now then, what time are you meeting your father? And where are you eating?'

'He's coming to the hotel at eight-thirty and I don't know where he's taking me. I know it's not here.'

'Excellent. The last thing you need is the rest of us gawping at you both whilst you're trying to catch up.' He raised his glass. 'Here's to tonight. May it turn out just as you want. And if you need anyone to talk to afterwards, just knock on my door.'

She tapped her glass lightly against his. 'You're a diamond of a fella, Mac. You'd have made a wonderful father, you know. Why didn't you ever marry and do the whole family thing?'

'Because I was a driven and determined whippersnapper who turned into a selfish old git who didn't want to be tied down. Ask Conrad.'

Mac thought about this as he waited for their food to arrive, whilst watching the excruciating interplay between Conrad and Helen. They were acting like strangers and hardly speaking to each other.

Driven and determined he may have been as a young man when he'd wanted to get on and prove himself in the world, but refusing to be tied down had never been an issue for Mac. He would have willingly given up everything to be with Hannah. He'd have cast aside all his ambition to have her say the words he longed to hear: 'I'm leaving my husband for you.'

He was brought out of his thoughts by Helen asking him if he was all right. 'You're very quiet tonight, Mac,' she said. 'Everything okay?'

'Nothing that a good meal won't put right,' he said. 'I'm famished.

It must be all the walking we've done today. Have you heard from Hunter yet? Has he arrived safely?'

Helen looked at her watch. 'He'll still be in the air. But he's going to be furious with himself. I found his mobile on the bedside table when I got back to the room earlier. He'll be lost without it.'

Their food arrived at last and after the obligatory black pepper and parmesan had been proffered, Mac said, 'So where did you two end up going for a drink?'

'A bar called the San Remo,' Conrad said. 'You should have come with us.'

Mac added salt to his artichoke soup in a quantity that would have Conrad mentally tutting. 'Oh, I imagine you two probably had a far more enjoyable time without me tagging along for the ride.' He didn't doubt it for a minute. They'd made polite noises about him joining them, but he'd decided to bow out and let them get on with breaking one another's hearts. He couldn't protect them any longer. If they were hell bent on making life unbearable for themselves, then they had to learn the hard way. Just as he had.

He changed the subject and said, 'I wonder how Lucy's faring.' Having already obtained Lucy's permission to explain to Conrad and Helen where she'd been that afternoon – knowing that the question would come up during dinner – he'd given them a glossed-over version of her activities, saying only that she'd wanted time to think and had gone exploring on her own. But before either Helen or Conrad had a chance to reply to his remark, a murmur went round the restaurant and heads turned. Aha! thought Mac with a wry smile: the piano player makes his grand entrance once again.

The atmosphere became even more party-like as the evening wore on and they were treated to a selection of popular classics by Cole Porter, Gershwin, the Beatles, Lloyd Webber, Burt Bacharach, Henry Mancini, and all those numbers made famous by the likes of Frank Sinatra, Judy Garland, Elvis, Aretha Franklin, Tony Bennett, Dean Martin, and Ella Fitzgerald. A space had been cleared to make an impromptu dance floor and a few couples were showing off their dancing skills and shimmying elegantly. Others were approaching Alessio with requests – and discreetly folded Euros – and all the time he smiled and played, he didn't have a sheet of music in front of him. Mac couldn't help but respect the young man. But step out of line with Lucy, he thought, and you'll have me to answer to.

And probably her father, he added as an afterthought.

Marcus had never been so terrified. When he'd met Lucy in the foyer at the Hotel Villa Rosa, his mind had been a jumble of confused thoughts, of words he wanted to say, of memories he wanted to share, and some he wanted desperately to forget. The last meal he'd shared with Lucy had been that day in Fulham when he'd told her of his plans to be with Francesca. He'd been sick with nerves that tonight could end the same way, with Lucy running out on him again.

'I've booked us a table at the Serbelloni,' he'd said when they were descending the flight of steps to join the main street. A strange look on her face made him say, 'Is that all right with you, or would you prefer somewhere else? Somewhere less formal?'

'I don't know anywhere else in Bellagio. I'm sure the Serbelloni will be fine.'

She hadn't sounded sure to him as they walked along the Piazza Mazzini, passing the bars, shops and restaurants of the popular arcade. When they were shown to their table, he'd wondered if she despised him for his choice as if he were trying to impress her with a show of grandeur. His doubts were confirmed when she asked him if he ate here regularly. 'Once a month, with a friend,' he'd told her. 'Francesca and I—' His voice had broken off. He hadn't wanted to ram Francesca down her throat too much, too soon. 'We often eat at the Hotel Villa Rosa and our local restaurant, the Pergola in Pescallo, where we live,' he'd said. He'd watched her face and waited to see if she would say that she'd been in Pescallo that afternoon.

What she'd actually said was, 'It's okay, you can say Francesca's name without me throwing a hissy fit.'

This had been the turning point, when he began to relax and his fear subsided sufficiently to allow him to think there was a real chance of them making their peace.

They were now waiting for their main course to arrive. The waiters, who all knew him well and had reserved a table outside on the terrace with a lakeside view, had given Lucy more than a few passing looks of interest. He couldn't say he blamed them. She looked lovely this evening. Her long, wavy blonde hair shone in the candlelight and her face, barely touched with make-up, had a healthy natural glow that would be the envy of most of the overly made-up women around them. He wondered if some of the waiters were putting two and two together and coming up with a lot more than four. It wouldn't surprise him at all if by breakfast time tomorrow morning, Bellagio was rife with the news that Marcus Gray was cheating on his wife with a beautiful girl young enough to be his daughter!

'You're smiling, Dad. Something amusing you?'

He hadn't been conscious that he was, and was about to explain when he stopped in his tracks. 'You called me Dad.'

'So I did.'

They stared in embarrassed silence at one another. 'I suppose I shouldn't have commented on it,' he said at length. 'That was clumsy of me. Only, it sounded so strange after all this time.'

'Weird strange?' she asked.

'No. Good strange. Definitely good. I'm so pleased you phoned me. I was beginning to think you might not.'

She twirled her wine glass round on the table. 'I knew I would, I just didn't know when. And then my day got kind of skewed. I spent the afternoon with someone you know. He's sort of related to Francesca.'

Marcus pretended not to know who she was talking about. 'Oh? Who's that?'

'Alessio Trentini. He's working as a pianist at the Hotel Villa Rosa.'

'Ah yes, that's right, I'd heard he was to be the in-house entertainment for the rest of the season.'

'He told me he's recuperating here after nearly dying from meningitis.'

Did he also tell you he breaks hearts for fun? was on the tip of Marcus's tongue. 'Alessio gave the family quite a scare when he was ill,' he said more equably. 'Everyone was very worried about him. So how did you get to know Alessio? You've been here so little time.'

'He introduced himself last night after dinner, then I bumped into him today. He took me to Pescallo for lunch.' She laughed. 'He's quite something, isn't he?'

'No question about that,' Marcus said lightly. 'Have you seen where I live?'

'I've seen the village. Alessio wanted to show me your house, but I ... I wasn't ready.'

'Do you think you might be tomorrow?'

'Will Francesca be there?'

'Would you rather she wasn't?'

'I think it's time to stop pussy-footing about, don't you, Dad?'

Their main course arrived. The waiters put the plates in front of them, lifted the silver domed covers off with a perfectly synchronized theatrical flourish and then left them alone.

'You're sure you're ready for all this, Lucy?'

'Trust me, I can tuck this away no problem. I'm starving.'

He smiled. 'I was talking about seeing where I live and meeting Francesca.'

She laughed, embarrassed. 'You're not worried I'll savage Francesca, are you?' she asked some minutes later.

'Will you?'

'I don't think so. Unless she starts on me first, of course.'

'There's no chance of that happening. She's been a strong guiding force in not letting me give up on you.' Too late he realized his mistake.

'You thought of giving up on me?'

He decided to be honest with her. 'Yes. Sometimes it was just too painful to think of you living in England and hating me so much you couldn't bring yourself to reply to any of my letters. It hurt deeply.'

'And how about the hurt you caused us when you left Mum and me?'

Now they were down to it. There was no hiding behind hesitant small-talk or honey-coated rhetoric. 'I never wanted to hurt anyone,' he said, 'least of all you. However, I did, and I've never pretended otherwise. When I fell in love with Francesca my life changed for ever and I had to accept the consequences. Perhaps one day you'll fall in love and—' He held himself in check. He sounded pompous, as if he was lecturing Lucy. 'I'm sorry,' he said, 'sorry for going on, and more importantly, sorry for every second of pain I ever caused you. I can't take any of it back, but if we could be friends now, then maybe I could start to make it up to you in some—'

She raised her hand to interrupt him. 'Answer this one question for me. If you could live your life over again, would you change any of it?'

'You're asking if I would put my family first, before giving up everything for the love of my life?'

'Yes.'

He shook his head wearily. 'I can't answer that.'

'You just did.'

So that was it. He'd blown it. One tiny lie was all it would have taken. Why couldn't he have said it?

Because that would be the biggest lie and act of betrayal he could ever commit.

Chapter Fifty

Once again Lucy had been given it straight, that she just wasn't quite good enough. Nothing new there. No point in arguing the toss either. 'Sorry, Miss Gray,' the peaked-cap official in the sky who arranged these things would say, 'but you are, according to our records, destined to be an also-ran. Your potential for loser status was spotted the day you were born and as far as we can see, you will always be denied access to the winner's enclosure. Carry on; you're doing a splendid job of always coming in second!'

It hurt knowing that she could never make the grade in the eyes of those who had once meant so much to her. But then what misguided hope had entered her head to think it could be otherwise? Her father was bound to say that he loved Francesca more than her. And what fool would have thought that Orlando could view her as anything but a friend when there was Savannah spinning in his orbit?

But hey, no hard feelings! That's the way it was. She could cope. She was tougher than the lot of them. Hadn't she proved that already by coming here in the first place?

All this she thought as her father dutifully walked her back to her hotel. 'There's no need,' she'd told him when they left the Serbelloni and the waiters were wishing them goodnight. 'I know my way.'

'But I'd like to.'

They walked in silence along the main street where the shops, bars and restaurants were still buzzing with activity. A number of people they passed, including an elderly couple drinking tiny cups of espresso and shots of grappa, smiled and exchanged friendly greetings with her father. It surprised her to hear him replying in Italian. It was like being with a stranger.

She wondered why she had forced him into the corner that she had during dinner. Things had been going all right up until then. They'd been close to enjoying themselves. But then maybe that was why she'd done it. To let him know that he wasn't off the hook that easily. Her forgiveness couldn't be acquired so cheaply. Do that and it would make a nonsense of everything; it would devalue the effort she'd put into coping with her mother. Of coping with herself, for that matter. Laughing it off as though it were nothing but a trifling inconvenience was not something she could ever do.

Perhaps what hurt most was that he didn't even try to back-pedal his way out of what he'd said. Okay, he didn't look too happy about it, and the conversation never fully recovered – for something to say he'd even tried to warn her off Alessio, saying that he had a reputation when it came to girls – right, like she hadn't worked that out for herself! But her father had said what he'd said. He'd as good as admitted that he'd do the same thing over again, that he'd treat her as a disposable daughter whom she could pick up and put down when the mood took him.

Well, no way would she let him see how upset she was. Let him think it was water off the proverbial duck's back, that he meant buttons to her. As much as she did to him. Alessio had been wrong. Very wrong. He was probably looking at the situation through his spectacularly sexy but seriously blinkered Italian eyes, imagining that all families were like his: a happy and loving Waltons extravaganza of make-believe.

A group of Americans were checking in at the Hotel Villa Rosa when they arrived back. An enormous pile of luggage took up most of the space in the foyer and Lucy and her father had to pick their way through and over the suitcases. Having successfully circumnavigated the chaos, Lucy could hear piano music coming from the restaurant upstairs.

Alessio.

He suddenly seemed the perfect pick-me-up after the evening she'd had. She hoped her father wasn't expecting her to offer him a drink so that he could meet her friends from England. 'I suppose you want to dash off home to Francesca?' she said.

'I haven't got to dash anywhere,' he replied.

So he *was* expecting things to drag on. A round of applause from the restaurant decided it for her. In her current frame of mind she didn't want to introduce her father to anyone. What she did fancy was sitting with a whopping great drink and listening to

Alessio tinkling the ivories. 'I think I'll call it a night,' she said. 'It's been a long day.' She faked a stifled yawn.

Her father took the hint. 'Of course. I'm sorry to have kept you up so late.'

'I'll call you again tomorrow,' she said.

'Do you still want to meet Francesca?'

'Yes. Why wouldn't I?'

He looked uncomfortable. And so he should after what he'd said to her. 'I was worried you might have changed your mind,' he said.

How satisfying it would be to say, I think you'll find you're the fickle one, Dad, not me. But determined to show him that there was nothing petty about her, she said, 'I'll call you tomorrow so that we can fix a time. Thank you for dinner. It was great.' She couldn't bring herself to give him a daughterly peck on the cheek. That would be expecting too much of her limited acting abilities. This time when they parted she didn't look back. She wasn't making that mistake again.

As she entered the dining room, where a lone couple was dancing, she willed herself not to glance over towards Alessio. Eyes straight ahead. No turning to the left. Keep going straight on to the bar. One foot in front of the other. Nice and cool. Nice and steady. 'I'll have a Jack Daniels, please,' she said when she was perched on a bar stool. Only when she had the drink in her hand did she casually swivel round to glance equally casually over to where Alessio was playing. She gave him a look that was supposed to imply, 'Oh, so you're here, are you?'

He stared straight back at her, a wide smile brightening his face. He winked and mouthed 'Ciao,' to her. Her stomach – that great betrayer of her emotions – responded by performing a neat little somersault. People were turning to see who was on the receiving end of his greeting. She surreptitiously peered round the bar and restaurant to see if anyone from home was watching. The only people she recognized were a foursome from the Gatwick contingent who were playing cards at one of the tables. She wondered where everyone else was. Outside in the garden, perhaps? She leaned sideways off her stool, craning her neck to see if she could see Mac and the others out in the candlelit garden. She drew a blank again. And very nearly toppled off the stool. So much for nice and cool! When she'd righted herself, she saw that Alessio's eyes were still on her. Her stomach flipped over again.

She swivelled her stool round to face the bar. This was getting silly. Totally out of hand. She swirled her drink in the glass, making the ice cubes rattle, then took a large mouthful. Setting the glass down in front of her she saw herself in the mirror behind the bar. There was something different about her. She turned to the right, then back to the left. Definitely different. Sort of glowing. She must have caught the sun that afternoon at Pescallo.

She took another mouthful of Jack Daniels. From behind her came the sound of 'Lady in Red'. She smiled. It didn't matter where in the world you were, that bloody Lady in Red would be there waiting for you! Minutes later Alessio had moved onto another cheesy old favourite: 'Yesterday'. It really was extraordinary how well he played. And all from memory. She didn't know how he did it. But then the pinnacle of her musical career had been a virtuoso performance of bashing out 'Jingle Bells' on the triangle at a primary-school nativity play. She could still remember the embarrassment of dropping the triangle and then losing her halo of tinsel as she scrabbled on the floor for it. She could also remember her father swinging her round in his arms afterwards and telling her what a star she was.

No! No more thoughts about her father. 'Yesterday' had finished – how appropriate! – and now Alessio was playing something else. She suddenly pricked up her ears. Could it be? Surely not? She swivelled round so fast on her stool she slopped some of her drink down her front. It was 'Cowboys and Angels', her all-time favourite George Michael song. George had always been a shameful vice for her. At school she'd taken a vow that she would never listen to anything sappy or sentimental. If it wasn't Gun'n'Roses, U2, The Smiths, Joy Division, New Order, then it was crap. No soft-in-the-head rubbish for her! But some years later, during one long, hot summer when she thought she was in love, George slipped under the wire. She became hooked and started listening to him in secret.

Now here was Alessio playing the very song that she used to put on continuous play for hours at a time. It wasn't the same without George or the strings and saxophone, but it had to be said, Alessio's version had a quality all of its own. She closed her eyes and listened, letting the hypnotically seductive melody carry her off on a daydream of ... of dancing close and personal with Alessio. When she opened her eyes she found that he was looking straight at her again. He wasn't smiling. He wasn't playing to the crowd. He was just staring at her in the most intense and mesmerizing way imaginable. She tried not to meet his gaze, but inevitably she did and when the connection was made, her heart jolted and she felt the room spin. I've drunk too much, she thought. But she knew she hadn't. She knew too that she had experienced something completely unknown to her. Inexplicably, she wanted to burst into tears.

No longer looking at her, Alessio now had his head bent over the keys of the piano, his hair hiding his face, his shoulders slightly hunched. He's so beautiful, she thought with an ache in her heart. So exquisitely, so unfairly beautiful. The threat of tears was gaining momentum. She had to get out of here. And fast. But in her current state, the walk across the restaurant to make her escape would be like crossing a tightrope in high heels. The garden. That's where she would go. It was deserted. She'd be safe there.

She slipped off the stool and somehow made it outside. She went and stood at the far end of the garden, having trouble breathing. What was wrong with her? Why did she feel that someone had just thumped her hard in the chest?

She hoped it wasn't what she thought it was. That would be just plain crazy. But even as she tried to deny the obvious, she felt her heart surge again as she thought of Alessio. How could it have happened? A tear slid down her cheek. She pushed it away with her hand. Stupid, stupid, *stupid* girl! You're twenty-nine years old. Not a teenage girl at her first disco nursing a crush on the DJ!

'Lucia?'

Oh, God, it was him! 'Alessio. Shouldn't you be hard at work on the piano?'

He tapped his watch. 'It's midnight. I have finished work for today.' He came towards her, but then stopped short. 'Lucia, you are crying. What is it? Did your evening with your father not go well?'

'It was fine,' she said, taking a step back to put some distance between them.

He moved in closer. 'You have made it up with him?'

'Not quite.'

'And is that what is upsetting you?'

'I'm not upset.'

He was standing next to her now, just inches away. He put a hand out to her, his fingers lightly grazing her cheek. She shivered at his touch. He then examined his fingers. 'You have definitely been crying, Lucia. See? Tears.'

She said nothing. Just stood there staring at him as he contemplated her so fully. She then made the mistake of letting her eyes slowly drift down to his neck, where his shirt was open. The sight of that small area of bare, smooth skin was her undoing and unable to stop herself, she closed the gap between them and kissed him. It felt just as it had that afternoon, the perfect rightness of it. And as their mouths found their own harmonious rhythm, and their arms held each other tightly, Lucy could only wonder at the connection she was experiencing. A connection that defied all logical reason.

Eventually Alessio's mouth broke away from hers and he started kissing her neck and throat, whispering her name as he tilted her head back. '*Lucia mia, ti voglio. Ti voglio. Non voglio perderti.*'

She didn't know what he was saying, but she didn't care. So long as he kept on kissing her, he could say what he wanted. She wanted to lose herself in his embrace. But then he said something she did understand: 'Come to my room.'

'People will talk.'

'Let them. I don't care if anyone sees us sitting here holding hands, Helen, the rules of engagement have changed. I thought we'd established that this afternoon.'

How Helen wanted to believe Conrad. How she wanted to believe that she could stay here on this seat with this wonderful man looking out over the lake and everything would always feel this good. That it would always be midnight with the moon and stars looking down on her from a sky of black velvet, and she would never have to feel the weight of shame and disillusionment that now eclipsed her true self.

But her desire to keep things wrapped in this perfect moment was another example of her cowardice. She simply wasn't brave enough to take the step Conrad wanted her to. She just couldn't do it. Somehow she had to make him understand this. Which was why she'd agreed to join him for a walk after dinner. It wasn't fair to let him go on living in false hope. His declaration of love this afternoon, followed by his extraordinary suggestion that he should take care of her was proof enough that things had gone too far. She had no idea how she was going to bear the next few days when he would no longer want to be in the same room as her, never mind think that he loved her, but it was the only way.

She had reached this conclusion during dinner – an agonizing couple of hours spent looking at him across the table and thinking of what it could be like between them. She had pictured them in bed together, knowing that the intimacy they would share would be the antithesis of what she had with Hunter. She had thought of the respect she had for him, and of the refreshing honesty that would be the backbone of their relationship. Why had fate done this to her? Why couldn't she have met Conrad before Hunter?

But she hadn't. And that was an end to it.

She carefully extracted her hand from Conrad's. 'Conrad,' she said, 'the rules of engagement, as you call them, haven't changed. Whatever you think we have, or could have, is all inside your head. There can never be anything between us for the simple reason that I'm pregnant.'

She saw the look of shock on his face and knew that she would never stop hating herself for what she was doing to him. She willed her voice not to betray her and said, 'I think even you would agree that that puts a different light on things.'

Chapter Fifty-one

'But you can't be!'

'I'm sorry, but I am. Despite being what the experts would call a geriatric mother.'

'But how? I mean ...' Conrad ran out of words. And comprehension. He felt as if a cruel trick had been played on him. How could she have kept something so fundamentally important like this from him? 'When did you know?' he asked at last.

'Last week.'

Last week! He'd never felt so betrayed. 'Was it planned?'

'No.'

'Does Hunter know?'

She shook her head. 'He's going to be as surprised as I was.'

'And you didn't think to mention it before now?'

'I was waiting for the right moment.'

'And this was? After everything I said to you this afternoon and you'd given me—' Once more he found himself unable to speak.

'I've given you nothing but friendship, Conrad,' she murmured. 'You said that yourself.'

'No,' he said sharply. 'You gave me more than that. You gave me hope that there might be something meaningful between us. You spoke so honestly with me this afternoon. What was that all about, if not to give me hope that there might be something meaningful between us one day?'

She looked at him, her face deathly pale. 'I should never have told you all those things.'

'But you did. And you did it for a reason.'

'I ... I was upset and you pushed me. You kept on and on until I gave in.'

He stood up, went over to the railing, and looked down onto the shore of the lake. Every now and then a flash of silver appeared in the moonlight as a fish came to the dark, glutinous surface of the water then disappeared with a flip of its tail. Conrad gripped the metal railing. The thought of Helen misleading him was almost as abhorrent as the idea of her making love with Hunter and conceiving his child.

'This is what you want, then?' he said, turning to face her. 'A child with Hunter.'

She didn't falter. 'A baby will bring us closer together.'

'Yeah, that's right, like some magic wonder glue,' he said savagely. Disbelief had now turned to anger. Anger that she'd played him for a fool. Anger too that once again Mac would be proved right. Of course Helen had had no intention of leaving Hunter. Like the lovesick fool he was, he'd been at the mercy of his subconscious desires, and just as blood flowed through his veins, so had the belief that she would one day appreciate how much better her life could be if it was spent with him. Perhaps, after all, he was just as arrogant and egotistical as Hunter.

And what of Hunter's unfaithfulness? What if he blurted that out, told Helen what he knew? Would it make her reconsider that she was wrong to think a baby would change the man to whom she was married? But what would that gain him? She would still be pregnant with Hunter's child. And he would still feel she hadn't been straight with him. 'That's quite a challenge you're setting the poor little sod when it's born,' he said nastily. 'I hope he or she is up to the task of fixing your marriage.'

He saw in her face that the vehemence of his words had hit home and she was hurt. Good! Because he was more than hurt. He was crushed. He waited for her to respond, so that he could take pleasure in lashing out at her again. But she didn't. She merely stared down at her hands in her lap. Perhaps she was thinking of the baby inside her. The baby he'd just used as a weapon to hurt her. Shame hit him. What kind of a man did that? He suddenly thought of the child he and Sam would have had. He remembered the shortlist of names they'd finally settled on: Noah if it was a boy, and Louisa for a girl. He pictured the nursery they'd decorated together with its blue and yellow frieze of sailing boats, the white furniture they'd spent hours at Ikea choosing and even longer assembling. He thought of the curtains Sam had insisted on making, despite her never having touched a needle and thread since she'd been at school. The curtains had turned out perfectly, just as everything did when Sam put her mind to it. She'd wanted everything to be perfect for their first child. Just one thing she'd got wrong. That fucking dressing gown.

Conrad looked back at Helen. 'I'm sorry,' he forced himself to say. 'I hope you're right, and that a child makes all the difference for you and Hunter. You deserve to be happy.'

'So do you,' she said quietly.

He pushed his hands into his trouser pockets. 'It would seem not.'

Chapter Fifty-two

There was something about the early morning light here. It put everything into soft focus, took away all the nasty harsh edges. Lucy thought it was a shame life couldn't feel this good all the time.

She stretched languidly, then turning her back on the view of rooftops and chimneys, she rolled over. Alessio was still sleeping peacefully beside her. If it was possible, he looked even more gorgeous asleep. Unlike herself, she thought ruefully, running a hand through her tangled hair.

The decision to go to bed with Alessio had not been a difficult one. Under normal circumstances, she didn't do one-night stands or holiday flings. Yet with Alessio, she had dispensed with the rule book. There had been a moment when she'd brought him back to her room – not his, as he'd originally suggested – when she had wondered how she might feel in the morning. Would she regret her rashness? The truth was she didn't. How could she regret something that felt so utterly right? She had no need to justify her actions to herself, not when all it took was one look at him to make her heart swell. If she was shocked by anything at all, it was the intensity of her emotions. She had never been in this situation before and hardly dared to think what it might mean. As Alessio had undressed her last night, he'd told her he would never forget this moment. She had no idea if he'd meant what he said, but she for one knew she would always remember it. He'd been a confident and attentive lover, which hadn't surprised her. What had surprised her, though, was how gloriously uplifting their lovemaking had been. He had stroked and caressed every part of her body, saying how he adored the paleness of her skin, the fullness of her breasts, or the curve of her hips. She loved how he expressed himself, the way no Englishman ever could. His spontaneous, uninhibited adoration of her body was unlike anything she had ever known before. Perhaps it was simply the Italian way of doing things.

On the verge of quietly slipping out of bed to go to the bathroom and tidy herself up, a hand grabbed her by the wrist, making her jump. 'Oh, no you don't!'

Laughing, she tried to wriggle out of his grasp. 'Alessio, I need a shower.'

He ignored her and manoeuvred her in one fluid motion so that her naked body was lying on top of his. He held her face in his hands. 'We will shower together. Later.'

'You were pretending to be asleep, weren't you?'

'Yes. Earlier I was watching you while you were staring out of the window. What were you thinking?'

'It's private.'

'Were you thinking of your father?'

'My father? Are you mad?'

'You have not spoken of him yet.'

'That's because I've had something far more interesting on my mind. You.'

He smiled and stroked her hair, taking it in one hand and holding it at the nape of her neck. 'Please, I want to hear how your meeting with Marcus went. Did you talk honestly with him?' His tone was soft. Concerned, even.

'If you must know, we spoke a little too honestly.' She slid to his side, and resting her head on his shoulder, she told him what she'd asked her father and what he'd said. When she'd finished speaking, Alessio said nothing, just ran his fingers slowly down her spine as if playing an arpeggio. More slowly his strong fingers worked their way back up to her neck. She shivered with desire, her father once again forgotten. Alessio turned to face her and kissed her deeply.

'You wouldn't have the energy,' she teased, when before long he made his intentions clear. 'You're recuperating. Remember?'

'In that case, I will lie back and let you do all the work.'

She laughed. 'I'd love to, but I don't have the time. Have you forgotten I'm here to sightsee? I'm visiting the Villa Balbi-something-or-other this morning.'

'Villa del Balbianello can wait. I can't. *Ti voglio.*'

She frowned. 'You said that last night. What does it mean?'

'It means I want you.' He suddenly threw aside the bedclothes and began covering her neck and breasts with slow, lingering kisses. He moved further down her body, his mouth making her skin tingle. When he parted her legs, she closed her eyes and felt the world slide.

Orlando was awake early and thinking that he was having the worst time of his life. And not just because his head thumped to the beat of the most impressive hangover he'd had in years.

He and Savannah had argued again last night. Their worst to date. Although he suspected Savannah was easily capable of topping her behaviour in the bar last night. He'd never known anyone who could so entirely flip from happy bunny to miserable cow in one easy step. Had he had the slightest inkling that she could be like this, he would never have got involved with her.

With his hands clasped behind his head as he lay back against the pillow and stared at the ceiling, he tried to remember what the attraction had been in the first place. Whatever it was, it was long gone. All that remained of the person he'd thought he'd been crazy about was a selfish, possessive girl who had yet to grow up.

Or perhaps he was being too harsh. After all, Savannah was only twenty, and given her upbringing, in particular that father of hers, it was hardly surprising that she could lapse into sulky, selfish brat territory at the flick of a switch. He could make all the excuses in the world for her, but the bottom line was he didn't want or need the hassle. Didn't need it at all. Which put him squarely in Division One of the All Men Are Selfish Bastards league.

What had triggered things last night had been Savannah's irritating wheedling that he should have supported her at lunch. Granted she'd had a fair bit to drink by this time, and so had he, but he wasn't in the mood for compromise. He'd done enough of that when she'd apologized to him in the afternoon. He'd swallowed back her words for the sake of peace, as well as suggesting she should say sorry to Helen and Conrad and Mac, but her dragging the subject up again had lit the touchpaper. 'Do you have any idea how upset I was when you went off to find Lucy?' she'd asked him.

'No,' he'd said. 'But do you have any idea how much you must have upset Lucy with your remarks about her father?'

'Here we go again. Lucy, bloody Lucy! What is it with that frigging girl? Why are you always rushing to defend her?'

'You know perfectly well that she's my oldest friend and friends always look out for each other. And for the record, it was you who brought up Lucy, not me.'

She'd drained her glass of grappa and jabbed a finger a few inches from his face. 'Seeing as I have, I'm gonna ask you this. Why don't you just put her out of her misery and screw her? You know she's gagging for it.'

'What the hell are you on about now?'

'Oh, don't be a numb-nuts! You know exactly what I'm talking about. And do you know what I think?'

'Astound me.'

'My money's on you enjoying keeping her dangling. Yeah, the more I think about it, the more I think you get off on the fact that she'd do anything to get into bed with you. What an ego boost that must be for you.' She flicked him on the end of his nose. 'You're a tease, Orlando. A shitty tease. If she wasn't such a whingeing sad case, I'd almost feel sorry for the poor bitch. But I'll give her this. She's not wasted any time since coming here. I even admire her taste. I wouldn't mind making a play for him myself.'

Stunned, all Orlando had managed to say was, 'You've had too much to drink.'

'Who the hell are you suddenly? My dad?' Savannah's voice was raised now and people were looking their way.

'I know how you love to be the centre of attention at all times,' he'd muttered, 'but find the volume control, will you? Everyone's staring at us.'

'And why don't you get out of my face!' she'd shouted. 'You were annoying me before, now you're scaring me. You sound as pathetically old as the rest of the crowd on this trip. I don't know why I bothered to come. The whole thing's been a big bastard yawn from the moment we arrived. I'd have had more fun at home having a bikini wax.'

'Then do us all a favour and bugger off home early!'

'Don't worry. I fully intend to.'

He'd watched her stumble out of the bar, cursing the day he'd ever set eyes on her. He should have gone after her and made sure, in her drunken state, that she got back to the hotel okay, but he didn't. Instead, he'd ordered another beer and put her as far from his mind as he could.

Out of bed now, and in the shower, he thought of when he'd first met Savannah in the garden at the Old Rectory and later when she'd appeared on his doorstep soaked to the skin. He then recalled the afternoon when he'd found her naked in his bed. He had the feeling that she'd cleverly orchestrated their every meeting. Turning his face up towards the shower head and letting the powerful jets blast at his skin, he wondered how he could have been so stupid.

And hadn't Lucy warned him? Hadn't she said that Savannah was trouble?

He thought of what Savannah had said about Lucy and in particular the bit about Lucy wanting to go to bed with him. He didn't know where Savannah had got that idea from but it wasn't true. Lucy had never once shown the slightest interest in him, other than close friendship. Which, a long time ago, had been a problem for him. It had happened at his twenty-first birthday party. Lucy had been wearing the most amazingly tight white jeans with a simple black strappy top. She hadn't been wearing a bra and when he was dancing with her he had felt her breasts rubbing against his chest. Suddenly he'd had to arch his body away from hers. He would never have heard the last of it if she'd known she'd given him an erection. But then she'd gone and made it worse by whispering in his ear that she wasn't wearing any knickers either. 'These jeans are so tight, there just wasn't room,' she'd laughed. For weeks afterwards he'd lain in bed at night fantasizing about her. He'd finally plucked up the courage to talk to her – to tell her that it was possible that his feelings for her were more than just friendly feelings – when she phoned him to say that she'd just met this fantastic bloke called Steve. Steve came and went in about the same length of time it took for Orlando to come to terms with the fact that Lucy would never view him as a potential boyfriend. To this day he was just plain old Orlando to her. Sometimes he regretted it couldn't be otherwise. But mostly he accepted the situation for what it was.

Moreover, it was laughable what Savannah had suggested, that he was leading Lucy on. She had been talking paranoid nonsense because she was childishly jealous of the closeness he had with Lucy.

Yet the more he reasoned with the situation the more he began to wonder if Savannah hadn't been entirely wrong. Was it possible that Lucy had taken a violent dislike against Savannah because she was jealous of the girl? If that was so, could he really have been so blind? Surely he would have known if Lucy regarded him as more than a friend?

Stepping out of the shower and rubbing himself down with a towel, Orlando replayed something else Savannah had said last night. How Lucy hadn't wasted any time since coming here. It was a cheap shot, but not without an element of truth. Just thinking of Lucy with that sickeningly smooth Italian was enough to make Orlando feel the way he had when Steve had appeared on the scene all those years ago – if he couldn't have Lucy, then no one could. He wiped the condensation away from the mirror with a hand towel and stared at his reflection. Have you changed? he asked himself.

He thought hard before answering and came to the only conclusion he could. No, he hadn't changed. He wasn't even shocked. It was as if deep down he'd always known that the rightful way of the world was for him and Lucy to be together.

'Then it's time to do something about it,' he said aloud.

First, there was Savannah to deal with. Whilst shaving, he started rehearsing what he was going to say when he saw her at breakfast. He would explain that it really would be better if they ended things between them, just in case she was harbouring any thoughts about them kissing and making up. Somehow he doubted that even she would want that now.

But there was no sign of Savannah at breakfast. Or of Lucy and Helen. He sat at a table with Mac and Conrad and pretended to be interested in what Mac was reading to them from his guide book about the villa they were visiting that morning.

'Apparently the Villa Balbianello is situated on the rocky tip of a promontory so there's not much of a garden to see,' Mac told his two gloomy breakfast companions. 'Makes you wonder why it's on the itinerary if that's the case.'

When neither responded, Mac rolled his eyes and helped himself to some more coffee. Some holiday this was turning out to be!

It wasn't until they'd finished breakfast and were leaving the terrace garden, Orlando having already gone on ahead, that Mac decided to say something. He was concerned about Conrad. He hadn't seen him looking this glum in a long while. 'Has your mood got anything to do with the fact that Helen is a no show for breakfast?' he asked.

'Not even close.'

'What, then?'

'It's none of your business.'

They were waiting for the lift. No one else was about. Mac pressed the lift button again. 'If you're not careful, Conrad, you're going to turn into me.' The lift seemed to be stuck on the top floor. Mac gave the button another jab. 'So what's the problem?'

'Is there any point in asking you to leave it?'

'No. Believe it or not, you mean too much to me to stand back and watch you do this to yourself.'

Conrad fiddled with the buttons on his cuffs, undoing them and then rolling up the sleeves to his elbows. 'And what exactly am I doing to myself?'

'I won't even dignify that with an answer.'

The lift arrived and they stepped inside. As the doors closed, Conrad said, 'If it makes you feel any better, you were right about Helen. She'll never leave Hunter.'

Mac stared at Conrad's morose reflection. It seemed safer than turning to look him in the eye. 'What's happened to make you reach this conculsion?'

'She's pregnant.'

'Good God!'

'Good God, indeed.'

'It's not yours, is it?'

'Haven't you listened to anything I've told you? It's Hunter's.'

The lift stopped. They'd arrived at their floor. 'Do you want to come to my room and finish off this conversation, or shall we dance around it for the rest of the day?'

Conrad glanced at his watch. 'We have to be down in the foyer in twenty minutes.'

'Time enough.'

Letting them into his room – the chambermaid had been and gone, leaving the place spick and span – Mac gestured for Conrad to sit down. But Conrad shook his head and remained standing, looking out at the lake. 'She's known for a week,' he said. 'A whole bloody week and she didn't say anything.'

'She must have had her reasons.'

Conrad spun round. 'What? Like sticking the knife in me and twisting it round a couple of turns for fun?'

'Helen isn't that kind of a woman. There's not a malicious bone in her body.'

'I thought that once, but right now I don't know what to think of her.'

'It's odd that Hunter wasn't bragging about being a father all over again during lunch yesterday. It would have been just his style, don't you agree?'

'Helen says she hasn't told him yet.'

Mac frowned. 'I wonder why.'

Conrad seemed not to hear him. He said, 'What really gets to me is that Helen is trying to convince herself that this baby's going to be a magic wand for her marriage. She doesn't love Hunter. I know she doesn't. She told me only yesterday that the only reason she married him was so that her grandmother could be taken better care of.'

'She told you that?'

'As good as. If we're to believe what she says, the old lady had been abused at a previous nursing home and Hunter with all his booty was their knight in shining armour.'

As shocking as this was, Mac wasn't too surprised. Not that the old lady had been ill-treated, but that Helen had seized an opportunity. There would be those who would no doubt view her actions as calculating and devious, but he'd experienced enough of life to see it differently. Sometimes enormous sacrifices and compromises had to be made for the good of those one loved, and it wasn't ever fair to judge. But the baby was another matter. Admittedly Helen had known she was pregnant for only a week, but why, when she knew how Conrad felt about her, hadn't she said something to him before now? Mac began to feel angry that Helen hadn't been more honest with Conrad. But now wasn't the time to get steamed up. It would only make Conrad feel worse.

'Look, Conrad,' he said in a placatory tone, 'for the baby's sake, Helen now has to try and make a go of her marriage. You have to put her out of your mind.'

'Easier said than done. Especially with what else I know.'

'Which is?'

'Hunter's having an affair. He's not in Dubai. He's with a woman somewhere. I overheard him talking to her on his mobile at Villa Carlotta yesterday morning.'

Mac sighed and sat down heavily on the edge of the bed. He was beginning to regret having instigated the conversation. 'Do you think Helen knows?'

'I haven't a clue. She's clearly capable of playing her cards pretty close to her chest. If she does know, then I'm afraid I feel even less for her. Where's her self-respect?'

Mac snorted. 'That's harsh. And not without a good dose of hypocrisy, given that you, if she'd not been the woman she is, would have pushed her into having an affair with you.'

'It's not the same. I loved Helen. Whereas all Hunter's doing is screwing around.'

'Who knows, you may be right. But one thing that is patently obvious is that you have to back off from Helen now. Would you rather we cut short the holiday and flew home early?'

A glimmer of a smile appeared on Conrad's face. 'And deprive you of your gardens? I'd never hear the last of it.'

Mac smiled. 'In that case, we'd better get a move on. Our presence is required downstairs. I wonder if we'll have that rather attractive Italian woman as our guide today. I do hope so.'

Chapter Fifty-three

With a trembling hand, Francesca switched off her mobile. She had just received the news that confirmed what she'd known ever since she had found that first terrifying lump. She was dying. And from the very same disease that had taken her mother. Lymphatic cancer.

Somehow she had found the strength to stay calm and matter of fact whilst the doctor broke the news and asked her to make a return visit to see him so that he could run some further tests. But now the fear and panic that she had been keeping at bay were threatening to break free and overwhelm her. She tried to stop it, to think about the day ahead, of the tour group she was taking to Villa Balbianello. But she couldn't do it, and feeling nauseous, she crossed the kitchen, unlocked the door and went outside. Standing at the top of the garden and looking down the gentle slope of lawn, she began to cry. She didn't want to die. She didn't want to leave Marcus. Or her family. Through tear-filled eyes, she stared up at the sky and the God who was punishing her. First he'd denied her the children she'd craved, now this. And all because she'd made the mistake of falling in love with Marcus and destroying his family. Why did anyone believe in a God who could be so vindictive?

She wrapped her arms around her body to stop it from shaking. Weak with shock, she forced her legs and feet to move and slowly made her way down to the bottom of the garden. There on the wooden seat that overlooked the lake, where she and Marcus so often sat with a glass of wine whilst catching up on the day, she wept until exhaustion shuddered through her. She hadn't bargained on this, that having her fears unequivocally confirmed would leave her feeling so utterly spent. As if the fight for her life was already over.

Dead. The word echoed cruelly inside her head. It was no longer a maybe; it was really going to happen, and there wasn't a thing she could do to stop it. There had been moments of hope, desperate shards of belief that this couldn't happen to her. How easy it was to believe in one's invincibility. She had prayed so hard for a miracle, not so much for her own sake, but for Marcus's.

Her darling Marcus. How on earth was she going to tell him? She thought of all the petty arguments they'd had lately – his anger over Lucy and Alessio, then his reaction last night when he'd returned home after his dinner with Lucy and she'd admitted that she had been with the Gardens of Delight group that afternoon. 'But why didn't you tell me?' he'd demanded.

'I thought you'd try and stop me. I know how you wanted to keep me in the background.'

'It's not that. I just don't want to rush things.'

You might have to, she had wanted to say. 'As it turned out there was no one of Lucy's age in the party,' she'd explained to him, 'so I concluded she wasn't there.'

'She wasn't,' he'd said grimly. 'Alessio had seen to that. They were together all afternoon.'

Recalling the terseness of Marcus's words, and his obvious disappointment that she'd gone behind his back, Francesca drew her knees up to her chest and cried even more. I must tell him, she thought. There must be no more secrets between us. Somehow she would get through today and she would tell him tonight. She would bring him out here and they would sit and watch the sun go down and she'd tell him that they had to make the most of their time together. Ten months at best, the doctor had said. Probably less.

From their bedroom window, Marcus looked down at his wife at the end of the garden and knew with absolute certainty that their marriage was over. He could only guess from the way she was sitting with her back to him – her shoulders hunched, her legs drawn up with her arms clasped around her knees – that she was figuring out how to tell him she was leaving him.

Everything added up: the absences, the long silences, the distracted behaviour, the jumping whenever the phone rang and the most telling of all, her withdrawal from him in bed on several occasions recently when he'd tried to make love to her.

He'd been in the bathroom when he had caught the sound of her mobile ringing. He'd heard her hurrying downstairs to take the call, obviously wanting to be alone, away from the danger of being overheard. He sensed now, as he pressed his forehead against the glass and stared at the isolated figure of his wife, that whatever had just passed between Francesca and her lover, a point of no return had been reached. It was crunch time.

As extraordinary as it was, he loved her so much, he couldn't bear to see her going through this agony. He felt compelled to go to her and help make the decision for her. He would rather she was happy with someone else than this wretched with him. It was the ultimate test of loving someone, letting that person go if that's what they wanted.

It was what he'd done with Lucy.

Last night, after he'd walked Lucy back to the Hotel Villa Rosa, he had driven the short distance home hoping she would understand that by being totally honest with her about his love for Francesca he had been showing her that his affair had been no piffling matter. He had wanted her to know that only something that important to him would have caused him to take the steps he had. Before the conversation had taken the nosedive it had, Lucy had seemed prepared to come here to Pescallo and meet Francesca. He remembered how happy this had instantly made him feel, but now it seemed unlikely it would ever take place. For all he knew, Francesca could be gone by the end of the day. Perhaps she already had a suitcase filled, had it hidden somewhere in the house ready for her escape.

The thought filled him with such sadness that it was all he could do to keep standing. When he'd recovered himself, he decided to go to his office in Milan. He had planned to work from home again today, in the hope that Lucy would want to see him, but he needed to get away. He needed to have his mind fully occupied. And only work could do that.

With their guide from yesterday leading the way towards the landing stage, Mac deliberately slowed his step so that he could trail behind and make his observations. Olivia and her new chum – a seventy-three-year-old widower from Cirencester who was a Gardens of Delight veteran, this being his fifth trip with them – were up at the front of the group with Francesca. Vi and Barbara had been shrugged off like an unwanted cardigan on a hot summer's day. Conrad was making polite conversation with Colin Campbell and pretending to admire his new digital camera. And Helen, looking like she hadn't slept that night, was talking to

Orlando – there was no sign of Savannah. As for Lucy, well, God bless the girl! The smile on her face could stretch from here to Swanmere. And little wonder. They'd all just witnessed her being kissed by her handsome beau, Alessio. The pair of them had been in the lift, so engrossed in what they were doing – Alessio had her pressed against the back of it – they weren't aware the doors had opened and everyone in the foyer had front-row seats. It had been a real all-singing, all-dancing, show-stopping kiss and had provoked a spontaneous round of applause. But the look on Orlando's face had made Mac pity him. Poor devil, he'd thought. He's catching on to what might have been. Welcome to the club of Screwed Up and Lost Out, young man!

Once again they were crossing the flat, calm lake, this time bound for Lenno, and as the *traghetto* pulled into the landing stage at Tremezzo for people to disembark for Villa Carlotta, Mac sought out Helen. She was sitting alone, her eyes closed, a pale cream silk scarf fluttering in the breeze at her neck. 'Not interested in the view?' he asked as he plonked himself into the seat next to her.

She started. 'Mac! I was miles away.'

'I bet you were. Picking out baby clothes I shouldn't wonder.' His voice resonated with anger and he could feel his temple pulsing with the need to vent his feelings. Up until now, so as not to add further fuel to Conrad's disappointment, he'd kept his mouth shut. But now that he'd had time to stew, he was ready to let rip. He wanted Helen to know just how much havoc she was wreaking. He saw the colour rise to her face.

'Conrad told you?' she murmured.

'Too right he did. Why didn't you tell him before? Why put him through all this? You haven't played fair, Helen. I don't think I'll ever forgive you for that.'

'I never meant for things to get so complicated.'

'Well they have and I'm telling you, Conrad is devastated. God help him, but you're the first woman for whom he's allowed himself to feel anything.'

'Stop it, Mac. Please. Don't you think I know this? I'm not completely heartless.'

But Mac had the bit between his teeth. Not since Sam's death had he felt so protective of Conrad. 'So what are you going to do about it?'

'What *can* I do?'

'You and your charmless husband could leave Swanmere. That would certainly be an expeditious move on your part.'

She looked at him aghast, a hand raised to her mouth. 'You hate me, don't you, Mac?'

'Right now, I think I do.'

Francesca could do these tours in her sleep, which was just as well. They had arrived in Lenno, and on autopilot she was instructing the group to walk along the main road of the pretty lakeside town, urging them to take care when they climbed into the small boat that would take them across to the Punta Balbianello. She counted everyone in and when the skipper of the boat, Roberto, who had been at school with her brothers, had pushed them away from the jetty, she took the last remaining seat next to an attractive auburn-haired woman, who, for a woman on holiday, looked remarkably unhappy. In Francesca's line of work, most of the people she encountered were relaxed and carefree, glad to be away from all the stresses and strains of home and work. But then who knew what problems this woman was coping with? Any more than anyone would guess that an hour and a half ago Francesca had been given her official death sentence.

But the woman sitting next to her was not who Francesca was really interested in. She had spotted Lucy straight away. It hadn't been difficult. Along with everyone else back at the hotel, she had seen Alessio and Lucy in the lift in the foyer. Same old Alessio, Francesca had thought with amused affection as she'd discreetly hidden herself behind a pillar so that he wouldn't spot her. She hadn't wanted him blurting out to Lucy who she was at that point.

Now, hiding behind her sunglasses, Francesca gave Marcus's daughter her full attention. As pretty as Lucy was, Francesca was intrigued: what exactly was it about her that had caught Alessio's eye? His track record in the last five years revealed a fondness for the smart-set girls of Milan and Rome. His last girlfriend, before he'd nearly died from meningitis, had been the daughter of a wealthy industrialist from Piedmont. In contrast, Lucy was as natural as the breeze blowing at her long, crinkly blonde hair. With her unadorned complexion and simple clothes – peach-coloured linen skirt, white top and flip-flops – there was a fresh wholesomeness to her that was as English as tea and scones and cricket on the village green. Perhaps that was the attraction for Alessio?

Putting Alessio's preferences aside, Francesca continued to study her husband's daughter. *Her step-daughter*. She didn't look the sort of girl who would bear malice. Far from it. Sitting next to an elderly gentleman and talking to him most animatedly, she gave the impression of being an open-hearted young woman with a spirited sense of fun. Seeing Lucy in the flesh after more than a decade of imagining what she might be like pained Francesca all the more when she thought how Marcus had been denied the pleasure of having his daughter in his life. But it wasn't just Marcus who had lost out; Lucy had too. She had been deprived of a father who had never stopped loving her.

It was all such a waste. And would never have happened if Francesca hadn't gone to London as a student and if Marcus hadn't knocked her off her bicycle. She had always believed that he'd paid an unfairly high price for her, but never more so than now with his precious daughter sitting just a few feet away. If it was the last thing she did, Francesca knew that she would have to be the one to make good the damage she had inflicted on these two people. More than that, she wanted to make her own peace with Lucy Gray.

At some stage during the course of their visit to the Villa Balbianello, she would make herself known to Lucy. Unlike yesterday, when she'd met the group for the first time, this morning she hadn't bothered to mention her name again, so it was quite possible that Lucy hadn't made the association. Certainly there was nothing in the girl's manner to suggest that she had put two and two together and was sizing her up.

As she assisted Roberto with helping everyone off the boat, she thought how surreal it was that her brain could so easily distract itself. But then she had amazed herself at home earlier when she had calmly watched Marcus leave the house for Milan. Lucy's unexpected presence in Bellagio was obviously having an unsettling effect on him for he didn't seem to notice that she'd been crying. Grateful for this, she had kept quiet about her plans for the day, that once again she would be the tour guide for the Gardens of Delight group. She was grateful too that she had work to occupy her. Had she been forced to spend the day alone, she would have given into self-pity. So long as she had the strength, she knew she would have to keep herself busy. It was what her mother had tried to do. It had worked for several months – she had busied herself with the grandchildren, scolding Francesca's brothers for working too hard, praising her daughters-in-law for putting up with the men they'd married – but then one morning it was as if she had simply run out of energy. Once she was admitted to hospital, the end came fast. Too fast. None of them, despite knowing that death was imminent, had been prepared for it. Francesca had been the least able to cope with the loss of her mother. She had leant on Marcus heavily during that shattering period of grief.

She swallowed and pursed her lips, wondering who Marcus would lean on when she died.

Lucy. It would have to be Lucy.

Chapter Fifty-four

Lucy hopped onto the jetty with a spring in her step, waving aside the offers of help from the skipper of the boat and their guide. Never had she experienced such happiness before. And what girl wouldn't feel the same?

In the shower earlier, when Alessio had been soaping her back, he had asked if he could see her again after he'd finished work. She had teased him that she would need an early night and didn't he have another girl lined up anyway? He'd turned her round to face him. 'Why do you say that? Why would I want to see anyone else?'

'Because you're an Italian sex god, and that's what sex gods do,' she'd joked. And this wonderful moment will have soon run its course, she'd thought more seriously.

He'd rubbed his hand across his face, wiping water from his eyes. 'Lucy, don't make fun of me. *Ti prego*. From the second I saw you, I wanted to see only you. No one else.' He'd tilted her face up towards his – letting the water from the shower wash over it – then covered her mouth with his. It had been a deeply erotic kiss and as Lucy thought of it now – and his words – she felt the powerful magnetic pull of him.

No man had ever had this effect on her. She had only to think of Alessio's sinewy body against hers and she felt a rush of desire. She now knew what the expression to be knocked off one's feet really meant.

Trailing behind the rest of the group as they followed their guide away from the landing stage and then progressed to climbing up a steep, winding path, passing plane trees that had been pruned to within an inch of their lives, Lucy knew that everyone would be thinking she had fallen, like countless others before her, for the romantic charm of a sweet-talking foreigner. And so what if she had? There were far worse crimes she could commit. Life was just too short, she'd decided, to deprive oneself of a little fun.

Ahead of her the group had come to a stop: everyone had their cameras out. When Lucy saw the view she reached for hers as well. With Bellagio no more than a hazy outline in the distance, the shimmering radiance of the lake in all its splendour was before them. Touched by the serene beauty of it, she envied those who lived here. Yesterday Alessio had told her that some of his favourite and most vivid childhood memories were of visiting Bellagio, especially during the winter, when the snow-capped mountains rose mysteriously through the ghostly mist that covered the lake. 'When I was very young, I remember fearing that there were monsters who lived at the bottom of the lake,' he'd told her. 'I was convinced they came to the surface at night and swam to the shore looking for bad children to eat. Naturally, my parents encouraged me to believe this; it was the only way they could stop me from being too naughty.' She had laughed and wondered just how naughty a child he had been.

The sun was burning hotly from a cloudless sky of eggshell blue, and Lucy stepped into the shade to enjoy the view. How different her father's life must have become when he left England for this. A pang of regret tweaked at her heart. She shouldn't have left things as she had with him last night. She had been so sure that it would make her feel better to keep reminding him of what he'd done, but she couldn't in all honesty say that it did.

'Having a good holiday?'

To her surprise, it was Orlando. These were the first words he'd uttered to her since ... since for ever. When was the last time they'd spoken to each other since arriving in Italy? When was the last time she had even thought of him? 'I'm having a great holiday,' she said, thinking of Alessio. It wouldn't have taken much for her to confide in Orlando, just like old times. But how serious he looked. And how stolid. There was no joy in his face; not a flicker. Just a mask of cool indifference. How could he be surrounded by so much beauty and not be affected by it? Had Alessio been here he probably would have been flinging his arms out wide and bursting into song. It was his passionate, uninhibited nature that she found so refreshingly appealing. He might well have an unrealistic live-for-the-moment philosophy, but she sensed his rapturous zest for life was rubbing off on her.

The group was gathering around their guide to hear what she was saying, something about the last owner of the villa – a Count called Guido Monzino who had led expeditions to Everest and the North Pole – but Lucy stayed where she was. As interesting and enthusiastic as the Italian guide was, Lucy wanted to go on enjoying the stunning view. When Orlando didn't move away either, she said, 'So how's your holiday going?'

'Do you really need to ask?'

She blinked. 'I'm sorry. Have I missed something?'

'It's Savannah. She and I ... Oh, I'm sure you've guessed; it's turning out to be a disaster.'

Now there's a surprise! Lucy resisted the temptation to crow. 'Oh,' she said. 'Where is Savannah?'

'I haven't a clue. The last time I saw her was last night. We had a row.' He sighed. 'Another row. I don't seem to be able to say the right thing to her at the moment.'

'It'll pass, I'm sure.'

He looked at Lucy steadily. 'That's not what I want. I'm going to end it with her.'

Two days ago this would have been all Lucy would have wanted to hear. Yet now she received the news with an equanimity she wouldn't have believed herself capable of. 'That's a shame. You were so happy with her.'

He looked embarrassed. 'I got caught up in the heat of the moment.' He hesitated. A nervous smile appeared on his face. 'A bit like you and your new friend, the pianist.'

Lucy caught the pointed significance of his remark and didn't like it. She smiled tightly. 'Looks like everyone's moving on to the next part of the tour. We'd better join them.'

But Orlando stayed where he was. 'He doesn't really seem your sort, Luce.'

'I have a sort?'

'You know what I mean. And you do seem to have rushed into things with him.'

'Is there any other way?' She was being flippant, but really, what else could she say? Who did Orlando think he was? And to think she had imagined herself in love with him! She must have been crazy.

'You spent the night with him, didn't you?'

'And what if I did? What business is it of yours or anyone else's for that matter?'

'But you hardly know him!'

'Then sleeping with him will go a long way to getting to know him better!'

'Doesn't it bother you that you're probably nothing more than this week's hot chick? That the minute you leave, he'll be working his charm on some other witless victim?'

That did it! Her patience had been stretched too far. 'I am not some witless victim,' she said with enormous control. 'I know exactly what I'm doing. I'm having fun, which is clearly more than you are. Now if you don't mind, I'd like to catch up with the rest of the group and look round the garden.'

As he watched Lucy walk away, Orlando regretted every word that had just spewed out of his mouth. How could he have got it so wrong? He'd done nothing but antagonize Lucy. All he'd wanted to do was let her know how much he cared about her. He'd even forgotten to ask about her father. What a pillock he'd been!

Jealousy. That's what had done it for him. He couldn't stand the thought of Lucy being with that Italian. Of her being taken in by him and getting hurt. His only consolation was that he knew he would be there for her when that did happen.

And the worst of it was, it was all his fault. He'd been the one who had pushed to make her come here. If only he'd left well alone.

He stared out at the lake. Was anyone else having as bad a holiday as he was?

'God, I can't tell you what a crap time I'm having!'

The seriously good-looking man opposite Savannah frowned. 'But why? Bellagio is a lovely place to visit.'

'It might be for the over fifties, but as far as I can see there's nothing to do for people my age.' She laughed. 'That's probably why you've been entertaining yourself with Lucy, isn't it?'

He lowered his gaze and added a cube of sugar to his ridiculously tiny cup of black coffee. Savannah took a sip of her cappuccino and searched Alessio's face for some clue as to what he might say next. Disappointingly, his expression was blank.

When she'd eventually surfaced for breakfast, with a stinker of a hangover, she'd come across Alessio in the dining room; he was sitting at the piano. He wasn't playing the kind of music she'd heard him play before. This was heavy classical stuff he was bashing out with scary concentration, his hands flying over the keys, his black hair flapping like a curtain in the wind as his head thrashed from side to side. She'd grimaced at the God-awful noise and was relieved when he noticed her and stopped. 'Can I help you?' he'd asked.

'You can if you can point me in the direction of some breakfast,' she'd said.

'I'm afraid you're too late.' He'd cast his eyes around the empty dining room where two waiters were changing tablecloths. 'Breakfast finished over an hour ago.'

With his dead sexy accent and cracking good looks, he was a pretty neat package. If nothing else, Lucy had taste: first Orlando, now this guy. That was when an idea occurred to Savannah. An idea that would give her something interesting to do while she waited for Orlando to pull his finger out and do some grovelling. 'Oh, that's too bad,' she'd said. 'Perhaps if I ask nicely I could get some coffee.'

'I'm sure that could be arranged.'

'And would it be all right if I drink it here and listen to you play? You play very well. Or would it put you off?'

Seeming to consider her suggestion for a long moment, he'd then carefully closed the lid of the piano. 'I have finished for the morning,' he'd said.

Better and better. Now she wouldn't have to endure any more of that ear-splitting racket. 'In that case, why don't you join me?'

He'd smiled. '*Grazie*, but I need to rest now.'

She'd smiled back. 'From what I hear from Lucy, I'm not surprised.' His perfectly arched eyebrows had shot up at this. *Yes!* Just as she'd thought it would, that had got his attention. Now the fun would start.

He'd come over at that. 'Lucy has spoken to you of me?'

'Oh, yes. Lucy and I are the best of friends; we tell each other everything. You're quite a hit with her. And I can quite understand why.' She'd let her eyes do the talking by looking him up and down.

'A hit? What is that? A punch?'

Oh, God, she'd thought, don't you just love it when these simple foreign guys can't speak English! 'Have some coffee with me and I'll tell you,' she'd said. 'My name's Savannah, by the way.'

He took her to a nearby bar, in the arcade of shops and restaurants, where he'd said she would be able to eat the best croissants in Bellagio.

'So,' Savannah said now, having demolished two croissants stuffed with apricots and a piece of toast – her hangover fast disappearing. 'What would you like to know about Lucy?'

He drank his coffee in one mouthful. After he'd replaced the cup in its saucer, he stretched out his legs to one side of the table and fixed his amazing eyes on hers. 'Nothing,' he said softly. 'I'm much more interested in you. Why don't you tell me everything about *you*?'

Score! Just as she'd thought. A randy Italian who was always up for it. Wait till she told Lucy that he'd tried it on with her as well! That would take the smug look off her face for sure.

The day had just got supremely better.

Chapter Fifty-five

Helen felt horribly sick. She should have forced herself to eat something at breakfast, but it had been beyond her; all she'd been able to stomach was a cup of coffee, which she'd had in her room. Now, as she sat apart from the rest of group at the front of the boat for the return journey to Bellagio, she tried not to think how queasy she was feeling. But it wasn't working. Just as it was futile to try and forget that awful conversation she'd had earlier with Mac.

Several times during the tour of the Villa del Balbianello she had caught him looking at her and each time it had made her want to shrivel up and die. The worst moment had been when they were standing in the shade of the loggia – with Tremezzina behind them and the stretch of water towards Isola Comacina in front of them – and their guide had been describing how Cardinal Durini, the original owner of the villa, had had the loggia built with two rooms either side of it, a library and a music room. 'It was in these two rooms,' their guide explained, 'that Cardinal Durini spent most of his time with his closest friends. Some of them were the greatest intellects of their day.'

It was at the mention of the word 'friends' that Mac had looked directly at Helen, his face displaying withering contempt. In that one look of his she imagined she saw a lifetime of animosity distilled. She felt weak, as though he'd struck her. How she had wanted to throw herself at him and beg his forgiveness! But it could never be. The two people who had come to mean so much to her since moving to Swanmere – Mac and Conrad – hated her and she couldn't blame them. She was the author of her own predicament. Consequently, she would never know their kindness again. Their friendship was over and she would regret that for ever.

The feeling of nausea was getting worse now. For something to do, she opened her handbag for Hunter's mobile so that she could ring the nursing home and check on Emma. She'd brought Hunter's phone with her because she'd forgotten to recharge the battery of her own mobile overnight. Hunter's mobile was a far more expensive and complicated piece of technology than her simple old thing and so she took a few minutes to familiarize herself with how it worked. Once she had, she scrolled through the menu, looking for Hunter's address book, hoping that he would have added the number she wanted. His address book was extensive, as she'd guessed it would be; most of the names were completely unknown to her. But there was one name and number that she did recognize. She stared at it for a couple of seconds. Why? Why would Hunter have that particular number stored on his phone? She continued to stare at the small screen and then she mentally flipped a coin.

Heads: it meant nothing and she was being paranoid.

Tails: it meant something and she should take it further.

She took it further.

Within seconds she'd accessed Hunter's text messages. It took even less time for suspicion to collide with truth. It was all there in that childish language of abbreviation and misspelling that she'd naively thought was the preserve of teenagers. Hunter was having an affair. And with all people, the woman she'd counted on as a best friend. Annabel.

When the *traghetto* pulled into the landing stage at Bellagio, Helen couldn't get off the boat fast enough. The hubbub of voices and the smell of diesel were closing in on her, making her stomach heave. She began to worry that she wouldn't make it back to the hotel in time. With a hand pressed to her mouth, her pulse racing and her head spinning, she moved fast, rudely pushing her way through the crowds. How could Annabel do this to her? Hunter she could almost understand. But Annabel? She was her friend. She was the one who had encouraged her to go out with Hunter in the first place. 'Don't let him slip through your hands,' she'd said.

She was almost across the Piazza Mazzini in front of the Hotel du Lac when her body just seemed to give up. Her legs went from beneath her and the sky began to whirl. Then it went black. The last thing she was aware of was an ear-piercing screech of brakes and people gasping.

Conrad was first to reach Helen. It had all happened so fast. One minute he'd been watching her hurrying off the boat, and the next she was a crumpled heap on the ground, a car with its front tyre just inches from her body.

He dropped to his knees and spoke her name softly, fearfully. 'Helen. Can you hear me? Helen?' Getting no response, he put a hand to her throat, moving aside the silk scarf that was tied there. A crowd had now gathered around them.

'*Dottore!*' someone shouted.

'*Ambulanza!*'

'*Polizia!*'

'*Infarto!*'

As far as Conrad knew, *infarto* meant heart attack, and he was sure that wasn't what had felled Helen. Above the rising mayhem, he heard Mac telling everyone to get back. One man ignored him; he was the driver of the car and he was in a voluble state of wild agitation, gesticulating frantically, his eyes wide. '*Non ha guardato!*' he yelled, pointing down at Helen. '*Non ho avuto tempo di fermarmi! Dio mio!*'

'Okay, okay,' shouted Conrad at the man. 'She didn't look and you didn't have time to stop. Now shut up!' In the sudden hush, and as Francesca took the driver to one side, Conrad tried again to feel for a pulse. All the while he tried hard not to let himself be reminded of another time, another place. He closed his eyes. *Come on, Helen,* he willed her. *Don't do this to me. Not you as well.* He fought to focus his concentration, to ignore his heart pounding painfully in his chest. Sweat was pooling between his shoulder blades and a paralysing fear was threatening to engulf him.

Then suddenly he felt it. It was faint, but it was a pulse all the same. He snapped his eyes open. Alive! Thank God!

'How's she doing?'

He looked up to see Mac crouching beside him. Orlando and Lucy were behind him. 'She's alive. More than that I don't know. Has anyone actually called for an ambulance?'

A young waiter said, '*Sì*, there is one on its way.'

'Do you think we should risk moving her?' Mac asked gruffly.

Conrad shook his head. 'No. We've no idea what damage may have been done. Does anyone know if the car hit her?'

'I don't think it could have.'

This was from Orlando.

'You saw it happen?' Conrad demanded.

'Not exactly. I'm just guessing. But going by the close proximity of where she's lying to where the car is, I doubt it. She would have taken a real flyer if the car had made any contact. What's more, there doesn't appear to be a dent in the bonnet of car. Or the bumper.'

Conrad winced. 'Can you check with the driver?' He looked at Francesca. But before Francesca had a chance to say anything, the circle of onlookers moved to let someone through. It was Savannah. With her was Alessio, the pianist from the hotel.

'Bloody hell!' Savannah exclaimed. 'It's Helen! She's not dead, is she?'

Mac stood up and held her back. 'We're waiting for an ambulance. It should be here any minute.'

Francesca came over to Conrad. 'The driver says it happened so fast he doesn't know for sure if he made contact with her.'

The sound of a siren made everyone turn to look up the busy road. Conrad felt a wave of relief. But it was short-lived. It wasn't the ambulance, it was the *polizia*. Two officers stepped out of the Alfa Romeo and immediately began trying to disperse the crowd of onlookers. They seemed to add to the commotion, instead of easing it.

'Would you like me to handle this?' Francesca asked when the officers started questioning people, including the driver of the car who, now he had an official audience, had erupted again with a babbling torrent of arm-waving, eye-rolling incomprehensibility.

Only too willing to let their guide take charge, Conrad nodded. All he cared about was Helen. She was still motionless. Still out cold. He felt so helpless. The thought that she might never come round filled him with such pain he could hardly breathe. How would he ever live with himself knowing that their last conversation had been so acrimonious? 'Oh, Helen,' he whispered, bending closer to her so that his mouth was almost touching her ear. 'Forgive me, please. I didn't mean half of what I said.' He jerked back from her. Had he just imagined it, or had she moved? 'Helen?'

Her eyes flickered open. Closed. Then opened again. 'Conrad?'

Relief surged through him. 'Yes,' he murmured, 'it's me.'

She squinted in the bright sunlight. 'What's happened? Why are all these people staring at me?'

'We're not entirely sure, but you're currently the star attraction in Bellagio. How do you feel?'

'Awful. My head hurts.'

'Concussion very likely. I wouldn't try—'

Too late. She raised her head from the ground and then he saw the blood on the tarmac beneath her. 'Hold it there,' he said. Very carefully he untied the silk scarf from around her neck and placed it gently under her head. 'I hope that wasn't too expensive,' he said. 'I'll buy you a new one if you like.'

She smiled weakly. 'I'm sorry, Conrad. I'm sorry for everything I've said and done. I shouldn't have lied to you. Forgive me, please.' Her smile faded and a tear spilled out from her eye; it slid slowly down her cheek.

He stroked it away. 'Nothing to forgive,' he said softly. And meaning it. 'Everything's going to be all right.'

She closed her eyes and her face dimmed. 'Tell Mac I'm sorry too. I didn't mean to make him hate me.'

'You can tell him yourself. He's right here. Helen? *Helen*, can you hear me?'

But he knew the answer. She couldn't hear anything more. She'd slipped back into unconsciousness. He gripped her hand, wrapping his fingers around hers.

Seconds later another siren sounded. This time it was the ambulance.

Chapter Fifty-six

An assumption had been made that Conrad was Helen's husband, and as a consequence he was invited to go in the ambulance with her to the hospital. Francesca had explained that the hospital was in Lecco, about twenty-five minutes away. 'I'll meet you there so I can help with any language difficulties you might encounter,' she'd told Conrad. It was at this point that Mac had asked Francesca if he could tag along with her. He'd never forgive himself if Helen died without him being able to make amends. His behaviour that morning had been nothing short of despicable. He'd treated her shabbily; no two ways about it. And now he might never get the chance to explain his reasons for speaking out the way he did. He hadn't known her for long, but when he thought of all the enjoyable times they'd spent together, his throat constricted. Her quiet, benign company had been a soothing balm to his infernal mood swings. So often she'd lifted his spirits with her unexpected flashes of humour and perceptiveness. She'd even played along with his flirting games, making an old man feel young again. Stupid old fool that he was!

He dashed away the tears from his eyes with the palm of his hand, grateful that Francesca was too preoccupied with negotiating the winding road to notice.

Back at the Hotel Villa Rosa, sitting in the terrace garden with Orlando, Lucy and Alessio, Savannah was trying to get hold of her father. Because he didn't have his mobile with him, she had no way of getting in touch with him directly, so she was ringing Clancy. Clancy always knew what to do. He'd know where Dad was staying and they'd be able to ring the hotel.

As she waited for her step-brother to answer his phone, Savannah couldn't wait to offload onto him. She wanted to see how he'd react to the news that he wasn't the only one with a baby on the way. When the paramedics had been loading Helen onto the ambulance, she'd overheard Conrad telling them that she was pregnant. *Pregnant!* She couldn't believe it. The whole bastard idea was disgusting. The last thing she wanted was a baby brother or sister. The thought of her father fawning over the little brat filled her with hatred.

At last she heard Clancy's voice. 'Hi, Savannah,' he said. 'How's Italy? I hope the weather's better there than it is here.'

She quickly told him what had happened and that she couldn't get in touch with their father in Dubai.

'Dubai?' he repeated. 'What's Dad doing there?'

'I haven't a clue. Hang on. Didn't you know he was there? He got a call yesterday morning and he was gone by the afternoon.'

'It's news to me. But don't panic, I'll get onto his PA, Judith. She'll know where he is. Savannah, you didn't say, but how is Helen?'

'I don't know. She was unconscious when they put her in the ambulance.'

'Are you at the hospital with her?'

'No.'

'She's there alone?'

Savannah heard the disbelief in her step-brother's voice. Also its edge of criticism. Clancy had always got along with Helen. 'Don't be stupid,' she said defensively, 'of course she isn't alone. Some friends are there with her.'

'Good. Now sit tight and I'll get back to you. Okay?'

Minutes later, Savannah's phone rang. Clancy sounded puzzled. 'Judith doesn't know anything about Dubai,' he said. 'She was under the impression Dad was still in Italy with you and Helen.'

'But that's crazy. You know how Dad always jokes that he could cover his tracks with twelve coats of paint and Judith would still be able to find him.'

'It sounds odd, I'll grant you. The good news is that she knows the hotels he normally uses and is ringing round. We'll be in contact with him within the hour, I'm sure. Do you want me to fly over?'

'No. You stay there. As soon as I hear anything from the hospital, I'll let you know.' She ended the call. Only then did she remember that she'd forgotten to tell him that Helen was pregnant.

Whilst she'd been having this conversation the others had moved away to another table to give her some privacy, but now they drifted back to hear what she had to say. Despite their big bust-up last night, Orlando was actually being nice to her. A shame he couldn't have got his act together sooner.

Lucy listened to Savannah's explanation about Hunter's PA back in England now being on the case to locate her father and knew that something didn't add up. She could clearly remember on the boat yesterday morning – when they were crossing the lake to Tremezzo – that Hunter had said his assistant was checking the flight availability to Dubai. '*As we speak*,' his actual words had been. She had a bad feeling about all this.

Something else she had a bad feeling about was what she'd seen just seconds before the accident. Across the Piazza Mazzini, and beneath the awning of one of the bars, she had clearly seen Savannah and Alessio sitting at a table together.

Orlando's words at Villa del Balbianello came back to haunt her – '*Doesn't it bother you that you're probably nothing more than this week's hot chick?*' Could she really have been so stupid as to think that what she and Alessio had been experiencing was anything other than a two-second holiday fling? What hurt most was how he'd made her feel. Special. Adored. Wanted. Desired. Now she knew every word he'd uttered had been a well-practised sham. Nothing more than the means to keep himself amused until the next girl came along. Couldn't he have had the decency to wait until she'd gone home?

And did it have to be Savannah?

How she hated that girl!

It was selfish of her to be so caught up in her own thoughts when poor Helen was being rushed to hospital, but it was all Lucy could do to keep herself from slapping Savannah across the face and then kicking Alessio somewhere painful. How satisfying that would be!

She moved away from the group, just in case she did give in to the urge to teach Savannah and Alessio a lesson they wouldn't forget. She walked to the end of the terrace and watched a woman on a nearby balcony watering the pots of flowers. She suddenly wanted to be back in Swanmere watering her own garden. She thought of Dan and pictured him in his smelly old jacket, leaning on a hoe and chatting with Bill and Joe. How straightforward his life was compared to hers. He got up in the morning, pottered about at home and then spent the rest of the day working his plot.

Perhaps when she reached that age her own life would be as calm and uncomplicated.

'Lucia?'

It could only be Alessio.

She whirled round. 'Don't call me that!' she fired back at him. 'In fact, don't say anything to me ever again.'

Twenty-two kilometres away in Lecco, Conrad thought he was in hell. The waiting was unbearable. For too long there had been no word on Helen's condition. No news is good news, he kept reminding himself.

Thank God he had Mac with him. And Francesca. She'd been a great support, helping with the formality of the paperwork and translating when needed. She was outside at the moment, on her mobile to her husband. Who, it turned out, was none other than Lucy's father. Francesca had been quick to say that Lucy was still in ignorance of this.

'Why don't you sit down?' Conrad said to Mac, who had been pacing the waiting room now for the last ten minutes. 'You'll wear yourself out.'

Mac grunted. 'That's the least of my worries.' He paced some more, then came to a stop in front of Conrad. 'The thing is, I did something terrible this morning. Something I'll always regret.'

Conrad raised his head. 'Would a confession help?'

'I think it might.'

'Then fire away.'

'I ... I told Helen that she and Hunter should move out of Swanmere.'

Conrad frowned, but kept quiet.

'It gets worse. I told her I hated her.'

Now Conrad was appalled. 'Why? Why would you say a thing like that to Helen? You adore her.'

Mac's shoulders slumped and he looked forlorn. 'I was angry. I was furious at what she was doing to you.'

'You shouldn't have got involved. I'm more than old enough to fight my own battles.'

'I know. Call it protective love.' He exhaled deeply. 'You mean the world to me, Conrad. And I know this might not seem the right time to tell you this, but I'm going to say it anyway. I've wanted to for some—'

He got no further. A woman in a white coat – presumably a

doctor – appeared in the doorway of the waiting room. '*Signor Madison-Tyler?*'

Conrad sprang to his feet. '*Sono il Signor Truman. Un amico.*'

A frown wrinkled the woman's brow. It made her look even more serious than she already did. '*Dov'e il marito?*'

Good bloody question, thought Conrad. Hunter could be any-where. '*Non lo so,*' he answered. His basic knowledge of Italian wasn't going to get him much further. He wished Francesca would return.

'Please,' said Mac, taking the classic British way of handling matters, that of annunciating very slowly and clearly in what used to pass for BBC English. 'What ... can ... you ... tell ... us ... about ... Helen?'

The doctor finally smiled, causing Conrad to feel a flicker of hope. '*La Signora* Madison-Tyler is awake now. She is suffering from concussion but she will be fine.'

'Thank God!' Conrad let out. Just as relief kicked in, he saw Mac close his eyes as if in prayer, but then he swayed and sud-denly he was no longer vertical. The old man's knees buckled and Conrad leapt to break his fall.

Chapter Fifty-seven

Groggy with shock and pain, Helen thought how odd it was that the flotsam of one's childhood should come to the surface at the unlikeliest of times. She was remembering being nine years old and finding a dead bird in the garden.

It was autumn and after two days of stormy weather, the wind and rain had shaken the leaves from the trees and left them covering the lawn and flowerbeds in a thick multi-layered blanket. Helen was helping her grandfather rake the leaves into wet slippery piles when she found the remains of a bird. It was no more than a skeleton and its skull was bashed in. She wasn't scared by it. As with most young children, morbid fascination outweighed any fear and she'd got down onto her knees in the sodden grass to get a better look. She called to her grandfather to come and see. 'Do you suppose it flew into a tree and knocked itself out?' she asked him. Last summer a blackbird had flown into the kitchen window after the window cleaner had been and it had lain on the ground for ages before it managed to pick itself up and fly off. 'It must have been flying very fast to smash its head like that.'

'More likely its skull was crushed after it died,' her grandfather said.

'You mean someone might have trodden on it?' she asked. Somehow this didn't seem fair to the poor little thing.

'These things happen,' her grandfather had said as he added the remains of the bird to one of the piles of leaves.

For weeks afterwards Helen had watched where she stepped in the garden.

If only she had been as careful today, she thought. If she hadn't been so upset and made herself sick with worry and needed to rush back to the hotel, she wouldn't feel as though her own skull had been crushed by a careless boot.

So long as she didn't move the pain was bearable, but the slightest movement caused an explosion to go off inside her head. If she had understood the doctor correctly, she must have fainted and cracked her head when she hit the ground. She was to be kept in overnight for observation, and providing nothing was amiss, she would be discharged tomorrow. What happened then was anyone's guess.

There was a faint knock at the door. 'All right to come in?'

She made the mistake of instinctively twisting her head towards the door that was opening. Bang! She closed her eyes at the pain. When it had subsided, she opened her eyes and saw Conrad hovering in the doorway. She motioned for him to come into the room.

He came and stood by the side of the bed. 'How're you doing?'

'I've been better.'

'You gave us all a terrible scare.'

'I scared myself. Why don't you sit down?'

He pulled up a chair and leant forward so that he was resting an elbow on the bed. The concern on his face touched her so tangibly she reached out to him. He took her hand and held it gently in his. She had so much to say to him. So much to straighten out. It was then that she noticed how pale and strained he looked. 'Conrad, are you okay?'

'Hey, that's not how this works. I'm the one sitting comfortably in the chair and you're the one in the bed with a head covered in a bandage.'

She sensed he was prevaricating, but her brain was too foggy to get to the bottom of it. What was of paramount importance to her now was what she had to tell him. 'Conrad,' she began, 'What I said to you—'

'It doesn't matter,' he interrupted her. 'I don't care any more that you kept your pregnancy from me.'

'Please, Conrad, let me speak.'

'Helen, it's okay. Really. It's not important to me. All I want is for you to be happy.'

'But I lied. I lied when I said I was pregnant.'

She saw the confusion in his eyes. 'But why? Why did you say that you were?'

'To put an end to ... to us. I was desperate. It was all I could think to say that would make you hate me. I've been sick with regret ever since.'

'Oh, Helen. I could never hate you.'

'And there's something else you should know. I'm leaving Hunter.'

'You are?'

'He's been having an affair. I'm not trying to claim any moral high ground, but enough's enough. It's not what I want for Emma, but I can't go on.'

'When did you know about the affair?'

'I found out this morning, on the boat coming back from Lenno. I tried to use Hunter's mobile and discovered an exchange of text messages with ... with a friend of mine. That's why I wasn't looking where I was going when I crossed that road. All I could think of was my friend's betrayal.'

He squeezed her hand. 'You know that Hunter's with her now, don't you?'

She did a double take. 'You knew?'

He nodded.

'But how?'

'I didn't believe the unexpected need to rush off to Dubai so I checked with the airlines. There was no flight for the time he claimed to be travelling. And I overheard him talking to the woman on his mobile at Villa Carlotta.'

'You should have told me.'

'I couldn't do it.'

'I don't understand.'

'I didn't want to take the risk that you'd get involved with me just to get back at your husband. It had to be real between us.'

'It's always been real between us, Conrad. That's what's been the trouble. Right from the word go.' Exhaustion crept up on her and she closed her eyes briefly. When she opened them, Conrad was standing over her. He looked as if he was about to bend down and kiss her. But a knock at the door had him glancing over his shoulder.

Conrad tried to read the expression on Francesca's face as she appeared in the doorway. Good news or bad news, he couldn't tell.

'Sorry to disturb you,' she said quietly, 'but the doctor says your uncle is asking for you.'

He turned to Helen to indicate he'd return when he could, and seeing the alarm in her face, he added, 'I'll explain later.' And then he was out of the door and moving at full speed. He hoped to God it wasn't another stroke. He knew the chance of it happening was high, but if there was any justice in the world Mac would be spared a second stroke. Especially a massive, debilitating one.

He'd tried to give the staff as many details as he could about Mac's medical history while his uncle was being lifted onto the bed, but they soon made it clear that his presence was not required.

He had deliberately not mentioned anything to Helen about Mac collapsing because he knew she would only worry. Also, he didn't think he had the strength to pretend he wasn't scared to death that Mac might be about to die on him.

'He's in here,' Francesca said, coming to a stop in front of a closed door. 'I'll go and see if there's anything Helen needs.'

'Thank you. Just one thing, though. Please try to put Helen's mind at rest about Mac. Don't let her think there's anything seriously wrong. She's had enough shocks for one day.'

He watched Francesca go back the way they'd just come, then taking a deep breath he knocked on the door and pushed it open. Grey-faced, Mac was propped up in bed. His chest was bare and dotted with sensor pads that led to a monitoring device on a nearby trolley. He looked dazed and frail, as if he had aged by about ten years. His lips were moving, as though he was talking in his sleep. Conrad was glad Mac's eyes were closed; it meant he couldn't see the shock he was feeling. A nurse was studying the monitoring device and after she had made an adjustment to it, she smiled at Conrad. She then very lightly touched Mac on the forearm. 'Signor Truman, your son, he is here now. Didn't I tell you he would come?'

Conrad approached the bed cautiously, his eyes glued to Mac's, which were now fluttering open.

'Ten minutes only,' the nurse instructed, 'your father needs much rest.'

'He's not my father,' he corrected her absent-mindedly. 'He's my—' But he stopped himself short. As his unfinished sentence hung in the air, the nurse shrugged and left the room. For what felt like for ever, he stood watching the door slowly close behind her with a whispering swish.

Could it be true? But even as he asked himself the question, he knew the answer. Perhaps he'd always known. Myriad images from his childhood came before him, and one by one, they assembled an altogether different picture from the one that he was familiar with. In an instant the past was recreated. There was no shock to this discovery; it simply made sense.

Going over to the bed, Conrad once more pulled up a chair. Once more he asked the same question: 'How're you doing?'

'Bugger me if I know,' Mac said weakly, his voice sounding slightly strangulated. 'Nobody tells me anything.'

At least he was coherent, Conrad thought. 'No mention of a stroke, then?'

'Not so far. But then how would I know with everyone gabbling on in Italian?'

Conrad managed a smile. Same old Mac.

Except he wasn't the same old Mac. Everything had changed. And all because of a perfectly reasonable misunderstanding. *Signor Truman, your son, he is here ... your father needs much rest.* He repeated the words over and over. Oh, yes, it certainly made sense. The wonder was he'd never made the connection before. 'Do you have enough energy to talk?' he asked Mac.

Mac nodded. 'How's Helen?'

'She's fine.'

'Really?'

'Yes.'

'And the baby? Has that come to any harm?'

'There is no baby.' Conrad gave Mac an edited version of what Helen had told him.

'So it was a ruse to throw you off the scent. Damned near worked, too, didn't it?'

'Not when I thought she was dying,' Conrad said. 'In that moment I knew I could forgive her anything.'

From nowhere, a stagnant silence descended on them. Noises from beyond the room – voices, shrill and insistent, a telephone ringing, a child crying – filtered through to magnify the booming resonance of the deathly hush. A frown began to gather on Mac's brow. He glanced away, then looked back at Conrad. 'Do the same rules apply for me? Would you forgive me anything?'

'In a blink of an eye.'

Mac's hands trembled and the frown deepened. 'Even if you discovered you'd been lied to all your life?'

'Does this have anything to do with what you started to tell me in the waiting room earlier?'

'Yes.'

'You're my father, aren't you? Edwin Truman brought me up, but you're my biological father.'

Tears filled Mac's bloodshot eyes. 'I made your mother a promise. And by God, as hard as it was, I kept it all these years.'

'Until today. Why?'

'What with Helen, I'd thought you'd been lied to enough. Suddenly, all I could think of was me dying and you never knowing the truth. I needed you to know everything. Even though it was breaking my promise to your mother.'

'Why didn't you say anything when you had your stroke? Surely you felt more at risk then?'

'I don't know. Perhaps I was a different man then. Not so defeated. All I know now is that I couldn't take the secret to my grave. Truth is, I think that day is coming sooner than I'd like. I've been having these dizzy turns.'

'Why the hell didn't you tell me?'

'I didn't want to cause a fuss and get you in a lather. You can be the very devil for that.'

Conrad passed a hand over his face. He suddenly felt bone-weary. 'Now isn't the time, but when you're feeling stronger, I'd like to know the truth. About you and my mother.'

'No! It has to be now. I might not get another chance.'

'Nonsense. You're match fit, Mac. You're going to be fine.'

'Don't patronize me! Anything but that!'

Worried that if he went against Mac's wishes any more he might bring on another collapse, Conrad gave in. 'Okay,' he said. 'But don't exhaust yourself. The nurse said you needed to rest.'

Mac scowled, and after seeming to rummage in his thoughts, he began his story.

'Your father was never particularly robust, physically or mentally, but the war was his undoing. He should never have been allowed to join the RAF as a bomber pilot. He should have had a safe desk job. If only fate had seen fit to make me the older brother instead of Edwin, then I would have been the one to endure what he did. As it was, I was born too late and Edwin too early. He wasn't able to put the horror of it behind him and afterwards he went into the Church to make some kind of atonement. Except it didn't work. The way he saw it, he couldn't ever be forgiven for dropping bombs on all those innocent people. He couldn't see that it was a means to a justified end. Sometimes, it was as though he wanted to put names and faces to all those unknown people he'd killed. The guilt tore at his guts. I suppose he was what you'd call, in modern parlance, a functioning depressive. He could keep it under control. Just.'

'But what about when he married my mother? Surely that changed things for him?'

'It did. For a time. But then after years of trying for a child, the depression took hold of him again. He started to believe that it was a punishment sent from God for what he'd done in the war. That's when your mother needed someone to turn to.'

'You?'

'We never intended for things to go the way they did, but we fell in love. It wasn't a sordid affair, if that's what you're thinking. It was love. I'd have done anything for her. Which I did. I gave her a child. You.'

'I was planned?'

'Oh, yes. Hannah wanted children as much as Edwin did and so I gave her what he couldn't. But on the understanding that I was never to tell anyone. I would have no claim. I would only ever be your uncle. Hannah made me swear to that.'

'That's quite a sacrifice.'

'The alternative was far worse, seeing Hannah miserable. This way at least the woman I loved would raise my child. There wasn't another woman on the planet with whom I would have wanted a family.'

'How did my father … Edwin, greet the news that my mother was pregnant?'

'He was overjoyed.'

'And Susan? Are you her father as well?'

Mac slowly shook his head. 'No. Nature intervened. Hannah always claimed that once Edwin believed in his ability to father a child, it would happen naturally for him. She was right.' Mac finally raised his eyes and looked directly at Conrad. 'You mustn't think badly of your mother. She was a good woman. The best. She never wanted to hurt your father. She loved him. And as I'm sure you remember, he wasn't the easiest of men to love. Or to live with.'

'I'm not judging you, Mac. Or my mother. I'd never do that.'

Mac sighed. 'She was so lonely. And so very tired of making do. Just about any money that came into the house, your father gave away. It was all I could do not to take a fist to him when I saw how difficult life was for Hannah. When things were really tight, I gave her money that your father never knew about. He was so wrapped up in himself, he hardly seemed to be aware of what was going on in his own home.'

'You think he never knew?'

'I'm sure of it. We were always very careful. Hannah made me promise that I would never jeopardize your father's happiness. He had experienced so little of it in his life, she used to say.'

'But why didn't she leave him and give them both a chance to start afresh?'

'I begged her to. But she wouldn't. It broke my heart. I would have done anything to have her to myself. But she wouldn't leave Edwin. "He's not as strong as you, Mac," she once said. "He doesn't have your resilience."'

Mac exhaled deeply and sank back further into the pillows behind him. 'So you see, Conrad,' he said tiredly, his eyelids drooping, 'when I was warning you off Helen, I knew what I was talking about. I spent a lifetime chasing a dream that never came true.'

'Yet you still held on to that dream, didn't you?'

'I had no choice in the matter. That's what love – real love – does to you. And now, if you don't mind, I think I'd like to rest.'

He drifted off to sleep, and as it so often was, Hannah's beautiful face was before him.

Chapter Fifty-eight

Francesca had given Conrad Truman her mobile phone number and told him to ring if he needed anything. She had offered to stay but he'd assured her he could manage from here on.

Desperate to go home, she was grateful for his assurance. It had been a long and eventful day. Eventful! That was one way to describe it. But before she could go home and prepare herself for the evening's ordeal with Marcus, she had to return to the Hotel Villa Rosa. She hoped that the members of the Gardens of Delight tour group wouldn't be too disappointed by her not being able to accompany them on their afternoon's visit to Villa d'Este at Cernobbio. She knew that for a lot of British and American tourists, the hotel and its beautiful Italianate garden was the highlight of any trip to Lake Como. Before leaving for the hospital in Lecco she had telephoned the agency and explained the situation. With the English guide still too ill to do her job and no one else available, Francesca had had no choice but to tell the members of the group who were still hanging around the Piazza Mazzini that if they wanted to visit the gardens at Villa d'Este they would have to go alone. There had been a few noticeable grumbles but on the whole the news had been accepted without complaint. Given the circumstances, it would have shown a lack of consideration on their part to act otherwise.

Now, though, Francesca knew it would be unprofessional of her not to call in at the Hotel Villa Rosa and see if anyone needed advice or assistance. She knew how helpless some tourists became when they were without their guide.

More importantly, with Alessio's help, she hoped to find Lucy at the hotel. The time had come.

She parked her car in the first available space she came across on Via Garibaldi and took the steps down to the hotel. She wasn't at all nervous. With a death sentence hanging over her, she had developed a sharpened sense of perspective. What did she have to lose by introducing herself to Lucy? So what if the girl was rude to her and told her to get lost? So what if Marcus accused her of interfering? What did any of it matter now?

Lucy had chosen not to go to Cernobbio on the hydrofoil to see the Villa d'Este. Instead she had spent the afternoon alone wandering round the shops in Bellagio buying presents to take home.

Now, against her better judgement, she was having a drink with Alessio in the garden at the Hotel Villa Rosa. Sipping a cold beer, she was determined not to make a fool of herself by giving Alessio the satisfaction of thinking that she cared what he'd been up to. If he wanted to come on to Savannah behind her back than that was his business. It was no concern of hers. But as he continued to look at her, his eyes so dark and compelling, she wanted to scream and shout with jealous rage. Why her? Why Savannah-bloody-Tyler?

When she'd lost her temper with him earlier, and had told him never to speak to her again, she had taken herself off to her room. He hadn't followed her and nor had he been waiting for her when she eventually came out an hour later. Relieved he wasn't going to pester her, she'd found herself a lakeside bar for a late lunch and had then gone shopping. It was when she was returning to the hotel that she found him leaning nonchalantly against the marble desk in the reception area and talking to the pretty receptionist. 'Lucia,' he'd exclaimed loudly, taking her by the arm. 'Come and have a drink with me. *Ciao!*' he said to the receptionist who was now smiling at him as Lucy struggled to break free of his grasp. All he did was hold her even more firmly. Only when he'd led her upstairs to the roof garden and he'd manhandled her into a chair had he let go of her.

'Lucia,' he said now, 'five minutes we have been sitting here and not a word have you said. What is the matter?'

'I'm upset about Helen,' she said, speaking the truth. 'I'd have thought that would be obvious.'

'Yes,' he said, 'of course.' He was quiet for a minute, whilst he drank some of his beer. 'But earlier, when I tried to speak to you when Savannah and Orlando were here, you were very angry with me. Why?'

'I wasn't,' she lied.

'*Sì.* You raised your voice at me. And then you ran off.'

'Why would I be sitting here having a drink with you if I was cross with you?'

He slid his chair back, crossed his legs and drummed the long, elegant fingers of his right hand on his knee. 'I think you're here with me against your wishes. I think you would rather be anywhere but here. I'm right, aren't I?'

She tore her eyes away from his fingers which were still moving rhythmically. She thought how they'd brought her to a mind-blowing climax only that morning, and swallowed. 'Have you given me any reason to be angry with you?' she asked. Good question, she congratulated herself with a swell of pride. Let's see him wriggle out of that one!

'Yes, it is possible that I have.'

What a cool customer he was! 'Really?' she asked, doing her best to stay calm and play along. 'What have you done?'

'I took Savannah for a cup of coffee.'

'Is that it?' she said with what she hoped was just the right amount of incredulous disbelief. 'Is that what you think has made me cross?'

She obviously didn't get it right for he suddenly snapped forward in his seat. '*Lucia! Ti prego!* Be honest with me. Stop playing these games. I know you saw me with Savannah. And I know too what you have been thinking ever since. But you are wrong. Very wrong. *Credi mi. Ti prego!*'

'Oh, don't go all Italian on me, Alessio, please.'

He looked at her, his eyes wide. 'You will have to forgive me, but I *am* Italian!'

'I mean, don't start speaking in Italian. You know I can't understand you when you do that.'

'The real problem is you don't understand me. Not the first thing about me.'

'Oh, I understand you all right. You come on to me, have sex with me, then move on to the next conquest before I've even left town. Where I come from we call that bad manners!'

'*Merda!* I knew that was what you were thinking all along.' He leaned even further forward and one of his elegant hands reached out for hers. 'Listen to me, Lucia. I want you to know that what you saw was not what you thought it was.'

She snatched her hand away. 'Please don't insult my intelligence.'

'That is something I will only do if you refuse to let me speak.

And in case you were wondering, the receptionist I was talking to a few moments ago is my cousin, Antonia.'

The arrogance of the man! As if it had even crossed her mind! 'Okay, speak. But don't expect me to be interested in anything you have to say. Especially if you're going to talk about Savannah.'

'But you would agree with me, wouldn't you, if I were to say that she is a most cunning girl?'

'No argument there!'

'Good. I am pleased we agree on that point. *Allora*. This morning when I was practising at the piano she asked me to join her for a cup of coffee. She was not subtle. She made it very clear what her game was.'

'Takes one to know one,' Lucy muttered.

Ignoring her, he carried on. 'I decided to find out what she was up to. You see, she mentioned you and said what good friends the two of you were, and how you told her everything.'

'The liar!' burst out Lucy. 'I never tell her anything.'

He nodded. 'I knew that. I remembered how you spoke about the girl. It was not in her favour. It was then I knew for sure what game she was playing, so I went along with her, just to see what she was prepared to do. *Dio mio!* Lucia, I swear to you, she is the work of the devil. But she told me something that upsets me. She said that you were only interested in me to make Orlando jealous. She said you—'

Lucy cut him off. 'I think I've heard enough of what that little bitch has to say.'

'But do you believe me? Do you believe that I am telling you the truth?'

God help her, but Lucy did. There was such a ring of truth to everything Alessio had told her that it was all too easy to picture Savannah doing exactly what Alessio had described. The girl just couldn't stop herself.

'Lucia?' he prompted her. 'You haven't answered me.'

'I'm sorry,' she said. 'Yes, I do believe you.'

'Really?'

'Although why it should matter, I don't know.'

'It matters a great deal to me.'

She shrugged. 'I leave here the day after tomorrow. I don't suppose we will ever meet again.'

He was frowning now. 'Is that what you want? Never to see me again?'

'I'm being practical.'

'It seems to me that maybe Savannah was right. You have used me. I have just been a holiday amusement to you, a way to score a point against the man you love, but who loves another.'

She looked at him in astonishment. 'That's not true! And if it were, why was I so upset at the thought of you and Savannah?' She instantly regretted her words. She had laid her feelings bare, had made herself vulnerable. And all for what?

'Do you love Orlando?' he asked. Alessio's expression was suddenly intensely earnest.

The question, so plainly put, made her think about her answer. 'Yes,' she said, after a brief pause. 'I do. I think I always have.' She might have been wrong, but she thought she saw disappointment in Alessio's face. 'Let me explain what I mean,' she said. 'I love Orlando like a brother. For years now, we've been inseparable. I couldn't imagine it being any other way.'

'You know what you two should do?'

So caught up in their conversation, Lucy had forgotten where they were and together with Alessio, they both turned at the sound of a deep, raspy voice with an American accent. Looming over their table was a large woman dressed in a powder-blue jogging suit. It was an unfortunate choice of outfit for it resembled a romper suit and made her look like a grotesquely overweight baby. Her hair was startlingly blonde and sat atop her head in a weirdly elaborate fashion. 'My friend and I,' – she pointed to a diminutive woman at a nearby table – 'couldn't help but overhear what you were saying, and we both think you should simply kiss and make up. We think you make a great-looking couple.'

Lucy was too stunned to speak, but Alessio said, '*Grazie signora. Tante grazie.*'

'Don't mention it, honey. My mother always used to say advice comes free. It's when we ignore it that it costs us.'

They watched her waddle back to her friend and when she'd parked her enormous powder-blue bottom on the chair, Alessio whispered, 'Shall we?'

'Shall we what?'

'Take their advice and kiss.'

'Could it be as simple as that?'

'*Mia* Lucia, unless we try we will never know.'

She looked into those soft dark eyes and couldn't help herself. They were mid-delicious kiss when once more they were interrupted, this time by an attractive woman clearing her throat. With the colour rising to her cheeks, Lucy recognized the woman as their guide from that morning's excursion. Alessio stood up and to Lucy's surprise greeted the woman warmly. '*Ciao. Comé sta?*' After an exchange of cheek-kissing, and some rapid-fire talk, he offered her a chair. Alessio, also sitting down now, spoke to Lucy. 'Lucia,' he said, 'let me introduce you to your step-mother, Francesca Gray.'

Chapter Fifty-nine

Francesca wasn't at all what Lucy had expected. She looked nothing like the woman she had hated since she was fourteen years old. Only that morning, during the tour of the Villa del Balbianello, she had thought what a pleasant, friendly woman their guide was. She had been impressed, too, by how efficiently she had dealt with things this afternoon. Now, as Lucy remembered Francesca's reassuring presence, how she had quietly taken charge – talking to the police and paramedics, and keeping the group informed of what was going on – she recalled a small exchange between the woman and Alessio. She hadn't thought about it at the time, but she wondered now if this meeting had been planned.

'Why didn't you introduce yourself to me this morning?' she asked eventually.

'I wanted to but it didn't feel right. I made up my mind to say something when we arrived back at Bellagio. I was going to offer to take you for a drink. But then everything changed and I had to go to Lecco with Mrs Madison-Tyler.'

Concern for Helen instantly put all other thoughts aside. 'God, yes! How is Helen?'

'Despite suffering a nasty bang to the head, she was making a good recovery when I saw her last. The doctor indicated that she would be discharged tomorrow. Mr Truman was going to stay for the evening.'

'With his uncle, Mac?'

'Oh … perhaps you don't know. Mr Truman's uncle was taken ill at the hospital.'

Lucy shot forward in her seat, nearly knocking over her drink. 'Mac? Is he okay?' She had a sudden flash of recall – their first evening here when Mac had stumbled in the lift before dinner. Vertigo, he'd claimed.

'Again, the last I heard was that he was all right, but he was having a series of tests carried out on him. I believe he had a stroke a few years ago. That seemed to be his nephew's main concern, that it might be a second stroke.'

'Poor Mac. Maybe I should go to the hospital myself. I could keep Conrad company.'

'Yes, that might be a good idea. I would drive you there, but I have to—'

'That's okay, Francesca,' cut in Alessio, 'I can drive Lucia there myself.'

Grateful for his offer, Lucy said, 'But haven't you got to work this evening?'

'There is plenty of time to get you to Lecco and for me to come back before eight o'clock.' He got to his feet, spoke briefly in Italian to Francesca, and then to Lucy he said, 'I will leave you two to talk.' With a quick glance at his watch, he added, '*Allora*, I shall meet you in the foyer in an hour. If that is convenient to you?'

Lucy nodded her thanks.

When they were alone, Francesca said, 'I'm glad you've had a chance to get to know Alessio. He's an engaging young man.'

'I'm aware of his reputation, if that's what you're getting at. My father warned me.'

Seeming to choose her words with care, Francesca said, 'Marcus has not always been Alessio's number one fan. He disapproves of Alessio's love of ...' she hesitated. 'Of his love of falling in love.'

'My father's a fine one to talk.'

With a dark, unblinking gaze, the other woman stared at Lucy.

'I'm not going to take that back,' Lucy said defiantly.

'I wouldn't expect you to. You must speak your mind. I want you to feel you can be honest with me. Because I certainly intend to be honest with you.'

After all these years, Lucy felt as if she had finally locked horns with the cause of all the bitterness and pain she had been forced to endure. But she found she wasn't in the mood for confrontation. After the tumult of emotions she'd experienced today – her humiliating jealous anger with Alessio, her anxiety for Helen and now Mac – the fight had gone out of her. She sighed. 'Look, I don't want to argue with you. When it comes down to it, I don't know the first thing about you. Only that you're married to my father. I can't say that I'm over the moon to meet you. But then equally so, I'm not sitting here hating you.'

'That's more than I had hoped for.'

'But I really don't know what you think we can achieve by meeting like this.'

'If I hope to achieve anything, Lucy, it's this. I want you to change your view of your father. I want you to forgive Marcus.'

Lucy snorted. 'You're not asking for much, are you?'

'Would it be *that* difficult for you?'

Lucy thought of when she saw her father last night at the Serbelloni, when once more she'd felt the sting of his rejection. 'I was close to it during dinner last night,' she admitted.

'What stopped you?'

'I asked my father if he would change what he did if he had his time over again. He made it very clear he would choose you over me.'

Francesca looked shocked. 'He said that?'

'More or less.'

'*Che pazzo!* The idiot!'

'You should be flattered. He must love you an awful lot.'

'I can only imagine that he was trying to prove to you the gravitas of the situation. Even so, he should not have been so brutal. It wasn't fair to you. I'm so sorry, Lucy. I can't imagine how you must have felt. It was most insensitive of him. You should have thrown your glass of wine in his face. That's what I would have done. Then I would have walked out on him, making sure everyone was staring and wondering what kind of a devil he was. Believe me; I would have caused a scene he would not have forgotten in a hurry!'

Lucy smiled. Against all the odds, she decided she liked this woman. They had something in common: a temper. 'How old are you?' she asked.

'I'm forty-two. Fifteen years younger than your father.'

'And thirteen years older than me. You don't look your age.'

'I assure you I feel it today. Every year. And some more.'

Lucy took a moment to reflect on their conversation and drained the last of her glass of beer. She came to another decision. 'I don't know what time I'll be back from the hospital this evening, but if it isn't too late, could I visit you and Dad at home tonight?'

Francesca shook her head. 'I'm afraid that isn't a very good idea.'

'Oh.' Lucy felt let down.

'Please, let me explain. I have to talk to your father this evening.

There's something very important I have to tell him. Can you keep a secret, Lucy?'

'Um ... well, yes, I suppose so.'

'I was told this morning that I have lymphatic cancer. Marcus doesn't know. Not yet.' She took a deep breath. 'I have to tell your father that I'm dying, Lucy.'

'Dying? Are you sure?' Then realizing how crass she sounded, she said, 'Isn't it treatable?' Lucy found it hard to believe that this vibrant woman sitting opposite her could be dying. Even harder to believe was that she seemed so calm.

'In my case, no. My mother died of the same thing three years ago.'

'How long do you have?'

Francesca smiled ruefully. 'Not nearly long enough. This Christmas will be my last.'

'But how will Dad cope?'

'That's where I need your help, Lucy. When I'm no longer around, I want you to be the one Marcus turns to.'

'This is bloody ridiculous!' yelled Savannah. She was getting more and more frustrated and she didn't care who knew it. Let them stare! Sitting in a bar overlooking the lake, she was talking to Clancy on her mobile.

'It's as though he's disappeared off the face of the earth,' Clancy said. 'Judith can't understand it. We can't even locate the taxi driver who took him to the airport.'

'She's not the only one who can't understand it. What the hell is Dad playing at? Why did he lie to me? Why did he say he was going to Dubai when he wasn't?'

'I've no idea. I've phoned round everyone I can think of in Dubai but they haven't heard from him.'

'What if he's had an accident as well as Helen? Do you think we should get the police involved?'

'No. Dad would hate that. As for an accident, I think you're overreacting. It was only yesterday afternoon that he left Bellagio. Maybe he'll ring this evening. Are you sure you don't want me to fly over?'

'No, you might just as well stay there.'

'Give my best to Helen, won't you?'

'Yeah. Whatever.'

Savannah switched off her mobile and tossed it onto the table.

What the bastard hell was she supposed to do now? What a night-mare this holiday was turning into!

Back from using the loo inside the bar, Orlando sat down next to Savannah. 'Any news?' he asked.

'Nothing. Clancy's come up with a big zero. I mean, how difficult can it be to find our father? You'd think he was deliberately hiding from us.'

'Maybe he is.'

'Why ever would he do that?'

'I don't know; perhaps he's got some secret deal he's trying to pull off.'

'He's a businessman not a bloody secret agent! Oh, look, there's Lucy's lover-boy. Let's invite him to join us. Alessio!'

Great! Just what Orlando needed. Bad enough that in view of today's events he'd decided to put his goodbye speech to Savannah on hold, now he was to be subjected to the company of Lucy's holiday fling. If it was any consolation to him, Alessio didn't look too happy when he clocked who was calling out to him. All the same, he came over. '*Ciao*,' he said stiffly.

'Why don't you join us for a drink?' Savannah said. 'I could do with being cheered up.' She gave Orlando a pointed look.

'Thank you, but I can't. I am on my way back to the hotel. I'm taking Lucy to the hospital.'

'What for?' asked Savannah.

Alessio frowned. 'She is worried about her friend.'

'Hey, we're all worried about Helen, but cluttering up the hospital won't help anyone. My step-mother needs rest, not a party.'

'No. It is Signor Mac Truman Lucy is concerned about.'

'Mac? What's wrong with him?' Orlando asked.

'Apparently he was taken ill at the hospital.'

'Seriously?'

'I'm sorry, I don't know. Would you like me to ask Lucy to ring you so that she can tell you what is happening?'

Putting his animosity aside, Orlando said, 'Yes. Thanks. I'd really appreciate that.'

'Unless you would like to come with us?'

Orlando was about to say no, when Savannah said, 'Maybe we should go, Orlando. Perhaps I'm wrong about Helen and she would appreciate some company.'

The thing about Savannah, Orlando now understood – since the scales had fallen from his eyes – was that she never did anything unless there was something to be gained from the situation. He suspected that not to be outdone by Lucy's proposed visit to the hospital, she was about to embark on a major face-saving exercise. How bad would it look if everyone but Savannah went to see Helen?

Sometimes things happen out of order. People fall in love with the wrong people at the wrong time. It was something that would go on happening for as long as the world kept spinning.

This was the conclusion Conrad had reached while he watched his uncle – he stopped and corrected himself – as he watched his *father* sleep. It seemed so obvious now, that his mother and Mac had had an affair. All those occasions when Mac came to stay and the atmosphere in the house immediately underwent a dramatic change. It was always as if someone had found the light switch and the darkness that was Edwin Truman was extinguished. Mac effortlessly radiated a much-needed cheerfulness into their dull lives. His company was always invigorating and genial, and it was not an exaggeration to say that Conrad had worshipped the ground Mac walked on. When they were young, Conrad and his sister used to hover in the hall when they knew their uncle's arrival was imminent. They would sit at the bottom of the stairs speculating about what new game he would play with them, or what presents he would pull out from his enormous and well-travelled suitcase. One year, following a visit to North Africa, Mac had given them each a bright red fez. They had worn the hats all day, including during supper that evening. Only when they were rebuked by their father for impersonating Tommy Cooper whilst he said grace did they reluctantly remove the hats.

Undoubtedly, and unusually for an older brother, Edwin had lived permanently in Mac's awesome shadow, and given that combined with the aftermath of his wartime experiences, Conrad thought it unlikely that he had ever been happy or known peace of mind. Having experienced his own period of hell with Sam's death, he could sympathize. And despite what Mac had said, Conrad had a feeling that his father – the man who had raised him – might well have known that his wife and brother were having an affair and had stoically turned a blind eye to it so as not to risk bringing matters to a head and losing his wife altogether.

Conrad would never know for sure if this was the case, but one thing he did know was that just as Mac had been prepared to do anything for the woman he loved, so was he.

Marcus's hands were shaking as Francesca took hold of them. 'I'm so sorry *caro mio*,' she whispered, resting against him and brushing her lips against his cheek.

'We'll get a second opinion. That's what we'll do. These doctors don't always get it right. They don't know everything.'

She leaned away from him and shook her head sadly. 'It won't change anything. The diagnosis will still be the same.'

'You can't know that. Not for sure.'

'Marcus, please don't make it any worse for me. We need to accept it, not deny it. There can be no pretence.'

He let out a half-stifled groan, then turned to stare at the lake in the growing darkness. She watched him trying desperately to keep his composure, but his trembling lips gave him away. 'I knew something was wrong,' he murmured. 'But not this … never this. I thought you were planning to leave me for another man.' He swallowed loudly and returned his gaze to her. 'I was even prepared to let you go. I thought that if I was making you miserable it would be better to let you be happy with someone else.' Tears filled his eyes and he tried to blink them away, but they rolled unbidden down his cheeks. 'Oh, God, Francesca, what can I do to make this go away for you?'

Tears were spilling down her own cheeks now. 'You can't make it go away, my darling, but you can be strong for me. I'm going to need you more than I've ever needed you before.'

Chapter Sixty

Helen woke to the sound of squeaking. After taking a few moments to orientate herself, she identified it as the sound of rubber-soled shoes hurrying on the floor at the end of her bed. She had been moved to a regular ward last night and unbelievably she had slept, despite the constant noise and activity that seemed to go on around her.

She lay very still, afraid to move lest she was rewarded with an explosion inside her skull. She blinked a couple of times to see what harm that would do.

Nothing. That was good. It was progress.

She raised a hand to her head and tentatively touched the bandaged area. It was still there in one piece, which was as far as her medical opinion stretched. Another few minutes and she'd risk moving. For now she was content to lie back and wait to be told when she could leave. But getting out of here was dependent not just on her condition, but also on how well Mac was doing. After Conrad had told her what had happened to his uncle, she had promised to stay with him until they knew for sure what was wrong with Mac.

Conrad had kept her company for most of yesterday evening whilst Mac had slept, and he'd been particularly helpful when to their surprise Lucy, Orlando and Savannah had shown up. 'Savannah is the last person I want to see at the moment,' she'd told Conrad.

'I'll say you're not well enough to see them,' he'd said, 'that you're still feeling a bit groggy.'

He'd returned shortly with a bunch of flowers.

'I guarantee they're not from Savannah,' Helen had remarked as she watched Conrad put them on her bedside locker.

'They're from Lucy,' he answered. 'She had some for Mac as well.'

'That was sweet of her.'

'It was. I felt sorry for her; she was so worried about you and Mac. I let her look in on him just to convince her that he was still breathing.'

'Have they gone back to Bellagio now?'

'Yes.'

'Did Savannah say anything?'

'Quite a lot. She wanted to know when the baby was due.'

'What did you tell her?'

'I said I didn't have a clue. I'm afraid that's something you'll have to sort out yourself.'

'Did she say anything about Hunter?'

'A fair bit. She and her step-brother, back in Cheshire, have been trying to locate him but he seems to have disappeared. She seemed pretty stroppy abut the whole business.'

'She doesn't like to be thwarted. She'll take it all as a personal slight against her.'

'So what are you going to do about Hunter? I don't mean in the long term, I mean right now. You're the only one who can track him down. You can ring the woman he's with and make him squirm.'

But Helen wasn't ready to get in touch with Hunter yet. She wasn't even sure that she wanted to make him squirm. What was to be gained from that?

Her thoughts were cut short by the sound of squeaking shoes again. A young nurse appeared at the side of her bed. '*Buongiorno, Signora*. You have a special visitor. One you will be very glad to see I think.' Helen watched her pull the curtains around the bed and thinking that perhaps the nurse had been joking, that her visitor was going to be some burly, moustachioed woman with a cold, wet sponge to give her a bed bath, she waited with trepidation to see who would appear.

'*Mac!*' She winced at the loudness of her voice.

'Steady on, old thing,' he said as he parted the curtains and planted a kiss on her cheek. He was wearing an unflattering hospital gown that was much too small. 'Sorry about the state of me,' he said, when he had positioned a chair and sat down, 'but it's the best I could do under the circumstances. How are you feeling?'

'Better for seeing you. But how are you, Mac?'

'I'm fine. Apparently I've been taking the wrong tablets and my blood pressure's been lower than it should be. Comes to something when a foreign quack has to correct the mistake my own doc at home made. Although to be fair, it was the ten-year-old locum who made the error. If the health service wasn't in such a shambles I'd sue. Knowing my luck I'd be dead before the case went to court.'

Helen smiled. 'Then you'll just have to settle for being alive now.'

He smiled too. 'That's my girl. Politely putting me in my place as usual. Seriously, though, I'm delighted to see you looking so much better than yesterday. For a nasty moment, I thought … Well, never mind what I thought. I'm just relieved that I now have the opportunity to ask you to forgive me.'

'What for?'

'For what I said to you yesterday morning on the boat. I wasn't much of a gentleman, was I?'

'It's okay, Mac. I know why you said what you did. You were angry on Conrad's behalf.'

'But I went too far.'

'No. It was me who went too far. Has Conrad told you that I lied to him about being pregnant?'

'Yes. I don't wish to poke and pry, but how long did you think you'd be able to get away with lying to him? And to everyone else?'

'It wasn't something I'd really thought through. All I could think of was trying to make Conrad hate and despise me. It sounds a bit half-cocked, doesn't it? I've been very foolish. Maybe this bang to my head will have knocked some sense into me.'

'Don't be too hard on yourself, Helen. And for the record, I don't think Conrad is capable of hating you. He tells me Hunter's been having an affair and that you're leaving him.'

'Yes, but the affair isn't the sole reason.'

'It doesn't matter what your reasons are, so long as you're sure you'll be happy. At the risk of being impertinent—'

She raised a hand to stop him. 'Please don't ask me anything to do with Conrad.'

Mac looked affronted. 'I wasn't going to. I was thinking of what's going to happen to you when you leave Hunter. Where will you live?'

'I still have my little house in Crantsford. Only trouble is, the tenants are there for another three months. In the long term, I will probably have to sell it to help fund my grandmother's care in a new nursing home. It's the last thing I wanted to happen, moving her again, but I don't have a choice.'

'Meanwhile, in the short term, you need a roof over your head. Maybe Conrad might like a lodger.'

'No. Don't even think it.'

'It could be the answer, just until you get yourself straight.'

'Absolutely not. I've taken enough liberties with Conrad as it is. Where is he, by the way?'

'Sound asleep. He must be exhausted. I'm told that he was awake for most of the night, keeping a vigil at my bedside, just in case I dared to give up the ghost and popped my clogs.'

'Don't joke like that, Mac. Conrad's a good nephew to you. You should treat him more kindly. Just occasionally.'

Mac suddenly looked perturbed. Seconds passed, and then he cleared his throat. 'Actually, regarding my nephew, there's something I'd like to tell you.'

Slumped at the kitchen table, an untouched cup of coffee before him, Marcus didn't think he would ever be free of the gut-wrenching pain that had kept him awake all night.

Fresh tears filled his eyes as he thought of Francesca lying upstairs in bed. How had she borne the suspicion of what was wrong with her, on her own? How had she carried on with her work yesterday, knowing what she then knew? She had more courage than he did. She had made him promise not to tell anyone yet, not until she had told her family, which she intended to do in a few days' time. 'I need to adjust to the news myself before I speak to them,' she had said in the early hours of the morning. 'I need to feel that I'm in control of this for as long as possible,' she'd added.

He knew that she was dreading her family's reaction; even now her brothers were still so protective of her. He didn't know how he would do it, but somehow he would help and support her all he could. By focusing on her needs, he might just survive. But what would happen to him when she was gone? She was his world. He would be lost without her.

'Selfish bastard!' He cried out aloud. 'Stop thinking about yourself!' In despair, he raked his hands through his hair. This wasn't about him. It was about Francesca. He suddenly felt sick, and it was no passing queasiness. He jumped to his feet and made it to the sink just in time to retch violently. His shoulders heaved and his vision became blurred with tears. It was then that he heard a knock at the door. He did his best to get rid of the revolting mess in the sink, splashed cold water onto his face, and grabbing the hand towel, he went to see who it was.

It was the last person on earth he expected to see.

Lucy took one look at her father and knew that Francesca must have told him. All she could think to say was, 'Dad, are you okay?'

'Yes. No.' He rubbed his unshaven face roughly and sniffed. 'No, I'm not all right. We've had some bad news. Perhaps ... perhaps now isn't a good time for you to visit.'

He stood barring her way, his bloodshot gaze skimming the top of her head. He looked awful. She could feel the sorrow emanating from him. 'Please, Dad,' she said, 'don't push me away.' She was going to say, 'again', but held back. It had taken so much courage to keep the promise she'd made to Francesca yesterday, that she would come here this morning. She had slept hardly at all last night. Lying in the darkness with Alessio, she kept thinking how fragile life was. Helen could so nearly have died if that car hadn't stopped in time, and for all she knew, despite Conrad's assurances at the hospital that his uncle was okay, Mac may well have passed away in the night. And now here was her father trying to cope with the knowledge that his wife was dying. It really hadn't been her intention to confide in Alessio, but as the night wore on and still she couldn't sleep, he had switched on the bedside lamp and said, 'I know there is something troubling you, *cara*. Is it your friends, Helen and Mac?'

After making him swear that he wasn't to say anything to anyone, she had told him about Francesca. His reaction had been to hold her tightly and when he pulled away his eyes were moist. 'The family will be devastated by this,' he said. 'Francesca is loved by everyone.' His concern had then turned to Lucy's father. 'O Dio, your poor father, he will never survive this. He is devoted to her. His heart will surely break.' Alessio had surprised her yet further by going on to say, 'Lucia, Marcus will need you. He will need your love. You must go to him tomorrow morning, just as Francesca has asked you to. You must bury the past and be his friend and daughter.'

'He may not want me,' she'd said doubtfully. 'I might not be what he needs.'

Alessio had tutted and placed a finger to her lips. '*Mia Lucia*, you are exactly what he needs. You are *famiglia*.'

'Will you come with me? I don't even know where he lives.'

'I will draw you a map. And while you are there I will go to *San Giaccomo* and light a candle for Francesca. Don't look so surprised. I may not behave like a choir boy, but like most Italians, I have my faith.'

'Do you go to confession as well?'

'Occasionally. Why do you ask? Or are you thinking that I have much to confess?'

'Something like that.'

'And you have nothing to confess? Ever? You are *perfetta*?'

'Not by a long way. But confessing seems so superficial and ineffectual.'

'I find it helps to say sorry sometimes.'

'Even if you go on committing the same sin?'

'We are only human, Lucia. God knows our strengths and our weaknesses.' His words had revealed a side to his character that she would never have guessed at.

Now, though, as her father continued to stand his ground and not let her over the threshold, Lucy doubted Alessio's wisdom – Francesca's too – that she would be able to help her father. She had never felt more inadequate. What strengths did she have at a time like this?

'Marcus, why aren't you letting Lucy in? Why are you keeping her on the doorstep?'

They both looked to see Francesca standing behind Marcus. Ironically, thought Lucy, she looked better than he did. Her father's gaze swivelled between the two of them.

'I invited her to come here, Marcus,' Francesca said.

His arm dropped away from the door. 'Really?'

Francesca nodded. '*Sì*. She knows about … about my illness. I told her yesterday.'

'You told her before me?'

But before Francesca was able to answer, Lucy said, 'Dad, does it matter?'

He stared at her for the longest moment and as his eyes filled and he put a trembling hand to his mouth, both Lucy and Francesca moved simultaneously to embrace him.

Chapter Sixty-one

It had just turned four o'clock when the taxi dropped the three of them off in the Piazza Mazzini. With Conrad and Mac either side of her – Mac had a hand under her elbow and Conrad a hand gently resting on the small of her back – they climbed the narrow passageway of steps to Hotel Villa Rosa. 'You don't have to help me,' Helen said, noticing that passers-by were staring. 'I can manage, really.'

'Quiet, girl!' Mac growled. 'Accept our help or pay the consequences.'

Secretly Helen was enjoying the attention. She felt anchored and protected by their solicitude. Even so, she couldn't stop herself from saying, 'But you're making me feel such a fraud. I only bumped my head; I didn't lose the ability to walk.'

'Keep this up and I'll move that bandage from your head to your mouth.'

'He's all charm, isn't he?' Conrad said when they'd made it to the glass doors of the hotel and he was pushing them open. The man behind the desk – one of the owners, Helen recalled – immediately rushed forward to see if there was anything he could do.

'What a terrible holiday this has become for you!' he cried out. 'Alessio kept us informed of events, but we were so worried for you. Please, allow me to bring you some coffee to your rooms? Or would you prefer tea?'

'I'd prefer something stronger,' Mac said. 'A double Scotch would hit the spot.'

'Not with those new tablets you won't,' Conrad interceded. His voice was stern but his face was benign.

'I'd love a cup of tea,' Helen said. 'But not in my room. I've been cooped up for too long. I'd like to sit in the garden, please.'

'Better make that tea for three,' Conrad said.

'*Piacere*. Go and make yourselves comfortable and I will see to your drinks at once.'

To Helen's relief, there was no one about. She had been dreading coming back and having to face a barrage of questions and sympathy. There was also Savannah and all that pregnancy nonsense to explain away.

The day was beautifully warm, and despite the dull ache in her head – her skull felt as if it had shrunk and was pressing on her brain – and what the last twenty-four hours had thrown at her, she was unexpectedly calm. Sitting in the afternoon sunshine, looking out over the rooftops at the lake, she was imbued with a comfortable numbness. Her future had never seemed more uncertain but somehow it didn't matter. Maybe it was the knowledge that she could so easily have died – if the car had actually hit her – that was giving her a new perspective. Or maybe it was no more than the effect of the painkillers she was taking.

Their drinks arrived. When they were alone, Conrad poured their tea and Helen took the cup he offered her. 'I've made a decision,' she said. 'I'm going to speak to Hunter.'

'And say what?'

'Mac, that's none of our business,' Conrad said.

'You might not think it is, but I do. I don't want that swine upsetting Helen.'

'He won't,' Helen said firmly.

When she decided the time had come to make the call, Helen went upstairs to her room. The battery of her own mobile was still dead, so she took Hunter's mobile out of her handbag and sat on the end of the bed. She scrolled through the address book until she came to Annabel's number. She was about to make the connection when she changed her mind. An element of surprise was called for. If she used Hunter's phone, Annabel would be forewarned. Going over to the telephone on the dressing table, she tapped in the number and waited. She wondered where they were. On a sandy beach somewhere? Annabel would love that. But Hunter wouldn't. He preferred his holidays to have more purpose to them – like proposing in a hot air balloon, or sizing up a potential property investment. It was a mystery to Helen why he'd insisted on coming to Italy with her. He'd said it was because Marcia wanted him to keep an eye on Savannah, but that really didn't ring true. And then it struck her: Hunter was probably here with Annabel in Italy.

Helen was still waiting for Annabel to answer her mobile when she recalled her friend's long weekend away with 'the girls' and how tired she had looked when she was back in the office. Another piece of the puzzle slotted into place. That was when Hunter had been in Dubai. Presumably the girls' weekend away had been a lie and Annabel had been in Dubai too. How many other lies had there been?

A voice in her ear roused her. 'Hello?'

'Annabel. It's Helen. I wonder if I could speak to my husband, please.'

There was a stunned silence, followed by, 'It's a terrible line, Helen – what did you say?'

'I asked to speak to my husband.'

'Is this some kind of a joke?'

'Do you hear me laughing?'

'No ... but ... surely he's with you in Italy?'

'Don't make this any sillier than it already is, Annabel. Just go and tell Hunter I'd like to speak to him.'

There was another silence, during which Helen could hear murmured voices, the rustle of a newspaper, and then: 'How did you know where to find me?'

How typical of the man. No attempt to deny or bluster his way out of a difficult situation. 'Your mobile; I tried to use it yesterday.'

'You don't sound very cross.'

'I'm not.' She had a feeling her flat response would penetrate his ego deeper than any spite-filled accusation. 'I'm just calling to let you know that I fainted yesterday and ended up in hospital. Savannah and Clancy have been trying to get hold of you. You might like to ring them and explain where you are, if only to put their minds at rest.'

She let this sink in before saying, 'Where exactly are you? I know you're not in Dubai.'

'I'm still here on Lake Como. I'm at the Villa D'Este.'

She whistled. 'Lucky old Annabel. But very risky on your part, seeing as the hotel and gardens are part of the Gardens of Delight tour.' When he didn't reply, she said, 'I should have known better. You're not scared of anything, are you? A day not taking a risk is a wasted day as far as you're concerned, isn't it?'

'Do you think we could discuss this when we're back in England?'

She detected irritation in his voice. 'Of course, I'm sorry. It must be difficult for you, what with Annabel being there.'

'Please don't be sarcastic, Helen.'

'I'm not.' She sighed, suddenly tired. Tired of it all. 'I'm returning to England tomorrow,' she said. 'As originally planned.'

'What do you want me to do?'

'I'd like some time alone to sort things out.'

'What things?'

'Such as how quickly I can extricate myself from our marriage, Hunter.'

'There's no need to do anything hasty, Helen. Why don't I come over to Bellagio and we'll talk about this?'

'That's hardly fair to Annabel, is it? And please, remember what I said about wanting some time alone. Don't try ringing me, either.'

She ended the call and went outside onto the small balcony. Her legs were a bit wobbly and her heart was pounding, but apart from that she was all right.

Staring out at the lake and watching the hydrofoil churn up the water, she took stock. She had always known deep down what kind of a man Hunter was, but she had kidded herself that it wouldn't matter, that she would adapt and compromise to suit the situation.

How wrong could she have been?

About as wrong as her motives for marrying Hunter in the first place.

With enormous relief, she took off her wedding ring and engagement ring. There was no going back now.

Savannah couldn't believe what she was hearing. How dare her father tell her to mind her own business! 'Look, Dad, Clancy and I were dead worried about you. We didn't have a clue where you were. I was beginning to think you'd had an accident. Where the hell are you?'

'It doesn't matter where I am; the important thing is—'

She cut him short. 'I don't get it. Why are you being so secretive? What's the big deal?'

'I don't have to tell you everything I do. And as I was just about to say, I'll be—'

'Oh, save it for someone who cares! You know what? I don't give a shit where you are. But answer me this: did you know that Helen is pregnant?' She heard the intake of breath down the line and smiled. 'Yeah, I didn't think so. It's just a thought, Dad, but I wouldn't be too sure that you're the father.'

Before he could respond, Savannah cut the call and switched off her mobile. 'Now see how it feels,' she muttered under her breath.

SWANMERE

Chapter Sixty-two

It was raining hard in Swanmere.

The ferocious downpour had started at about four in the morning. It hadn't woken Lucy; restless and unable to sleep, she had already been awake for an hour. Now, dressed in her bathrobe, she stared out of her bedroom window, watching the leaden sheets of rain slash at the glass, obscuring the view of the garden. It was a miserable day to match her miserable mood.

She had been home for a day and a half and there had been no word from Alessio. He had said he would ring her, but he hadn't. Common sense told her she shouldn't be surprised, but it didn't lessen the disappointment. When he had told her he would call as soon as she was home, she had so badly wanted to believe him. She knew, though, that she would have to grit her teeth and consign him to the graveyard of that was then, this is now. She brushed away a tear and tried to make herself feel angry. Not just with Alessio but with herself, for being gullible and too keen to believe that he had meant any of what he'd said.

But it was too soon for anger. It would come. Just not yet. She still wanted to believe in the magic of him. To live the dream.

She closed her eyes, as if to picture every detail of him more clearly. Letting the memories blend into one seamless sensation of bittersweet pleasure, she felt weak with longing. What wouldn't she give to hear his voice, to hear him say how much he desired and wanted her. Never before had she received such intense declarations of adoration. That, she knew, had been her mistake. She had been too quick to take him seriously and bask in his attention.

On their last morning together he had played the piano for her. The waiters had finished clearing the dining room after breakfast and he had asked her if she would sit with him while he did his morning practice session. Watching him play had been one of the most erotic and mesmerizing experiences of her life. Just thinking now about the intensity of his concentration caused a shiver to run up and down her spine.

She opened her eyes. The time would come when she would have to stop torturing herself with these memories, but for now she wanted to hang onto them, to believe that her mobile would ring and it would be Alessio saying *Ciao, Lucia!*

The only calls she had received since coming home had been from her mother and her father. The conversation with her mother had been a minefield of explosive pauses. Having not even mentioned to Fiona that she was going to Italy, she had to give her mother the full story of not just meeting her father, but of being reconciled with him. Fiona had listened in stony silence and Lucy had felt cold reproach. A lifetime of being allies in their loathing of the despicable Marcus Gray had just been wiped away in one clean sweep. It was a betrayal that would be difficult, if not impossible, for Fiona to come to terms with. And whilst Lucy didn't consider her father to be a saint all of a sudden, she could finally admit that he wasn't entirely to blame. No one knew better than Lucy that Fiona wasn't an easy woman to live with, but of course that had been a large part of the problem. She had held her father responsible for the mess he had left behind him, namely a neurotic mother who couldn't cope. Everything wrong in their lives had to be down to him. Who else's fault could it be?

At no stage during the stilted exchange did Lucy tell Fiona about Francesca's illness. Knowing how vindictive she could be, Lucy hadn't trusted her mother to react appropriately.

The conversation with her father had been no less fraught, for the simple reason she had never thought to hear his voice whilst standing in the kitchen of Church View. She'd had tears in her eyes when she'd put the phone down afterwards.

Their parting in Pescallo had been equally emotional. As he'd kissed her goodbye, she had promised to come back as soon as she could. 'May I ring you tonight?' he'd asked. 'Just to know you arrived home safely.'

'Please, Dad,' she'd said, 'you don't have to ask my permission for anything. I've given you my number because I want you to call me.'

They'd hugged again and then Francesca had stepped forward. They'd embraced each other cautiously. Francesca had said, 'Are we friends now, Lucy?'

'Yes. Of course.'

'Come back soon,' Francesca had said softly. She had then looked Lucy in the eye as if to say, Don't leave it too late.

Stiff from standing so long at the window, Lucy moved away. She had to get ready for work – her first day back since coming home.

Downstairs in the kitchen Orlando was already dressed and eating a slice of toast, at the same time spooning coffee into a mug. He immediately offered to make her a drink when he saw her.

'It's okay, I'll do it,' she said. Poor Orlando, he'd been so sweet to her. He knew that she was upset over Alessio and he had gone out of his way to cheer her up. Not once had he uttered the words 'I told you so', but she could see it in his face and in his every kind gesture. Last night he'd cooked one of her favourite meals for her – sausage, egg and chips. 'Comfort food,' he'd said. 'Just what you need.' Afterwards, he'd even run a bath for her and lit some candles in the bathroom.

'I'll make you some toast,' he said now, already loading slices of bread into the toaster.

'It's me who should be doing this for you,' she said. 'It's you who's gone through the official break-up.'

'Do I look like I'm heartbroken?'

'No. But it can't have been easy for you.'

'Call me a ruthless bastard, but finishing with Savannah was the easiest thing I ever did.'

'Do you think that's what Alessio's thinking about me?'

He pushed the lever down on the toaster. 'I don't know, Luce.'

She smiled. 'Thanks.'

'For what?'

'For not bullshitting me. He's not going to ring, is he?'

'You could try calling him.'

'What, and look like I don't know how the game's played? It was a holiday romance that I took a bit too seriously. I got carried away and didn't know when to stop. It's my own fault. I'll soon forget all about him.'

So why does my heart feel like it's cracking in two? she asked herself.

Orlando couldn't bear to see Lucy so miserable. He'd do anything to make her happy again. He'd even phone the hotel in Bellagio and demand to speak to Alessio. He'd tell him to do the decent

393

thing and put Lucy out of her misery by ringing her to say it was over. Leaving her dangling like this was too cruel.

He himself had never been accused of cruelty, not until Savannah had levelled this criticism at him. It was just one of many that she'd fired off when he'd told her it was over between them. He had intended to keep quiet until they were home but on their last night in Bellagio, when they were having a drink in one of the lakeside bars, she'd pushed his patience with the inevitable result that he'd lost his temper. It had all started when she was being rude about Helen. 'So what do you make of all this business with Helen?' she'd said. 'One minute she's pregnant and then she's not.'

'I'd say it's between her and her husband,' he'd said guardedly.

'Aren't you forgetting who her husband is? As his daughter I have a right to know what the hell's going on. And if you ask me, Bitch Queen Helen is way too cosy with that Conrad Truman. Have you seen the way he looks at her?'

Orlando had noticed something, but he wasn't going to speculate.

'I wouldn't be at all surprised if they've been at it on the sly,' Savannah had gone on to say. 'I hinted as much to Dad on the phone earlier.'

'You did what?'

'Don't look so shocked. I didn't really mean it. I just said it to kick Dad up the arse. Seeing as he's acting like one.'

'He's not the only one.'

'And what's that supposed to mean?'

'That – not for the first time – your mouth's got ahead of itself. Do you ever think before you speak?'

From then on it was open warfare. She called him every name under the sun, much to the amusement of everybody sitting nearby, and when she'd hit the pause button long enough for him to take a turn, he'd said, 'I take it from that outburst that we're done here. Oh, and to clarify the situation; consider yourself free of any contractual obligations we previously had regarding your employment with me. You're sacked!' He'd then pushed back his chair before she thought to throw the remains of her drink in his face. A middle-aged couple at a table next to them had actually applauded when he'd walked away. He didn't feel proud of himself, though. He should have been smart enough to avoid getting into anything so doomed.

In the short time since they'd all come home from Italy, he'd heard from Helen that Savannah had packed up her things and left Swanmere. She was now back in Crantsford with her mother. He doubted their paths would ever cross again.

When Lucy arrived for work, Angie and Hugh were both waiting to hear how her holiday had gone. 'Hasn't Orlando told you?' Lucy said, handing them their presents from Bellagio – a bottle of red wine for Hugh and a handmade alabaster picture frame for Angie. She knew that Orlando had phoned his parents yesterday and so assumed Hugh would be up to speed with all there was to know.

Hugh shook his head. 'I asked him, but he said it wasn't his place to tell me anything. He can be annoyingly discreet when he chooses to be. Gets it from his mother.'

'Not from you, Hugh?' smirked Angie. 'You do surprise me.'

He shook his head. 'She's been unbearable, Lucy.'

It was good to be back. Back amongst the familiar. That was what she had to concentrate on. She then told them all they wanted to know about Lake Como, editing heavily where necessary. Namely avoiding any reference to Alessio.

Much later in the morning, when the rain had finally stopped and Lucy was tidying up the plants that had been toppled by the deluge, she thought how grateful she was to Orlando that he hadn't mentioned Alessio to his father. The fewer people who knew, the better. It was a pity she couldn't trust Olivia Marchwood and her cronies to keep their mouths shut as well. Perhaps she should have done with it and simply post the news on the parish noticeboard outside the church.

Hugh appeared just as she'd finished doing the rounds of the plants. 'I'm glad it went well with you and your dad, Lucy,' he said.

'Thanks. It feels weird, but it's as if I've suddenly discovered I have this whole other life to explore. It's been just Mum and me for all these years; now I have a new family to get to know.'

'That's a great way to look at it. I've been thinking about your dad, and what he'll be going through, and if you need time off to visit him, just say the word.' He had almost turned to leave her when he said, 'Orlando says he's finished with Savannah. Apparently she's left Swanmere.'

'That's right.'

'Don't suppose there's any chance of—'

'Forget it, Hugh. Orlando and I are destined always to be just good friends.'

'You don't know that for sure.'

Oh, yes I do, thought Lucy. They were both on the rebound. If anything happened between them now it would be a disaster.

The solicitor passed the letter across his desk. Helen read it through for herself, despite the fact that the solicitor had read it out to her. It was too extraordinary.

'I don't know what to say,' she said. 'I don't deserve it, that much I do know. And if people think I coerced it out of her, it could all get very unpleasant. Perhaps it would be better not to accept it.' As she placed the letter back on the desk, she wondered if the solicitor was thinking that she probably had coerced poor Mrs Jenkins. He might even think she'd bumped the poor old lady off! Thank God she'd been in Italy when Mrs Jenkins had passed away in her sleep.

'Mrs Jenkins was very clear on that point,' he said, cutting into her panicky thoughts. 'She wrote a letter to me only last month, stating very clearly that you had no knowledge of what she planned to do.'

'But surely there'll be someone who will contest it.'

'There's no one. Mrs Jenkins was all alone in this world. In her letter to me she wrote very movingly of you, stressing just how fond she was of you and how much you helped her.'

'But I didn't do anything special. I just did what anyone would have done.'

'Be that as it may, you are the sole beneficiary of Mrs Jenkins' will. She's left you her house and a not inconsiderable amount of money. Would you like me to tell you how much?'

Expecting a couple of thousand pounds, Helen nodded. When the solicitor told her the amount, she asked him to repeat it.

'I said it was a not inconsiderable sum, didn't I?'

'But she lived so frugally! She gave no indication that she had that kind of money.'

'It's so often the way. Life is full of surprises, Mrs Madison-Tyler, and trust me, I've seen many an expression of disbelief in this office. Often it's outrage that the relatives are getting their hands on so little, but in this instance, I'm delighted the way things have turned out. There's the process of probate to work through, but

I don't envisage too many problems with that.' He straightened a pile of paperwork. 'You mentioned earlier that coincidentally you were in need of a solicitor for an entirely different matter. Can I be of assistance?'

'Yes, I need someone to handle my divorce.'

An hour later, with the sun breaking through the clouds and creating great shafts of light, Helen drove on to see her grandmother. It was her second visit since coming back from Lake Como. Today she was able to drive herself – yesterday Conrad had insisted that he should be her chauffeur. He'd said he would wait in the car for her, but remembering how good he'd been with Emma at Wollerton, she invited him to come inside with her. Emma had no recollection of him, though, and thought he was a doctor. She kept telling Helen to wait outside while the doctor checked her over. It was some time before she noticed the dressing Helen still had on her head and then became obsessed with it and wanted to know if that was why the doctor was here with them.

Now as Helen parked the car and looked up at the ivy-clad building, she thought of Isobel Jenkins' totally unexpected act of benevolence. She had often chatted to Isobel about her grandmother and how close they were, and it had even crossed her mind to bring Isobel here to meet Emma. She would miss the old lady. And would be for ever grateful for her generosity. Never in her wildest dreams could she have foreseen this turn of events. It meant the world to her that Emma's future would be secure now.

Emma dozed fitfully for most of Helen's visit and when she eventually fell into a deep sleep, Helen kissed her goodbye and drove on to Swanmere. She was officially of no fixed abode, having moved out of The Old Vicarage yesterday morning, hot on the heels of Savannah's departure. However, she wasn't without a roof over her head. She had eventually taken Conrad up on his offer of a place to stay until the lease came to an end on her house in Crantsford and the tenants moved out. She had taken some persuading. 'Who cares what anyone thinks of the situation?' Mac had waded in. 'You're a friend and we've invited you to stay with us. You're not afraid of Hunter, are you?'

'I'm afraid of what he might think of Conrad,' she admitted.

'Do you think Conrad gives a damn?'

'No, but that's why I should care. I don't want him involved.'

'Too late for that, Helen. He's involved already.'

And so she had moved in with them and taken over their spare room. Within minutes the whole village must have known – Evie had been the first to know of the arrangements.

She parked alongside Conrad's Saab and was just switching off the engine when a car pulled in behind her. There was no mistaking the Mercedes, or its driver. It was Hunter.

Despite Helen asking him to leave her alone, he had phoned her as soon as she was back at the Old Rectory. He'd threatened to come home immediately unless she spoke to him, so she'd given in and answered his questions as honestly as she could. His first question had been about her pregnancy. 'I'm afraid you've been misinformed,' she'd said. 'Presumably it was Savannah who told you.'

'It doesn't matter who told me. What matters is that you kept it from me. Are you or are you not pregnant? And am I the father?'

'I'm not pregnant. I never was.'

'So why the hell did Savannah say that you were? And more importantly, why did she suggest I was being made a monkey of?'

'You'll have to take that up with her. Perhaps you might like to consider the possibility that your daughter is a manipulative, lying troublemaker who might have turned out better if you'd taken not just a firmer line, but some genuine interest in her. And if anyone's been made to feel foolish, I'd say it was me. How's Annabel?'

'She's just a fling, Helen. She doesn't mean anything. It's just sex.'

Amazed that he hadn't reacted to her criticism of Savannah, she said, 'I hope Annabel can't hear you.'

'She's not with me.'

'Where are you?'

'I'm with Clancy. I want to see you, Helen. I want to make sure you don't do anything rash. You need me. You know that.'

She'd rung off then and unplugged the answerphone.

'How did you know I'd be here?' she said now as she watched Hunter get out of his car and come towards her.

'It wasn't difficult. Where else would you have been? With Olivia Marchwood? I don't think so. And please don't insult my intelligence by pretending there's been nothing going on between you and Conrad. Your act of self-righteousness just won't cut it, Helen.'

'Everything okay, Helen?'

Mac and Conrad appeared round the side of the house. They must have been in the garden and heard voices. Fritz was with them. When the dog saw Hunter he gave off a low growl.

'Everything's fine, Conrad.' She turned back to Hunter. 'Why don't we go for a drink and discuss this?'

Hunter glared at Conrad. 'I'm happy to stay here.'

'No,' said Helen. 'I'm not dragging anyone else into this.'

'I'd have thought you'd done that already.' Still staring at Conrad, he sneered. 'I hope you can afford her. She has expensive tastes.'

Conrad stepped forward but Helen put a hand out to him. 'Hunter,' she said, 'why exactly did you marry me? I'm not much of a trophy wife, am I? Okay, I'm younger than you, but you could have had anyone you wanted. Why me?'

Rarely had Helen seen Hunter wrongfooted, but the question seemed to disarm him. He looked disconcerted. Helen almost felt sorry for him. 'I ... I thought you'd be different,' he said. 'I thought you'd really need me. But you're just like the rest. Once you've got what you want, you start trying to pull the strings.'

Helen was shocked. 'Do you really believe that?'

'I've never met a woman who doesn't do it. You're all the same. I knew when you agreed to marry me what your game was. And I was happy to go along with it. It seemed a fair enough arrangement. But then you stopped playing fair. You started to question me.' Hunter's voice had turned steely now. Out of the corner of her eye, Helen could see both Mac and Conrad moving towards her. Later she would think that perhaps they'd had an inkling of what was about to happen, but she didn't. Suddenly Hunter's hand was raised and then she felt it strike her hard on the side of her face and he was calling her a heartless bitch. The blow was so hard she fell back against her car. For what seemed an eternity her head spun and she couldn't see. She was vaguely aware of the pandemonium going on around her: Conrad had thrown himself at Hunter, Fritz was barking furiously and Mac was asking her if she could stand. 'I'm fine,' she said. But she wasn't. She was back in Italy, lying in the gutter again.

Chapter Sixty-three

With her first day at work over, Lucy cycled home in double-quick time. She changed into a pair of old jeans and a T-shirt, grabbed the carrier bag she'd left hanging on the back of the kitchen door that morning and headed out. There was someone she was anxious to see.

This was her first opportunity since returning from Italy to see Dan and to thank him for taking care of her allotment whilst she was away. The sound of a horn pipping had her looking to the other side of the road. Orlando stopped his van and wound down the window. She went over to him. 'I'm going up to the allotments,' she said. 'How about you? Finished work for the day?'

'No. I'm just stopping off at home to grab a sandwich then going on to take a look at some woman's garden she wants revamping. Not sure what time I'll be finished. How was your day?'

'Fine. And no, he still hasn't called me. If it makes you feel better you now have my full permission to say you told me so.'

'I wouldn't do that to you, Luce. Look, I'd better go. But we'll talk properly tonight. How about I pick up a takeaway on my way home?'

'Good idea.'

'Say hi to Dan and the Boys from me.'

Dan, Bill and Joe greeted Lucy as though she'd just returned from navigating the world single-handedly in a leaking old bath-tub. 'Have you brought us back some presents?' Joe asked, eyeing the bag she was carrying. 'Sophia Loren would do for starters!'

'I've brought you some grappa,' she said, handing over two bottles to Bill and Joe. To Dan, who was strictly teetotal, she gave a wrapped, box-shaped present.

'Why does he always get special treatment?' Joe remarked.

'Because he deserves it.'

Dan put his arm around Lucy and guided her up the path. 'Do you want to go and check on your plot while I put the kettle on?' he asked.

'No, I'll check it out later. Why don't I make the drinks and you open your present?'

'There was no need for you to buy me anything,' he said when she went inside his shed and struck a match to the stove.

'I know, but I wanted to. Go on, unwrap it.'

He did. Seconds later he was admiring a china mug with a picture of Bellagio and the lake printed on it. 'Looks right fancy where you went,' he said after he'd thanked her and she'd made his tea in it. 'So how did it go?'

Sitting next to him, she took a deep breath and told him all about her father, and then Francesca.

'I take it you liked her in the end?' he said.

'I did, Dan. She was lovely. She couldn't have been nicer to me. And I've thought so ill of her all these years. I turned her into a monster.'

'Yes, but that's all behind you now. No point in beating yourself up over what's in the past. You've got to look ahead.'

Lucy took a long, thoughtful sip of her tea. 'That's what Alessio said to me.'

'Oh, aye? And who's Alessio when he's at home?'

'Someone I met. He's the same age as me and a musician. A classically trained pianist.'

'And?'

'And I saw quite a lot of him during my stay. We sort of clicked, if you know what I mean.'

Dan smiled. 'Well, I'll be damned. That wasn't how I saw things turning out. Will you be seeing him again?'

'No.'

'You seem very sure. Why's that?'

She then told him everything: how she'd fallen for him and how Orlando had even warned her to be careful. 'But I was anything but careful, Dan. I lost myself completely. Now I feel so confused. You see, before I went to Italy, I thought ... well, I think I con-vinced myself that I loved Orlando. It was the reason I was crying like a banshee that night and you were so sweet to me. Do you remember?'

He nodded. 'I'd heard talk that he'd been seeing some other girl. That young thing up at the Old Rectory.'

'He was. It's over between them now.'

'That was quick. And now you're wondering whether you and he should get—'

'No!' she blurted out. 'No. I think the only reason I thought I loved him was because I was insanely jealous of him being attracted to someone I hated. I just couldn't understand what he saw in Savannah. She was so transparent.'

'To a smart girl like you, maybe. But us chaps are simple folk. When it comes to women, we see only what we want to see. So tell me about this Alessio.'

'Oh, Dan. What can I say? There was a magic about him. I've never experienced anything like it before.'

'Sounds like he dazzled you.'

'Blinded me, more like it.'

'It doesn't matter what fancy tags you want to put to it, the thing is you had a great time together and that's something to be treasured.'

'Even if I feel he used me?'

'Did you feel used when you were with him?'

She thought about this. 'No,' she said. 'No I didn't.'

'Then my advice is to remember the happy times you had with him.'

'I just wish he'd ring, even if it's to confirm that it's all over.'

'He said he'd call you?'

'Yes.'

Dan seemed to mull this over. He slurped his drink noisily. 'For all you know there may be a jolly good reason why he hasn't phoned. Nice cup of tea by the way. You've not lost your touch.'

Lucy closed her eyes. How good it was to be here with Dan. He was always so positive. She was so busy judging herself for her recklessness that she had lost sight of what was important. Why spoil what had been a great time in Bellagio by demonizing Alessio? Hadn't she learned anything from all her years of misplaced anger towards her father and Francesca?

The sound of her mobile going off in her jeans pocket made her start. It was probably Orlando to say that there'd been a change of plan.

'*Ciao, Lucia!* It's me, Alessio.'

The colour rushed to her face. Every hope that had nearly died in her sprang to life. Her heart instantly went into overdrive. She put down her mug of tea and after exchanging a look with Dan, she moved away up the path. 'Alessio. How are you?'

'Oh, Lucia, forgive me for not ringing before now. I have been so cross with myself. I lost your number. I had it written down, but then I could not find it anywhere. I found it eventually, between the pages of some music. *Sono stupido!*'

Her heart soared. But she quickly reigned herself in. Perhaps he was lying. 'Why didn't you speak to my father?' she asked. 'He would have given you my number.'

'You know how he feels about me. Not only that, he and Francesca are going through such a difficult time. She was at the hospital yesterday for more tests. I couldn't bother them. But Lucia, why did you not ring *me*?'

'Because ...' Her voice tailed off.

'Lucia?'

'I wasn't sure ... I thought it was over. That it was just a holiday thing.'

'What can I do to prove to you that it isn't?'

Before she had a chance to reply, the connection was lost. She groaned with frustration. The reception was always a bit hit and miss up here. Something to do with all the trees. Before ringing him back, she waited to see if he would call her first. She pictured them ringing each other all evening and getting a permanently engaged tone.

'*Cara mia*, does this prove anything to you?'

She spun round and got the surprise of her life. There, looking as gorgeous, as impossibly attractive as he always did, was Alessio. Dressed in a smart black suit with a blue-and-white open-necked shirt, he could not have appeared more wildly out of place. 'Alessio! What the ... what are you doing here?'

He took off his sunglasses and slipped them into his jacket pocket. 'I came to see you, of course.'

'But how did you know how to find me?'

'Please, these questions can wait. For now I would like my reward for coming all this way.'

She smiled. 'And that would be what, exactly?'

He came in close. '*Questo.*' He took her in his arms and kissed her for so long she half expected the sun to have set and the moon to be shining down on them when they finally pulled apart. Unable to speak, she gazed at him in wonder. Her heart felt as if it was overflowing with love for him. He too seemed lost for words

403

and when she looked into his eyes and saw the loving tenderness contained in them, she had to steady herself against him. Just as she'd thought before, there was no denying the connection they had. It was as though they had never been strangers.

A volley of loud whistling had them both turning round. Not for the first time they had attracted an audience. Dan had his mug of tea raised to her, whilst Bill and Joe were embellishing their whistles with a selection of obscene hand gestures. Standing alongside the Old Boys was Orlando. He was almost smiling. But not quite.

BELLAGIO

Chapter Sixty-four

A month had passed since Hunter had confirmed for Conrad what he'd always suspected, that Hunter was an unscrupulous, ruthless man with a dangerously vicious side to him. In other words, he was a short-arsed, tyrannical thug.

Yet even though he'd had his suspicions, Conrad had still been shocked and disgusted that Hunter had lost control the way he did. At least he hadn't driven off unscathed. As a result of the two well-landed punches that Conrad had unleashed on him, he'd left with a bleeding mouth and a potentially very black eye. In view of the head injury Helen already had, Conrad had been all for taking her to hospital, but she had refused, insisting she was more shaken than hurt. Mac had poured out three glasses of medicinal whisky and Helen had surprised them by raising her glass and saying, 'To my impending divorce. And my new life.' She had then told them about her visit to the solicitor's office in Crantsford. Conrad had never heard of this Mrs Jenkins, but he could imagine Helen's surprise when she'd received the news. Helen's concerns for her grandmother were now over. She was free. And free to be herself. Conrad didn't think there was a better gift anyone could receive. Once or twice Helen had hinted that maybe she shouldn't accept the bequest, but Conrad had overheard Mac being firm with her. He'd told her that Mrs Jenkins had clearly valued their relationship, even if it had been a professional one, and this was her way of thanking Helen.

The following day, late in the afternoon, Helen had arrived back from her first day at work and knocked at his office door to ask if she could talk to him. It was the first time she had been inside his office and he had liked her presence there. As she'd perched on the window ledge overlooking the garden, her hair the colour of translucent amber with the sunlight streaming in behind her, she'd said, 'Annabel didn't come to work today. Instead she sent a letter.

She says that under the circumstances she doesn't feel it would be appropriate to work with me any more.'

'Seems reasonable,' Conrad had said, at the same time thinking he'd never seen Helen looking more beautiful. Her face was clear and untroubled. There was a new confidence to her. An inner peace, he supposed.

'Even more reasonable,' she said, 'is that because thirty per cent of the funding comes from Hunter, I'm going to have to shut up shop.'

'That's a shame.'

'Unless I accept the offer Mac made me last night. That's what I wanted to talk to you about. He wants to help. He says with all his years in the world of banking, drumming up funding would be child's play for him. He says he's very good at twisting arms.'

'He's good at Chinese burns, too.'

She'd smiled. 'What do you think?'

Getting up from his chair – how could he resist that smile? – Conrad had joined her at the window and looked down onto the garden, where Mac was sitting in a deckchair applying himself to *The Times* crossword: Fritz was at his feet. 'My father's always had a brilliant mind for business. Accept his offer of help, Helen. It'll give him something worthwhile to do.'

'I thought you'd say that. But it needs a great deal of thought. I'll only be able to carry on with Companion Care if I can make it pay me a decent wage. Expansion might be the answer. Does it feel weird referring to Mac as your father?'

Aware that she'd changed the subject, and knowing that her independence was a sensitive area, he let it go. 'Sometimes it does,' he said. 'Other times it's a wonder it hasn't slipped off my tongue before.'

She looked out of the window again, her attention caught by Mac throwing a ball for Fritz. Without thinking, Conrad put a hand to Helen's cheek and with the back of his fingers, he stroked her smooth, pale skin. She turned and with her eyes on his, she kissed his palm. He bent his head and kissed her softly on the mouth. Very slowly. Very carefully. It seemed impossible that it was their first kiss.

'That was nice,' she said, when she tipped her head back and held his gaze.

'It was, wasn't it? Would you like me to do it again?'

'I don't want to distract you from your work.'

'Too late for that.' He kissed her again. And again.

'Do you ever get the feeling that everything that has gone before has been a series of clues leading us to this point?'

They were on the stone steps of what had once been the landing stage for the Hotel Villa Cipressi, and with his head resting in Helen's lap, Conrad opened his eyes. Relinquishing the pleasant memory of that first kiss was a fair exchange for the sight of the lovely face above him. 'Could you be more specific, please?' he said, despite knowing exactly what Helen was asking. It was one of the many things about their relationship he liked: the way they were so in tune with each other. She always seemed to know what he was thinking. To his delight, though, he was still able to surprise her. As he had with this return trip to Lake Como. He'd decided last week that they needed to get away, and aware how disappointed Helen had been not to visit Varenna and the gardens here in September, he had booked for them to stay at the Hotel Villa Cipressi. The only change to the itinerary that she requested, once she knew what he'd done, was to suggest that Mac join them. It made him love her even more.

Stroking his forehead, she looked down at him. 'If love is supposed to blind you, why is it that when I'm with you, I feel that I'm seeing my life clearly for the first time ever?'

'You make me sound like an optician.'

'I'm being serious. My life suddenly seems so uncomplicated. There's no sense of dread each day. I get up in the morning and I'm happy. It's as simple as that. I no longer feel as if I'm swimming against the tide.'

He thought of that day at Villa Carlotta when he'd recognized the statue from the Hermitage Museum – 'Amore and Psyche Reclining' – and how, in the story Sam had told him, love had won out in the end. It had been a hell of a struggle along the way, but from the moment Helen moved in with him at Chapel House, the future had seemed crystal clear.

'Let's go for a swim,' he said.

They stripped off their clothes down to their swimming suits, and stepped into the cool water. It was the first week of October, but the weather was still warm. Their waitress at breakfast had said it was going to be twenty-four degrees today. To Helen, the mornings were even more beautiful than when they'd been here in September. Everything looked exquisitely enchanting in the soft light. Or was that because she was here with Conrad?

She watched Conrad swim away from the shore. How did I get to be so lucky? she thought. And why couldn't she have met him in her twenties and spent a lifetime of loving this special man?

From the many conversations she'd had with Mac, she had learned that he could teach her a lot about love. His affair with Conrad's mother had taught him that love is wildly indiscriminate. 'The blow strikes where it strikes,' he'd told Helen. 'It may not be convenient. It may not appear right. But there's damn all you can do about it. It was coming to terms with this that made me able to deal with the guilt I felt towards my brother.'

Helen no longer felt guilty about Hunter. She just felt enormous relief that she had ended things when she had. She had no idea if she was the first woman he'd ever hit, but it wasn't a question to which she needed an answer. All she knew was that it was the one and only time it would happen to her. Much to her solicitor's disapproval, she wasn't asking for any kind of a settlement. She didn't want a penny of Hunter's money. She felt tainted enough by him. She still cringed when she remembered how she'd allowed herself to be used by him, when the only way he could be sexually satisfied had been to dominate and overpower her. She would never be sure, but it was possible, from what he'd said that day when he'd hit her, that it was when he perceived a shift in power in their relationship that things had started to go badly wrong. He'd said that she had begun to question him. How sad that something as insignificant as that should have such an effect on him. It said a lot about his ego. And it said a lot about her own character that she had made all those excuses for him when he stopped bothering her in bed altogether. Tired and overworked, she'd thought, when all the time he'd gone elsewhere – to Annabel, who doubtless stroked that ego of his instead of ruffling it as she had begun to do. Hunter had only wanted Helen because he saw in her a person who would for ever be in his debt, and would therefore show him due respect and reverence.

But none of that was important now. Now she knew that she was loved by a man whom she trusted implicitly. Conrad would never hurt her. He would never cheat on her. Nor would he ever manipulate her. There was no side to him.

They had made no definite plans for the future, other than that they wanted to spend their every waking moment together. The details, as Conrad had said, would be filled in later. There was no hurry. Life, they were finding, had a habit of shaping itself.

Slowly, step by tiny step, Lucy was beginning to trust her feelings for Alessio. And his for her. It had not been an easy journey. There were times when they argued – the rows were fiery, contradictory and irrational – but the disagreements were always followed by an impassioned declaration of love on Alessio's part. He could be irrepressible and charmingly childlike, but never dull. She didn't know anyone else like him. Often she would panic and wonder what she was getting in to. But then she would picture his handsome face, or he would phone her and his voice would wash away her doubts and concerns. Nothing had prepared her for the changes he had wrought in her. When they were apart – which was too often – she veered from tearful heartbreak to a warm glow of just knowing that he had travelled all the way to Swanmere to tell her he loved her. *Ti amo, Lucia. Ti amo molto.* He was full of drama, she was finding.

That extraordinary evening when he had surprised her at the allotments, he had turned up in Swanmere, found where she lived, only then to discover that she wasn't there. Apparently Orlando had not been the friendliest of people when he'd opened the door to Alessio. But he'd thawed when Alessio had made it clear that he wasn't leaving until he'd spoken to Lucy. Orlando had then offered to take him to the allotments. 'Lucia, he has it bad for you,' Alessio had said later that evening, when Orlando had discreetly left them alone, going to spend the night at his parents' house. 'He wants you nearly as much as I do. I can see it in his eyes. Should I be jealous?' Her initial response was to say that Alessio was reading it all wrong, but whenever she thought of Orlando's expression when he'd been with Dan and the Old Boys and he couldn't quite muster a smile, she knew there was more than a little truth in what Alessio was saying. Poor Orlando. How had that happened? How had their wires become so crossed?

Two nights ago, Orlando had asked her what she really knew of Alessio. Or of Italian men in general. 'Not much,' she had admitted as they sat opposite each other at the kitchen table. 'Other than what my father has told me. According to him, Italian men stay spoilt Mama's boys until the natural order of things is changed and their mothers die. Only then do they grow up. He also said that sex is a matter of honour to them, with whoever it is: a wife, a girlfriend, or a mistress. Oh, and apparently they can't stay faithful. They lack the fidelity gene.'

'And that doesn't worry you?' Orlando had asked.

'Be fair, Orlando, that could describe any number of British men. I also think my father was trying to put me off Alessio. To protect me.'

'He just wants you to be happy. As do I.'

'I am happy. Unbelievably happy.'

'But he's made you cry. I've seen and heard you.'

'He makes me laugh more.'

'You're sure?'

'Oh, yes. The good stuff easily outweighs the bad.'

Forty-eight hours on and Lucy was trying to hang on to this thought: the good outweighs the bad. She was staying with her father and Francesca in Pescallo. It was her second visit – she had taken Hugh at his word about being able to take time off – and already she could see a change for the worse in Francesca. She was pale with dark, bruising shadows under her eyes and she'd lost weight.

With a mutual love of gardening, and Lucy's desire to learn Italian so that she could prove she was no slouch with Alessio, they had become firm friends. That was definitely the good bit. The flip side was knowing that their growing closeness would make Francesca's death that much harder to bear. Lucy now felt as though her childhood grievances were a long way behind her. All those hurts and grudges – her closest of friends – had been banished for ever.

She was in the garden with Francesca now. Francesca was taking a rest in a chair in the shade of the gazebo, which was covered with a magnificent Rosa mulliganii, while Lucy was setting out flutes of Prosecco on a white-clothed table. Inside the house, Mac was helping her father choose the wine.

'What time did Alessio think he would make it?' Francesca asked her.

Lucy thought before she answered. '*Alle due*. At two.'

'*Bravissima!* You're learning fast. But then you have such motivation.'

'I don't like Alessio to outsmart me too often.'

Francesca smiled. 'I strongly approve of that. He's a clever young man, but occasionally he needs reminding that he is not perfect and that others are equally as clever.'

The last of the glasses neatly set out, Lucy came and sat next to

Francesca on the soft, spongy grass. 'Is there any chance that my father might change his mind and actually approve of Alessio?'

'Don't worry. If it's the last thing I do, I shall make sure he sees the good in my nephew.'

It was only an expression – *if it's the last thing I do* – but Lucy winced at Francesca's words. In the short time she had known her step-mother, she had learnt what a kind and forgiving woman she was. She was a determined woman too – as evidenced by her defying her family to marry Marcus. 'Francesca, can I talk to you about Alessio?'

'Of course. What is it?'

'He's asked me to move here so we can spend more time to-gether.'

'Here in Pescallo?'

'Not Pescallo specifically. Maybe Bellagio.'

'And do you want to do that?'

'When I'm with him I can't think of anything I'd like more. But when we're apart, when I try to think straight, my head tells me it would be crazy.'

'Because you've known each other for so little time? Is that it?'

'Exactly. It's such a risk. I have a good job at home. And home is Swanmere. It's where all my friends are. What would I do here when Alessio is back in Milan playing with the orchestra?'

In an elegant, sweeping gesture Francesca swatted the question away with her hand. 'Let me ask you something important. Despite knowing Alessio for just over a month, do you love him?'

'Yes.' The admission slipped off her tongue before Lucy could stop it. How dangerous it sounded, that one small word.

But Francesca clapped her hands and smiled. 'You see! You didn't even have to think about it. And there is the answer to your question.'

'What if it fizzles out?'

'What if it does? So what if it is a transient period? Everything is transient. You have to live, Lucy. You have to make the most of every good thing that comes your way.'

Lucy smiled. 'You're like Alessio; you make everything sound so simple.'

'It's fear that complicates things. Look at it from another angle. Would it be possible for you to walk away from Alessio now? Knowing how he feels about you, and yes, I have seen the way he looks at you; I know what is in his heart – it is there for all to see;

could you really turn your back on that? Would you really want to deny yourself that happiness, just because you're afraid of the unknown?'

Before Lucy could reply, Francesca was speaking again. 'I darcd to face the consequences of falling in love with your father; now you must do the same with Alessio. It is so much easier to walk away, to pretend that it is for the best. But Lucy, remember this: when it comes to love there is nothing so cowardly as a safe compromise. Life should be an adventure. There should be thrills. Risks. Where would be the thrill if you returned to England?'

Caught up in Francesca's enthusiasm, Lucy laughed. 'You're quite a motivator, aren't you?'

'Now that's something you should ask your father about.'

'Ask me what?'

Mac and Marcus were crossing the lawn towards them, each carrying a large tray of food that Lucy had helped prepare earlier with Francesca. While Mac and her father had been putting the world to rights over a glass or two of wine, Lucy and Francesca had washed, peeled, chopped, fried and baked. There were artichoke hearts in olive oil with tiny caramelized onions, prosciutto with figs and mozzarella, succulent lamb cutlets with lemon juice and thyme, baked aubergines with courgettes and yellow tomatoes, slices of peaches and melon, and a particular favourite of Lucy's that Alessio had introduced her to: cherries soaked in grappa. Her father and Mac put the trays on the table either side of the glasses.

'Marcus,' Francesca said, 'I was just talking to Lucy about *amore*.' She put a hand out to him. He took it and squeezed it gently. Lucy had to turn away. The look of sadness in her father's face was too much.

It wasn't a large gathering, just a small get-together so that Marcus could meet some of his daughter's friends from Swanmere who were here on holiday. Mac Truman had been with them since mid-morning and Marcus had taken an instant liking to the elderly gentleman. He was solid and reliable. It was very apparent that Mac was extremely fond of Lucy and Marcus was glad that Lucy counted him as a friend.

The first guest to arrive was Enrico Mosto. Having lost his own wife, Enrico was one of the few people in whom Marcus felt able to confide his fears for Francesca. And for himself when the end came.

Next to arrive was Mac's son, Conrad. With him was an attractive auburn-haired woman called Helen. They both apologized for being ten minutes late. 'We were having a swim and lost track of the time,' Helen explained.

'Which means you're all set to eat and drink long into the night,' Francesca greeted them warmly. 'Just as it should be. Come and have a glass of Prosecco.'

Marcus watched his wife acting as if she didn't have a care in the world. She was doing what she always did: sharing her love of life with those around her. He saw Lucy looking at him and went over to her.

'How are you doing, Dad?' she asked him.

He still got a kick out of hearing Lucy calling him Dad. 'I'm okay,' he said.

'Really?'

He swallowed. 'It doesn't seem to be getting any easier. I thought it might. But with each day that passes, I know it's a day nearer—' He stopped himself from going any further. It wouldn't be what Francesca would want. 'I have a surprise for you,' he said.

'For me?'

'Yes, someone I want you to meet. His name's Enrico Mosto. He's a very good friend of mine. How's your Italian coming along?'

She looked alarmed. 'Does he only speak Italian? Because if so, I won't be able to talk to him.'

Marcus smiled. 'I'm thinking long term.'

'You've lost me, Dad.'

'I was talking to Alessio yesterday. He told me that he's asked you to come and live here.'

The look of alarm returned. 'He shouldn't have said anything to you. It's much too soon. And I certainly—'

He put a hand on her arm, wanting to reassure her. 'Lucy, it's okay. Whatever I thought about Alessio is in the past. The very fact that he came to me to ask what I thought about his idea shows that he's changing for the better. Francesca has also taken me to task. She has reminded me quite forcibly of her family's intense disapproval of me when I came to live here with her. She asked me if I wanted to spoil our reconciliation over something that is entirely between you and Alessio. As ever, she is right.'

'I don't know what to say.'

'In that case, come and meet Enrico because he might be the one to convince you to say yes to Alessio.'

'But why?'

'He runs one of the largest plant nurseries in the area and he might be able to offer you a job.'

'A real job?'

'Yes.'

'And you really don't object to Alessio and me being together?'

'Not if it means I get to see more of you.'

Mac watched Lucy hugging her father. Now there was a sight to warm the coldest of hearts. It was good to see her looking so happy. But when seconds later Alessio appeared at her side, the joy on her face was complete. A long, long time ago, he had once told Hannah that a person in love was the most beautiful person in the world. And that, Mac could see, was Lucy to a tee right now. He'd never seen her looking so radiant. He watched the young pair exchange a few words and after Alessio had said something to Marcus, he suddenly lifted Lucy off the ground, swung her round, and then kissed her.

There was nothing as infectious as other people's happiness. It was the best tonic in the world. Looking across the garden to where Helen and Conrad were sitting on the grass, their heads almost touching, Mac felt a wave of love for them both. It had always been the same for him: if Conrad was happy, he was happy. It was as simple as that.

More laughter from Lucy and Alessio had him glancing back their way. How wrong he'd been about Lucy and Orlando. He'd thought they were made for each other, but seeing Lucy with Alessio, he didn't doubt that she had made the right choice. He'd never seen her sparkle with Orlando the way she did with this Italian chap. The time would soon come when they wouldn't be seeing too much of her back in Swanmere. He would miss her.

He felt a sudden pang of longing for the only woman other than Hannah to whom he had felt really close: Alice. How she would have enjoyed all this. 'Gardeners make the best lovers,' she once joked. 'With the exception of Olivia Marchwood,' she'd added wickedly. But rumour had it that Olivia had had company recently. Her gentleman widower friend from Cirencester – the Gardens of Delight veteran – had been observed arriving at her front door with a small suitcase. Well, good luck to the old trout!

Going over to sit in the shade of the gazebo, Mac thought of what he'd read last night in bed. Just before they'd set off for Italy, Helen had returned Alice's diaries to him and he'd finally decided he was ready to read them. Whereas before he'd found the journals too upsetting, now he found them a comfort.

There was one entry that had struck him as being particularly apposite and wise: 'A garden, like its creator, should have its secrets and surprises,' Alice had written. 'It should contain delights within delights and paths that make you want to follow them, even though they may not lead you anywhere in particular. On the other hand, they may lead you somewhere wonderfully unexpected.'

Mac took a sip of his Prosecco. 'How right you are, Alice,' he murmured.